W9-BOL-417

PENGUIN CLASSICS

THE STORY OF THE STONE

VOLUME I

ADVISORY EDITOR: BETTY RADICE

Cao Xueqin (1715?–63) was born into a family which for three generations held the office of Commissioner of Imperial Textiles in Nanking, a family so wealthy that they were able to entertain the Emperor Kangxi four times. But calamity overtook them and their property was confiscated. Cao Xueqin was living in poverty near Peking when he wrote his famous novel *The Story of the Stone*, of which this is the first volume. The four other volumes, *The Crab-Flower Club*, *The Warning Voice*, *The Debt of Tears* and *The Dreamer Awakes*, are also published in Penguin Classics.

•

David Hawkes was Professor of Chinese at Oxford University from 1959 to 1971 and a Research Fellow of All Souls College, from 1973 to 1983. He now lives in retirement in Wales.

THE STORY
OF THE STONE

A CHINESE NOVEL BY
CAO XUEQIN
IN FIVE VOLUMES

*

VOLUME I
'THE GOLDEN DAYS'

*

TRANSLATED BY
DAVID HAWKES

PENGUIN BOOKS

PENGUIN BOOKS

Published by the Penguin Group
Penguin Books Ltd, 80 Strand, London WC2R 0RL, England
Penguin Putnam Inc., 375 Hudson Street, New York, New York 10014, USA
Penguin Books Australia Ltd, 250 Camberwell Road, Camberwell, Victoria 3124, Australia
Penguin Books Canada Ltd, 10 Alcorn Avenue, Toronto, Ontario, Canada M4V 3B2
Penguin Books India (P) Ltd, 11 Community Centre, Panchsheel Park, New Delhi – 110 017, India
Penguin Books (NZ) Ltd, Cnr Rosedale and Airborne Roads, Albany, Auckland, New Zealand
Penguin Books (South Africa) (Pty) Ltd, 24 Sturdee Avenue, Rosebank 2196, South Africa

Penguin Books Ltd, Registered Offices: 80 Strand, London WC2R 0RL, England

www.penguin.com

This translation first published 1973
047

Copyright © David Hawkes, 1973
All rights reserved

Printed in England by Clays Ltd, St Ives plc
Set in Monotype Garamond

ISBN-13: 978-0-140-44293-9

www.greenpenguin.co.uk

MIX
Paper from
responsible sources
FSC **FSC® C018179**
www.fsc.org

Penguin Books is committed to a sustainable
future for our business, our readers and our planet.
This book is made from Forest Stewardship
Council™ certified paper.

TO DOROTHY AND JUNG-EN

CONTENTS

VOWELS AND DIPHTHONGS

i. Open Vowels

a   is a long *ah* like *a* in *father* (e.g. Jia)

e   on its own or after any consonant other than y is like the sound in French *oeuf* or the *er*, *ir*, *ur* sound of Southern English (e.g. Gao E, Jia She)

e   after y or a semivowel is like the *e* of *egg* (e.g. Qin Bang-ye, Xue Pan)

i   after b.d.j.l.m.n.p.q.t.x.y is the long Italian *i* or English *ee* as in *see* (e.g. Nannie Li)

i   after zh.ch.sh.z.c.s.r is a strangled sound somewhere between the *u* of *suppose* and a vocalized *r* (e.g. Shi-yin)

i   after semivowel u is pronounced like *ay* in *sway* (e.g. Li Gui)

o   is the *au* of *author* (e.g. Duo)

u   after semivowel i and all consonants except j.q.x.y is pronounced like Italian *u* or English *oo* in *too* (e.g. Bu Gu-xiu)

u   after j.q.x.y and ü after l or n is the narrow French *u* or German *ü*, for which there is no English equivalent (e.g. Bao-yu, Nü-wa)

ii. Closed Vowels

an   after semivowel u or any consonant other than y is like *an* in German *Mann* or *un* in Southern English *fun* (e.g. Yuan-chun, Shan Ping-ren)

an   after y or semivowel i is like *en* in *hen* (e.g. Zhi-yan-zhai, Jia Lian)

ang   whatever it follows, invariably has the long *a* of *father* (e.g. Jia Qiang)

en, eng   the e in these combinations is always a short, neutral sound like *a* in *ago* or the first *e* in *believe* (e.g. Cousin Zhen, Xi-feng)

in, ing   short *i* as in *sin*, *sing* (e.g. Shi-yin, Lady Xing)

ong   the o is like the short *oo* of Southern English *book* (e.g. Jia Cong)

un   the rule for the closed u is similar to the rule for the open one: after j.q.x.y it is the narrow French *u* of *rue*; after anything else it resembles the short English *oo* of *book* (e.g. Jia Yun, Ying-chun)

iii. Diphthongs

ai   like the sound in English *lie*, *high*, *mine* (e.g. Dai-yu)

ao   like the sound in *how* or *bough* (e.g. Bao-yu)

ei   like the sound in *day* or *mate* (e.g. Bei-jing)
ou   like the sound in *old* or *bowl* (e.g. Gou-er)

The syllable er, sometimes found as the second element in names, is a peculiarity of the Pekingese dialect which lies outside this system. It sounds somewhat like the word *err* pronounced with a broad West Country accent.

INTRODUCTION

It is a somewhat surprising fact that the most popular book in the whole of Chinese literature remained unpublished for nearly thirty years after its author's death, and exists in several different versions, none of which can be pointed to as definitively 'correct'.

From 1763, the year in which Cao Xueqin died, until the appearance of the first printed edition in January 1792,[1] *The Story of the Stone* circulated in manuscript copies, at first privately, among members of the Cao family and their friends, and then more widely, as copies began to find their way on to bookstalls at the temple markets of Peking. One such copy was bought in 1769 by a future Provincial Judge who happened to be staying in Peking at the time to sit for an examination. It was published in Shanghai in a somewhat garbled form a century and a half later.

These manuscript copies included a commentary consisting of the remarks, in many cases signed and dated, of two or three different commentators, evidently made over a period of years, and written, often in red ink, in the manuscripts' margins and in the spaces between the text. They circulated in several different versions, both the commentary and the text differing somewhat from copy to copy, but they all had two things in common: they were all entitled *Red Inkstone's Reannotated Story of the Stone*; and they all, to the intense disappointment of their readers, broke off at the end of chapter 80, just as the plot appeared to be drawing towards some sort of climax.

The appearance of a complete version in 120 chapters in Gao E and Cheng Weiyuan's first printed edition of 1792 did not immediately end the lucrative traffic in hand-written copies, because the first printed edition was an expensive one;

1. Chinese authorities mostly refer to this as 'the 1791 edition', though in point of fact it was not published until January of the following year.

but its subsequent pirating in cheaper reprints by other publishers did; and though a dwindling number of *cognoscenti* still clung to their Red Inkstones and denounced Gao E's edition as an impudent (or ignorant) imposture, the majority of readers were well satisfied with the completed version. No longer was the *Stone* to be found only in the drawing-rooms of Manchu noblemen. Soon everyone in Peking was reading and talking about it, and throughout the whole of the nineteenth century its popularity continued to grow and spread. Old gentlemen nearly came to blows over the relative merits of its two heroines and every languishing young lady imagined herself a Dai-yu.

As the Gao E version became more and more established, continuing to hold its own against a crop of competing but quite obviously spurious 'complete versions' – including one equipped with a forged testimonial by Xueqin's mother – so Red Inkstone and his commentaries were gradually forgotten. Indeed, people even forgot about Cao Xueqin; for although he mentions himself by name in the first chapter, he does so in a spoofing, ironical way which seems to imply that he was only the book's editor and not its author, and when Gao E and Cheng Weiyuan introduced the book to the general public in 1792 they told their readers that the author's name was unknown.

Once Cao Xueqin's authorship was forgotten, all sorts of fanciful theories about the author and his characters could flourish unchallenged. Readers assumed that the novel was a *roman à clef*, but now that they had ceased to know about Cao Xueqin and his family they had lost the key. *Stone* studies became a sort of literary hobby, like identifying Mr W. H. or proving that Bacon wrote Shakespeare.

In modern times such facts as we know about this novel have had to be laboriously rediscovered. The publication of the Judge's manuscript in 1912 was a beginning. Unfortunately the manuscript itself was burned only a few years later and the printed version was a somewhat garbled one. But since 1927, when an important fragment of Red Inkstone came to light, more and more manuscripts have emerged from obscurity, and by studying them and comparing what could be learned from them with such information as could be gleaned from eighteenth-century archives and from the letters and poems of the Caos and their friends, Chinese scholars have been able to reconstruct a fairly detailed picture of the novel's background. Much, however, still remains uncertain and mysterious. Opinions shift and change from year to year as more manuscripts and other new materials continue to come to light. New theories are continually being propounded and old ones heatedly defended or acrimoniously attacked, so that it is difficult to give an account of the novel that will not seem dated in a year or two's time.

In writing this account I have relied heavily on the published researches of Chinese scholars like Yu Pingbo, Zhou Ruchang, Wu Shichang and Zhao Gang – particularly the last, whose theories on a number of controversial issues seem to me the most convincing. Wu Shichang is the only one of these scholars whose work is available in English. His book *On 'The Red Chamber Dream'* was published in English by the Clarendon Press in 1961. Another English-language book I am greatly indebted to is Jonathan Spence's *Ts'ao Yin and the K'ang-hsi Emperor*, published by Yale University in 1966. This is an interesting and informative study of Cao Xueqin's grandfather which some readers may perhaps wish to consult for themselves.

The Chinese scholar's first reaction to the discovery of the Red Inkstone manuscripts was outright rejection of Gao E's completed 120-chapter version. It was clear that the anonymous person calling himself 'Red Inkstone' was in some way closely related to the author (brother, cousin, uncle, wife or best friend) and familiar with his intentions, and his references to future developments in the plot occurring after chapter 80 are almost invariably different from what is found in the last forty chapters of the Gao E version. Gao E, who claimed in his Preface to the novel that all he had done was to edit the very patchy and defective manuscript given him to work on by his bookseller friend Cheng Weiyuan, was branded as a bare-faced liar.

It seems a somewhat illogical reaction, since Gao E could just as well have been the innocent dupe of a forger as a liar and forget himself, and even those of his contemporaries who refused to accept the 120-chapter version as genuine gave him the benefit of the doubt to this extent; nevertheless a few years ago most people were willing to accept that Gao E was a liar. Now, however, as new evidence comes to light, it is becoming more and more probable that he was *not* – that he *did* only edit, not fabricate, the last forty chapters. Moreover, although the last forty chapters are not by Cao Xueqin himself, it is beginning to look more and more as though they were written by someone very close to Xueqin, probably a member of his family – someone who was familiar with his drafts and wanted a different ending but did not necessarily have any intention of passing off the new ending as the author's own work.

The novel we read today, then, is an incomplete novel by Cao Xueqin in eighty chapters with a supplement by an anonymous author in forty chapters which, though in many respects not what the author intended and perhaps inferior to what he would have written, is nevertheless, because of the inside knowledge of the person who wrote it, a vastly better ending than any of that mushroom crop which sprang up once the commercial possibilities of a completed edition had been established.

This translation, though occasionally following the text of one or other of the manuscripts in the first eighty chapters, will nevertheless be a translation of the whole 120 chapters of the Gao E edition. The title chosen for it, *The Story of the Stone*, is not, however, the one that Gao E gave to his completed 120-chapter version but the one used by Red Inkstone in the eighty-chapter manuscripts.

In the opening chapter of the novel the author himself mentions no less than five titles which he and the members of his family, who watched the novel grow and helped him with their suggestions, had at one time or another considered using:

1. *Shitouji* (The Story of the Stone)
2. *Qing seng lu* (The Passionate Monk's Tale)
3. *Fengyue baojian* (A Mirror for the Romantic)

4. *Hong lou meng* (A Dream of Red Mansions)
5. *Jinling shier chai* (Twelve Young Ladies of Jinling)

It was in fact the fourth of these titles that Gao E used for the printed edition. It is by that title that the novel is known in China today and by translations of that title that it is invariably referred to in other parts of the world:

> *The Dream of the Red Chamber*
> *Le rêve dans le pavillon rouge*
> *Der Traum der Roten Kammer*
> *Il sogno della camera rossa*
> *Son v krasnom teremye*, etc.

These translated titles are somewhat misleading. The image they conjure up – that of a sleeper in a crimson-coloured room – is a highly evocative one, full of charm and mystery; but unfortunately it is not what the Chinese implies. In old China storeyed buildings with red-plastered outer walls – this is the literal meaning of '*hong lou*' – were a sign of opulence and grandeur. (In Peking it is the former palaces, temples and yamens that have red walls; the habitations of commoners are for the most part grey.) But '*hong lou*' early acquired another, more specialized meaning. It came to be used specifically of the dwellings of rich men's daughters, or, by extension, of the daughters themselves. It follows from this that the fourth and fifth titles ('A Dream of Red Mansions' and 'Twelve Young Ladies of Jinling') represent somewhat different formulations of the same idea, just as the first and second titles ('The Story of the Stone' and 'The Passionate Monk's Tale') both refer to the fiction that the text of the novel started off as an immensely long inscription on a miraculous stone which was copied out by a visiting holy man and taken down into the world for publication.

A proof of this is the use of '*Hong lou meng*' in Bao-yu's dream in chapter 5 as the title of a cycle of twelve songs, each about one of the twelve principal female characters of the novel, whereas in an earlier part of the dream the same twelve characters are referred to as 'The Twelve Beauties of Jinling'. In chapter 5 I have translated the title of the song-cycle as

'A Dream of Golden Days'. Perhaps 'A Dream of Golden Girls' would have been a more accurate translation; but the vision of sun-tanned bathing belles which it evokes is too far a remove from the fragile blossoms of the novel for it to have been considered seriously. And in any case, the ambiguity of the title – in that 'A Dream of Red Mansions' can mean both a dream of delicately nurtured young ladies living in luxurious apartments *and* a dream of vanished splendour – is a deliberate one, as is made clear in an introduction to the first chapter written by the author's younger brother.

The frequent use of dream imagery in this novel, says the younger brother, is due to the fact that the glittering, luxurious world of his youth which the author was attempting to recall in it had vanished so utterly by the time he came to write it that it now seemed more like a dream or mirage than something he had experienced in reality. But he also tells us that the book originally grew out of his brother's desire to write something about the numerous girls who had surrounded him in his youth.

'Who are the characters in this book,' he asks, 'and what was the author's motive in writing it?' He answers the question by quoting Cao Xueqin's own words:

Having made an utter failure of my life, I found myself one day, in the midst of my poverty and wretchedness, thinking about the female companions of my youth. As I went over them one by one, examining and comparing them in my mind's eye, it suddenly came over me that those slips of girls – which is all they were then – were in every way, both morally and intellectually, superior to the 'grave and mustachioed signior' I am now supposed to have become. The realization brought with it an overpowering sense of shame and remorse, and for a while I was plunged in the deepest despair. There and then I resolved to make a record of all the recollections of those days I could muster – those golden days when I dressed in silk and ate delicately, when we still nestled in the protecting shadow of the Ancestors and Heaven still smiled on us. I resolved to tell the world how, in defiance of all my family's attempts to bring me up properly and all the warnings and advice of my friends, I had brought myself to this present wretched state, in which, having frittered away half a lifetime, I find myself without a single skill with which I could earn a decent living. I resolved that, however unsightly my own shortcomings might be, I must not, for the sake of keeping them hid, allow those wonderful girls to pass into oblivion without a memorial.

Reminders of my poverty were all about me: the thatched roof, the wicker lattices, the string beds, the crockery stove. But these did not need to be an impediment to the workings of the imagination. Indeed, the beauties of nature outside my door—the morning breeze, the evening dew, the flowers and trees of my garden – were a positive encouragement to write. I might lack learning and literary aptitude, but what was to prevent me from turning it all into a story and writing it in the vernacular? In this way the memorial to my beloved girls could at one and the same time serve as a source of harmless entertainment and as a warning to those who were in the same predicament as myself but who were still in need of awakening.

The question as to whether or not the Bao-yu of the novel is a portrait of the author as a boy will be dealt with later; but certainly this dejected middle-aged man who concludes that the girls he had known in his youth were all 'morally and intellectually [his] superior' has a good deal in common with the adolescent who thought that 'the pure essence of humanity was all concentrated in the female of the species and that males were its mere dregs and off-scourings', who once observed of his female cousins that 'if they, whose understanding was so superior, were manifestly still so far from Enlightenment, it was obviously a waste of time for *him* to go on pursuing it', and who, when he was a very little boy, used to maintain that 'girls are made of water and boys are made of mud', and that only when he was with girls did he feel 'fresh and clean'.

Whether or not Bao-yu represents the author, the girls in the novel are undoubtedly, in a majority of cases, portraits of the girls he had known in his youth. Quite apart from the author's own statement as quoted in his brother's introduction, there are the words spoken by the Stone in his argument with Vanitas in the allegorical opening of the novel's first chapter: 'Surely my "number of females", whom I spent half a lifetime studying with my own eyes and ears, are preferable to this kind of stuff? ...' And if this were not enough, we now have the commentaries of Red Inkstone, drooling in tearful nostalgia over the text: 'Ah yes. I remember her.' 'Yes, there was such a person.' 'Yes, it really happened.' 'A perfect likeness!' 'She was just like that.' And so on and so forth.

If *The Story of the Stone* is a sort of Chinese *Remembrance of Things Past*, it becomes doubly important to us to know as much as we can about the author's life. Unfortunately what little we know from direct evidence concerns only his last years. Of his childhood and early maturity we know virtually nothing. We do not even know with any certainty either when he was born or who his father was.

Cao Xueqin died on the 12 February 1763, the eve of the Chinese New Year.[2] His age at the time is referred to variously as 'in his forties' or 'less than fifty'. These statements, taken in conjunction with what is known of the Cao family's history a half-century before, make it seem highly probable that he was born in 1715, thus making him forty-eight when he died. His death is said to have been hastened by the loss of his only son a few months before. One of his friends mentions that he left a 'new wife' behind, which seems to imply that he was twice married and that the son he lost was his child by the first wife.

As regards appearance, there is a picture believed by some to be a portrait of Cao Xueqin which was painted by a well-known contemporary artist about a year before his death. It shows him reclining on the ground in the midst of a bamboo grove through which a fast-running stream is flowing. He is leaning on a large rock, and his *qin* (that adjunct of cultured ease as indispensable to the Chinese gentleman as was the lute to his Renaissance counterpart) is lying on another rock a yard or two away with a cloth-wrapped bundle of scrolls beside it. The carefully painted head on its impressionistic, unanatomical body looks for all the world like a photographic cut-out pasted on to a pen-and-wash cartoon. There can be little doubt that it is a genuine portrait, whose ever it is.

It is a large, fat, swarthy, rather heavy face. The eyebrows

2. Some scholars maintain that it was on New Year's Eve of the year following, but the evidence for the earlier date seems to me much stronger.

are high, far apart and downward-sloping, like a clown's. The eyes are tiny, humorous and twinkling. There is a large, spreading, bulbous, drinker's nose, a Fu Manchu moustache and a large, rather fleshy mouth. It is an ugly face, but kindly and humorous.

A description by the Manchu critic Yurui written, admittedly, a good few years after Cao Xueqin's death, but based on statements made by older members of his wife's family who had known the author personally, says that he was 'fat, swarthy and of low stature' – all of which sounds very much like the painting but not at all like the beautiful, moon-faced Bao-yu. Yurui's informants confirm the portrait's good humour. A wonderful, witty talker, they call him: 'Wherever he was, he made it spring.' There are also contemporary accounts of his holding forth, generally in a loud and excited voice, and particularly if wine could be procured, to a circle of delighted friends.

For about the last six years of his life – perhaps longer – Cao Xueqin was living in the Western Hills outside Peking in considerable poverty. A friend speaks of the whole family living on porridge – though to what extent this was because the money was all being spent on drink would be hard to say. Contemporaries make frequent mention of his heavy drinking and there are references to his obtaining wine on credit or borrowing money to buy it with.[3] A poem by the same friend who mentioned the porridge describes him 'discoursing of high, noble things while one hand hunts for lice'.

He was a versatile poet and an accomplished painter, specializing – rather appropriately, since 'rock' and 'stone' are the same word in Chinese – in rock-painting. Selling paintings was his one source of income that we know about. He might, like other impoverished Bannermen, have been receiving a tiny monthly allowance. He may have taught for a short while as a private tutor or schoolmaster. It is also possible that he may have sat for some examination at the age of about forty with a view to obtaining some sort of

3. Xueqin is reported to have said once, 'If anyone is in a hurry to read my novel, all he's got to do is keep me daily supplied with roast duck and good Shaoxing wine, and I'll be happy to oblige him.'

employment. But these are all conjectures based on the interpretation of cryptic allusions in the verses of his friends.

His friends all knew about his book. They encouraged
him to get on with it, even if the freedom to get on with it
meant poverty and hardship, and they advised him not to go
'knocking at rich men's doors' and subjecting himself to
the constrictions of patronage. They frequently refer to his
'dream of vanished splendour', the 'dream of his old home',
his 'dream of the South', and so on. (The novel contains
ample evidence that Cao Xueqin spoke like a Southerner.
To his dying day he was unable to distinguish between
'*qin*' and '*qing*'.)

What was this 'vanished splendour', this 'old home in the
South' which furnished the material for his 'Dream of Golden
Days'?

Until he was thirteen, the age he had reached when the
family fortunes crashed, Xueqin lived in Nanking. His
family, particularly his grandfather, were important people
whose names occur frequently in the official archives of the
period and in the writings of their contemporaries. For this
reason more is known about some of them than about
Xueqin himself. Indeed, so famous was Xueqin's grandfather
Cao Yin, that Xueqin was invariably introduced as 'Cao Yin's
grandson', with the result that the name of his father is
nowhere to be found.

In order to understand the somewhat peculiar position
occupied by the Caos until their dramatic fall in 1728 it is
necessary to know something of the Manchu banner system
to which they belonged.

The Manchus were a Tungusic people from Manchuria
who overthrew the native Chinese dynasty and set up their
own 'Qing' régime at Peking in 1644. They imposed the
'pigtail' on all male Chinese[4] and ruled over them, with

4. Female fashion remained unaffected by the conquest and Chinese
women continued to hobble about on artificially deformed feet. Manchu
women retained their unbound feet and distinctive national dress until the
end of the dynasty. Cao Xueqin tries as much as possible to present the
family in the novel as an aristocratic Chinese one. It is only occasionally
that he unintentionally lets slip some indication that its women are proud-
stepping Manchu dames.

growing incompetence, until the republican revolution of 1911.

In 1615, when the Manchus were still consolidating their position in Manchuria, they organized their state on military lines under eight 'banners', each consisting of so many companies of fighting men together with their families and dependants and having its own landholdings and investments. Later they extended this system to include allied races and defectors from the enemy. In 1634 they established eight Mongol banners and in 1642 eight Chinese ones.

It used to be thought that the Caos, who were known to be Bannermen but at the same time ethnically Chinese, belonged to this last category, but it is now known that Xueqin's ancestor, a Chinese colonist in Manchuria, was captured at the fall of Mukden in 1621 and made a slave, or 'bondservant', of the Plain White Banner. The Caos were therefore Manchu Bannermen with the status of Bondservant (Manchu *bōi*).

Being enslaved by the Plain White Banner turned out in the event to be a piece of good luck, because this was one of the three 'Upper Banners' which later came under the direct control of the Manchu ruler. When the Manchu ruler became the Great Qing Emperor, the Bondservants of these banners were institutionalized as the Imperial Household.

The Manchu conquest of China, particularly of the South, was a slow process extending over many years. At first, though the Manchus' inadequate command of Chinese prevented them from performing many of the more complicated administrative functions by themselves, they distrusted the Chinese bureaucrats whom they were obliged to make use of. At the same time they were deeply distrustful of that other great traditional stand-by of autocratic power in China, the eunuchs. Under the Ming dynasty, which the Manchus overthrew, the eunuchs had wielded enormous power as private instruments of the Emperor, operating outside the control of the normal civil and military agencies; but they had so greatly abused their power that Manchu emperors were wary of using them except in their original capacity of palace servants.

It was in these circumstances that the Bondservants of the

Imperial Household came to play an important part. In particular they were employed as Textile Commissioners and Salt Inspectors[5] in the great cultural and commercial centres of Nanking, Soochow and Hangchow in the South. A great-grandfather of Cao Xueqin, whose wife had nursed the Emperor Kangxi[6] in his infancy, was Textile Commissioner in Nanking from 1663 to 1684. His son Cao Yin was Textile Commissioner in Soochow from 1690 to 1692, and from 1692 until 1728, a period of thirty-six years, Cao Yin and his heirs held the post of Textile Commissioner in Nanking continuously. For much of this time Cao Yin's brother-in-law Li Xu was Textile Commissioner in Soochow. Li Xu's sister, who survived Cao Yin by many years, was almost certainly the model for Grandmother Jia in the novel.

The official duties of a Textile Commissioner were to manage the government-owned silk factories, each with their hundreds of skilled employees, to purchase the raw materials which supplied them, and to supervise the transport of finished products to the Imperial Court at Peking; but their actual duties were far more numerous. They were in fact the Emperor's 'men on the spot', charged with observing and reporting on the high-ranking officials in their area and keeping him privately informed on a variety of topics ranging from market fluctuations to the weather and amusing local scandal.

5. In Imperial China the salt monopoly was an important source of government revenue. Distribution was in the hands of contractors operating under government licence. Great fortunes were made in salt both by the merchant-contractors and by the Government Inspectors who controlled them.

6. Chinese emperors were in the habit of proclaiming 'eras' with grandiloquent titles. These era titles were used in dating events: thus the outbreak of the An Lu-shan rebellion occurred in the 'thirteenth year of the Heavenly Treasure era' and the Jürched sacked Kaifeng and carried the Chinese emperor into captivity in the era of Pacific Tranquillity. In the Ming and Qing dynasties it became the practice to have one era-name for the whole of the reign, as a consequence of which Chinese are in the habit of calling Ming and Qing emperors by the names of their eras. Strictly speaking we should say 'the Kangxi Emperor' or 'the Emperor of the Kangxi era', but it seems neater to follow Chinese colloquial practice. To avoid confusion, I later on refer to Kangxi's successor as 'Yongzheng' even before he became emperor, although this is really a solecism.

From time to time they would be given some special commission to execute, like purchasing foreign curios or supervising financial or cultural projects in which the Emperor had become interested. Cao Xueqin's grandfather, for whom the Emperor Kangxi seems to have had a real affection (he sent him little presents of the new wonder drug, quinine, and fussy notes telling him to look after himself when he was ill) was chosen to supervise the compiling and printing of the huge *Complete Poems of the Tang Dynasty*, comprising nearly fifty thousand poems by more than two thousand poets and still the standard work used by those studying the literature of the period.

Cao Yin acted as host to the Emperor and his vast retinue no less than four times when Kangxi visited Nanking in the course of his celebrated Southern Tours. This involved building a special palace with its own gardens in which to receive him – rather like the Separate Residence made for the Imperial Concubine's visit in the novel. There is a disguised reference to this in the conversation between Wang Xi-feng and Nannie Zhao in chapter 16.

A commissioner with two or three thousand persons in his employment, handling hundreds of thousands of silver taels a year and sending confidential reports to the Emperor in Peking was a rich and powerful person. Yet men like Cao Yin and his brother-in-law Li Xu, for all their power and magnificence, were still technically the Emperor's slaves and could be broken by him, immediately and totally, at his whim. Although in the novel the family are disguised as highborn aristocrats whose ancestors were ennobled for their military prowess, something of this terrible vulnerability comes through. Consider the family's anxiety, amounting to panic, when Jia Zheng is summoned to the Palace in chapter 16, or the cavalier way in which they are treated by the palace eunuchs. In chapter 18 the eunuchs, who are perfectly well aware when the Imperial Concubine will be arriving, allow the entire family, including its aged matriarch, to wait in the street from daybreak, not bothering to inform them, until forced to do so, that their visitor is unlikely to arrive before evening.

Cao Yin was fortunate in retaining the trust and affection of his Imperial master to the end of his life. He had in fact a combination of talents which fitted him almost ideally for his somewhat invidious role. A Manchu of the Manchus, he could ride and shoot with the best. Yet at the same time he was steeped in native Chinese culture. A passable poet, a connoisseur of fine art, a bibliophile, an amateur playwright who wrote a successful play, *From the Maw of the Tiger*, about the last days of the Ming dynasty, he was able to win the respect and, in a number of cases, the affection of the cultured Southern gentry, at this period by no means all reconciled to the foreign dynasty. The fall of the Bondservants in the next reign was at least partly due to the fact that the Manchus had themselves become more Chinesified and therefore more acceptable to the Chinese, with the result that these half-Chinese half-Manchu mediators had lost their function.

Under Cao Yin the Cao family attained the peak of its prosperity. The operations he was engaged in required a good deal of financial juggling however – juggling in which the other great Bondservant families played a part. (The court usher's talk in chapter 4 of the novel about the four great families of Jinling who stood or fell together is a fictionalized representation of this historical fact.) As long as the balls remained in the air all went well enough; but when Cao Yin died in 1712 he left a huge deficit behind him and only an inexperienced nineteen-year-old son to inherit it. It is an indication of Kangxi's deep regard for his old servant that he allowed Li Xu the means of paying off his deceased brother-in-law's debts for him and permitted the totally unqualified Cao Yong to inherit his father's post of Textile Commissioner in Nanking. Not only that, but when Cao Yong, to the utter dismay of the family, died only three years later, he allowed Cao Yin's nephew Cao Fu, a young man in his early twenties, to be adopted by old Lady Li as Cao Yin's posthumous 'son' and to succeed to the post of Textile Commissioner.

In spite of aid and advice from Li Xu (which may not, however, have been entirely disinterested) the Caos from this time on were in almost continuous trouble financially, and Kangxi's attitude of amused tolerance towards his youthful

Commissioners became at times a little strained. But the real troubles were to begin when Kangxi died in 1722.

The Emperor Yongzheng, who succeeded Kangxi, was an efficient but ruthless and vindictive autocrat. He disliked the Bondservants, suspecting them, with some justification, of dishonesty and incompetence. As informants he despised them, preferring his own highly organized army of secret agents; and as old servants of his father they were under suspicion of being well-disposed towards the princes whom his father had favoured: for Yongzheng had not been expected to succeed the old Emperor and had only done so by means of a *coup d'état*.

Of Kangxi's twenty sons it was the fourteenth, Yinti, hero of the Eleuth War and conqueror of Tibet, who was expected to succeed the old Emperor. Unfortunately he was away at the front when his father died, giving Yongzheng in Peking the chance to forestall him. Yet though he spent most of Yongzheng's reign in confinement, for some reason it was not on him but on the eighth and ninth brothers, Yinsi and Yintang, that the full weight of the Emperor's malice descended. Even their names were taken from them. Yinsi was renamed 'Acina', which in Manchu means 'Cur', and Yintang became 'Seshe' or 'Swine'.

Yongzheng did not at once proceed to extremes against his brothers. They had powerful supporters in the provinces and his doubtful accession made consolidation a necessity. But his dissatisfaction with the Bondservants showed itself immediately. The first to fall was Li Xu, now a man in his sixties. The post of Textile Commissioner in Soochow, which he had held for more than thirty years, was taken from him and his stewardship made the subject of an official inquiry which stripped him of most of his wealth. And though he emerged from his ordeal physically unscathed, he was not to remain at liberty for very long. To the Caos, who in the years since Cao Yin's death had depended on him so much, his fall must have come as a very great blow, and they must have wondered how long their own turn would be in coming.

The purge of the princes and their followers began less than three years later. In January 1726 Nian Gengyao, a high-ranking official who had played an important part in Yinti's Tibetan campaign but had subsequently been treated by Yongzheng with pretended favour, was suddenly degraded and impeached on ninety-two counts, some of them very trifling. He was believed to have been corresponding with Yintang (the Swine). Nian himself was allowed to commit suicide, but one of his sons was beheaded and the rest banished to the frontier.

Two months later the man who had succeeded Li Xu as Textile Commissioner in Soochow and who happened to be a brother-in-law of Nian Gengyao was dismissed from his post and his estate confiscated. He and his wife and concubine all hanged themselves.

Yinsi and Yintang, the unfortunate Cur and Swine, themselves both died in prison after months of sadistic maltreatment in September of this year.

In March of the following year (1727) Li Xu was arrested and imprisoned for the crime of having once offered Yinsi a present of Soochow sing-song girls. His fate is unknown, but it seems probable that he died in prison.

In January of 1728 (a grim New Year's present) Cao Fu and Sun Wencheng — the latter had been Textile Commissioner in Hangchow since 1706[7] — were both dismissed and their estates confiscated.

That these confiscations could be brutal and frightening affairs seems to be indicated by the frequency with which those who were subjected to this favourite punishment of Yongzheng's committed suicide. The victim's property would be surrounded in a surprise raid by the military, his senior servants would be carried off for questioning, and the house sealed and no one allowed in or out while the investigating officials ransacked it from top to bottom and wrote down their inventory of its contents.

Cao Fu's own dismissal does not appear to have been directly connected with the purge of the Princes' party, though a belated attempt was made to implicate him with it when the investigating officer discovered two gilt lions belonging to Yin-

7. Cao Yin's mother, the old lady who was once Kangxi's nurse, was a Sun and may have belonged to the same family.

tang in the Cao family temple. Cao Fu had been manifestly too young for his post and it was certainly more on the grounds of incompetence than anything else that he was dismissed in the first instance, whatever else may have emerged against him subsequently. Nevertheless it is important to remember that the dismissal occurred in the latter stages of a major political purge. For two years before the axe fell upon the Caos themselves heads had been falling to left and right of them, and the doom-laden atmosphere which from time to time obtrudes itself upon the innocent frivolities of the novel is not necessarily a literary device, but the faithful portrayal of a tension that was actually felt.

We know that the Caos had a house or houses in Peking which they were allowed to keep and that some of them moved to Peking after their Fall. We also know that there was a branch of the family that had been in Peking all along – including the three elder brothers of Cao Fu with whom he had always been on bad terms. The novel contains a number of passages in which poor relations are humiliated by their more fortunate kinsmen, as for example Jia Yun's treatment in chapter 24 at the hands of his uncle Bu Shi-ren (a name that could be roughly anglicized as Mr Hardleigh Hewmann). In commenting on such passages Red Inkstone darkly observes that only those who have experienced this kind of thing can possibly know how bad it is; so it seems safe to assume that the Nanking Caos met with some sort of rebuff from their relations at the capital. The latter may, in any case, have felt that Yongzheng's victims were too dangerous to help. The fact of the matter is, however, that we simply do not know. Having become 'unpersons', the Caos now disappear almost completely from the records.

There is no doubt about Cao Xueqin's intention of making the history of his own family's decline and fall the general background of the novel; but the exact relationship existing between the characters of the novel and the various members of the Cao family is much less certain. Some scholars like Zhou Ruchang have striven to establish a precise parallelism between the two, but the case for this is extremely flimsy. The commentaries establish beyond doubt that many of the characters are portraits of real people, but it does not follow that the re-lationships between the different characters in the novel were those of the people in real life whom they represent. All the evidence goes to show that Xueqin deliberately mixed the generations up as a means of disguising the facts. We know, for example, that one of Cao Yin's daughters who married the Manchu prince Nersu was probably the model for the Imperial Concubine (her up-grading in the novel is typical); and the Manchu Yurui expressly says that Bao-yu's 'sisters' were really portraits of the author's aunts.

In any attempt to relate the characters and events of the novel to the persons and events of Xueqin's childhood the identification of the novel's main character, Bao-yu, is crucial. Bao-yu is an almost clinical picture[8] of the kind of child whom old ladies refer to in lowered voices as 'a very strange little boy'. Yet for all the portrait's objectiveness, the struggle towards emotional maturity is recorded with such a wealth of detail and understanding that it is hard to believe that the inner side at least of the character is not a chronicle of the author's own experience. It used, in fact, until quite recently, to be assumed as a matter of course that Bao-yu was a self-portrait of the author. But this assumption naturally raises the other question: who was Xueqin?

The likeliest hypothesis until recently (or so it seemed to me) was that Cao Xueqin was the posthumous child of Cao Yin's only son Cao Yong – the young man who inherited Cao Yin's place as Textile Commissioner and died only three years later. It is known from the archives that Cao Yong's wife was seven months pregnant when he died. Assuming that the child was a boy and survived, he would have been just thirteen in 1728 when the big crash came – the age of Bao-yu throughout quite a large section of the novel.

8. Xueqin's eighteenth century insights can be quite startling. Consider this passage from chapter 3:

' "None of the girls has got one," said Bao-yu, his face streaming with tears and sobbing hysterically. "Only I have got one. It always upsets me. And now this new cousin comes here who is as beautiful as an angel and she hasn't got one either, so I *know* it can't be any good." '

I do not think the fact that he is actually referring to his jade talisman makes this passage psychologically any the less interesting.

Admittedly Cao Xueqin is known to have had a younger brother, and Cao Yong's posthumous child could only have had one in the – in those days – highly improbable event of his mother's remarriage. But the Chinese word for 'brother' can also be used to indicate the sons of paternal uncles, so the objection is not an insuperable one. Another objection might be that in the novel *both* Bao-yu's parents are living. But then how puzzling is Bao-yu's relationship with those parents! He lives not with them but with his Grannie; and although they all inhabit the same mansion, whole weeks seem to go by without his seeing his father Jia Zheng at all.

If Cao Xueqin was really Cao Yong's posthumous child, it would be quite natural for him to live with Grannie and quite natural for Grannie, who had lost her husband and her only son within a few years of each other, to dote upon this last male survivor of the line as her 'precious jewel' (which is what 'Bao-yu' means) and to look with indifference, if not positive resentment, on Cao Fu, her adopted 'son' by Imperial fiat, who had inherited the business and usurped the position of her darling boy. Equally, it would be quite natural for Cao Fu to look upon Cao Xueqin as a spoilt little brat in need of a good hiding – which is precisely Jia Zheng's attitude towards Bao-yu in the novel – and to feel terrified of the consequences when he at last succeeded in giving him one and Grannie, as a reprisal, threatened to withdraw her patronage.

As for 'the girls', they would be the unmarried daughters of Cao Yin, probably still spry enough in his sixties to have fathered one or two children on his concubines. In the novel two out of the Three Springs are in fact concubine's children, and Grandmother Jia's somewhat casual treatment of this luckless trio would be a reflection of Grannie Cao's attitude to her husband's daughters by another woman.

Unfortunately for this splendid theory, a clan register of the Liaodong branch of the Cao family came to light in Peking a few years ago which, if it is genuine, makes it clear that Cao Yong's posthumous son was *not* Cao Xueqin but a person called Cao Tianyou, who at one period during his life held a small government appointment.

Turning for enlightenment to Red Inkstone's commentary,

we find that it abounds in what appear to be clues to Xueqin's paternity, if only we knew how to use them. He is constantly telling us of experiences that he shared with the author or with Bao-yu or with both – for example, when he says of a passage in which Bao-yu is shown in a particularly unflattering light: 'I felt quite angry with the author when I first read this, but then I realized that in this instance he was probably talking about himself'; or when he apostrophizes the author in connection with a passage in chapter 8 in which Grandmother Jia gives a First Meeting present to Bao-yu's schoolboy friend Qin Zhong (evidently modelled on a real person): 'Do you still remember about that little gold charm? Objects bring back their memories. You tear my heart!' It seems from this highly probable that Red Inkstone was about the same age as Cao Xueqin and that the two of them went to school together. If the relationship between the two of them was so close, clearly the problem of identifying one will be closely bound up with the problem of the other one's identity.

One of the difficulties of identifying Red Inkstone is the question of 'Odd Tablet'. This is a signature which begins to replace that of Red Inkstone on comments dating from a year or two before Cao Xueqin's death. All the latest signed comments are Odd Tablet ones. The full signature is 'Old Man Odd Tablet' or 'Old Odd Tablet'. Sometimes he refers to himself as 'The Old Crock' or 'Old Useless'.

Until recently it was widely believed that Red Inkstone and Odd Tablet were one and the same person. Odd Tablet shows the same familiarity with the author and his family affairs; he writes in pretty much the same style; he refers to Red Inkstone comments of an earlier date much as if he had written them himself. It was assumed by those who believed them to be the same person that Red Inkstone had at some stage begun to feel his age and decided on a change of pseudonym. There were certain difficulties about this. The 'Old Man' part of the signature presented peculiar difficulties to those like Zhou Ruchang who thought that Red Inkstone was a lady, and 'Old Crock' suggested an advanced stage of decrepitude which seemed unlikely in one whose commentary at times made him appear no older than the author. But people *do* gives themselves peculiar pseudonyms, and these difficulties were not as a rule felt to be insuperable.

Then a new Red Inkstone manuscript turned up in the possession of an old Manchu family in Nanking. Unfortunately it very soon disappeared again; but in the interim it had been seen and described by an expert, who copied out and published a number of the more important-looking comments. If we accept his testimony, we are obliged to admit that Red Inkstone and Odd Tablet *must* be two people. The evidence consists of two parts:

(1) The first section of chapter 1 ends with the following quatrain:

> Pages full of idle words
> Penned with hot and bitter tears:
> All men call the author fool;
> None his secret message hears.

The Red Inkstone manuscript discovered in 1927 contains the following comment on these verses in the upper margin above them:

Only one who understood the secret message of this book *could* have the hot and bitter tears with which to finish it. Xueqin, having run out of tears, departed this life on the last day of *ren-wu* (12 February 1763) leaving his book unfinished. I have wept so much for Xueqin that I fear I too shall soon run out of tears. I often wish that I could find where that Greensickness Peak is so that I could ask Brother Stone about his story. What a pity there is no scabby-headed monk to take me there! If only the Creator would produce another Xueqin and another Red Inkstone to complete this book, how happy the two of us would be, down there together in the World of Shades!

> Written in tears,
> eighth month of *jia-wu* (September 1774)

This used to be one of the most important bits of evidence in support of the view that Red Inkstone and Odd Tablet were the same person, since it seemed to show that Red Inkstone survived Xueqin by many years and continued to comment on the manuscript during all the years that Odd Tablet was doing so. But the recently-discovered Nanking manuscript gave the date of this comment not as *jia-wu* but as *jia-shen* (the characters for *wu* and *shen* are not greatly dissimilar when written in a cursive hand) – i.e. not as 1774 but as 1764, only a year and a half after Xueqin's death.

(2) On a passage in chapter 22 in which Xi-feng is shown choosing plays, a manuscript which first came to light in the thirties has two rather cryptic comments by Odd Tablet, evidently written at some interval of time. The first says:

> Re Xi-feng choosing plays, Red Inkstone doing the writing, etc.: not many of us still left who know about this. Alas!

(Odd Tablet has a great weakness for mournful expletives.) The second says:

> Last time I read through this section I wrote "not many of us still left who know about this". Now – Summer, *ding-hai* (1767) – this Old Crock is the only one surviving. A painful thought!

In the newly-found Nanking manuscript the second of these comments was found in a much expanded form:

> Last time I read through this section I wrote "not many of us still left who know about this". Since then, in only a few years, Xueqin, Red Inkstone and Almond have all successively passed on, leaving – Summer, *ding-hai* – this Old Crock as the only survivor. A painful thought!

Putting these two bits of new evidence together, it now looks as if Red Inkstone must have died some time between 1764 and 1767, only a year or two after Xueqin – as he seems himself to have predicted.

Zhiyanzhai, the Chinese name I have translated 'Red Inkstone', strictly speaking means 'Carmine Inkstone' or 'Rouge Inkstone', *zhi* being the name of the unguent which Chinese ladies once used for reddening their cheeks and lips with. There have been many theories about the significance of this pseudonym. Those who favoured a female commentator thought it an appropriate one for a lady. Those who favoured a male one thought it just the kind of pseudonym that an *homme galant* would choose (dashing off a comment or two with a lady's lipstick, perhaps, in between sips of champagne from her slipper).

Zhao Gang, however, has demonstrated that 'Carmine Inkstone' was probably the name of a greatly prized antique inkstone belonging to Cao Yin. As a family heirloom it would have passed successively to his son Cao Yong, and, after Cao Yong's death, to his grandson Cao Tianyou. The latter might well have salvaged some such tiny treasure from the ruin of his house and clung to it when all else was lost. And that he should have called himself 'the Master of the Red Inkstone' in later life would seem reasonable enough, seeing that he was master of very little else. In short Zhao Gang believes that Red Inkstone was Cao Yong's posthumous son Cao Tianyou, from which it would follow by a simple process of deduction that Xueqin must almost certainly have been the son of Cao Fu, that nephew of Cao Yin's who became his posthumously adopted son after Cao Yong's death.

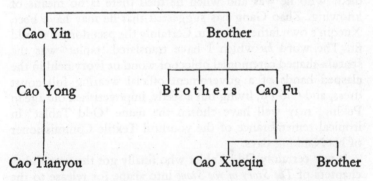

As a child Cao Xueqin's given name was not 'Xueqin' but 'Zhan', which means 'favour'. 'Tianyou' – Red Inkstone's name – means 'Heaven succours us'. It seems highly probable that just as Tianyou's name records the gratitude of Cao Yin's family for the birth of a male child to carry on the line after the death of its only heir, so Cao Zhan's name records Cao Fu's gratitude for the imperial favour which made him Cao Yin's heir and allowed him to succeed his cousin as Textile Commissioner in Nanking.

Bao-yu, then, as I think Wu Shichang was the first to point out, must be a composite portrait. It is a portrait based partly on the author himself and partly on his cousin and brother-by-adoption, Cao Tianyou.[9] Born in the same year, brought up in the same household and dying only a couple of years after him, it is scarcely surprising that Red Inkstone should seem so knowing both about the author and about his character Bao-yu, when so often he is commenting on a shared experience. It was he who made the fair copies of Xueqin's drafts – much as a friend or relation might type someone's manuscript for him today – reading through them afterwards and noting down comments, queries and suggestions to be discussed later by Xueqin, Xueqin's younger brother and the other members of the little family group who were privy to the great enterprise.

One member – clearly a somewhat older one – of this little group was Odd Tablet, and it was he who carried on the work of editing, annotating and recopying after Red Inkstone had died. Who he was and when he died there is no means of knowing. Zhao Gang has suggested that he may have been Xueqin's own father, Cao Fu. Certainly the pseudonym would fit. The word *hu* which I have translated 'tablet' was the spatula-shaped ceremonial object of wood or ivory held in the clasped hands of a government official wearing full court dress, and Cao Fu, living out a seedy, impoverished old age in Peking, may well have chosen the name 'Odd Tablet' in ironical remembrance of the youthful Textile Commissioner of his Nanking days.

It was certainly Odd Tablet who finally got the first eighty chapters of *The Story of the Stone* into shape for release to the public. By the end of the sixties manuscript copies were already coming onto the book market; and though they were still entitled *Red Inkstone's Reannotated Story of the Stone*, Red Inkstone had by then been dead for some years and the title was preserved merely out of respect for his memory. Odd Tablet himself preferred the title *A Dream of Red Mansions* and used this title at the head of his 'Advice to the Reader' which follows the title page. Some very late manuscripts may even have borne the *Dream* title on their title page as well.

[9] Mr Wu in fact identified Red Inkstone with one of Xueqin's uncles, but he also made the important point that Bao-yu is a composite of Xueqin and Red Inkstone.

Why did none of the Red Inkstone manuscripts go beyond the novel's eightieth chapter? It used to be assumed that Cao Xueqin died before he had time to write any more, but all the evidence is against this. All the evidence suggests that he finished the novel long before he died and was merely revising and correcting during his final years. It was the revising and the filling in of various missing bits, particularly poems, which was unfinished at his death. In the manuscript copy of chapter 22 the last page or two is missing and there is a marginal note by Red Inkstone explaining that the pages had got torn off and lost and that he was waiting for Xueqin to supply him with fresh copy. This is followed by a separate sheet which contains, among other things, the following comment:

Xueqin died before this chapter could be completed. Alas! Summer, 1767. Old Odd Tablet.

Clearly 'unfinished' can mean rather different things. Dying before you have rewritten a lost page is rather a different sort of 'unfinished' from dying before you have got to the end of your book.

That the unfinished state of the novel was to some extent due to the almost insane carelessness with which Xueqin's manuscripts were treated is shown by the following comment on a passage in chapter 20:

Snowpink comes into the story again in the section about the Temple of the Prison God. This side of Aroma's nature was developed in the later chapter 'Aroma is Determined to See Things Through'. I only saw it once, when I was making the fair copy. That and five or six other chapters, including 'A Sympathizer Consoles Bao-yu in the Temple of the Prison God' were all lost by someone who borrowed the manuscript to read.

Presumably it would not have been beyond the competence of Odd Tablet to patch up the remaining drafts somehow or other and present the small and select public who were reading the novel in manuscript with the ending they so much longed to see. That he did not do so may have been due to the fact that he was deliberately suppressing it.

There would have been a good reason for this. From clues

found in the commentaries and in the text itself, we can tell that Xueqin's dénouement must have been far more harrowing than the somewhat bland ending the novel is given in Gao E's version; and even though it could not conceivably have contained overt criticism of the Emperor who ordered the family's downfall, a sensitive autocrat might well see implied criticism in a too harrowing description of the hardships attendant on a confiscation. It was precisely during the seventies and eighties of the century – the interval between the author's death and the appearance of the novel's first printed edition – that the prolonged literary witch-hunt occurred which is generally referred to as 'Qianlong's Literary Inquisition'. During this period many an author had his writings burned and his bones disinterred for much less than Cao Xueqin had written.

The notion that anyone could ever have thought of the *Stone* as seditious may strike the modern reader as fanciful; but there is good contemporary evidence that the novel *was* regarded as potentially dangerous. The following is a marginal comment written by the poet's uncle above a set of *In Memoriam* poems about Xueqin in a book by the Manchu poet Yongzhong (1735–93):

> The poems are excellent: but I have no wish to read this 'Dream of Red Mansions'. It is an unpublished novel which might, I fear, contain indiscretions.

Whoever wrote the last forty chapters of Gao E's version was taking no chances. It ends amidst almost deafening praises of the Emperor's clemency.

Who was this person?

At first sight Odd Tablet seems the obvious guess. It was he who took over sole responsibility for the novel after Red Inkstone's death. It was he who prepared the first eighty chapters for the public. He had, as we shall see later, seen fit to subvert the author's intentions on at least one occasion during his lifetime. We know that he preferred *Hong lou meng* as a title, and that was the title which appeared on a 120-chapter manuscript version supposed to have been seen in 1790 and on Gao E's 120-chapter edition of 1792.

The drawback about this theory is that before undergoing Gao E's editing, the manuscript of the last forty chapters appears to have contained many features which imply ignorance of Xueqin's later revisions and Red Inkstone and Odd Tablet's later editorial changes. In other words, in order to believe that Odd Tablet wrote the last forty chapters, you would have to assume that he deliberately ignored his own work on the first eighty, which is clearly an impossibility.

My own guess is that there is an illiterate Manchu widow somewhere at the bottom of this mystery – either Red Inkstone's or Odd Tablet's, or (much more likely) Cao Xueqin's 'new wife'. She had this hoard of ageing manuscripts which she asked some male relation or family friend to 'do something with', and the result, a pretty botched job by all accounts, was the manuscript which Cheng Weiyuan bought and Gao E was asked to edit. And Gao E's job, as a conscientious scholar, was to bring the text of this newly discovered last third of the book into line with the text of the Red Inkstone manuscript he used for the first eighty chapters. A brief study of the pains he took over this exasperating task at once reveals how little he deserved those decades of execration as 'liar' and 'cheat'.[10]

But the problem of inconsistency which preoccupied Gao E and continues to trouble translators is by no means all due to the anonymous author of the last forty chapters. Cao Xueqin himself must be held responsible for quite a few of the novel's minor inconsistencies. This is partly due to the elaborate devices he used for disguising the facts of his family history – switching generations, substituting Peking for Nanking, and so forth – which make him peculiarly susceptible to slips about ages, dates, places, and the passage of time. As regards place, for example: the novel is quite obviously set in Peking. The interiors with their 'kangs'[11] are clearly Nor-

10. A clearer impression of the nature of Gao E's work on this novel has become possible since the publication in Peking in 1963 of a much-corrected draft which he evidently used at some stage in his preparation of the first printed edition.

11. The kang was a brick platform, often carpeted and cushioned and furnished with low tables and other small furniture, which could be

thern. The Imperial Palace is near at hand. There are even one or two Peking street-names scattered about the novel. Yet in chapter 4 the family are 'the Nanking Jia' and in chapter 5 the young ladies of the household are referred to as the 'Twelve Beauties of Jinling' (Jinling is an old name for Nanking), even though elsewhere in the novel Nanking is 'down South' and people travel on long journeys from or to it. As regards ages and dates – indeed, almost anything at all in which numbers are involved – Xueqin is a translator's despair, probably, I suspect, because he was just not very good at figures – the sort of person who can never count his change.

These minor inconsistencies, which probably give trouble only to Chinese scholars and English translators and are not even noticed by the majority of readers, result mainly from a clash between the remembered fact and the demands of fiction. But the novel contains another kind of inconsistency which came about in quite a different way. I shall demonstrate it with the most notable example.

Qin-shi, the little wife of Cousin Zhen's son Jia Rong, is apparently a character modelled on a real person. From the words spoken by the drunken retainer in chapter 7 and from Cousin Zhen's extraordinary behaviour after her death in chapter 13, it appears that she was involved in an incestuous liaison with her father-in-law. In chapter 5 both the riddle and painting about her in the *Twelve Beauties of Jinling* album and the song about her in the *Dream of Golden Days* song-cycle imply that she hanged herself when her adultery with Cousin Zhen was discovered. Yet in all extant versions of the novel, including all the manuscripts, Qin-shi dies in her bed after a mysterious illness.

The explanation of this inconsistency is found in a note by Odd Tablet at the end of chapter 13 in one of the manuscripts, in which he says that he 'ordered' Xueqin to excise a passage of eight or nine pages describing Qin-shi's suicide in the Celestial Fragrance Pavilion – presumably because he found it too upsetting.

It would be naïve to suppose that Xueqin simply overlooked

heated from underneath in winter. It provided a place to work, lounge or eat on during the daytime and a place to sleep on at night.

the discrepancy. It is much more likely that he made the alteration in chapter 13 very unwillingly and carried it out in a half-hearted manner and that his failure to make the necessary adjustments in chapter 5 was deliberate. If, as Zhao Gang has suggested, Odd Tablet was Xueqin's own father Cao Fu, the unfinished state in which Xueqin left the novel may well have been due to the despair he felt at not being allowed to publish it and instead being repeatedly ordered to rewrite and alter it in ways he knew in his bones to be artistically wrong.

But for all the little hair-cracks that the scholar's magnifying-glass reveals, The Story of the Stone is an amazing achievement and the psychological insight and sophisticated humour with which it is written can often delude a reader into judging it as if it were a modern novel. In fact neither the idea that fiction can be created out of the author's own experience, nor the idea that it can be concerned as much with inner experience – with motives, attitudes and feelings – as with outward events, both of which are a commonplace with us, had been so much as dreamed of in Xueqin's day. His numerous re-writings and the various mythopoeic 'devices' with which his novel is littered all testify to his struggle to find some sort of framework on which to arrange his inchoate material. At one point, so Red Inkstone tells us, he even thought of aban-doning the traditional romance-form altogether[12] and writing a verse drama instead. Certainly he was influenced much more by the techniques of drama (which he loved) and painting (which he practised)[13] than by any of the pre-existing works of Chinese prose fiction, which on the whole he rather des-pised.

Tang Xianzu of Linchuan, the great playwright of the

12. The extremely superficial nature of Xueqin's use of this form – one based on the methods of the professional story-teller, with each chapter arranged in imitation of the storyteller's 'session' to end at a point of suspense – can be judged from his statement in chapter 1 that the division into chapters and the composition of chapter-headings took place *after the novel had been completed*. In some manuscripts chapters 17 and 18 are in fact still undivided.

13. This is not only my opinion. Red Inkstone constantly makes use of the technical vocabulary of Chinese painting in discussing the novel and insists that Xueqin's technique as a novelist is essentially a painterly one.

poetical, romantic drama of the sixteenth century in which Cao
Xueqin was steeped, was, like Xueqin, preoccupied with the
interplay between dream and reality. His four most famous
plays are often referred to as 'Linchuan's Four Dreams'.
We may be sure that Xueqin's play, if he had written it, would
have been called 'A Dream of Red Mansions'. It is even
possible that the 'Dream of Golden Days' song-cycle in
chapter 5 was written at a time when he was still toying with
the idea of writing a play.

As regards the various 'devices' which Xueqin employs
for converting remembered fact into artistic fiction, one he
makes persistent use of throughout the novel is the antinomy
of *zhen* and *jia*, meaning respectively 'real' and 'imaginary',
but both regarded by Xueqin as being different parts of a
single underlying Reality:

> *Jia zuo zhen shi zhen yi jia*
> *Wu wei you chu you huan wu*
> Truth becomes fiction when the fiction's true
> Real becomes not-real when the unreal's real

is the inscription written up over the gateway to the Land of
Illusion which we pass through at the beginning of the novel.

'Jia', the surname of the family in the novel, looks, in
Chinese script, a little bit like the character for Cao; but it is
also a pun on this other *jia* which means 'fictitious'. The Jias
of the novel are connected in various ways with a mysterious
family in Nanking called the Zhens – another word-play –
who are a sort of mirror-reflection of the Jia family. There is
even a Zhen Bao-yu. One day Bao-yu has a dream about him
from which he wakes up in tears calling out 'Come back,
Bao-yu! Come back, Bao-yu!' and finds himself looking at his
own reflection in the dressing-mirror beside his bed.

A Mirror for the Romantic was, as we have seen already, one
of the titles once considered for the novel by Xueqin and his
family. It appears from Red Inkstone's commentary that this
was in fact the name of an earlier, probably much shorter
draft of the novel which Xueqin subsequently discarded.
Parts of it may be incorporated in the novel as it is today, like
the Jia Rui episode in chapter 12 in which the magic mirror

makes its appearance and which still, on close inspection, shows signs of tailoring. It is easy to imagine that many of the *Stone*'s 'devices' had their genesis at this stage: the presentation of fiction and reality or reality and illusion or the waking world and the dreaming world as opposite sides of a sort of single super-reality, for example – like the two worlds one on each side of the mirror.

The idea that the worldling's 'reality' is illusion and that life itself is a dream from which we shall eventually awake is of course a Buddhist one; but in Xueqin's hands it becomes a poetical means of demonstrating that his characters are both creatures of his imagination and at the same time the real companions of his golden youth. To that extent it can be thought of as a literary device rather than as a deeply held philosophy, though it is really both.

Such devices play a functional part in the structure of the novel; but many of the symbols, word-plays and secret patterns with which the novel abounds seem to be used out of sheer ebullience, as though the author was playing some sort of game with himself and did not much care whether he was observed or not. Chinese devotees of the novel often continue to read and reread it throughout their lives and to discover more of these little private jokes each time they read it. Many such subtleties will, I fear, have vanished in translation. Alas! – as Odd Tablet would have said.

One bit of imagery which *Stone*-enthusiasts will miss in my translation is the pervading *redness* of the Chinese novel. One of its Chinese titles is red, to begin with, and red as a symbol – sometimes of spring, sometimes of youth, sometimes of good fortune or prosperity – recurs again and again throughout it. Unfortunately – apart from the rosy cheeks and vermeil lip of youth – redness has no such connotations in English and I have found that the Chinese reds have tended to turn into English golds or greens ('spring the green spring' and 'golden girls and boys' and so forth). I am aware that there is some sort of loss here, but have lacked the ingenuity to avert it.

In translating this novel I have felt unable to stick faithfully to any single text. I have mainly followed Gao E's version of the first chapter as being more consistent, though less interesting, than the other ones; but I have frequently followed a manuscript reading in subsequent chapters, and in a few, rare instances I have made small emendations of my own. My one abiding principle has been to translate *everything* – even puns. For although this is, in the sense I have already indicated, an 'unfinished' novel, it was written (and rewritten) by a great artist with his very lifeblood. I have therefore assumed that whatever I find in it is there for a purpose and must be dealt with somehow or other. I cannot pretend always to have done so successfully, but if I can convey to the reader even a fraction of the pleasure this Chinese novel has given me, I shall not have lived in vain.

DAVID HAWKES

CHAPTER I

Zhen Shi-yin makes the Stone's
acquaintance in a dream
And Jia Yu-cun finds that poverty is not incompatible
with romantic feelings

GENTLE READER,

What, you may ask, was the origin of this book?

Though the answer to this question may at first seem to border on the absurd, reflection will show that there is a good deal more in it than meets the eye.

Long ago, when the goddess Nü-wa was repairing the sky, she melted down a great quantity of rock and, on the Incredible Crags of the Great Fable Mountains, moulded the amalgam into thirty-six thousand, five hundred and one large building blocks, each measuring seventy-two feet by a hundred and forty-four feet square. She used thirty-six thousand five hundred of these blocks in the course of her building operations, leaving a single odd block unused, which lay, all on its own, at the foot of Greensickness Peak in the aforementioned mountains.

Now this block of stone, having undergone the melting and moulding of a goddess, possessed magic powers. It could move about at will and could grow or shrink to any size it wanted. Observing that all the other blocks had been used for celestial repairs and that it was the only one to have been rejected as unworthy, it became filled with shame and resentment and passed its days in sorrow and lamentation.

One day, in the midst of its lamentings, it saw a monk and a Taoist approaching from a great distance, each of them remarkable for certain eccentricities of manner and appearance. When they arrived at the foot of Greensickness Peak, they sat down on the ground and began to talk. The monk, catching sight of a lustrous, translucent stone – it was in fact the rejected building block which had now shrunk itself to the

size of a fan-pendant and looked very attractive in its new
shape – took it up on the palm of his hand and addressed it
with a smile:

'Ha, I see you have magical properties! But nothing to
recommend you. I shall have to cut a few words on you so that
anyone seeing you will know at once that you are something
special. After that I shall take you to a certain

> brilliant
> successful
> poetical
> cultivated
> aristocratic
> elegant
> delectable
> luxurious
> opulent
> locality on a little trip'.

The stone was delighted.

'What words will you cut? Where is this place you will
take me to? I beg to be enlightened.'

'Do not ask,' replied the monk with a laugh. 'You will know
soon enough when the time comes.'

And with that he slipped the stone into his sleeve and set off
at a great pace with the Taoist. But where they both went to
I have no idea.

*

Countless aeons went by and a certain Taoist called Vanitas
in quest of the secret of immortality chanced to be passing
below that same Greensickness Peak in the Incredible Crags of
the Great Fable Mountains when he caught sight of a large
stone standing there, on which the characters of a long inscription were clearly discernible.

Vanitas read the inscription through from beginning to end
and learned that this was a once lifeless stone block which had
been found unworthy to repair the sky, but which had magi-
cally transformed its shape and been taken down by the
Buddhist mahāsattva Impervioso and the Taoist illuminate
Mysterioso into the world of mortals, where it had lived

out the life of a man before finally attaining nirvana and returning to the other shore. The inscription named the
country where it had been born, and went into considerable
detail about its domestic life, youthful amours, and even the
verses, mottoes and riddles it had written. All it lacked was the
authentication of a dynasty and date. On the back of the stone
was inscribed the following quatrain:

> Found unfit to repair the azure sky
> Long years a foolish mortal man was I.
> My life in both worlds on this stone is writ:
> Pray who will copy out and publish it?

From his reading of the inscription Vanitas realized that this
was a stone of some consequence. Accordingly he addressed
himself to it in the following manner:

'Brother Stone, according to what you yourself seem to
imply in these verses, this story of yours contains matter of
sufficient interest to merit publication and has been carved
here with that end in view. But as far as I can see (a) it has no
discoverable dynastic period, and (b) it contains no examples
of moral grandeur among its characters – no statesmanship,
no social message of any kind. All I can find in it, in fact, are
a number of females, conspicuous, if at all, only for their
passion or folly or for some trifling talent or insignificant
virtue. Even if I were to copy all this out, I cannot see that it
would make a very remarkable book.'

'Come, your reverence,' said the stone (for Vanitas had been
correct in assuming that it could speak) 'must you be so
obtuse? All the romances ever written have an artificial
period setting – Han or Tang for the most part. In refusing to
make use of that stale old convention and telling my *Story of
the Stone* exactly as it occurred, it seems to me that, far from
depriving it of anything, I have given it a freshness these other
books do not have.

'Your so-called "historical romances", consisting, as they
do, of scandalous anecdotes about statesmen and emperors of
bygone days and scabrous attacks on the reputations of long-
dead gentlewomen, contain more wickedness and immorality
than I care to mention. Still worse is the "erotic novel", by

whose filthy obscenities our young folk are all too easily corrupted. And the "boudoir romances", those dreary stereotypes with their volume after volume all pitched on the same note and their different characters undistinguishable except by name (all those ideally beautiful young ladies and ideally eligible young bachelors) – even they seem unable to avoid descending sooner or later into indecency.

'The trouble with this last kind of romance is that it only gets written in the first place because the author requires a framework in which to show off his love-poems. He goes about constructing this framework quite mechanically, beginning with the names of his pair of young lovers and invariably adding a third character, a servant or the like, to make mischief between them, like the *chou* in a comedy.

'What makes these romances even more detestable is the stilted, bombastic language – inanities dressed in pompous rhetoric, remote alike from nature and common sense and teeming with the grossest absurdities.

'Surely my "number of females", whom I spent half a lifetime studying with my own eyes and ears, are preferable to this kind of stuff? I do not claim that they are better people than the ones who appear in books written before my time; I am only saying that the contemplation of their actions and motives may prove a more effective antidote to boredom and melancholy. And even the inelegant verses with which my story is interlarded could serve to entertain and amuse on those convivial occasions when rhymes and riddles are in demand.

'All that my story narrates, the meetings and partings, the joys and sorrows, the ups and downs of fortune, are recorded exactly as they happened. I have not dared to add the tiniest bit of touching-up, for fear of losing the true picture.

'My only wish is that men in the world below may sometimes pick up this tale when they are recovering from sleep or drunkenness, or when they wish to escape from business worries or a fit of the dumps, and in doing so find not only mental refreshment but even perhaps, if they will heed its lesson and abandon their vain and frivolous pursuits, some small arrest in the deterioration of their vital forces. What does your reverence say to that?'

For a long time Vanitas stood lost in thought, pondering this speech. He then subjected the *Story of the Stone* to a careful second reading. He could see that its main theme was love; that it consisted quite simply of a true record of real events; and that it was entirely free from any tendency to deprave and corrupt. He therefore copied it all out from beginning to end and took it back with him to look for a publisher.

As a consequence of all this, Vanitas, starting off in the Void (which is Truth) came to the contemplation of Form (which is Illusion); and from Form engendered Passion; and by communicating Passion, entered again into Form; and from Form awoke to the Void (which is Truth). He therefore changed his name from Vanitas to Brother Amor, or the Passionate Monk, (because he had approached Truth by way of Passion), and changed the title of the book from *The Story of the Stone* to *The Tale of Brother Amor*.

Old Kong Mei-xi from the homeland of Confucius called the book *A Mirror for the Romantic*. Wu Yu-feng called it *A Dream of Golden Days*. Cao Xueqin in his Nostalgia Studio worked on it for ten years, in the course of which he rewrote it no less than five times, dividing it into chapters, composing chapter headings, renaming it *The Twelve Beauties of Jinling*, and adding an introductory quatrain. Red Inkstone restored the original title when he recopied the book and added his second set of annotations to it.

This, then, is a true account of how *The Story of the Stone* came to be written.

> Pages full of idle words
> Penned with hot and bitter tears:
> All men call the author fool;
> None his secret message hears.

*

The origin of *The Story of the Stone* has now been made clear. The same cannot, however, be said of the characters and events which it recorded. Gentle reader, have patience! This is how the inscription began:

Long, long ago the world was tilted downwards towards the south-east; and in that lower-lying south-easterly part of the earth there is a city called Soochow; and in Soochow the district around the Chang-men Gate is reckoned one of the two or three wealthiest and most fashionable quarters in the world of men. Outside the Chang-men Gate is a wide thoroughfare called Worldly Way; and somewhere off Worldly Way is an area called Carnal Lane. There is an old temple in the Carnal Lane area which, because of the way it is bottled up inside a narrow *cul-de-sac*, is referred to locally as Bottle-gourd Temple. Next door to Bottle-gourd Temple lived a gentleman of private means called Zhen Shi-yin and his wife Feng-shi, a kind, good woman with a profound sense of decency and decorum. The household was not a particularly wealthy one, but they were nevertheless looked up to by all and sundry as the leading family in the neighbourhood.

Zhen Shi-yin himself was by nature a quiet and totally unambitious person. He devoted his time to his garden and to the pleasures of wine and poetry. Except for a single flaw, his existence could, indeed, have been described as an idyllic one. The flaw was that, although already past fifty, he had no son, only a little girl, just two years old, whose name was Ying-lian.

Once, during the tedium of a burning summer's day, Shi-yin was sitting idly in his study. The book had slipped from his nerveless grasp and his head had nodded down onto the desk in a doze. While in this drowsy state he seemed to drift off to some place he could not identify, where he became aware of a monk and a Taoist walking along and talking as they went.

'Where do you intend to take that thing you are carrying?' the Taoist was asking.

'Don't you worry about him!' replied the monk with a laugh. 'There is a batch of lovesick souls awaiting incarnation in the world below whose fate is due to be decided this very day. I intend to take advantage of this opportunity to slip our little friend in amongst them and let him have a taste of human life along with the rest.'

'Well, well, so another lot of these amorous wretches is about to enter the vale of tears,' said the Taoist. 'How did all this begin? And where are the souls to be reborn?'

'You will laugh when I tell you,' said the monk. 'When this stone was left unused by the goddess, he found himself at a loose end and took to wandering about all over the place for want of better to do, until one day his wanderings took him to the place where the fairy Disenchantment lives.

'Now Disenchantment could tell that there was something unusual about this stone, so she kept him there in her Sunset Glow Palace and gave him the honorary title of Divine Luminescent Stone-in-Waiting in the Court of Sunset Glow.

'But most of his time he spent west of Sunset Glow exploring the banks of the Magic River. There, by the Rock of Rebirth, he found the beautiful Crimson Pearl Flower, for which he conceived such a fancy that he took to watering her every day with sweet dew, thereby conferring on her the gift of life.

'Crimson Pearl's substance was composed of the purest cosmic essences, so she was already half-divine; and now, thanks to the vitalizing effect of the sweet dew, she was able to shed her vegetable shape and assume the form of a girl.

'This fairy girl wandered about outside the Realm of Separation, eating the Secret Passion Fruit when she was hungry and drinking from the Pool of Sadness when she was thirsty. The consciousness that she owed the stone something for his kindness in watering her began to prey on her mind and ended by becoming an obsession.

' "I have no sweet dew here that I can repay him with," she would say to herself. "The only way in which I could perhaps repay him would be with the tears shed during the whole of a mortal lifetime if he and I were ever to be reborn as humans in the world below."

'Because of this strange affair, Disenchantment has got together a group of amorous young souls, of which Crimson Pearl is one, and intends to send them down into the world to take part in the great illusion of human life. And as to-day happens to be the day on which this stone is fated to go into the world too, I am taking him with me to Disenchantment's tribunal for the purpose of getting him registered and sent down to earth with the rest of these romantic creatures.'

'How very amusing!' said the Taoist. 'I have certainly never heard of a debt of tears before. Why shouldn't the two of us take advantage of this opportunity to go down into the world ourselves and save a few souls? It would be a work of merit.'

'That is exactly what I was thinking,' said the monk. 'Come with me to Disenchantment's palace to get this absurd creature cleared. Then, when this last batch of romantic idiots goes down, you and I can go down with them. At present about half have already been born. They await this last batch to make up the number.'

'Very good, I will go with you then,' said the Taoist. Shi-yin heard all this conversation quite clearly, and curiosity impelled him to go forward and greet the two reverend gentlemen. They returned his greeting and asked him what he wanted.

'It is not often that one has the opportunity of listening to a discussion of the operations of *karma* such as the one I have just been privileged to overhear,' said Shi-yin. 'Unfortunately I am a man of very limited understanding and have not been able to derive the full benefit from your conversation. If you would have the very great kindness to enlighten my benighted understanding with a somewhat fuller account of what you were discussing, I can promise you the most devout attention. I feel sure that your teaching would have a salutary effect on me and – who knows – might save me from the pains of hell.'

The reverend gentlemen laughed. 'These are heavenly mysteries and may not be divulged. But if you wish to escape from the fiery pit, you have only to remember us when the time comes, and all will be well.'

Shi-yin saw that it would be useless to press them. 'Heavenly mysteries must not, of course, be revealed. But might one perhaps inquire what the "absurd creature" is that you were talking about? Is it possible that I might be allowed to see it?'

'Oh, as for that,' said the monk: 'I think it is on the cards for you to have a look at *him*,' and he took the object from his sleeve and handed it to Shi-yin.

Shi-yin took the object from him and saw that it was a clear, beautiful jade on one side of which were carved the words 'Magic Jade'. There were several columns of smaller characters on the back, which Shi-yin was just going to examine more closely when the monk, with a cry of 'Here we are, at the frontier of Illusion', snatched the stone from him and disappeared, with the Taoist, through a big stone archway above which

THE LAND OF ILLUSION

was written in large characters. A couplet in smaller characters was inscribed vertically on either side of the arch:

> Truth becomes fiction when the fiction's true;
> Real becomes not-real where the unreal's real.

Shi-yin was on the point of following them through the archway when suddenly a great clap of thunder seemed to shake the earth to its very foundations, making him cry out in alarm.

And there he was sitting in his study, the contents of his dream already half forgotten, with the sun still blazing on the ever-rustling plantains outside, and the wet-nurse at the door with his little daughter Ying-lian in her arms. Her delicate little pink-and-white face seemed dearer to him than ever at that moment, and he stretched out his arms to take her and hugged her to him.

After playing with her for a while at his desk, he carried her out to the front of the house to watch the bustle in the street. He was about to go in again when he saw a monk and a Taoist approaching, the monk scabby-headed and barefoot, the Taoist tousle-haired and limping. They were behaving like madmen, shouting with laughter and gesticulating wildly as they walked along.

When this strange pair reached Shi-yin's door and saw him standing there holding Ying-lian, the monk burst into loud sobs. 'Patron,' he said, addressing Shi-yin, 'what are you doing, holding in your arms that ill-fated creature who is destined to involve both her parents in her own misfortune?'

Shi-yin realized that he was listening to the words of a madman and took no notice. But the monk persisted:

'Give her to me! Give her to me!'

Shi-yin was beginning to lose patience and, clasping his little girl more tightly to him, turned on his heel and was about to re-enter the house when the monk pointed his finger at him, roared with laughter, and then proceeded to intone the following verses:

> 'Fond man, your pampered child to cherish so –
> That caltrop-glass which shines on melting snow!
> Beware the high feast of the fifteenth day,
> When all in smoke and fire shall pass away!'[1]

Shi-yin heard all this quite plainly and was a little worried by it. He was thinking of asking the monk what lay behind these puzzling words when he heard the Taoist say, 'We don't need to stay together. Why don't we part company here and each go about his own business? Three *kalpas* from now I shall wait for you on Bei-mang Hill. Having joined forces again there, we can go together to the Land of Illusion to sign off.'

'Excellent!' said the other. And the two of them went off and soon were both lost to sight.

'There must have been something behind all this,' thought Shi-yin to himself. 'I really ought to have asked him what he meant, but now it is too late.'

He was still standing outside his door brooding when Jia Yu-cun, the poor student who lodged at the Bottle-gourd Temple next door, came up to him. Yu-cun was a native of Hu-zhou and came from a family of scholars and bureaucrats which had, however, fallen on bad times when Yu-cun was born. The family fortunes on both his father's and mother's side had all been spent, and the members of the family had themselves gradually died off until only Yu-cun was left. There were no prospects for him in his home town, so he had set off for the capital, in search of fame and fortune. Unfortunately he had got no further than Soochow when his funds

1. See Appendix, p. 528.

ran out, and he had now been living there in poverty for a year, lodging in this temple and keeping himself alive by working as a copyist. For this reason Shi-yin saw a great deal of his company.

As soon as he caught sight of Shi-yin, Yu-cun clasped his hands in greeting and smiled ingratiatingly. 'I could see you standing there gazing, sir. Has anything been happening in the street?'

'No, no,' said Shi-yin. 'It just happened'that my little girl was crying, so I brought her out here to amuse her. Your coming is most opportune, dear boy. I was beginning to feel most dreadfully bored. Won't you come into my little den, and we can help each other to while away this tedious hot day?'

So saying, he called for a servant to take the child indoors, while he himself took Yu-cun by the hand and led him into his study, where his boy served them both with tea. But they had not exchanged half-a-dozen words before one of the servants rushed in to say that 'Mr Yan had come to pay a call.' Shi-yin hurriedly rose up and excused himself: 'I seem to have brought you here under false pretences. I do hope you will forgive me. If you don't mind sitting on your own here for a moment, I shall be with you directly.'

Yu-cun rose to his feet too. 'Please do not distress yourself on my account, sir. I am a regular visitor here and can easily wait a bit.' But by the time he had finished saying this, Shi-yin was already out of the study and on his way to the guest-room.

Left to himself, Yu-cun was flicking through some of Shi-yin's books of poetry in order to pass the time, when he heard a woman's cough outside the window. Immediately he jumped up and peered out to see who it was. The cough appeared to have come from a maid who was picking flowers in the garden. She was an unusually good-looking girl with a rather refined face: not a great beauty, by any means, but with something striking about her. Yu-cun gazed at her spellbound.

Having now finished picking her flowers, this anonymous member of the Zhen household was about to go in again when, on some sudden impulse, she raised her head and caught sight of a man standing in the window. His hat was frayed and his clothing threadbare; yet, though obviously poor, he had a fine, manly physique and handsome, well-proportioned features.

The maid hastened to remove herself from this male presence; but as she went she thought to herself, 'What a fine-looking man! But so shabby! The family hasn't got any friends or relations as poor as that. It must be that Jia Yu-cun the master is always on about. No wonder he says that he won't stay poor long. I remember hearing him say that he's often wanted to help him but hasn't yet found an opportunity.' And thinking these thoughts she could not forbear to turn back for another peep or two.

Yu-cun saw her turn back and, at once assuming that she had taken a fancy to him, was beside himself with delight. What a perceptive young woman she must be, he thought, to have seen the genius underneath the rags! A real friend in trouble!

After a while the boy came in again and Yu-cun elicited from him that the visitor in the front room was now staying to dinner. It was obviously out of the question to wait much longer, so he slipped down the passage-way at the side of the house and let himself out by the back gate. Nor did Shi-yin invite him round again when, having at last seen off his visitor, he learned that Yu-cun had already left.

But then the Mid Autumn festival arrived and, after the family convivialities were over, Shi-yin had a little dinner for two laid out in his study and went in person to invite Yu-cun, walking to his temple lodgings in the moonlight.

Ever since the day the Zhens' maid had, by looking back twice over her shoulder, convinced him that she was a friend, Yu-cun had had the girl very much on his mind, and now that it was festival time, the full moon of Mid Autumn lent an inspiration to his romantic impulses which finally resulted in the following octet:

'Ere on ambition's path my feet are set,
Sorrow comes often this poor heart to fret.
Yet, as my brow contracted with new care,
Was there not one who, parting, turned to stare?

> Dare I, that grasp at shadows in the wind,
> Hope, underneath the moon, a friend to find?
> Bright orb, if with my plight you sympathize,
> Shine first upon the chamber where she lies.'

Having delivered himself of this masterpiece, Yu-cun's thoughts began to run on his unrealized ambitions and, after much head-scratching and many heavenward glances accompanied by heavy sighs, he produced the following couplet, reciting it in a loud, ringing voice which caught the ear of Shi-yin, who chanced at that moment to be arriving:

> 'The jewel in the casket bides till one shall come to buy.
> The jade pin in the drawer hides, waiting its time to fly.'[2]

Shi-yin smiled. 'You are a man of no mean ambition, Yu-cun.'

'Oh no!' Yu-cun smiled back deprecatingly. 'You are too flattering. I was merely reciting at random from the lines of some old poet. But what brings you here, sir?'

'Tonight is Mid Autumn night,' said Shi-yin. 'People call it the Festival of Reunion. It occurred to me that you might be feeling rather lonely here in your monkery, so I have arranged for the two of us to take a little wine together in my study. I hope you will not refuse to join me.'

Yu-cun made no polite pretence of declining. 'Your kindness is more than I deserve,' he said. 'I accept gratefully.' And he accompanied Shi-yin back to the study next door.

Soon they had finished their tea. Wine and various choice dishes were brought in and placed on the table, already laid out with cups, plates, and so forth, and the two men took their places and began to drink. At first they were rather slow and ceremonious; but gradually, as the conversation grew more animated, their potations too became more reckless and uninhibited. The sounds of music and singing which could now be heard from every house in the neighbourhood and the full moon which shone with cold brilliance overhead seemed to

2. Yu-cun is thinking of the jade hairpin given by a visiting fairy to an early Chinese emperor which later turned into a white swallow and flew away into the sky. Metaphors of flying and 'climbing the sky' were frequently used for success in the Civil Service examinations.

increase their elation, so that the cups were emptied almost as soon as they touched their lips, and Yu-cun, who was already a sheet or so in the wind, was seized with an irrepressible excitement to which he presently gave expression in the form of a quatrain, ostensibly on the subject of the moon, but really about the ambition he had hitherto been at some pains to conceal:

> 'In thrice five nights her perfect O is made,
> Whose cold light bathes each marble balustrade.
> As her bright wheel starts on its starry ways,
> On earth ten thousand heads look up and gaze.'

'Bravo!' said Shi-yin loudly. 'I have always insisted that you were a young fellow who would go up in the world, and now, in these verses you have just recited, I see an augury of your ascent. In no time at all we shall see you up among the clouds! This calls for a drink!' And, saying this, he poured Yu-cun a large cup of wine.

Yu-cun drained the cup, then, surprisingly, sighed:

'Don't imagine the drink is making me boastful, but I really do believe that if it were just a question of having the sort of qualifications now in demand, I should stand as good a chance as any of getting myself on to the list of candidates. The trouble is that I simply have no means of laying my hands on the money that would be needed for lodgings and travel expenses. The journey to the capital is a long one, and the sort of money I can earn from my copying is not enough—'

'Why ever didn't you say this before?' said Shi-yin interrupting him. 'I have long wanted to do something about this, but on all the occasions I have met you previously, the conversation has never got round to this subject, and I haven't liked to broach it for fear of offending you. Well, now we know where we are. I am not a very clever man, but at least I know the right thing to do when I see it. Luckily, the next Triennial is only a few months ahead. You must go to the capital without delay. A spring examination triumph will make you feel that all your studying has been worth while. I shall take care of all your expenses. It is the least return I can make for your friendship.' And there and then he instructed his boy to go with all speed and make up a parcel of fifty taels of the best refined silver and two suits of winter clothes.

'The almanac gives the nineteenth as a good day for travelling,' he went on, addressing Yu-cun again. 'You can set about hiring a boat for the journey straight away. How delightful it will be to meet again next winter when you have distinguished yourself by soaring to the top over all the other candidates!'

Yu-cun accepted the silver and the clothes with only the most perfunctory word of thanks and without, apparently, giving them a further moment's thought, for he continued to drink and laugh and talk as if nothing had happened. It was well after midnight before they broke up.

After seeing Yu-cun off, Shi-yin went to bed and slept without a break until the sun was high in the sky next morning. When he awoke, his mind was still running on the conversation of the previous night. He thought he would write a couple of introductory letters for Yu-cun to take with him to the capital, and arrange for him to call on the family of an official he was acquainted with who might be able to put him up; but when he sent a servant to invite him over, the servant brought back word from the temple as follows:

'The monk says that Mr Jia set out for the capital at five o'clock this morning, sir. He says he left a message to pass on to you. He said to tell you, "A scholar should not concern himself with almanacs, but should act as the situation demands," and he said there wasn't time to say good-bye.'

So Shi-yin was obliged to let the matter drop.

*

It is a true saying that 'time in idleness is quickly spent'. In no time at all it was Fifteenth Night, and Shi-yin sent little Ying-lian out, in the charge of one of the servants called Calamity, to see the mummers and the coloured lanterns. It was near midnight when Calamity, feeling an urgent need to relieve his bladder, put Ying-lian down on someone's doorstep while he went about his business, only to find, on his return, that the child was nowhere to be seen. Frantically he searched for her throughout the rest of the night; but when day dawned and he had still not found her, he took to his heels, not daring to face his master and mistress, and made off for another part of the country.

Shi-yin and his wife knew that something must be wrong when their little girl failed to return home all night. Then a search was made; but all those sent out were obliged in the end to report that no trace of her could be found.

The shock of so sudden a loss to a middle-aged couple who had only ever had the one daughter can be imagined. In tears every day and most of the night, they almost lost the will to go on living, and after about a month like this first Shi-yin and then his wife fell ill, so that doctors and diviners were in daily attendance on them.

Then, on the fifteenth of the third month, while frying cakes for an offering, the monk of Bottle-gourd Temple carelessly allowed the oil to catch alight, which set fire to the paper window. And, since the houses in this area all had wooden walls and bamboo fences – though also, doubtless, because they were doomed to destruction anyway – the fire leaped from house to house until the whole street was blazing away like a regular Fiery Mountain; and though the firemen came to put it out, by the time they arrived the fire was well under way and long past controlling, and roared away all night long until it had burnt itself out, rendering heaven knows how many families homeless in the process.

Poor Zhens! Though they and their handful of domestics escaped unhurt, their house, which was only next door to the temple, was soon reduced to a heap of rubble, while Shi-yin stood by helpless, groaning and stamping in despair.

After some discussion with his wife, Shi-yin decided that they should move to their farm in the country; but a series of crop failures due to flooding and drought had led to widespread brigandage in those parts, and government troops were out everywhere hunting down the mutinous peasants and making arrests. In such conditions it was impossible to settle on the farm, so Shi-yin sold the land and, taking only two of the maids with them, went with his wife to seek refuge with his father-in-law, Feng Su.

This Feng Su was a Ru-zhou man who, though only a farmer by calling, had a very comfortable sufficiency. He was somewhat displeased to see his son-in-law arriving like a refugee on his doorstep; but fortunately Shi-yin had on him the money he had realized from the sale of the farm, and this he now entrusted to his father-in-law to buy for him, as and when he could, a house and land on which he could depend for his future livelihood. Feng Su embezzled about half of this sum and used the other half to provide him with a ruinous cottage and some fields of poor, thin soil.

A scholar, with no experience of business or agricultural matters, Shi-yin now found himself poorer after a year or two of struggle than when he had started. Feng Su would treat him to a few pearls of rustic wisdom whenever they met, but behind his back would grumble to all and sundry about 'incompetents' and 'people who liked their food but were too lazy to work for it', which caused Shi-yin great bitterness when it came to his ears. The anxieties and injustices which now beset him, coming on top of the shocks he had suffered a year or two previously, left a man of his years with little resistance to the joint onslaught of poverty and ill-health, and gradually he began to betray the unmistakable symptoms of a decline.

One day, wishing to take his mind off his troubles for a bit, he had dragged himself, stick in hand, to the main road, when it chanced that he suddenly caught sight of a Taoist with a limp – a crazy, erratic figure in hempen sandals and tattered clothes, who chanted the following words to himself as he advanced towards him:

> 'Men all know that salvation should be won,
> But with ambition won't have done, have done.
> Where are the famous ones of days gone by?
> In grassy graves they lie now, every one.

> Men all know that salvation should be won,
> But with their riches won't have done, have done.
> Each day they grumble they've not made enough.
> When they've enough, it's goodnight everyone!

Men all know that salvation should be won,
But with their loving wives they won't have done.
The darlings every day protest their love:
But once you're dead, they're off with another one.

Men all know that salvation should be won,
But with their children won't have done, have done.
Yet though of parents fond there is no lack,
Of grateful children saw I ne'er a one.'

Shi-yin approached the Taoist and questioned him. 'What is all this you are saying? All I can make out is a lot of "won" and "done".'

'If you can make out "won" and "done",' replied the Taoist with a smile, 'you may be said to have understood; for in all the affairs of this world what is won is done, and what is done is won; for whoever has not yet done has not yet won, and in order to have won, one must first have done. I shall call my song the "Won-Done Song".'

Shi-yin had always been quick-witted, and on hearing these words a flash of understanding had illuminated his mind. He therefore smiled back at the Taoist: 'Wait a minute! How would you like me to provide your "Won-Done Song" with a commentary?'

'Please do!' said the Taoist; and Shi-yin proceeded as follows:

'Mean hovels and abandoned halls
Where courtiers once paid daily calls:
Bleak haunts where weeds and willows scarcely thrive
Were once with mirth and revelry alive.
Whilst cobwebs shroud the mansion's gilded beams,
The cottage casement with choice muslin gleams.
Would you of perfumed elegance recite?
Even as you speak, the raven locks turn white.
Who yesterday her lord's bones laid in clay,
On silken bridal-bed shall lie today.
Coffers with gold and silver filled:
Now, in a trice, a tramp by all reviled.
One at some other's short life gives a sigh,
Not knowing that he, too, goes home – to die!
The sheltered and well-educated lad,
In spite of all your care, may turn out bad;

And the delicate, fastidious maid
End in a foul stews, plying a shameful trade.
The judge whose hat is too small for his head
Wears, in the end, a convict's cangue instead.
Who shivering once in rags bemoaned his fate,
Today finds fault with scarlet robes of state.
In such commotion does the world's theatre rage:
As each one leaves, another takes the stage.
In vain we roam:
Each in the end must call a strange land home.
Each of us with that poor girl may compare
Who sews a wedding-gown for another bride to wear.'

'A very accurate commentary!' cried the mad, lame Taoist, clapping his hands delightedly.

But Shi-yin merely snatched the satchel that hung from the other's shoulder and slung it from his own, and with a shout of 'Let's go!' and without even waiting to call back home, he strode off into the wide world in the company of the madman.

This event made a great uproar in the little town, and news of it was relayed from gossip to gossip until it reached the ears of Mrs Zhen, who cried herself into fits when she heard it. After consulting her father, she sent men out to inquire everywhere after her husband; but no news of him was to be had.

It was now imperative that she should move in with her parents and look to them for support. Fortunately she still had the two maids who had stayed on with her from the Soochow days, and by sewing and embroidering morning, noon and night, she and her women were able to make some contribution to her father's income. The latter still found daily occasion to complain, but there was very little he could do about it.

One day the elder of the two maids was purchasing some silks at the door when she heard the criers clearing the street and all the people began to tell each other that the new mandarin had arrived. She hid in the doorway and watched the guards and runners marching past two by two. But when the mandarin in his black hat and scarlet robe of office was borne past in his great chair, she stared for some time as though puzzled. 'Where have I seen that mandarin before?' she wondered. 'His face looks extraordinarily familiar.' But presently she went into the house again and gave the matter no further thought.

That night, just as they were getting ready for bed, there was suddenly a great commotion at the door and a confused hubbub of voices shouting that someone was wanted at the *yamen* for questioning, which so terrified Feng Su that he was momentarily struck dumb and could only stare.

If you wish to know what further calamity this portended, you will have to read the following chapter.

CHAPTER 2

A daughter of the Jias ends her days
in Yangchow city
And Leng Zi-xing discourses on the Jias of
Rong-guo House

Hearing the clamour of yamen runners outside, Feng Su hurried to the door, his face wreathed in smiles, to ask what they wanted. 'Tell Mr Zhen to step outside,' they were shouting. 'Hurry!'

Feng Su's smile became even more ingratiating. 'My name is Feng, not Zhen. My son-in-law's name is Zhen, but he left home to become a Taoist more than a year ago. Could he be the one you want?'

'"Feng" or "Zhen", it's all the same to us,' said the runners; 'but if you're his father-in-law you'd better come along with us to see the magistrate.' And they hustled him off, leaving the entire household in a state of panic, quite at a loss to know what the trouble could be.

It was ten o'clock before Feng Su returned, and everyone pressed him to give a full account of what had transpired.

'It seems that the new mandarin is a Hu-zhou man called Jia. He used to be an acquaintance of Shi-yin's in the old days. He guessed that Shi-yin must have moved to these parts when he saw our Lucky in the doorway buying silks. That's why he sent the runners here. I explained what had happened to Shi-yin, and he seemed very upset. Then he asked me about Ying-lian, and I said she was lost while out watching the lanterns. "Never mind," he said, "wait till I send some people out to look for her. We shall have her back in no time." Then we chatted a bit longer, and just as I was going, he gave me two taels of silver.'

Mrs Zhen could not help being affected by this account. But the rest of that night we pass over in silence.

Early next day a messenger arrived from Yu-cun bearing two packets of silver and four bolts of silk brocade for Mrs

Zhen as a token of the sender's gratitude. There was also a confidential letter for Feng Su commissioning him to ask Mrs Zhen for Lucky's hand as Yu-cun's second wife. Enraptured at the prospect of doing a good turn for a mandarin, Feng Su hastened to urge upon his daughter the importance of complying with this request, and that very night Lucky was bundled into a small covered chair and carried off to the yamen. Yu-cun's delight goes without saying. Another hundred taels of silver were despatched to Feng Su, together with a number of good things for Mrs Zhen, to cheer and sustain her until such time as her daughter's whereabouts could be discovered.

Lucky was, of course, the maid who had once turned back to look at Yu-cun when they were living at the house in Soochow. She could scarcely have foreseen at the time what singular good fortune that one glance would procure for her. But she was destined to be doubly fortunate. She had not been with Yu-cun more than a year when she gave birth to a son; and a mere six months later Yu-cun's first wife died, whereupon Lucky was promoted to fill her place and became Her Ladyship. As the proverb says,

> Sometimes by chance
> A look or a glance
> May one's fortune advance.

*

When Yu-cun received the gift of money from Zhen Shi-yin he had left for the capital on the day after the festival. He had done well in the Triennial examination, passing out as a Palace Graduate, and had been selected for external service. And now he had been promoted to the magistracy of this district.

But although his intelligence and ability were outstanding, these qualities were unfortunately offset by a certain cupidity and harshness and a tendency to use his intelligence in order to outwit his superiors; all of which caused his fellow-officials to cast envious glances in his direction, with the result that in less than a year an unfavourable report was sent in by a senior official stating that his 'seeming ability was no more than a mask for cunning and duplicity' and citing one or two instances in which he had aided and abetted the peculations of his underlings or allied himself with powerful local interests in order to frustrate the course of justice.

The imperial eye, lighting on this report, kindled with wrath. Yu-cun's instant dismissal was commanded. The officials at the Prefecture, when notice that he was to be cashiered arrived from the Ministry, rejoiced to a man. But Yu-cun, in spite of all the shame and chagrin that he felt, allowed no glimmer of resentment to appear on his face. Indeed, he joked and smiled as before, and when the business of handing over was completed, he took his wife and family and the loot he had accumulated during his years of office and having settled them all safely in his native Hu-zhou, set off, free as the air, on an extended tour of some of the more celebrated places of scenic interest in our mighty empire.

One day Yu-cun chanced to be staying in the Yangchow area when he heard that the Salt Commissioner for that year was a certain Lin Ru-hai. This Lin Ru-hai had passed out Florilege, or third in the whole list of successful candidates, in a previous Triennial, and had lately been promoted to the Censorate. He was a Soochow man and had not long taken up his duties in Yangchow following his nomination by the emperor as Visiting Inspector in that area.

Lin Ru-hai came of an aristocratic family and was himself fifth in line since his ancestor's ennoblement. The original patent had been inheritable only up to the third generation, and it was only through the magnanimity of the reigning sovereign that an exceptional act of grace had extended it for a further generation in the case of Lin Ru-hai's father. Lin Ru-hai himself had therefore been obliged to make his way up through the examination system. It was fortunate for him that, though the family had up to his time enjoyed hereditary emoluments, it had nevertheless enjoined a high standard of education on all of its members.

Lin Ru-hai was less fortunate, however, in belonging to a family whose numbers were dwindling. He could still point to several related households, but they were all on the distaff side. There was not a single relation in the direct line who bore his name. Already he was fifty, and his only son had died the year before at the age of three. And although he kept several concubines, he seemed fated to have no son, and had all but resigned himself to this melancholy fact.

His chief wife, who had been a Miss Jia, had given him a daughter called Dai-yu. Both parents doted on her, and because she showed exceptional intelligence, conceived the idea of giving her a rudimentary education as a substitute for bringing up a son, hoping in this way somewhat to alleviate the sense of desolation left by the death of their only heir.

Now Jia Yu-cun had had the misfortune to catch a severe chill while staying in his lodgings at Yangchow, and after his recovery, found himself somewhat short of cash. He was therefore already looking around for some more permanent haven where he could rest and recuperate, when he chanced to run into two old friends who were acquainted with the new Salt Commissioner and who, knowing that the latter was looking for a suitable tutor for his daughter, took Yu-cun along to the yamen and introduced him, with the result that he was given the job.

Since Yu-cun's pupil was both very young and rather delicate, there were no regular hours of instruction; and as she had only a couple of little maids studying with her for company who stayed away when she did, Yu-cun's employment was far from arduous and left ample time for convalescence.

A year or more passed uneventfully and then, quite unexpectedly, Lin Ru-hai's wife took ill and died. Yu-cun's little pupil helped with the nursing throughout her mother's last illness and mourned for her bitterly after her death. The extra strain this placed on her always delicate constitution brought on a severe attack of a recurrent sickness, and for a long time she was unable to pursue her lessons.

Bored by his enforced idleness, Yu-cun took to going for walks as soon as lunch was over whenever the weather was warm and sunny.

One day a desire to savour country sights and sounds led him outside the city walls, and as he walked along with no fixed destination in mind, he presently found himself in a place ringed with hills and full of murmuring brooks and tall stands of bamboo where a temple stood half-hidden among the trees. The walled approach to the gateway had fallen in and parts of the surrounding wall were in ruins. A board above the gate announced the temple's name:

THE TEMPLE OF PERFECT KNOWLEDGE

while two cracked and worn uprights at the sides of the gate were inscribed with the following couplet:

(on the right-hand side)

As long as there is a sufficiency behind you, you press greedily forward.

(on the left-hand side)

It is only when there is no road in front of you that you think of turning back.

'The wording is commonplace to a degree,' Yu-cun reflected, 'yet the sentiment is quite profound. In all the famous temples and monasteries I have visited, I cannot recollect having ever seen anything quite like it. I shouldn't be surprised to find that some story of spectacular downfall and dramatic conversion lay behind this inscription. It might be worth going in and inquiring.'

But when he went inside and looked around, he saw only an ancient, wizened monk cooking some gruel who paid no attention whatsoever to his greetings and who proved, when Yu-cun went up to him and asked him a few questions, to be both deaf and partially blind. His toothless replies were all but unintelligible, and in any case bore no relation to the questions.

Yu-cun walked out again in disgust. He now thought that in order to give the full rural flavour to his outing he would treat himself to a few cups of wine in a little country inn and accordingly directed his steps towards the near-by village. He had scarcely set foot inside the door of the village inn when one of the men drinking at separate tables inside rose up and advanced to meet him with a broad smile.

'Fancy meeting you!'

It was an antique dealer called Leng Zi-xing whom Yu-cun had got to know some years previously when he was staying in the capital. Yu-cun had a great admiration for Zi-xing as a practical man of business, whilst Zi-xing for his part was tickled to claim acquaintanceship with a man of Yu-cun's great learning and culture. On the basis of this mutual admiration the two of them had got on wonderfully well, and Yu-cun now returned the other's greeting with a pleased smile.

'My dear fellow! How long have you been here? I really had no idea you were in these parts. It was quite an accident that I came here today at all. What an extraordinary co-incidence!'

'I went home at the end of last year to spend New Year with the family,' said Zi-xing. 'On my way back to the capital I thought I would stop off and have a few words with a friend of mine who lives hereabouts, and he very kindly invited me to spend a few days with him. I hadn't got any urgent business waiting for me, so I thought I might as well stay on a bit and leave at the middle of the month. I came out here on my own because my friend has an engagement today. I certainly didn't expect to run into *you* here.'

Zi-xing conducted Yu-cun to his table as he spoke and ordered more wine and some fresh dishes to be brought. The two men then proceeded, between leisurely sips of wine, to relate what each had been doing in the years that had elapsed since their last meeting.

Presently Yu-cun asked Zi-xing if anything of interest had happened recently in the capital.

'I can't think of anything particularly deserving of mention,' said Zi-xing. 'Except, perhaps, for a very small but very unusual event that took place in your own clan there.'

'What makes you say that?' said Yu-cun, 'I have no family connections in the capital.'

'Well, it's the same name,' said Zi-xing. 'They must be the same clan.'

Yu-cun asked him what family he could be referring to.

'I fancy you wouldn't disown the Jias of the Rong-guo mansion as unworthy of you.'

'Oh, you mean them,' said Yu-cun. 'There are so many members of my clan, it's hard to keep up with them all. Since the time of Jia Fu of the Eastern Han dynasty there have been branches of the Jia clan in every province of the empire. The Rong-guo branch is, as a matter of fact, on the same clan register as my own; but since they are exalted so far above us socially, we don't normally claim the connection, and nowadays we are completely out of touch with them.'

Zi-xing sighed. 'You shouldn't speak about them in that way, you know. Nowadays both the Rong and Ning mansions are in a greatly reduced state compared with what they used to be.'

'When I was last that way the Rong and Ning mansions both seemed to be fairly humming with life. Surely nothing could have happened to reduce their prosperity in so short a time?'

'Ah, you may well ask. But it's a long story.'

'Last time I was in Jinling,' went on Yu-cun, 'I passed by their two houses one day on my way to Shi-tou-cheng to visit the ruins. The Ning-guo mansion along the eastern half of the road and the Rong-guo mansion along the western half must between them have occupied the greater part of the north side frontage of that street. It's true that there wasn't much activity outside the main entrances, but looking up over the outer walls I had a glimpse of the most magnificent and imposing halls and pavilions, and even the rocks and trees of the gardens beyond seemed to have a sleekness and luxuriance that were certainly not suggestive of a family whose fortunes were in a state of decline.'

'Well! For a Palace Graduate Second Class, you ought to know better than that! Haven't you ever heard the old saying, "The beast with a hundred legs is a long time dying"? Although I say they are not as prosperous as they used to be in years past, of course I don't mean to say that there is not still a world of difference between *their* circumstances and those you would expect to find in the household of your average government official. At the moment the numbers of their establishment and the activities they engage in are, if anything, on the increase. Both masters and servants all lead

lives of luxury and magnificence. And they still have plenty
of plans and projects under way. But they can't bring themselves to economize or make any adjustment in their accustomed style of living. Consequently, though outwardly
they still manage to keep up appearances, inwardly they are
beginning to feel the pinch. But that's a small matter. There's
something much more seriously wrong with them than that.
They are not able to turn out good sons, those stately houses,
for all their pomp and show. The males in the family get more
degenerate from one generation to the next.'

'Surely,' said Yu-cun with surprise, 'it is inconceivable that
such highly cultured households should not give their children
the best education possible? I say nothing of other families,
but the Jias of the Ning and Rong households used to be
famous for the way in which they brought up their sons.
How could they come to be as you describe?'

'I assure you, it is precisely those families I am speaking of.
Let me tell you something of their history. The Duke of
Ning-guo and the Duke of Rong-guo were two brothers by
the same mother. Ning-guo was the elder of the two. When he
died, his eldest son, Jia Dai-hua, inherited his post. Dai-
hua had two sons. The elder, Jia Fu, died at the age of eight
or nine, leaving only the second son, Jia Jing, to inherit.
Nowadays Jia Jing's only interest in life is Taoism. He spends
all his time over retorts and crucibles concocting elixirs, and
refuses to be bothered with anything else.

'Fortunately he had already provided himself with a son,
Jia Zhen, long before he took up this hobby. So, having set
his mind on turning himself into an immortal, he has given
up his post in favour of this son. And what's more he refuses
outright to live at home and spends his time fooling around
with a pack of Taoists somewhere outside the city walls.

'This Jia Zhen has got a son of his own, a lad called Jia
Rong, just turned sixteen. With old Jia Jing out of the way
and refusing to exercise any authority, Jia Zhen has thrown
his responsibilities to the winds and given himself up to a life
of pleasure. He has turned that Ning-guo mansion upside
down, but there is no one around who dares gainsay
him.

'Now I come to the Rong household – it was there that this strange event occurred that I was telling you about. When the old Duke of Rong-guo died, his eldest son, Jia Dai-shan, inherited his emoluments. He married a girl from a very old Nanking family, the daughter of Marquis Shi, who bore him two sons, Jia She and Jia Zheng.

'Dai-shan has been dead this many a year, but the old lady is still alive. The elder son, Jia She, inherited; but he's only a very middling sort of person and doesn't play much part in running the family. The second son, though, Jia Zheng, has been mad keen on study ever since he was a lad. He is a very upright sort of person, straight as a die. He was his grand-father's favourite. He would have sat for the examinations, but when the emperor saw Dai-shan's testamentary memorial that he wrote on his death bed, he was so moved, thinking what a faithful servant the old man had been, that he not only ordered the elder son to inherit his father's position, but also gave instructions that any other sons of his were to be pre-sented to him at once, and on seeing Jia Zheng he gave him the post of Supernumerary Executive Officer, brevet rank, with instructions to continue his studies while on the Minis-try's payroll. From there he has now risen to the post of Under Secretary.

'Sir Zheng's lady was formerly a Miss Wang. Her first child was a boy called Jia Zhu. He was already a Licensed Scholar at the age of fourteen. Then he married and had a son. But he died of an illness before he was twenty. The second child she bore him was a little girl, rather remarkable because she was born on New Year's day. Then after an interval of twelve years or more she suddenly had another son. He was even more remarkable, because at the moment of his birth he had a piece of beautiful, clear, coloured jade in his mouth with a lot of writing on it. They gave him the name "Bao-yu" as a consequence. Now tell me if you don't think that is an extraordinary thing.'

'It certainly is,' Yu-cun agreed. 'I should not be at all surprised to find that there was something very unusual in the heredity of that child.'

'Humph,' said Zi-xing. 'A great many people have said

that. That is the reason why his old grandmother thinks him such a treasure. But when they celebrated the First Twelvemonth and Sir Zheng tested his disposition by putting a lot of objects in front of him and seeing which he would take hold of, he stretched out his little hand and started playing with some women's things – combs, bracelets, pots of rouge and powder and the like – completely ignoring all the other objects. Sir Zheng was very displeased. He said he would grow up to be a rake, and ever since then he hasn't felt much affection for the child. But to the old lady he's the very apple of her eye.

'But there's more that's unusual about him than that. He's now rising ten and unusually mischievous, yet his mind is as sharp as a needle. You wouldn't find one in a hundred to match him. Some of the childish things he says are most extraordinary. He'll say, "Girls are made of water and boys are made of mud. When I am with girls I feel fresh and clean, but when I am with boys I feel stupid and nasty." Now isn't that priceless! He'll be a lady-killer when he grows up, no question of that.'

Yu-cun's face assumed an expression of unwonted severity. 'Not so. By no means. It is a pity that none of you seem to understand this child's heredity. Most likely even my esteemed kinsman Sir Jia Zheng is mistaken in treating the boy as a future libertine. This is something that no one but a widely read person, and one moreover well-versed in moral philosophy and in the subtle arcana of metaphysical science could possibly understand.'

Observing the weighty tone in which these words were uttered, Zi-xing hurriedly asked to be instructed, and Yu-cun proceeded as follows:

'The generative processes operating in the universe provide the great majority of mankind with natures in which good and evil are commingled in more or less equal proportions. Instances of exceptional goodness and exceptional badness are produced by the operation of beneficent or noxious ethereal influences, of which the former are symptomatized by the equilibrium of society and the latter by its disequilibrium.

'*Thus,*

> Yao,
> Shun,
> Yu,
> Tang,
> King Wen,
> King Wu,
> the Duke of Zhou,
> the Duke of Shao,
> Confucius,
> Mencius,
> Dong Zhong-shu,
> Han Yu,
> Zhou Dun-yi,
> the Cheng brothers,
> Zhu Xi and
> Zhang Zai

– all instances of exceptional goodness – were born under the influence of benign forces, and all sought to promote the well-being of the societies in which they lived; whilst

> Chi You,
> Gong Gong,
> Jie,
> Zhou,
> the First Qin Emperor,
> Wang Mang,
> Cao Cao,
> Huan Wen,
> An Lu-shan and
> Qin Kuai

– all instances of exceptional badness – were born under the influence of harmful forces, and all sought to disrupt the societies in which they lived.

'*Now*, the good cosmic fluid with which the natures of the exceptionally good are compounded is a pure, quintessential humour; whilst the evil fluid which infuses the natures of the exceptionally bad is a cruel, perverse humour.

'*Therefore*, our age being one in which beneficent ethereal influences are in the ascendant, in which the reigning dynasty is well-established and society both peaceful and prosperous, innumerable instances are to be found, from the palace down to the humblest cottage, of individuals endowed with the pure, quintessential humour.

'*Moreover*, an unused surplus of this pure, quintessential humour, unable to find corporeal lodgement, circulates freely abroad until it manifests itself in the form of sweet dews and balmy winds, asperged and effused for the enrichment and refreshment of all terrestial life.

'*Consequently*, the cruel and perverse humours, unable to circulate freely in the air and sunlight, subside, by a process of incrassation and coagulation, into the bottoms of ditches and ravines.

'*Now*, should these incrassate humours chance to be stirred or provoked by wind or weather into a somewhat more volatile and active condition, it sometimes happens that a stray wisp or errant flocculus may escape from the fissure or concavity in which they are contained; and if some of the pure, quintessential humour should chance to be passing overhead at that same moment, the two will become locked in irreconcilable conflict, the good refusing to yield to the evil, the evil persisting in its hatred of the good. And just as wind, water, thunder and lightning meeting together over the earth can neither dissipate nor yield one to another but produce an explosive shock resulting in the downward emission of rain, so does this clash of humours result in the forcible downward expulsion of the evil humour, which, being thus forced downwards, will find its way into some human creature.

'Such human recipients, whether they be male or female, since they are already amply endowed with the benign humour before the evil humour is injected, are incapable of becoming either greatly good or greatly bad; but place them in the company of ten thousand others and you will find that they are superior to all the rest in sharpness and intelligence and inferior to all the rest in perversity, wrongheadedness and eccentricity. Born into a rich or noble household they are likely to become great lovers or the occasion of great love in others; in a poor but well-educated household they will

become literary rebels or eccentric aesthetes; even if they are
born in the lowest stratum of society they are likely to become
great actors or famous *hetaerae*. Under no circumstances will
you find them in servile or menial positions, content to be at
the beck and call of mediocrities.

'For examples I might cite:

> Xu You,
> Tao Yuan-ming,
> Ruan Ji,
> Ji Kang,
> Liu Ling,
> the Wang and Xie clans of the Jin period,
> Gu Kai-zhi,
> the last ruler of Chen,
> the emperor Ming-huang of the Tang dynasty,
> the emperor Hui-zong of the Song dynasty,
> Liu Ting-zhi,
> Wen Ting-yun,
> Mi Fei,
> Shi Yan-nian,
> Liu Yong and
> Qin Guan;

or, from more recent centuries:

> > Ni Zan,
> > Tang Yin and
> > Zhu Yun-ming;

or again, for examples of the last type:

> > Li Gui-nian,
> > Huang Fan-chuo,
> > Jing Xin-mo,
> > Zhuo Wen-jun,
> > Little Red Duster,
> > Xue Tao,
> > Cui Ying-ying and
> > Morning Cloud.

All of these, though their circumstances differed, were
essentially the same.'

'You mean,' Zi-xing interposed,

> 'Zhang victorious is a hero,
> Zhang beaten is a lousy knave?'

'Precisely so,' said Yu-cun. 'I should have told you that during the two years after I was cashiered I travelled extensively in every province of the empire and saw quite a few remarkable children in the course of my travels; so that just now when you mentioned this Bao-yu I felt pretty certain what type of boy he must be. But one doesn't need to go very far afield for another example. There is one in the Zhen family in Nanking – I am referring to the family of the Zhen who is Imperial Deputy Director-General of the Nanking Secretariat. Perhaps you know who I mean?'

'Who doesn't?' said Zi-xing. 'There is an old family connection between the Zhen family and the Jias of whom we have just been speaking, and they are still on very close terms with each other. I've done business with them myself for longer than I'd care to mention.'

'Last year when I was in Nanking,' said Yu-cun, smiling at the recollection, 'I was recommended for the post of tutor in their household. I could tell at a glance, as soon as I got inside the place, that for all the ducal splendour this was a family "though rich yet given to courtesy", in the words of the Sage, and that it was a rare piece of luck to have got a place in it. But when I came to teach my pupil, though he was only at the first year primary stage, he gave me more trouble than an examination candidate.

'He was indeed a comedy. He once said, "I must have two girls to do my lessons with me if I am to remember the words and understand the sense. Otherwise my mind will simply not work." And he would often tell the little pages who waited on him, "The word 'girl' is very precious and very pure. It is much more rare and precious than all the rarest beasts and birds and plants in the world. So it is most extremely important that you should never, never violate it with your coarse mouths and stinking breath. Whenever you need to say it, you should first rinse your mouths out with clean water and scented tea. And if ever I catch you slipping up, I shall

have holes drilled through your teeth and lace them up
together."

'There was simply no end to his violence and unruliness.
Yet as soon as his lessons were over and he went inside to
visit the girls of the family, he became a completely different
person – all gentleness and calm, and as intelligent and well-
bred as you please.

'His father gave him several severe beatings but it made no
difference. Whenever the pain became too much for him he
would start yelling "Girls! girls!" Afterwards, when the girls
in the family got to hear about it, they made fun of him. "Why
do you always call to us when you are hurt? I suppose you
think we shall come and plead for you to be let off. You ought
to be ashamed of yourself!" But you should have heard his
answer. He said, "Once when the pain was very bad, I thought
that perhaps if I shouted the word 'girls' it might help to ease
it. Well," he said, "I just called out once, and the pain really
was quite a bit better. So now that I have found this secret
remedy, I just keep on shouting 'Girls! girls! girls!' whenever
the pain is at its worst." I could not help laughing.

'But because his grandmother doted on him so much, she
was always taking the child's part against me and his father.
In the end I had to hand in my notice. A boy like that will
never be able to keep up the family traditions or listen to the
advice of his teachers and friends. The pity of it is, though,
that the girls in that family are all exceptionally good.'

'The three at present in the Jia household are also very
fine girls,' said Zi-xing. 'Sir Jia Zheng's eldest girl, Yuan-
chun, was chosen for her exceptional virtue and cleverness to
be a Lady Secretary in the Imperial Palace. The next in age
after her and eldest of the three still at home is called Ying-
chun. She is the daughter of Sir Jia She by one of his secondary
wives. After her comes another daughter of Sir Zheng's, also
a concubine's child, called Tan-chun. The youngest, Xi-chun,
is sister-german to Mr Jia Zhen of the Ning-guo mansion.
Old Lady Jia is very fond of her granddaughters and keeps
them all in her own apartments on the Rong-guo side. They
all study together, and I have been told that they are doing
very well.'

'One of the things I liked about the Zhen family,' said Yu-cun, 'was their custom of giving the girls the same sort of names as the boys, unlike the majority of families who invariably use fancy words like "*chun*", "*hong*", "*xiang*", "*yu*", and so forth. How comes it that the Jias should have followed the vulgar practice in this respect?'

'They didn't,' said Zi-xing. 'The eldest girl was called "Yuan-chun" because she was in fact born on the first day of spring. The others were given names with "*chun*" in them to match hers. But if you go back a generation, you will find that among the Jias too the girls had names exactly like the boys'.

'I can give you proof. Your present employer's good lady is sister-german to Sir She and Sir Zheng of the Rong household. Her name, before she married, was Jia Min. If you don't believe me, you make a few inquiries when you get home and you'll find it is so.'

Yu-cun clapped his hands with a laugh. 'Of course! I have often wondered why it is that my pupil Dai-yu always pronounces "*min*" as "*mi*" when she is reading and, if she has to write it, always makes the character with one or two strokes missing. Now I understand. No wonder her speech and behaviour are so unlike those of ordinary children! I always supposed that there must have been something remarkable about the mother for her to have produced so remarkable a daughter. Now I know that she was related to the Jias of the Rong household, I am not surprised.

'By the way, I am sorry to say that last month the mother passed away.'

Zi-xing sighed. 'Fancy her dying so soon! She was the youngest of the three. And the generation before them are all gone, every one. We shall have to see what sort of husbands they manage to find for the younger generation!'

'Yes, indeed,' said Yu-cun. 'Just now you mentioned that Sir Zheng had this boy with the jade in his mouth and you also mentioned a little grandson left behind by his elder son. What about old Sir She? Surely he must have a son?'

'Since Sir Zheng had the boy with the jade, he has had another son by a concubine,' said Zi-xing, 'but I couldn't tell you what he's like. So at present he has two sons and one grandson. Of course, we don't know what the future may bring.

'But you were asking about Sir She. Yes, he has a son too, called Jia Lian. He's already a young man in his early twenties. He married his own kin, the niece of his Uncle Zheng's wife, Lady Wang. He's been married now for four or five years. Holds the rank of a Sub-prefect by purchase. He's another member of the family who doesn't find responsibilities congenial. He knows his way around, though, and has a great gift of the gab, so at present he stays at home with his Uncle Zheng and helps him manage the family's affairs. However, ever since he married this young lady I mentioned, everyone high and low has joined in praising *her*, and he has been put into the shade rather. She is not only a *very* handsome young woman, she also has a very ready tongue and a very good head – more than a match for most men, I can tell you.'

'You see, I was not mistaken,' said Yu-cun. 'All these people you and I have been talking about are probably examples of that mixture of good and evil humours I was describing to you.'

'Well, I don't know about that,' said Zi-xing. 'Instead of sitting here setting other people's accounts to rights, let's have another drink!'

'I am afraid I have drunk quite a lot while we were busy talking,' said Yu-cun.

Zi-xing laughed. 'There's nothing like a good gossip about other people's affairs for making the wine go down! I'm sure an extra cup or two won't do us any harm.'

Yu-cun glanced out of the window. 'It's getting late. We must be careful we don't get shut out of the city. Why not continue the conversation on our way back? Then we can take our time.'

The two men accordingly rose from their seats, settled the bill for the wine, and were just about to start on their way, when a voice from behind called out, 'Yu-cun, congratulations! I've got some good news for you.'

Yu-cun turned to look.

But if you wish to know who it was, you will have to read the next chapter.

CHAPTER 3

Lin Ru-hai recommends a private tutor
to his brother-in-law
And old Lady Jia extends a compassionate welcome
to the motherless child

When Yu-cun turned to look, he was surprised to see that it was Zhang Ru-gui, a former colleague who had been cashiered at the same time and for the same reason as himself. Zhang Ru-gui was a native of these parts, and had been living at home since his dismissal. Having just wormed out the information that a motion put forward in the capital for the reinstatement of ex-officials had been approved, he had been dashing about ever since, pulling strings and soliciting help from potential backers, and was engaged in this activity when he unexpectedly ran into Yu-cun. Hence the tone of his greeting.

As soon as they had finished bowing to each other, Zhang Ru-gui told Yu-cun the good news, and after further hurried conversation they went their separate ways.

Leng Zi-xing, who had overheard the news, proposed a plan. Why should not Yu-cun ask his employer Lin Ru-hai to write to his brother-in-law Jia Zheng in the capital and enlist his support on his, Yu-cun's, behalf? Yu-cun agreed to follow this suggestion, and presently the two friends separated.

Back in his quarters, Yu-cun quickly hunted out a copy of the *Gazette*, and having satisfied himself that the news was authentic, broached the matter next day with Lin Ru-hai.

'It so happens that an opportunity of helping you has just presented itself,' said Ru-hai. 'Since my poor wife passed on, my mother-in-law in the capital has been worried about the little girl having no one to look after her, and has already sent some of her folk here by barge to fetch her away. The only reason she has so far not gone is that she has not been quite recovered from her illness. I was, however, only just now thinking that the moment to send her had arrived. And as I have still done nothing to repay you for your kindness in tutoring her for me, you may be sure that now this opportunity has presented itself I shall do my very best to help you.

'As a matter of fact, I have already made a few arrangements. I have written this letter here entrusting my brother-in-law with your affair, explaining my indebtedness to you and urging him to see it properly settled. I have also made it quite clear in my letter that any expenses which may be involved are to be taken care of; so you have nothing to worry about on that account.'

Yu-cun made an elaborate bow to his patron and thanked him profusely. He then ventured a question.

'I am afraid I do not know what your relation's position is at the capital. Might it not be a little embarrassing for a person in my situation to thrust himself upon him?'

Ru-hai laughed. 'You need have no anxiety on that score. My brothers-in-law in the capital are your own kinsmen. They are grandsons of the former Duke of Rong-guo. The elder one, Jia She, is an hereditary official of the First Rank and an honorary colonel; the younger one, Jia Zheng, is an Under Secretary in the Ministry of Works. He takes very much after his late grandfather: a modest, generous man, quite without the arrogance of the pampered aristocrat. That is why I have addressed this letter to him. If I did not have complete confidence in his willingness to help you, I should not have put your honour at risk by soliciting him; nor, for that matter, should I have taken the trouble to write the letter.'

Yu-cun now knew that what Zi-xing had told him was the truth and he thanked Lin Ru-hai once again.

'I have fixed the second day of next month for my little girl's journey to the capital,' said Ru-hai. 'If you cared to travel with her, it would be convenient for both of us.'

Yu-cun accepted the suggestion with eager deference. Everything, he thought to himself, was turning out very satisfactorily. Ru-hai for his part set about preparing presents for his wife's family and parting gifts for Yu-cun, all of which Yu-cun in due course took charge of.

At first his little pupil could not be persuaded to part from her father; but her grandmother was insistent that she should go, and Ru-hai added his own reasons.

'I'm half a century old now, my dear, and I have no intention of taking a second wife; so there will be no one here to act as a mother to you. It isn't, either, as if you had sisters who could help to take care of you. You know how often you are poorly. And you are still very young. It would be a great weight off my mind to know that you had your Grandmother Jia and your uncles' girls to fall back on. I really think you ought to go.'

After this Dai-yu could only take a tearful leave of her father and go down to the boat with her nurse and the old women from the Rong mansion who had been sent to fetch her. There was a separate boat for Yu-cun and a couple of servant-boys to wait on him, and he too now embarked in the capacity of Dai-yu's escort.

In due course they arrived in the capital, and Yu-cun, dressed in his best and with the two servant-boys at his heels, betook himself to the gate of the Rong mansion and handed in his visiting-card, on which he had been careful to prefix the word 'kinsman' to his own name. By this time Jia Zheng had already seen his brother-in-law's letter, and accorded him an interview without delay.

Yu-cun's imposing looks and cultivated speech made an excellent impression on Jia Zheng, who was in any case always well-disposed towards scholars, and preserved much of his grandfather's affability with men of letters and readiness to help them in any sort of trouble or distress. And since his own inclinations were in this case reinforced by his brother-in-law's strong recommendation, the treatment he extended to Yu-cun was exceptionally favourable. He exerted himself on his behalf to such good effect that on the very day his petition was presented Yu-cun's reinstatement was approved, and before two months were out he was appointed to the magistracy of Ying-tian-fu in Nanking. Thither, having chosen a suitable day on which to commence his journey, and having first taken his leave of Jia Zheng, he now repaired to take up his duties.

But of him, for the time being, no more.

*

On the day of her arrival in the capital, Dai-yu stepped ashore to find covered chairs from the Rong mansion for her and her women and a cart for the luggage ready waiting on the quay.

She had often heard her mother say that her Grandmother Jia's home was not like other people's houses. The servants she had been in contact with during the past few days were comparatively low-ranking ones in the domestic hierarchy, yet the food they ate, the clothes they wore, and everything about them was quite out of the ordinary. Dai-yu tried to imagine what the people who employed these superior beings must be like. When she arrived at their house she would have to watch every step she took and weigh every word she said, for if she put a foot wrong they would surely laugh her to scorn.

Dai-yu got into her chair and was soon carried through the city walls. Peeping through the gauze panel which served as a window, she could see streets and buildings more rich and elegant and throngs of people more lively and numerous than she had ever seen in her life before. After being carried for what seemed a very great length of time, she saw, on the north front of the east-west street through which they were passing, two great stone lions crouched one on each side of a triple gateway whose doors were embellished with animal-heads. In front of the gateway ten or so splendidly dressed flunkeys sat in a row. The centre of the three gates was closed, but people were going in and out of the two side ones. There was a board above the centre gate on which were written in large characters the words:

NING-GUO HOUSE
Founded and Constructed by
Imperial Command

Dai-yu realized that this must be where the elder branch of her grandmother's family lived. The chair proceeded some distance more down the street and presently there was another triple gate, this time with the legend

RONG-GUO HOUSE

above it.

Ignoring the central gate, her bearers went in by the

western entrance and after traversing the distance of a bow-shot inside, half turned a corner and set the chair down. The chairs of her female attendants which were following behind were set down simultaneously and the old women got out. The places of Dai-yu's bearers were taken by four handsome, fresh-faced pages of seventeen or eighteen. They shouldered her chair and, with the old women now following on foot, carried it as far as an ornamental inner gate. There they set it down again and then retired in respectful silence. The old women came forward to the front of the chair, held up the curtain, and helped Dai-yu to get out.

Each hand resting on the outstretched hand of an elderly attendant, Dai-yu passed through the ornamental gate into a courtyard which had balustraded loggias running along its sides and a covered passage-way through the centre. The foreground of the courtyard beyond was partially hidden by a screen of polished marble set in an elaborate red sandalwood frame. Passing round the screen and through a small reception hall beyond it, they entered the large courtyard of the mansion's principal apartments. These were housed in an imposing five-frame building resplendent with carved and painted beams and rafters which faced them across the courtyard. Running along either side of the courtyard were galleries hung with cages containing a variety of different-coloured parrots, cockatoos, white-eyes, and other birds. Some gaily-dressed maids were sitting on the steps of the main building opposite. At the appearance of the visitors they rose to their feet and came forward with smiling faces to welcome them.

'You've come just at the right time! Lady Jia was only this moment asking about you.'

Three or four of them ran to lift up the door-curtain, while another of them announced in loud tones,

'Miss Lin is here!'

As Dai-yu entered the room she saw a silver-haired old lady advancing to meet her, supported on either side by a servant. She knew that this must be her Grandmother Jia and would have fallen on her knees and made her kotow, but before she could do so her grandmother had caught her in her arms and pressing her to her bosom with cries of 'My pet!' and 'My poor lamb!' burst into loud sobs, while all those present wept in sympathy, and Dai-yu felt herself crying as though she would never stop. It was some time before those present succeeded in calming them both down and Dai-yu was at last able to make her kotow.

Grandmother Jia now introduced those present.

'This is your elder uncle's wife, Aunt Xing. This is your Uncle Zheng's wife, Aunt Wang. This is Li Wan, the wife of your Cousin Zhu, who died.'

Dai-yu kotowed to each of them in turn.

'Call the girls!' said Grandmother Jia. 'Tell them that we have a very special visitor and that they need not do their lessons today.'

There was a cry of 'Yes ma'am' from the assembled maids, and two of them went off to do her bidding.

Presently three girls arrived, attended by three nurses and five or six maids.

The first girl was of medium height and slightly plumpish, with cheeks as white and firm as a fresh lychee and a nose as white and shiny as soap made from the whitest goose-fat. She had a gentle, sweet, reserved manner. To look at her was to love her.

The second girl was rather tall, with sloping shoulders and a slender waist. She had an oval face under whose well-formed brows large, expressive eyes shot out glances that sparkled with animation. To look at her was to forget all that was mean or vulgar.

The third girl was undersized and her looks were still somewhat babyish and unformed.

All three were dressed in identical skirts and dresses and wore identical sets of bracelets and hair ornaments.

Dai-yu rose to meet them and exchanged curtseys and introductions. When she was seated once more, a maid served tea, and a conversation began on the subject of her mother: how her illness had started, what doctors had been called in, what medicines prescribed, what arrangements had been made for the funeral, and how the mourning had been observed. This conversation had the foreseeable effect of upsetting the old lady all over again.

'Of all my girls your mother was the one I loved the best,' she said, 'and now she's been the first to go, and without my even being able to see her again before the end. I can't help being upset!' And holding fast to Dai-yu's hand, she once more burst into tears. The rest of the company did their best to comfort her, until at last she had more or less recovered.

Everyone's attention now centred on Dai-yu. They observed that although she was still young, her speech and manner already showed unusual refinement. They also noticed the frail body which seemed scarcely strong enough to bear the weight of its clothes, but which yet had an inexpressible grace about it, and realizing that she must be suffering from some deficiency, asked her what medicine she took for it and why it was still not better.

'I have always been like this,' said Dai-yu. 'I have been taking medicine ever since I could eat and been looked at by ever so many well-known doctors, but it has never done me any good. Once, when I was only three, I can remember a scabby-headed old monk came and said he wanted to take me away and have me brought up as a nun; but of course, Mother and Father wouldn't hear of it. So he said, "Since you are not prepared to give her up, I am afraid her illness will never get better as long as she lives. The only way it might get better would be if she were never to hear the sound of weeping from this day onwards and never to see any relations other than her own mother and father. Only in those conditions could she get through her life without trouble." Of course, he was quite crazy, and no one took any notice of the things he said. I'm still taking Ginseng Tonic Pills.'

'Well, that's handy,' said Grandmother Jia. 'I take the Pills myself. We can easily tell them to make up a few more each time.'

She had scarcely finished speaking when someone could be heard talking and laughing in a very loud voice in the inner courtyard behind them.

'Oh dear! I'm late,' said the voice. 'I've missed the arrival of our guest.'

'Everyone else around here seems to go about with bated

breath,' thought Dai-yu. 'Who can this new arrival be who is so brash and unmannerly?'

Even as she wondered, a beautiful young woman entered from the room behind the one they were sitting in, surrounded by a bevy of serving women and maids. She was dressed quite differently from the others present, gleaming like some fairy princess with sparkling jewels and gay embroideries.

Her chignon was enclosed in a circlet of gold filigree and clustered pearls. It was fastened with a pin embellished with flying phoenixes, from whose beaks pearls were suspended on tiny chains.

Her necklet was of red gold in the form of a coiling dragon.

Her dress had a fitted bodice and was made of dark red silk damask with a pattern of flowers and butterflies in raised gold thread.

Her jacket was lined with ermine. It was of a slate-blue stuff with woven insets in coloured silks.

Her under-skirt was of a turquoise-coloured imported silk crêpe embroidered with flowers.

She had, moreover,

> eyes like a painted phoenix,
> eyebrows like willow-leaves,
> a slender form,
> seductive grace;
> the ever-smiling summer face
> of hidden thunders showed no trace;
> the ever-bubbling laughter started
> almost before the lips were parted.

'You don't know her,' said Grandmother Jia merrily. 'She's a holy terror this one. What we used to call in Nanking a "peppercorn". You just call her "Peppercorn Feng". She'll know who you mean!'

Dai-yu was at a loss to know how she was to address this Peppercorn Feng until one of the cousins whispered that it was 'Cousin Lian's wife', and she remembered having heard her mother say that her elder uncle, Uncle She, had a son called Jia Lian who was married to the niece of her Uncle Zheng's wife, Lady Wang. She had been brought up from earliest childhood just like a boy, and had acquired in the schoolroom the somewhat boyish-sounding name of Wang Xi-feng. Dai-yu accordingly smiled and curtseyed, greeting her by her correct name as she did so.

Xi-feng took Dai-yu by the hand and for a few moments scrutinized her carefully from top to toe before conducting her back to her seat beside Grandmother Jia.

'She's a beauty, Grannie dear! If I hadn't set eyes on her today, I shouldn't have believed that such a beautiful creature could exist! And everything about her so *distingué*! She doesn't take after your side of the family, Grannie. She's more like a Jia. I don't blame you for having gone on so about her during the past few days – but poor little thing! What a cruel fate to have lost Auntie like that!' and she dabbed at her eyes with a handkerchief.

'I've only just recovered,' laughed Grandmother Jia. 'Don't you go trying to start me off again! Besides, your little cousin is not very strong, and we've only just managed to get *her* cheered up. So let's have no more of this!'

In obedience to the command Xi-feng at once exchanged her grief for merriment.

'Yes, of course. It was just that seeing my little cousin here put everything else out of my mind. It made me want to laugh and cry all at the same time. I'm afraid I quite forgot about you, Grannie dear. I deserve to be spanked, don't I?'

She grabbed Dai-yu by the hand.

'How old are you dear? Have you begun school yet? You musn't feel homesick here. If there's anything you want to eat or anything you want to play with, just come and tell me. And you must tell me if any of the maids or the old nannies are nasty to you.'

Dai-yu made appropriate responses to all of these questions and injunctions.

Xi-feng turned to the servants.

'Have Miss Lin's things been brought in yet? How many people did she bring with her? You'd better hurry up and get a couple of rooms swept out for them to rest in.'

While Xi-feng was speaking, the servants brought in tea and various plates of food, the distribution of which she proceeded to supervise in person.

Dai-yu noticed her Aunt Wang questioning Xi-feng on the side:

'Have this month's allowances been paid out yet?'

'Yes. By the way, just now I went with some of the women to the upstairs storeroom at the back to look for that satin. We looked and looked, but we couldn't find any like the one you described yesterday. Perhaps you misremembered.'

'Oh well, if you can't find it, it doesn't really matter,' said Lady Wang. Then, after a moment's reflection, 'You'd better pick out a couple of lengths presently to have made up into clothes for your little cousin here. If you think of it, send someone round in the evening to fetch them!'

'It's already been seen to. I knew she was going to arrive within a day or two, so I had some brought out in readiness. They are waiting back at your place for your approval. If you think they are all right, they can be sent over straight away.'

Lady Wang merely smiled and nodded her head without saying anything.

The tea things and dishes were now cleared away, and Grandmother Jia ordered two old nurses to take Dai-yu round to see her uncles; but Uncle She's wife, Lady Xing, hurriedly rose to her feet and suggested that it would be more convenient if she were to take her niece round herself.

'Very well,' said Grandmother Jia. 'You go now, then. There is no need for you to come back afterwards.'

So having, together with Lady Wang, who was also returning to her quarters, taken leave of the old lady, Lady Xing went off with Dai-yu, attended across the courtyard as far as the covered way by the rest of the company.

A carriage painted dark blue and hung with kingfisher-blue curtains had been drawn up in front of the ornamental gateway by some pages. Into this Aunt Xing ascended hand in hand with Dai-yu. The old women pulled down the carriage blind and ordered the pages to take up the shafts, the pages drew the carriage into an open space and harnessed mules to it, and Dai-yu and her aunt were driven out of the west gate, eastwards past the main gate of the Rong mansion, in again through a big black-lacquered gate, and up to an inner gate, where they were set down again.

Holding Dai-yu by the hand, Aunt Xing led her into a courtyard in the middle of what she imagined must once have been part of the mansion's gardens. This impression was strengthened when they passed through a third gateway into the quarters occupied by her uncle and aunt; for here the smaller scale and quiet elegance of the halls, galleries and loggias were quite unlike the heavy magnificence and imposing grandeur they had just come from, and ornamental trees and artificial rock formations, all in exquisite taste, were to be seen on every hand.

As they entered the main reception hall, a number of heavily made-up and expensively dressed maids and concubines, who had been waiting in readiness, came forward to greet them.

Aunt Xing asked Dai-yu to be seated while she sent a servant to call Uncle She. After a considerable wait the servant returned with the following message:

'The Master says he hasn't been well these last few days, and as it would only upset them both if he were to see Miss Lin now, he doesn't feel up to it for the time being. He says, tell Miss Lin not to grieve and not to feel homesick. She must think of her grandmother and her aunts as her own family now. He says that her cousins may not be very clever girls, but at least they should be company for her and help to take her mind off things. If she finds anything at all here to distress her, she is to speak up at once. She mustn't feel like an outsider. She is to make herself completely at home.'

Dai-yu stood up throughout this recital and murmured polite assent whenever assent seemed indicated. She then sat for about another quarter of an hour before rising to take her leave. Her Aunt Xing was very pressing that she should have a meal with her before she went, but Dai-yu smilingly replied that though it was very kind of her aunt to offer, and though she ought really not to refuse, nevertheless she still had to pay her respects to her Uncle Zheng, and feared that it would be disrespectful if she were to arrive late. She hoped that she might accept on another occasion and begged her aunt to excuse her.

'In that case, never mind,' said Lady Xing, and instructed

the old nurses to see her to her Uncle Zheng's in the same carriage she had come by. Dai-yu formally took her leave, and Lady Xing saw her as far as the inner gate, where she issued a few more instructions to the servants and watched her niece's carriage out of sight before returning to her rooms.

Presently they re-entered the Rong mansion proper and Dai-yu got down from the carriage. There was a raised stone walk running all the way up to the main gate, along which the old nurses now conducted her. Turning right, they led her down a roofed passage-way along the back of a south-facing hall, then through an inner gate into a large courtyard.

The big building at the head of the courtyard was connected at each end to galleries running through the length of the side buildings by means of 'stag's head' roofing over the corners. The whole formed an architectural unit of greater sumptuousness and magnificence than anything Dai-yu had yet seen that day, from which she concluded that this must be the main inner hall of the whole mansion.

High overhead on the wall facing her as she entered the hall was a great blue board framed in gilded dragons, on which was written in large gold characters

THE HALL OF EXALTED FELICITY

with a column of smaller characters at the side giving a date and the words '. . . written for Our beloved Subject, Jia Yuan, Duke of Rong-guo', followed by the Emperor's private seal, a device containing the words 'kingly cares' and 'royal brush' in archaic seal-script.

A long, high table of carved red sandalwood, ornamented with dragons, stood against the wall underneath. In the centre of this was a huge antique bronze *ding*, fully a yard high, covered with a green patina. On the wall above the *ding* hung a long vertical scroll with an ink-painting of a dragon emerging from clouds and waves, of the kind often presented to high court officials in token of their office. The *ding* was flanked on one side by a smaller antique bronze vessel with a pattern of gold inlay and on the other by a crystal bowl. At each side of the table stood a row of eight yellow cedar-wood armchairs with their backs to the wall; and above the chairs

hung, one on each side, a pair of vertical ebony boards inlaid
with a couplet in characters of gold:

(on the right-hand one)

May the jewel of learning shine in this house more effulgently than
the sun and moon.

(on the left-hand one)

May the insignia of honour glitter in these halls more brilliantly
than the starry sky.

This was followed by a colophon in smaller characters:

> With the Respectful Compliments of your Fellow-
> Student, Mu Shi, Hereditary Prince of Dong-an.

Lady Wang did not, however, normally spend her leisure
hours in this main reception hall, but in a smaller room on the
east side of the same building. Accordingly the nurses conducted Dai-yu through the door into this side apartment.

Here there was a large kang underneath the window, covered
with a scarlet Kashmir rug. In the middle of the kang was a
dark-red bolster with a pattern of medallions in the form of
tiny dragons, and a long russet-green seating strip in the same
pattern. A low rose-shaped table of coloured lacquer-work
stood at each side. On the left-hand one was a small, square,
four-legged *ding*, together with a bronze ladle, metal chopsticks, and an incense container. On the right-hand one was a
narrow-waisted Ru-ware imitation *gu* with a spray of freshly
cut flowers in it.

In the part of the room below the kang there was a row of
four big chairs against the east wall. All had footstools in front
of them and chair-backs and seat-covers in old rose brocade
sprigged with flowers. There were also narrow side-tables on
which tea things and vases of flowers were arranged, besides
other furnishings which it would be superfluous to enumerate.

The old nurses invited Dai-yu to get up on the kang; but
guessing that the brocade cushions arranged one on each side
near the edge of it must be her uncle's and aunt's places, she
deemed it more proper to sit on one of the chairs against the
wall below. The maids in charge of the apartment served tea,

and as she sipped it Dai-yu observed that their clothing, make-up, and deportment were quite different from those of the maids she had seen so far in other parts of the mansion.

Before she had time to finish her tea, a smiling maid came in wearing a dress of red damask and a black silk sleeveless jacket which had scalloped borders of some coloured material.

'The Mistress says will Miss Lin come over to the other side, please.'

The old nurses now led Dai-yu down the east gallery to a reception room at the side of the courtyard. This too had a kang. It was bisected by a long, low table piled with books and tea things. A much-used black satin back-rest was pushed up against the east wall. Lady Wang was seated on a black satin cushion and leaning against another comfortable-looking back-rest of black satin somewhat farther forward on the opposite side.

Seeing her niece enter, she motioned her to sit opposite her on the kang, but Dai-yu felt sure that this must be her Uncle Zheng's place. So, having observed a row of three chairs near the kang with covers of flower-sprigged brocade which looked as though they were in fairly constant use, she sat upon one of those instead. Only after much further pressing from her aunt would she get up on the kang, and even then she would only sit beside her and not in the position of honour opposite.

'Your uncle is in retreat today,' said Lady Wang. 'He will see you another time. There is, however, something I have got to talk to you about. The three girls are very well-behaved children, and in future, when you are studying or sewing together, even if once in a while they may grow a bit high-spirited, I can depend on them not to go too far. There is only one thing that worries me. I have a little monster of a son who tyrannizes over all the rest of this household. He has gone off to the temple today in fulfilment of a vow and is not yet back; but you will see what I mean this evening. The thing to do is never to take any notice of him. None of your cousins dare provoke him.'

Dai-yu had long ago been told by her mother that she had a boy cousin who was born with a piece of jade in his mouth and who was exceptionally wild and naughty. He hated study and liked to spend all his time in the women's apartments with the girls; but because Grandmother Jia doted on him so much, no one ever dared to correct him. She realized that it must be this cousin her aunt was now referring to.

'Do you mean the boy born with the jade, Aunt?' she asked. 'Mother often told me about him at home. She told me that he was one year older than me and that his name was Bao-yu. But she said that though he was very wilful, he always behaved very nicely to girls. Now that I am here, I suppose I shall be spending all my time with my girl cousins and not in the same part of the house as the boys. Surely there will be no danger of *my* provoking him?'

Lady Wang gave a rueful smile. 'You little know how things are here! Bao-yu is a law unto himself. Because your grandmother is so fond of him she has thoroughly spoiled him. When he was little he lived with the girls, so with the girls he remains now. As long as they take no notice of him, things run quietly enough. But if they give him the least encouragement, he at once becomes excitable, and then there is no end to the mischief he may get up to. That is why I counsel you to ignore him. He can be all honey-sweet words one minute and ranting and raving like a lunatic the next. So don't believe anything he says.'

Dai-yu promised to follow her aunt's advice.

Just then a maid came in with a message that 'Lady Jia said it was time for dinner', whereupon Lady Wang took Dai-yu by the hand and hurried her out through a back door. Passing along a verandah which ran beneath the rear eaves of the hall they came to a corner gate through which they passed into an alley-way running north and south. At the south end it was traversed by a narrow little building with a short passage-way running through its middle. At the north end was a white-painted screen wall masking a medium-sized gateway leading to a small courtyard in which stood a very little house.

'That,' said Lady Wang, pointing to the little house, 'is where your Cousin Lian's wife, Wang Xi-feng, lives, in case you want to see her later on. She is the person to talk to if there is anything you need.'

There were a few young pages at the gate of the courtyard

who, when they saw Lady Wang coming, all stood to attention with their hands at their sides.

Lady Wang now led Dai-yu along a gallery, running from east to west, which brought them out into the courtyard behind Grandmother Jia's apartments. Entering these by a back entrance, they found a number of servants waiting there who, as soon as they saw Lady Wang, began to arrange the table and chairs for dinner. The ladies of the house themselves took part in the service. Li Wan brought in the cups, Xi-feng laid out the chopsticks, and Lady Wang brought in the soup.

The table at which Grandmother Jia presided, seated alone on a couch, had two empty chairs on either side. Xi-feng tried to seat Dai-yu in the one on the left nearer to her grandmother – an honour which she strenuously resisted until her grandmother explained that her aunt and her elder cousins' wives would not be eating with them, so that, since she was a guest, the place was properly hers. Only then did she ask permission to sit, as etiquette prescribed. Grandmother Jia then ordered Lady Wang to be seated. This was the cue for the three girls to ask permission to sit. Ying-chun sat in the first place on the right opposite Dai-yu, Tan-chun sat second on the left, and Xi-chun sat second on the right.

While Li Wan and Xi-feng stood by the table helping to distribute food from the dishes, maids holding fly-whisks, spittoons, and napkins ranged themselves on either side. In addition to these, there were numerous other maids and serving-women in attendance in the outer room, yet not so much as a cough was heard throughout the whole of the meal.

When they had finished eating, a maid served each diner with tea on a little tray. Dai-yu's parents had brought their daughter up to believe that good health was founded on careful habits, and in pursuance of this principle, had always insisted that after a meal one should allow a certain interval to elapse before taking tea in order to avoid indigestion. However, she could see that many of the rules in this household were different from the ones she had been used to at home; so, being anxious to conform as much as possible, she accepted the tea. But as she did so, another maid proferred a spittoon, from which she inferred that the tea was for rinsing her mouth with. And it was not, in fact, until they had all rinsed out their mouths and washed their hands that another lot of tea was served, this time for drinking.

Grandmother Jia now dismissed her lady servers, observing that she wished to enjoy a little chat with her young grandchildren without the restraint of their grown-up presence.

Lady Wang obediently rose to her feet and, after exchanging a few pleasantries, went out, taking Li Wan and Wang Xi-feng with her.

Grandmother Jia asked Dai-yu what books she was studying.

'*The Four Books*,' said Dai-yu, and inquired in turn what books her cousins were currently engaged on.

'Gracious, child, they don't study books,' said her grandmother; 'they can barely read and write!'

While they were speaking, a flurry of footsteps could be heard outside and a maid came in to say that Bao-yu was back.

'I wonder,' thought Dai-yu, 'just what sort of graceless creature this Bao-yu is going to be!'

The young gentleman who entered in answer to her unspoken question had a small jewel-encrusted gold coronet on the top of his head and a golden headband low down over his brow in the form of two dragons playing with a large pearl.

He was wearing a narrow-sleeved, full-skirted robe of dark red material with a pattern of flowers and butterflies in two shades of gold. It was confined at the waist with a court girdle of coloured silks braided at regular intervals into elaborate clusters of knotwork and terminating in long tassels.

Over the upper part of his robe he wore a jacket of slate-blue Japanese silk damask with a raised pattern of eight large medallions on the front and with tasselled borders.

On his feet he had half-length dress boots of black satin with thick white soles.

As to his person, he had:

a face like the moon of Mid-Autumn,
a complexion like flowers at dawn,
a hairline straight as a knife-cut,
eyebrows that might have been painted by an artist's brush,
a shapely nose, and

eyes clear as limpid pools,
    that even in anger seemed to smile,
        and, as they glared, beamed tenderness the while.

Around his neck he wore a golden torque in the likeness of
a dragon and a woven cord of coloured silks to which the
famous jade was attached.

Dai-yu looked at him with astonishment. How strange! How
very strange! It was as though she had seen him somewhere
before, he was so extraordinarily familiar. Bao-yu went straight
past her and saluted his grandmother, who told him to come
after he had seen his mother, whereupon he turned round and
walked straight out again.

Quite soon he was back once more, this time dressed in a
completely different outfit.

The crown and circlet had gone. She could now see that his
side hair was dressed in a number of small braids plaited with
red silk, which were drawn round to join the long hair at the
back in a single large queue of glistening jet black, fastened at
intervals from the nape downwards with four enormous
pearls and ending in a jewelled gold clasp. He had changed his
robe and jacket for a rather more worn-looking rose-coloured
gown, sprigged with flowers. He wore the gold torque and his
jade as before, and she observed that the collection of objects
round his neck had been further augmented by a padlock-
shaped amulet and a lucky charm. A pair of ivy-coloured
embroidered silk trousers were partially visible beneath his
gown, thrust into black and white socks trimmed with
brocade. In place of the formal boots he was wearing thick-
soled crimson slippers.

She was even more struck than before by his fresh complexion. The cheeks might have been brushed with powder
and the lips touched with rouge, so bright was their natural
colour.

His glance was soulful,
    yet from his lips the laughter often leaped;
        a world of charm upon that brow was heaped;
        a world of feeling from those dark eyes peeped.

In short, his outward appearance was very fine. But appearances can be misleading. A perceptive poet has supplied two

sets of verses, to be sung to the tune of *Moon On West River*, which contain a more accurate appraisal of our hero than the foregoing descriptions.

I

Oft-times he sought out what would make him sad;
Sometimes an idiot seemed and sometimes mad.
Though outwardly a handsome sausage-skin,
He proved to have but sorry meat within.
A harum-scarum, to all duty blind,
A doltish mule, to study disinclined;
His acts outlandish and his nature queer;
Yet not a whit cared he how folk might jeer!

2

Prosperous, he could not play his part with grace,
Nor, poor, bear hardship with a smiling face.
So shamefully the precious hours he'd waste
That both indoors and out he was disgraced.
For uselessness the world's prize he might bear;
His gracelessness in history has no peer.
Let gilded youths who every dainty sample
Not imitate this rascal's dire example!

'Fancy changing your clothes before you have welcomed the visitor!' Grandmother Jia chided indulgently on seeing Bao-yu back again. 'Aren't you going to pay your respects to your cousin?'

Bao-yu had already caught sight of a slender, delicate girl whom he surmised to be his Aunt Lin's daughter and quickly went over to greet her. Then, returning to his place and taking a seat, he studied her attentively. How different she seemed from the other girls he knew!

Her mist-wreathed brows at first seemed to frown, yet were not frowning;

Her passionate eyes at first seemed to smile, yet were not merry.

Habit had given a melancholy cast to her tender face;

Nature had bestowed a sickly constitution on her delicate frame.

Often the eyes swam with glistening tears;

Often the breath came in gentle gasps.
In stillness she made one think of a graceful flower reflected
    in the water;
In motion she called to mind tender willow shoots caressed by
    the wind.
She had more chambers in her heart than the martyred Bi Gan;
And suffered a tithe more pain in it than the beautiful Xi
Shi.

Having completed his survey, Bao-yu gave a laugh.

'I have seen this cousin before.'

'Nonsense!' said Grandmother Jia. 'How could you possibly have done?'

'Well, perhaps not,' said Bao-yu, 'but her face seems so
familiar that I have the impression of meeting her again after
a long separation.'

'All the better,' said Grandmother Jia. 'That means that you
should get on well together.'

Bao-yu moved over again and, drawing a chair up beside
Dai-yu, recommenced his scrutiny.

Presently: 'Do you study books yet, cousin?'

'No,' said Dai-yu. 'I have only been taking lessons for a
year or so. I can barely read and write.'

'What's your name?'

Dai-yu told him.

'What's your school-name?'

'I haven't got one.'

Bao-yu laughed. 'I'll give you one, cousin. I think
"Frowner" would suit you perfectly.'

'Where's your reference?' said Tan-chun.

'In the *Encyclopedia of Men and Objects Ancient and Modern* it
says that somewhere in the West there is a mineral called "dai"
which can be used instead of eye-black for painting the eyebrows with. She has this "dai" in her name and she knits her
brows together in a little frown. I think it's a splendid name
for her!'

'I expect you made it up,' said Tan-chun scornfully.

'What if I did?' said Bao-yu. 'There are lots of made-up
things in books – apart from the *Four Books*, of course.'

He returned to his interrogation of Dai-yu.

'Have you got a jade?'

The rest of the company were puzzled, but Dai-yu at once divined that he was asking her if she too had a jade like the one he was born with.

'No,' said Dai-yu. 'That jade of yours is a very rare object. You can't expect everybody to have one.'

This sent Bao-yu off instantly into one of his mad fits. Snatching the jade from his neck he hurled it violently on the floor as if to smash it and began abusing it passionately.

'Rare object! Rare object! What's so lucky about a stone that can't even tell which people are better than others? Beastly thing! I don't want it!'

The maids all seemed terrified and rushed forward to pick it up, while Grandmother Jia clung to Bao-yu in alarm.

'Naughty, naughty boy! Shout at someone or strike them if you like when you are in a nasty temper, but why go smashing that precious thing that your very life depends on?'

'None of the girls has got one,' said Bao-yu, his face streaming with tears and sobbing hysterically. 'Only I have got one. It always upsets me. And now this new cousin comes here who is as beautiful as an angel and she hasn't got one either, so I *know* it can't be any good.'

'Your cousin did have a jade once,' said Grandmother Jia, coaxing him like a little child, 'but because when Auntie died she couldn't bear to leave her little girl behind, they had to let her take the jade with her instead. In that way your cousin could show her mamma how much she loved her by letting the jade be buried with her; and at the same time, whenever Auntie's spirit looked at the jade, it would be just like looking at her own little girl again.

'So when your cousin said she hadn't got one, it was only because she didn't want to boast about the good, kind thing she did when she gave it to her mamma. Now you put yours on again like a good boy, and mind your mother doesn't find out how naughty you have been.'

So saying, she took the jade from the hands of one of the maids and hung it round his neck for him. And Bao-yu, after reflecting for a moment or two on what she had said, offered no further resistance.

At this point some of the older women came to inquire what room Dai-yu was to sleep in.

'Move Bao-yu into the closet-bed with me,' said Grandmother Jia, 'and put Miss Lin for the time being in the green muslin summer-bed. We had better wait until spring when the last of the cold weather is over before seeing about the rooms for them and getting them settled permanently.'

'Dearest Grannie,' said Bao-yu pleadingly, 'I should be perfectly all right next to the summer-bed. There's no need to move me into your room. I should only keep you awake.'

Grandmother Jia, after a moment's reflection, gave her consent. She further gave instructions that Dai-yu and Bao-yu were each to have one nurse and one maid to sleep with them. The rest of their servants were to do night duty by rota in the adjoining room. Xi-feng had already sent across some lilac-coloured hangings, brocade quilts, satin coverlets and the like for Dai-yu's bedding.

Dai-yu had brought only two of her own people with her from home. One was her old wet-nurse Nannie Wang, the other was a little ten-year-old maid called Snowgoose. Considering Snowgoose too young and irresponsible and Nannie Wang too old and decrepit to be of much real service, Grandmother Jia gave Dai-yu one of her own maids, a body-servant of the second grade called Nightingale. She also gave orders that Dai-yu and Bao-yu were to be attended in other respects exactly like the three girls: that is to say, apart from the one wet-nurse, each was to have four other nurses to act as chaperones, two maids as body-servants to attend to their washing, dressing, and so forth, and four or five maids for dusting and cleaning, running errands and general duties.

These arrangements completed, Nannie Wang and Nightingale accompanied Dai-yu to bed inside the tent-like summer-bed, while Bao-yu's wet-nurse Nannie Li and his chief maid Aroma settled him down for the night in a big bed on the other side of the canopy.

Like Nightingale, Aroma had previously been one of Grandmother Jia's own maids. Her real name was Pearl. Bao-yu's grandmother, fearful that the maids who already waited on her darling boy could not be trusted to look after him properly, had picked out Pearl as a girl of tried and conspicuous fidelity and put her in charge over them. It was Bao-yu who was responsible for the curious name 'Aroma'. Discovering that Pearl's surname was Hua, which means 'Flowers', and having recently come across the line

> The flowers' aroma breathes of hotter days

in a book of poems, he told his grandmother that he wanted to call his new maid 'Aroma', so 'Aroma' her name thenceforth became.

Aroma had a certain dogged streak in her nature which had made her utterly devoted to Grandmother Jia as long as she was Grandmother Jia's servant, but which caused her to become just as exclusively and single-mindedly devoted to Bao-yu when her services were transferred to him. Since she found his character strange and incomprehensible, her simple devotion frequently impelled her to remonstrate with him, and when, as invariably happened, he took not the least notice of what she said, she was worried and hurt.

That night, when Bao-yu and Nannie Li were already asleep, Aroma could hear that Dai-yu and Nightingale on their side of the canopy had still not settled down, so, when she had finished taking down her hair and making herself ready for bed, she tiptoed through the muslin curtains and in a friendly way inquired what was the matter. Dai-yu invited her to sit down, and when she had seated herself on the edge of the bed, Nightingale proceeded to tell her what was troubling her new mistress.

'Miss Lin is all upset. She has just been crying her eyes out because she says she only just arrived here today, and yet already she has started young hopeful off on one of his turns. She says if that jade had been really smashed, it would have been all her fault. That's what she's so upset about. I've had no end of a job trying to comfort her.'

'You mustn't take on so, Miss,' said Aroma. 'You'll see him do much stranger things than that before he's finished. If you allow yourself to feel hurt every time he carries on like that, he will always be hurting you. Try not to be so sensitive, Miss!'

Dai-yu thanked her and promised to bear in mind what she had said, and after talking a little longer, they all settled down and went to sleep.

*

Rising early next day, they visited Grandmother Jia to wish her a good morning and then went over to Lady Wang's. They found her closeted with Wang Xi-feng, deep in discussion of a letter which had just arrived from Nanking, and attended by two women who had come with a message from Lady Wang's elder brother and sister-in-law. Tan-chun and the girls told Dai-yu, who knew nothing of the matter under discussion, that they were talking about Xue Pan, the son of their Aunt Xue who lived in Nanking.

It seemed that Xue Pan, relying on wealth and family pull to protect him from the consequences, had taken another man's life. The case was at present under investigation by the Ying-tian-fu yamen. Their uncle Wang Zi-teng had been informed of it, and had sent these messengers to the members of the family in the Rong mansion to suggest that they should invite Xue Pan to the capital.

But the outcome of this discussion will be dealt with in the following chapter.

CHAPTER 4

*The Bottle-gourd girl meets an
unfortunate young man
And the Bottle-gourd monk settles a
protracted lawsuit*

When Dai-yu and the girls went to call on Lady Wang, they found her in the midst of discussing family affairs with the messengers from her elder brother and his wife and heard talk of their aunt's family in Nanking being involved in a case of manslaughter. Since Lady Wang was obviously preoccupied with this matter, the girls went off to call on Li Wan.

Li Wan's husband Jia Zhu had died young, but fortunately not without issue. He left her a son called Jia Lan who was now just five years old and had already begun his schooling. Like most of the Jia women, Li Wan was the daughter of a distinguished Nanking official. Her father, Li Shou-zhong, had been a Director of Education.

Up to Li Shou-zhong's time, all members of the clan, including the women, had been given a first-class education; but when Li Shou-zhong became head of the family, he founded his educational policy for girls on the good old maxim 'a stupid woman is a virtuous one' and, when he had a daughter of his own, refused to let her engage in serious study. She was permitted to work her way through *The Four Books for Girls* and *Lives of Noble Women*, so that she might be able to recognize a few characters and be familiar with some of the models of female virtue of former ages; but overriding importance was to be attached to spinning and sewing, and even her name 'Wan', which means a kind of silk, was intended to symbolize her dedication to the needle.

Thanks to her upbringing, this young widow living in the midst of luxury and self-indulgence was able to keep herself like the 'withered tree and dead ashes' of the philosopher, shutting out everything that did not concern her and attending only to the duties of serving her husband's parents and bring-

ing up her child. Whatever leisure this left her was devoted to
her little sister-in-law and cousins, accompanying them at their
embroidery or hearing them recite their lessons.

With such gentle companions to console her, Dai-yu,
though a stranger and far from home, soon had nothing apart
from her old father that she need worry about.

*

Let us now turn to the affairs of Jia Yu-cun, newly installed
in the yamen at Ying-tian-fu.

No sooner had he arrived at his new post than a case involving manslaughter was referred to his tribunal. It concerned two parties in dispute over the purchase of a slave-girl.
Neither had been willing to give way to the other, and in the
ensuing affray one of the parties had been wounded and had
subsequently died. After reading the papers in the case, Yu-cun
summoned the plaintiff for questioning and received from him
the following account of what had happened:

'The murdered man was my master, Your Honour. Although
he did not realize it at the time, the girl he purchased had been
kidnapped by the man who was selling her. My master paid
him in advance, and arranged to receive the girl into his house
three days from the date of purchase, the third day being a
lucky day. The kidnapper, having already pocketed my young
master's money, then quietly went off and sold her again to
Xue. When we found this out, we went along to seize him and
to collect the girl.

'But unfortunately this Xue turned out to be a powerful
Nanking boss, who evidently thought that by money and
influence he could get away with anything. He set a crowd of
his henchmen on to my young master and beat him up so
badly that he died.

'Xue and his henchmen have now disappeared without
trace, leaving only a few retainers who were not involved in
the crime. But though it is a year since I first brought this
charge, no one has yet done anything to help me. I beseech
Your Honour to arrest the criminals and to uphold the course
of justice! Both the living and the dead will be everlastingly
grateful to you if you do!'

'This is monstrous!' said Yu-cun in a towering rage. 'Am I to understand that a man can be beaten to death and the murderer walk off scot-free with nobody lifting a finger to arrest him?' and he took up a warrant and was on the point of sending his runners to seize the murderer's dependants and bring them to court so that they might be put to the torture, when he observed one of the ushers signalling to him with his eyes not to issue the warrant. His resolution somewhat shaken, he put it down again and adjourned to his private chambers, dismissing everyone except the usher, whom he ordered to remain behind in attendance.

When they were alone together the usher, with a broad smile on his face, came forward and touched his hand and knee to the ground in the Manchu salute.

'Your Honour has gone a long way up in the world during these past eight or nine years! I don't expect you would remember me!'

'Your face is certainly familiar,' said Yu-cun, 'but for the moment I simply can't place it.'

The usher smiled again. 'Has Your Honour forgotten the place you started from? Do you remember nothing of the old times in Bottle-gourd Temple?'

With a start of recognition, Yu-cun remembered. The usher had been a little novice in the temple where he once lodged.

Finding himself homeless after the fire, and bethinking himself that a post in a yamen was a fine, gentlemanly way of earning a living, and being furthermore heartily sick of the rigours of monastic life, the little novice had taken advantage of his youth to grow his hair again and get himself a post as an usher. Small wonder that Yu-cun had failed to recognize him!

'Ah, so it *was* an old acquaintance!' said Yu-cun, grasping him warmly by the hand and urging him to sit down for a chat. But the usher would not be seated.

'Come,' said Yu-cun, 'as a friend of my early, hard-up days you are entitled to. After all, this is a private room. Why not?'

The usher permitted himself to perch one of his haunches sideways on the edge of a chair.

'Tell me,' said Yu-cun, 'why did you stop me issuing that warrant just now?'

'Your Honour is new to this post. Surely you must have provided yourself before you left with a copy of the *Mandarin's Life-Preserver* for this province?'

'What is the *Mandarin's Life-Preserver*?' Yu-cun inquired curiously.

'Nowadays every provincial official carries a private hand-list with the names of all the richest, most influential people in his area. There is one for every province. They list those families which are so powerful that if you were ever to run up against one of them unknowingly, not only your job, but perhaps even your life might be in danger. That's why they are called "life-preservers".

'Now take this Xue you were dealing with just now. Your Honour couldn't possibly try conclusions with *him*! Why do you suppose this case has remained unsettled for so long? It's a straightforward enough case. The reason is simply that none of your predecessors dared touch it because of the unpleasant-ness and loss of face it would have caused them.'

While he was speaking he had been fishing for a copy of the *Mandarin's Life-Preserver* in his pocket. This he now presented to Yu-cun for his inspection. It contained a set of doggerel verses in which were listed the big families and most powerful magnates of the area in which he was working. It went some-thing like this:

> Shout hip hurrah
> For the Nanking Jia!
> They weigh their gold out
> By the jar.
>
> The Ah-bang Palace
> Scrapes the sky,
> But it could not house
> The Nanking Shi.
>
> The King of the Ocean
> Goes along,
> When he's short of gold beds,
> To the Nanking Wang.
>
> The Nanking Xue
> So rich are they,
> To count their money
> Would take all day . . .

Before Yu-cun had time to read further, a warning chime from the inner gate and a shout outside the door announced the arrival of a Mr Wang on an official call. Yu-cun hastily donned the hat and robe of office which he had temporarily laid aside and went out to meet the visitor. About the length of time it would take to eat a meal elapsed before he returned and resumed his conversation with the usher.

'Those four families,' said the usher in answer to a question from Yu-cun, 'are all closely connected with each other. A loss for one is a loss for all. A gain for one is a gain for all. The Xue who has been charged with the manslaughter is one of the "Nanking Xue so rich are they". Not only can he count on the support of the other three Nanking families, he also has any number of family friends and connections of his own both at the capital and in the provinces. *Now* who are you going to arrest?'

'That's all very well,' said Yu-cun with an uneasy laugh, 'but how am I going to settle this case? Incidentally, I assume you know perfectly well where the criminal is hiding?'

'I wouldn't deceive Your Honour,' replied the usher with a grin, 'not only do I know where the criminal has gone but I also know who the kidnapper is and all about the poor devil who was killed. Let me tell you the whole story.

'The man who was killed was a poor country squire's son called Feng Yuan. His father and mother were both dead and he had no brothers. He lived off the income of a very small estate. He was eighteen or nineteen when he died. He was a confirmed queer and not interested in girls. Which shows that the whole business must have been fated, because no sooner did he set eyes on this girl than he at once fell in love with her – swore he would never have anything more to do with boys and never have any other woman but her. That was the idea of this waiting three days before she came to him. To make it seem more like a wedding and less like a sale.

'What he couldn't foresee, of course, was that the kidnapper would use this interval to resell her on the sly to Xue, hoping to pocket the money from both parties and then do a flit. Only he didn't get away with it. The two parties nabbed him before he could disappear and beat the daylights out of

him. Both refused to take back their money, and both insisted
that they wanted the girl. It was at this point that our young
friend Xue called for his roughs to get to work on Feng Yuan.
They beat him till he was hardly recognizable. Then they
picked him up and carried him home. He died three days
later.

'Now long before any of this happened, young Xue had
made arrangements for a journey to the capital. So after killing
Feng and carrying off the girl, he set off with his family, calm
as you please, on the appointed day. There was no question of
his running away because of the killing. In his eyes a trifling
matter like taking another man's life was something for his
junior clansmen or the servants to clear up in his absence.

'But never mind him. Who do you think the slave-girl is?'

'How in the world should I know?' said Yu-cun.

The usher smiled maliciously. 'You ought to, Your
Honour! She is your great benefactress – Ying-lian, the little
daughter of Mr Zhen, who used to live next door to
Bottle-gourd Temple.'

'Good gracious!' said Yu-cun in astonishment. 'I had heard
that she was kidnapped at the age of five. But how did she
come to be sold so long after the kidnapping?'

'This type of kidnapper specializes in kidnapping very
young girls and rearing them until they are twelve or thirteen
for sale in other parts of the country. When she was little we
used to play with Ying-lian at the temple nearly every day, so
I knew her very well; and when I saw her again, even though
it was after an interval of seven or eight years, I could tell it
was her. She'd grown into a little woman in the meantime, but
her features were still the same; and to confirm it there was a
tiny red birthmark right in the middle of her brow which I
remembered.

'By a strange coincidence the kidnapper had rented one of
my rooms, and one day when he was out I put it to her who
she was. But she said she was scared of being beaten and
nothing would induce her to talk. She just kept insisting that
the kidnapper was her real father, selling her because he had
no money to pay his debts with. I kept on at her, cajoling and
persuading, and in the end she broke down and cried. Said she

didn't remember anything about her childhood. But there's no doubt in my mind. It's her, all right.

'The day young Feng met her and paid out the money for her, the kidnapper got drunk, and she opened up to me a bit. She was feeling very relieved. She said, "Today I think my tribulations are at last coming to an end." But then later, when she heard that she wasn't to be installed until after another three days, she began to look worried and despondent again. I felt truly sorry for her, and sent the wife round to have a talk with her while the kidnapper was out and give her a bit of encouragement.

'The wife said to her, "Mr Feng's insistence on waiting three days before taking you in shows that he doesn't intend to treat you like a servant. Besides," she said, "he's a very nice, handsome gentleman, and quite comfortably off. Normally he doesn't like the fair sex, yet here he is spending everything he has on your purchase. You can tell from that," she said, "how much he must care for you. You only have to be patient for another day or two," she said. "You've no cause to be downcast."

'Well, that seemed to cheer her up a bit, and she began to feel that life was going to be worth living.

'But only the day after that, by the most accursed stroke of bad luck which no one could possibly have foreseen, she was sold to Xue. Now if it had been anyone else, it wouldn't have mattered so much, but this young Xue, whose nickname is the Oaf King, is the world's most bad-tempered bully; and having spent money like water on buying the girl only to find that she wasn't willing, he knocked her about until she was half unconscious and dragged her off with him more dead than alive. Whether she's alive or dead now, I have no idea.

'And young Feng is really to be pitied! After a brief moment of happiness, before anything had come his way, he spent all his money and laid down his life for nothing!'

Yu-cun sighed sympathetically. 'Their meeting cannot have been coincidental. It must have been the working out of some destiny. An atonement. Otherwise, how is one to account for Feng Yuan's sudden affection for that particular girl?

'And Ying-lian, after all those years of ill-treatment at the

hands of her kidnapper, suddenly seeing a road to freedom
opening in front of her – for she was a girl of feeling, and there
is no doubt that they would have made a fine couple if they
had succeeded in coming together – and then for this to have
happened!

'And even though Xue may be far wealthier and better-
placed than Feng was, a man like that is sure to have numbers
of concubines and paramours and to be licentious and de-
bauched in his habits – quite incapable of concentrating all his
affections on one girl as Feng Yuan would have done.

'A real case of an ideal romance on the one hand and a pair
of unlucky young things on the other adding up to make a
tragedy!

'But a truce to this discussion of other people's affairs! Let
us rather consider how this case is to be settled!'

'Your Honour used to be decisive enough in the old days,'
said the usher with a smile. 'What has become of your old
resolution today? Now, I was told that your promotion to this
post was due to the combined influence of the Jias and the
Wangs; and this Xue Pan is related to the Jias by marriage.
Why not trim your sails to the wind in your handling of this
case? Why not make a virtue of necessity by doing them a
favour which will stand you in good stead next time you see
them?'

'What you say is, of course, entirely correct,' said Yu-cun.
'But there is, after all, a human life involved in this case; and
you have to remember that I have only just been restored to
office by an act of Imperial clemency. I really cannot bring
myself to pervert justice for private ends at the very moment when I ought to be doing my utmost to show my
gratitude.'

The usher smiled coldly. 'What Your Honour says is no
doubt very right and proper, but it won't wash. Not the way
things are in the world today! Haven't you heard the old saying "The man of spirit shapes his actions to the passing
moment"? And there's another old saying: "It is the mark of
a gentleman to avoid what is inauspicious". If you were to act
in accordance with what you have just said, not only would
you *not* be able to show your gratitude to the Emperor, but

also you would probably put your own life in danger. If I were you, I should think very carefully before you do anything.'

Yu-cun lowered his head in thought. After a very long pause he asked, 'What do *you* think I ought to do?'

'I've thought of a very good solution,' said the usher. 'When you open court tomorrow, you should make a great display of authority. Send out writs, issue warrants for arrest, and so forth. You won't, of course, be able to arrest the culprits, and the plaintiffs will certainly not allow the matter to rest there; so what you do then is to arrest some of Xue's clansmen and servants for questioning. But in the meantime I shall have got to work on them on the side and arranged for them to report that Xue has died of sudden illness. This can be supported by the affidavits of the whole Xue clan and the people living in the neighbourhood.

'Then Your Honour has it put about that you have a gift for the planchette. You have an altar set up in the court and a planchette board installed on it and you issue an open invitation to any members of the public who want to to attend a séance. Then you say, "The spirit control gives judgment as follows:

' "The dead man, Feng Yuan, owed a debt of *karma* to Xue Pan from a former life and 'meeting his enemy in a narrow way', paid for it with his life. The sudden, unexplained illness which struck down Xue Pan was caused by the vengeful ghost of Feng Yuan come to claim its own. Since the tragedy was entirely due to the behaviour of the kidnapper, the kidnapper should be dealt with according to the full rigour of the law; but apart from him, all other parties are exonerated ..." and so on and so forth.

'I shall secretly instruct the kidnapper to make a full confession, and when the public see that the judgment given by the planchette tallies with the confession made by the kidnapper, they will naturally have no suspicions.

'Then you award the Fengs compensation to cover funeral expenses and so on. And since the Xues are rolling in money, you can say anything you like. Five hundred, a thousand – it doesn't matter. There's no one of any importance on the Feng side, and in any case they're mainly in this for the money. So once they have got their compensation, they shouldn't give you any further trouble.

'What about that for a plan, Your Honour? You just think it over!'

Yu-cun laughed. 'Too risky! Let me turn it over in my mind a little longer. The main thing is to think of something that will stop people talking.'

And with this observation the two men concluded their discussion.

At next day's session a group of well-known associates of the wanted man were brought in and subjected by Yu-cun to careful questioning. It emerged, as the usher had said, that the Fengs were few in number and had brought this action solely in the hope of gaining some compensation, and that it was only because the Xues had, with the arrogance of the very rich and very powerful, refused to pay a penny, that the case had been brought to a standstill.

By a judicious bending of the law to suit the circumstances, Yu-cun managed to arrive at some sort of judgment whereby the plaintiffs received substantial compensation and went off tolerably well satisfied. He then hurriedly drafted and sent off two letters, one to Jia Zheng and one to Wang Zi-teng, Commandant, Metropolitan Barracks, in which he merely stated that their 'nephew's affair had been settled and there was no further cause for concern'.

Fearful that the now usher and quondam novice of Bottle-gourd Temple might talk to others about the days when he was an obscure and impoverished student, Yu-cun for some time went about in great discomfort of mind. Finally, however, he managed to catch him out in some misdemeanour or other and have him drafted for military service on a frontier outpost, after which he felt able to breathe freely again.

*

But now no more of Yu-cun. Let us turn instead to Young Xue, the man who purchased Ying-lian and had Feng Yuan beaten to death. He was a native of Nanking and came of a refined and highly cultivated family, but having lost his father in infancy and been, as sole remaining scion of the stock, excessively indulged by a doting widowed mother, he had grown up into a useless lout. The family was immensely wealthy. As one of the official Court Purveyors they received money from the Privy Purse with which to make purchases for the Imperial Household.

Xue Pan, to give him his full name, was a naturally extravagant young man with an insolent turn of speech. He had been educated after a fashion, but could barely read and write. He devoted the greater part of his time to cock-fighting, horse-racing, and outings to places of scenic interest. Though an Imperial Purveyor, he was wholly innocent of business skill and *savoir-faire*; and though, for his father's and grandfather's sake, he was allowed to register at the Ministry and receive regular payments of grain and money, everything else was looked after for him by the clerks and factors of the family business.

Xue Pan's widowed mother was a younger half-sister of Wang Zi-teng, at that time Commandant of the Metropolitan Barracks, and younger sister of Lady Wang, the wife of Jia Zheng of the Rong mansion. She was now around fifty and had only the one son. Besides Xue Pan she had a daughter two years his junior called Bao-chai, a girl of flawless looks and great natural refinement. While her father was still alive she had been his favourite and had been taught to read and write and construe – all of which she did ten times better than her oafish brother; but when he died and her brother proved incapable of offering their mother any comfort, she laid aside her books and devoted herself to needlework and housewifely duties in order to take some of the burden off her mother's shoulders.

The well-known interest always shown by our present sovereign in literature and the arts, and the widespread recruitment of talent that this has stimulated, had recently, at the time of which we speak, led to an unprecedented act of Imperial grace whereby daughters of hereditary officials and distinguished families, apart from the possibility of being recruited to the Imperial seraglio by the customary procedures, were permitted to have their names sent in to the

Ministry for selection as study-companions, with the rank and title of Maid of Honour or Lady-in-waiting, of the Imperial princesses and the daughters of princes of the blood.

This circumstance, coupled with the fact that, since the death of his father, the managers, clerks, and factors of the family business in its various agencies throughout the provinces had profited from Xue Pan's youth and ignorance of affairs to feather their own nests at the firm's expense, and even the family's enterprises in the capital, of which there were several, had shown a gradual falling-off, provided Xue Pan, who had long heard of the rich pleasures of the metropolis and was agog to taste them, with excuses for realizing his cherished ambition, viz:

1. They must go to the capital because he had to present his sister to the Ministry for selection.

2. They must go to the capital to look up their kinsfolk there.

3. They must go to the capital so that he might clear his accounts with the Ministry and take receipt of a new instalment of funds.

(Needless to say, the sole substantial reason for going to the capital, Xue Pan's desire to see the sights, was unexpressed.)

Accordingly, their baggage had long been packed and souvenirs of Nanking for their friends and relations in the capital long been selected and a date for their departure long been decided on, when Xue Pan encountered the kidnapper and Ying-lian and, as Ying-lian was an uncommonly attractive slave-girl, resolved to purchase her and make her his concubine.

Then Feng and his servants came to seize the girl and Xue Pan, confident in his superior forces, shouted the command to his attendant roughs which was to have such fatal consequences for poor Feng Yuan.

Entrusting everything to his clansmen and a few old and trusty retainers, he then proceeded to depart according to schedule, in company with his mother and sister, on the long journey to the capital, accounting the charge of manslaughter a mere bagatelle which the expenditure of a certain amount of coin could confidently be expected to resolve.

Of the journey our story gives no record, except to say that on the last day, when they were about to enter the capital, they heard news that Xue Pan's uncle Wang Zi-teng had just been promoted C.-in-C. Northern Provinces with instructions to leave the capital on a tour of frontier inspection. The news secretly delighted Xue Pan.

'Just as I was worrying about Uncle cramping my style when we got to the capital and preventing me from having a really good fling,' he reflected, 'the old boy obligingly gets himself popped out of the way. Fortune is on my side!'

He then proceeded to reason as follows with his mother:

'We've got several houses in the capital, but it's all of ten years since anyone has been to stay in them, so you can bet that the housekeepers will have let all the rooms out on the sly. We shall have to send someone on ahead to get things straightened out for us.'

'Whyever should we go to any such trouble?' said his mother. 'I thought the main purpose of our coming here in the first place was to see our relations. There must be lots and lots of spare room at your Uncle Wang's and at your Uncle Jia's place. Surely it would be much more sensible to stay with one of them first? There will be plenty of time to send our people to get a place of our own ready after we are there.'

'But Uncle's just been promoted to the Northern Provinces,' Xue Pan expostulated. 'They will all be making frantic preparations for him to go. What sort of stupid idiots shall we look like if we come scooting along with all our bag and baggage just at the very moment when he wants to leave?'

'Suppose your Uncle Wang *has* been promoted to another place,' said his mother. 'There is still your Uncle Jia. Besides, Uncle Wang and Auntie Jia have for years been sending us letters inviting us to come and stay with them. Now that we are here, even though Uncle Wang is busy getting ready to go, Auntie Jia will probably be only too glad to have us. I'm sure she would be most offended if we were to go rushing off to get our own house ready.

'But I know perfectly well what's in your mind. You think that if we are staying with your uncle or aunt you will be too restricted, and that if we were living in our own place you would be freer to do just as you liked. Very well then. Why don't you go off and choose a house for yourself to live in and let me and your sister go to Auntie's without you? I haven't seen her or the girls for years and years, and I intend to spend a few days with them now we are here.'

Experience taught Xue Pan that his mother was in an obstinate mood and not to be shaken from her purpose, so he resignedly gave orders to the porters to make straight for the Rong mansion.

*

Lady Wang had just breathed a sigh of relief on learning that the affair of Xue Pan's manslaughter charge had been retrieved through the good offices of Jia Yu-cun, when the news that her elder brother had been promoted to a frontier post plunged her once more in gloom at the prospect of losing her main source of contact with the members of her own family. Several days passed in despondency, and then suddenly the servants announced that her sister, bringing her son and daughter and all her household with her, had arrived in the capital and was at that very moment outside the gate dismounting from her carriage.

Delightedly she hurried with her women to the entrance of the main reception hall and conducted Aunt Xue and her party inside. The sudden reunion of the two sisters was, it goes without saying, an affecting one in which joy and sorrow mingled. After an exchange of information about the years of separation, and after they had been taken to see Grandmother Jia and made their reverence to her, and after the gifts of Nanking produce had been presented and everyone had been introduced to everyone else, there was a family party to welcome the new arrivals.

Xue Pan, meanwhile, had paid his respects to Jia Zheng and Jia Lian and been taken to see Jia She and Cousin Zhen. Jia Zheng now sent a servant round to Lady Wang with the following message:

'Your sister is getting on in years and our nephew is very young and seems rather inexperienced and, I fear, quite capable of getting into a scrape again if they are going to live outside. Pear Tree Court in the north-east corner of our property is lying completely unoccupied at the moment and has quite a sizeable amount of room in it. Why not invite your sister and her children to move in there?'

Lady Wang had wanted all along to ask her sister to stay. Grandmother Jia had sent someone round to tell her that she should 'ask Mrs Xue to stay with us here, so that we can all be close to one another.' And Aunt Xue for her own part had been wanting to stay so that some sort of check could be kept on her son. She was sure that if they were to be on their own somewhere else in the city his unbridled nature would precipitate some fresh calamity. She therefore accepted the invitation with alacrity, privately adding the proviso that she could only contemplate a long stay if it was on the understanding that they were themselves to be responsible for all their expenses. Lady Wang knew that money was no problem to them, so she readily consented, and Aunt Xue and her children proceeded there and then to move into Pear Tree Court.

This Pear Tree Court had been the Duke of Rong-guo's retreat during the last years of his life. Its buildings totalled not much more than ten frames; but though small and charming, it was complete in every respect, with a little reception room in the front and all the usual rooms and offices behind. It had its own outer door on to the street, through which Xue Pan and the menservants could come and go, and another gate in the south-west corner giving on to a passage-way which led into the courtyard east of Lady Wang's compound.

Through this passage-way Aunt Xue would now daily repair, either after dinner or in the evening, to gossip with Grandmother Jia or reminisce with her sister, Lady Wang. Bao-chai for her part spent her time each day in great contentment, reading or playing Go or sewing with Dai-yu and the three girls.

The only dissatisfied member of the party – to begin with, at any rate – was Xue Pan. He had not wanted to stay in the Jia household, fearing that his uncle's control would prevent him from enjoying himself, but what with his mother's obstinacy and the insistence of the Jias themselves, he was obliged to acquiesce in settling there for the time being, contenting himself with sending some of his people to clean up one of their houses outside so that he would be able to move there later on.

But, to his pleasant surprise, he discovered that the young males of the Jia establishment, half of whom he was already on familiar terms with before he had been there a month, were of the same idle, extravagant persuasion as himself and thought him a capital fellow and boon companion. And so he found himself meeting them for a drinking-party one day, for theatre-going the next, on a third day perhaps gambling with them or visiting brothels. For there were no limits to the depravity of their pleasures, and Xue Pan, who was bad enough to start with, soon became ten times worse under their expert guidance.

It was not that Jia Zheng was a slack disciplinarian, incapable of keeping his house in order; but the clan was so numerous that he simply could not keep an eye on everyone at once. And in any case the nominal head of the family was not Jia Zheng but Cousin Zhen who, as eldest grandson of the senior, Ning-guo branch, had inherited the founder's office and emoluments and was therefore officially in charge of all the clan's affairs.

Besides, Jia Zheng was kept busy with public and private business of his own and, being by nature a quiet, retiring man who attached little importance to mundane affairs, tended to use whatever leisure time he had for reading and playing Go.

Then again, the Pear Tree Court was two courtyards away from Jia Zheng's compound and had its own private door onto the street by which Xue Pan could come and go as he pleased, so that he and his young cronies could enjoy themselves to their heart's content with no one being any the wiser.

Under these agreeable circumstances Xue Pan gradually abandoned all thought of moving out.

But as to the outcome of these capers: that will be told in a later chapter.

CHAPTER 5

Jia Bao-yu visits the Land of Illusion
And the fairy Disenchantment performs the
'Dream of Golden Days'

From the moment Lin Dai-yu entered the Rong mansion, Grandmother Jia's solicitude for her had manifested itself in a hundred different ways. The arrangements made for her meals and accommodation were exactly the same as for Bao-yu. The other three granddaughters, Ying-chun, Tan-chun and Xi-chun, were relegated to a secondary place in the old lady's affections, and the objects of her partiality themselves began to feel an affection for each other which far exceeded what they felt for any of the rest. Sharing each other's company every minute of the day and sleeping in the same room at night, they developed an understanding so intense that it was almost as if they had grown into a single person.

And now suddenly this Xue Bao-chai had appeared on the scene – a young lady who, though very little older than Dai-yu, possessed a grown-up beauty and aplomb in which all agreed Dai-yu was her inferior. Moreover, in contrast to Dai-yu with her air of lofty self-sufficiency and total obliviousness to all who did not move on the same exalted level as herself, Bao-chai had a generous, accommodating disposition which greatly endeared her to subordinates, so that even the tiniest maid looked on Miss Bao-chai as a familiar friend. Dai-yu could not but feel somewhat put out by this – a fact of which Bao-chai herself, however, was totally unaware.

As for Bao-yu, he was still only a child – a child, moreover, whom nature had endowed with the eccentric obtuseness of a simpleton. Brothers, sisters, cousins, were all one to him. In his relationships with people he made no distinction between one person and another. If his relationship with Dai-yu was exceptional, it was because greater proximity – since she was living with him in his grandmother's quarters – made her more familiar to him than the rest; and greater familiarity bred greater intimacy.

And of course, with greater intimacy came the occasional tiffs and misunderstandings that are usual with people who have a great deal to do with each other.

One day the two of them had fallen out over something or other and the argument had ended with Dai-yu crying alone in her room and Bao-yu feeling remorsefully that perhaps he had spoken too roughly. Presently he went in to make his peace with her and gradually, very gradually, Dai-yu's equanimity was restored.

The winter plum in the gardens of the Ning Mansion was now at its best, and this particular day Cousin Zhen's wife, You-shi, had some wine taken into the gardens and came over in person, bringing her son Jia Rong and his young wife with her, to invite Grandmother Jia, Lady Xing and Lady Wang to a flower-viewing party.

Grandmother Jia and the rest went round as soon as they had finished their breakfast. The party was in the All-scents Garden. It began with tea and continued with wine, and as it was a family gathering confined to the ladies of the Ning and Rong households, nothing particularly worth recording took place.

At one point in the party Bao-yu was overcome with tiredness and heaviness and expressed a desire to take an afternoon nap. Grandmother Jia ordered some of the servants to go back to the house with him and get him comfortably settled, adding that they might return with him later when he was rested; but Qin-shi, the little wife of Jia Rong, smilingly proposed an alternative.

'We have got just the room here for Uncle Bao. Leave him to me, Grannie dear! He will be quite safe in my hands.'

She turned to address the nurses and maidservants who were in attendance on Bao-yu.

'Come, my dears! Tell Uncle Bao to follow me.'

Grandmother Jia had always had a high opinion of Qin-shi's trustworthiness – she was such a charming, delightful little creature, the favourite among her great-granddaughters-in-law – and was quite content to leave the arrangements to her.

Qin-shi conducted Bao-yu and his little knot of attendants to an inner room in the main building. As they entered, Bao-yu glanced up and saw a painting hanging above them on the opposite wall. The figures in it were very finely executed. They represented Scholarly Diligence in the person of the Han philosopher Liu Xiang at his book, obligingly illuminated for him by a supernatural being holding a large flaming torch. Bao-yu found the painting – or rather its subject – distasteful. But the pair of mottoes which flanked it proved the last straw:

True learning implies a clear insight into human activities.
Genuine culture involves the skilful manipulation of human relationships.

In vain the elegant beauty and splendid furnishings of the room! Qin-shi was given to understand in no uncertain terms that her uncle Bao-yu wished to be out of it *at once*.

'If this is not good enough for you,' said Qin-shi with a laugh, 'where *are* we going to put you? – unless you would like to have your rest in my bedroom.'

A little smile played over Bao-yu's face and he nodded. The nurses were shocked.

'An uncle sleep in the bedroom of his nephew's wife! Who ever heard of such a thing!'

Qin-shi laughed again.

'He won't misbehave. Good gracious, he's only a little boy! We don't have to worry about that sort of thing yet! You know my little brother who came last month: he's the same age as Uncle Bao, but if you stood them side by side I shouldn't be a bit surprised if he wasn't the taller of the two.'

'Why haven't I seen your brother yet?' Bao-yu demanded. 'Bring him in and let me have a look at him!'

The servants all laughed.

'Bring him in? Why, he's ten or twenty miles away! But I expect you'll meet him one of these days.'

In the course of this exchange the party had made its way to Qin-shi's bedroom. As Bao-yu entered, a subtle whiff of the most delicious perfume assailed his nostrils, making a sweet stickiness inside his drooping eyelids and causing all the joints in his body to dissolve.

'What a lovely smell!'

He repeated the words several times over.

Inside the room there was a painting by Tang Yin entitled 'Spring Slumber' depicting a beautiful woman asleep under a crab-apple tree, whose buds had not yet opened. The painting was flanked on either side by a pair of calligraphic scrolls inscribed with a couplet from the brush of the Song poet Qin Guan:

(on one side)

The coldness of spring has imprisoned the soft buds in a wintry dream;

(on the other side)

The fragrance of wine has intoxicated the beholder with imagined flower-scents.

On a table stood an antique mirror that had once graced the tiring-room of the lascivious empress Wu Ze-tian. Beside it stood the golden platter on which Flying Swallow once danced for her emperor's delight. And on the platter was that very quince which the villainous An Lu-shan threw at beautiful Yang Gui-fei, bruising her plump white breast. At the far end of the room stood the priceless bed on which Princess Shou-yang was sleeping out of doors under the eaves of the Han-zhang Palace when the plum-flower lighted on her forehead and set a new fashion for coloured patches. Over it hung a canopy commissioned by Princess Tong-chang entirely fashioned out of ropes of pearls.

'I like it here,' said Bao-yu happily.

'My room,' said Qin-shi with a proud smile, 'is fit for an immortal to sleep in.' And she unfolded a quilted coverlet, whose silk had been laundered by the fabulous Xi Shi, and arranged the double head-rest that Hong-niang once carried for her amorous mistress.

The nurses now helped Bao-yu into bed and then tiptoed out, leaving him attended only by his four young maids: Aroma, Skybright, Musk, and Ripple. Qin-shi told them to go outside and stop the cats from fighting on the eaves.

As soon as Bao-yu closed his eyes he sank into a confused

sleep in which Qin-shi was still there yet at the same time seemed to be drifting along weightlessly in front of him. He followed her until they came to a place of marble terraces and vermilion balustrades where there were green trees and crystal streams. Everything in this place was so clean and so pure that it seemed as if no human foot could ever have trodden there or floating speck of dust ever blown into it. Bao-yu's dreaming self rejoiced. 'What a delightful place!' he thought. 'If only I could spend all my life here! How much nicer it would be than living under the daily restraint of my parents and teachers!'

These idle reflections were interrupted by someone singing a song on the other side of a hill:

> 'Spring's dream-time will like drifting clouds disperse,
> Its flowers snatched by a flood none can reverse.
> Then tell each nymph and swain
> 'Tis folly to invite love's pain!'

It was the voice of a girl. Before its last echoes had died away, a beautiful woman appeared in the quarter from which the voice had come, approaching him with a floating, fluttering motion. She was quite unlike any earthly lady, as the following poem will make clear:

She has left her willow-tree house, from her blossoming bower
　　stepped out;
For the birds betray where she walks through the trees that cluster
　　about,
And a shadow athwart the winding walk announces that she is near,
And a fragrance of musk and orchid from fluttering fairy sleeves,
And a tinkle of girdle-gems that falls on the ear
At each movement of her dress of lotus leaves.
A peach-tree blossoms in her dimpling cheek;
Her cloud-coiled tresses are halcyon-sleek;
And she reveals, through parted cherry lips,
Teeth like pomegranate pips.
Her slim waist's sinuous swaying calls to mind
The dance of snowflakes with the waltzing wind;
Hair ornaments of pearl and halcyon blue
Outshine her painted forehead's golden hue.
Her face, through blossoms fleetingly disclosed,

To mirth or ire seems equally disposed;
And as by the waterside she goes,
Hovering on light-stepping toes,
A half-incipient look of pique
Says she would speak, yet would not speak;
While her feet, with the same irresolution,
Would halt, yet would not interrupt their motion.
I contemplate her rare complexion,
Ice-pure and jade-like in perfection;
I marvel at her glittering dress,
Where art lends grace to sumptuousness;
I wonder at her fine-cut features –
Marble, which fragrance marks as one with living creatures;
And I admire her queenly gait,
Like stately dance of simurgh with his mate.
Her purity I can best show
In plum-trees flowering in the snow;
Her chastity I shall recall
In orchids white at first frost-fall;
Her tranquil nature will prevail,
Constant as lone pine in an empty vale;
Her loveliness as dazzled make
As sunset gilding a pellucid lake;
Her glittering elegance I can compare
With dragons in an ornamental mere;
Her dreamy soulfulness most seems
Like wintry waters in the moon's cold beams.
The beauties of days gone by by her beauty are all abashed.
Where was she born, and from whence descended?
Immortal I judge her, fresh come from fairy feastings by the
  Jasper Pool,
Or from fluting in starry halls, some heavenly concert ended.

Observing delightedly that the lady was a fairy, Bao-yu
hurried forward and saluted her with a smile.

'Madam Fairy, I don't know where you have come from or
where you are going to, but as I am quite lost in this place,
will you please take me with you and be my guide?'

'I am the fairy Disenchantment,' the fairy woman replied.
'I live beyond the Realm of Separation, in the Sea of Sadness.
There is a Mountain of Spring Awakening which rises from
the midst of that sea, and on that mountain is the Paradise of

the Full-blown Flower, and in that paradise is the Land of Illusion, which is my home. My business is with the romantic passions, love-debts, girlish heartbreaks and male philanderings of your dust-stained, human world. The reason I have come here today is that recently there has been a heavy concentration of love-*karma* in this area, and I hope to be able to find an opportunity of distributing a quantity of amorous thoughts by implanting them in the appropriate breasts. My meeting you here today is no accident but a part of the same project.

'This place where we are now is not so very far from my home. I have not much to offer you, but would you like to come back with me and let me try to entertain you? I have some fairy tea, which I picked myself. You could have a cup of that. And I have a few jars of choice new wine of my own brewing. I have also been rehearsing a fairy choir and a troupe of fairy dancers in a twelve-part suite which I recently composed called "A Dream of Golden Days". I could get them to perform it for you. What do you think?'

Bao-yu was so excited by this invitation that he quite forgot to wonder what had become of Qin-shi in his eagerness to accompany the fairy. As he followed her, a big stone archway suddenly loomed up in front of them on which

THE LAND OF ILLUSION

was written in large characters. A couplet in smaller characters was inscribed on either side of the arch:

> Truth becomes fiction when the fiction's true;
> Real becomes not-real when the unreal's real.

Having negotiated the archway, they presently came to the gateway of a palace. The following words were inscribed horizontally above the lintel:

SEAS OF PAIN AND SKIES OF PASSION

whilst the following words were inscribed vertically on the two sides:

> Ancient earth and sky
>   Marvel that love's passion should outlast all time.
> Star-crossed men and maids
>   Groan that love's debts should be so hard to pay.

'I see,' said Bao-yu to himself. 'I wonder what the meaning of "passion that outlasts all time" can be. And what are "love's debts"? From now on I must make an effort to understand these things.'

He could not, of course, have known it, but merely by thinking this he had invited the attentions of the demon Lust, and at that very moment a little of the demon's evil poison had entered Bao-yu's body and lodged itself in the innermost recesses of his heart.

Wholly unconscious of his mortal peril, Bao-yu continued to follow the fairy woman. They passed through a second gateway, and Bao-yu saw a range of palace buildings ahead of them on either hand. The entrance to each building had a board above it proclaiming its name, and there were couplets on either side of the doorways. Bao-yu did not have time to read all of the names, but he managed to make out a few, viz:

DEPARTMENT OF FOND INFATUATION
DEPARTMENT OF CRUEL REJECTION
DEPARTMENT OF EARLY MORNING WEEPING
DEPARTMENT OF LATE NIGHT SOBBING
DEPARTMENT OF SPRING FEVER
DEPARTMENT OF AUTUMN GRIEF

'Madam Fairy,' said Bao-yu, whose interest had been whetted by what he had managed to read, 'couldn't you take me inside these offices to have a look around?'

'In these offices,' said the fairy woman, 'are kept registers in which are recorded the past, present and future of girls from all over the world. It is not permitted that your earthly eyes should look on things that are yet to come.'

Bao-yu was most unwilling to accept this answer, and begged and pleaded so persistently that at last Disenchantment gave in.

'Very well. You may make a very brief inspection of this office here.'

Delighted beyond measure, Bao-yu raised his head and read the notice above the doorway:

DEPARTMENT OF THE ILL-FATED FAIR

The couplet inscribed vertically on either side of the doorway was as follows:

> Spring griefs and autumn sorrows were by yourselves provoked.
> Flower faces, moonlike beauty were to what end disclosed?

Bao-yu grasped enough of the meaning to be affected by its melancholy.

Passing inside, he saw a dozen or more large cupboards with paper strips pasted on their doors on which were written the names of different provinces. He was careful to look out for the one belonging to his own area and presently found one on which the paper strip said 'Jinling, Twelve Beauties of, Main Register'. Bao-yu asked Disenchantment what this meant, and she explained that it was a register of the twelve most outstanding girls of his home province.

'People all say what a big place Jinling is,' said Bao-yu. 'Surely there should be more than just twelve names? Why, even in my own home, if you count the servants, there must be altogether several hundred girls.'

'Certainly there are a great many girls in the whole province,' said Disenchantment with a smile, 'but only the most important ones have been selected for recording in this register. The registers in the cupboards on either side contain two other selections from the same area. But of the host of ordinary girls outside those three dozen we keep no records.'

Bao-yu glanced at the other two cupboards referred to by Disenchantment. One was labelled 'Jinling, Twelve Beauties of, Supplementary Register No. 1'; the other was labelled 'Jinling, Twelve Beauties of, Supplementary Register No. 2'. Stretching out his hand he opened the door of the second one, took out Supplementary Register No. 2, which was like a large album, and opened it at the first page.

It was a picture, but not of a person or a view.[1] The whole page was covered with dark ink washes representing storm-clouds or fog, followed on the next page by a few lines of verse:

> Seldom the moon shines in a cloudless sky,
> And days of brightness all too soon pass by.

1. See Appendix, p. 527.

> A noble and aspiring mind
> In a base-born frame confined,
> Your charm and wit did only hatred gain,
> And in the end you were by slanders slain,
> Your gentle lord's solicitude in vain.

Bao-yu could not make much sense of this, and turned to the next page. It was another picture, this time of a bunch of fresh flowers and a worn-out mat, again followed by a few lines of verse.

> What price your kindness and compliance,
> Of sweetest flower the rich perfume?
> You chose the player fortune favoured,
> Unmindful of your master's doom.

Bao-yu was even more mystified by this than by the first page, and laying the album aside, opened the door of the cupboard marked 'Supplementary Register No. 1' and took out the album from that.

As in the previous album, the first page was a picture. It represented a branch of cassia with a pool underneath. The water in the pool had dried up and the mud in the bottom was dry and cracked. Growing from it was a withered and broken lotus plant. The picture was followed by these lines:

> Your stem grew from a noble lotus root,
> Yet your life passed, poor flower, in low repute.
> The day two earths shall bear a single tree,
> Your soul must fly home to its own country.

Once more failing to make any sense of what he saw, Bao-yu picked up the Main Register to look at. In this album the picture on the first page represented two dead trees with a jade belt hanging in their branches and on the ground beneath them a pile of snow in which a golden hairpin lay half-buried. This was followed by a quatrain:

> One was a pattern of female virtue,
> One a wit who made other wits seem slow.
> The jade belt in the greenwood hangs,
> The gold pin is buried beneath the snow.

Still Bao-yu was unable to understand the meaning. He would have liked to ask, but he knew that Disenchantment would be unwilling to divulge the secrets of her immortal world. Yet though he could make no sense of the book, for some reason he found himself unable this time to lay it down, and continued to look through it to the end.

The picture that followed was of a bow with a citron hanging from it, followed by what looked like the words of a song:

You shall, when twenty years in life's hard school are done,
In pomegranate-time to palace halls ascend.
Though three springs never could with your first spring compare,
When hare meets tiger your great dream shall end.

Next was a picture of two people flying a kite. There was also a large expanse of sea with a boat in it and a girl in the boat who had buried her face in her hands and appeared to be crying. This was followed by a quatrain:

> Blessed with a shrewd mind and a noble heart,
> Yet born in time of twilight and decay,
> In spring through tears at river's bank you gaze,
> Borne by the wind a thousand miles away.

The next picture showed some scudding wisps of cloud and a stretch of running water followed by these words:

> What shall avail you rank and riches,
> Orphaned while yet in swaddling bands you lay?
> Soon you must mourn your bright sun's early setting.
> The Xiang flows and the Chu clouds sail away.

Next was a picture showing a beautiful jade which had fallen into the mud, followed by words of judgement:

> For all your would-be spotlessness
> And vaunted otherworldliness,
> You that look down on common flesh and blood,
> Yourself impure, shall end up in the mud.

Next was a striking picture of a savage wolf pursuing a beautiful girl. He had just seized her with his jaws and appeared to be about to eat her. Underneath it was written:

> Paired with a brute like the wolf in the old fable,
> Who on his saviour turned when he was able,
> To cruelty not used, your gentle heart
> Shall, in a twelvemonth only, break apart.

After this was an old temple with a beautiful girl sitting all on her own inside it reading a Buddhist sūtra. The words said:

> When you see through the spring scene's transient state,
> A nun's black habit shall replace your own.
> Alas, that daughter of so great a house
> By Buddha's altar lamp should sleep alone!

Next was an iceberg with a hen phoenix perched on the top of it, and these words:

> This phoenix in a bad time came;
> All praised her great ability.
> 'Two' makes my riddle with a man and tree:
> Returning south in tears she met calamity.

Next was a cottage in a deserted village inside which a beautiful girl sat spinning, followed by these words:

> When power is lost, rank matters not a jot;
> When families fall, kinship must be forgot.
> Through a chance kindness to a country wife
> Deliverance came for your afflicted life.

This was followed by a picture of a vigorously growing orchid in a pot, beside which stood a lady in full court dress. The words said:

> The plum-tree bore her fruit after the rest,
> Yet, when all's done, her Orchid was the best.
> Against your ice-pure nature all in vain
> The tongues of envy wagged; you felt no pain.

The picture after that showed an upper room in a tall building in which a beautiful girl was hanging by her neck from a beam, having apparently taken her own life. The words said:

> Love was her sea, her sky; in such excess
> Love, meeting with its like, breeds wantonness.
> Say not our troubles all from Rong's side came;
> For their beginning Ning must take the blame.

Bao-yu would have liked to see some more, but the fairy woman, knowing how intelligent and sharp-witted he was, began to fear that she was in danger of becoming responsible for a leakage of celestial secrets, and so, snapping the album shut, she said with a laugh, 'Come with me and we will do some more sight-seeing. Why stay here puzzling your head over these silly riddles?'

Next moment, without quite knowing how it happened, Bao-yu found that he had left the place of registers behind him and was following Disenchantment through the rear parts of the palace. Everywhere there were buildings with ornately carved and painted eaves and rafters, their doorways curtained with strings of pearls and their interiors draped with embroidered hangings. The courtyards outside them were full of deliciously fragrant fairy blooms and rare aromatic herbs.

> Gleam of gold pavement flashed on scarlet doors,
> And in jade walls jewelled casements snow white shone.

'Hurry, hurry! Come out and welcome the honoured guest!' he heard Disenchantment calling to someone inside, and almost at once a bevy of fairy maidens came running from the palace, lotus-sleeves fluttering and feather-skirts billowing, each as enchantingly beautiful as the flowers of spring or the autumn moon. Seeing Bao-yu, they began to reproach Disenchantment angrily.

'So this is your "honoured guest"! What do you mean by making us hurry out to meet *him*? You told us that today at this very hour the dream-soul of our darling Crimson Pearl was coming to play with us, and we have been waiting I don't know how long for her arrival. And now, instead, you have brought this disgusting creature to pollute our pure, maidenly precincts. What's the idea?'

At these words Bao-yu was suddenly overwhelmed with a sense of the uncleanness and impurity of his own body and sought in vain for somewhere to escape to; but Disenchantment held him by the hand and advanced towards the fairy maidens with a conciliatory smile.

'Let me tell you the reason for my change of plan. It is true that I set off for the Rong mansion with the intention of fetching Crimson Pearl, but as I was passing through the Ning mansion on my way, I happened to run into the Duke of Ning-

guo and his brother the Duke of Rong-guo and they laid a
solemn charge on me which I found it hard to refuse.

' "In the hundred years since the foundation of the present
dynasty," they said, "several generations of our house have
distinguished themselves by their services to the Throne and
have covered themselves with riches and honours; but now
its stock of good fortune has run out, and nothing can be done
to replenish it. And though our descendants are many, not one
of them is worthy to carry on the line. The only possible
exception, our great-grandson Bao-yu, has inherited a perverse,
intractable nature and is eccentric and emotionally unstable;
and although his natural brightness and intelligence augur
well, we fear that owing to the fated eclipse of our family's
fortunes there will be no one at hand to give the lad proper
guidance and to start him off along the right lines.

' "May we profit from the fortunate accident of this encounter, Madam, to entreat you to take the boy in hand for us?
Could you perhaps initiate him in the pleasures of the flesh
and all that sort of thing in such a way as to shock the silli-
ness out of him? In that way he might stand a chance of
escaping some of the traps that people fall into and be able to
devote himself single-mindedly to the serious things of life. It
would be such a kindness if you would do this for us. "

'Hearing the old gentlemen so earnest in their entreaty, I
was moved to compassion and agreed to bring the boy here.
I began by letting him have a good look at the records of the
three grades of girls belonging to his own household; but the
experience did not bring any awareness; and so I have brought
him to this place for another attempt. It is my hope that a full
exposure to the illusions of feasting, drinking, music and
dancing may succeed in bringing about an awakening in him
some time in the future.'

Having concluded her explanation, she led Bao-yu indoors.
At once he became aware of a faint, subtle scent, the source of
which he was quite unable to identify and about which he felt
impelled to question Disenchantment.

'How could you possibly know what it was,' said Disenchantment with a somewhat scornful smile, 'since this perfume is not to be found anywhere in your mortal world? It is

made from the essences of rare plants found on famous mountains and other places of great natural beauty, culled when they are new-grown and blended with gums from the pearl-laden trees that grow in the jewelled groves of paradise. It is called "*Belles Se Fanent*".'

Bao-yu expressed his admiration.

The company now seated themselves, and some little maids served them with tea. Bao-yu found its fragrance fresh and clean and its flavour delicious, totally unlike those of any earthly blend he knew. He asked Disenchantment for the name.

'The leaves are picked in the Paradise of the Full-blown Flower on the Mountain of Spring Awakening,' Disenchantment informed him. 'It is infused in water collected from the dew that lies on fairy flowers and leaves. The name is "Maiden's Tears".'

Bao-yu nodded attentively and commended the tea.

Looking around the room he noticed various musical instruments, antique bronzes, paintings by old masters, poems by new poets, and other hallmarks of gracious living. He was particularly delighted to observe some rouge-stained pieces of cotton-wool lying on the window-sill – evidently the aftermath of some fairy-woman's toilet. A pair of calligraphic scrolls hung on the wall, making up the following couplet:

> Earth's choicest spirits in the dark lie hid:
> Heaven ineluctably enforced their fate.

After reading the scrolls, Bao-yu asked to be introduced to the fairy maidens. They had a strange assortment of names. One was called Dream-of-bliss, another was called Loving-heart, a third Ask-for-trouble, a fourth Past-regrets, and the rest all had names that were equally bizarre.

Presently the little maids came in again and proceeded to arrange some chairs around a table and to lay it with food and wine for a feast. In the words of the poet,

> Celestial nectar filled the crystal cup,
> And liquid gold in amber goblets glowed.

The wine's bouquet was delectable, and once again Bao-yu could not resist asking about it.

'This wine,' said Disenchantment, 'is made from the petals of hundreds of different kinds of flowers and extracts from thousands of different sorts of trees. These are blended and fermented with kylin's marrow and phoenix milk. Hence its name, "*Lachrymae Rerum*".'

Bao-yu praised it enthusiastically.

As they sat drinking wine, a troupe of twelve dancers entered and inquired what pieces they should perform for the company's entertainment.

'You can do the twelve songs of my new song-and-dance suite "A Dream of Golden Days",' said Disenchantment.

At once the sandalwood clappers began, very softly, to beat out a rhythm, accompanied by the sedate twang of the *zheng*'s silver strings and by the voice of a singer.

'When first the world from chaos rose. . .'

The singer had got no further than the first line of the first song when Disenchantment interrupted.

'This suite,' she told Bao-yu, 'is not like the music-dramas of your earthly composers in which there are always the fixed parts of *sheng*, *dan*, *jing*, *mo* and so on, and set tunes in the various Northern and Southern modes. In my suite each song is an elegy on a single person or event and the tunes are original compositions which we have orchestrated ourselves. You need to know what the songs are about in order to appreciate them properly. I should not imagine you are very familiar with this sort of entertainment; so unless you read the libretto of the songs first before listening to them, I fear you may find them rather insipid.'

Turning to one of the maids, she ordered her to fetch the manuscript of her libretto of 'A Dream of Golden Days' and gave it to Bao-yu to read, so that he could listen to the songs with one eye on the text. These were the words in Disenchantment's manuscript:

Prelude: *A Dream of Golden Days*[2]

When first the world from chaos rose,
Tell me, how did love begin?
The wind and moonlight first did love compose.

2. See Appendix, p. 528.

Now woebegone
And quite cast down
In low estate
I would my foolish heart expose,
And so perform
This *Dream of Golden Days*,
And all my grief for my lost loves disclose.

First Song: *The Mistaken Marriage*

Let others all
Commend the marriage rites of gold and jade;
I still recall
The bond of old by stone and flower made;
And while my vacant eyes behold
Crystalline snows of beauty pure and cold,
From my mind can not be banished
That fairy wood forlorn that from the world has vanished.
How true I find
That every good some imperfection holds!
Even a wife so courteous and so kind
No comfort brings to my afflicted mind.

Second Song: *Hope Betrayed*

One was a flower from paradise,
One a pure jade without spot or stain.
If each for the other one was not intended,
Then why in this life did they meet again?
And yet if fate had meant them for each other,
Why was their earthly meeting all in vain?
In vain were all her sighs and tears,
In vain were all his anxious fears:
All, insubstantial, doomed to pass,
As moonlight mirrored in the water
Or flowers reflected in a glass.
How many tears from those poor eyes could flow,
Which every season rained upon her woe?

Third Song: *Mutability*

In the full flower of her prosperity
Once more came mortal mutability,
Bidding her, with both eyes wide,
All earthly things to cast aside,
And her sweet soul upon the airs to glide.

So far the road back home did seem
That to her parents in a dream
Thus she her final duty paid:
'I that now am but a shade,
Parents dear,
For your happiness I fear:
Do not tempt the hand of fate!
Draw back, draw back, before it is too late!'

Fourth Song: *From Dear Ones Parted*

Sail, boat, a thousand miles through rain and wind,
Leaving my home and dear ones far behind.
I fear that my remaining years
Will waste away in homesick tears.
Father dear and mother mild,
Be not troubled for your child!
From of old our rising, falling
Was ordained; so now this parting.
Each in another land must be;
Each for himself must fend as best he may;
Now I am gone, oh do not weep for me!

Fifth Song: *Grief Amidst Gladness*

While you still in cradle lay,
Both your parents passed away.
Though born to silken luxury,
No warmth or kind indulgence came your way.
Yet yours was a generous, open-hearted nature,
And never could be snared or soured
By childish piques and envious passions –
You were a crystal house by wind and moonlight scoured.
Matched to a perfect, gentle husband,
Security of bliss at last it seemed,
And all your childish miseries redeemed.
But soon alas! the clouds of Gao-tang faded,
The waters of the Xiang ran dry.
In our grey world so are things always ordered:
What then avails it to lament and sigh?

Sixth Song: *All at Odds*

Heaven made you like a flower,
With grace and wit to match the gods,
Adding a strange, contrary nature
That set you with the rest at odds.
Nauseous to you the world's rank diet,
Vulgar its fashion's gaudy dress:
But the world envies the superior
And hates a too precious daintiness.
Sad it seemed that your life should in dim-lit shrines be wasted,
All the sweets of spring untasted:
Yet, at the last,
Down into mud and shame your hopes were cast,
Like a white, flawless jade dropped in the muck,
Where only wealthy rakes might bless their luck.

Seventh Song: *Husband and Enemy*

Zhong-shan wolf,
Inhuman sot,
Who for past kindnesses cared not a jot!
Bully and spendthrift, reckless in debauch,
For riot or for whoring always hot!
A delicate young wife of gentle stock
To you was no more than a lifeless block,
And bore, when you would rant and rave,
Treatment far worse than any slave;
So that her delicate, sweet soul
In just a twelvemonth from its body stole.

Eighth Song: *The Vanity of Spring*

When triple spring as vanity was seen,
What use the blushing flowers, the willows green?
From youth's extravagance you sought release
To win chaste quietness and heavenly peace.
The hymeneal peach-blooms in the sky,
The flowering almond's blossoms seen on high
Dismiss, since none, for sure,
Can autumn's blighting frost endure.
Amidst sad aspens mourners sob and sigh,
In maple woods the poor ghosts thinly cry,

And under the dead grasslands lost graves lie.
Now poor, now rich, men's lives in toil are passed
To be, like summer's pride, cut down at last.
The doors of life and death all must go through.
Yet this I know is true:
In Paradise there grows a precious tree
Which bears the fruit of immortality.

Ninth Song: *Caught By Her Own Cunning*

Too shrewd by half, with such finesse you wrought
That your own life in your own toils was caught;
But long before you died your heart was slain,
And when you died your spirit walked in vain.
Fall'n the great house once so secure in wealth,
Each scattered member shifting for himself;
And half a life-time's anxious schemes
Proved no more than the stuff of dreams.
Like a great building's tottering crash,
Like flickering lampwick burned to ash,
Your scene of happiness concludes in grief:
For worldly bliss is always insecure and brief.

Tenth Song: *The Survivor*

Some good remained,
Some good remained:
The daughter found a friend in need
Through her mother's one good deed.
So let all men the poor and meek sustain,
And from the example of her cruel kin refrain,
Who kinship scorned and only thought of gain.
For far above the constellations
One watches all and makes just calculations.

Eleventh Song: *Splendour Come Late*

Favour, a shadow in the glass;
Fame, a dream that soon would pass:
The blissful flowering-time of youth soon fled,
Soon, too, the pleasures of the bridal bed.
A pearl-encrusted crown and robes of state
Could not for death untimely compensate;

And though each man desires
Old age from want made free,
True blessedness requires
A clutch of young heirs at the knee.
Proudly upright
The head with cap and bands of office on,
And gleaming bright
Upon his breast the gold insignia shone.
An awesome sight
To see him so exalted stand! –
Yet the black night
Of death's dark frontier lay close at hand.
All those whom history calls great
Left only empty names for us to venerate.

Twelfth Song: *The Good Things Have An End*

Perfumed was the dust that fell
From painted beams where springtime ended.
Her sportive heart
And amorous looks
The ruin of a mighty house portended.
The weakness in the line began with Jing;
The blame for the decline lay first in Ning;
But retribution all was of Love's fashioning.

Epilogue: *The Birds Into The Wood Have Flown*

The office jack's career is blighted,
The rich man's fortune now all vanished,
The kind with life have been requited,
The cruel exemplarily punished;
The one who owed a life is dead,
The tears one owed have all been shed.
Wrongs suffered have the wrongs done expiated;
The couplings and the sunderings were fated.
Untimely death sin in some past life shows,
But only luck a blest old age bestows.
The disillusioned to their convents fly,
The still deluded miserably die.
Like birds who, having fed, to the woods repair,
They leave the landscape desolate and bare.

Having reached the end of this suite, the singers showed signs of embarking on another one. Disenchantment observed with a sigh that Bao-yu was dreadfully bored.

'Silly boy! You still don't understand, do you?'

Bao-yu hurriedly stopped the girls and told them that they need not sing any more. He felt dizzy and his head was spinning. He explained to Disenchantment that he had drunk too much and would like to lie down.

At once she ordered the remains of the feast to be removed and conducted Bao-yu to a dainty bedroom. The furnishings and hangings of the bed were more sumptuous and beautiful than anything he had ever seen. To his intense surprise there was a fairy girl sitting in the middle of it. Her rose-fresh beauty reminded him strongly of Bao-chai, but there was also something about her of Dai-yu's delicate charm. As he was pondering the meaning of this apparition, he suddenly became aware that Disenchantment was addressing him.

'In the rich and noble households of your mortal world, too many of those bowers and boudoirs where innocent tenderness and sweet girlish fantasy should reign are injuriously defiled by coarse young voluptuaries and loose, wanton girls. And what is even more detestable, there are always any number of worthless philanderers to protest that it is woman's beauty alone that inspires them, or loving feelings alone, unsullied by any taint of lust. They lie in their teeth! To be moved by woman's beauty is itself a kind of lust. To experience loving feelings is, even more assuredly, a kind of lust. Every act of love, every carnal congress of the sexes is brought about precisely because sensual delight in beauty has kindled the feeling of love.

'The reason I like you so much is because you are full of lust. You are the most lustful person I have ever known in the whole world!'

Bao-yu was scared by the vehemence of her words.

'Madam Fairy, you are wrong! Because I am lazy over my lessons, Mother and Father still have to scold me quite often; but surely that doesn't make me *lustful*? I'm still too young to know what they do, the people they use that word about.'

'Ah, but you *are* lustful!' said Disenchantment. 'In principle, of course, all lust is the same. But the word has many different meanings. For example, the typically lustful man in the common sense of the word is a man who likes a pretty face, who is fond of singing and dancing, who is inordinately given to flirtation; one who makes love in season and out of season, and who, if he could, would like to have every pretty girl in the world at his disposal, to gratify his desires whenever he felt like it. Such a person is a mere brute. His is a shallow, promiscuous kind of lust.

'But your kind of lust is different. That blind, defenceless love with which nature has filled your being is what we call here "lust of the mind". "Lust of the mind" cannot be explained in words, nor, if it could, would you be able to grasp their meaning. Either you know what it means or you don't.

'Because of this "lust of the mind" women will find you a kind and understanding friend; but in the eyes of the world I am afraid it is going to make you seem unpractical and eccentric. It is going to earn you the jeers of many and the angry looks of many more.

'Today I received a most touching request on your behalf from your ancestors the Duke of Ning-guo and the Duke of Rong-guo. And as I cannot bear the idea of your being rejected by the world for the greater glory of us women, I have brought you here. I have made you drunk with fairy wine. I have drenched you with fairy tea. I have admonished you with fairy songs. And now I am going to give you my little sister Two-in-one – "Ke-qing" to her friends – to be your bride.

'The time is propitious. You may consummate the marriage this very night. My motive in arranging this is to help you grasp the fact that, since even in these immortal precincts love is an illusion, the love of your dust-stained, mortal world must be doubly an illusion. It is my earnest hope that, knowing this, you will henceforth be able to shake yourself free of its entanglements and change your previous way of thinking, devoting your mind seriously to the teachings of Confucius and Mencius and your person wholeheartedly to the betterment of society.'

Disenchantment then proceeded to give him secret instruc-

tions in the art of love; then, pushing him gently inside the
room, she closed the door after him and went away.

Dazed and confused, Bao-yu nevertheless proceeded to
follow out the instructions that Disenchantment had given
him, which led him by predictable stages to that act which
boys and girls perform together – and which it is not my intention to give a full account of here.

Next morning he lay for a long time locked in blissful
tenderness with Ke-qing, murmuring sweet endearments in
her ear and unable to tear himself away from her. Eventually
they emerged from the bedroom hand in hand to walk together
out-of-doors.

Their walk seemed to take them quite suddenly to a place
where only thorn-trees grew and wolves and tigers prowled
around in pairs. Ahead of them the road ended at the edge of
a dark ravine. No bridge connected it with the other side.
As they hesitated, wondering what to do, they suddenly
became aware that Disenchantment was running up behind
them.

'Stop! Stop!' she was shouting. 'Turn back at once! Turn
back!'

Bao-yu stood still in alarm and asked her what place this
was.

'This is the Ford of Error,' said Disenchantment. 'It is ten
thousand fathoms deep and extends hundreds of miles in either
direction. No boat can ever cross it; only a raft manned by a
lay-brother called Numb and an acolyte called Dumb. Numb
holds the steering-paddle and Dumb wields the pole. They
won't ferry anyone across for money, but only take those who
are fated to cross over.

'If you had gone on walking just now and had fallen in, all
the good advice I was at such pains to give you would have
been wasted!'

Even as she spoke there was a rumbling like thunder from
inside the abyss and a multitude of demons and water monsters
reached up and clutched at Bao-yu to drag him down into its
depths. In his terror the sweat broke out over his body like
rain and a great cry burst from his lips,

'Ke-qing! Save me!'

Aroma and his other maids rushed upstairs in alarm and clung to him.

'Don't be frightened, Bao-yu! We are here!'

But Qin-shi, who was out in the courtyard telling the maids to be sure that the cats and dogs didn't fight, marvelled to hear him call her name out in his sleep.

' "Ke-qing" was the name they called me back at home when I was a little girl. Nobody here knows it. I wonder how he could have found it out?'

If you have not yet fathomed the answer to her question, you must read the next chapter.

CHAPTER 6

Jia Bao-yu conducts his first experiment
in the Art of Love
And Grannie Liu makes her first entry into the
Rong-guo mansion

Qin-shi was surprised to hear Bao-yu call out her childhood
name in his sleep, but did not like to pursue the matter. As
she stood wondering, Bao-yu, who was still bemused after
his dream and not yet in full possession of his faculties, got out
of bed and began to stretch himself and to adjust his clothes,
assisted by Aroma. As she was doing up his trousers, her hand,
chancing to stray over his thigh, came into contact with something cold and sticky which caused her to draw it back in
alarm and ask him if he was all right. Instead of answering, he
merely reddened and gave the hand a squeeze.

Aroma had always been an intelligent girl. She was, in any
case, a year or two older than Bao-yu and had recently begun
to have some understanding of the facts of life. Observing
the condition that Bao-yu was in, she therefore had more than
an inkling of what had happened. Abandoning her question,
she busied herself with his clothes, her cheeks suffused by a
crimson blush of embarrassment. When he was properly
dressed, they went to rejoin Grandmother Jia and the rest.
There they bolted a hurried supper and then slipped back to
the other house, where Aroma profited from the absence of
the nurses and the other maids to take out a clean under-
garment for Bao-yu to change into.

'Please, Aroma,' Bao-yu shamefacedly entreated as she
helped him change, '*please* don't tell anyone!'

Equally ill at ease, Aroma giggled softly.

'Why did you . . . ?' she began to ask. Then, after glancing
cautiously around, began again.

'Where did that stuff come from?'

Bao-yu blushed furiously and said nothing. Aroma stared at
him curiously and continued to giggle. After much hesitation

he proceeded to give her a detailed account of his dream. But when he came to the part of it in which he made love to Two-in-one, Aroma threw herself forward with a shriek of laughter and buried her face in her hands.

Bao-yu had long been attracted by Aroma's somewhat coquettish charms and tugged at her purposefully, anxious to share with her the lesson he had learned from Disenchantment. Aroma knew that when Grandmother Jia gave her to Bao-yu she had intended her to belong to him in the fullest possible sense, and so, having no good reason for refusing him, she allowed him, after a certain amount of coy resistance, to have his way with her.

From then on Bao-yu treated Aroma with even greater consideration than before, whilst Aroma for her part redoubled the devotion with which she served him. But of this, for the time being, no more.

*

The inhabitants of the Rong mansion, if we include all of them from the highest to the humblest in our total, numbered more than three hundred souls, who produced between them a dozen or more incidents in a single day. Faced with so exuberant an abundance of material, what principle should your chronicler adopt to guide him in his selection of incidents to record? As we pondered the problem *where to begin*, it was suddenly solved for us by the appearance as it were out of nowhere of someone from a very humble, very insignificant household who, on the strength of a very tenuous, very remote family connection with the Jias, turned up at the Rong mansion on the very day of which we are about to write.

Their name was Wang and they were natives of these parts. A grandfather had held some very small official post in the capital and had there become acquainted with Wang Xi-feng's grandfather, the father of Lady Wang. Conceiving an admiration for the power and prestige of this greater namesake, he had sought to link his family with the latter's clan by becoming his adoptive nephew. Only Lady Wang and her elder brother – Wang Xi-feng's father – who chanced at that time to be staying with their parent on his tour of duty at the capital, knew anything about this. The other members of the clan were unaware that any such relationship existed.

The grandfather had long since died, leaving an only son called Wang Cheng who, having fallen on hard times, had moved back into the countryside somewhere outside the capital. Wang Cheng in his turn had died leaving a son called Gou-er, who had married a girl from a family called Liu and now had two children, a son called Ban-er and a daughter called Qing-er. The four of them depended on agriculture for their living, and since, with Gou-er himself busy most of the day on the land and his wife busy about the farm drawing water, pounding grain, and the like, there was no one to look after Qing-er and her little brother, Gou-er invited his mother-in-law, old Grannie Liu, to come and live with them.

This Grannie Liu was an ancient widow-woman, rich in experience of the world, who, having no son or daughter-in-law to cherish her, eked out her solitary existence by scratching a livelihood from a miserable half-acre of land. She therefore embraced her son-in-law's invitation with alacrity and threw herself enthusiastically into the business of helping the young couple to make a living.

The season was now at the turn between autumn and winter. The cold weather was beginning, but none of the preparations for winter had yet been made. By drinking to allay his anxiety, Gou-er merely put himself more out of temper. He returned home to vent some of his spleen on his long-suffering wife. Grannie Liu could eventually stomach no more of his wife-baiting and intervened on her daughter's behalf.

'Now look here, son-in-law: probably you will think me an interfering old woman; but we country folk have to be grateful for what is in the pot and cut down our appetites to the same measure. When you were little your Ma and Pa could afford to indulge you; so now you're grown-up you spend all your money as soon as you've got any, without stopping to count the cost; then, when it's all gone, you start making a fuss. But what sort of way is that for a grown man to behave?

'Now where we live may be out in the country, but it's still "in the Emperor's shadow", as they say. Over there in the

city the streets are paved with money just waiting for someone to go and pick it up. What's the sense in rampaging
around here at home when you could go out and help yourself?'

'It's easy for you to sit on your backside and talk,' said
Gou-er rudely, 'but what do you expect me to do? Go out
and rob?'

'No one's asking you to rob,' said Grannie Liu. 'But can't
we all sit down peaceably and think of a way? Because if we
don't, the money isn't going to come walking in the door of
its own accord.'

Gou-er snorted sarcastically. 'If there were a way, do you
suppose I should have waited till now before trying it out?
There are no tax-collectors in my family and no mandarins
among my friends. What way *could* there be of laying my hands
on some money? Even if I did have rich friends or relations,
I'm not so sure they would want to be bothered with the likes
of us.'

'I wouldn't say that,' said Grannie Liu. 'Man proposes,
God disposes. It's up to us to think of something. We must
leave it to the good Lord to decide whether He'll help us or
not. Who knows, He might give us the opportunity we are
looking for.

'Now I can think of a chance you might try. Your family
used to be connected with the Wang clan of Nanking. Twenty
years ago the Nanking Wangs used to be very good to you
folk. It's only because of late years you have been too stiff-
necked to approach them that they have become more distant
with you.

'I can remember going to their house once with my
daughter. The elder Miss Wang was a very straightforward
young lady, very easy to get on with, and not at all high and
mighty. She's now the wife of the younger of the two Sir
Jias in the Rong mansion. They say that now she's getting
on in years she's grown even more charitable and given to
good works than she was as a girl. Her brother has been
promoted; but I shouldn't be surprised if she at least didn't
still remember us. Why don't you try your luck with *her*? You
never know, she might do something for you for the sake of

old times. She only has to feel well disposed and a hair off her arm would be thicker than a man's waist to poor folks like us!'

'That's all very well, Mother,' put in Gou-er's wife, 'but just take a look at us! What sort of state are we in to go calling on great folks like them? I doubt the people at the door would bother to tell them we were there. Who's going to all that trouble just to make a fool of themselves?'

Gou-er's cupidity, however, had been aroused by the words of his mother-in-law, and his reaction to them was less discouraging than his wife's.

'Well, if it's as you say, Grannie, and being as you've already seen this lady, why not go there yourself and spy out the land for us?'

'Bless us and save us!' said Grannie Liu. 'You know what they say: "A prince's door is like the deep sea." What sort of creature do you take me for? The servants there don't know me; it would be a journey wasted.'

'That's no problem,' said Gou-er. 'I'll tell you what to do. You take young Ban-er with you and ask for Old Zhou that stayed in service with your lady after she married. If you tell them you've come to see him, it will give you an excuse for the visit. Old Zhou once entrusted a bit of business to my father. He used to be very friendly with us at one time.'

'I knew all about that,' said Grannie Liu. 'But it's a long time since you had anything to do with him and hard to say how he may prove after all these years. Howsomever. Being a man, you naturally can't go in your present pickle; and a young married woman like my daughter can't go gallivanting around the countryside showing herself to everybody. But as my old face is tough enough to stand a slap or two, it's up to me to go. So be it, then. If any good does come of the visit, we shall all of us benefit.'

And so, that very evening, the matter was settled.

Next day Grannie Liu was up before dawn. As soon as she had washed and done her hair, she set about teaching Ban-er a few words to say to the ladies at the great house – an exercise to which he submitted cheerfully enough, as would any little

boy of four or five who had been promised an outing to the
great city. That done, she set off on her journey, and in due
course made her way to Two Dukes Street. There, at each
side of the stone lions which flanked the gates of the Rong
Mansion, she saw a cluster of horses and palanquins. Not
daring to go straight up, she first dusted down her clothes and
rehearsed Ban-er's little repertoire of phrases before sidling
up to one of the side entrances.

A number of important-looking gentlemen sat in the gateway sunning their bellies and discoursing with animated
gestures on a wide variety of topics. Grannie Liu waddled up
to them and offered a respectful salutation. After looking her
up and down for a moment or two, they asked her her business.
Grannie Liu smiled ingratiatingly.

'I've come to see Old Zhou that used to be in service with
Her Ladyship before she married. Could I trouble one of
you gentlemen to fetch him out for me?'

The gentlemen ignored her request and returned to their
discussion. After she had waited there for some considerable
time one of them said, 'If you stand at that gate along there on
the corner, someone from inside the house should be coming
out presently.'

But a more elderly man among them protested that it was 'a
shame to send her on a fool's errand', and turning to Grannie
Liu he said, 'Old Zhou is away in the South at the moment,
but his missus is still at home. She lives round at the back.
You'll have to go from here round to the back gate in the other
street and ask for her there.'

Grannie Liu thanked him and trotted off with little Ban-er
all the way round to the rear entrance. There she found a
number of sweetmeat vendors and toy-sellers who had set
their wares down outside the gate and were being beseiged
by a crowd of some twenty or thirty noisy, yelling children.
She grabbed a small urchin from their midst and drew him
towards her.

'Tell me, sonny, is there a Mrs Zhou living here?'

The urchin stared back at her impudently.

'Which Mrs Zhou? There are several Mrs Zhous here.
What's her job?'

'She's the Mrs Zhou that came here with Her Ladyship when she was married.'

'That's easy,' said the urchin. 'Follow me!'

He led Grannie Liu into a rear courtyard. 'That's where she lives,' he said, pointing in the direction of a side wall. Then, bawling over the wall, 'Mrs Zhou, there's an old woman come to see you!'

Zhou Rui's wife came hurrying out and asked who it was.

'How are you, my dear?' said Grannie Liu, advancing with a smile. Zhou Rui's wife scrutinized her questioningly for some moments before finally recognizing her.

'Why, it's Grannie Liu! How are you? It's so many years since I saw you last, I'd forgotten all about you! Come in and sit down!'

Grannie Liu followed her cackling.

'You know what they say: "Important people have short memories." I wouldn't expect you to remember the likes of us!'

When they were indoors, Zhou Rui's wife ordered her little hired help to pour out some tea.

'And hasn't Ban-er grown a big boy!' said Zhou Rui's wife; then, after a few inquiries about the various things that had happened since they last met, she asked Grannie Liu about her visit.

'Were you just passing by, or have you come specially?'

'Well, of course, first and foremost we came to see you,' replied Grannie Liu mendaciously, 'but we were also hoping to pay our respects to Her Ladyship. If you could take us to see her, that would be very nice; but if that's not possible, perhaps we could trouble you just to give her our regards.'

From the tone of this reply Zhou Rui's wife was already able to make a pretty good guess as to the real purpose of the old woman's visit; but because some years previously her husband had received a lot of help from Gou-er's father in a dispute over the purchase of some land, she could not very well reject Grannie Liu now, when she came to her as a suppliant. She was, in any case, anxious to demonstrate her own importance in the Jia household; and so the answer she gave her was a gracious one.

'Don't you worry, Grannie! After you've made such a long pilgrimage, we won't let you go home without seeing a real Buddha! By rights, of course, Callers and Visitors has nothing to do with me. You see, we each have our own jobs here. My man's is collecting the half-yearly rents in the spring and autumn; and when he's not doing that, he takes the young masters out when they go on visits. That's all he ever does. Now my job is to attend to their ladyships and the young mistresses when *they* go out. But being as how you are a relation of Her ladyship, and since you've put your confidence in me and turned to me to help you, I don't mind breaking the rules for once and taking in a message.

'There's only one thing, though. I don't expect you know, but things here are very different from what they were five years ago. Nowadays Her Ladyship doesn't run things here any longer. It's Master Lian's wife who does all the managing – You'll never guess who that is: Her Ladyship's niece Wang Xi-feng. You know, Her Ladyship's eldest brother's daughter, that we used to call "Feng-ge" when she was a child.'

'Bless you, my dear, for being such a help!' said Grannie Liu.

'Oh Grannie, how can you say such a thing?' said Zhou Rui's wife demurely. 'You know what the old saying is, "He who helps others helps himself." It's only a question of saying a few words. No trouble at all.'

So saying, she instructed the little maid to slip quietly round to the back of old Lady Jia's quarters and ask if they were serving lunch yet. The little maid departed on her errand and the two women resumed their conversation.

'This Mrs Lian,' said Grannie Liu: 'she can't be more than eighteen or nineteen years old. She must be a very capable young woman. Fancy her being able to run a great household like this!'

'Oh Grannie, you have no idea!' said Zhou Rui's wife. 'Mrs Lian may be young, but when it comes to doing things, she's got an older head on her shoulders than any *I've* ever come across. She's grown up to be a real beauty too, has Mrs Lian. But sharp! Well, if it ever comes to a slanging match, she can talk down ten grown men any day of the week! Wait till you meet her, and you'll see what I mean. There's only one thing, though. She's a bit too strict with those beneath her.'

As she was speaking, the little maid came back, her errand completed.

'They've finished serving lunch at Her Old Ladyship's. Mrs Lian is still there.'

Zhou Rui's wife hurriedly rose to her feet and urged Grannie Liu to do likewise.

'Quick! After she comes out from there she'll be free for a few minutes while she has her meal. We must try and catch her then. If we delay a moment longer, people will start coming in with messages and we shan't have a chance to speak to her. And once she goes off for her afternoon nap, we've really lost her!'

Grannie Liu got off the kang, adjusted her clothing, conducted Ban-er through a rapid revision of his little stock of phrases and followed Zhou Rui's wife through various twists and turns to Jia Lian's quarters. Just before they reached them, Zhou Rui's wife planted them both in a covered passage-way while she went on ahead round the screen wall and into the gate of the courtyard. First ascertaining that Wang Xi-feng had not yet left Lady Jia's, she sought out Xi-feng's chamber-maid and principal confidante, Patience, and primed her with a full account of Grannie Liu's antecedents.

'She has come all this way today to pay her respects,' she concluded. 'At one time Her Ladyship used to see quite a lot of her, which is why I thought it would be in order for me to bring her in. I thought I would wait for the young mistress to come back and explain it all to her. I hope she won't be angry with me for pushing myself forward.'

Patience at once made up her mind what to do.

'Let them come in here. They can sit here while they are waiting.'

Zhou Rui's wife went off again to fetch her charges. As they ascended the steps to the main reception room, a little maid lifted up the red carpet which served as a portière for them to enter. A strange, delicious fragrance seemed to reach forward and enfold them as they entered, producing in Grannie

Liu the momentary sensation that she had been transported bodily to one of the celestial paradises. Their eyes, too, were dazzled by the bright and glittering things that filled the room. Temporarily speechless with wonder, Grannie Liu stood wagging her head, alternating clicks of admiration with pious ejaculations.

From the glittering reception room they passed to a room on the east side of it in which Jia Lian's baby daughter slept. Patience, who was standing by the edge of the kang, made a rapid assessment of Grannie Liu and judged it sufficient to greet her with a civil 'how-do-you-do' and an invitation to be seated.

Grannie Liu looked at the silks and satins in which Patience was dressed, the gold and silver ornaments in her hair, her beauty of feature which in every respect corresponded with what she had been told of Wang Xi-feng, and taking the maid for the mistress, was on the point of greeting her as 'Gou-er's aunt', when Zhou Rui's wife introduced her as 'Miss Patience'. Then, when Patience shortly afterwards addressed Zhou Rui's wife as 'Mrs Zhou', she knew that this was no mistress but a very high-class maid. So Grannie Liu and Ban-er got up on the kang at one side, while Patience and Zhou Rui's wife sat near the edge of it on the other, and a little maid came in and poured them all some tea.

Grannie Liu's attention was distracted by a persistent *tock tock tock tock* not unlike the sound made by a flour-bolting machine, and she could not forbear glancing round her from time to time to see where it came from. Presently she caught sight of a sort of boxlike object fastened to one of the central pillars of the room, and a thing like the weight of a steelyard hanging down from it, which swung to and fro in ceaseless motion and appeared to be the source of the noise which had distracted her.

'I wonder what that can be,' she thought to herself, 'and what it can be used for?'

As she studied the strange box, it suddenly gave forth a loud *dong!* like the sound of a bronze bell or a copper chime, which so startled the old lady that her eyes nearly popped out of her head. The *dong!* was followed in rapid succession by eight or nine others, and Grannie Liu was on the point of asking what it meant, when all the maids in the house began scurrying about shouting, 'The mistress! The mistress! She'll be coming out now!' and Patience and Zhou Rui's wife hurriedly rose to their feet.

'Just stay here, Grannie,' they said. 'When it is time for you to see her, we shall come in and fetch you'; and they went off with the other servants to greet their mistress.

As Grannie Liu sat in silence, waiting with bated breath and head cocked to one side for her summons, she heard a far-off sound of laughter, followed presently by a sound of rustling dresses as between ten and twenty women entered the reception room and passed from it into the room beyond. Then two or three women bearing large red lacquer boxes took up their positions on the side nearest the room in which she sat and stood there waiting to be called. A voice in the far room called out, 'Serve now, please!' at which, to judge from the noises, most of the women scuttled off, leaving only the few who were waiting at table. A long silence ensued in which not so much as a cheep could be heard; then two women came in bearing a small, low table which they set down on the kang. It was covered with bowls and dishes containing all kinds of meat and fish, only one or two of which appeared to have been touched. At the sight of it Ban-er set up a clamour for some meat and was silenced by Grannie Liu with a resounding slap.

Just at that moment Zhou Rui's wife appeared, her face all wreathed in smiles, and advanced towards Grannie Liu beckoning. Grannie Liu slipped off the kang, lifted down Ban-er, and exchanged a few hurried whispers with her in the reception room before waddling into the room beyond.

A dark-red patterned curtain hung from brass hooks over the doorway. Inside, under the window in the south wall, there was a kang covered with a dark-red carpet. At the east end of the kang, up against the wooden partition wall, were a back-rest and bolster, both covered in gold brocade, and a large flat cushion for sitting on, also glittering with gold thread. Beside them stood a silver spittoon.

Wang Xi-feng had on a little cap of red sable, which she

wore about the house for warmth, fastened on with a pearl-studded bandeau. She was dressed in a sprigged peach-pink gown, with an ermine-lined skirt of dark-red foreign crêpe underneath it, and a cloak of slate-blue silk with woven coloured insets and lining of grey squirrel around her shoulders. Her face was exquisitely made-up. She was sitting on the edge of the kang, her back straight as a ramrod, with a diminutive pair of tongs in her hand, removing the spent charcoal from a portable hand-warmer. Patience stood beside her carrying a covered teacup on a tiny inlaid lacquer tray. Xi-feng appeared not to have noticed her, for she neither reached out for the cup nor raised her head, but continued picking absorbedly at her hand-warmer. At last she spoke:

'Why not ask them in, then?'

As she did so, she raised her head and saw Zhou Rui's wife with her two charges already standing in front of her. She made a confused movement as if to rise to her feet, welcomed the old lady with a look of unutterable benevolence, and almost in the same breath said rather crossly to Zhou Rui's wife, 'Why didn't you tell me?'

By this time Grannie Liu was already down on her knees and had touched her head several times to the floor in reverence to her 'Aunt Feng'.

'Stop her, Zhou dear!' said Xi-feng in alarm. 'She mustn't do that, I am much too young! In any case, I don't know her very well. I don't know what sort of relations we are and what I should call her.'

'This is the Grannie Liu I was just telling you about,' said Zhou Rui's wife.

Xi-feng nodded, and Grannie Liu sat herself down on the edge of the kang. Ban-er at once hid himself behind her back and neither threats nor blandishments would induce him to come out and make a bow to his 'Auntie'.

'Relations don't come to see us much nowadays,' said Xi-feng affably. 'We are getting to be quite strangers with everybody. People who know us realize that it is because you are tired of us that you don't visit us oftener; but some spiteful people who don't know us so well think it's our fault, because we have grown too proud.'

Grannie Liu invoked the Lord Buddha in pious disavowal of so shocking a view.

'It's hard times that keeps us away. We can't *afford* to visit. We are afraid that if we came to see you looking the way we are, you would disown us; and even the people at the gate might think we were tramps!'

'Now you are really being too hard on us! What if Grandfather did make a little bit of a name for himself and we do hold some miserable little appointment? What does it all amount to? It's all empty show, really. You know what they say: "Even the Emperor has poor relations." It would be strange indeed if *we* didn't have a few!'

She turned to Zhou Rui's wife.

'Have you told Her Ladyship yet?'

'No, ma'am. I was waiting for your instructions.'

'Go and have a look, then. If she has anyone with her, you had better leave it; but if she is free, tell her about their visit and see what she says.'

Zhou Rui's wife departed on her errand.

Xi-feng told one of the servants to give Ban-er a handful of sweets, and had just begun a desultory conversation with Grannie Liu when a number of domestics and underlings of either sex arrived to report on their duties.

'I am entertaining a guest,' said Xi-feng to Patience when she came in to announce their arrival. 'Let them leave it until this evening. But if anyone has important business, bring them in and I will deal with it now.'

Patience went out and returned a minute later to say that she had asked them and no one had any business of special importance, so she had sent them all away. Xi-feng nodded.

At this point Zhou Rui's wife returned with a message for Xi-feng.

'Her Ladyship says she isn't free today, but that if you will entertain them for her, it will be just the same as if she were to receive them herself. She says please thank them very much for coming. And she says if it's just an ordinary visit she has nothing more to add; but if they have anything particular to say, she says tell them that they can say it to you instead.'

'I hadn't anything particular in mind,' said Grannie Liu.

'Only to look in on Her Ladyship and your mistress. Just a visit to relations.'

'Well all right then, if you are sure you have nothing to say. But if you *have* got anything to say, you really ought to tell the mistress. It will be just the same as if you were to say it to Her Ladyship.' Zhou Rui's wife darted a meaningful look at Grannie Liu as she said this.

Grannie Liu perfectly well understood the significance of this look, and a blush of shame overspread her face. Yet if she did not speak up now, what would have been the purpose of her visit? She forced herself to say something.

'By rights I ought not to mention it today, seeing that this is our first meeting: but as I have come such a long way to see you, it seems silly not to speak . . .'

She had got no further when the pages from the outer gate announced the arrival of 'the young master from the Ning mansion' and Xi-feng gestured to her to stop.

'It's all right. There is no need to tell me.' She turned to the pages. 'Where is Master Rong, then?'

A man's footstep sounded outside and a fresh-faced, willowy youth of seventeen or eighteen in elegant and expensive-looking winter dress came into the room.

Grannie Liu, acutely embarrassed in this male presence, did not know whether to sit or stand, and looked round her in vain for somewhere to hide herself. Xi-feng laughed at her discomfiture.

'Don't mind him; just stay where you are! It's only my nephew.'

With a good deal of girlish simpering Grannie Liu sat down again, perching herself obliquely on the extreme edge of the kang.

Jia Rong saluted his aunt Manchu fashion.

'My father is entertaining an important visitor tomorrow and he wondered if he might borrow the little glass screen that your Uncle Wang's wife gave you, to put on our kang while he is there. We can let you have it back again as soon as he has gone.'

'You are too late,' said Xi-feng. 'I lent it yesterday to someone else.'

Jia Rong flashed a winning smile at her and half-knelt on the side of the kang.

'If you won't lend it, my father will say that I didn't ask properly and I shall get a beating. Come on, Auntie, be a sport! Just for my sake!'

Xi-feng smiled maliciously.

'I don't know what's so special about my family's things. Heaven knows, you have enough stuff of your own over there; yet you have only to set eyes on anything of ours, and you want it for yourselves.'

Jia Rong's smile flashed again.

'Please, Auntie! Be merciful!'

'If it's the tiniest bit chipped,' said Xi-feng, 'I'll have the hide off you!'

She ordered Patience to take the key of the upstairs room and get some reliable servants to carry it over. Delighted with his good luck, Jia Rong hurriedly forestalled her.

'I'll get some of my own people to carry it. Don't put yours to a lot of trouble!' and he hurried out.

Xi-feng suddenly seemed to remember something, and called to him through the window, 'Rong, come back!'

Servants in the yard outside dutifully took up the cry, 'Master Rong, you're wanted back again!'

Jia Rong came hurrying back, wreathed in smiles, and looked at Xi-feng with eyebrows arched inquiringly.

Xi-feng, however, sipped very intently from her teacup and mused for a while, saying nothing. Suddenly her face flushed and she gave a little laugh:

'It doesn't matter. Come back again after supper. I've got company now, and besides, I don't feel in the mood to tell you.'

'Yes, Aunt,' said Jia Rong, and pursing his lips up in a complacent smile he sauntered slowly out of the room.

Having all this while had time to collect herself, Grannie Liu began her speech again:

'The real reason I have brought your little nephew here today is because his Pa and Ma haven't anything in the house to eat, and the weather is getting colder, and – and – I thought I'd bring him here to see you ...' She gave Ban-er a despairing push. 'What did your Pa tell you to say when we got here? What was it he sent us for? Look at you! All you can do is sit there eating sweets!'

It was abundantly clear to Xi-feng that the old lady was too embarrassed to go on, and she put her out of her misery with a gracious smile.

'It's quite all right. There is no need to tell me. I quite understand.' She turned to Zhou Rui's wife. 'I wonder if Grannie has eaten yet today?'

'We were on our way first thing this morning,' Grannie Liu chimed in. 'There was no time to think about eating.'

Xi-feng gave orders for a meal to be brought in, and Zhou Rui's wife went out and presently reappeared with a guest's portion of various choice dishes on a little table, which she set down in the east wing, and to which she then conducted Grannie Liu and Ban-er for their meal.

'Zhou, dear,' said Xi-feng, 'will you keep them company and see that they have enough to eat? I shan't be able to sit with them myself.' Then calling her aside for a moment she asked, 'What did Her Ladyship say when you went to report about them just now?'

'She said they don't really belong to the family but were adopted into the clan years ago when your grandfather and theirs were working in the same office. She said they haven't been round much of late years, but in the old days when they used to visit us we never sent them back empty-handed. She said it was nice of them to come and see us today and we should be careful to treat them considerately. And she said if they appear to want anything, she would leave it to you to decide what we should do for them.'

'No wonder!' exclaimed Xi-feng when she had heard this account. 'I couldn't understand how they could be really related to us if I had never even heard of them.'

While they were talking, Grannie Liu came back from the other room having already finished eating, smacking her lips and sucking her teeth appreciatively, and voicing her thanks for the repast.

'Sit down,' said Xi-feng with a smile. 'I have something to say to you. I quite understand what you were trying to tell me just now. As we are relations, we ought by rights not to wait for you to come to our door before helping you when you are in trouble; but there are so many things to attend to in this family, and now that Her Ladyship is getting on a bit she doesn't always remember them all. And since I took over the management of the household, I find there are quite a lot of relations that I don't even know about. And then again, of course, though we may look thriving enough from the outside, people don't realize that being a big establishment like ours carries its own difficulties. They won't believe it if you tell them, but it's true. However, since you have come such a long way, and since this is the first time you have ever said a word about needing help, we obviously can't let you go back empty-handed. Fortunately it so happens that I still haven't touched any of the twenty taels of silver that Her Ladyship gave me the other day to make clothes for the maids with. If you don't mind it being so little, you are very welcome to take it.'

When Grannie Liu heard Xi-feng talk about 'difficulties' she concluded that there was no hope. Her delight and the way in which her face lit up with pleasure when she heard that she was, after all, to be given twenty taels of silver can be imagined.

'We knew you had your troubles,' she said, 'but as the saying goes, "A starved camel is bigger than a fat horse." Say what you like, a hair plucked from your arm is thicker than a man's waist to folks like us!'

Horrified by the crudity of these expressions, Zhou Rui's wife, who was standing by, was meanwhile signalling frantically to the old lady to stop. But Xi-feng laughed quite unconcernedly and told Patience to wrap up the silver and also to fetch a string of cash to go with it. The money was set down in front of Grannie Liu.

'Here is the twenty taels of silver,' said Xi-feng. 'Take this for the time being to make some winter clothes for the children with. Some time later on, when you have nothing better to do, look in on us for a day or two for kinship's sake. It's late now, so I won't try to keep you. Give our regards to everybody who ought to be remembered when you get back!'

She rose to her feet, and Grannie Liu, with heartfelt expressions of gratitude, picked up the money and followed Zhou Rui's wife out of the room.

'My dear good woman,' said the latter when they were out of earshot, 'whatever came over you? First, when you met her, you couldn't get a word out; then, when you did start talking, it was all "your nephew" this and "your nephew" that! I hope you won't mind my saying so, but even if the child was a real nephew you would still need to go a bit easy on the familiarities. Now Master Rong, he is her *real* nephew. That's the sort of person a lady like that calls "nephew". Where she would come by a nephew like *this* one, I just do not know!'

'My dear,' replied Grannie Liu with a laugh, 'when I saw the pretty little darling sitting there, I took such a liking to her that my heart was too full to speak.'

Back in Zhou Rui's quarters the two women sat talking for a while. Grannie Liu wanted to leave a piece of silver to buy something for the Zhou children with, but Zhou Rui's wife said she wouldn't hear of it and refused absolutely to accept anything. And so, with many expressions of gratitude, the old lady took her leave and set out once more through the back gate of the mansion.

And if you want to know what happened after she had left, you will have to read the next chapter.

CHAPTER 7

*Zhou Rui's wife delivers palace flowers and finds Jia
Lian pursuing night sports by day
Jia Bao-yu visits the Ning-guo mansion and has an
agreeable colloquy with Qin-shi's brother*

When Zhou Rui's wife had finished seeing off Grannie Liu,
she went to Lady Wang's place to report. Lady Wang, however, was not in her apartment. The maids said that she had
gone off to visit Aunt Xue. Zhou Rui's wife accordingly
went out by the gate in the east corner of the compound,
crossed the eastern courtyard, and made her way to Pear
Tree Court. As she reached the gate of the Court, she came
upon Lady Wang's maid, Golden, playing on the front steps
with a young girl. Golden realized that Zhou Rui's wife must
have come with a message for Lady Wang and indicated that
her mistress was inside by turning her chin towards the house
and shooting out her lips.

Zhou Rui's wife gently raised a side of the portière and
entered. She found the two sisters in the midst of a seemingly
interminable discussion of some domestic odyssey. Not
daring to interrupt it, she passed on into the inner room,
where Xue Bao-chai, dressed in workaday clothes, her hair
unadorned and twisted in a knot on top of her head, sat with
her maid Oriole over a little table towards the back of the
kang, tracing a pattern for her embroidery. Seeing Zhou
Rui's wife enter, she laid down her tracing brush, turned
towards her with a smile, and invited her to sit with them.

'How are you, Miss?' asked Zhou Rui's wife, returning her
smile and sitting down on the edge of the kang. 'I haven't
seen you over our side these last two or three days. Has
Master Bao been upsetting you?'

'Good gracious, no!' said Bao-chai with a laugh. 'I've
had an attack of my old sickness again and thought I had
better rest quietly at home for a day or two. That's the only
reason.'

'Very sensible!' said Zhou Rui's wife. 'But what is this sickness of yours, Miss? Oughtn't you to call in a doctor and get it properly seen to? It's no joke when a young person of your age lets an illness get its grip on them.'

'Oh, don't talk about my illness!' said Bao-chai. 'I don't know how many doctors we must have consulted about it, and how many medicines I must have swallowed, or how much money we must have spent on it – all without any benefit whatsoever. In the end we were fortunate enough to hear of a monk who specialized in treating illnesses that other people couldn't diagnose and asked him to have a look at me. He said that I had a congenital tendency to overheatedness, but that fortunately, as my constitution was a strong one, it wasn't serious. He said the usual medicines wouldn't do it any good, and he gave us a prescription supposed to have been handed down from the Immortals of the Islands. He also gave us a packet of powder with a very unusual fragrance which he said was to be used as the base. He said that if each time I had a turn I took just one of the pills made up from this prescription, the sickness would go away. And the remarkable thing is that they really have proved quite effective.'

'What was this prescription, Miss? If you will tell me, I shall try to remember it so that I can pass it on to others. If I ever met anyone else who had the same sort of illness, I could do them a charity, couldn't I?'

'You don't know what you are asking,' said Bao-chai. 'It's such a finicky prescription, it would drive anyone mad trying to make it up. It's not so much the materials. There is, after all, a limit to the number of drugs from one part of the world or another that are available. It's the *timing* involved that is so difficult.

'You have to take twelve ounces of stamens of the spring-flowering white tree-peony, twelve ounces of stamens of the summer-flowering white water-lily, twelve ounces of stamens of the autumn-flowering white lotus, and twelve ounces of stamens of the winter-flowering white plum and dry them all in the sun on the day of the spring equinox of the year immediately following the year you picked them in. Then you have to mix them with the powder I told you about and pound

them all up together in a mortar. Then you must take twelve
drams of rain water that fell on the Rain Days in the second
month . . .'

Zhou Rui's wife laughed.

'Why, that's already three years it would take! And suppose
it didn't rain that year on the Rain Days?'

'Exactly,' said Bao-chai. 'Rain is seldom so obliging. You
would just have to wait till the next year. Then you have to
collect twelve drams of dew on the day White Dew in the
ninth month, twelve drams of frost at Frost Fall in the tenth,
and twelve drams of snow at Lesser Snow in the last month of
the year, stir these four kinds of water into the mixture, make
it up into pills about the size of a longan, and store the pills in
an old porcelain jar. The jar is supposed to be buried in a
flower bed and only dug up when you have an attack of the
illness. Then one of the pills is taken out and swallowed in hot
water into which one and a quarter drams of tincture of
phellodendron has been stirred.'

'God bless my soul!' Zhou Rui's wife exclaimed. 'You
would certainly need some patience! Why, you might wait
ten years before getting all those things at the proper times!'

'Well,' said Bao-chai, 'we were lucky. Within only a year
or two of the monk's visit we had managed to get all the
ingredients together and were able to make up the pills
without trouble. We brought them with us when we came to
live here and have buried them under one of the pear-trees in
the garden.'

'Has this medicine got a name?' Zhou Rui's wife asked.

'Yes,' said Bao-chai. 'The monk said the pills are called
"Cold Fragrance Pills".'

Zhou Rui's wife nodded appreciatively.

'Tell me, Miss, what exactly *is* this illness of yours?'

'It doesn't really bother me very much. It makes me cough
and wheeze a bit. But as soon as I have taken one of the pills,
it goes away.'

Zhou Rui's wife was about to ask something else when they
were interrupted by a call from Lady Wang:

'Who have you got in there?'

She hurried back into the outer room to make her report

on Grannie Liu. Having finished it, she waited for some comment from Lady Wang, but finding that none was forthcoming, was on the point of withdrawing when Aunt Xue smilingly enjoined her to stay.

'Just a moment! There is something I should like you to take for me.'

She called to someone outside.

'Caltrop!'

The rings of the portière rattled and the young girl whom Zhou Rui's wife had seen a few minutes before playing on the steps with Golden came into the room.

'You called, Madam?'

'Bring me that box with the flowers in!'

Caltrop went into a side room and returned with a small embroidered box.

'There are twelve artificial flowers in here,' said Aunt Xue. 'They were made in the Imperial Palace, all in the latest fashion. I suddenly thought to myself yesterday what a pity it was to leave them lying around here doing nothing, and how much nicer it would be to give them to the girls to wear. I meant to send them round yesterday but forgot. It's lucky that you came here today, because you will be able to take them for me. There are two each for each of the Jia girls. That leaves six. Then two for Miss Lin, and the remaining four for Mrs Lian.'

'Keep them for Bao-chai to wear,' said Lady Wang. 'What do you want to go bothering about our girls for?'

'You don't know our Bao-chai. She is funny about these things. She has never liked ornaments or make-up or anything of that sort.'

Zhou Rui's wife took up the box and went out into the courtyard, where she came once more upon Golden, sunning herself on the steps.

'Tell me,' she asked her, 'is that little Caltrop the one they are always talking about who was bought just before they came to the capital? The one they had the murder trial about?'

'That's her,' said Golden.

At that moment Caltrop herself came skipping up with a sunny smile on her face, and Zhou Rui's wife took her by the hand and studied her curiously. Then she turned to Golden again.

'You know, there's something about this child's face that reminds me of Master Rong's wife over at the Ning mansion.'

'That's just what I've said,' Golden agreed.

Zhou Rui's wife asked Caltrop how old she was when she became a slave. Then she asked her where her parents were, what her age was, and what part of the country she came from. But to all of these questions Caltrop only shook her head and said that she didn't remember.

Zhou Rui's wife and Golden exchanged glances and sighed sympathetically.

Bearing her box of flowers, Zhou Rui's wife presently came to the part of the house behind Lady Wang's quarters. Grandmother Jia had recently decided that her granddaughters were becoming too numerous and declared that she would retain only Bao-yu and Dai-yu in her own apartments to keep her amused. Ying-chun, Tan-chun and Xi-chun were to move out into the penthouse behind Lady Wang's, with Li Wan to supervise them and keep them company. Thither, accordingly, Zhou Rui's wife now directed her steps.

A number of little maids were sitting under the eaves there waiting to be called, and just as she arrived, Ying-chun's maid Chess and Tan-chun's maid Scribe came through the portière, each carrying a teacup on a tray, from which she deduced that the two cousins must be inside together.

On entering the room, Zhou's wife found Ying-chun and Tan-chun sitting by the window playing Go. She presented the flowers and explained who they were from, and the two girls stopped their game for a moment to bow their thanks, and gave orders to the maids to take charge of them.

'Where is Miss Xi-chun?' Zhou Rui's wife inquired.

'Isn't she in the next room?' said the maids; and there in fact she proved to be, playing with the little nun Sapientia from Water-moon Priory. She asked Zhou Rui's wife what she had come for, and when Zhou Rui's wife took the flowers from the box and explained, she laughed:

'I was telling Sapientia that one of these days I am going to have my hair shaved and go off with her to be a nun, when just at that very moment you came in with these flowers. What shall I do with flowers when I have no hair to stick them in?'

Further pleasantries followed from the others present.

Xi-chun told one of the maids to take the flowers and look after them.

'When did you arrive?' Zhou Rui's wife asked Sapientia. 'And where's that precious Mother Superior of yours gone off to, bald-headed old mischief?'

'We arrived first thing this morning,' said Sapientia. 'Mother Euergesia went off to visit the Yu mansion after she had seen Her Ladyship. She told me to wait for her here.'

'Have you had this month's donation yet?' said Zhou Rui's wife. 'It was due on the fifteenth.'

Sapientia said that she didn't know.

'Who looks after the monthly donations nowadays?' asked Xi-chun.

'Yu Xin,' said Zhou Rui's wife.

'That explains it. As soon as Mother Euergesia arrived, Yu Xin's wife was in here like a shot and they were chattering together for ages. I expect that's what it was about.'

After gossiping a bit longer with Sapientia, Zhou Rui's wife made her way to Xi-feng's quarters. To get there she had to go down a passage-way between two walls, under the windows at the back of Li Wan's apartments, along the foot of an ornamental wall, and through a gateway in the western corner of the compound. When she entered Xi-feng's reception room, a maid sitting on the threshold of the inner room hurriedly waved her away and told her to go across to the other side of the house. Taking the hint, Zhou Rui's wife tiptoed quietly into the room opposite, where she found the baby's nurse patting her rhythmically to make her sleep.

'Is the mistress taking her afternoon nap?' she asked the nurse in a low whisper. 'I think you'll have to wake her, even if she is.'

The nurse smiled, grimaced, and shook her head. Zhou Rui's wife was about to ask her what she meant when she heard a low laugh in what was unmistakably Jia Lian's voice from the room opposite. It was followed almost immediately by the sound of the door opening, and Patience came out carrying a large copper basin which she asked one of the maids to fetch water in.

'Ah, Mrs Zhou!' she said, catching sight of Zhou Rui's wife and crossing into the room opposite. 'What brings you back again?'

Zhou Rui's wife hastily rose to her feet and picking up the box, proferred it to Patience and explained her mission. Patience opened the lid, selected four of the flowers, and slipped away again for several minutes. She came back with two still in her hand, which she gave to a little page called Sunshine.

'Take these to Master Rong's wife over in the Ning mansion and tell her they are for her to wear,' she said. Then turning to Zhou Rui's wife she asked her to convey Xi-feng's thanks to the donor.

Zhou Rui's wife now made her way towards Grandmother Jia's apartments. Just as she was coming out of the covered passage-way, she ran head-on into her daughter, all dressed up in her best clothes having just arrived on a visit from her mother-in-law's.

'What's suddenly brought you here at a time like this?' she asked her daughter.

'How have you been keeping, Mother? I've been waiting at your place for hours for you to come back. What's been keeping you all this time? I got tired of waiting. I thought I'd go and say "hullo" to Her Old Ladyship, and now I was just on my way to see Her Ladyship. Have you still not finished then? What's that you've got in your hand?'

Zhou Rui's wife laughed.

'Today is not my lucky day! First of all someone called Grannie Liu turned up, so like a fool I spend half the day rushing around with her. Then, as if that wasn't enough, Her Ladyship's sister sees me and gets me delivering flowers to the young ladies. I haven't finished yet. Now what have you come here today for? Something's gone wrong, I'll be bound!'

'I don't know how you always manage to guess, Mother, but you're right: it has. I'll be honest with you. My man had a cup too much to drink the other day and got into a fight with someone, and now, out of spite, they are trying to stir up trouble for him. They say his papers aren't in order, and they've reported him to the yamen and want to get him deported back South to his old village. So I thought I'd come and ask your advice, Mother, and see if you couldn't get someone here to put in a word for him. Do you think there's anyone who would be able to help?'

'I knew it would be something like this,' said Zhou Rui's wife. 'Well, cheer up, it's not so serious as all that! You just go back and wait while I take these flowers to Miss Lin. You can't see Her Ladyship now. She and the young mistress are both busy.'

The daughter obediently turned back to her mother's quarters. As she went, she said pleadingly,

'Be as quick as you can, Mother, won't you?'

'Yes, yes, yes. I'll be as quick as I can! You young people take everything so tragically! Lack of experience, that's what it is!' said Zhou Rui's wife, and moved on to Dai-yu's room.

Dai-yu was not in her own room, but with Bao-yu, trying to undo metal puzzles.

'Miss Lin,' said Zhou Rui's wife with a smile, 'Mrs Xue asked me to give you these flowers.'

'What flowers?' said Bao-yu. 'Let me see!'

He stretched out his arm, took the box from Zhou Rui's wife, and looked. Two artificial flowers, exquisitely fashioned by Palace craftsmen out of silk gauze, lay inside it. Dai-yu glanced over his arm into the box.

'Am I the only one getting these, or have the others had some too?'

'All the young ladies are getting them,' said Zhou Rui's wife. 'These two are for you, Miss.'

'I thought as much,' said Dai-yu sneeringly. 'I get the leavings when everyone else has had their pick.'

Zhou Rui's wife received this sally in silence, not daring to retort.

'What were you doing at my aunt's place, Zhou?' Bao-yu asked.

'Her Ladyship was there, and I had something to tell her.

Then while I was over there, Mrs Xue took the opportunity of giving me these flowers to deliver for her.'

'Was Miss Bao-chai there?' Bao-yu asked. 'Why hasn't she been round these last few days?'

'She's not very well.'

Bao-yu turned to his maids.

'Which of you will go and see Miss Bao-chai for me? Say that Miss Lin and I send our regards to her and her mother, and ask her if her illness is any better and what she's taking for it. Say that I really ought to go myself, but that as I've just got back from my lessons and have caught a bit of a cold, I shall be coming round another day.'

Snowpink said that she would go, and she and Zhou Rui's wife left the room together and went their separate ways.

This son-in-law of Zhou Rui's who had got himself into trouble was none other than Jia Yu-cun's old friend, Leng Zi-xing. He had recently become involved in a lawsuit arising out of the sale of some antiques, and had asked his wife to get strings pulled for him at the mansion. Zhou Rui's wife made light of the affair, confident of her employers' power to influence. A word to Xi-feng in the evening, and it would be as good as settled.

*

At lighting-up time that evening Xi-feng came in partial négligé (having removed her ornaments for the night) to report on the day's affairs to Lady Wang.

'Today I received the things sent us by the Zhen family. The Zhens have their own boat delivering seasonal produce for the New Year, so I have given their people our presents to the Zhens to take back on their return journey.'

Lady Wang nodded.

'I've got our birthday presents ready for the Earl of Lin-an's mother,' continued Xi-feng. 'Who would you like us to send with them?'

'Just see which women are free and send four of them,' replied Lady Wang. 'You don't have to ask me about things like that!'

'Today Cousin Zhen's wife invited me to spend tomorrow

with them at the other house,' Xi-feng continued. 'Is there anything tomorrow that needs doing here?'

'Whether there is or not,' said Lady Wang, 'I don't see that it matters. Generally when she brings an invitation it is for all of us, and you are naturally too busy to go. This time the invitation is to you personally, which shows that she had deliberately arranged this in order to give you a rest. The thought is a kind one, and it would be ungrateful to refuse. I think you ought to go.'

By now Li Wan and the three girls had also arrived for their evening duty, and when all had wished Lady Wang good night they departed to their different rooms.

Next day, as soon as Xi-feng had completed her toilet, she first reported to Lady Wang and then went to take her leave of Grandmother Jia. Hearing that she was going to the other house, Bao-yu said he wanted to go too, and Xi-feng was obliged to say that she would take him and to stand waiting for him while he changed his clothes. The two then got into a mule-cart and were soon inside the Ning-guo mansion, where Cousin Zhen's wife You-shi, her son Jia Rong, her little daughter-in-law Qin-shi, and a large number of women attendants and maids were standing outside the inner gate ready to welcome them.

You-shi's encounters with Xi-feng were always the occasion of good-humoured banter. Taking Bao-yu by the hand and chatting to Xi-feng, she conducted them both into the main reception room, where they all sat down and were served tea by Qin-shi.

'Well,' said Xi-feng, 'what have you asked me here for? Something nice, I hope! If it's a present, you'd better bring it now; I'm a busy woman!'

Before You-shi could think of a suitable retort, one of the women attendants replied for her:

'You ought not to have come, Mrs Lian! Now that you're here, we've got you in our power and you'll have to do what *we* say for a change!'

At that moment Jia Rong came in and paid his respects to the visitors. Bao-yu asked what had happened to Cousin Zhen.

'He's gone into the country to see Father,' said You-shi.

Then she added, 'It's not much fun for you sitting here. Why don't you go off and amuse yourself inside?'

'You've chosen a good day to come, Uncle Bao,' said little Qin-shi. 'Last time you were here you wanted to see my brother. Well, today he's here. He's sitting in the study at this very moment. Why don't you go in and see him?'

Bao-yu was for rushing off straight away. You-shi hurriedly ordered some servants to go after him in discreet attendance.

'Well now, just a minute!' said Xi-feng. 'Why not ask him in here so that I can see him too?'

'Oh dear, I don't think that would do at all!' said You-shi. 'Some people's children aren't used to rackety ways like ours. Some people's children are quiet and refined. If they were to meet a termagant like you, they might die of laughing.'

'He'll be lucky if *I* don't laugh at *him*,' said Xi-feng cheerfully. 'He'd better not try laughing at *me*!'

'He's very, very shy, Auntie,' said Jia Rong. 'We are afraid that if you saw him it might only irritate you.'

'Fiddlestick!' said Xi-feng. 'I don't care if he's a three-faced wonder with eight arms, I still want to see him. Stop farting about and bring him in, or I'll box your ears!'

Jia Rong cringed in mock alarm.

'Yes, Auntie! No need to get so fierce! We'll bring him in straight away.'

They both laughed, and Jia Rong disappeared for a while and presently came back leading a youth who, though somewhat thinner than Bao-yu, was more than his equal in freshness and liveliness of feature, in delicacy of complexion, handsomeness of figure, and grace of deportment, but whose painful bashfulness created a somewhat girlish impression. He approached Xi-feng and made his bow with a shy confusion which delighted her.

'You've met your match!' she said to Bao-yu with a laugh, nudging him playfully. Then, leaning forward and gripping the boy's hand in her own, she drew him down beside her and proceeded in a very deliberate manner to ask him how old he was, what books he was reading, and various other matters — among them his name, which was Qin Zhong.

When the maids and womenfolk in attendance on Xi-feng

realized that she was about to meet Qin Zhong and that they had come without the requisite material for a First Meeting present, they had sent some of their number back to consult Patience in the other house. Patience had, at her own discretion, selected a suitable length of material and two little 'Top of the List' solid gold medallions to give the messengers. These gifts now arrived for Xi-feng (who thought them somewhat on the meagre side) to give to Qin Zhong. When he and his sister had formally thanked her, the company sat down to lunch, after which You-shi, Xi-feng and Qin-shi settled down to a game of cards, while Bao-yu and Qin Zhong left the table to converse elsewhere.

When Bao-yu first set eyes on Qin Zhong it had been as though part of his soul had left him. For a while he stared blankly, oblivious to all around him, while a stream of idle fancies passed through his mind.

'How perfect he is! Who would have believed there could be such perfection? Now that I have seen him I know that I am just a pig wallowing in the mud, a mangy dog! Why, why did I have to be born in this pretentious *aristocratic* household? Why couldn't I have been born in the family of some poor scholar or low-grade clerk? Then I could have been near him and got to know him, and my life would have been worth living. Though I am so much richer and more nobly born than he, what use are my fine clothes but to cover up the dead and rotten wood beneath? What use the luxuries I eat and drink but to fill the cesspit and swell the stinking sewer of my inside? O rank and riches! How you poison everything!'

At the same time Qin Zhong, struck by Bao-yu's rare good looks and princely bearing and – even more perhaps – by the golden coronet and embroidered clothing and the train of pretty maids and handsome pages who attended him, was thinking:

'No wonder my sister raves about him whenever his name is mentioned! Why did I have to be born in a poor *respectable* family? How I should have liked to get to know him: to have shared moments of warmth and affection with him! But it was not to be!'

Each, plunged in reverie, for a while said nothing. Then

Bao-yu asked Qin Zhong about his reading, and Qin Zhong replied – a full, frank reply, without the trappings of politeness: and presently they were in the midst of a delightful conversation and were already like old friends.

After a while tea and various confections were brought in.

'We two shan't be drinking any wine,' Bao-yu said to the ladies. 'May we have a plate or two of these things set out on the little kang in the other room? We can talk in there without disturbing you,'

The two boys moved into the inner room for their tea.

In between plying Xi-feng with wine and delicacies, Qin-shi slipped in for a word with Bao-yu.

'My brother's quite young, Uncle Bao. Please, for my sake, don't mind him if he does anything to offend you! He may be shy, but he's got quite a nasty temper. He's not really easy to get on with at all.

'You go along!' said Bao-yu with a smile. 'We shall be all right!'

After a few admonitory words to her brother, Qin-shi went back to look after Xi-feng.

Some minutes later Xi-feng and You-shi sent a servant in to inquire whether the boys would like anything else to eat, adding that they had only to ask if they wanted anything. Bao-yu promised that they would; but his mind was not on eating and drinking, and he continued to question Qin Zhong about his life at home.

'My private tutor resigned last year,' Qin Zhong told him. 'Father is quite old, and as his health is not very good and his job keeps him terribly busy, he hasn't been able to do anything yet about getting me another one. At the moment I am just going over old lessons on my own at home. The trouble is, though, that if you want to get on in a subject, you really need one or two like-minded people to study with you, so that every so often you can all discuss what you have been reading . . .'

'Exactly!' Bao-yu put in eagerly, not waiting for him to finish. 'We have a private school in our family to which any members of the clan who can't manage private tuition may send their children, and boys from related families who aren't

in the clan can also be admitted. I have been at a loose end
ever since my tutor went home on leave, and Father would
have liked me to go to this school for revision until he gets
back next year and I can be taught privately again. But
Grandmother said that with so many boys in the school I
should be sure to get up to mischief, and it would do me more
harm than good. She also said I couldn't in any case go then,
because I'd only just recovered after several days in bed. And
so it got put off.

'From what you say, your father is worried about the same
problem as mine; so why not tell him about this school when
you get back today and ask him if you can join? I should be
there to keep you company, and we could both help each
other. I think it would be a marvellous idea.'

'The other day when the question of engaging a tutor
came up, Father mentioned this school of yours as a possible
alternative,' said Qin Zhong. 'He was going to come over and
have a word with my sister's father-in-law about it and get
him to recommend me; but they were busy here at the time
and it didn't seem the right moment to bother them with a
little thing like this. However, if you are really of the opinion
that I could be of some service to you, even if it's only grinding
your ink or cleaning your ink-stone, do please arrange it as
soon as you can, before we both get too rusty! We should be
relieving our parents of an anxiety and having the pleasure
of each other's company at one and the same time; so it would
be a good arrangement from every point of view.'

'Don't worry!' said Bao-yu. 'I'll tell Cousin Lian's wife
presently, when we join the others. Then when we get back
home tonight, *you* must tell your father and *I* shall tell my
grandmother. There's no reason that I can see why this
shouldn't be settled immediately.'

They had concluded their discussion in gathering dusk, and
now moved back into the lamplit outer room and watched the
ladies at their cards for a while. When the latter had finished
and had added up their scores, it appeared that Qin-shi and
You-shi had lost to Xi-feng and owed her a dramatic entertainment at which the players and the drinks were to be
provided at their expense. In the course of dinner, which was

now served and at which they were joined by the two boys, it was decided that this should take place in two days' time.

As it was now quite dark, You-shi gave her women orders to see that two menservants were detailed to attend Qin Zhong on his way back home. The women were gone on their errand an unusually long time and eventually Qin Zhong rose to take his leave.

'Who has been chosen to go with him?' You-shi asked.

'They have asked Big Jiao,' said the women, 'but it seems that he is terribly drunk and swearing at everybody.'

You-shi and Qin-shi were indignant.

'Whatever did they want to go and ask *him* for? Any of the younger ones would have done. What was the point of provoking *him*?'

'I always said you were too soft with people,' said Xi-feng. 'You really mustn't let servants get away with it like this. I never heard of such a thing!'

'You don't know Big Jiao,' said You-shi. 'Even Father couldn't do anything with him, let alone Zhen. When he was young he went with Grandfather on three or four of his campaigns and once saved his life by pulling him from under a heap of corpses and carrying him to safety on his back. He went hungry himself and stole things for his master to eat; and once when he had managed to get half a cupful of water, he gave it to his master and drank horse's urine himself. Because of these one or two acts of heroism he was always given special treatment during Grandfather's lifetime; so naturally we don't like to upset him now. But since he's grown old he has let himself go completely. He drinks all the time, and when he's drunk he starts abusing everybody – literally *everybody*. I've repeatedly told the steward not to give him jobs to do – to behave exactly as though he were dead and ignore him completely. Why on earth should he have chosen him today?'

'I know this Big Jiao all right,' said Xi-feng, 'and I still say that you are too weak. You ought to send him away. Right away. Send him to live on one of your farms: that would put a stop to his nonsense!' She turned to the women and asked if her own carriage was ready yet. The women replied that it was waiting, and she rose to take her leave and, taking Bao-yu by the hand, went out on to the steps, attended by You-shi and the rest.

In the flickering light of many lanterns the pages stood stiffly to attention on the pavement below, while Big Jiao, encouraged by Cousin Zhen's absence to indulge his talent for drunken abuse, was getting to work on the Chief Steward, Lai Sheng, accusing him of being unfair, of always dropping on the weakest, and so on and so forth.

'If there's a cushy job going you give it to someone else, but when it's a question of seeing someone home in pitch bloody darkness, you pick on me. Mean, rotten bugger! Call yourself a steward? Some steward! Don't you know who Old Jiao is? I can lift my *foot* up higher than your head! Twenty years ago I didn't give a damn for *anybody*, never mind a pack of little misbegotten abortions like you!'

He was just getting into his stride when Jia Rong came out to see Xi-feng off in her carriage. The servants shouted to Big Jiao to stop, but without success. Impatient of the old man's insolence, Jia Rong cursed him angrily.

'Tie him up,' he said to the servants. 'We shall see if he is still so eager for death tomorrow morning, when he has sobered up a bit.'

But Big Jiao was not to be intimidated by such as Jia Rong. On the contrary, he staggered up to him and bellowed even louder.

'Oh ho! Little Rong, is it? Don't you come the Big Master stuff with me, sonny boy! Never mind a little bit of a kid like you, even your daddy and your granddaddy don't dare to try any funny stuff with Old Jiao. If it wasn't for Old Jiao, where would you lot all be today, with your rank and your fancy titles and your money and all the other things you enjoy? It was your great-granddad, whose life I saved when he was given up for dead, that won all this for you, by the sweat of his brow. And what reward do I get for saving him? Nothing. Instead you come to me and you put on your Big Master act. Well, I'll tell you something. You'd better watch out. Because if you don't, you're going to get a shiny white knife inside you, and it's going to come out red!'

'You'd better hurry up and send this unspeakable creature about his business,' said Xi-feng to Jia Rong from her carriage. 'It's positively dangerous to keep a man like this on the premises. If any of our acquaintance get to know that a family like ours can't keep even a semblance of discipline about the place, we shall become a laughing-stock.'

Jia Rong assented meekly.

Several of the servants, seeing that Big Jiao had got quite out of hand and that something had to be done at all costs, rushed up and overpowered him, and throwing him face downward on the ground, frog-marched him off to the stables. By now even Cousin Zhen was being included in his maledictions, which became wilder and noisier as he shouted to his captors that he wanted to go to the ancestral temple and weep before the tablet of his old Master.

'Who would ever have believed the Old Master could spawn this filthy lot of animals?' he bawled. 'Up to their dirty little tricks every day. *I* know. Father-in-law pokes in the ashes. Auntie has it off with nevvy. Do you think I don't know what you're all up to? Oh, we "hide our broken arm in our sleeve"; but you don't fool me.'

Terrified out of their wits at hearing a fellow-servant utter such enormities, the grooms and pages tied him up and stuffed his mouth with mud and horse-dung.

Big Jiao's last words had been clearly audible to Xi-feng and Jia Rong, though they were a considerable distance away, but they both pretended not to have heard. Bao-yu, sitting in the carriage with Xi-feng, was less inhibited.

'Feng, what did he mean when he said "Father-in-law pokes in the ashes"?'

'Hold your tongue!' Xi-feng snapped back at him, livid. 'It's bad enough for a person in your position to even listen to such drunken filth, but to go asking questions about it, really! Just wait till I tell your mother! You're going to get the biggest hiding you've ever had in your life!'

Terrified by her vehemence, Bao-yu implored forgiveness.

'Please, Feng, don't tell her! I promise never to say those words again.'

Xi-feng's manner at once became soothing and indulgent.

'That's my good little cuzzy! When we get back I must tell Grandma to make them explain to the school about Qin Zhong and arrange for him to be admitted soon.'

As they talked, the carriage bore them back into Rong-guo House. But what happened there will be told in the chapter which follows.

CHAPTER 8

*Jia Bao-yu is allowed to see the strangely
corresponding golden locket
And Xue Bao-chai has a predestined encounter
with the Magic Jade*

When Bao-yu and Xi-feng were back and had seen the others, Bao-yu told Grandmother Jia of his wish to have Qin Zhong admitted to the clan school. He pointed out that a congenial study-companion would stimulate him to greater effort and gave her a glowing account of Qin Zhong's amiable qualities. Xi-feng was at hand to lend her support. She told Grandmother Jia that Qin Zhong would be calling on her within a day or two to pay his respects. Their infectious enthusiasm put the old lady in a high good humour, which Xi-feng took advantage of to ask if she would accompany her to the dramatic entertainment which her opponents had promised in two days' time.

In spite of her years Grandmother Jia loved any kind of excitement and when, two days later, You-shi came to fetch Xi-feng, the old lady did in fact accompany them, taking Lady Wang, Dai-yu and Bao-yu as well. By about noon, however, she was ready to go back and rest, and Lady Wang, who disliked noise and excitement, took the opportunity to leave with her. This left Xi-feng as principal guest, and she moved into the place of honour and stayed there for the rest of the day, enjoying herself immensely and not returning until late in the evening.

After accompanying Grandmother Jia back to her apartment and seeing her safely settled down for her nap, Bao-yu would have liked to go back and watch some more plays but was afraid that his presence would be an inconvenience to Qin-shi and his other 'juniors'. Remembering that Bao-chai had been at home unwell during the past few days and that he had still not been to see her, he thought he would go there instead and pay her a call, but fearing that if he went the quickest way through the corner gate behind the main hall he might meet with some entanglement on the way or, worse, run into his father, he decided to go by a more circuitous route.

The maids and nurses who attended him had been expecting him to change into his everyday clothes, but seeing him go out of the inner gate again without doing so, followed after him, assuming that he was going back to the other mansion to watch the plays. To their surprise, however, he turned left when he reached the covered passage-way instead of going straight on, and made off in a north-easterly direction.

But he was out of luck, for as he did so he found himself facing Zhan Guang and Shan Ping-ren, two of the literary gentlemen patronized by his father, who were walking towards him from the opposite direction. They descended on him gleefully, one of them clasping him round the waist, the other taking him by a hand.

'Angelic boy! How seldom one has the pleasure! Is it really you, or is this some delightful dream?'

They prattled on for what seemed an age before finally releasing him. As they were going, one of the old nurses detained them a moment longer.

'Have you two gentlemen just come from the Master's?'

The two gentlemen nodded and smiled conspiratorially:

'Sir Zheng is in his little study in the Su Dong-po Rooms, having his afternoon nap. All is well!'

They hurried off. Bao-yu smiled too, relieved that his father was safely out of the way. Turning once again, this time north-wards, he made his way swiftly towards Pear Tree Court.

Once more he was unlucky. The Clerk of Stores Wu Xin-deng, a man called Dai Liang who was foreman at the granary, and five other foremen were just at that moment coming out of the counting-house together and, catching sight of Bao-yu, at once stood respectfully to attention. One of their number, a buyer called Qian Hua who had not seen Bao-yu for some considerable time, hurried forward, dropped on his right knee, and touched his hand to the ground in the Manchu salute. Bao-yu smilingly extended a hand to raise him up. The men all relaxed in smiles.

'I saw some of your calligraphy in town the other day, Master Bao,' said one of them. 'It's getting really good! When are you going to give us a few sheets for ourselves, to put up on the wall?'

'Where did you see it?' Bao-yu asked.

'Any number of places,' the men told him. 'Everyone has been praising it no end. They even come to us asking for specimens.'

'You can have some easily enough if you really want to,' Bao-yu said. 'You have only to ask one of my boys.'

He hurried on. The men waited for him to pass before dispersing about their business.

To omit further details of his progress, Bao-yu came at last to Pear Tree Court, and going first into Aunt Xue's room, found her giving instructions to her maids about some embroidery. Her response to his greeting was to draw him towards her and clasp him to her bosom in an affectionate embrace.

'What a nice, kind boy to think of us on a cold day like this! Come up on the kang and get warm!'

She ordered a maid to bring him some 'boiling hot tea'.

Bao-yu inquired whether Cousin Pan was at home. Aunt Xue sighed.

'Pan is like a riderless horse: always off enjoying himself somewhere or other. He won't spend a single day at home if he can help it.'

'What about Bao-chai? Is she quite better?'

'Ah yes, of course!' said Aunt Xue. 'You sent someone to ask about her the other day, didn't you? That was very thoughtful of you. I think she's inside. Go in and have a look! It's warmer in there than here. You go in and sit down, and I'll be with you in a moment when I've finished tidying up.'

Bao-yu got down from the kang and going to the doorway of the inner room, lifted up the rather worn-looking red silk curtain which covered it. Bao-chai was sitting on the kang inside, sewing. Her lustrous black hair was done up in a simple bun without any kind of ornament. She was wearing a honey-coloured padded gown, a mulberry-coloured sleeveless jacket with a pattern in gold and silver thread, and a greenish-yellow padded skirt. All her clothing had the same sensible, rather well-worn look about it.

He saw no hint of luxury or show,
only a chaste, refined sobriety;
to some her studied taciturnity
might seem to savour of duplicity;
but she herself saw in conformity
the means of guarding her simplicity.

'Have you quite recovered, cousin?' Bao-yu asked.

Raising her head, Bao-chai saw Bao-yu enter the room. She rose quickly to her feet and smiled at him.

'I am quite better now. It was nice of you to think of me.'

She made him sit on the edge of the kang and ordered Oriole to pour him some tea. Then she proceeded to ask him first about Grandmother Jia, then about Lady Wang and then about the girls, while her eye took in the details of his dress.

He had a little jewel-encrusted coronet of gold filigree on the top of his head and a circlet in the form of two dragons supporting a pearl round his brow. He was dressed in a narrow-sleeved, full-skirted robe of russet-green material covered with a pattern of writhing dragons and lined and trimmed with white fox-fur. A butterfly-embroidered sash with fringed ends was fastened round his waist, and from his neck hung a padlock-shaped amulet, a lucky charm, and the famous jade said to have been inside his mouth when he was born.

Bao-chai's eye came to rest on the jade.

'I am always hearing about this famous stone of yours,' she said smilingly, 'but I have never yet had a chance of examining it really closely. Today I think I should like to have a look.'

She moved forward as she spoke, and Bao-yu too leaned towards her, and taking the stone from his neck, put it into her hand.

Looking at it as it lay on her palm, she saw a stone about the size of a sparrow's egg, glowing with the suppressed, milky radiance of a sunlit cloud and veined with iridescent streaks of colour.

Reader, you will, of course, remember that this jade was a

transformation of that same great stone block which once lay at the foot of Greensickness Peak in the Great Fable Mountains. A certain *jesting poet* has written these verses about it:

> Nü-wa's stone-smelting is a tale unfounded:
> On such weak fancies our Great Fable's grounded.
> Lost now, alack! and gone *my* heavenly stone –
> Transformed to this vile bag of flesh and bone.
> For, in misfortune, gold no longer gleams;
> And bright jade, when fate frowns, lack-lustre seems.
> Heaped charnel-bones none can identify
> Were golden girls and boys in days gone by.

The words which the scabby-headed monk had incised on the stone when he found it lying in its diminished shape under Greensickness Peak were as follows.

(On the front side)

MAGIC JADE

> Mislay me not, forget me not,
> And hale old age shall be your lot.

(On the reverse side)

> 1. Dispels the harms of witchcraft.
> 2. Cures melancholic distempers.
> 3. Foretells good and evil fortune.

When Bao-chai had looked at the stone all over, she turned back to the inscription on the front and repeated it a couple of times to herself out loud:

> 'Mislay me not, forget me not,
> And hale old age shall be your lot.'

'Why aren't you pouring the tea?' she asked Oriole. 'What are you standing there gawping for?'

Oriole laughed.

'Because those words sounded like a perfect match to the ones on your necklace.'

'So you have an inscription, too?' said Bao-yu pricking up his ears. 'I must have a look.'

'Don't take any notice of her!' said Bao-chai. 'There is no inscription.'

'Cousin, cousin,' said Bao-yu entreatingly, '*you*'ve had a look at *mine*. Be fair!'

Bao-chai could not escape the logic of this entreaty.

'There is a motto on it which someone gave us once for luck and which we had engraved on it,' she admitted. 'That's the only reason I always wear it; otherwise it would be too tiresome to have a heavy thing like this hanging round one's neck all the time.'

As she was speaking she undid the top buttons of her jacket and gown and extracted the necklace that she was wearing over the dark red shift beneath. Its pendant was a locket of shining solid gold, bordered with sparkling gems. There was a line of writing engraved on either side of it which together made up the words of a charm:

> Ne'er leave me, ne'er abandon me:
> And years of health shall be your fee.

He recited them a couple of times and then recited the words of his own inscription a couple of times.

'Why, yes!' he cried delightedly. 'The two inscriptions are a perfect match!'

'A scabby-headed old monk gave Miss Bao-chai the words,' said Oriole. 'He said they must be engraved on something made of gold . . .'

Bao-chai angrily cut her short, telling her to mind her business and pour the tea. To change the subject she asked Bao-yu where he had just come from.

Bao-yu was now sitting almost shoulder to shoulder with her and as he did so became aware of a penetrating fragrance that seemed to emanate from her person.

'What incense do you use to scent your clothes with, cousin?' he asked. 'I have never smelt such a delicious perfume.'

'I can't stand incense perfumes,' said Bao-chai. 'I could never see the point of smoking perfectly good, clean clothes over an incense-pot.'

'In that case, what *is* this perfume I can smell?'

Bao-chai thought for a moment.

'I know! It must be the Cold Fragrance Pill I took this morning.'

'What's a Cold Fragrance Pill?' said Bao-yu with a laugh. 'Won't you give me one to try?'

'Now you're being silly again. Medicine isn't something to be taken for amusement.'

Just at that moment the servants outside announced 'Miss Lin' and almost simultaneously Dai-yu came flouncing into the room. Catching sight of Bao-yu she let out a wail of mock dismay.

'Oh dear! I *have* chosen a bad time to come!'

The others rose and invited her to be seated.

'Why did you say that?' Bao-chai asked her.

'If I had known *he* was coming, I shouldn't have come myself.'

'What exactly do you mean by that?'

'What do I mean by that?' said Dai-yu. 'I mean that if I only come when he does, then when I don't come you won't have any visitors. Whereas if we space ourselves out so that he comes one day and I come the next, it will never get either too lonely or too noisy for you. I shouldn't have thought that needed much explaining.'

Observing that Dai-yu was wearing a greatcoat of red camlet over her dress, Bao-yu asked whether it was snowing outside.

'It's been snowing for some time,' said one of the old women standing below the kang.

Bao-yu asked someone to go and fetch his winter cape.

'You see!' said Dai-yu. 'When I come, he has to go!'

'Who said anything about going?' said Bao-yu. 'I just want them to have it ready for me.'

'It's no time to go now, while it's still snowing,' said Bao-yu's old nurse, Nannie Li. 'Much better stay here and play with your cousins. In any case, I think your Aunt Xue is getting tea ready for you. I'll send a maid to fetch your cape. Shall I tell the boys outside they can go?'

Bao-yu nodded, and Nannie Li went outside and dismissed the pages.

By now Aunt Xue had finished laying tea, which included a number of delicious-looking things to eat, and invited the cousins to partake. While they were doing so, Bao-yu happened to mention the excellent goose-foot preserve made by his Cousin Zhen's wife that he had eaten at the Ning mansion only two days previously. Aunt Xue at once hurried out and fetched some of her own for him to try.

'This really needs to be eaten with wine,' said Bao-yu.

Aunt Xue gave orders for some of the best wine to be decanted; but Nannie Li disapproved.

'He shouldn't have wine, Mrs Xue.'

'Oh go on, Nannie!' Bao-yu pleaded good-humouredly. 'I shall only drink one cup.'

'It's no good!' said Nannie Li. 'I don't mind if you drink a hogshead as long as your grandmother or your mother is there. But look at the trouble I got into the other day just because when I had my back turned for a moment some wretched person who ought to have known better gave you a sip or two to humour you! I didn't hear the end of it for days after.

'You don't know how wild he can be, Mrs Xue,' she continued. 'And he gets even worse when he's had something to drink. With Her Old Ladyship you can never tell. One day when she's feeling high-spirited she'll let him drink as much as he likes; other days she won't let him touch a drop. But come what may, I'm always the one that gets into trouble.'

'Poor old thing!' said Aunt Xue with a laugh. 'Have a drink yourself and stop worrying! I'll see that he doesn't drink too much. And if Lady Jia *does* say anything, I shall take full responsibility.' She turned to one of the maids: 'Come on, now! Pour Nannie a nice warm cup of wine to keep the cold out!'

Nannie Li could scarcely sustain her objection after this and went off with the other servants to have her drink.

'Don't bother to heat the wine for me,' said Bao-yu. 'I prefer it cold.'

'Good gracious, that will never do!' said Aunt Xue. 'You mustn't drink wine cold, or when you write your hand will shake!'

'I'm surprised at you, Cousin Bao!' said Bao-chai with a smile. 'With all your enthusiasm for out-of-the-way learning, fancy not knowing a thing like that! Wine has an exceptionally fiery nature, and therefore must be drunk warm in order to be quickly digested. If it is drunk cold, it congeals inside the body and harms it by absorbing heat from the internal organs. From this day on you must reform! No more cold wine!'

Dai-yu, who sat cracking melon-seeds between her teeth throughout this homily, smiled ironically. Just at that moment her maid Snowgoose came hurrying in with a little hand-warmer for her.

'Who told you to bring this?' Dai-yu asked her. 'Very kind of them, I am sure. But I was not actually freezing to death here.'

'Nightingale told me to bring it, Miss. She was afraid you might be cold.'

'I am glad you are so ready to obey her. Generally when *I* tell you to do anything it goes in one ear and out the other; yet anything *she* tells you to do is followed out more promptly than an Imperial Edict!'

Bao-yu knew perfectly well that these words were really intended for him, but made no reply, beyond laughing good-humouredly. Bao-chai, long accustomed to Dai-yu's peculiar ways, also ignored them. But Aunt Xue protested.

'You've always been rather delicate and you've always felt the cold badly. Surely it was nice of them to think of you?'

'You don't understand, Aunt,' said Dai-yu. 'It doesn't matter here, with you; but some people might be deeply offended at the sight of one of my maids rushing in with a hand-warmer. It's as though I thought my hosts couldn't supply one themselves if I needed it. Instead of saying how thoughtful the maid was, they would put it down to my arrogance and lack of breeding.'

'You are altogether too sensitive, thinking of things like that,' said Aunt Xue. 'Such a thought would never have crossed my mind!'

Bao-yu had soon finished his third cup of wine and Nannie Li once more came forward to restrain him. But Bao-yu, who was now warm and happy and in the midst of a hilarious conversation with his cousins, was naturally unwilling to stop, and pleaded humbly with the old lady for a reprieve.

'Nannie darling, just two more cups and then I'll stop!'

'You'd better look out,' said Nannie Li. 'Your father's at home today. He'll be asking you about your lessons before you know where you are.'

At these words all Bao-yu's happiness drained away. Slowly he set down his cup and bowed his head in dejection.

'Don't spoil everyone's enjoyment,' said Dai-yu. 'Even if Uncle *does* call for you, you can always say that Aunt Xue is keeping you. I think that old Nannie of yours has had a cup too many and is looking for a bit of excitement at our expense.' She gave him a gentle nudge to encourage a more valiant spirit in him, muttering, as she did so, 'Take no notice of the old fool! Let's go on enjoying ourselves and not mind about her!'

Nannie Li knew only too well what Dai-yu was capable of.

'Now Miss Lin,' she said, 'don't *you* go taking his part! If *you* encourage him he's only too likely to do what you say!'

Dai-yu smiled dangerously. 'Take his part? Why should *I* want to encourage him? You are over-cautious, my dear Nannie. After all, Lady Jia often lets him drink; why should it matter if Mrs Xue lets him have a cup or two? I suppose you think he can't be trusted to drink here because Mrs Xue is not one of us?'

Nannie Li did not know whether to feel upset or amused.

'Really, Miss Lin. Some of the things you say cut sharper than a knife!'

Bao-chai could not suppress a giggle. She pinched Dai-yu's cheek playfully.

'Really, Miss Frowner, the things you say! One doesn't know whether to grind one's teeth or laugh!'

Aunt Xue laughed too.

'Don't be afraid, my boy! Heaven knows I've got little enough to offer you when you come to see me. You mustn't get upset over a small thing like this, or I shall feel quite uncomfortable. Drink as much as you like; I'll look after you! You may as well stay to supper, in any case; and even if you *do* get drunk, you can always spend the night here.' She told a maid to heat some more wine. 'There! Auntie will drink a cup or two with you, and then we shall have some supper.'

Bao-yu's spirits began to revive a bit under his aunt's encouragement.

'Keep an eye on him,' said Nannie Li to the maids. 'I'm just going back for a few minutes to change my clothes.' Then aside to Aunt Xue she said, 'Don't let him drink too much, Mrs Xue!' and went off home.

Although two or three old women still remained after her departure, none felt very much concern for Bao-yu, and as soon as Nannie Li was out of the way they quietly slipped off about their own concerns, leaving, of the attendants who had come with him, only two small maids, whose only anxiety was to please their young master by indulging him as much as possible.

Fortunately Aunt Xue, by exercising great tact and finesse, managed to spirit the wine away when Bao-yu had drunk only a few more cups, and to replace it with a hot, sour soup of pickled bamboo-shoots and chicken-skin. He drank several bowls of this with great relish and then ate half a bowl of green-rice gruel. After that, when Bao-chai and Dai-yu had finished eating, he drank several cups of very strong tea. At this point Aunt Xue felt sure that he would be all right.

As Snowgoose and the other maids had now finished supper too and were once more in attendance, Dai-yu asked Bao-yu if he was ready to go. He looked at her blearily through tired eyes.

'If you want to go, I will go with you.'

Dai-yu rose to her feet. 'We really ought to go. We've been here practically all day!'

The two of them began saying their good-byes.

A maid came forward with Bao-yu's rain-hat and he lowered his head slightly for her to put it on. Holding the brim of the great saucer-shaped red felt top, she jerked it up and prepared to bring it down, aiming the inside part at his crown.

'Stop!' he cried impatiently. 'You have got to go easy with a great clumsy thing like that! Haven't you ever seen anyone putting one of these things on before? You had better let me do it myself.'

'Come here!' said Dai-yu standing on the edge of the kang. 'I'll put it on for you!'

Bao-yu went and stood in front of her. Putting her two hands round the inner cap, Dai-yu eased it gently down until its rim fitted over his golden headband, so that the walnut-sized red woollen pompom of the headband was left quivering outside the cap on its flexible golden stem.

'There!' she said, after a few further adjustments. 'Now you can put on your cape.'

Bao-yu took the cape from his maid and fastened it himself.

'The nurses who came with you are still not back,' said Aunt Xue. 'Perhaps you had better wait a bit.'

'*We* wait for *them*?' said Bao-yu. 'We have got the maids. We shall be all right.'

But Aunt Xue was not satisfied, and ordered two of her own women to see the cousins home.

As soon as they were back they thanked the women for their trouble and went straight in to see Grandmother Jia, who had not yet had her supper. She was delighted to learn that they had been with Aunt Xue, and observing that Bao-yu, had had more than a little to drink, she told him to go and rest in his room and not come out again, and instructed the servants to keep a careful watch over him. Remembering which servants usually attended him, she asked what had become of Nannie Li. The maids dared not tell her the truth, which was that she had gone home.

'I think she must have had something to do,' said one of them. 'She came in when we did just now, but went out again almost immediately.'

'Why worry about her?' said Bao-yu over his shoulder, swaying slightly as he made his way to the bedroom. 'She's better looked after than you are! If it weren't for her I might live a few days longer!'

Inside his room he found a writing-brush and ink laid out on the desk. Skybright was the first to greet him.

'You're a nice one!' she said. 'You made me mix all this ink for you this morning, sat down in a state of great enthusiasm, wrote just three characters, threw down the brush again, rushed out, and left me waiting here all day for you to come back and finish. Now you just sit down here and use this ink up, and perhaps I'll let the matter pass!'

Skybright's words awoke in Bao-yu a recollection of the morning's events.

'What became of the three characters I wrote?'

Skybright laughed. 'You're really drunk, aren't you! This morning before you went to the other house you gave careful instructions that they were to be pasted up over the outside door. I was afraid that someone else might make a mess of it, so I got up on a ladder and spent half the morning sticking them up myself. My hands are still numb from doing it.'

'I'd forgotten.' Bao-yu smiled. 'If your hands are cold, I'll warm them for you.' He took both her hands in his own and led her outside to inspect the sheet of calligraphy newly pasted up over the doorway. Just then Dai-yu arrived.

'I want you to tell me honestly, cousin,' said Bao-yu. 'Which of these three characters do you think is the best?'

Dai-yu looked up at the three characters above the door:

RED RUE STUDY

'They are all equally good. I didn't know you could write so beautifully. You must do one for me some time!'

'You're just saying that to humour me,' said Bao-yu. 'Where is Aroma?' he asked Skybright.

Skybright shot out her lips and indicated the kang inside, on which Aroma, fully clothed, was lying fast asleep.

'Just look at that!' said Bao-yu with a laugh. 'It's a bit early for sleep, isn't it?'

He turned once more to Skybright. 'When I was having lunch at the other house today there was a plate of bean-curd dumplings. I remembered how fond you are of those things and asked Mrs Zhen if I could have some to eat in the evening. She had them sent over for me. Did you get them all right?'

'Don't talk to me about those dumplings!' said Skybright. 'As soon as they arrived I realized that they must be for me, but as I'd only just finished eating, I put them on one side meaning to eat them later. Then after a while Nannie Li came in and caught sight of them. "I don't expect Bao-yu will want these," she said. "I think I'll take them for my grand-children"; and she had them sent round to her house.'

While Skybright was talking, Snowpink came in carrying some tea on a tray. Bao-yu invited Dai-yu to have some, to the great merriment of the maids, who pointed out that she had slipped away some minutes before.

After drinking about half a cupful, Bao-yu suddenly thought of the tea he had drunk early that morning.

'When you made that Fung Loo this morning,' he said to Snowpink, 'I remember telling you that with that particular brand the full flavour doesn't come out until after three or four waterings. Why have you given me this other stuff? This would have been just the time to have the Fung Loo.'

'I *was* keeping it for you,' said Snowpink, 'but Nannie Li came and drank it all.'

With a flick of the wrist Bao-yu hurled the cup he was holding on to the floor, where it smashed noisily, breaking into innumerable pieces and showering Snowpink's skirt with hot tea. He jumped angrily to his feet.

'Is she your mistress that you should all treat her with such reverence? Merely because I drank her milk for a few days when I was a baby she is as spoiled and pampered as though she were some sort of divinity. Let's get rid of the old woman now and have done with it!'

And he strode off without more ado to tell Grandmother Jia that he wanted his old nurse dismissed.

All this time Aroma had been only pretending to sleep, hoping by this means to engage Bao-yu's attention and provoke some coquetry between them. As long as the talk dwelt on calligraphy and Skybright's dumplings there seemed no pressing need for her to get up; but when she heard him break a teacup and grow really angry she hurriedly rose to her feet and intervened to restrain him.

By this time someone had arrived from Grandmother Jia's room to inquire what all the noise was about. Aroma pre-tended that she had smashed the cup herself by slipping on some snow while fetching tea. Having disposed of the inquirer, she then proceeded to exhort Bao-yu.

'Dismiss her by all means, if you really want to! But we

should all like to leave with her; so while you are about it, why not make a clean sweep and dismiss the lot of us? I am sure you will find plenty of other good servants to replace us with.'

Bao-yu had nothing to say to this, and Aroma and the rest helped him onto the kang and started undressing him. He kept trying to tell them something as they did so, but an object seemed to impede his tongue and his eyelids were growing increasingly hot and heavy. Soon the maids had him lying down between covers. Aroma took off the 'Magic Jade', wrapped it in a piece of silk, and slipped it under the quilt, so that it should not be cold on his neck the next morning. By this time Bao-yu was already asleep, having dropped off as soon as his head touched the pillow.

While this was going on, Nannie Li and the other old women had arrived back at last. Learning that Bao-yu was drunk, they dared not approach him and soon went off again, having satisfied themselves by whispered exchanges that he was safely asleep.

*

Bao-yu awoke next morning to hear someone announcing that 'Master Rong from the other house' had brought Qin Zhong over to pay his respects. Bao-yu hurried out to receive them and conducted Qin Zhong into the presence of Grandmother Jia. Observing that Qin Zhong's good looks and gentle demeanour admirably qualified him to become Bao-yu's study-companion, Grandmother Jia was pleased, and made him stay for tea and then dinner, after which she sent him to be introduced to Lady Wang and the rest. Everybody loved Qin-shi and was delighted to meet this charming younger brother, and there were First Meeting presents from everybody waiting for him when he left. Grandmother Jia's was an embroidered purse enclosing a little God of Literature in solid gold to signify that literary success was 'in the bag'.

'Since your home is so far away,' she said to Qin Zhong as he was leaving, 'the weather may sometimes make it inconvenient for you to go back at night. In that case, do please stay here with us! And mind that you always keep with your

Uncle Bao and don't go getting into mischief with those young ragamuffins at the school!'

Qin Zhong received these admonitions with deference and then went home to report on the day's events to his father.

Qin Zhong's father, Qin Bang-ye, was one of the Secretaries in the Public Buildings Department of the Board of Works and a man in his middle sixties. He had lost his wife early, and finding himself still childless at the age of fifty, had adopted a boy and a girl from an orphanage. The boy had died, leaving only the girl Ke-er, or 'Ke-qing' as she was more elegantly renamed, who had grown up into an extremely charming and vivacious young woman and been married into the Jia family, with whom her adoptive father had long had a connection.

Qin Bang-ye fathered Qin Zhong when he was fifty-three and the boy was now twelve years old. His tutor had returned south the year before, and he had been revising old lessons at home ever since. Qin Bang-ye had himself been on the point of speaking to his daughter's in-laws about the possibility of getting Qin Zhong admitted into the Jia clan school as an external scholar when the happy accident of Qin Zhong's meeting with Bao-yu occurred. Bang-ye knew of Jia Dai-ru, the master in charge of the school, as one of the leading elder scholars of the day, under whose tutelage there would be every hope of Qin Zhong's making rapid strides in his education and eventually obtaining an advancement. He was therefore delighted that the matter had been so easily concluded.

There was only one difficulty. Knowing the sort of style in which the Jias lived, Bang-ye realized that he would have to dip deeply into his pocket, and his official salary left that pocket only meagrely supplied. However, since this was a matter which concerned the whole future of his son, there was nothing for it but to strain his credit to the utmost. By borrowing a bit here and a bit there he was able to get together a sum of twenty-four taels of silver which he made up into a packet and laid reverently before Jia Dai-ru when he took Qin Zhong to the old teacher's house to make his kotow. Nothing now remained but for Bao-yu to choose an auspicious day on which the two of them could begin school together.

Their entry into the school was the occasion of a tumultuous incident of which an account will be given in the following chapter.

CHAPTER 9

A son is admonished and Li Gui receives
an alarming warning
A pupil is abused and Tealeaf throws the
classroom in an uproar

In the last chapter we left Qin Bang-ye and his son waiting for a message from the Jia household to tell them when Qin Zhong was to begin school. Bao-yu was impatient to see Qin Zhong again and sent word to say that it was to be the day after next.

When the appointed day arrived, Bao-yu rose in the morning to find that Aroma had already got his books, brushes and other writing materials ready for him and was sitting disconsolately on the side of his bed. Seeing him get up, she roused herself and helped him to do his hair and wash. He asked her the cause of her despondency.

'What's upset you this time, Aroma? I can't believe you are worried about being left alone while I am at school.'

'Of course not!' said Aroma with a laugh. 'Learning is a very good thing. Without it you would fritter all your life away and never get anywhere. I only hope that you'll see to it that you *are* learning when you are meant to be and that, when you are not, you will be thinking about home and not getting into scrapes with the other boys; because then you would be in *real* trouble with your father. And though you talk a lot about the need for effort and self-improvement, it would really be better to do too little work than too much. For one thing you don't want to bite off more than you can chew; and for another you don't want your health to suffer. At least, that's how it seems to me, so you mustn't mind my saying so.'

Each time Aroma paused, Bao-yu answered 'Yes' or 'No'. She continued:

'I have packed your big fur gown for the pages to take. Mind you put it on if you find it cold at the school. It won't be like here, where there is always someone else to think of these things for you. I've also given them your foot-warmer and your hand-warmer. You'll have to see that they give the charcoal a stir from time to time. They're such a lazy pack of good-for-nothings, they'll be only too pleased to do nothing if you don't stand over them. You could freeze to death for all they cared.'

'Don't worry!' said Bao-yu. 'I know how to do it myself. And don't go getting gloomy, all of you, cooped up here while I am away. Try to spend as much time as you can with my Cousin Lin.'

His dressing was now completed and Aroma urged him to begin his visits to Grandmother Jia, Jia Zheng and Lady Wang. After a few parting instructions to Skybright and Musk, he went off to his grandmother's, where he had to listen to more admonitions, then on to Lady Wang's, and then outside to the study to see his father, Jia Zheng.

Jia Zheng was in conversation with his literary gentlemen when Bao-yu entered the room and made his salutation. Hearing him announce that he was off to school to resume his studies, Jia Zheng smiled sarcastically.

'I think you had better not use that word "studies" again in my hearing, unless you want to make me blush for you. In my opinion you might just as well be left to fool around as before, since that is all you seem fit for. At all events, I don't want you here. I find your presence in a place like this contaminating.'

The literary gentlemen rose to their feet with nervous laughter.

'Come, come, Sir Zheng! You are too hard on him! Two or three years from now our young friend will be carrying all before him! He has left his old, childish ways behind him now – haven't you boy? Quite reformed. Come!' – two of the older men took Bao-yu by the hands and hurried him from the room – 'I am sure it must be time now for your breakfast. To breakfast! To breakfast!'

Jia Zheng asked who was in attendance on Bao-yu. There was a ringing 'Sir!' from outside, and three or four strapping fellows entered the study and saluted Manchu fashion. Jia

Zheng recognized the foremost one as Li Gui, the son of Bao-yu's old wet-nurse, Nannie Li, and addressed himself to him.

'You have attended Bao-yu during all his lessons in the past. What precisely has he been doing? Stuffing his head with worthless nonsense and acquiring a fine new stock of knavish tricks, I shouldn't wonder! Wait until I have a little time to spare: I'll have your hide off first and then settle accounts with that good-for-nothing son of mine!'

'Sir!'

Li Gui sank terrified to his knees, snatched off his cap, and knocked the ground several times with his forehead.

'Master Bao has read the first three books of the *Poetry Classic*, sir, up to the part that goes

> Hear the happy bleeding deer
> Grousing in the vagrant meads . . .

That's the truth, sir. I wouldn't tell a lie.'

This novel version of the well-known lines provoked a roar of laughter from the literary gentlemen. Even Jia Zheng could not restrain a smile.

'If he read *thirty* books of the *Poetry Classic*,' said Jia Zheng, 'it would still be tomfoolery. No doubt he hopes to deceive others with this sort of thing, but he does not deceive me. Give my compliments to the Headmaster and tell him from me that I want none of this trifling with the *Poetry Classic* or any other ancient literature. It is of the utmost importance that he should thoroughly understand and learn by heart the whole *Four Books* before he attempts anything else.'

'Sir!'

Seeing that Jia Zheng had nothing more to say, Li Gui and the other servants rose to their feet again and withdrew.

All this time Bao-yu had been waiting for them in the courtyard outside, scarcely daring to breathe. As they came out, dusting their knees, Li Gui said,

'Did you hear that, young master? "Have my hide off first" he said. Some people's servants are respected for their masters' sakes, but not us. All we get is beatings and hard words. So spare a thought for us in future, will you?'

'Don't be upset, old chap!' said Bao-yu. 'Tomorrow I'll treat you all.'

'Little ancestor,' Li Gui replied, 'nobody's looking for treats. All we ask is that once in a while – just once in a while – you should do what you are told.'

They were now back at Grandmother Jia's apartment. Qin Zhong had already arrived and was engaged in conversation with the old lady. As soon as the two friends had greeted each other they took their leave.

Bao-yu suddenly remembered that he had not yet seen Dai-yu and hurried to her room to say good-bye. He found her by the window making herself up at the mirror. Her answer to his announcement that he was off to begin school was smiling but perfunctory:

'Good. I wish you every success. I'm sorry I can't see you off.'

'Wait till I get back and have had my supper, cousin,' said Bao-yu, 'and I will give you a hand with that rouge.'

He chatted with her for quite a bit longer before finally tearing himself away. As he was going she suddenly called after him so that he stopped:

'Aren't you going to say good-bye to your cousin Bao-chai?'

Bao-yu smiled but said nothing and went straight off to school with Qin Zhong.

*

The Jia clan school was situated at no great distance from Rong-guo House. It was a charitable foundation which had been established many years previously by the founder of the family and was designed for the sons and younger brothers of those members of the clan who could not afford to pay for private tuition. All members of the clan holding official posts were expected to contribute towards its expenses and members of advanced years and known integrity were chosen to be its masters. As soon as Bao-yu and Qin Zhong arrived they were introduced to the other students and then set to work at once on their lessons.

From now on the two friends were inseparable, arriving at

school and leaving school together and sitting beside each other in class. Grandmother Jia herself became very fond of Qin Zhong. She was always having him to stay for three or four nights at a time and treated him exactly as if he were one of her own great-grandchildren. And because she realized that his family was not very well off, she frequently helped out with clothes and the like. Within a month or two he was a familiar and accepted member of the Rong household.

Bao-yu had always been impatient of social conventions, preferring to let sentiment rather than convention dictate the terms of his relationships. It was this which now prompted him to make Qin Zhong the following proposal:

'You and I are schoolmates and pretty much the same age. Let us in future forget all this "uncle" "nephew" business and address each other exactly like friends or brothers!'

Qin Zhong was at first too timid to comply; but as Bao-yu persisted and went on calling him 'brother' or 'Jing-qing' (which was his school-name) whenever he spoke to him, Qin Zhong himself gradually fell into the habit of addressing Bao-yu as an equal.

All the pupils at the clan school were either members of the Jia clan or relations by marriage; but as the proverb rightly says, 'there are nine kinds of dragon and no two kinds are alike'. Where many are gathered together the wheat is sure to contain a certain amount of chaff; and this school was no exception in numbering some very ill-bred persons among its pupils.

The two new boys, Qin Zhong and Bao-yu, were both as beautiful as flowers; the other scholars observed how shrinking and gentle Qin Zhong was, blushing almost before you spoke to him and timid and bashful as a girl; they saw in Bao-yu one whom nature and habit had made humble and accommodating in spite of his social position, always willing to defer to others in the interest of harmony; they observed his affectionate disposition and familiar manner of speech; and they could see that the two friends were devoted to each other. Perhaps it is not to be wondered at that these observations should have given rise to certain suspicions in the minds of those ill-bred persons, and that both in school and out of it all kinds of ugly rumours should have circulated behind their backs.

When Xue Pan learned, some time after moving into his aunt's place in the capital, that the establishment included a clan school plentifully stocked with young males of a certain age, his old enthusiasm for 'Lord Long-yang's vice' was re-awakened, and he had hastened to register himself as a pupil. His school-going was, needless to say, a pretence – 'one day fishing and two days to dry the nets' as they say – and had nothing to do with the advancement of learning. Having paid a generous fee to Jia Dai-ru, he used his membership of the school merely as a means of picking up 'soul-mates' from among his fellow-students. It must with regret be recorded that a surprisingly large number of the latter were deluded into becoming his willing victims by the prospect of receiving those ample advances of money and goods which he was in a position to offer.

Among them were two amorous young creatures whose names and parentage escape us but who, because of their glamorous looks and affected manners, were universally known by the nicknames of 'Darling' and 'Precious'. Although their fellow-students much admired them and entertained towards them feelings not at all conducive to that health of mind which the Young Person should at all times endeavour to cultivate, they were deterred from meddling with them for fear of what Xue Pan might do.

When Qin Zhong and Bao-yu joined the school it was only to be expected that they too should fall under the spell of this charming pair; but like the rest they were inhibited from overt declaration of their feelings by the knowledge that Xue Pan was their 'friend'. Their feelings were reciprocated by Darling and Precious, and a bond of mutual attraction grew up be-tween the four, which nevertheless remained unexpressed, except for the significant looks that every day passed between them across the classroom, or the occasional rather too loud utterance to a neighbour of some remark really intended for the ears of the opposite pair.

They were persuaded that these cryptic communications had escaped the notice of their fellows; but they were wrong.

Certain young hooligans among their classmates had long since discerned the true nature of what was going on, and while the two handsome couples were engaged in their silent and (as they thought) secret communion, these others would be winking and leering behind their backs or becoming suddenly convulsed with paroxysms of artificial coughing.

It happened that one day Jia Dai-ru was called home on business and left the class with the first half of a fourteen word couplet to complete, telling them that he would be back on the morrow to take them over the next passage in their reading and putting his eldest grandson Jia Rui in charge of the school during his absence. Xue Pan had by now stopped coming in even for roll-call, and so on this occasion he too was out of the way. The opportunity was too good to miss, and Qin Zhong and Darling, after a preliminary exchange of glances, both asked to be excused and went round to the rear courtyard to converse.

'Does your father mind what friends you have?' Qin Zhong had got no further than this question when there was a cough behind them. The two boys spun round and saw that it came from their classmate 'Jokey' Jin. Darling had a somewhat impetuous nature which now, fired by a mixture of anger and shame, caused him to round sharply on the intruder.

'What's that cough supposed to mean? Aren't we allowed to talk if we want to?'

Jokey Jin leered: 'If you're allowed to talk, aren't I allowed to cough if I want to? What I'd like to know is, if you've got something to say to each other, why can't you say it out openly? Why all this guilty secrecy? But what's the good of pretending? It's a fair cop. You let me in on your game and I won't say anything. Otherwise there'll be trouble!'

With furious blushes the other two protested indignantly that they did not know what he was talking about.

Jokey Jin grinned. 'Caught you in the act, didn't I?' He began to clap his hands and chant in a loud, guffawing voice,

> 'Bum-cake!
> Bum-cake!
> Let's all have a
> Bit to eat!'

Angry and indignant, Qin Zhong and Darling hurried
back into the classroom and complained to Jia Rui that
Jokey Jin was persecuting them.

This Jia Rui was a spineless, unprincipled character who, as
a means of obliging the boys to treat him, always displayed
the most shameless favouritism in his settlement of classroom disputes. In return for money, drinks, and dinners, he
had lately given Xue Pan a free hand in his nefarious activities
– had, indeed, not only refrained from interfering with him,
but even 'aided the tyrant in his tyranny'.

Now Xue Pan was very inconstant in his affections, always
blowing east one day and west the next. He had recently
abandoned Darling and Precious in favour of some newly
discovered sweetheart, just as previously he had abandoned
Jokey Jin in favour of Darling and Precious. It followed that
in this present confrontation Jia Rui, to his chagrin, could not
hope to gain any rewards by the exercise of his usual partiality. Instead of blaming this vexatious state of affairs on
Xue Pan's fickleness, however, he directed all his resentment
against Darling and Precious, for whom he felt the same
unreasonable jealousy as motivated Jokey Jin and the rest.

Qin Zhong's and Darling's complaint at first put Jia Rui in
somewhat of a quandary, for he dared not openly rebuke
Qin Zhong. He could, however, give his resentment outlet
by making an example of Darling; so instead of dealing with
his complaint, he told him that he was a trouble-maker and
followed this up with so savage a dressing-down that even
Qin Zhong went back to his seat humiliated and crestfallen.

Jokey Jin, now thoroughly cock-a-hoop, wagged his head
and tutted in a most provoking manner and addressed wound-
ing remarks to no one in particular, which greatly upset
Darling and Precious for whose ears they were intended. A
furious muttered altercation broke out between them across
the intervening desks. Jokey Jin insisted that he had caught
Qin Zhong and Darling *in flagrante delicto*.

'I ran into them in the back courtyard, kissing each other
and feeling arses as plain as anything. I tell you they had it
all worked out. They were just measuring themselves for size
before getting down to business.'

Reckless in his hour of triumph, he made these wild allegations, unmindful of who might hear them. But one heroic soul was moved to mighty anger by his wanton words. This was Jia Qiang, a member of the Ning-guo branch of the family of the same generation as Jia Rong. He had lost both his parents when a small child and been brought up by Cousin Zhen. At sixteen he was even more handsome and dashing than Jia Rong and the two youths were inseparable friends.

Any establishment as large as the Ning household always contains a few disgruntled domestics who specialize in traducing their masters, and a number of disagreeable rumours concerning Jia Qiang did in fact begin to circulate among the servants which seem to have reached the ears of Cousin Zhen, for, partly in self-defence (since they involved him too), he moved Jia Qiang out of the house and set him up in a small establishment of his own somewhere in the city.

Jia Qiang possessed a very shrewd brain under his dazzlingly handsome exterior. His attendance at the school, however, was no more than a blind to his other activities, principal among which were cock-fighting, dog-racing, and botanizing excursions into the Garden of Pleasure; but with a doting Cousin Zhen to protect him on the one hand and Jia Rong to aid and comfort him on the other, there was no one in the clan who dared thwart him in anything he did.

Since Qin Zhong was the brother-in-law of his best friend, Jia Qiang was naturally unwilling to stand by and see him abused in so despiteful a manner without doing anything to help. On the other hand he reflected that there would be certain disadvantages in coming forward as his champion.

'Jokey Jin, Jia Rui, and that lot are all friends of Uncle Xue,' he thought. 'For that matter, I'm a friend of Uncle Xue myself. If I openly stick up for Qin Zhong and they go and tell old Xue, it'll make things rather awkward between us. On the other hand, if I don't interfere at all, Jokey Jin's rumours are going to get quite out of hand. This calls for a stratagem of some kind which will shut the little beast up without causing too much embarrassment afterwards.'

Having thought of a plan, he pretended that he wanted to be excused, and slipping round to the back, quietly called over Bao-yu's little page Tealeaf and whispered a few inflammatory words in his ear.

Tealeaf was the most willing but also the youngest and least sensible of Bao-yu's pages. Jia Qiang told him how Jokey Jin had been bullying Qin Zhong. 'And even Bao-yu came in for a share,' he said. 'If we don't take this Jin fellow down a peg, next time he is going to be quite insufferable.'

Tealeaf never needed any encouragement to pick a fight, and now, inflamed by Jia Qiang's message and open incitement to action, he marched straight into the classroom to look for Jokey Jin. And there was no 'Master Jin' when he saw him, either: it was 'Jin! Who do you think you are?'

At this point Jia Qiang began to scrape his boots on the floor and make a great business of straightening his clothes and glancing out of the window at the sky, muttering to himself as he did so, 'Ah, yes. Hmn. Must be about time.' Going up to Jia Rui, he informed him that he had an engagement which necessitated his leaving early, and Jia Rui, not having the courage to stop him, allowed him to slip away.

Tealeaf had by now singled out Jokey Jin and grabbed him by the front of his jacket.

'Whether we fuck arseholes or not,' he said, 'what fucking business is it of yours? You should be bloody grateful we haven't fucked your dad. Come outside and fight it out with me, if you've got any spunk in you!'

'Tealeaf!' Jia Rui shouted agitatedly. 'You are not to use such language in here!'

Jokey Jin's face turned pale with anger.

'This is mutiny! I don't have to take this sort of thing from a slave. I shall see your master about this' – and he shook himself free of Tealeaf and made for Bao-yu, intending to seize and belabour him.

As Qin Zhong turned to watch the onslaught, he heard a rushing noise behind his head and a square inkstone launched by an unseen hand sailed past it and landed on the desk occupied by Jia Lan and Jia Jun.

Jia Lan and Jia Jun belonged to the Rong-guo half of the clan and were in the same generation as the other Jia Lan, the little son of Li Wan and nephew of Bao-yu. Jia Jun had lost his father in infancy and was doted on by his widowed mother. Jia Lan was his best friend, which is why they always sat next to each other in school. Though Jia Jun was among the youngest in the class, his tiny body contained an heroic soul. He was extremely mischievous and completely fearless. With the impartial interest of an observer he had watched a friend of Jokey Jin's slyly aim the inkstone at Tealeaf; but when it fell short and landed right in front of him on his own desk, smashing a porcelain water-bottle and showering his books with inky water, his blood was up.

'Rotten swine!' he shouted. 'If this is a free-for-all, here goes!' and he grabbed at the inkstone intending to send it sailing back. But Jia Lan was a man of peace and held it firmly down.

'Leave it, old chap! It's none of our business,' he counselled.

Jia Jun was not to be restrained, however. Deprived of the inkstone, he picked up a satchel full of books and raising it in both hands above his head, hurled it in the direction of the assailant. Unfortunately his body was too small and his strength too puny for so great a trajectory, and the satchel fell on the desk occupied by Bao-yu and Qin Zhong. It landed with a tremendous crash, scattering books, papers, writing-brushes and inkstones in all directions and smashing Bao-yu's teabowl to smithereens so that tea flowed over everything round about. Nothing daunted, Jia Jun leaped out and rushed upon the thrower of inkstones to smite him.

Meanwhile Jokey Jin had found a bamboo pole which he flailed around him: a terrible weapon in so confined and crowded a space. Soon Tealeaf had sustained a blow from it and was bawling for reinforcements from outside. There were three other pages in attendance on Bao-yu besides himself, all equally inclined to mischief. Their names were Sweeper, Ploughboy and Inky. With a great· shout of 'To arms! To arms! Down with the bastards!' these three now came rushing like angry hornets into the classroom, Inky wielding a door-bar which he had picked up and Sweeper and Ploughboy brandishing horsewhips.

Jia Rui, in a frenzy of outraged authority, hopped from one to the other, alternately grabbing and cajoling, but none would take the slightest bit of notice. Disorder was now general. The more mischievous of the scholars mingled glee-fully in the fray, safe, in the general scrimmage, to land punches at chosen foes without fear of discovery or reprisal. The more timid crawled into places of safety. Others stood on their desks, laughing and clapping their hands and cheering on the combatants. The classroom was like a cauldron of still water that had suddenly come to the boil.

Li Gui and the other older servants, hearing the uproar from outside, now hurried in, and by concerted shouting eventually managed to call the boys to a halt. Li Gui asked them what they were fighting about. He was answered by a medley of voices, some saying one thing and some another. Unable to make sense of what he heard, he turned his attention to Tealeaf and the other pages, cursing them roundly and turning them out of the room.

Qin Zhong had fallen an early victim to Jokey Jin's pole, sustaining a nasty graze on the head which Bao-yu was at this very moment mopping with the flap of his gown. Seeing that Li Gui had succeeded in restoring some kind of order, he asked to be taken away.

'Pack up my books, Li Gui, and fetch the horse, will you? I am going to tell Great-uncle Dai-ru about this. We were shamefully insulted, and because we didn't want to start a quarrel, we went along in a perfectly polite and reasonable manner and reported the matter to Cousin Rui. But instead of doing anything about it, he gave *us* a telling-off, stood by while someone called us filthy names, and actually *encouraged* them to start hitting us. Naturally Tealeaf stuck up for us when he saw we were being bullied. What would you expect him to do? But they all ganged up on him and started hitting *him*, and even Qin Zhong's head was cut open. We can't go on studying here after this.'

Li Gui tried to calm him.

'Don't be hasty, young master! Your great-uncle has gone

home on business and if we go running after him to pester him about a little thing like this, he'll think we don't know how to behave. If you want my advice, the proper way to settle this affair is by dealing with it here, where it started. Not by rushing off and upsetting your poor old uncle.' He turned to Jia Rui. 'This is all your fault, Mr Rui, sir. While your granfer is away you are the head of the whole school and everyone looks to you to set an example. If anyone does anything they shouldn't, it's up to you to deal with it – give them a hiding, or whatever it is they need. Not sit by and let matters get out of hand to this extent.'

'I *did* tell them to stop,' said Jia Rui, 'but they wouldn't listen.'

'If you don't mind my saying so,' said Li Gui, 'it's because you've been to blame yourself on past occasions that these lads won't do what you tell them to now. So if this business today does get to the ears of your grandfather, you'll be in trouble yourself, along of all the rest. If I were you, sir, I should think of some way of sorting this out as quickly as possible.'

'Sort it out nothing!' said Bao-yu. 'I'm definitely going to report this.'

'If Jokey Jin stays here,' wailed Qin Zhong tearfully, 'I'm not studying in this school any longer.'

'There is no earthly reason to talk about leaving this school,' said Bao-yu. 'We have as much right to come here as anyone else. When I've explained to everyone exactly what happened, Jokey Jin will be expelled.

'Who is this Jokey Jin, any way?' he asked Li Gui.

Li Gui thought for a moment.

'Better not ask. If I told you, it would only make for more unpleasantness.'

Tealeaf's voice piped up from outside the window:

'He's the nephew of Mrs Huang on the Ning-guo side. Trash like that trying to scare us! I know your Auntie Huang, Jokey Jin! She's an old scrounger. I've seen her down on her knees in front of our Mrs Lian, begging for stuff so that she could go out and pawn it. What an aunt! I'd be ashamed to own an aunt like that!'

Li Gui shouted at him furiously.

'Detestable little varmint! Trust *you* to know the answer and spread your poison!'

Bao-yu sniffed contemptuously.

'So that's who he is! The nephew of Cousin Huang's wife. I'll go and speak to *her* about this.'

He wanted to go straight away, and called to Tealeaf to come inside and pack up his books.

'No need for you to go, Master Bao,' said Tealeaf as he swaggered in triumphantly to do his bidding. 'Let me go for you and save you the trouble. I'll just say that Lady Jia wants a word with her, hire a carriage, and bring her along myself. Then you can question her in front of Lady Jia.'

Li Gui was furious.

'Do you want to die? If you're not careful, my lad, when we get home I'll first thrash the living daylights out of you and then tell Sir Zheng and Lady Wang that Master Bao was put up to all this by your provocation. I've had trouble enough as it is trying to get these lads calmed down a bit without needing any fresh trouble from you. It was all of your making, this rumpus, in the first place. But instead of thinking about ways of damping it down, you have to go throwing more fat on the fire.'

After this outburst Tealeaf was at last silent.

Jia Rui was by now terrified lest the matter should go any further and his own far from clean record be brought to light. Fear made him abject. Addressing Qin Zhong and Bao-yu in turn, he humbly begged them not to report it. At first they were adamant. Then Bao-yu made a condition:

'All right, we won't tell. But you must make Jokey Jin apologize.'

At first Jokey Jin refused, but Jia Rui was insistent, and Li Gui added his own persuasion:

'After all, it started with you, so if you don't do what they say, how are we ever going to end it?'

Under their combined pressure Jokey Jin's resistance at last gave way and he locked hands and made Qin Zhong a bow. But Bao-yu said this was not enough. He insisted on a kotow. Jia Rui, whose only concern now was to get the matter

over with as quickly as possible, quietly urged him to comply:
'You know what the proverb says:

> He who can check a moment's rage
> Shall calm and carefree end his days.'

Did Jokey Jin comply? The following chapter will reveal.

CHAPTER 10

Widow Jin's self-interest gets the better of her
righteous indignation
And Doctor Zhang's diagnosis reveals the origin
of a puzzling disease

Outnumbered, and hard pressed by Jia Rui to apologize, Jokey Jin made a kotow to Qin Zhong, whereupon Bao-yu agreed to let the matter drop. Back in his own home, when school was over, he brooded with mounting anger on his humiliation.

'Qin Zhong is Jia Rong's brother-in-law: it's not as if he were one of the Jia clan. He's only an external scholar, the same as me; and it's only because he is friends with Bao-yu that he can afford to be so high and mighty. Well, in that case he ought to behave himself, then no one would have any cause to complain. But he's always carrying on in such a sneaky, underhand way with Bao-yu, as though he thought the rest of us were all blind and couldn't see what he was up to. And now today he's started making up to someone else and I happen to have found him out. So what if there *were* a row about this? I've got nothing to be afraid of.'

His mother, Widow Jin, overheard his muttering.

'What have you been getting up to this time?' she asked. 'Look at the job we had getting you into that school. All the talks I had with your aunt and the trouble she went to to see Mrs Lian about it. Suppose we hadn't had their help in getting you in there, we could never have afforded a tutor. What's more, you get free tea and free dinners there, don't you? That has meant a big saving for us during the two years you have been going there. And you're glad enough to have something decent to wear out of the money saved, aren't you? And another thing. If you hadn't been going to that school, how would you ever have met that Mr Xue of yours? Between seventy and eighty taels of silver we've had out of him during this past year. I can tell you this, my boy. If you get yourself thrown out of there, you needn't think you can get in anywhere else, because you could easier fly to the moon than find another place like that. Now you just play quietly for a bit and then go to bed like a good boy!'

Thus admonished, Jokey Jin swallowed his anger and fell silent. Before long he went to bed and to sleep, and next day was back at the school again as usual. Of him no more.

*

Jokey Jin's aunt was married to one Jia Huang, a member of the Jia clan in the same generation as Cousin Zhen and Jia Lian. It goes without saying, of course, that not all members of the clan lived in the sort of style maintained by the Ning and Rong households. Jia Huang and his wife had only the income from a very small property to live on, and it was only by dint of frequent visits to the Ning and Rong mansions, where their flattering attentions on Wang Xi-feng and You-shi earned them an occasional subsidy, that they were able to make ends meet.

Today the weather was fine and sunny and Mrs Huang had nothing particular to do at home, so taking an old serving-woman with her, she got into a cab and went off to pay a call on her sister-in-law and nephew.

In the course of conversation Widow Jin soon got on to the subject of yesterday's affair in the schoolroom and launched into a full account, from which no detail was omitted, of all those happenings. It would have been as well for her if she had not done so, for the effect was to kindle a dangerous anger in the bosom of her sister-in-law.

'That little beast Qin Zhong!' said Mrs Huang. 'He may be related to the Jias, by marriage, but then so is your boy. What business has he to go throwing his weight about like that, I should like to know? Especially after the disgusting things he had been doing himself. Considering what he'd been up to, even Bao-yu ought not to have sided with him to that extent. Let me go and see Mrs Zhen about this. I shall ask her to let me have it out with Qin Zhong's sister and see if we can't get some satisfaction.'

'Oh dear, I shouldn't talk so much! I never meant to tell you this. Please, my dear, I beg of you not to speak to them about it! Never mind the rights and wrongs of the case, if this all gets out, they will make it too hot for my boy to stay on at the school; and if he had to stop going to the school, we should never be able to afford a tutor for him, quite apart from all the extra expense I should have of feeding him during the day.'

'Never mind about all that!' said Mrs Huang. 'We'll worry about that after I've spoken to them and seen what happens.'

Dismissing her sister-in-law's entreaties, she sent the old servant-woman out for a cab, and getting inside, drove straight off to the Ning-guo mansion. But by the time she had reached it, driven in at the east end gate, dismounted from the carriage and gone in to see You-shi, the edge had already worn off her anger, and it was only after deferential inquiries about the health and comfort of her hostess and various other inconsequential matters that she got around to asking what had become of Qin-shi, who was usually in evidence during her visits.

'I don't know what's the matter with her lately,' said You-shi. 'It's been more than two months now since she had a period, yet the doctors say she isn't pregnant. And during the last few days she's been getting so tired and listless in the afternoons: doesn't feel like doing anything; doesn't even feel like talking; all the spirit seems to have gone out of her. I've said to her, "Never mind about wifely duties. Just forget about the morning and evening visits and concentrate on getting better. Even when relations call," I said, "I can see to them myself. And never mind what the older members of the family might say: I'll do all the explaining for you." I've spoken to Rong, as well. "You're not to tire her out," I told him, "and you're not to let her get upset! She must just rest quietly for a few days and look after herself. And if there's anything she fancies to eat, just come to my apartment to get it. Because if anything should happen to her," I said, "you wouldn't find another wife like that, with her looks and her good nature, if you took a lantern to look for her." She's such a sweet person, there isn't anyone among our relations or among the older members of the family who doesn't love her. I've been so worried on her account these last few days. And just to make matters worse, first thing this morning her young brother comes along – Silly little boy! he ought to have realized that his sister wasn't well and not in a condition to listen to such things, even if he'd suffered ten thousand times the injustice! – It seems that yesterday there was a fight at the school. One of the external students – I don't know which one it was – had been bullying him; and there were a lot of other very nasty things as well. So he had to go and tell all this to his sister. Well, you know how sensitive she is, my dear, in spite of the fact that she always seems so lively and full of fun to talk to. The slightest little thing can upset her and set her brooding on it for whole days and nights together. In fact, this illness has been brought on by too much worrying, I'm sure of it. Well, this morning when she heard that someone had been bullying her brother, it both upset her and at the same time made her angry. She was upset to think that those horrible boys at the school should be able to twist things round and say such terrible things about him, but she was also angry with *him*, because she said he must have been getting into bad ways and not giving his mind properly to his studies to have got into trouble of this sort in the first place. So of course, because of this upset she wouldn't have any breakfast. I've just been round there trying to calm her. I gave her brother a talking-to and sent him round to see Bao-yu, and I stood over her while she ate half a bowlful of bird's-nest soup. I've only just this minute got back. Oh, I'm so worried about her, my dear! We haven't got a good doctor at the moment, either. It pierces me to the heart when I think about that child's illness! I suppose *you* don't happen to know of a good doctor, do you?'

Mrs Huang's determination to have things out with Qin-shi, of which she had boasted so valiantly at her sister-in-law's, had, in the course of this outpouring, fled to the far kingdom of Java. She hastened to own that she knew of no good doctor.

'But hearing what you have said about this illness,' she added, 'I can't help wondering if it may not after all be pregnancy. You want to be careful they don't give her the wrong treatment. If they give her the wrong treatment for *that*, there will be real trouble!'

'I know,' said You-shi. 'That's what I say.'

While they were still talking, Cousin Zhen came in from

outside. 'Isn't this Cousin Huang's wife?' he asked You-shi, catching sight of the visitor. Mrs Huang dropped him a curtsey and a 'how-do-you-do'. 'You must ask our cousin to dinner,' he said, going on into the room beyond.

The original object of Mrs Huang's visit had of course been to complain to Qin-shi about Qin Zhong's treatment of her nephew. Hearing of Qin-shi's illness she had abandoned all thought of even mentioning the subject; and now that Cousin Zhen and You-shi were being so nice to her, her anger gradually gave way to pleasure, and after gossiping a while longer she went off home.

When she had gone, Cousin Zhen came in again and sat down.

'What did she come about today?' he asked You-shi.

'Oh,' said You-shi, 'nothing in particular. When she first came in she appeared to be upset about something or other, then after we'd been talking for some time and I mentioned that Rong's wife was ill, she gradually calmed down. When you invited her to dinner she knew she couldn't very well stay on with sickness in the house and left after chatting a few minutes longer. She didn't ask for anything before she went.

'But let's talk about that child's illness. The thing is, you really must find a good doctor to look at her, before it gets too late. This lot we have around the house at present are completely useless! Each one of them just listens to what you say and then gives it back to you with a few learned words thrown in. And they're so terribly conscientious about it! We have three or four of them coming by turns every day, and sometimes they'll take her pulse four or five times in the same day. Then they have long discussions while they decide on a prescription. None of the medicine does her any good, and the only consequence of all this is that she is having to change her clothes four or five times in a day and be constantly getting up and sitting down to see these doctors, which is no good at all for a person in her condition.'

'Oh, she's a silly child!' said Cousin Zhen. 'There's no *need* for all this dressing and undressing. Suppose she caught a chill on top of this other illness, that would be really frightful.

Never mind about the clothes, for goodness' sake, however good they are! It's the child's *health* that matters. Who cares if she has to have a completely new outfit every day? We can afford it.

'What I was going to tell you is that I've just had a visit from Feng Zi-ying. He noticed that something was bothering me, and when he asked me what it was I explained that our daughter-in-law isn't well and told him how worried we are because we haven't got a decent doctor who can tell us for sure whether it's pregnancy or disease, so that we don't even know how serious it is. Then Feng Zi-ying told me about a scholar friend of his called Zhang You-shi. He and Feng were at school together. He is a man of very wide learning including, apparently, an excellent knowledge of medicine and the ability to tell with certainty whether a disease is curable or not. He's up at the capital this year to purchase a place for his son and is at present staying in Feng Zi-ying's house. It looks as if in his hands she might stand a good chance of getting better. Anyway, I've already sent someone round with my card and and asked him to call. It's getting a bit late for him to come today, but he should definitely be round tomorrow. Feng Zi-ying promised to see him when he got back and put in a word for me to make quite sure that he agrees to come. So we'll just have to wait and see what this Dr Zhang says.'

You-shi was delighted with this news.

'And what are we going to do about Father's birthday?' she asked. 'It's the day after tomorrow.'

'I've just been out to see him,' said Cousin Zhen, 'and I took the opportunity while I was there of asking him if he would come over on his birthday to receive everyone's kotows, but he refused. He said, "I've got used to the peace and quiet of the monastery and I'm not willing to go back into your quarrelsome world again. If you insist on celebrating my birthday it would be a hundred times better to have my tract on *Divine Rewards* written out by a good calligrapher and cut on blocks for printing than to drag me back to your house for a lot of senseless head-knocking." He said, "If the family turn up tomorrow and the day after for my birthday, you can give them a party yourself. But don't go sending me any presents,"

he said, "and don't come yourself! If it will set your mind at
rest you can give me a kotow now and get it over with. But
if you come round here the day after tomorrow with a lot of
other people to pester me, I shall refuse to see you." Well,
after that I obviously can't go again on his birthday. We'd
better have Lai Sheng in and make arrangements for two days'
entertainment.'

You-shi called in Jia Rong.

'Tell Lai Sheng to prepare the usual two-day party for
Grandfather,' she said. 'Say we want a really good spread.
We shall be asking Lady Jia and Sir Zheng and Lady Wang and
your Auntie Lian from the other house: you can go round
yourself to invite them.

'And by the way: today your father heard of a good doctor
and has already sent someone to ask him round. He should be
coming tomorrow. When he does, you had better tell him
exactly what your wife's symptoms have been during the past
few days.'

Jia Rong promised to carry out his mother's instructions
and left the room, encountering, as he did so, the youth who
had been sent to Feng Zi-ying's house to request a call from
the doctor. He had just got back from delivering his message
and reported to Jia Rong as follows:

'I took the Master's card to the doctor at Mr Feng's house
and asked him to call. He said Mr Feng had already spoken to
him about it, but he had been out visiting all day and only just
got back and he simply didn't have the energy to go out any
more today. He said, "Even if I were to go round to your
house now I shouldn't be able to take the young lady's pulse.
It would take me all night to get my breathing regulated.
However," he said, "I shall definitely call round tomorrow."
And he said, "My knowledge of medicine is really too slight
for a consultation of this importance, but as your master and
Mr Feng are so pressing, I obviously cannot refuse. But I
hope you will explain this to your master." And he said,
"As for your master's card, that is an honour I really cannot
accept"; and he made me bring it back. Will you please pass
on this message for me, Master Rong?'

Jia Rong turned and went back into the room to tell his

parents. Going out once more, he summoned Lai Sheng and gave instructions for preparing a two-day birthday party, which Lai Sheng duly proceeded to put into operation. But of that no more.

About noon next day one of the servants at the gate came in to report:

'The Dr Zhang you sent for has arrived, sir'.

Cousin Zhen went out to receive the doctor and conducted him into the main reception room, where they both sat down. He waited until the doctor had taken tea before broaching the subject of his visit.

'Yesterday Mr Feng was telling me about your great learning,' said Cousin Zhen. 'I gather that it includes a profound knowledge of medicine. I assure you I was very much impressed.'

'I am only a very indifferent scholar,' replied Dr Zhang, 'and my knowledge is really extremely superficial. However, Mr Feng was telling me yesterday of the courteous and considerate patronage of scholars which is traditional in your family, so when I received your summons I felt unable to refuse. I must insist, though, that I am entirely lacking in real learning and am acutely embarrassed to think that this will all too soon become apparent.'

'My dear sir, you are altogether too modest,' said Cousin Zhen. 'Do you think I could ask you to go in now and have a look at my daughter-in-law? We are relying on your superior knowledge to put us out of our uncertainty.'

He left the doctor in the charge of Jia Rong, who conducted him through the inner part of the house to his own apartment, where Qin-shi was.

'Is this the lady?' asked the doctor.

'Yes, this is my wife,' Jia Rong replied. 'Do sit down! I expect you would like me to describe her symptoms first, before you take the pulse?'

'If you will permit me, no,' said the doctor. 'I think it would be better if I took the pulse first and asked you about the development of the illness afterwards. This is the first time I have been to your house, and as I am not a skilled practitioner and have only come here at our friend Mr Feng's insistence, I think I should take the pulse and give you my diagnosis first. We can go on to talk about her symptoms and discuss a course of treatment if you are satisfied with the diagnosis. And of course, it will still be up to you to decide whether or not the treatment I prescribe is to be followed.'

'You speak with real authority, doctor,' said Jia Rong. 'I only wish we had got to hear of you earlier. Take her pulse now, then, and let us know whether what she has can be cured, so that my parents may be spared further anxiety.'

At this point Qin-shi's women carried in a large arm-rest of the kind used in consultations, propped her forward with her arms across it, and drew back her sleeves, exposing both arms at the wrist. The doctor stretched out his hand and laid it on her right wrist, then, having first regulated his own breathing in order to be able to count the rate, he felt the pulses with great concentration for the space of several minutes, after which he transferred to the left wrist and spent an equal amount of time on that. This done, he proposed that they should withdraw to the outside room to talk.

Jia Rong accompanied him outside and sat with him on the kang. An old woman served tea, which Jia Rong invited the doctor to take, waiting until he had done so before asking him for his diagnosis.

'Tell me, doctor, from your reading of my wife's pulse, do you think she can be cured?'

'Well, the lower left distal pulse is rapid and the lower left median pulse is strong and full,' said the doctor. 'On the right side, the distal pulse is thin and lacks strength and the median pulse is faint and lacks vitality.

'Now, a rapid lower left-hand distal pulse means that a malfunction of the controlling humour of the heart is causing it to generate too much fire; and the strong lower median pulse means that the liver's humour is blocked, giving rise to a deficiency of blood. A thin, weak distal pulse on the right side indicates a gross deficiency of humour in the lungs; and a faint right median pulse lacking in vitality shows that the earth of the spleen is being subdued by the woody element of the liver.

'If the heart is generating fire, the symptoms should be irregularity of the menses and insomnia. A deficiency of blood and blockage of humour in the liver would result in pain and congestion under the ribs, delay of the menses beyond their term, and burning sensations in the heart. A deficiency of humour in the lungs would give rise to sudden attacks of giddiness, sweating at five or six in the morning, and a sinking feeling rather like the feeling you get in a pitching boat. And if the earth of the spleen is being subdued by the wood of the liver, she would undoubtedly experience loss of appetite, lassitude, and general enfeeblement of the whole body. If my reading of the lady's pulse is correct, she ought to be showing all these symptoms. Some people would tell you they indicated a pregnancy, but I am afraid I should have to disagree.'

'You must have second sight, doctor!' said one of the old women, a body-servant of Qin-shi's who was standing by. 'What you have said exactly describes how it is with her; there is no need for us to tell you anything more. Of all the doctors we've lately had around here to look at her none has ever spoken as much to the point as this. Some have said she's expecting; others have said it's illness; one says it's not serious; another only gives her till the winter solstice; not one of them tells you anything you can really rely on. Please doctor, *you* tell us: just how serious *is* this illness?'

'I am afraid my colleagues have allowed your mistress's condition to deteriorate,' said the doctor. 'If she had been given proper treatment at the very beginning, when she first started her courses, there is every reason to suppose that she would by now be completely cured. But the illness has been neglected for so long now, this breakdown was almost bound to happen. I would say that with proper treatment she has about a one in three chance of recovery. We shall just have to see how she responds to my medicine. If, after taking it, she can get a good night's sleep, her chances will be distinctly better: say fifty-fifty.

'From my reading of her pulse, I should expect your mistress to be a very highly strung, sensitive young woman. Sometimes, when people are over-sensitive, they find a good deal that is upsetting in what goes on around them; and of course, if things are upsetting them, they will tend to worry a lot. This illness has been caused by too much worry affecting the spleen and causing an excess of wood in the liver, with the result that the menstrual blood has been prevented from flowing at the proper times. If we were to ask your mistress about the dates of her courses, I am sure we should find that they tended to be on the late side, isn't that so?'

'Absolutely right,' the old woman replied. 'Her periods have never been early. Sometimes two or three days late, sometimes as much as ten days: but in any case, always late.'

'You see!' said the doctor. 'There is the cause of the trouble. If she could have been treated in time with something to fortify the heart and stabilize the humours, she would never have got into this present state. What we have now, I am afraid, is an advanced case of dehydration. Well, we shall have to see what my medicine can do for her.'

He wrote out the following prescription and handed it to Jia Rong:

For a decoction to increase the breath, nourish the heart, fortify the spleen and calm the liver

℞

Ginseng	2 drams
Atractylis (clay-baked)	2 drams
Lycoperdon	3 drams
Nipplewort (processed)	4 drams
Angelica	2 drams
White peony root	2 drams
Hemlock parsley	$1\frac{1}{2}$ drams
Yellow vetch root	3 drams
Ground root of nutgrass	2 drams
Hare's ear (in vinegar)	$\frac{3}{4}$ dram
Huaiqing yam	2 drams
Dong E ass's glue (prepn with powdered oyster-shell)	2 drams
Corydalis (cooked in wine)	$1\frac{1}{2}$ drams
Roast liquorice	$\frac{3}{4}$ dram

Adjuvant: Excoriate and remove pits from 7 lotus-seeds;
    Item 2 large jujubes.

'Most impressive!' said Jia Rong, glancing at the prescription. 'Tell me, though, doctor: just how serious *is* this illness? Is her life in danger?'

The doctor smiled. 'You are an intelligent young man, Mr Jia. When an illness has reached this stage, it is not going to be cured in an afternoon. We must see how she responds to medication. As I see it, there is no real danger this winter. I should say that if she can get past the spring equinox, you could look forward to a complete recovery.'

Jia Rong was intelligent enough to understand the real import of what the doctor was telling him and did not question him further. Having first seen him out, he went in to show the prescription and written summary of the diagnosis to Cousin Zhen and gave both his parents a full account of what the doctor had said.

'No other doctor has ever spoken so convincingly,' said You-shi, turning to Cousin Zhen. 'I am sure his medicine will do her good.'

Cousin Zhen smiled complacently.

'This man is no medical hack practising for a living,' he said. 'It's only because Feng Zi-ying is such a good friend of mine that he could be persuaded to come and see us. Perhaps with a man like this treating her our daughter-in-law stands some chance of getting better. I see there is ginseng in that prescription, by the way. You can use some of that pound of high-grade ginseng we bought the other day.'

Seeing that they had no more to say, Jia Rong went out and ordered the drugs for Qin-shi's medicine to be purchased and prepared. But you will have to read the next chapter if you want to know what effect the medicine had on her when she had taken it.

CHAPTER 11

Ning-guo House celebrates the birthday
of an absent member
And Jia Rui conceives an illicit passion
for his attractive cousin

Jia Jing's birthday had now arrived. Cousin Zhen packed
sixteen lacquer gift-boxes with the rarest and choicest delicacies and instructed Jia Rong to take a number of domestics
with him and deliver them to Jia Jing. He was to observe
carefully whether or not his grandfather was pleased, and
having made his kotow, was to deliver the following message:

'Because of your request, Father has not ventured to visit
you himself. Instead he will place himself at the head of the
entire family and lead them in prostrating themselves in your
direction.'

Having received his father's instructions, Jia Rong mus-
tered his band of servants and set out.

Back at home visitors gradually began to arrive. Jia Lian
and Jia Qiang were the first. Having inspected the various
seating arrangements, they inquired whether there was to be
entertainment of some kind.

'The Master had originally been reckoning on old Sir Jing
coming here today,' said one of the servants, 'so he didn't
arrange for any entertainment. But the day before yesterday
he learned that Sir Jing would not be coming, so he asked us
to find a troupe of actors and a band. They are at present on
the stage in the garden getting ready for the performance.'

Lady Xing, Lady Wang, Wang Xi-feng and Bao-yu arrived
next and were welcomed and conducted inside by Cousin
Zhen and You-shi. You-shi's mother was already there. She
was introduced to the new arrivals, who were then invited to
sit down and were served by Cousin Zhen and You-shi with
tea.

'We realize,' said Cousin Zhen, 'that Lady Jia is a generation
older than Father. Father is only her nephew, of course, and

strictly speaking it wasn't correct form to invite a person of her age at all. Nevertheless, since the weather is so fresh and nice just now and the chrysanthemums in the garden at their best, we had rather hoped that she might enjoy coming over for a bit and having all her children and grandchildren around her. That was our only motive in asking her. I'm sorry she decided not to honour us.'

'Up to yesterday,' Xi-feng put in hurriedly, not waiting for Lady Wang to reply, 'Grandmother had been intending to come. Then yesterday evening she saw Bao-yu eating some peaches and the greedy old thing couldn't resist trying one herself. She only ate about two thirds of a peach, but she had to get up twice running in the early hours, and this morning she still felt rather poorly and told me to tell you that she definitely wouldn't be able to come. But she said that if you have any specially nice things to eat she would like one or two kinds to try; only they must be soft and easy to digest.'

Cousin Zhen smiled with pleasure.

'Well, that's all right then. Knowing how much Grandma enjoys a bit of fun, I thought it didn't seem like her not to come today unless she had some good reason for not coming.'

'The other day Xi-chun was telling us that Rong's wife is not very well,' said Lady Wang. 'What exactly is wrong with her?'

'It's a very puzzling illness,' You-shi replied. 'At Mid-Autumn last month, when she got back from playing cards half the night with you and Lady Jia, she seemed perfectly all right. But from the twentieth onwards she seemed to get more and more tired and listless every day – too tired even to eat. She's been like that for more than a fortnight now, and it is two months since she had a period.'

'Couldn't she be expecting?' said Lady Xing.

They were interrupted by a servant from outside:

'Sir She and Sir Zheng and all the other gentlemen have arrived, sir. They are in the main reception room.'

Cousin Zhen hurried out.

'To begin with that's what some of the doctors told us,' said You-shi, resuming the conversation; 'but yesterday Feng Zi-ying introduced a doctor friend of his to us who is terribly good, someone he went to school with, and he said that she wasn't expecting at all. He said she was suffering from a serious illness. He wrote a prescription for her yesterday and she has already had one dose of the medicine. Today her giddiness is a bit better, but everything else is still pretty much the same.'

'There!' said Xi-feng. 'I thought it must be something quite serious to keep *her* away, especially on a day like this. I know she would have forced herself to come if she could have done.'

'You remember you saw her here on the third,' said You-shi. 'She had a terrible struggle to keep going on that occasion. It was only because the two of you have always been so close and she didn't want to miss you that she made the effort.'

Xi-feng's eyes became moist and for a moment she was too overcome to speak.

'I know "the weather and human life are both unpredictable",' she said at last, 'but she's only a child still. If anything should happen to her as a result of this illness, I think all the fun would go out of life!'

While she was speaking Jia Rong came in, and having greeted in turn first Lady Xing, then Lady Wang, and then Xi-feng, he turned to his mother:

'I've just delivered the food to Grandfather, and I told him that Father was entertaining all the men of the family at home and had not presumed to visit him because of what he said. Grandfather was very pleased. He said "That is exactly as it should be." He said I was to tell you and Father to see that my great-uncles and great-aunts are properly looked after, and he told me that I was to look after my uncles and aunts and cousins. He also said he wanted the blocks for *Divine Rewards* to be cut as quickly as possible and ten thousand copies printed for free distribution. I've already given this message to Father. Now I've got to hurry off again to look after the gentlemen while they have their dinner.'

'Rong, just a moment!' said Xi-feng as he was going. 'How is it really with your wife?'

Jia Rong's brows contracted in a worried frown.

'She's not at all well, Auntie. You'll know what I mean when you see her presently.'

He left without saying any more.

'Well, ladies!' said You-shi. 'Will you have dinner in here, or shall we eat in the garden? There are some actors in the garden preparing an entertainment.'

'In here would be all right, wouldn't it?' said Lady Wang with a glance in Lady Xing's direction.

You-shi at once gave orders to her women to serve. There was an answering cry from outside the door and a great flurry of domestics each bustling about her own contribution to the meal. In no time at all the table was laid and dinner ready. You-shi made Lady Xing and Lady Wang sit at the head with her mother, while she, Xi-feng and Bao-yu sat at the two sides.

Lady Xing and Lady Wang politely protested that they had come to offer birthday felicitations, not to eat a birthday feast.

'Yes,' said Xi-feng. 'After all these years of spiritual self-improvement, Uncle must by now be practically an Immortal. And with Immortals, as we all know, "it's the thought that counts and not the ceremony".'

The others all laughed.

You-shi's mother, Lady Xing, Lady Wang and Xi-feng, having finished their meal, rinsed out their mouths and washed their hands, had just announced their intention of going into the garden, when Jia Rong came in with a message for his mother.

'My great-uncles and all the other gentlemen have just finished their dinner. Great-uncle She says he has business at home, and Great-uncle Zheng doesn't like plays because he says he can't stand the noise; but all the others have gone with Uncle Lian and Cousin Qiang to watch the players.

'People have come with cards and birthday presents from the Prince of An-nan, the Prince of Dong-ping, the Prince of Xi-ning, the Prince of Bei-jing, the Duke of Zhen-guo and five others of the Niu clan and the Marquis of Zhong-jing and seven others of the Shi clan. The presents have all been received at the counting-house. They have been entered in the gift-book, and the people who brought them have been issued with thank-you cards. They have also been tipped the usual amounts and given a meal before leaving.

'And Father says will you please bring the great-aunts and Grandmother You and Auntie Feng to the garden now.'

'Yes, we've finished too,' said You-shi. 'We were about to come over when you arrived.'

'Aunt Wang,' said Xi-feng, 'may I go and see Rong's wife first? I can go on to the garden from there.'

'Certainly. You ought to go,' said Lady Wang. 'In fact, we should all like to go with you, but I am afraid it would be too much excitement for her. Please give her our love.'

'My dear,' said You-shi, 'I know she will always do anything *you* ask her to. See if you can talk her into a more cheerful frame of mind. It would be such a relief to me if you could. But join us in the garden as soon as you can!'

Bao-yu asked if he could go with Xi-feng to see Qin-shi.

'Yes,' said Lady Wang. 'She is your nephew's wife. I think you should. Just look in for a moment, though, and then join the rest of us.'

Thereupon You-shi invited Lady Wang, Lady Xing and old Mrs You to accompany her to the All-scents Garden, while Xi-feng and Bao-yu accompanied Jia Rong to Qin-shi's room.

Entering the door of the apartment, they tiptoed softly into the inner room. As soon as she saw them, Qin-shi attempted to rise, but Xi-feng would not let her.

'No, no, don't get up!' she said. 'You will make yourself giddy.'

In two rapid strides she was at her side and holding her by the hand.

'My dearest child! It's only a few days since last I saw you, but look how thin you have grown!'

She sat down beside her on the quilt on which she sat propped. Bao-yu, after greeting her, sat in a chair opposite.

'Pour out some tea,' said Jia Rong. 'Auntie Feng and Uncle Bao didn't get any after their dinner.'

Qin-shi grasped Xi-feng's hand and forced a smile to her wan face.

'It looks as though I wasn't *meant* to be happy, Auntie!' she said. 'This is such a lovely family to have married into. Rong's parents treat me as if I were their own daughter. Rong may be young, but he respects me, and I respect him;

there has never been a cross word between us. You, it goes without saying – but not only you, *all* the older members of the family – have always been goodness itself to me. I did so want to be worthy of all this kindness. But now this wretched illness has come along and taken away the chance. Now I shall never be able to be a good daughter to Rong's parents; and however badly I want to, I shall never be able to repay any of the love *you* have shown me. I have a feeling inside me, Auntie: I don't think I am going to last the year out.'

Bao-yu had been studying the 'Spring Slumber' painting on Qin-shi's wall all this time and re-reading the couplet by Qin Guan on the scrolls at each side of it:

The coldness of spring has imprisoned the soft buds in a wintry dream;
The fragrance of wine has intoxicated the beholder with imagined flower-scents.

As he did so, the memory returned of that earlier afternoon when he had slept in that very same room and dreamed about the Land of Illusion. He was musing on the contents of that dream when he suddenly became aware of the words that Qin-shi was saying. They pierced his heart like the points of a thousand arrows. Great tears welled up in his eyes and rolled down his cheeks. Xi-feng, seeing him, was herself deeply affected; but fearing that the sight of his grief might make Qin-shi even more distressed, whereas the declared purpose of their visit had been to cheer her up, she rallied him lightly on his tears.

'Don't be such a baby, Bao-yu! It's not really that serious: sick people always say things like that. Besides, she's still young, and when you are young you can shake an illness off in no time at all. – You mustn't let yourself think such stupid things,' she said, turning to Qin-shi. 'You'll make yourself worse.'

'If only she could get a bit of food inside her.' said Jia Rong. 'That's her real trouble: she won't eat anything.'

'Bao,' said Xi-feng, 'your mother told you not to stay long. If you're going to be like this, you will only upset her, and in any case I expect your mother is beginning to wonder about

you. – You go on ahead with Uncle Bao,' she said to Jia
Rong. 'I am going to sit a little longer with your wife.'

Jia Rong at once led Bao-yu away to join the others in the
All-scents Garden, while Xi-feng addressed some words of
encouragement to Qin-shi, after which, dropping her voice
to a murmur, she engaged in a long and intimate conversation
with her, ignoring two or three messages from You-shi urging
her to join the party. At last she felt unable to stay any longer.

'Look after yourself!' she said. 'I shall come again. I feel
sure that you are meant to get better. It can't have been an
accident that they found that doctor the other day; and now
that you've got him, there's really nothing to worry about.'

Qin-shi smiled.

'Even if he's a miracle-man, Auntie, "death's a sickness
none can cure", and I know that it's just a question of time
now.'

'If *will* go on talking like that, how can you possibly
get better?' said Xi-feng. 'If only you would try to look on
the bright side. Remember what the doctor said. He said that
if you weren't being properly treated, next spring would be
dangerous for you. If this were a household which couldn't
afford things like ginseng for your treatment, you might have
something to worry about. But now they know that you can
be cured, there's nothing Rong's parents wouldn't do and
nothing they couldn't afford to do for you. Never mind two
drams of ginseng a day; if you needed two *pounds* a day, they
would get it for you gladly. So do try and get better! I must
go over to the garden now.'

'Forgive me for not being able to see you out, Auntie,' said
Qin-shi. 'Please come again when you are free. We'll have a
nice talk together, just the two of us.'

There were tears in Xi-feng's eyes as she promised to come
often, whenever she was free. Then, followed by the women
who had accompanied her from the Rong mansion and a
number of female domestics belonging to the Ning household,
she made her way round to one of the side gates leading into
the gardens.

> Golden chrysanthemums covered the open spaces;
> Silvery willow-trees bordered the water's margins.

> The little bridge arched its span over a storied stream;
> The winding path made its way into a fairy hill.
> Crystal rills tinkled amidst the rocks.
> A quickset hedge recalled preautumnal fragrances.
> Crimson leaves fluttered upon the boughs.
> A wintry copse described calligraphic traceries.
> In the cold wind's more insistent blast
> The oriole's cry could still be heard.
> In the late sun's more infrequent warmth
> The cricket's chirp a while revived.
> At the far south-east end
> Pavilions nestled in artificial mountains.
> On the near north-west side
> Verandahs brooded on circumjacent waters.
> Music of little organs playing in the summer-house
> Increased the melancholy in the air.
> Glimpses of women's dresses flitting through the little wood
> Enhanced the delicacy of the scene.

Xi-feng was making her way through the garden, admiring the view as she went, when a figure suddenly stepped out from behind an artificial hill of rock and made its way towards her:

'How are you, cousin?'

Xi-feng gave a start of surprise and retreated a step.

'Isn't it Cousin Rui?'

'Don't you even know who I am, cousin?'

'It isn't that I don't know you,' said Xi-feng, 'but you did come up rather suddenly and I wasn't expecting to see you here.'

'We must have been fated to meet, cousin,' said Jia Rui. 'I had just slipped away from the party to take a little stroll in these peaceful surroundings. I never expected to meet my fair cousin here, but lo! So there must be a bond.'

He ogled her as he spoke with a fixed and meaningful stare.

Xi-feng's sharp intelligence enabled her to penetrate without much difficulty the little game he was playing, and feigning an interest she did not feel, she answered him with a smile.

'I can see why Lian is always speaking so highly of you. From seeing you today and just hearing you speak those few words I can tell at once that you are an intelligent, good-natured sort of person. At the moment I'm on my way to join my aunts, and I'm afraid that I can't stay and talk to you. Perhaps we could meet some other time when we are both free?'

'I should like to call on you when you are at home,' said Jia Rui, 'but I suppose a young person like your good self is not in a position to receive visitors of the other sex.'

Xi-feng feigned a laugh.

'We're all one family – all one flesh and blood. I don't see that age comes into it.'

Jia Rui was secretly delighted by this encouragement.

'I never dreamed today would bring a chance like this my way,' he thought, and the goatish eagerness of his expression grew even more repellent.

'You had better hurry back to the party,' said Xi-feng. 'If they catch you playing truant, you will find yourself being sconced!'

Jia Rui was by now scarcely in command of his own person. Slowly, very slowly he walked away, frequently turning back to gaze at Xi-feng as he did so. Xi-feng mischievously provoked him by deliberately slowing down the pace of her own progress through the garden.

'What an odious creature!' she thought to herself when there was some distance between them. 'Appearances certainly are deceptive! Who would have guessed he was that sort of person? Well, if he is, he had better look out! One of these days I'll settle his hash for him; then perhaps he will realize what sort of person he is up against!'

Xi-feng had resumed a normal pace and had just skirted the foot of a little hill, when she saw two or three old serving-women hurrying towards her in a state of great agitation.

'Oh, Mrs Lian,' said one of the old women with a smile, when they caught sight of her, 'our mistress has been getting into such a state because you didn't come! She's sent us to fetch you.'

'Just like your mistress!' said Xi-feng. 'Always in a lather about something or other!' and she sauntered on quite unconcernedly, talking to the old woman as she went.

'How many pieces have they done so far?'

'Eight or nine,' the old woman replied.

By this time they had arrived at the rear entrance of the two-storey Celestial Fragrance Pavilion, where they found Bao-yu playing with a group of maids.

'Mind you don't make a nuisance of yourself, Bao,' said Xi-feng.

'Lady Xing and Lady Wang are sitting upstairs watching,' said one of the maids. 'You can get up there from this side, madam.'

Lifting up her skirts, Xi-feng climbed slowly up the stairs. She found You-shi standing at the top waiting for her.

'You *are* an affectionate pair!' said You-shi with a smile. 'Once the two of you meet, there's no separating you. To-morrow you had better move in with her and set up house together! Come on, sit down! I'm going to drink a cup of wine with you!'

Xi-feng asked her two aunts for permission to sit. When she had done so You-shi held out the playbill and invited her to make a choice.

'It's not for me to choose when Mother and Aunt Wang are here,' said Xi-feng.

'Go ahead and choose!' said Lady Xing. 'Mrs You and your aunt and I have already chosen a number of plays. Now you pick out one or two good ones for us!'

Xi-feng politely rose to thank her, and taking the playbill from You-shi, scanned it through and picked out two of the items listed: one a scene from *The Return of the Soul* and the other 'Gui-nian Plays His Guitar' from *The Palace of Eternal Youth*.

'If they do these two after they have finished singing this scene from *Faithful Bi-lian*,' she said, handing the playbill back to You-shi, 'I think that will be just about enough for the day.'

'I'm sure it will,' said Lady Wang. 'We ought in any case to break up early, so that our hosts can get a good night's rest. They have had a lot on their minds lately.'

'It isn't often that you both come to see us,' said You-shi.

'Please stay as long as you can. It will be so much more fun. It's really quite early yet.'

'Where have all the gentlemen gone to?' inquired Xi-feng, who had got up from her seat and was peering down into the lower storey.

'They have gone off to the Frozen Sunlight Gallery to drink,' said one of the old women in attendance. 'They left only a moment ago. They've taken the band with them.'

'What was wrong with this place?' said Xi-feng, 'Heaven knows what they can be getting up to behind our backs!'

'We can't all be as strait-laced as you are,' said You-shi with a laugh.

As they laughed and chattered together, the actors eventually finished performing the second of the two pieces Xi-feng had selected, whereupon the wine was removed from the tables and rice served. When they had finished their meal, the company retired to the main reception room indoors and took tea there, after which carriages were called for and the other ladies took their leave of old Mrs You. You-shi stood at the head of all the concubines and female domestics of the Ning household to see them outside, while Cousin Zhen at the head of the junior male members of his family stood beside the waiting carriages.

'You must come again tomorrow, ladies,' said Cousin Zhen to Lady Xing and Lady Wang as they emerged from the house.

'I think not,' said Lady Wang. 'We have sat here the whole day being entertained and we are all rather tired now. I think tomorrow we should like a rest.'

Jia Rui was staring fixedly at Xi-feng throughout this exchange.

After Cousin Zhen had gone indoors again, Li Gui led out a horse and Bao-yu mounted on its back and rode off behind Lady Wang's carriage. Cousin Zhen and the other males then sat down to supper and, when it was over, the party broke up. Next day there was another day of feasting for the members of the clan, particulars of which, however, we omit from our record. We shall confine ourselves to observing that from that day on Xi-feng paid frequent calls on Qin-shi. Sometimes her illness seemed slightly better for a day or two, sometimes it seemed slightly worse. Cousin Zhen, You-shi and Jia Rong were acutely worried.

*

Jia Rui made several visits to the Rong mansion, but all his calls seemed to coincide with Xi-feng's visits to the Ning mansion to see Qin-shi.

The thirtieth day of the eleventh month, the day of the winter solstice, arrived. It was the turn of the season, and for several days before it Grandmother Jia, Lady Wang and Xi-feng had been sending messengers daily to inquire after Qin-shi. Each time the report they brought back was the same:

'She hasn't got any worse these last few days, but she doesn't seem to be very much better.'

'At this time of year,' said Lady Wang, 'it's a hopeful sign if an illness like hers *doesn't* get any worse.'

'Oh I do hope so!' said Grandmother Jia. 'That sweet child! If anything should happen to her, it would break my heart.'

A wave of bitterness passed over her.

'You and she have always been good friends,' she said, turning to Xi-feng. 'Tomorrow is the "First of the Last". Go and see her again some time after tomorrow. Have a very careful look and try to find out exactly how she is. If she seems a bit better, come and tell me when you get back. And if there is anything the dear child has ever fancied eating in the past, see that she is kept constantly supplied with it.'

Xi-feng promised to do as she had said, and on the second day of the next month she went over to the Ning-guo mansion as soon as she had finished her breakfast. Qin-shi's sickness appeared to be no worse than previously, but the flesh on her face and body was pitifully wasted. Xi-feng sat for a long time chatting with her, and once more urged her to take a more optimistic view of her illness.

'We shall know the worst when the spring comes,' said Qin-shi. 'At least I've got past the solstice without anything happening, so perhaps I *shall* get better. Give Grandma and Auntie Wang my regards, won't you. I've eaten one or two bits of that yam-cake with the date stuff inside that Grandma sent me yesterday. I found it quite easy to digest.'

'I'll send you some more tomorrow,' said Xi-feng. 'Now I must go and see your mother-in-law, and after that I have to hurry back and give my report on you to Grandma.'

'Give Grandma and Auntie Wang my love, Auntie.'

'I will,' said Xi-feng, and left her.

She went into You-shi's reception room and sat down.

'Tell me honestly,' said You-shi. 'What did you think of her?'

Xi-feng sat silent for some time with lowered head.

'There's no hope, is there? You'll have to start getting things ready for the end. Of course, it's always possible that doing so may break the bad luck.'

'I've already been quietly making a few preparations on the side,' said You-shi. 'The only thing we haven't yet got is the right timber for the you know what. But we're looking round all the time.'

Xi-feng had some tea and chatted a while longer with You-shi. Then she said:

'I must hurry back to report to Grandma.'

'Break it to her gently,' said You-shi. 'You don't want to give her a shock, at her age.'

'Of course,' said Xi-feng, and rising to her feet went straight back home and called on Grandmother Jia.

'Rong's wife asked me to give you her regards, Grandma. She sends you a kotow and she says she feels somewhat better. She begs you not to worry about her. And she says that when she's made a bit more progress she's going to come over to see you and make you a kotow in person.'

'How did you think she seemed?' said Grandmother Jia.

'For the time being there doesn't seem to be anything much to worry about,' said Xi-feng. 'She seems to be in quite good spirits.'

For a long time the old lady brooded in silence. Then, remembering Xi-feng, she told her to change her clothes and rest a while.

Xi-feng said yes, she would, and after calling on Lady Wang, went back to her own apartment, where Patience had warmed her everyday clothes for her to change into. When she had changed, she sat down and asked Patience if anything had happened during her absence.

'Nothing, really,' said Patience, handing her some tea. 'Brightie's wife came with the interest on the three hundred taels of silver and I received it for you. Oh, and Mr Rui sent someone to ask if you were in. He wants to pay you a call and talk about something.'

Xi-feng snorted.

'Horrible creature! he seems to be *looking* for trouble. Just let him come, then!'

'What does Mr Rui want?' asked Patience. 'Why does he keep coming like this?'

In reply Xi-feng gave her a full account of her encounter with him in the garden of the Ning-guo mansion and of the things he had said to her on that occasion.

'What a nasty, disgusting man!' said Patience. 'A case of "the toad on the ground wanting to eat the goose in the sky". He'll come to no good end, getting ideas like that!'

'Just wait till he comes!' said Xi-feng. 'I know how to deal with him.'

But if you wish to know the outcome of Jia Rui's visit, you will have to read the next chapter.

CHAPTER 12

*Wang Xi-feng sets a trap for her admirer
And Jia Rui looks into the wrong side of the mirror*

Jia Rui's arrival was announced while Xi-feng and Patience were still talking about him.

'Ask him in,' said Xi-feng.

Hearing that he was to be received, Jia Rui rejoiced inwardly. He came into the room wreathed in smiles and overwhelmed Xi-feng with civilities. With feigned solicitude she pressed him to be seated and to take tea. He became quite ecstatic at the sight of her informal dress.

'Why isn't Cousin Lian back yet?' he asked, staring with fascinated eyes.

'I don't know what the reason can be,' said Xi-feng.

'Could it be,' Jia Rui inquired archly, 'that Someone has detained him on his way home and that he can't tear himself away?'

'Men are all the same!' said Xi-feng. 'They have only to set eyes on a woman to begin another affair.'

'Ah, there you are wrong!' said Jia Rui. '*I* am not that sort of man.'

'But how many men are there like you?' said Xi-feng. 'I doubt you could find one in ten.'

At this last remark Jia Rui positively scratched his ears with pleasure.

'You must find it very dull here on your own every day,' he said.

'Yes, indeed!' said Xi-feng. 'If only there were someone who could come and talk to me and help me to pass the time!'

'Well,' said Jia Rui, 'I am always free. How would it be if *I* were to come every day to help you pass the time?'

'You must be joking!' said Xi-feng. 'What would you want to come here for?'

'I mean every word I say,' said Jia Rui. 'May I be struck by lightning if I don't! True, there was a time when I should have been scared to come, because people always told me what a holy terror you were and how dangerous it was to cross you; but now I know that in reality you are all gentleness and fun, there is nothing that could stop me coming. I would come now if it cost me my life.'

'It's true then,' said Xi-feng, smiling delightedly. 'You really are an *understanding* sort of person – so much more so than Rong or Qiang! I used to think that since they were such handsome and cultured-looking young men they must be understanding as well, but they turned out to be stupid brutes without the least consideration for other people's feelings.'

This little speech went straight to Jia Rui's heart, and unconsciously he began edging his seat nearer to Xi-feng's. He peered closely at an embroidered purse that she was wearing and expressed a strong interest in one of her rings.

'Take care!' said Xi-feng in a low tone. 'The servants might see you!'

Obedient to his goddess's command, Jia Rui quickly drew back again. Xi-feng laughed.

'You had better go!'

'Ah no, cruel cousin! Let me stay a little longer!'

'Even if you stay, it's not very convenient here in broad daylight, with people coming and going all the time. Go away now and come back later when it's dark, at the beginning of the first watch. You can slip into the gallery west of this apartment and wait for me there.'

Jia Rui received these words like someone being presented with a rare and costly jewel.

'Are you sure you're not joking?' he asked hurriedly. 'A lot of people must go through that way. How should we avoid being seen?'

'Don't worry!' said Xi-feng. 'I'll give the watchmen a night off. When the side gates are closed, no one else can get through.'

Jia Rui was beside himself with delight and hurriedly took his leave, confident that the fulfilment of all he wished for was now in sight. Having waited impatiently for nightfall, he groped his way into the Rong-guo mansion just before they closed the gates and slipped into the gallery, now totally deserted – as Xi-feng had promised it would be – and black as pitch.

The gate at the end of the alley-way opening on to Grandmother Jia's quarters had already been barred on the outer side; only the gate at the east end remained open. For a long time Jia Rui listened intently, but no one came. Suddenly there was a loud slam and the gate at the east end, too, banged shut. Alarmed, but not daring to make a sound, Jia Rui stealthily crept out and tried it. It was locked – as tight as a bucket. Now even if he wanted to get out he could not, for the walls on either side of the alley-way were too high to scale. Moreover the gallery was bare and draughty and this was the midwinter season when the nights are long and the bitter north wind seems to pierce into the very marrow of the bones. By the end of the night he was almost dead with cold.

When at last morning came, Jia Rui saw the gate at the east end open and an old woman pass through to the gate opposite and call for someone to open up. Still hugging himself against the cold, he sprinted out of the other gate while her back was towards him. Fortunately no one was about at that early hour, and he was able to slip out of the rear entrance of the mansion and run back home unseen.

Jia Rui had lost both of his parents in infancy and had been brought up under the sole guardianship of his grandfather Jia Dai-ru. Obsessed by the fear that once outside the house his grandson might indulge in drinking and gambling to the detriment of his studies, Dai-ru had subjected him since early youth to an iron discipline from which not the slightest deviation was tolerated. Seeing him now suddenly absent himself a whole night from home, and being incapable, in his wildest imaginings, of guessing what had really happened, he took it as a foregone conclusion that he had been either drinking or gaming and had probably passed the night in some house of prostitution – a supposition which caused the old gentleman to spend the whole night in a state of extreme choler.

The prospect of facing his grandfather on arrival made Jia Rui sweat. A lie of some sort was indispensable.

'I went to see Uncle yesterday,' he managed to say, 'and as it was getting dark, he asked me to stay the night.'

'I have always told you that you are not to go out of that gate without first informing me,' said his grandfather. 'Why then did you presume to go off on your own yesterday without saying a word to anybody? That in itself would constitute sufficient grounds for chastisement. But in addition to that you are lying!'

Thereupon he forced him to the ground, and, with the utmost savagery, dealt him thirty or forty whacks with the bamboo, after which he forbade him to eat and made him kneel in the open courtyard with a book in his hand until he had prepared the equivalent of ten days' homework.

The exquisite torments suffered by Jia Rui, as he knelt with an empty stomach in the draughty courtyard reciting his homework after having already been frozen all night long and then beaten, can be imagined.

Yet even now his infatuation remained unaltered. It never entered his mind that he had been made a fool of. And so two days later, as soon as he had some free time, he was back once more looking for Xi-feng. She deliberately reproached him for having failed her, thereby so exasperating him that he swore by the most terrible oaths that he had been faithful. Seeing him hurl himself so willingly into the net, Xi-feng decided that a further lesson would be needed to cure him of his folly and proposed another assignation.

'Only tonight,' she said, 'don't wait for me in that place again. Wait in the empty room in the little passage-way *behind* this apartment. But mind you don't run into anybody.'

'Do you really mean this?' said Jia Rui.

'If you don't believe me, don't come!'

'I'll come! I'll come!' said Jia Rui. 'Whatever happens, I shall be there.'

'Now I think you had better go.'

Confident of seeing her again in the evening, Jia Rui went off uncomplainingly, leaving Xi-feng time to muster her forces, brief her officers, and prepare the trap in which the luckless man was to be caught.

Jia Rui waited for the evening with great impatience. By a

stroke of bad luck some relations came on a visit and stayed to supper. It was already lamplight when they left, and Jia Rui then had to wait for his grandfather to settle down for the night before he could scuttle off to the Rong mansion and make his way to the room in the little passage-way where Xi-feng had told him to go. He waited there for her arrival with the frenzied agitation of an ant on a hot saucepan. Yet, though he waited and waited, not a human shape appeared nor a human sound was heard, and he began to be frightened and a little suspicious:

'Surely she won't fail me? Surely I shan't be made to spend another night in the cold . . . ?'

As he was in the midst of these gloomy imaginings, a dark figure glided into the room. Certain that it must be Xi-feng, Jia Rui cast all caution to the winds and, when the figure approached him, threw himself upon it like a hungry tiger seizing its prey or a cat pouncing on a harmless mouse.

'My darling, how I have waited for you!' he exclaimed, en-folding his beloved in his arms; and carrying her to the kang, he laid her down and began kissing her and tugging at her trousers, murmuring 'my sweetest darling' and 'my honey love' and other such endearments in between kisses. Through-out all of this not a single sound was uttered by his partner. Jia Rui now tore down his own trousers and prepared to thrust home his hard and throbbing member. Suddenly a light flashed – and there was Jia Qiang holding aloft a candle in a candlestick which he shone around:

'Who is in this room?'

At this the person on the kang gave a giggle:

'Uncle Rui is trying to bugger me!'

Horrors! The sight he saw when he looked down made Jia Rui want to sink into the ground. It was Jia Rong! He turned to bolt, but Jia Qiang held him fast.

'Oh no you don't! Auntie Lian has already told Lady Wang that you have been pestering her. She asked us to keep you here while she went to tell. When Lady Wang first heard, she was so angry that she fainted, but now she's come round again and is asking for you to be brought to her. Come along, then! Off we go!'

At these words Jia Rui's soul almost left its seat in his body.

'My dear nephew, just tell her that you didn't find me here!' he said. 'Tomorrow I will reward you handsomely.'

'I suppose I could let you go easily enough,' said Jia Qiang. 'The question is, how big would this reward be? In any case, just *saying* that you will give me a reward is no good. I should want a written guarantee.'

'But I can't put a thing like this down in writing!'

'No problem there,' said Jia Qiang. 'Just say that you've lost money gambling and have borrowed such and such an amount to cover your losses. That's all you need do.'

'I could do that, certainly,' said Jia Rui.

Jia Qiang at once disappeared and reappeared only a moment later with paper and a writing-brush which had evidently been made ready in advance. Writing at his dictation Jia Rui was compelled, in spite of protests, to put down fifty taels of silver as the amount on the IOU. The document, having been duly signed, was at once pocketed by Jia Qiang, who then pretended to seek the connivance of Jia Rong. But Jia Rong feigned the most obdurate incorruptibility and insisted that he would lay the matter next day before a council of the whole clan and see that justice was done. Jia Rui became quite frantic and kotowed to him. Finally, under pressure from Jia Qiang and in return for another IOU for fifty taels of silver made out in his favour, he allowed his scruples to be overcome.

'You realize, don't you,' said Jia Qiang, 'that I'm going to get into trouble for this? Now let's see. The gate leading to Lady Jia's courtyard was bolted some time ago, and Sir Zheng is at the moment in the main reception room looking at some stuff that has just arrived from Nanking, so you can't go through that way. The only way left would be through the back gate. The trouble is, though, that if you leave now, you might run into someone on the way, and then I should get into even worse trouble. You'd better let me scout around a bit first and come for you when the coast is clear. In the meantime you can't hide here, though, because they will shortly be coming in to store the stuff from Nanking here. I'll find somewhere else for you.'

He took Jia Rui by the arm, and having first blown the candle out, led him into the courtyard and groped his way round to the underside of the steps which led up to the terrace of the central building.

'This hollow under the steps will do. Crouch down there, and don't make a sound! You can go when I come for you.'

Jia Qiang and Jia Rong then went off leaving him to himself.

Jia Rui, by now a mere automaton in the hands of his captors, obediently crouched down beneath the steps and was just beginning a series of calculations respecting his present financial predicament when a sudden *slosh*! signalled the discharge of a slop-pail's stinking contents immediately above his head, drenching him from top to toe with liquid filth and causing him to cry out in dismay – but only momentarily, for the excrement covered his face and head and caused him to close his mouth again in a hurry and crouch silent and shivering in the icy cold. Just then Jia Qiang came running up:

'Hurry! hurry! You can go now.'

At the word of command Jia Rui bounded out of his hole and sprinted for dear life through the rear gate and back to his own home. It was now past midnight, and he had to shout for someone to let him in. When the servant who answered the gate saw the state he was in and asked him how it had happened, he had to pretend that he had been out in the darkness to ease himself and had fallen into the jakes. Then rushing into his own room he stripped off his clothes and washed, his mind running all the time on how Xi-feng had tricked him. The thought of her trickery provoked a surge of hatred in his soul; yet even as he hated her, the vision of her loveliness made him long to clasp her to his breast. Torn by these violent and conflicting emotions, he passed the whole night without a single wink of sleep.

From that time on, though he longed for Xi-feng with unabated passion, he never dared to visit the Rong-guo mansion again. Jia Rong and Jia Qiang, on the other hand, came frequently to his house to ask for their money, so that he was in constant dread of his grandfather finding out about the IOUs.

Unable, even now, to overcome his longing for Xi-feng, saddled with a heavy burden of debt, harassed during the daytime by the schoolwork set him by his exacting grandfather, worn-out during the nights by the excessive hand-pumping inevitable in an unmarried man of twenty whose mistress was both unattainable and constantly in his thoughts, twice frozen, tormented and forced to flee – what constitution could withstand so many shocks and strains without succumbing in the end to illness? The symptoms of Jia Rui's illness – a palpitation in the heart, a loss of taste in the mouth, a weakness in the hams, a smarting in the eyes, feverishness by night and lassitude by day, albumen in the urine and blood-flecks in the phlegm – had all manifested themselves within less than a year. By that time they had produced a complete breakdown and driven him to his bed, where he lay, with eyes tight shut, babbling deliriously and inspiring terror in all who saw him. Physicians were called in to treat him and some bushels of cinnamon bark, autumn root, turtle-shell, black leek and Solomon's seal must at one time and another have been infused and taken without the least observable effect.

Winter went and spring came and Jia Rui's sickness grew even worse. His grandfather Dai-ru was in despair. Medical advice from every quarter had been taken and none of it had proved effective. The most recent advice was that the patient should be given a pure decoction of ginseng without admixture of other ingredients. So costly a remedy was far beyond Dai-ru's resources and he was obliged to go to the Rong-guo mansion to beg. Lady Wang ordered Wang Xi-feng to weigh out two ounces for him from their own supplies.

'The other day when we were making up a new lot of pills for Grandmother,' said Xi-feng, 'you told me to keep any of the remaining whole roots for a medicine you were sending to General Yang's wife. I sent her the medicine yesterday, so I am afraid we haven't any left.'

'Well, even if *we* haven't got any,' said Lady Wang, 'you can send to your mother-in-law's for some; and probably they will have some at your Cousin Zhen's. Between you you ought somehow or other to be able to raise enough to give him. If you can save a man's life by doing so, you will have performed a work of merit.'

But though Xi-feng pretended to do as Lady Wang suggested, in fact she made no such inquiries. She merely scraped a few drams of broken bits together and sent them to Dai-ru with a message that 'Lady Wang had instructed her to send this, and it was all they had.' To Lady Wang, however, she reported that she had asked the others and altogether obtained more than two ounces of ginseng which she had sent to Dai-ru.

Jia Rui now wanted desperately to live and eagerly swallowed every medicine that they offered him; but all was a waste of money, for nothing seemed to do him any good. One day a lame Taoist appeared at the door asking for alms and claiming to be able to cure retributory illnesses. Jia Rui, who chanced to overhear him, called out from his bed:

'Quick, tell the holy man to come in and save me!' and as he called, he kotowed with his head on the pillow. The servants were obliged to bring the Taoist into the bedroom. Jia Rui clung to him tenaciously.

'Holy one, save me!' he cried out again and again.

The Taoist sighed.

'No medicine will cure your sickness. However, I have a precious thing here that I can lend you which, if you will look at it every day, can be guaranteed to save your life.'

So saying, he took from his satchel a mirror which had reflecting surfaces on both its sides. The words A MIRROR FOR THE ROMANTIC were inscribed on the back. He handed it to Jia Rui.

'This object comes from the Hall of Emptiness in the Land of Illusion. It was fashioned by the fairy Disenchantment as an antidote to the ill effects of impure mental activity. It has life-giving and restorative properties and has been brought into the world for the contemplation of those intelligent and handsome young gentlemen whose hearts are too susceptible to the charms of beauty. I lend it to you on one important condition: you must only look into the back of the mirror. Never, never under any circumstances look into the front. Three days hence

I shall come again to reclaim it, by which time I guarantee that your illness will have gone.'

With that he left, at a surprising speed, ignoring the earnest entreaties of those present that he should stay longer.

'This is intriguing!' Jia Rui thought to himself when the Taoist gave him the mirror. 'Let me try looking into it as he says,' and holding it up to his face he looked into the back as instructed and saw a grinning skull, which he covered up hastily with a curse:

'Silly old fool, to scare me like that! – But let me see what happens when I look into the other side!'

He turned the mirror round and looked, and there inside was Xi-feng beckoning to him to enter, and his ravished soul floated into the mirror after her. There they performed the act of love together, after which she saw him out again. But when he found himself once more back in his bed he stared and cried out in horror: for the mirror, of its own accord, had turned itself round in his hand and the same grinning skull faced him that he had seen before. He could feel the sweat trickling all over his body and lower down in the bed a little pool of semen that he had just ejaculated.

Yet still he was not satisfied, and turned the face of the mirror once more towards him. Xi-feng was there beckoning to him again and calling, and again he went in after her. He did this three or four times. But the last time, just as he was going to return from the mirror, two figures approached him holding iron chains which they fastened round him and by which they proceeded to drag him away. He cried out as they dragged him:

'Wait! Let me take the mirror with me . . .!'

Those were the last words he ever uttered.

To those who stood around the bed and watched him while this was happening he appeared first to be holding up the mirror and looking into it, then to let it drop; then to open his eyes in a ghastly stare and pick it up again; then, as it once more fell from his grasp, he finally ceased to move.

When they examined him more closely they found that his breathing had already stopped and that underneath his body there was a large, wet, icy patch of recently ejaculated semen.

At once they lifted him from the bed and busied themselves with the laying-out, while old Dai-ru and his wife abandoned themselves to a paroxysm of grief. They cursed the Taoist for a necromancer and ordered the servants to heap up a fire and cast the mirror upon the flames. But just at that moment a voice was heard in the air saying, 'Who told him to look in the front? It is you who are to blame, for confusing the unreal with the real! Why then should you burn my mirror?'

Suddenly the mirror was seen to rise up and fly out of the room, and when Dai-ru went outside to look, there was the lame Taoist asking for it back. He snatched it as it flew towards him and disappeared before Dai-ru's very eyes.

Seeing that there was to be no redress, Dai-ru was obliged to set about preparing for the funeral and began by announcing his grandson's death to everybody concerned. Reading of the sūtras began on the third day and on the seventh the coffin was drawn in procession to temporary lodging in the Temple of the Iron Threshold to await future reburial. The various members of the Jia family all came in due course to offer their condolences. From the Rong-guo side Jia She and Jia Zheng each gave twenty taels of silver and from the Ning-guo side Cousin Zhen also gave twenty taels. The other members of the clan gave amounts varying from one to four taels according to their means. A collection made among the parents of the dead man's fellow-students raised an additional twenty or thirty taels. Although Dai-ru's means were slender, with so much monetary help coming in he was able to perform the whole business in considerable style.

*

Towards the end of the year in which Jia Rui's troubles started Lin Ru-hai fell seriously ill and wrote a letter asking to see Dai-yu again. Though Grandmother Jia was plunged into deepest gloom by the letter, she was obliged to prepare with all possible expedition for her granddaughter's departure. And Bao-yu, though he too was distressed at the prospect of Dai-yu's leaving him, could scarcely seek to interfere in a matter affecting the natural feelings of a father and his child. Grandmother Jia insisted that Jia Lian should accompany

Dai-yu and see her safely there and back. The various gifts to be taken and the journey-money were, it goes without saying, duly prepared. A suitable day on which to commence the journey was quickly determined and Jia Lian and Dai-yu took leave of all the rest and, embarking with their attendants, set sail for Yangchow.

If you wish for further details, you may learn them in the following chapter.

CHAPTER 13

Qin-shi posthumously acquires the status
of a Noble Dame
And Xi-feng takes on the management
of a neighbouring establishment

After Jia Lian's departure for Yangchow Xi-feng felt bored and unhappy, particularly in the evenings when, apart from chatting with Patience, there seemed little to do but sleep. On the occasion of which we write she had sat beside the lamp with Patience until late into the evening; then, the bedding having been well warmed, the two women had gone to bed, where they lay until after midnight discussing the stages of Jia Lian's journey and attempting to calculate what point he was likely to have reached in it. By this time Patience was fast asleep and Xi-feng herself was on the point of dropping off when she became dimly aware that Qin-shi had just walked into the room from outside.

'So fond of sleep, Auntie?' said Qin-shi with a gentle smile. 'I shall have to begin my journey today without you to see me off. But never mind! Since you cannot come to me, I have come to you instead. We two have always been so close, I could not have borne to leave you without saying good-bye. Besides, I have a last wish that you alone must hear, because I cannot trust anyone else with it.'

'What is your wish?' Xi-feng heard herself asking. 'You can trust me to carry it out for you.'

'Tell me, Auntie,' said Qin-shi, 'how is it that you who are such a paragon among women that even strong men find more than their match in you can yet be ignorant of the simple truths expressed in homely proverbs? Take this one:

> The full moon smaller grows,
> Full water overflows.

Or this:

> The higher the climb, the harder the fall.

Our house has now enjoyed nearly a century of dazzling success. Suppose one day "joy at its height engenders sorrow". And suppose that, in the words of another proverb, "when the tree falls, the monkeys scatter". Will not our reputation as one of the great, cultured households of the age then turn into a hollow mockery?'

Qin-shi's question made Xi-feng feel uneasy, though at the same time inspiring a deep respect in her for her niece's foresight.

'You are quite right to show concern,' she said. 'Is there any means by which we can keep permanently out of danger?'

'Now you are being silly, Auntie!' said Qin-shi somewhat scornfully. ' "The extreme of adversity is the beginning of prosperity" – and the reverse of that saying is also true. Honour and disgrace follow each other in an unending cycle. No human power can arrest that cycle and hold it permanently in one position. What you *can* do, however, is to plan while we are still prosperous for the kind of heritage that will stand up to the hard times when they come.

'At the moment everything seems well looked after; but in fact there are still two matters that have not been properly taken care of. If you will deal with them in the way that I shall presently suggest, you will be able to face the future without fear of calamity.'

'What two matters?' Xi-feng asked her.

'Though the seasonal offerings at the ancestral burial-ground are at present regularly attended to,' said Qin-shi, 'no special income has been set aside to pay for them. That is the first matter. The second matter concerns the clan school. There again, there is no fixed source of income. Obviously there will be no lack of funds either for the seasonal offerings or for the school as long as we enjoy our present prosperity. But where is the money for them coming from in the future, when the family has fallen on hard times?

'I am convinced that the only way of dealing with these two matters is to invest now, while we are still rich and powerful, in as much property as possible – land, farms, and houses – in the area around the burial-ground, and to pay for the seasonal offerings and the running of the school entirely out of the income from this property. Moreover the school itself ought to be situated on it. The whole clan, old and young alike, should be convened and a set of regulations drawn up whereby each family is made to administer the estate and look after the financing of the seasonal offerings and the clan school for one year in turn. By making the responsibility rotate in a fixed order you will remove the possibility of quarrels about it and also lessen the danger of the property getting mortgaged or sold.

'Then even if the clan gets into trouble and its possessions are confiscated, this part of its property, as charitable estate, will escape confiscation; and when the family's fortunes are in decline, it will be a place where the young people can go to farm and study, as well as a means of maintaining the ancestral sacrifices in unbroken succession. To refuse to take thought for the morrow on the grounds that our present prosperity is going to last for ever would be extremely short-sighted.

'Quite soon a happy event is going to take place in this family, bringing it an even greater glory than it has enjoyed up to now. But it will be a glory as excessive and as transitory as a posy of fresh flowers pinned to an embroidered dress or the flare-up of spilt cooking-oil on a blazing fire. In the midst of that brief moment of happiness never forget that "even the best party must have an end". For if you do, and if you fail to take precautions in good time, you will live to regret it bitterly when it is already too late.'

'What is this happy event you speak of?' Xi-feng asked her eagerly.

'That is a secret which may not be revealed to mortal ears. However, for the sake of our brief friendship on this earth, I leave you these words as my parting gift. Be sure that you remember them well!

When the Three Springs have gone, the flowering time will end,
And each one for himself as best he may must fend.'

Xi-feng was about to ask her another question when she was interrupted by the sound of the iron chime-bar which hung in the inner gate.

Four strokes. The signal of death!

She woke with a start to hear a servant announcing, 'Mrs Rong of the Ning-guo mansion is dead.' A cold sweat broke out over her body and for a while she lay too stunned to move. Then forcing herself to get up she pulled on her clothes and went round to Lady Wang's.

By this time the entire household had heard the news. All seemed bewildered by it and all were in one way or another deeply distressed. Those older than Qin-shi thought of how dutiful she had always been; those in her own generation thought of her warmth and friendliness; her juniors remembered how kindly and lovingly she had treated them; even the servants, irrespective of sex and age, remembering her compassion for the poor and humble and her gentle concern for the old and the very young, all wept and lamented as loud and bitterly as the rest.

But we digress.

During the last few days, since Dai-yu's return to her father had deprived him of her companionship, Bao-yu, far from seeking diversion in the company of the others, had kept to himself, going to bed early every night and sleeping disconsolately on his own. The news of Qin-shi's death came to him in the midst of his dreams, causing him to start up in bed with a jerk. A sudden stabbing pain shot through his heart. He retched involuntarily and spat out a mouthful of blood. Aroma and the maids clung to him, terrified, and asked him what was the matter. They wanted to tell Grandmother Jia and ask her to send for a doctor; but Bao-yu would not hear of it.

'Don't worry, it's of no consequence!' he told them. 'Something that happens when a sudden rush of fire to the heart prevents the blood from getting back into the right channels.'

He climbed out of bed as he spoke and told them to bring him some clean clothes, so that he could see his grandmother and then go straight on to the other house. Aroma was still concerned for him, but seeing him so determined, allowed him to have his way.

Grandmother Jia did not want him to go, either.

'It won't be clean there,' she said, 'with her scarcely yet

cold. And besides, there's a nasty wind at this time of night. It will be soon enough if you go there first thing tomorrow.'

But Bao-yu would not be gainsaid, so she gave instructions for a carriage to be made ready for him and a numerous retinue of servants to attend him there.

Arriving in haste at the entrance of the Ning-guo mansion, they found the gates flung wide open and lanterns on either side turning the night into noonday. Despite the hour, a multitude of people were hurrying through it in both directions, while from inside the house issued a sound of lamentation that seemed to shake the very buildings to their foundations.

Alighting from his carriage, Bao-yu hurried through to the room in which Qin-shi lay and wept there for a while very bitterly. He then went to call on You-shi, whom he found ill in bed, struck down by a sudden attack of some gastric trouble from which she had occasionally suffered in the past. After leaving You-shi, he went to look for Cousin Zhen.

By now Jia Dai-ru, Jia Dai-xiu, Jia Chi, Jia Xiao, Jia Dun, Jia She, Jia Zheng, Jia Cong, Jia Bin, Jia Heng (I), Jia Guang, Jia Chen, Jia Qiong, Jia Lin, Jia Qiang, Jia Chang, Jia Ling, Jia Yun, Jia Qin, Jia Jin, Jia Ping, Jia Zao, Jia Heng (II), Jia Fen, Jia Fang, Jia Lan, Jia Jun and Jia Zhi had all arrived, and Bao-yu found Cousin Zhen in their midst addressing them, though well-nigh choked with tears:

'Everyone, young or old, kinsman or friend, knows that my daughter-in-law was ten times better than any son. Now that she has been taken from us it's plain to see that this senior branch of the family is doomed to extinction!' and he broke down once more into incontrollable weeping.

The men present tried to console him:

'Now that she's gone, crying isn't going to bring her back again. The important thing now is to make your plans for the funeral.'

'Plans? What plans?' Cousin Zhen cried, somewhat theatrically. 'Just take everything I have – everything!'

As he was speaking Qin Bang-ye and Qin Zhong arrived, and various members of You-shi's family, including her two younger sisters. Cousin Zhen deputed Jia Qiong, Jia Chen,

Jia Lin and Jia Qiang from among the younger men present to look after them and any other guests who might arrive.

He also instructed someone to invite an expert from the Board of Astronomy to select dates for the funeral and the ceremonies preceding it. With the approval of this official it was decided that the lying in state should be for forty-nine days and that the notification of bereavement indicating the family's readiness to receive official visits of condolence should be made in three days' time. A hundred and eight Buddhist monks were engaged to perform a Grand Misericordia for the salvation of all departed souls in the main reception hall of the mansion during these forty-nine days, while at the same time ninety-nine Taoist priests of the Quanzhen sect were to perform ceremonies of purification and absolution at a separate altar in the Celestial Fragrance pavilion. These arrangements having been made, the body was moved to a temporary shrine in another pavilion of the All-scents Garden. Fifty high-ranking Buddhist monks and fifty high-ranking Taoist priests took turns in chanting and intoning before it on every seventh day.

Nothing would induce old Jia Jing to return home when he learned of the death of his grandson's wife. Immortality was within his grasp and he was not going to impair his hard-won sanctity with the taint of earthly pollution. Accordingly he left all these matters to Cousin Zhen to order as he wished.

Free to indulge his own extravagant tastes, Cousin Zhen had inspected several sets of deal coffin-boards without finding any to his liking. Xue Pan heard of his problem when he came round to condole.

'We've got a set in our timber-yard,' he told Cousin Zhen. 'It's in a wood supposed to have come from the Iron Net Mountains. They say that a coffin made from it will last for ever without rotting. It was brought here years ago by my father. Prince Zhong-yi was going to have it, but when he came unstuck it didn't get used. It's still locked up in store because no one has ever been found who could afford to buy it. If you are interested, I can have it carried round for you to look at.'

Cousin Zhen was delighted, and the timber was brought

over at once for everyone to inspect. The planks for the base and sides were at least eight inches thick. The wood had a grain like areca palm and a fragrance suggestive of musk and sandalwood. When rapped with the knuckles it gave off a hard, ringing sound like jade or stone. Everyone was impressed and Cousin Zhen eagerly inquired the price. Xue Pan laughed.

'I doubt you could buy a set like this for a thousand taels of silver cash down,' he said. 'Blow the price! Give the workmen a couple of taels for carrying it here and it's yours.'

Cousin Zhen thanked him profusely and at once gave orders for the planks to be sawn up and made into a coffin. Jia Zheng doubted the propriety of using such material for the burial of a person not of royal blood and insisted that it would be sufficient to use the best quality deal; but Cousin Zhen refused to listen.

News was suddenly brought that Qin-shi's little maid Gem, on hearing that her mistress was dead, had taken her own life by dashing her head against a pillar. Such rare devotion excited the wondering admiration of the entire clan. Cousin Zhen at once had her laid out and encoffined with the rites appropriate to a granddaughter and ordered her coffin to be placed in the Ascension Pavilion of the All-scents Garden side by side with Qin-shi's.

As Qin-shi had died without issue, another of her little maids called Jewel volunteered to stand in as her daughter and perform the chief mourner's duties of smashing the bowl when the bearers came in to take up the coffin and walking in front of it in the funeral procession. Cousin Zhen was very pleased and gave orders that thenceforth everyone was to address her as '*Miss* Jewel' just as if she were Qin-shi's real daughter. In the meantime she installed herself by the coffin and, comporting herself in the manner prescribed for an unmarried daughter, wept and wailed until she had almost lost her voice.

Following these preliminaries, the rest of the clan together with the family servants all proceeded to carry out their mourning duties according to long-established precedents and in a correct and orderly manner. The family's respect for tradition was, however, a source of great unease to Cousin Zhen when he reflected on Jia Rong's status: for Jia Rong was only an Imperial College Student – an absurdly insignificant title to write on a funeral banner; and the insignia to which Qin-shi was entitled would make a very poor showing when borne in the funeral procession.

By a stroke of luck the fourth day of the first seven-day period – the day on which official condolences were scheduled to begin – brought a visit from Dai Quan, the Eunuch Chamberlain of the Da-ming Palace. Having sent his representative along well in advance with offerings for the departed spirit, he presently arrived himself, seated in a great palanquin and preceded by criers and men with gongs clearing the streets before him, to present his offerings in person. Cousin Zhen at once made up his mind to take advantage of the visit.

As soon as Dai Quan had made his offering, Cousin Zhen ushered him into the Honey Bee Gallery, invited him to be seated, and served him with tea. Then, entering into conversation with his guest, he quickly found occasion to mention the fact that he was thinking of purchasing a place for his son Jia Rong. The eunuch guessed what was in his mind, and laughingly inquired whether it was not with a view to adding a little pomp to the funeral that he had conceived this notion.

'My dear Chamberlain,' Cousin Zhen readily agreed, 'you have hit the nail on the head!'

'Well, by a lucky coincidence,' said Dai Quan, 'there is rather a good place going at this very moment. The Corps of Officers of the Imperial Guard, which has an establishment of three hundred, has got two vacancies in it. Yesterday Lord Xiang-yang's younger brother "Sannikins" begged me for one of them and sent fifteen hundred taels of silver round to my house to pay for it. He and I have always been good friends, as you know, and in any case I felt I had to do something, for his Grandpa's sake; so I couldn't very well refuse. "Piggy" Feng, the Military Governor of Yong-xing, has asked me if he can buy the remaining place for his son, but I haven't yet had time to give him a reply. If our young friend here wants it, why not jot down his particulars and I'll see what I can do.'

Cousin Zhen at once ordered someone to write out Jia Rong's name, age and lineage on a sheet of red paper. The

following description was hurriedly prepared and handed to
Dai Quan for his inspection:

Name: JIA RONG

Place of Origin: (County) Kiangning; (Prefecture) Ying-tian-fu;
(Province) Kiangnan.

Status: Imperial College Student

Age: 20

Great-grandfather: General Jia Dai-hua, C.-in-C. Metropolitan
Barracks, hereditary noble of the first rank.

Grandfather: Jia Jing, Palace Graduate of the year 17—.

Father: Hon. Colonel Jia Zhen, third rank (hereditary).

After glancing through it quickly, Dai Quan handed it into
the keeping of a young eunuch secretary at his side.

'When we get back,' he said to the latter, 'give this to old
Zhao, the President of the Board of Revenue, with my compliments, and ask him if he would kindly make out a commission
for a captain in the Imperial Guard, fifth rank, and also the
papers to go with it with these particulars filled in. Tell him
I'll call round tomorrow to pay in the money.'

The young eunuch bowed, and Dai Quan rose to go. Seeing
that he could no longer detain him, Cousin Zhen showed him
out as far as the main gate. As the eunuch was getting into his
palanquin, Cousin Zhen asked him whether he should take
the money to the Ministry or bring it round to Dai Quan's
own house.

'Better bring a thousand taels, standard weight, to my
house. If you go to the Ministry, they're sure to fleece you.'

Cousin Zhen thanked him warmly.

'When the period of mourning is over,' he said, 'I shall
bring the young fellow round to your house to kotow his
thanks.'

With that they parted. But no sooner had the eunuch gone
than the sound of criers was once more heard in the street,
this time heralding the arrival of the Marchioness of Zhong-
jing, wife of Grandmother Jia's nephew Shi Ding, with her
little niece Shi Xiang-yun. Lady Wang, Lady Xing and Wang
Xi-feng received them in Cousin Zhen's drawing-room.

Offerings from the Marquises of Jin-xiang and Chuan-ning
and the Earl of Shou-shan were now on display, and those

three gentlemen were shortly to be observed alighting from their palanquins outside. Cousin Zhen went out to meet them and conducted them up the steps into the main reception hall.

From then on there was a continuous stream of arrivals, and throughout the whole forty-nine-day period the street in front of the Ning-guo mansion was thronged with family mourners in white and mandarins in their colourful robes of office, milling in and out and to and fro all day long.

The day after Dai Quan's visit Cousin Zhen made Jia Rong change out of mourning into a court dress and go to collect his commission. The furnishings and insignia in the shrine were all rearranged in a manner befitting a person of the fifth rank. The wording on the spirit tablet which stood on the table of offerings at the foot of the coffin now read:

Spirit tablet of the Lady Qin-shi of the Jia family
Gentlewoman of the Fifth Rank by Imperial Patent

The gate of the All-scents Garden opening on to the street was thrown wide open and booths for musicians were erected on either side of it, in which black-coated funeral bands played at fixed times throughout the day. To either side of them were displayed the insignia of rank: glittering rows of axes and halberds arranged in wooden stands. At each side of the gateway vermilion-painted boards inscribed in large golden characters boldly announced the status of the bereaved:

Honorary Captain of the Imperial Bodyguard
Inner Palace, Northern Capital Division

Inside the gateway, facing the street, a high staging was constructed on which Buddhist monks and Taoist priests sat on opposite sides of an altar intoning their sacred texts. In front of the staging was a notice on which was written in large characters:

FUNERAL OBSEQUIES
OF
THE LADY QIN-SHI

Senior great-great-granddaughter-in-law of
Jia Yan, Hereditary Duke of Ning-guo, and
wife of the *Right Honourable Jia Rong*, Captain
in the Imperial Bodyguard, Inner Palace:

WHEREAS

in this favoured *Country*, situate in the centremost part of the four continents of the earth,
on which it has pleased Heaven to bestow the
blessings of everlasting prosperity and peace,

WE,

The Very Reverend *Wan-xu*, Co-President of
the Board of Commissioners having authority over all monks and clergy of the Incorpor-
eal, Ever-tranquil Church of the *Lord Buddha*,

and

the Venerable *Ye-sheng*, Co-President of the
Board of Commissioners having authority
over all priests and practitioners of the Primordial, All-unifying Church of the *Heavenly
Tao*,

HAVE,

with all due reverence and care, prepared
offices for the salvation of all departed
souls, supplicating *Heaven* and calling upon
the Name of the *Lord Buddha* . . .

NOW,

earnestly praying and beseeching the Eighteen Guardians of the Sangha, the Warlike
Guardians of the Law, and the Twelve
Guardians of the Months mercifully to ex-
tend their holy compassion towards us, but
terribly to blaze forth in divine majesty
against the powers of evil, we do solemnly
perform for nine and forty days the Great
Mass for the purification, deliverance and
salvation of all souls on land and on sea . . .

– and a great deal more on those lines which it would be
tedious to repeat.

*

Although Cousin Zhen now had every reason to feel satisfied
with his arrangements, there was still one matter which caused

him uneasiness. You-shi's unfortunate illness meant that she was unable to discharge any of her social obligations, and he was mortally afraid that with so many great ladies coming to the house on visits of condolence, some breach of etiquette might occur which would cause the family to look ridiculous.

Bao-yu once chanced to be sitting next to him when his mind was dwelling on this problem, and observing the gloomy and preoccupied expression on his cousin's face, asked him why he should still be worried now that everything had been so excellently taken care of. Cousin Zhen explained that it was the present lack of a responsible female head of household which was the cause of his concern.

'That's no problem!' said Bao-yu encouragingly. 'I know just the person for this. Put her in temporary control here for a month, and I guarantee that you will have nothing further to worry about.'

'Who?' inquired Cousin Zhen eagerly.

Bao-yu deemed it imprudent to mention her name out loud in the hearing of so many friends and relations, so leaning across he whispered it in Cousin Zhen's ear. Cousin Zhen's reaction was ecstatic.

'Yes, absolutely the right person!' he cried. 'Let's see about it straight away!'

And seizing Bao-yu by the hand, he excused himself to the company and hurried round to the reception room in his own apartment.

It so happened that this day was not one of the seven on which masses were said, so visitors from outside the family were fairly few. In the inner apartments there was only a handful of lady visitors, all of them close connections of the Jia family, whom Lady Xing, Lady Wang, Wang Xi-feng and various female members of the clan were keeping company. When a servant announced 'The Master is here', all these females jumped up with little shrieks of alarm and rushed off to hide themselves – all, that is, except Xi-feng, who rose slowly to her feet and imperturbably stood her ground.

Cousin Zhen had of late been feeling far from well. The debility his sickness caused him had been further aggravated by excessive grief and obliged him to support himself with a staff. Lady Xing was concerned to see the pitiful· figure he presented as he entered the room.

'You are not well,' she said, 'and you have been doing too much now for days. You ought to be getting some rest. What do you want to come in here for?'

Clutching his staff in his hand, Cousin Zhen struggled down on to his knees, and having made his duty to his aunts, began thanking them for all their trouble. Lady Xing hurriedly ordered Bao-yu to raise him up and commanded a chair to be moved forward for him to sit on. But Cousin Zhen refused to be seated.

'I have come to ask you three ladies a favour,' he said, forcing his woebegone features into a smile.

'What is it you want?' Lady Xing asked him.

'As you doubtless know,' said Cousin Zhen, 'my wife has been ill in bed ever since our daughter-in-law's death, and with no one to run her side of the household it has been getting into a pretty deplorable state. I should like to ask Cousin Feng if she could possibly see her way to running things here for us during the coming month. It would be a great relief to me if she could.'

'So that's what you want!' said Lady Xing with a smile. 'Feng is now part of your Aunt Wang's establishment. You'd better talk to *her* about it.'

'She's only a child yet, you know,' Lady Wang put in hastily. 'What experience has she ever had of *this* kind of thing? Suppose she proved not quite up to the task. We should all be made to look ridiculous. I think you had better trouble someone else.'

'I can easily guess what is in your mind, Aunt,' said Cousin Zhen. 'You are afraid we should overwork her. For I assure you there is no question of her not being a good enough manager. Even in her childhood games, Cousin Feng had the decisiveness of a little general, and since she's married and had some experience of running things next door, she is a thoroughly seasoned campaigner. I've thought the matter over carefully these past few days and am quite convinced that apart from Cousin Feng there really isn't anyone else I can ask. If you won't let her do this for my sake or my wife's sake, at least won't you let her for the sake of the one who has just died?'

And at this point he burst into tears.

Lady Wang's only concern had been lest Xi-feng, who had had no experience of large-scale funerals, might find the task too big for her and perhaps end up by making a fool of herself. But Cousin Zhen's moving plea caused her attitude to soften considerably and she eyed Xi-feng thoughtfully as though struggling to make up her mind. Xi-feng for her part had always loved managing things and enjoyed showing off her ability to do so. When Cousin Zhen first made his request, her mind had at once consented; and now, observing that Lady Wang appeared to be already half persuaded, she hastened to complete the process.

'Cousin Zhen has spoken so eloquently. Oughtn't we perhaps to agree, Aunt?'

'Do you think you can do it?' Lady Wang asked her in a low aside.

'I don't see why not,' said Xi-feng. 'Cousin Zhen has already seen to all the outside arrangements himself. It's only a question of looking after the domestic side for a bit. And even if there is anything I don't know about, I can always ask you.'

This seemed reasonable enough to Lady Wang, so she said nothing. Seeing that Xi-feng herself appeared to be willing, Cousin Zhen turned to her with a smile.

'Actually there isn't so very much to do,' he said. 'You really must let us persuade you to take this on. Let me make you a reverence now, to show my gratitude. Then, when this is all over, I shall come round to your place to thank you properly.'

So saying, he clasped his hands before him and made her a formal bow. Xi-feng hurriedly curtseyed back.

Cousin Zhen now ordered someone to fetch the tallies for the entire Ning-guo household and instructed Bao-yu to hand them to Xi-feng.

'I want you to manage things whatever way you like,' he told her. 'Anything you want you can get by using one of these. There is no need to ask me for it. I have only two requests to make of you. First that you should dismiss from your mind any idea of trying to save me any money. The important thing is to put on a good show: the expense doesn't matter. And secondly that you should treat our people here exactly as you treat the members of your own household. Don't be afraid of upsetting them. Provided that you will observe those conditions, I leave everything in your hands with the utmost confidence.'

Xi-feng watched Lady Wang, not daring to accept the tallies without her approval.

'You hear what your cousin says,' said Lady Wang. 'You had better do as he asks. Only do not take too much upon yourself. If there are any decisions to make, be sure to ask Cousin Zhen or his wife first.'

Bao-yu had already received the tallies from Cousin Zhen and now thrust them at Xi-feng. For politeness' sake she feigned a certain amount of reluctance, but was soon prevailed upon to accept them.

'Will you stay here with us,' Cousin Zhen asked her, 'or will you be coming over every day from the other house? If you intend to come over from the other house every day, it will greatly add to your burdens. We have an apartment here with its own courtyard which we can very quickly place at your disposal. If you would care to move in for the next week or two, I am sure we could make you comfortable.'

'Thank you, but it won't be necessary,' said Xi-feng with a smile. 'I am needed at the other house too, so it will be best if I come here every day.'

Having accomplished his mission, Cousin Zhen stayed chatting a little longer and then left. Presently, when the visiting ladies had dispersed, Lady Wang asked Xi-feng what her plans were for the rest of the day.

'Please go on without me, Aunt,' said Xi-feng. 'Before I go back myself I must first try to sort out exactly what this job is going to entail.'

Lady Wang accordingly left without more delay in the company of Lady Xing, and the two ladies returned to the Rong-guo mansion, where we must now leave them.

Alone at last, Xi-feng wandered into a sort of penthouse

building where she sat down and tried to formulate the task that lay ahead. Five major abuses, long habitual in the Ning-guo establishment, presented themselves to her mind as being specially in need of attention, viz:

1. Because it was so large and so motley an establishment, things were always getting lost.

2. Because there was no rational division of labour, it always seemed to be someone else's responsibility whenever a job needed to be done.

3. Because the household's expenditure was so lavish, money was always getting misappropriated or misspent.

4. Because no distinctions were made between one job and another, the rewards and hardships were unfairly distributed.

5. Because the servants were so arrogant and undisciplined, those with 'face' could brook no restraint and those without could win no advancement.

If you want to know how Xi-feng dealt with these abuses, you will have to read the chapter which follows.

CHAPTER 14

*Lin Ru-hai is conveyed to his last
resting-place in Soochow
And Jia Bao-yu is presented to the Prince of
Bei-jing at a roadside halt*

When Lai Sheng, the Chief Steward of the Ning-guo mansion, learned that Xi-feng had been invited to take on the management of the household, he called his cronies together and addressed them in the following terms:

'Well lads, it seems that they've called in Mrs Lian from the other house to run things here for a bit; so if she should happen to come round asking for anything or have occasion to talk to you about anything, be sure to do what she says, won't you? During this coming month we shall all have to start work a bit earlier and knock off a bit later than usual. If you'll put up with a little extra hardship just for this month, we can make up for it by taking things easy when it's over. Anyway, I'm relying on you not to let me down. She's well known for a sour-faced, hard-hearted bitch is this one, and once she's got her back up, she'll give no quarter, no matter who you are. So be careful!'

There was a chorus of agreement from the rest. One of them did observe, half-jokingly, that 'by rights they could do with someone like her to straighten things up a bit, considering the state they had got into'. But just at that moment Brightie's wife arrived on a mission from Xi-feng. She was to take receipt of some ledger-paper, buckram, and book-labels, and had a tally in her hand and a slip of paper specifying the quantities required. The men pressed round her offering her a place to sit and a cup of tea to drink while one of them hurried off with the list to fetch the needed items. Not only that, but, having fetched them, he carried them for her all the way to the inner gate of the mansion, only handing them to her then so that she could take them in to Xi-feng by herself. Xi-feng at once ordered Sunshine to make them up into stout workbooks for use in the office. At the same time she sent for Lai Sheng's wife and asked her for the register of the household staff. She also told her to get in touch with all the married females on the staff and arrange for them to assemble first thing next morning to be told their new duties. Then, after roughly checking through the numbers in the 'establishment' sheet and questioning Lai Sheng's wife on a few points, she got into her carriage and drove back home.

At half past six next morning she was back at the Ning-guo mansion. By this time all the married women on the staff had been assembled. Not daring to go in, they hung about outside the window listening to Xi-feng discussing work-plans with Lai Sheng's wife inside the office. 'Now that I'm in charge here', they heard her telling the latter, 'I won't promise to make myself agreeable. I haven't got a sweet temper like your mistress, you know. You won't find *me* letting you do everything just as it suits you. So don't let me hear anyone saying "We don't do it that way here"! From now on, whatever it is, you do it the way I tell you to, and anyone who departs by as much as a hair's breadth from what I say is for it good and proper, no matter how senior or how important she thinks she is!'

Having delivered herself of this formidable preliminary she ordered Sunshine to call the roll. One by one the women stepped into the office to be looked at. When she had looked at them all, Xi-feng proceeded to make her dispositions.

'This twenty here. I want you to divide yourselves into two shifts of ten. Your job every day will be to look after lady visitors and serve them tea. That's all you have to do. Nothing else.

'This twenty here. I want you divided into two shifts like the others. Your job will be serving tea and meals to the family. Nothing else.

'These forty. Again, two shifts. Your job is to look after the shrine: lighting fresh joss-sticks, keeping the lamps in oil, changing the drapes. You will also take turns by the spirit tablet, making offerings of rice and tea, kotowing when the visitors kotow, wailing when they wail. That is your job and nothing else besides.

'You four are to look after the cups and plates and so forth in the ladies' tea-room. If anything is missing, you share the responsibility between you and a quarter of the cost will be stopped out of each of your wages.

'You four here are to look after the dinner-ware: bowls, wine-cups and the like. Anything missing will be stopped out of your wages.

'This eight here. I want you to take charge of all funeral offerings sent in from outside.

'This eight. I want you to look after oil, candles, and paper-offerings. I'm going to put the whole lot in your charge; then whenever any is needed somewhere, you must go to wherever it is and supply them with whatever amount I tell you to.

'This twenty here. I want you doing night duty by rota. You are to see that all the gates are locked and keep a look-out for fires. You'll also be responsible for keeping the outside properly swept.

'The rest of you are to be divided up between the different apartments. Each of you will be responsible for the things in your own apartment, from furniture and antique ware down to spittoons and dusters. If the tiniest sliver gets lost or broken, you will be held responsible and will be expected to make it good.

'Lai Sheng's wife will make a general inspection every day, and if she catches anyone idling or gambling or drinking or fighting or being difficult, she will at once bring them to me for dealing with. And there will be no favouritism. If I find you've done something wrong, I shan't care whether you've been in service here for three or four generations, it will make no difference to me.

'Well, now you all know the rules. From now on whenever any trouble occurs I shall know exactly who to hold respon-sible.

'Those who are used to working with me at the other place always have a watch handy, and everything they do, no matter how small a thing it is, is done at a fixed time. You may not have watches, but at least there is a clock in your master's drawing-room you can look at. So here are the main times to remember. At half past six I shall come over to hear the roll-call. At ten o'clock I take my lunch. I shall see people with reports to make or tallies to collect up to, but not after, eleven o'clock. At seven in the evening, as soon as the paper-offerings have been burnt, I shall make a personal tour of inspection; and when I get back from it, I shall issue those on night duty with their keys. Then next day I shall be back here again at half past six.

'I dare say we are all going to be a bit overworked during the days ahead, but I am sure your master will want to reward you all for your trouble when this is over.'

Xi-feng now proceeded to supervise the distribution of supplies of tea, oil, candles, feather-dusters, and brooms to some of her work-parties, and to issue others with table-cloths, chair-covers, cushions, mats, spittoons, footstools, and other furnishings, an entry of the amount supplied being made in the book as each consignment was handed over.

A clear record now existed of what individuals were in charge of which parts of the household, what items they were responsible for, and what duties they were expected to per-form. Gone now were the days when everyone picked the easiest tasks to do first and the less popular ones never got carried out; gone the convenient disorder in which objects had so easily strayed (no one ever knew how) from the rooms where they belonged. Even with the greatly increased coming and going occasioned by the bereavement, it was quieter now than it had been before, when muddle and confusion still pre-vailed. And the old idling and pilfering appeared to have been eradicated completely. Secure in her authority, respected and obeyed by all, Xi-feng might be forgiven for contemplating her achievement with a certain amount of satisfaction.

Meanwhile You-shi was still unwell and Cousin Zhen too crushed by his somewhat disproportionate grief to think much about eating and drinking. Xi-feng accordingly had all sorts of invalid slops for You-shi and tempting little delicacies for Cousin Zhen prepared in the kitchens of the Rong-guo man-sion and sent over each day to the prostrate couple. Cousin Zhen reciprocated by instructing his own cooks to prepare dishes of the very highest quality exclusively for Xi-feng and having them carried round to her in her little penthouse office.

Xi-feng seemed quite tireless in the discharge of her extra

duties. Every morning she would be over at the appointed hour to hear the roll-call and would sit there alone in her office, never once emerging to mix with the young Ning-guo women of her own generation. Even when lady visitors arrived she remained in the office and took no part in their reception.

The Thirty-fifth had now arrived – an important day in the penitential cycle of seven times seven days preceding the funeral – and the monks in the main hall had reached a particularly dramatic part of their ceremonies. Having opened up a way for the imprisoned souls, the chief celebrant had succeeded by means of spells and incantations in breaking open the gates of hell. He had shone his light (a little hand-mirror) for the souls in darkness. He had confronted Yama, the Judge of the Dead. He had seized the demon torturers who resisted his progress. He had invoked Kṣitigarbha, the Saviour King, to aid him. He had raised up a golden bridge, and now, by means of a little flag which he held aloft in one hand, was conducting over it those souls from the very deepest pit of hell who still remained undelivered.

Meanwhile the ninety-nine Taoists in the Celestial Fragrance Pavilion were on their knees offering up a written petition to the Three Pure Ones and calling on the Jade Emperor himself in his heavenly palace. Outside, on their high staging, with swinging of censers and scattering of little cakes for the hungry ghosts to feed on, Zen monks were performing the great Water Penitential. And in the shrine where the coffin stood, six young monks and six young nuns, magnificently attired in scarlet slippers and embroidered copes, sat before the spirit tablet quietly murmuring the *dharani* that would assist the soul of the dead woman on the most difficult part of its journey into the underworld. Everywhere there was a hum of activity.

Knowing that the day would be a busy one bringing a greater than usual number of visitors, Xi-feng had risen at four o'clock in the morning to begin her toilet. By the time she had completed it, paid her daily tribute to nature, washed her hands, drunk a few mouthfuls of milk, and rinsed out her mouth, it was already half past six and Brightie's wife, at the head of the other female domestics, had been waiting for some considerable time in the courtyard outside. At last she emerged and stepped into the waiting carriage. Two horn lanterns inscribed in large characters with the words

RONG-GUO HOUSE

were borne before her as she went.

The great gate of the Ning-guo mansion was hung with lanterns and there were rows of identical standard lanterns on each side of the gateway illuminating the entrance with the brightness of noonday and eerily emphasizing the whiteness of the mourning-clothes worn by the menservants lined up to receive the carriage. At their invitation it was drawn in through the centremost of the three gates. Then the menservants retired and Xi-feng's own women hurried forward and raised the curtain of the carriage for her to descend. She did so, leaning on the shoulder of her maid Felicity, and the two women with the lanterns led her in, lighting the way for her as they went, while her other women closed in behind her and the women of the Ning-guo household advanced to meet her, curtseyed, and chorused their morning greetings.

Xi-feng walked slowly through the All-scents Garden until she came to the shrine in the Ascension Pavilion. As soon as she caught sight of the coffin the tears, like pearls from a broken necklace, rolled in great drops down her cheeks. A number of pages were standing stiffly in the courtyard outside awaiting the command to set fire to the paper offerings. Xi-feng gave orders for them to begin and for tea to be offered up inside the shrine. At once there was a clash of cymbals followed by the mournful strains of a funeral band. An armchair had already been called for and set down facing the spirit tablet. In this Xi-feng now sat, and raising her voice to a shrill pitch, wept with abandon, whereupon the entire household, high and low, male and female, indoors and out, responded by breaking into loud and prolonged lamentation.

Presently a representative of Cousin Zhen and You-shi arrived and begged Xi-feng to desist. Brightie's wife poured out a cup of tea for her to rinse her mouth with, and when she had sufficiently recovered herself she rose to her feet once more, took leave of various members of the clan who were present, and went off to her office in the penthouse.

An inspection of the roster showed that all the members of her work-parties were present except for one woman belonging to the group responsible for the reception of friends of the family. Someone was sent to fetch her, and presently the woman arrived, flustered and fearful.

'So it is you!' said Xi-feng with a chilling smile. 'I suppose you thought that because you have a somewhat more lady-like job than the rest, you could afford to disobey my orders!'

'Oh no, madam, indeed not!' said the woman. 'I've been coming extra early every day. It's only today, because I overslept, that I'm a bit late. Please let me off this once, madam! It really is the first time.'

Just at that moment Xi-feng observed Wang Xing's wife from the Rong-guo mansion, peeping round the door as if looking for a chance to speak to her.

'Yes, what is it?' she asked, turning away from the offender but giving her no indication that she might go.

Wang Xing's wife approached and said that she wanted a tally authorizing the purchase of silk cord to be made up into carriage trimmings for the funeral. She handed Xi-feng a slip of paper on which the order was written. It specified the number of network trimmings that would be required for two large sedans, four small sedans, and four carriages, and the number of pounds of silk cord that would be required for that amount of network. Xi-feng made Sunshine read it out to her, and having satisfied herself that the figures were correct, told him to enter them in his book and to issue Wang Xing's wife with one of the Rong-guo tallies, whereupon the latter hurried off to complete her mission.

Xi-feng was about to address the latecomer when four more servants from the Rong-guo mansion came in asking for tallies. She told them to hand over the order-slips and made Sunshine read them out to her. Two of them contained errors, and Xi-feng flung them down and told the bearers to 'go away and come back when they had got their figures right'. The two of them went off crestfallen.

Xi-feng next observed Zhang Cai's wife hovering about at the edge of the room and asked her what she wanted.

'It's those carriage curtains, ma'am. We want the money for the tailor who made them up.'

Xi-feng took the bill and told Sunshine to enter the figures from it in his book. But she would not authorize Zhang Cai's wife to pay for the tailoring until Wang Xing's wife had returned the tally for the material used and the buyer's receipt. There was a second piece of paper which Sunshine now read, requesting permission to purchase paper for the windows of Bao-yu's outer study, which had just been redecorated. This too Xi-feng kept, and made Sunshine enter the amount in his book. She told Zhang Cai's wife that the goods must be supplied first before any payment could be authorized.

'Tomorrow another one will be late and the day after that it will be someone else,' said Xi-feng turning to the still waiting offender, 'and before we know where we are we shall have no one turning up at all. I should have liked to let you off, but if I'm lenient with you the first time, it will be that much harder for me to deal with someone else the second time; so I am obliged to make an example of you.' Her face hardened as she pronounced sentence: 'Take her out and give her twenty strokes of the bamboo!'

Seeing that Xi-feng was really angry, the servants dared not show themselves slack in executing her command. The wretched woman was half-dragged from the room and the flogging administered in full view of the waiting throng, after which they came in again, the executioners to report that they had discharged their duty and their victim to thank Xi-feng for her punishment. Xi-feng threw down one of the Ning-guo tallies.

'Take this to Lai Sheng and tell him to stop a month's pay from her wages. If anyone is late tomorrow they will get forty strokes and the day after that it will be sixty. So if you enjoy being beaten you have only to come late for roll-call. Dismiss.'

The servants, including the shamefaced and silently weeping victim, trooped off to their various duties.

Now began a steady stream of servants from both households collecting and returning tallies, each of whom Xi-feng attended to in a brisk and efficient manner.

From that day onwards the staff of the Ning-guo mansion

realized just how formidable Xi-feng could be and went about their duties in fear and trembling, not daring to idle or delay.

*

But let us now turn to Bao-yu.

On this particular occasion, fearing that with so great an influx of visitors Qin Zhong might find himself somewhat overwhelmed, Bao-yu brought him round to Xi-feng's office for a quiet chat.

'Did you smell the food?' said Xi-feng with a laugh. (She was halfway through her lunch when they entered.) 'Come up on the kang and have some!'

'Thank you, but we have already eaten,' said Bao-yu.

'Here, or in the other house?'

'Catch me eating here with those clowns!' said Bao-yu. 'No, back at home, with Grandmother.'

He and Qin Zhong sat down, and presently Xi-feng finished her lunch. Just then a woman came in asking for a tally with which to obtain a fresh supply of oil for the altar lamps.

'I calculated that you would be needing some by now,' said Xi-feng with a smile. 'I thought you must have forgotten. If you *had* forgotten, you'd have had to pay for it yourself. That would have suited me down to the ground!'

'Oh no, madam! As you say, I just forgot. I only thought of it a moment ago, and I realized that if I didn't hurry I should be too late to get a tally.'

So saying, she took her tally and went. For a short while longer the handing over of tallies and registering of amounts continued.

'Both your houses use these tallies for everything,' said Qin Zhong, who had been watching these transactions with some interest. 'Suppose some outsider were to forge one and use it to get a lot of money with?'

'Not everyone is as crooked as you are!' said Xi-feng good-humouredly.

'How is it that there is no one from *our* place coming in for tallies?' Bao-yu asked.

'At the time when *they* come,' Xi-feng replied, 'you are still fast asleep in bed. Now let me ask *you* something. When are you going to begin studying at night?'

'I should like nothing better than to begin today,' said Bao-yu. 'But what can I do if they won't get on with my study?'

'If you were to ask me nicely,' said Xi-feng jovially, 'I think *I* could undertake to hurry them up for you.'

'Oh, *you're* no good,' said Bao-yu, 'no more than any of the rest. They'll get round to it in time. It's just a question of waiting till they do.'

'Whether they get round to it or not,' said Xi-feng, 'they still need materials for the job, and they can't get the materials if I don't choose to give them the tallies – I can tell you that for sure!'

As soon as he heard this, Bao-yu twined himself round Xi-feng and began coaxing and wheedling her to give the workmen the tallies that would enable them to begin work on his study.

'Stop it! Stop it!' cried Xi-feng. 'I am so tired that my bones ache. How can I stand up to being mauled about by a great ape like you? You needn't worry. They've just been round to see about paper for the windows. It would look pretty stupid if you were to send them off for something they have already got.'

Bao-yu refused to believe her until she made Sunshine look up the entry in his book and show it to him.

While Bao-yu was inspecting the book, a servant announced the arrival of Shiner, one of the boys who had accompanied Jia Lian to Yangchow. Xi-feng eagerly ordered him in. Shiner louted to his mistress in the Manchu fashion and hoped that she was well.

'Why have you come back?' said Xi-feng.

'The Master sent me, ma'am. Mr Lin died on the third at ten in the morning and the Master and Miss Lin are taking him to Soochow to be buried. They expect to be home by the end of the spring. The Master told me to bring back the news and to give everyone his regards, and he said I was to ask Her Old Ladyship for instructions. He also told me to see if you were getting on all right, ma'am; and he said would I take some fur-lined gowns back with me for winter wear.'

'Have you seen anyone else yet?' Xi-feng asked him.

'Yes, everyone,' said Shiner, and withdrew.

Xi-feng turned to Bao-yu with a smile:

'It looks now as if your Cousin Lin will be staying with us permanently.'

'Poor thing!' said Bao-yu. 'How she must have cried and cried during this past week or so!' The thought of her crying made him knit his brows and sigh.

Now that Shiner was back, Xi-feng was all agog to question him about Jia Lian but could not do so in any detail in front of the others. She would have liked to follow him back home, but her duties were by no means over, and she was obliged to hold out until evening. Then, back in her own apartment, she summoned him to her and asked him for full particulars of the journey. She looked out all Jia Lian's furs, and she and Patience sat up into the night getting them ready and packing them – together with anything else which careful thought suggested might be needed – for Shiner to take back with him to his Master. Xi-feng gave Shiner minute instructions concerning his conduct towards the latter:

'Mind you look after your master properly away from home, now. Try not to make him angry. And do always be on at him not to drink too much. And don't encourage him to get mixed up with bad women. If, when you get back, I find out that you *have* done, I'll break your legs!'

Shiner laughingly agreed to abide by all her instructions. By the time they got to bed it was well past one in the morning. To Xi-feng it seemed as though she had barely lain down to sleep when it was dawn once more and time to get up again and wash and dress for another round of duties at Ning-guo House.

The day of the funeral was now approaching and Cousin Zhen took an expert in geomancy with him in his carriage and drove out to the Temple of the Iron Threshold to inspect the terrain and personally assist in the selection of a suitable resting-place for Qin-shi's coffin. He gave detailed instructions to the monk-in-charge, Father Sublimitas, for the provision of a completely new set of hangings and altar furnishings for the funeral, and for the engagement of as many fashionable monks as he could think of to participate in the ceremony of receiving the coffin.

Sublimitas hurriedly prepared a vegetarian supper for his visitors; but Cousin Zhen had little heart for eating, and, as it was by now too late to return to the city, presently retired to a bed that had been made up for him in the monk's quarters, leaving first thing next morning in order to press on with arrangements for the funeral. On his return he sent some workmen out to the temple to refurbish the place he had chosen for the coffin. They were instructed to work on the job throughout the night in order to make sure that it was finished in time. He also sent out a number of kitchen staff to cater for the funeral party on its arrival.

Xi-feng, too, began to make her own careful preparations as the day of the funeral drew near. On the one hand she had to select coachmen and bearers from the Rong-guo staff for the carriages and sedans that Lady Wang and the other Rong-guo ladies would ride in in the procession. On the other hand, as she fully intended to take part in it herself, she had to find herself somewhere to stop at on the way as well as accommodation for the night after the funeral.

The Dowager-duchess of Shan-guo happened to die just about this time and Xi-feng had to make the arrangements for Lady Xing and Lady Wang when they paid their visits of condolence and later when they attended the funeral. She had to see about birthday presents for the Princess of Xi-an. She had to write to her parents and get things ready to send to them when her elder brother Wang Ren returned with his wife and children to the South. And when on top of all this Jia Lian's young sister Ying-chun fell ill and needed doctors' visits and medicines every day, it was Xi-feng who had to puzzle over the diagnostic reports, discuss the patient's symptoms with the learned physicians, and decide on the relative merits of rival prescriptions.

Indeed, so multifarious had her activities become that it would be impossible to list them all. As a consequence she was far too busy to pay much attention to eating and drinking and could hardly sit or lie down for a moment in peace. When she went to the Ning-guo mansion she was followed around all the time by people from the Rong-guo mansion, and when she went back to Rong-guo House, members of the Ning-guo establishment would trail after her. Yet although she was so busy, a passion to succeed and a dread of being criticized enabled her to summon up reserves of energy, and she managed to plan everything with such exemplary thoroughness that every member of the clan was loud in her praises.

Wake night arrived – the night when no one in the family may go to bed – and Ning-guo House was crowded with friends and relations. Since You-shi was still confined to her room, it was left entirely to Xi-feng to do the honours. There were, to be sure, a number of other young married women in the clan, but all were either tongue-tied or giddy, or they were so petrified by bashfulness or timidity that the presence of strangers or persons of higher rank threw them into a state of panic. Xi-feng's vivacious charm and social assurance stood out in striking contrast – 'a touch of scarlet in a field of green'. She was in her element, and if she took any notice at all of her humbler sisters it was only to throw out an occasional order or to bend them in some other way to her imperious will.

Throughout the whole of that night the Ning-guo mansion was ablaze with lights. There was a constant bustle of guests being welcomed or seen off the premises and all the liveliness and excitement that is customary on occasions of this sort.

With the dawning of the day and the arrival of the hour deemed auspicious for its departure, sixty-four green-coated bearers arrived for the coffin, preceded by a great funeral banner bearing the following inscription:

Mortal Remains
of the
Much Lamented
LADY QIN-SHI
of the
House of Jia,
Senior Great-great-granddaughter-in-law
of the
Duke of Ning-guo,
Nobleman of the First Rank by Imperial Patent,
and Wife of the
Right Honourable Jia Rong,

Honorary Captain in the Imperial Bodyguard,
Inner Palace, Northern Capital Division.

The costumes, insignia, and funeral trappings were all glitteringly new, having been specially made for the occasion.

Jewel, acting in the capacity of unmarried daughter of the deceased, smashed a bowl on the floor at the foot of the coffin and as they bore it out walked in front with an impressive display of grief.

Among the distinguished guests taking part in the procession were:

Niu Ji-zong (earl, hereditary first rank), grandson of Niu Qing, Duke of Zhen-guo,

Liu Fang (viscount, hereditary first rank), grandson of Liu Biao, Duke of Li-guo,

Chen Rui-wen (Maj.-General), grandson of Chen Yi, Duke of Qi-guo,

Ma Shang-de (Maj.-General), grandson of Ma Kui, Duke of Zhi-guo,

Hou Xiao-kang (viscount, hereditary first rank), grandson of Hou Xiao-ming, Duke of Xiu-guo.

The grandfathers of the above, together with the Duke of Shan-guo, whose grandson Shi Guang-zhu was in mourning for the Dowager-duchess and unable to attend, and the Dukes of Rong-guo and Ning-guo, had formed the well-known group often referred to by their contemporaries as the 'Eight Dukes'.

The other mourners included:

The grandson of H.H. the Prince of Nan-an,

The grandson of H.H. the Prince of Xi-ning,

Shi Ding, Marquis of Zhong-jing, nephew of old Lady Jia,

Jiang Zi-ning (baron, hereditary second rank), grandson of the Marquis of Ping-yuan,

Xie Kun (baron, hereditary second rank, and lieutenant-colonel, Metropolitan Barracks), grandson of the Marquis of Ding-cheng,

Qi Jian-hui (baron, hereditary second rank), grandson of the Marquis of Xiang-yang,

Qiu Liang (Chief Commissioner of Police, Metropolitan Area), grandson of the Marquis of Jing-tian.

Also present were the Marquis of Jin-xiang's son Han Qi,

General Feng's son Feng Zi-ying, General Chen's son Chen Ye-jun, General Wei's son Wei Ruo-lan, and a large number of other young gentlemen of distinguished parentage.

As for lady guests, there were ten or so large and thirty or forty small palanquins, which together with the palanquins and carriages of the Jia ladies brought the total number of equipages to at least a hundred and ten. These, with the innumerable bearers of insignia and other funeral trappings up at the front, formed a procession altogether more than a mile long.

The procession had not advanced very far when it began to pass the decorated 'funeral bowers' and tables of offerings put up along the sides of the street by friends and well-wishers of the family. From some of them the strains of funeral music struck up as it approached.

The first of these bowers was the Princess of Dong-ping's, the second was the Prince of Nan-an's, the third was the Prince of Xi-ning's, and the fourth that of the Prince of Bei-jing.

Of the original holders of these four titles the Prince of Bei-jing had been highest in imperial favour by virtue of his great services to the Crown. As a consequence, the title and the style of 'prince' had been retained by his descendants. The present holder of the title, Shui Rong, was a youth still in his teens – a young man of great personal beauty and a modest and unaffected disposition. On receiving the announcement of the premature demise of the wife of one of the Duke of Ning-guo's descendants, Shui Rong was reminded of the friendship that had formerly existed between the Duke of Ning-guo and his own ancestor – both having fought in the same campaigns and shared hardships and triumphs together – and resolved to lay aside all considerations of rank in demonstrating his sympathy for the bereaved. Two days previously he had paid a visit of condolence and made inquiries about the funeral arrangements, and now, today, intending to make a libation to the coffin as it went by, he had had his booth constructed at the roadside and had instructed a number of his staff to wait there in readiness for his arrival.

At four o'clock that morning the prince had had to be present at the imperial palace for the early levée; but, as soon as his business there was over, he changed out of court dress and into mourning and after getting into his great palanquin, was borne through the streets, preceded by gongs and umbrellas of state, to the place where his funeral bower had been erected. There his palanquin was set down and the gentlemen of his household ranged themselves on either side of it. The street was kept clear of traffic and pedestrians while he waited.

Presently the procession came in sight, advancing from the north end of the street like a great river, the hearse itself looking like some great silver mountain that crushed the earth beneath it as it moved. In a trice the forerunners had reported back to Cousin Zhen, who at once gave orders to the insignia bearers to halt, and hurrying forward with his Uncles Jia She and Jia Zheng, saluted the prince with full court etiquette. The prince received their prostrations with a gracious smile and a slight inclination of his person inside the palanquin, and when he spoke to them it was not as a prince to a subject, but using the form of address he employed when speaking to family friends.

'Your Highness, I am quite overwhelmed by the honour you do us in graciously condescending to be present at the funeral of my daughter-in-law,' said Cousin Zhen.

'My dear friend,' said the Prince of Bei-jing, 'your excessive modesty does us both an injustice.'

Thereupon he turned to the chamberlain of his household and ordered him to make offerings on his behalf. Cousin Zhen and his uncles made the correct ritual responses while this official performed them, then returned to the palanquin and bowed their thanks to the prince. The prince received their thanks with a most becoming modesty and by way of conversation asked Jia Zheng a question about Bao-yu:

'Which is the boy who was born with a stone in his mouth? I have long looked forward to the pleasure of meeting him. I am sure he must be here today. Can you not bring him to see me?'

Jia Zheng at once withdrew to fetch Bao-yu. He made him first change into court dress before leading him forward to meet the prince.

Bao-yu had often heard about the Prince of Bei-jing. He had heard that he was very clever. He had also heard that he was as handsome as he was clever and that he was a quite jolly, unconventional sort of person who refused to let either his royal birth or the conventions of official life constrain him. He had often wanted to meet him, but had been deterred by his father's strictness from doing so. And now here was the Prince of Bei-jing asking to see *him*! A feeling of pleasant anticipation filled him as he hurried forward with his father. He peeped up at the prince as they advanced and saw that he was, as report had painted him, an extremely good-looking young man.

But if you want to know about his interview with the handsome prince, you will have to read about it in the next chapter.

CHAPTER 15

At Water-moon Priory Xi-feng finds how much profit may be procured by the abuse of power
And Qin Zhong discovers the pleasures that are to be had under the cover of darkness

Looking up, Bao-yu saw that Shui Rong's princely headgear was embellished by way of mourning with white bands, a white hatpin, and filigree silver 'wings'. As a further token of mourning his robe, though heavily bordered with a 'tooth and wave' design of rainbow-coloured stripes and gold-emblazoned with the royal five-clawed dragon, was of a white material. It was confined at the waist by a red leather belt, studded with green jade. The splendid costume, the luminous eyes, the finely chiselled features really did make him an arrestingly handsome young man. Bao-yu started forward impulsively to make his salutation, but the prince extended an arm from the palanquin and prevented him from kneeling.

Bao-yu was wearing a little silver coronet on the top of his head and a silver headband round his brow in the form of two dragons emerging from the sea. He had on a narrow-sleeved, full-skirted robe of white material and a silver belt inlaid with pearls. After studying these and admiring the flowerlike face and coal-black eyes, the prince's face broke into a smile.

'If "Bao-yu" means "precious jade", you are appropriately named,' he said. 'But where is the famous stone you were born with?'

Bao-yu hurriedly extracted the jade from inside his clothing and taking it off, handed it to the prince, who scrutinized it carefully, reciting the words of the inscription as he deciphered them.

'And does it really have these powers?' he asked.

'It is only alleged to,' Jia Zheng put in hastily. 'We have never put them to the test.'

The prince pronounced the stone a great wonder and with his own hands refastened its plaited silken cord round Bao-yu's neck. Then, taking one of Bao-yu's hands in his own, he asked him how old he was, what books he was studying, and other such questions, to all of which Bao-yu gave prompt replies.

Delighted that everything Bao-yu said was so clear and to the point, the prince observed to Jia Zheng that 'the young phoenix was worthy of his sire'.

'I trust I shall not offend you by saying so to your face,' he said, 'but I venture to prophesy that this fledgling of yours will one day "sing sweeter than the parent bird".'

Jia Zheng smiled politely.

'My son is doubtless unworthy of the compliment Your Highness is good enough to pay him. If, thanks to your encouragement, he turns out as you say, we shall count ourselves truly fortunate.'

'There is only one drawback in possessing such charm,' said the prince. 'I am sure it must make his grandmother dote upon him; and, unfortunately, being the object of too much affection is very bad for people of our years. It leads us to neglect our studies. This used at one time to be the case with me, and I suspect is now the case with your son. If he *does* find difficulty in working at home, he would be very welcome to come round to my palace. I do not pretend to be a gifted person myself, but I am fortunate in counting distinguished writers from all over the empire among my acquaintances, and my palace is a rendezvous for them when they are in the capital, so that I never want for intellectual company. By constantly mixing and conversing with such people at my palace, your son could do much to improve his education.'

'Yes.' Jia Zheng bowed deferentially.

The Prince of Bei-jing removed a rosary from his wrist and handed it to Bao-yu.

'Today is our first meeting, but as it was an unforeseen one, I have not come prepared with a suitable gift. All I can offer you is this rosary made of the aromatic seeds of some Indian plant. It was given me by His Imperial Majesty. I hope you will accept it as a little token of my esteem.'

Bao-yu took the rosary and turning back offered it respectfully to Jia Zheng, who made his son join him in formally thanking the prince for his gift.

At this point Jia She and Cousin Zhen knelt before the prince and invited him to return.

'The Departed is now in paradise,' said the prince. 'Though I enjoy imperial favour and princely rank, I would not presume to go past her carriage. Heavenly honours take precedence over earthly ones!'

When they saw that the prince was adamant, Jia She and the rest bowed their thanks, then, having ordered the musicians to vail their instruments and march by in silence, they caused the front part of the procession and the hearse to pass over the junction. As soon as the hearse had gone over, the prince and his retinue crossed in the other direction, after which the rear part of the procession moved forward and caught up with the rest.

*

The liveliness which attended the procession during the whole of its progress through the city reached a climax as it approached the city gate, for it was along this last stretch that the colleagues and office juniors of Jia She, Jia Zheng and Cousin Zhen had arranged their bowers, and it was necessary to stop and thank each one of them as they made their offerings to the passing hearse. They did at last succeed in getting out of the city gate, however, after which a clear road lay ahead all the way to the Temple of the Iron Threshold. Cousin Zhen went round with Jia Rong to the senior men among the mourners and invited them to proceed from there onwards by the transport provided. The upshot was that those of Jia She's generation got into carriages and sedans, while Cousin Zhen and the younger men mounted on horseback.

Xi-feng was worried about Bao-yu. Out in the country, she thought, he was liable to become wild and disobedient. She felt sure that he would get up to some kind of mischief now that he was removed from Jia Zheng's restraint. Accordingly she sent one of her pages to summon him, and presently he rode up to her carriage.

'Bao dear,' said Xi-feng, 'a person of your refinement belongs here with us. You don't want to go clomping around the countryside like apes on horseback with those horrid men!

Why not get in with me? The two of us will keep each other company.'

Bao-yu at once dismounted and climbed up into the carriage, and the two of them drove on, laughing and chattering as they went. They had not been driving very long when two horse-men galloped up beside them, dismounted, and leaning into the carriage, informed Xi-feng that they were now near her stopping-place, in case she wished to get out and 'stretch her legs'. Xi-feng sent them on ahead to ask Lady Xing and Lady Wang for instructions. The latter sent back word that they had no desire to stop, themselves, but that Xi-feng was wel-come to do so if she wished. Xi-feng accordingly gave orders for a short halt. At once the pages led the horses out of the main stream of traffic and headed northwards down a small side-road.

Bao-yu hurriedly sent someone off to fetch Qin Zhong, who was riding along behind his father's sedan. As the page came hurrying up and asked him to stop with Bao-yu for a little refreshment, he turned round and saw Bao-yu's horse in the distance, jogging along in a northerly direction with an empty saddle on its back behind Xi-feng's carriage, and he realized that Bao-yu must be inside the carriage with Xi-feng. Turning his horse's head about, he hurried after, and followed them into the gateway of a farm.

Apart from the barns and outhouses, the farmhouse con-sisted of little more than a single large room, so that there was nowhere the farmer's womenfolk could go to be out of the way of the visitors. The sudden appearance in their midst of Xi-feng, Bao-yu and Qin Zhong with their fashionable clothes and delicate city faces seemed to these simple countrywomen more like a celestial visitation than a human one.

As soon as they were inside the thatched central building, Xi-feng asked the boys to amuse themselves outside. Bao-yu realized that she needed to be alone, and conducted Qin Zhong and the pages on a tour of the farmyard. He had never in his life seen any of the farming implements before, and was very curious. One of his pages who had some experience of country matters was able to name each implement for him and explain its functions. Bao-yu was impressed.

'Now I can understand the words of the old poet,' he said:

> 'Each grain of rice we ever ate
> Cost someone else a drop of sweat.'

At that moment they came to an outhouse in which was a kang with a spinning-wheel on it. Bao-yu was even more intrigued.

'That's for spinning yarn with to make cloth out of,' said the pages.

Bao-yu at once got up on the kang and had just started to turn it when a country lass of seventeen or eighteen summers came running up:

'Don't! You'll spoil it!'

She was shouted at fiercely by the pages, but Bao-yu had already stayed his hand.

'I'm sorry. I've never seen one before. I was just turning it for fun, to see how it works.'

'You don't know how to turn it properly,' said the girl. 'Let me show you how 'tis done.'

Qin Zhong gave Bao-yu a sly tug:

'A comely damosel, thinkest thou nottest?'

'Shut up, or I'll clout you!' said Bao-yu, pushing him.

During this muttered exchange the girl had begun spinning. She did, indeed, make a charming picture as she bent over her work. Suddenly an old woman's voice called out from the other side of the yard:

'Ertie! Come here at once my gal.'

The girl jumped up from her spinning and hurried over. Bao-yu's spirits were quite dashed by her abrupt departure.

But just then someone came from Xi-feng inviting the boys indoors. They found her washed and changed. She asked them if they wanted to 'change' too, but Bao-yu replied that they did not. Then a variety of cakes and sweets were brought in by the servants, and fragrant tea was poured for them to drink. When the three had taken their fill of these refreshments and everything had been cleared away and re-packed by the servants, they rose up and got back into their carriage.

Outside in the yard Brightie handed the farmer's family their payment, which he had brought with him ready-wrapped in coloured paper, and the womenfolk hurried up to the carriage to express their thanks. Bao-yu scanned their faces carefully, but could not see his spinning-girl amongst them. They had not driven far, however, when he caught sight of her at the end of the village. She was standing watching for him beside the road, a baby brother in her arms and two little girls at her side. Bao-yu could not repress a strong emotion on seeing her, but sitting there in the carriage there was not much he could do but gaze back at her soulfully; and soon, as the carriage bowled along at a smarter pace, Ertie was lost to sight for ever.

With talk and laughter to beguile them, the journey passed quickly. Soon they had caught up with the main procession; soon the sound of drums and cymbals was heard and they could see ahead of them the banners and umbrellas of the monks from the Temple of the Iron Threshold who had come out in procession and lined either side of the road to welcome them; and soon they were inside the temple, where further ceremonies awaited them, a new staging having been erected for this purpose. The coffin was installed in one of the side-chapels leading off the inner hall, and Jewel arranged her sleeping-quarters near by to continue her watch over it.

In the outer hall Cousin Zhen was busy attending to his guests, some of whom were staying on, while others wished to leave immediately. To each he tendered formal thanks for their trouble in coming. They left in order of seniority; duke's kin going first, then those of marquises, then those of earls, then those of viscounts, then those of barons, and so on downwards. It was three o'clock by the time the last of them had gone.

Xi-feng received the lady guests inside. They, too, left in order of precedence and had not finally dispersed until around two o'clock. Only members of the clan and a few very close friends stayed behind to see the ceremonies through to their conclusion two days later.

Lady Xing and Lady Wang were among those who left. They could see that Xi-feng would be unable to return that day and wanted to take Bao-yu back with them into town. But Bao-yu, after his first taste of the countryside, was extremely loth to return and begged to stay with Xi-feng; so Lady Wang went without him, leaving him in Xi-feng's charge.

The Temple of the Iron Threshold was a private foundation of the Dukes of Ning-guo and Rong-guo which still had some land of its own in which members of the clan who died in the capital could be given temporary burial. The thoughtful Dukes had provided accommodation not only for the dead but also for the living, in the form of guest-rooms in which mourners might temporarily reside until their funereal business was over. What the old gentlemen had not foreseen was that their multitudinous progeny would come in time to exhibit differences of wealth and temperament so extreme as often to render their possessors mutually intolerable and that, whereas the more hard-up members of the clan gladly occupied the accommodation provided, the more affluent or pretentious found it 'inconvenient' to stay there and preferred to seek alternative accommodation in the farmsteads and convents round about.

Xi-feng was among those who found the Iron Threshold accommodation 'inconvenient'. Some time previously she had sent someone to Wheatcake Priory to make arrangements on her behalf with the prioress Euergesia, and the old nun had turned out several rooms in readiness for her arrival. 'Wheatcake Priory' (so-called because of the excellent steamed wheatbread made in its kitchens) was the popular name for Water-moon Priory, an offshoot of Water-moon Abbey situated at no great distance from the Temple of the Iron Threshold.

Presently, when the monks had finished their service and the evening offering of tea had been made, Cousin Zhen sent Jia Rong in to Xi-feng with a message inviting her to retire. Having first glanced round to ascertain that a sufficient number of Jia ladies were present to look after the still remaining guests, Xi-feng bade the company good night and left for Wheatcake Priory with Bao-yu and Qin Zhong. Qin Zhong had attached himself to the other two when his father Qin Bang-ye, unable by reason of his age and frail state of health to risk a night away from home, had gone back to the city, leaving him to await the conclusion of the requiem services on his own.

They soon arrived at the priory and were met by Euergesia, who had brought her two little disciples Benevolentia and Sapientia to welcome them. As soon as the first greetings were over, Xi-feng retired to her room to wash and change. Emerging refreshed, she observed how much taller Sapientia had grown and how radiantly good-looking, and inquired of Euergesia why she and her two charges had lately not been into town to see them.

'It is on account of Mr Hu's good lady,' said the old nun. 'She has lately been brought to bed of a boy, and sent us ten taels of silver for a three-day recital of the *Lake of Blood* sūtra by some of the sisters to purge the stain of childbirth. We have been so busy with the arrangements that we haven't had time to call.'

Let us leave Xi-feng in conversation with the prioress and turn to the other two.

Qin Zhong and Bao-yu were amusing themselves in the main hall of the priory when Sapientia happened to pass through.

'Here's Sappy,' said Bao-yu with a meaningful smile.

'Well, what about it?' said Qin Zhong.

'Now, now, stop play-acting!' said Bao-yu. '*I* saw you holding her that day at Grandma's when you thought nobody else was about. You needn't think you can fool me after *that*!'

'I don't know what you're talking about.'

'All right then. Never mind whether you know what I'm talking about or not. Just ask her to pour me out a cup of tea, will you, and then we'll let the subject drop.'

'What sort of joke is this? Why can't you ask her yourself? She'd pour it out just the same for you. Why ask *me* to tell her?'

'I couldn't do it with the same feeling as you. There'll be much more feeling in it if you ask her.'

He finally prevailed upon Qin Zhong to make the request.

'Oh, all right! – Sappy, pour us a cup of tea, will you?'

Sapientia had been a regular visitor at the Rong-guo mansion ever since she was a little girl and was familiar with all its inmates. The innocence of her childish rompings with Bao-yu and Qin Zhong had latterly, however – now that she had reached adolescence – given way to a more mature emotion. She had fallen in love with Qin Zhong, whose every feature and lineament now inspired her with romantic feelings; and Qin Zhong, captivated by her developing charms, had responded by loving her back. Although nothing serious had as yet passed between them, in their inclinations and affections they were already united.

Sapientia hurried out and returned with a cup of tea.

'Give it to me, Sappy!' said Qin Zhong.

'No, give it to me, Sappy!' said Bao-yu.

She stood between them, pouting prettily, and gave a little laugh:

'Surely you're not going to fight over a cup of tea? I must have honey on my hands!'

Bao-yu snatched the cup before Qin Zhong could do so and began drinking. He was about to say something when Benevolentia came in and fetched Sapientia away to help her lay the table. She was back again presently to invite the two boys to tea and cakes; but neither of them felt much enthusiasm for such feminine repasts, and after sitting a short while for the sake of politeness, were soon off to amuse themselves elsewhere.

Xi-feng, too, soon left, and retired to her private room to rest, Euergesia accompanying her. By this time the older servants, seeing that there was nothing further for them to do, had one by one drifted off to bed, leaving only a few personal maids, all of whom were in Xi-feng's confidence, in attendance. The old nun deemed it safe to broach a private matter in their hearing.

'There is something I have been meaning to call at your house and ask Her Ladyship about, but I should like to have your opinion on it first before I see her.'

'What do you want to ask her?' said Xi-feng.

'Bless his Holy Name!' the prioress began piously. 'When I was a nun at the Treasures in Heaven Convent in Chang-an, one of the convent's benefactors was a very wealthy man called Zhang, who had a daughter called Jin-ge. A certain young Mr Li, who is brother-in-law to the Governor of Chang-an, met her once when she was making an incense-offering in our temple and took a violent liking to her. He at once sent someone to the parents to ask for her hand in marriage, but unfortunately she was already betrothed to the son of a captain in the Chang-an garrison and the betrothal-presents had already been accepted. The Zhangs would have liked to cancel the betrothal but were afraid that the captain would object, so they told Li's matchmaker that the girl was already engaged. But oh dear! young Mr Li wouldn't take no for an answer, and the Zhangs were quite at their wit's end, being now in trouble with both parties. You see, when the captain got to hear of these goings-on he was most unreasonable. He came rushing along in a great rage and made a most terrible scene. "Just how many young men is this girl betrothed to?" he said, and so on and so forth. He refused outright to take back the betrothal-gifts and straightway began an action for breach of promise. By now the Zhangs were really upset and sent to the capital for some moral support – for they are now quite determined to break off their daughter's engagement, seeing that the captain has been so unreasonable.

'Well, it occurred to me that the Area Commander for Chang-an, General Yun, is on very good terms with your husband's family, and I thought I might try to find some way of persuading Her Ladyship to talk to Sir Zheng about this and get him to write a letter to General Yun and ask him to have a word with this captain. It is hardly likely that he would refuse to obey his commanding officer. The Zhangs would gladly pay *anything* – even if it meant bankrupting themselves – in return for this kindness.'

Xi-feng laughed.

'It doesn't sound very difficult. The only difficulty is that Lady Wang doesn't touch this kind of thing any more.'

'If Her Ladyship won't, what about you, Mrs Lian?'

Xi-feng laughed again.

'I'm not short of money; and besides, I don't touch that sort of thing either.'

Euergesia's face assumed an expression of great benignity. After sitting for a while in silence she sighed.

'It's a pity I let the Zhangs know that I was going to talk to you about this,' she said. '*Now* if you don't do this favour for them, they will never believe that it is because you haven't the time or don't want the money; they will take it as a sign that you are not able.'

This put Xi-feng on her mettle.

'You've known me a long time,' she said. 'You know that I've never believed all that talk about hell and damnation. If I decide that I want to do something I do it, no matter what it is. Tell them that if they are prepared to pay out three thousand taels of silver, I will undertake to relieve them of their trouble.'

The prioress was delighted.

'They will! They will! No doubt about it!'

'Mind you,' said Xi-feng, 'I'm not one of your money-grubbing run-of-the-mill go-betweens. I'm not doing this for the money. Every bit of this three thousand taels will go into the pockets of my boys or towards their expenses. *I* shan't touch a penny of it. If it was money I wanted, I could lay my hands on *thirty* thousand taels at this very moment.'

'Well, that's nicely settled!' said the prioress. 'So can we look forward to your kind help in this matter tomorrow? We may as well get it over and done with.'

'You can see how busy I am and how impossible it is for me to get away,' said Xi-feng. 'I've told you I'll do it, and so I will – in my own time. Surely that is enough for you?'

'A little thing like this might seem a great deal of trouble to some people,' said the old nun artfully, 'but even if it involved more than it does, it would still be nothing to a capable person like you, Mrs Lian. You know what they say: "The able man gets little leisure" – that's why Her Ladyship leaves everything to you. She knows how capable you are. Of course, you have to be careful that you don't overtax yourself. Your health is precious!'

Soothed by such flatteries, Xi-feng forgot her weariness, and the conversation continued with animation.

Meanwhile Qin Zhong had taken advantage of the darkness and the fact that there was no one much about to prosecute his designs on Sapientia. He found her on her own in one of the rooms at the back of the priory washing up tea-things. Throwing his arms around her from behind, he gave her a kiss. Sapientia stamped with vexation:

'What are you doing? Stop it!'

She was about to call out, but Qin Zhong spoke entreatingly:

'Darling Sappy! I want you so desperately! If you won't let me, I'll just lie down and die!'

'If you want me,' said Sapientia, 'you must first get me out of this hole and away from these people. Then you can do what you like.'

'That's easy,' said Qin Zhong. 'But "distant water is no cure for a present thirst" . . .'

And with that he blew out the light, plunging the room into inky darkness, and carried Sapientia on to the kang. She struggled hard to get up – though still not daring to call out; but soon, almost before she knew it, her breech-clout was off and the ship was in the harbour.

Suddenly, in less time than it takes to tell, a third person bore down on them from above and held them fast. The intruder made no sound, and for some moments the other two lay underneath his weight, half dead with fright. Then there was a splutter of suppressed laughter and they knew that it was Bao-yu.

'What do you think you're playing at?' said Qin Zhong crossly, as he scrambled to his feet.

'If you won't let me, darling,' Bao-yu mimicked, 'I'll call out!'

Poor Sapientia was so overcome with shame that she slipped away in the dark. Bao-yu hauled Qin Zhong from the room.

'Now,' he said: 'are you *still* going to pretend that Sappy means nothing to you?'

'Look, be a good chap! I'll do anything you say as long as you promise not to shout.'

'We won't say any more about it just now,' said Bao-yu

genially. 'Wait until we are both in bed and I'll settle accounts with you then.'

Bedtime soon came and they partially undressed and settled down for the night, Xi-feng in an inner room and Bao-yu and Qin Zhong in an outer room adjoining it. As there were numerous old women on night duty lying about everywhere on the floor wrapped up in their bedding, Xi-feng was afraid that the 'Magic Jade' might disappear in the course of the night; so as soon as Bao-yu was in bed she sent someone to fetch it from him, and put it under her own pillow for safety.

As for the 'settling of accounts' that Bao-yu had proposed to Qin Zhong, we have been unable to ascertain exactly what form this took; and as we would not for the world be guilty of a fabrication, we must allow the matter to remain a mystery.

Next day someone arrived from Grandmother Jia and Lady Wang to see how Bao-yu was getting on. He was counselled to dress up well against the cold and to come back home if there was nothing further to do. Bao-yu was most unwilling to return on his own account, and his unwillingness was reinforced by the promptings of Qin Zhong, who was anxious to see more of Sapientia and urged him to ask Xi-feng for another day.

Xi-feng reflected a little. The main business of the funeral was now over, but a sufficient number of minor matters still remained to be done to justify their staying on another day if they wanted to. Three arguments in favour of staying presented themselves to her mind:

1. It would be a gesture of considerateness to Cousin Zhen which would increase his indebtedness to her.

2. It would give her a breathing-space in which to get Euergesia's business attended to.

3. It would make Bao-yu happy, which would put her in good odour with Grandmother Jia.

Having now made her mind up, Xi-feng acceded to Bao-yu's request in the following terms:

'My own business here is all finished now, but if you want to amuse yourselves a bit longer, I suppose I must resign myself to staying. However, we definitely *must* go back tomorrow.'

When Bao-yu heard this it was all 'dearest Feng' this and 'darling Feng' that, and he promised faithfully to return on the morrow without demur. Accordingly it was settled that they should stay for one more night.

Xi-feng immediately sent someone in great secrecy to explain Euergesia's business to Brightie. Brightie grasped the situation at once, hurried into town, sought out a public letter-writer, had a letter written in Jia Lian's name to the captain's commanding officer, and set off for Chang-an overnight bearing the spurious missive with him.

Chang-an is only thirty or so miles from the capital, so that Brightie could finish his business and be back again within a couple of days. The general's name was Yun Guang. He was indebted to the Jia family for a number of past kindnesses and was only too pleased to be of service to them in a matter of such trifling importance. He said as much in the letter of reply which he gave Brightie to carry back with him. But that part of his mission is omitted from our story.

When their second day at the priory was over, Xi-feng and the boys took leave of Euergesia, and as she said good-bye, Xi-feng told the prioress to call at the Rong-guo mansion in two days' time to hear the news from Chang-an.

This parting was an unbearably painful one for Sapientia and Qin Zhong, and all sorts of secret vows were exchanged and whispered contracts made before they could tear themselves apart. We omit all details of that harrowing scene.

Xi-feng called in at the Temple of the Iron Threshold on the way back to see that everything was in order. Jewel, it seemed, refused absolutely to go back home, and Cousin Zhen was obliged to leave a woman or two at the temple to keep her company.

Their return, and the events which followed it, will be dealt with in the following chapter.

CHAPTER 16

*Jia Yuan-chun is selected for glorious promotion
to the Imperial Bedchamber
And Qin Zhong is summoned for premature departure
on the Journey into Night*

Xi-feng, Qin Zhong and Bao-yu, as we have said, called in at
the Temple of the Iron Threshold on their way home. After
looking round for a while, the three of them got back into
their carriage and continued their journey into the city. Home
once more, they first called on Grandmother Jia and Lady
Wang and then went off to their several rooms. But of the rest
of that day and the night which followed, our story says
nothing.

Next morning Bao-yu found that his outer study had now
been finished and was ready for use. He looked forward to
beginning night-work in it with Qin Zhong, in accordance
with a promise they had made each other. But unfortunately
Qin Zhong's always sickly constitution had been much
neglected during their two-day excursion into the country,
and the unwonted exposure to wind and cold and immoderate
indulgence in secret frolic with Sapientia had resulted on his
return in a cough and chill accompanied by total loss of
appetite. Altogether he presented so sorry a spectacle that
study was quite out of the question and they were obliged to
send him back home to bed. Although Bao-yu was very dis-
appointed, there was nothing at all he could do but wait for
his friend to get better.

Xi-feng had now received Yun Guang's reply to the bogus
letter, expressing his readiness to comply with her (or, as he
supposed, Jia Lian's) request. Euergesia communicated this
information to the Zhangs; and soon the captain, swallowing
his anger and resentment as best he could, was obliged to
receive back the betrothal gifts he had sent them on behalf of
his son. But Jin-ge possessed a far nobler spirit than might
have been expected in the daughter of such mercenary parents.

On learning that her affianced had been sent packing, she quietly went off and hanged herself in her scarf. The captain's son, too, turned out to be a young person of unexpectedly romantic notions, for on hearing that Jin-ge had hanged herself, he promptly threw himself into a river and was drowned. The Zhangs and the Lis were thus left in a very unenviable situation:

'the maid and eke the money gone'

in the words of the poet. The only gainer was Xi-feng, who now had three thousand taels of silver to sit back and enjoy at her leisure. Not an inkling of this affair reached the ears of Lady Wang.

Emboldened by this taste of success, Xi-feng from now on undertook many more ventures of a similar nature – far more than we could give an account of in this history.

*

The day of Jia Zheng's birthday arrived and all the members of the Ning-guo and Rong-guo households were gathered together to celebrate it. Just as the festivities were at their height, one of the janitors from the main gate burst in on the assembled company:

'The Master of the Imperial Bedchamber Mr Xia is on his way, sir, with an announcement from His Majesty the Emperor!'

Jia She, Jia Zheng and the rest were taken completely by surprise, quite unable to guess what the meaning of this visitation could be. Hurriedly giving orders for the players to halt their performance and for all traces of the feast to be cleared away, they caused a table with burning incense (which would be required for the reading of the Proclamation, if there was one) to be set down in its place. Then, throwing open the centre of the three main gates, they knelt down in the entrance of the mansion to receive their visitor.

Soon Xia Bing-zhong, the Eunuch Master of the Bed-chamber, arrived on horseback with a retinue of eunuchs at his back. He appeared to have no Imperial Proclamation or other document on his person, for instead of dismounting, as etiquette prescribed that he should if he was carrying a Written Instrument, he rode straight on to the foot of the main hall. There, with beaming countenance, he got down from his horse, climbed the steps, faced south and gave utterance to the following announcement:

'By order of His Imperial Majesty:

Jia Zheng is commanded to present himself at court immediately for private audience with His Imperial Majesty in the Hall of Reverence.'

Having delivered this message he got straight back on to his horse without staying for so much as a cup of tea and rode away. Still no wiser, Jia Zheng hurried into his court dress and hastened to the Palace, leaving Grandmother Jia and the rest in an extreme state of alarm which they endeavoured (unsuccessfully) to allay by dispatching a regular stream of mounted couriers post-haste to the Palace to inquire for news.

About four hours later Lai Da, the Chief Steward of the Rong-guo mansion, and three or four other stewards came panting into the inner gate and gasped out congratulations.

'Master's orders,' said Lai Da between breaths: 'will Her Old Ladyship please bring Their Ladyships to the Palace to give thanks to His Majesty for the great favour he has shown us!'

Unable in her agitated state to remain indoors, Grandmother Jia had been waiting outside in the loggia, whither the others – Lady Xing, Lady Wang, You-shi, Li Wan, Xi-feng, Aunt Xue and the girls – had also congregated to await news of Jia Zheng. Grandmother Jia called Lai Da inside to explain his cryptic message in somewhat greater detail.

'We servants were all waiting in an anteroom,' Lai Da told her, 'and we had no idea what was going on inside. Eventually Mr Xia came out and saw us waiting there. "Congratulations!" he said. "Your eldest young lady has been appointed Chief Secretary to the Empress and is to become an Imperial Concubine." Then after that Master came out, too, and told us the same thing. "I have to go off to the East Palace now," he said, "to see the Prince. But you must hasten back as quick as you can and tell Their Ladyships to come to the Palace and give thanks."'

Lai's Da information at once dispelled the anxiety that Grandmother Jia and the others had all this time been feeling, and the worried looks on their faces quickly gave way to smiles of pleasure. Now a great dressing-up began as each lady robed herself in the costume appropriate to her rank. Then off they went to the Palace in four sedans one behind the other: Grandmother Jia's at the head, then Lady Xing's, then Lady Wang's, and then You-shi's. Jia She and Cousin Zhen also changed into court dress, and taking Jia Rong and Jia Qiang with them, accompanied Grandmother Jia to the Palace as her male escort.

There was one person who did not share the unbounded delight now general among the members of the Ning-guo and Rong-guo households – who behaved, indeed, almost as if he had not heard the news at all. This person was Bao-yu. What was the reason for his unsociable lack of enthusiasm on this occasion?

A short time previously the little nun Sapientia had absconded from Water-moon Priory and made her way into the city to look for Qin Zhong. Qin Bang-ye had discovered her, driven her from the house, and given Qin Zhong a beating. The shock and anger of the discovery had brought on an attack of the illness from which the old gentleman was a chronic sufferer, and within only four or five days he had breathed his last. Qin Zhong had always been of a weak and nervous disposition and had still not fully recovered from his sickness when these events occurred. The severe beating followed by the overwhelming grief and remorse attendant on the death of his father from anger which he had himself provoked led to serious complications in his illness.

This, then, was the reason for Bao-yu's unseasonable melancholy – a melancholy which the news of his sister Yuan-chun's dazzling promotion was powerless to dispel. Grandmother Jia's visit to the Palace to give thanks, her return home, the visits of friends and relations to congratulate the family, the unwontedly cheerful bustle of the Ning and Rong households during the days that followed, the general satisfaction that everyone in those households now seemed to feel – as far as Bao-yu was concerned these things might just as well not have been: he viewed them with the eyes of an outsider. The rest of the family merely laughed at him, seeing in this behaviour only further confirmation of their belief that he was 'a bit touched'.

But then there was Jia Lian's and Dai-yu's homecoming to look forward to. The advent of the messenger sent on ahead to announce that they would be arriving next day produced the first glimmer of cheerfulness that Bao-yu had so far shown. On being questioned for further details the messenger told them that Jia Yu-cun was also returning to the capital to have an audience with the Emperor. This was the doing of Wang Zi-teng, who had recommended him in a report to the throne for promotion to a metropolitan post. As he was both a cousin (albeit a remote one) of Jia Lian and also Dai-yu's former teacher, it had been resolved that he should travel with them. Lin Ru-hai having been laid with his ancestors in the family burying-ground and his obsequies duly concluded, they would, if they had proceeded to the capital by the usual stages, have been arriving back some time in the following month; but when Jia Lian heard the news about Yuan-chun's elevation, they had decided to make greater speed, travelling by night as well as by day. The journey had been smooth and uneventful.

Bao-yu merely asked if Dai-yu was all right, and on being assured that she was, paid no further attention to the man's news.

Having waited with great impatience until the early afternoon of the following day, Bao-yu and the rest were rewarded with the announcement 'Mr Lian and Miss Lin have just arrived!' The joy of their reunion was, however, tempered with grief, because of the two deaths that had occurred since their parting, and for a while there was much loud weeping on either side. Then there were words of comfort and congratulation to exchange and Bao-yu had an opportunity of studying Dai-yu more carefully. He recognized the same ethereal quality he had always known in her, but it seemed to have deepened and intensified during her absence.

She had brought a lot of books back with her and was soon busy superintending the sweeping out of her bedroom to accommodate them and arranging various *objets d'art* around it which had also formed part of her luggage. She had salvaged some paper, writing-brushes and other articles of stationery from her old home which she distributed as presents to Bao-chai, Ying-chun, Bao-yu and the rest. Bao-yu for his part hunted up the rosary of fragrant Indian beads given him by the Prince of Bei-jing and offered it as a gift to Dai-yu; but she flung it back at him disdainfully:

'What, carry a thing that some coarse *man* has pawed over? *I* don't want it!'

So Bao-yu was compelled to take it back again.

But let us now turn to Jia Lian.

When he had finished seeing everyone in the family, Jia Lian returned at last to his own apartment. Xi-feng, though still so busy that she had not a moment's leisure, had somehow contrived to find time to welcome back her wandering lord.

'Congratulations, Imperial Kinsman!' she said with a smile when, except for the servants, they were at last alone together. 'You have had a tiring journey, Imperial Kinsman. Yesterday when the courier gave notice of your arrival, I prepared a humble entertainment to celebrate your homecoming. Will the Imperial Kinsman graciously condescend to take a cup of wine with his handmaid?'

Jia Lian replied in the same vein:

'Madam, you are too kind! I am your most *oble-e-eged* and humble servant, ma'am!'

As they joked together, Patience and the other maids came forward to welcome their Master back, after which they served them both with tea. Jia Lian asked Xi-feng about the events that had occurred during his absence and thanked her for looking after things so well while he was away.

'I am not much of a manager really,' said Xi-feng. 'I haven't got the knowledge, and I'm too poor at expressing myself and too simple-minded – always inclined to "take a ramrod for a needle", as they say. Besides, I'm too soft-hearted for the job. Anyone who says a few kind words can get the better of me. And my lack of experience makes me so nervous. Aunt Wang only had to be the slightest bit displeased and I would get so upset that I couldn't sleep at night. I begged her not to make me do all these things, but she insisted. She said I only refused out of laziness and unwillingness to learn. I don't think she realizes even now the state I have been in – too scared to move or even to open my mouth for fear of saying or doing something wrong. And you know what a difficult lot those old stewardesses are. The tiniest mistake and they are all laughing at you and making fun; the tiniest hint of favouritism and they are grumbling and complaining. *You* know their way of "cursing the oak-tree when they mean the ash". Those old women know just how to sit on the mountain-top and watch the tigers fight; how to murder with a borrowed knife, or help the wind to fan the fire. They will look on safely from the bank while you are drowning in the river. And the fallen oil-bottle can drain away: *they* are not going to pick it up. On top of that, as I am so young, I haven't got much authority over them; so it was all I could do to prevent them from ignoring me altogether. And to crown it all, when Rong's wife died Cousin Zhen kept coming round to see Aunt Wang and begging her on his knees to let me help out for a day or two next door. I said again and again that I couldn't do it; but Aunt Wang agreed just to please him, so there was nothing for it but to do as I was told. I'm afraid I made a terrible mess of it – even worse than I did here. And now it seems Cousin Zhen is beginning to grumble and says he wishes he had never asked me. When you see him tomorrow, do please try to make it up with him. Tell him it's because I'm young and inexperienced. You might even hint that it's his own fault for having asked me in the first place!'

While she was saying this there was a sound of talking in the next room.

'Who is it?' said Xi-feng.

Patience came in to reply.

'Mrs Xue sent Caltrop over to ask me about something. I've already given her an answer and sent her back.'

'Ah yes!' said Jia Lian, apparently pleased by the recollection. 'When I went to call on Aunt Xue just now to tell her I was back, I ran into such a pretty young woman! I couldn't place her as any of the girls in our household, so in the course of conversation I asked Aunt Xue who she was. It seems that she's the little maid they had that lawsuit about. Cal— something. Caltrop. She's finally been given as "chamber-wife" to that idiot Xue. Now that she has been plucked and painted like a grown-up woman she really does look most attractive! What a waste to throw away a beautiful girl on that great booby!'

Xi-feng made a little moue.

'I should have thought that having just got back from Hangchow and Soochow and seen something of the world, you would have settled down a bit; but I see you are still the same greedy-guts as ever. Well, if you want her, there's nothing simpler: I'll exchange our Patience for her. You know what Cousin Xue is like: always "one eye on the dish and the other on the saucepan". Throughout the whole of this last year there have been I don't know how many alarms and excursions between him and poor Aunt Xue because she wouldn't let him get his hands on Caltrop. It wasn't just her looks that made her concerned for the girl. Everything about her is so unusual. She is so gentle and so quiet. Even among our own young ladies there is scarcely her equal. In the end Aunt Xue decided that if she couldn't stop him having her, at least she could make sure that the thing was done properly, with a party and invitations and all the rest of it. So that's what she did, and made her his chamber wife. But would you believe it, before a fortnight had gone by he had completely lost interest . . .!'

She was interrupted by an announcement from one of the pages on the inner gate:

'Mr Zhen wants you, sir. He's waiting for you in the larger study.'

At once Jia Lian did up his gown and hurried out.

'What on earth did Mrs Xue want, sending Caltrop here like that?' Xi-feng asked Patience as soon as he had gone.

'It wasn't Caltrop!' said Patience. 'I had to make *something* up and hers was the first name that came to mind. That wife of Brightie's is such a stupid woman! Just imagine' – she drew closer to Xi-feng's ear and lowered her voice – 'of all the times she could have chosen to bring you the interest on that money, she had to pick on the very moment when the Master has just got home! It's lucky I was in the outside room when she came, otherwise she might have come blundering in here and Master would have heard her message. And we all know what Master is like where money is concerned: he'd spend the fat in the frying-pan if he could get it out! Once he found out that you had savings, he'd pluck up courage to spend them in 'no time. Anyway, I took the money from her quickly and gave her a piece of my mind – which I am afraid you must have heard. That's why I had to say what I did. I'd never have mentioned Caltrop in the Master's presence otherwise!'

Xi-feng laughed.

'I was going to say! Why, for no apparent reason, should Mrs Xue choose a chamber-wife to send here the moment Master gets back? So it was you up to your tricks, you little monkey!'

At this point Jia Lian came in again and Xi-feng ordered her maids to serve the wine and various choice dishes to go with it. Husband and wife sat cross-legged at opposite sides of the low table on the kang and began their drinking – Xi-feng with some restraint, although she was normally a fairly hard drinker, in view of the occasion.

They had not been drinking long when Jia Lian's old wet-nurse, Nannie Zhao, walked in. The young couple at once invited her to drink with them and tried to make her join them on the kang. This last honour she would under no circumstances accept, and Patience and the girls laid a little table for her at the side of the kang and set a little stool beside it, on which she sat down very contentedly. Jia Lian made a selection with his chopsticks from the dishes on the table, and after heaping up two platefuls, set them down on Nannie Zhao's own little table for her to eat there by herself. Xi-feng was critical:

'Nannie can't chew stuff like that. She'll break her teeth on it!' She turned to Patience. 'That piece of boiled gammon in the bowl I said this morning was so tender: that would be just the thing for Nannie. Why don't you run round to the kitchen and ask them to heat it up for her? – Nannie,' she said, addressing the old woman, 'you must try some of the rice wine your Lian brought back with him from the South!'

'Ooh yes!' said Nannie Zhao, 'I must try some of that! And you must have some too, Mrs Lian. Never fear! As long as you don't drink too much, 'twill do you good. But I didn't come all the way here for vittles and drink, bless you. I came on more serious business. And you heed my words, Mrs Lian, and stick up for me; because that Master Lian of yours he always *says* he'll do something, but when you go to see him later, he's clean forgot all about it! To think I reared you up on the milk of my own bosom, Master Lian! And a fine young man you've growed into, thanks be! Well, I'm old and of no account now. But there are these two sons of mine, d'ye see? If only you would be more like a foster-brother to them and look after them a bit, no one would dare say a word agen them. But dearie me! I've asked you again and again to help them, and you always says yes; yet to this very day nothing has ever come of it. Well, what I thought was this, Mrs Lian. With this great blessing of Heaven that's come on the family on account of your eldest young lady, surely, I thought to myself, there must be jobs in this for *someone*? I'll talk to Mrs Lian about it, I said to myself; because if I rely on Master Lian to help us, we'll starve to death for certain sure!'

Xi-feng laughed.

'Leave your two boys to me, Nannie. I'll look after them! You know all about Lian's little ways because you nursed him when he was a baby: he'll give the dearest thing he has to some nobody he's picked up outside, yet his own two foster-brothers who are much nicer young men than any of his favourites he neglects completely. If only you would take a bit of interest in *them*, Lian, you wouldn't hear a word of complaint from anyone, instead of wasting your kindnesses on those – those little *male misses* of yours! I shouldn't have called them "misses", though. You treat the *misses* as your *missus* and give me the *miss*!'

There was a loud laugh from everyone present, including Nannie Zhao, who concluded her cackles with a pious invocation:

'Bless his Holy Name! Here at last comes a just judge to set all things to rights – But oh Mrs Lian, those naughty things you said about "misses": that's not my Master Lian. It's just that he's so soft-hearted he can't bring himself to say "no" to anyone who spins him a tale.'

'Soft-hearted with his boy friends, maybe,' said Xi-feng with a lubricious smile; 'but when he has to do with us women he is hard enough.'

'Tee, hee, hee, what a one you are, Mrs Lian! I don't know when I was last so merry. Come on, let's have another cup of that good wine! – Now that I've got Mrs Lian to stand up for me I shall have no more worries!'

Jia Lian was by now thoroughly embarrassed and laughed sheepishly.

'Stop all this nonsense now and serve the rice! I've still got to go round to Cousin Zhen's after this to discuss things.'

'Ah yes,' said Xi-feng. 'We mustn't make you late for that. What did Cousin Zhen want you for just now?'

'It was about the visitation business,' said Jia Lian.

'Has it been settled, then?'

'Well, not absolutely. Eight or nine parts settled, you might say.'

'That's a great favour of the Emperor's, isn't it?' said Xi-feng. 'Something you don't hear of even in plays and stories about the olden days.'

'Very true!' chimed in Nannie Zhao. 'But I must be getting old and stupid, for everywhere these last few days have been a-buzz with talk of "visitations", but blessed if I can make head or tail of it. You tell us now: just what manner of thing *is* this "visitation"?'

Jia Lian undertook to do so.

'Our present Emperor, who has always had a great sympathy for the common man, believes that the filial affection of a child for its parents is the most important thing in the world, and that family feeling is the same everywhere, irrespective of social rank. He has found that in his own case, even after seeing the Ex-Emperor and Ex-Empress morning, noon and night every day of his life, he is still unable to express more than a fraction of the devotion he feels for them; and this has led him to think of all those concubines and maids of honour and other court ladies, taken from their homes and shut up in the Palace for years and years on end, and to realize how much they must miss *their* parents. And from there he got to thinking of the parents themselves, how they must long for the daughters they can never see again. And then he thought what a crime against Nature it would be if any of those parents were to become ill as a result of not seeing their daughters. And so he addressed a Memorial to the Ex-Emperor and Ex-Empress requesting permission to allow the families of palace ladies to visit them in the Palace on the twelfth day of every month. When Their Old Majesties saw this Memorial they were very pleased and praised the Emperor for his piety and goodness – "doing Heaven's work among men" they called it. But they pointed out in their Rescript that when the families of court ladies entered the Palace on these visits, they would inevitably be hampered by the restrictions of court etiquette in the expression of their natural feelings. So in the end, by an act of supreme generosity, the Emperor issued a special decree in which he said that, apart from allowing the families of court ladies to visit their daughters in the Palace on the twelfth day of each month, he would allow any family which had a separate house or annexe capable of being maintained in the degree of security specified for a Temporary Imperial Residence to make written application for permission to receive a Visitation in their own home, where the pleasures of reunion could be enjoyed in an atmosphere of intimacy and affection. The proclamation of this decree has created quite a stir. The Imperial Concubine Lady Zhou's father already has the builders at work on a special wing for visitations in his house, and Lady Wu's father, Wu Tian-you, has been outside the city looking for a site. So it's already eight or nine parts settled, as I said.'

'Bless my soul!' said Nannie Zhao. 'So that's what it is! Well, I suppose in that case we shall soon be getting ready to receive *our* young lady?'

'Of course,' said Jia Lian. 'What else do you think we're all so busy about?'

'If we *do* receive her,' said Xi-feng, 'it should be an experience worth remembering. I've often wished I'd been born twenty or thirty years earlier so that the old folk wouldn't be able to look down on me for having missed so much. To hear them talk about the Emperor Tai-zu's Southern Progress is better than listening to a story-teller. How I wish I'd been there to see it all!'

'Ah, now!' said Nannie Zhao. '*That*'s the sort of thing that scarce comes once in a thousand years! I was not so young then that I can't still remember. The head of the Jia family in those days was Superintendant of Shipyards and Harbour Maint'nance in the Soochow-Yangchow area and was chosen to receive the Emperor on one of his visits. The way they spent silver on that visit, why, it was like pouring out salt sea water! I call to mind . . .'

Xi-feng in her eagerness cut her short:

'We Wangs received the Emperor on one of his visits, too. At that time my grandfather was in charge of all the foreign tribute and the embassies going up to Court. Whenever any foreigners arrived, it was always my family that put them up. All the goods brought by the foreign ships to the seaports in Kwangtung, Fukien, Yunnan and Chekiang passed through our hands.'

'Everybody knows that,' said Nannie Zhao. 'There's even a rhyme about it:

> The King of the Ocean
> Goes along,
> When he's short of gold beds,
> To the Nanking Wang.

That's your family: the "Nanking Wangs". But then there's the Zhens, who still live down that way in Kiangnan. My word! There's riches for you! That family alone received the Emperor *four times*! If I hadn't seen with my own two eyes, I don't care who told me, I wouldn't have credited it, the sights I saw then! Never mind silver. Silver was just dirt to them. Every precious thing in the world you can think of they had there in mountains! Words like "save" and "spare" they just didn't seem to know the meaning of!'

'I believe you,' said Xi-feng. 'I've heard my grandfather talk about it, and he said it was just like that. But it still amazes me that a single family could have so much wealth.'

'I'll tell you something, Mrs Lian,' said the knowledgeable Nannie. ''Twere no more than paying for the Emperor's entertainment with the Emperor's own silver. No family that ever lived had money enough of its own to pay for such spectacles of vanity!'

While they were chatting, Lady Wang sent someone round to see if Xi-feng had finished her dinner yet. Xi-feng realized that there must be something which demanded her attention and, finishing hurriedly, rinsed out her mouth and prepared to go. Before she could leave, however, the pages from the second gate announced the arrival of Jia Rong and Jia Qiang from the Ning-guo mansion next door. Jia Lian had just finished rinsing his mouth and was washing his hands in a basin held out for him by Patience when the two young men came into the room.

'What is your message?' he asked them.

Xi-feng, curious, stayed to hear.

'Father sent us to tell you that the uncles have already reached a decision,' said Jia Rong. 'They have measured off an area just over a quarter of a mile square which takes in a part of our grounds, including the All-scents Garden, on the east side, and the north-west corner of your grounds on the west, to be turned into a Separate Residence for the Visitation. They've already commissioned someone to draw a plan, which should be ready tomorrow. Father says as you've just got home he's sure you must be tired, so don't bother to come round tonight. If there's anything to discuss, you can tell him about it first thing tomorrow.'

'Thank your father for me very much,' said Jia Lian with a grateful smile. 'It is very good of him to let me off tonight, and I shall do as he says and not go over until tomorrow. I think the great advantage of this proposal is that it is so economical and makes the job of construction so much easier. It would mean very much more trouble if we were to build on land out-side, yet at the same time we should lose the convenience this present scheme gives us of a single layout. Tell him when you get back that I think it is an excellent proposal, and that I leave it to him to protest in any way he thinks fit if the others show signs of going back on it. The one thing we must under no circumstances do is to go looking for land outside. Anyway,

I shall be round to see him first thing tomorrow and we can talk about it in detail then.'

Jia Rong promised to retail this message.

Jia Qiang now stepped forward with a message of his own:

'Uncle Zhen has given me the job of going to Soochow to engage music and drama teachers and to buy girl players and instruments and costumes so. that we can have our own theatricals for the visitation. I'm to take Lai Sheng's two sons with me; and two of Great-uncle Zheng's gentlemen, Dan Ping-ren and Bu Gu-xiu, are coming as well. Uncle said I ought to have a word with you about it before I go.'

Jia Lian looked the youth up and down appraisingly and laughed:

'Do you think you are qualified for the job? It may not be a very big one, but I should say the pickings would be pretty good for someone who knew the ropes.'

Jia Qiang laughed too.

'I shall have to learn as I go along!'

Jia Rong, who was standing somewhat away from the light, availed himself of the shadow's concealment to give Xi-feng's dress a surreptitious tug. She understood perfectly well what his meaning was, but pretended not to, dismissing him with a curt wave of the hand and addressing herself instead to Jia Lian:

'Don't be so officious, Lian! Cousin Zhen is no less capable of choosing the right person for the job than we are. What do you mean by asking the boy if he's qualified? He's as much qualified as any of the rest of us. He's old enough to have seen a pig run, even if he's not old enough to have eaten pork! In any case, I'm sure Cousin Zhen only chose him as a figurehead. You don't seriously suppose that he'll be the one to discuss prices and deal with the business side of the expedition? – *I* think myself it's a very good choice!'

'Of course it is,' said Jia Lian. 'I don't dispute it. I merely thought we ought to do a few of his sums for him before he goes. Where is the money for this coming from?' he asked Jia Qiang.

'We were discussing that just now,' said Jia Qiang. 'Gaffer Lai says that there's no point in taking money with us from here. He says the Zhens of Kiangnan hold fifty thousand taels of ours on deposit and he can give us a letter of credit to take to them when we go. We'll draw out thirty thousand first and leave the rest to buy lanterns, lamps, and curtains with later on.'

Jia Lian nodded appreciatively.

'Good idea.'

'Well, if that's all settled,' Xi-feng put in quickly, 'I've got two very reliable young men for you to take with you, Qiang. I'm sure you'll find them extremely useful.'

'What a coincidence!' said Jia Qiang. 'I was just about to ask if you could recommend a couple of helpers!'

He asked for their names, and Xi-feng turned to Nannie Zhao to supply them. But the old nurse was so bemused by all this talk of policy and high finance that she appeared to be in a sort of coma, which it took a sharp nudge from Patience to rouse her from. When she answered it was in a gabble, to make up for the awkward pause.

'One of them is called Zhao Tian-liang, the other is called Zhao Tian-dong.'

'Mind you don't forget!' said Xi-feng. 'Now I'm off to see to my own affairs.' And she left the room.

Jia Rong slipped out after her.

'If you will make a list of all the things you want,' he said, smilingly and softly, 'I'll see that he gets them for you, gracious lady.'

'Gracious arsehole!' said Xi-feng. 'Do you think you can buy my favour with a few knick-knacks? I don't like all this whispering in corners.'

She walked away without giving him a chance to reply.

Meanwhile Jia Qiang was making a somewhat similar proposal to Jia Lian.

'If there's anything I can get for you while I'm away, Uncle, I shall be glad to wangle it.'

'My, my!' said Jia Lian. 'Let's not get carried away, then! I must say, for one who's only just started, you certainly haven't lost much time in picking up the tricks of the trade! Yes, I dare say I shall write and let you know if I find I'm short of anything.'

With these words he sent the two young men back to the other house. Their departure was followed by a succession of three or four visits by servants reporting on household matters, after which he felt so exhausted that he instructed the servants on the inner gate to refuse admittance to any others and to inform them that he would deal with their business next day. It was midnight by the time Xi-feng got back to bed.

But the affairs of that night are no part of our story.

Rising early next morning, Jia Lian first called on his father and uncles and then went to the Ning-guo mansion, where, with Cousin Zhen, he joined a group consisting of the older stewards and domestics and a few friends and clients of the family in making a complete survey of the Ning-guo and Rong-guo properties with a view to deciding where the various buildings of the Separate Residence should be sited. He also helped them interview the craftsmen who would undertake the work.

After the assembling of builders and artisans the assembling of materials began: a continuous flow of supplies converging on the site from every direction, from precious consignments of gold, silver, copper and tin, to huge, bulky loads of builder's clay, timber, bricks and tiles.

Various walls, including the surrounding walls of the All-scents Garden, and some of the garden's pavilions were demolished so that the north-west part of the Ning-guo property and the large open court on the north-east side of Rong-guo House were thrown into a single site. A range of servants' quarters on the east side of the Rong-guo grounds had already been demolished. The Ning-guo and Rong-guo properties had previous to this been divided by an alley-way running from north to south between them, but as it was not a public thoroughfare, no problem was involved in closing it and incorporating part of it in the rest of the new site.

The All-scents Garden had been watered by a stream led in by a culvert which ran under a corner of the north wall. Now that the garden was being integrated in the larger site, it was no longer necessary to lead the water in at this point.

The artificial hills, rocks, trees and shrubs of All-scents Garden were, of course, insufficient for the whole of the new site; but the area occupied by Jia She was the original garden of Rong-guo House and plentifully supplied with bamboos, trees, rocks, pavilions, kiosks and pergolas capable of being moved elsewhere. By pooling the resources of these two gardens – the All-scents Garden of Ning-guo House and the original Rong-guo garden where Jia She lived – and redistributing them over a single area, it would be possible to make great economies in both labour and materials, and when the estimates came to be made it was found that the requirements, in terms of completely new materials, would be comparatively modest.

The conception as a whole and the designs for its execution were alike the work of a well-known landscape gardener familiar to all and sundry by the sobriquet of 'Horticultural Hu'.

Jia Zheng was unused to matters of a practical nature and left the management of men and the control of operations to a consortium consisting of Jia She, Cousin Zhen and Jia Lian, the stewards Lai Da, Lai Sheng and Lin Zhi-xiao, the Clerk of Stores Wu Xin-deng, and two of his literary gentlemen, Zhan Guang and Cheng Ri-xing. The digging of pools, the raising of hills, the siting and erection of lodges and pavilions, the planting of bamboos and flowers – in a word, all matters pertaining to the landscaping and layout of the gardens, were planned and supervised by Horticultural Hu. Jia Zheng would merely drop in occasionally when he got back from Court and look around. On any important matters he sought the advice of Jia She and the rest.

Jia She led a life of cultured ease and never did anything. On routine matters of no great importance Cousin Zhen would either report to him in person or send him a brief note when the thing was done. If consultation was unavoidable, he would send along Lai Da or one of the others for a reply.

Jia Rong's sole task was to supervise the making of objects in gold and silver.

Jia Qiang had already left for Soochow.

Cousin Zhen, Lai Da and the rest were the ones who did most of the real work. It was they who hired workmen, kept accounts, and supervised and inspected each job as it was undertaken.

The amount of noise and activity generated by these operations could not be described in a few words, and for the time being we shall not attempt the task.

The family's recent preoccupation with these important developments had released Bao-yu from his father's periodical quizzing about the progress of his studies. Unfortunately the relief of mind which this would otherwise have afforded him was displaced by a grave concern for Qin Zhong, whose sickness seemed to be daily worsening. Under such circumstances it was impossible for him to feel happy about anything else.

One morning, just as he had finished washing and dressing and was thinking of going round to Grandmother Jia to ask if he might pay Qin Zhong another visit, he caught sight of Tealeaf dodging about behind the screen wall of the inner gate and evidently trying to catch his attention. Bao-yu hurried over to him.

'What is it?'

'Master Qin. He's dying!'

Bao-yu was stunned.

'*Dying*? When I saw him yesterday he seemed quite lucid. How can he be dying so soon?'

'I don't know,' said Tealeaf. 'But that's what the old gaffer said just now who came round to tell me.'

Bao-yu hurried back and told Grandmother Jia. She instructed some of the more reliable servants to go with him and briefly admonished him before he went:

'When you get there you may stay with him to the end, since you have been such good friends; but you must come back as soon as it is over. Don't hang about!'

Bao-yu hurried off to change, only to find, on re-emerging, that the carriage was still not ready. Anxious lest he should arrive too late, he ran up and down the courtyard in a frenzy of impatience, imploring the servants to make haste; and when it at last arrived, he flung himself in it and drove off at great speed, hotly pursued by Li Gui, Tealeaf and the others attending him.

The house, when they reached it, appeared silent and deserted. Entering together in a tight little knot, master and servants surged through like swarming bees to the inner apartment at the back where Qin Zhong lay, causing great consternation among the two aunts and half-dozen girl cousins who were tending him and who were unable to conceal themselves before the advent of this masculine invasion.

At this stage Qin Zhong had already lost consciousness several times and, in accordance with the Northern custom which forbids a sick man to breathe his last on the kang, had some time since been lifted on to a trestle bed to die. Bao-yu gave an involuntary cry when he saw where he was lying and broke into noisy weeping. He was quickly restrained by Li Gui:

'You know how delicate Master Qin is. I expect the kang was too hard for him and they have put him here so that he can lie a bit more easy. You mustn't cry like that or you will make him worse!'

Bao-yu held back his sobs and drew close to his dying friend. Qin Zhong's face was waxen. His eyes were closed tight and he seemed to breathe with difficulty, twisting his head from side to side on the pillow.

'Jing-qing, old fellow! It's me! It's Bao-yu!' – He called him several times, but Qin Zhong seemed unaware of his presence. Again he called:

'It's Bao-yu!'

In point of fact Qin Zhong's soul had already left his body and the few faint gasps of breath in his failing lungs were the only life that now remained in it. The ministers of the underworld, armed with a warrant and chains to bind him with, were at that very moment confronting him; but his soul was refusing to go quietly. Remembering that he left no one behind him to look after his family's affairs, and bethinking him of poor Sapientia whose whereabouts were still unknown, he entreated them most piteously to spare him. But the infernal visitants had no ear for his entreaties and silenced him with angry rebuke:

'You're an educated young fellow: haven't you heard the saying

> If Yama calls at midnight hour
> No man can put off death till four – ?

We ministers of the nether world, from the highest down to the lowest, all have unbending iron natures and – unlike the officials of the mortal world, who are always doing kindnesses and showing favours and inventing little tricks and dodges for frustrating the course of justice – we are incapable of showing partiality.'

Suddenly, above their angry shouting, Qin Zhong heard a tiny cry:

'It's Bao-yu!'

At once he renewed his entreaties:

'Good gentlemen, be merciful! Give me just a moment for a few words with a very dear friend of mine, and I'll be back directly!'

'What is it now?' asked the demons. 'What friend?'

'I won't deceive you, gentlemen. It's a descendant of the Duke of Rong-guo. His name is Bao-yu.'

'*What*?' screamed the officer in charge of the party in great alarm. He turned angrily on his demon minions:

'I *told* you we ought to let him go back for a bit, but you wouldn't listen. Now look what's happened! He's gone and called up a person full of life and health to come here right in our midst! This is terrible!'

The demons showed signs of disarray on observing their leader to be so affected, and there was some angry muttering:

'Yer Honour was putting on a brave enough show a short while ago. Why should the name "Bao-yu" throw you into such a state of commotion? If you ask us, seeing that he's upper world and we're lower world, there's nothing to be afraid of. We might just as well carry this one off now and have done with it.'

The trepidation of their leader, who was perhaps thinking more of Bao-yu's demon-repelling talisman than of its wearer, was far from comforted by this reflection.

'No! No! No!' he shouted, and compelled them to let the soul return to its body.

With the return of his soul Qin Zhong regained consciousness and opened his eyes. He could see Bao-yu standing beside him; but his throat was so choked with phlegm that he was unable to utter a word. He could only fasten his eyes on him and slowly shake his head. Then there was a rasping sound in his throat and he slid once more into the dark.

What followed will be told in the following chapter.

CHAPTER 17

*The inspection of the new garden becomes
a test of talent
And Rong-guo House makes itself ready for
an important visitor*

Now that Qin Zhong was indisputably dead, Bao-yu wept long and bitterly, and it was some time before Li Gui and the rest could calm him. Even after their return he continued tearful and distressed. Grandmother Jia contributed thirty or forty taels towards Qin Zhong's funeral expenses and made additional provision for offerings to the dead. Bao-yu condoled and sacrificed, and on the seventh day followed his friend's coffin to the grave. He continued in daily grief for Qin Zhong for a very long time afterwards. But grief cannot mend our losses, and a day did at last arrive when he had ceased to mourn.

*

One day Cousin Zhen came to Jia Zheng with his team of helpers to report that work on the new garden had been completed.

'Uncle She has already had a look,' said Cousin Zhen. 'Now we are only waiting for you to look round it to tell us if there is anything you think will need altering and also to decide what inscriptions ought to be used on the boards everywhere.'

Jia Zheng reflected a while in silence.

'These inscriptions are going to be difficult,' he said eventually. 'By rights, of course, Her Grace should have the privilege of doing them herself; but she can scarcely be expected to make them up out of her head without having seen any of the views which they are to describe. On the other hand, if we wait until she has already visited the garden before asking her, half the pleasure of the visit will be lost. All those prospects and pavilions – even the rocks and trees and flowers will seem somehow incomplete without that touch of poetry which only the written word can lend a scene.'

'My dear patron, you are so right,' said one of the literary gentlemen who sat with him. 'But we have had an idea. The inscriptions for the various parts of the garden obviously cannot be dispensed with; nor, equally obviously, can they be decided in advance. Our suggestion is that we should compose provisional names and couplets to suit the places where inscriptions are required, and have them painted on rectangular paper lanterns which can be hung up temporarily – either horizontally or vertically as the case may be – when Her Grace comes to visit. We can ask her to decide on the permanent names after she has inspected the garden. Is not this a solution of the dilemma?'

'It is indeed,' said Jia Zheng. 'When we look round the garden presently, we must all try to think of words that can be used. If they seem suitable, we can keep them for the lanterns. If not, we can call for Yu-cun to come and help us out.'

'Your own suggestions are sure to be admirable, Sir Zheng,' said the literary gentlemen ingratiatingly. 'There will be no need to call in Yu-cun.'

Jia Zheng smiled deprecatingly.

'I am afraid it is not as you imagine. In my youth I had at best only indifferent skill in the art of writing verses about natural objects – birds and flowers and scenery and the like; and now that I am older and have to devote all my energies to official documents and government papers, I am even more out of touch with this sort of thing than I was then; so that even if I were to try my hand at it, I fear that my efforts would be rather dull and pedantic ones. Instead of enhancing the interest and beauty of the garden, they would probably have a deadening effect upon both.'

'That doesn't matter,' the literary gentlemen replied. 'We can *all* try our hands at composing. If each of us contributes what he is best at, and if we then select the better attempts and reject the ones that are not so good, we should be able to manage all right.'

'That seems to me a very good suggestion,' said Jia Zheng.

'As the weather today is so warm and pleasant, let us all go and take a turn round the garden now!'

So saying he rose to his feet and conducted his little retinue of literary luminaries towards the garden. Cousin Zhen hurried on ahead to warn those in charge that they were coming.

As Bao-yu was still in very low spirits these days because of his grief for Qin Zhong, Grandmother Jia had hit on the idea of sending him into the newly made garden to play. By unlucky chance she had selected this very day on which to try out her antidote. He had in fact only just entered the garden when Cousin Zhen came hurrying towards him.

'Better get out of here!' said Cousin Zhen with an amused smile. 'Your father will be here directly!'

Bao-yu streaked back towards the gate, a string of nurses and pages hurrying at his heels. But he had only just turned the corner on coming out of it when he almost ran into the arms of Jia Zheng and his party coming from the opposite direction. Escape was impossible. He simply had to stand meekly to one side and await instructions.

Jia Zheng had recently received a favourable report on Bao-yu from his teacher Jia Dai-ru in which mention had been made of his skill in composing couplets. Although the boy showed no aptitude for serious study, Dai-ru had said, he nevertheless possessed a certain meretricious talent for versification not undeserving of commendation. Because of this report, Jia Zheng ordered Bao-yu to accompany him into the garden, intending to put his aptitude to the test. Bao-yu, who knew nothing either of Dai-ru's report or of his father's intentions, followed with trepidation.

As soon as they reached the gate they found Cousin Zhen at the head of a group of overseers waiting to learn Jia Zheng's wishes.

'I want you to close the gate,' said Jia Zheng, 'so that we can see what it looks like from outside before we go in.'

Cousin Zhen ordered the gate to be closed, and Jia Zheng stood back and studied it gravely.

It was a five-frame gate-building with a hump-backed roof of half-cylinder tiles. The wooden lattice-work of the doors and windows was finely carved and ingeniously patterned. The whole gatehouse was quite unadorned by colour or gilding, yet all was of the most exquisite workmanship. Its walls stood on a terrace of white marble carved with a pattern of passion-flowers in relief, and the garden's whitewashed circumference wall to left and right of it had a footing made of black-and-white striped stone blocks arranged so that the stripes formed a simple pattern. Jia Zheng found the unostentatious simplicity of this entrance greatly to his liking, and after ordering the gates to be opened, passed on inside.

A cry of admiration escaped them as they entered, for there, immediately in front of them, screening everything else from their view, rose a steep, verdure-clad hill.

'Without this hill,' Jia Zheng somewhat otiosely observed, 'the whole garden would be visible as one entered, and all its mystery would be lost.'

The literary gentlemen concurred. 'Only a master of the art of landscape could have conceived so bold a stroke,' said one of them.

As they gazed at this miniature mountain, they observed a great number of large white rocks in all kinds of grotesque and monstrous shapes, rising course above course up one of its sides, some recumbent, some upright or leaning at angles, their surfaces streaked and spotted with moss and lichen or half concealed by creepers, and with a narrow, zig-zag path only barely discernible to the eye winding up between them.

'Let us begin our tour by following this path,' said Jia Zheng. 'If we work our way round towards the other side of the hill on our way back, we shall have made a complete circuit of the garden.'

He ordered Cousin Zhen to lead the way, and leaning on Bao-yu's shoulder, began the winding ascent of the little mountain. Suddenly on the mountainside above his head, he noticed a white rock whose surface had been polished to mirror smoothness and realized that this must be one of the places which had been prepared for an inscription.

'Aha, gentlemen!' said Jia Zheng turning back to address the others who were climbing up behind him. 'What name are we going to choose for this mountain?'

'Emerald Heights,' said one.

'Embroidery Hill,' said another.

Another proposed that they should call it 'Little Censer' after the famous Censer Peak in Kiangsi. Another proposed 'Little Zhong-nan'. Altogether some twenty or thirty names were suggested – none of them very seriously, since the literary gentlemen were aware that Jia Zheng intended to test Bao-yu and were anxious not to make the boy's task too difficult. Bao-yu understood and was duly grateful.

When no more names were forthcoming Jia Zheng turned to Bao-yu and asked him to propose something himself.

'I remember reading in some old book,' said Bao-yu, 'that "to recall old things is better than to invent new ones; and to recut an ancient text is better than to engrave a modern". We ought, then, to choose something old. But as this is not the garden's principal "mountain" or its chief vista, strictly speaking there is no justification for having an inscription here at all – unless it is to be something which implies that this is merely a first step towards more important things ahead. I suggest we should call it "Pathway to Mysteries" after the line in Chang Jian's poem about the mountain temple:

A path winds upwards to mysterious places.

A name like that would be more distinguished.'

There was a chorus of praise from the literary gentlemen:

'Exactly right! Wonderful! Our young friend with his natural talent and youthful imagination succeeds immediately where we old pedants fail!'

Jia Zheng gave a deprecatory laugh:

'You mustn't flatter the boy! People of his age are adept at making a little knowledge go a long way. I only asked him as a joke, to see what he would say. We shall have to think of a better name later on.'

As he spoke, they passed through a tunnel of rock in the mountain's shoulder into an artificial ravine ablaze with the vari-coloured flowers and foliage of many varieties of tree and shrub which grew there in great profusion. Down below, where the trees were thickest, a clear stream gushed between the rocks. After they had advanced a few paces in a somewhat northerly direction, the ravine broadened into a little flat-bottomed valley and the stream widened out to form a pool. Gaily painted and carved pavilions rose from the slopes on either side, their lower halves concealed amidst the trees, their tops reaching into the blue. In the midst of the prospect below them was a handsome bridge:

> In a green ravine
> A jade stream sped.
> A stair of stone
> Plunged to the brink.
> Where the water widened
> To a placid pool,
> A marble baluster
> Ran round about.
> A marble bridge crossed it
> With triple span,
> And a marble lion's maw
> Crowned each of the arches.

Over the centre of the bridge there was a little pavilion, which Jia Zheng and the others entered and sat down in.

'Well, gentlemen!' said Jia Zheng. 'What are we going to call it?'

'Ou-yang Xiu in his *Pavilion of the Old Drunkard* speaks of "a pavilion poised above the water",' said one of them. 'What about "Poised Pavilion"?'

'"Poised Pavilion" is good,' said Jia Zheng, 'but *this* pavilion was put here in order to dominate the water it stands over, and I think there ought to be some reference to water in its name. I seem to recollect that in that same essay you mention Ou-yang Xiu speaks of the water "gushing between twin peaks". Could we not use the word "gushing" in some way?'

'Yes, yes!' said one of the literary gentlemen. '"Gushing Jade" would do splendidly.'

Jia Zheng fondled his beard meditatively, then turned to Bao-yu and asked him for *his* suggestion.

'I agreed with what you said just now, Father,' said Bao-yu, 'but on second thoughts it seems to me that though it may have been all right for Ou-yang Xiu to use the word "gushing" in describing the source of the river Rang, it doesn't really suit the water round this pavilion. Then again, as this is a Separate Residence specially designed for the reception of a royal personage, it seems to me that something rather formal is called for, and that an expression taken from the *Drunkard's Pavilion* might seem a bit improper. I think we should try to find a rather more imaginative, less obvious sort of name.'

'I hope you gentlemen are all taking this in!' said Jia Zheng sarcastically. 'You will observe that when we suggest something original we are recommended to prefer the old to the new, but that when we *do* make use of an old text we are "improper" and "unimaginative"! – Well, carry on then! Let's have your suggestion!'

'I think "Drenched Blossoms" would be more original and more tasteful than "Gushing Jade".'

Jia Zheng stroked his beard and nodded silently. The literary gentlemen could see that he was pleased and hastened to commend Bao-yu's remarkable ability.

'That's the two words for the framed board on top,' said Jia Zheng. '*Not* a very difficult task. But what about the seven-word lines for the sides?'

Bao-yu glanced quickly round, seeking inspiration from the scene, and presently came up with the following couplet:

> 'Three pole-thrust lengths of bankside willows green,
> One fragrant breath of bankside flowers sweet.'

Jia Zheng nodded and a barely perceptible smile played over his features. The literary gentlemen redoubled their praises.

They now left the pavilion and crossed to the other side of the pool. For a while they walked on, stopping from time to time to admire the various rocks and flowers and trees which they passed on their way, until suddenly they found themselves at the foot of a range of whitewashed walls enclosing a small retreat almost hidden among the hundreds and hundreds of green bamboos which grew in a dense thicket behind them. With cries of admiration they went inside. A cloister-like covered walk ran round the walls from the entrance to the back of the forecourt and a cobbled pathway led up to the steps of the terrace. The house was a tiny three-frame one, two parts latticed, the third part windowless. The tables, chairs and couches which furnished it seemed to have been specially made to fit the interior. A door in the rear wall opened onto a garden of broad-leaved plantains dominated by a large flowering pear-tree and overlooked on either side by two diminutive lodges built at right angles to the back of the house. A stream gushed through an opening at the foot of the garden wall into a channel barely a foot wide which ran to the foot of the rear terrace and thence round the side of the house to the front, where it meandered through the bamboos of the forecourt before finally disappearing through another opening in the surrounding wall.

'This must be a pleasant enough place at any time,' said Jia Zheng with a smile. 'But just imagine what it would be like to sit studying beside the window here on a moonlight night! It is pleasures like that which make a man feel he has not lived in vain!'

As he spoke, his glance happened to fall on Bao-yu, who instantly became so embarrassed that he hung his head in shame. He was rescued by the timely intervention of the literary gentlemen who changed the subject from that of study to a less dangerous topic. Two of them suggested that the name given to this retreat should be a four-word one. Jia Zheng asked them what four words they proposed.

' "Where Bends the Qi" ' said one of them, no doubt having in mind the song in the *Poetry Classic* which begins with the words

> See in that nook where bends the Qi,
> The green bamboos, how graceful grown!

'No,' said Jia Zheng. 'Too obvious!'

' "North of the Sui",' said the other, evidently thinking of the ancient Rabbit Garden of the Prince of Liang in Suiyang – also famous for its bamboos and running water.

'No,' said Jia Zheng. 'Still too obvious!'

'You'd better ask Cousin Bao again,' said Cousin Zhen, who stood by listening.

'He always insists on criticizing everyone else's suggestions before he will deign to make one of his own,' said Jia Zheng. 'He is a worthless creature.'

'That's all right,' said the others. 'His criticisms are very good ones. He is in no way to blame for making them.'

'You shouldn't let him get away with it!' said Jia Zheng. 'All right!' he went on, turning to Bao-yu. 'Today we will indulge you up to the hilt. Let's have your criticisms, and after that we'll hear your own proposal. What about the two suggestions that have just been made? Do you think either of them could be used?'

'Neither of them seems quite right to me,' said Bao-yu in answer to the question.

'In what way "not quite right"?' said Jia Zheng with a scornful smile.

'Well,' said Bao-yu, 'This is the first building our visitor will enter when she looks over the garden, so there ought to be some word of praise for the Emperor at this point. If we want a classical reference with imperial symbolism, I suggest "The Phoenix Dance", alluding to that passage in the *History Classic* about the male and female phoenixes alighting "with measured gambollings" in the Emperor's courtyard.'

'What about "Bend of the Qi" and "North of the Sui"?' said Jia Zheng. 'Aren't they classical allusions? If not, I should like to know what they are!'

'Yes,' said Bao-yu, 'but they are too contrived. "The Phoenix Dance" is more fitting.'

There was a loud murmur of assent from the literary gentlemen. Jia Zhong nodded and tried not to look pleased.

'Young idiot! – A "small capacity but a great self-conceit", gentlemen – All right!' he ordered: 'now the couplet!'

So Bao-yu recited the following couplet:

'From the empty cauldron the steam still rises after the brewing of tea.
By the darkening window the fingers are still cold after the game of Go.'

Jia Zheng shook his head:

'Nothing very remarkable about *that*!'

With this remark he began to move on, but thought of something just as they were leaving, and stopped to ask Cousin Zhen:

'I see that the buildings in this garden have their proper complement of chairs and tables and so forth. What about blinds and curtains and flower-vases and all that sort of thing? Have they been selected to suit the individual rooms?'

'As regards ornaments,' Cousin Zhen replied, 'we have already got in quite a large stock, and when the time comes we shall naturally select from it what is suitable for each individual room. As regards drapes and hangings, Cousin Lian told me yesterday that there are quite a lot yet to come. What we did was to take the measurements from the plans drawn up for the carpenters and put the work in hand straight away, even before the buildings were finished. As far as I know, up to yesterday we had received about half of what was ordered.'

From the way Cousin Zhen spoke, Jia Zheng gathered that this was not his responsibility and sent someone to summon Jia Lian. He arrived within moments, and Jia Zheng questioned him about the types and quantities ordered and the figures for what had already been received and what was still to come.

In response to his inquiry Jia Lian extracted a wallet from the leg of his boot, and glancing at a folded schedule inside it, summarized its contents as follows:

'Curtains, large and small, in various silks and satins – flowered, dragon-spot, sprigged, tapestry, panelled, ink-splash: one hundred and twenty. – Eighty of those were delivered yesterday. That leaves forty to come. – Blinds: two hundred. – Yes. They all arrived yesterday. But then there are the special ones. – Blinds, scarlet felt: two hundred. Speckled bamboo: one hundred. Red lacquered bamboo with gold fleck: one hundred. Black lacquered bamboo: one hundred. Coloured net: two hundred. – We now have half of each of those four kinds. The other half is promised by the end of autumn. – Chair-covers, table-drapes, valances, tablecloths: one thousand two hundred of each. – Those we already have.'

They had been moving on as he spoke, but were presently brought to a halt by a steeply sloping hill which rose up in front of them. Having negotiated its foot, they could see, almost concealed in a fold half-way up the other side of it, a dun-coloured adobe wall crowned with a coping of rice-straw thatch. Inside it were several hundred apricot trees, whose flowering tops resembled the billowing rosy clouds of some vegetable volcano. In their midst stood a little group of reed-thatched cottages. Beyond the wall, with a barred gate dividing it in the middle, a loose hedge of irregular shape had been made by weaving together the pliant young shoots of the mulberry, elm, hibiscus, and silkworm thorn trees which grew outside it. Between this hedge of trees and the lower slope of the hill was a rustic well, furnished with both well-sweep and windlass. Below the well, row upon row of miniature fields full of healthy-looking vegetables and flowers ran down in variegated strips to the bottom.

'Ah, now here is a place with a purpose!' said Jia Zheng with a pleased smile. 'It may have been made by human artifice, but the sight of it is none the less moving. In me it awakens the desire to get back to the land, to a life of rural simplicity. Let us go in and rest a while!'

They were just on the point of entering the gate in the hedge when they observed a stone at the side of the pathway leading up to it which had evidently been put there in order that the name of the place might be inscribed upon it.

'What a brilliant idea!' the literary gentlemen exclaimed. 'If they had put a board up over the gate, the rustic atmosphere would have been completely destroyed, whereas this stone actually enhances it. This is a place which calls for the bucolic talent of a Fan Cheng-da to do it justice!'

'What shall we call it, then?' asked Jia Zheng.

'Just now our young friend was saying that to "recall an old thing is better than to invent a new one",' said one of the literary gentlemen. 'In this case the ancients have already provided the perfect name: "Apricot Village".'

Jia Zheng knew that he was referring to the words of the fainting traveller in Du Mu's poem:

> 'Where's the tavern?' I cry, and a lad points the way
> To a village far off in the apricot trees.

He turned to Cousin Zhen with a smile:

'Yes. That reminds me. There's just one thing missing here: an inn-sign. Tomorrow you must have one made. Nothing fancy. Just an ordinary inn-sign like the ones you see in country villages outside. And it should hang from a bamboo pole above the tree-tops.'

Cousin Zhen promised to see this done and added a suggestion of his own:

'The birds here, too, ought to be ordinary farmyard ones – hens, ducks, geese, and so on – to be in keeping with the surroundings.'

Jia Zheng and the rest agreed enthusiastically.

'The only trouble with "Apricot Village",' said Jia Zheng, '– though it would suit the place very well – is that it is the name of a real village; so we should have to get official permission first before we could use it.'

'Ah, yes,' said the others. 'That means we still have to think of something for a temporary name. Now what shall it be?'

While they were all still thinking, Bao-yu who had already had an idea, was so bursting with eagerness that he broke in, without waiting to be invited by his father:

'There is an old poem which has the lines

> Above the flowering apricot
> A hopeful inn-sign hangs.

For the inscription on the stone we ought to have "The Hopeful Sign".'

'"The Hopeful Sign",' echoed the literary gentlemen admiringly. 'Very good! The hidden allusion to "Apricot Village" is most ingenious!'

'Oh, as for the name of the village,' said Bao-yu scornfully, '"Apricot Village" is much too obvious! Why not "Sweet-rice Village" from the words of the old poem:

> A cottage by the water stands
> Where sweet the young rice smells?'

The literary gentlemen clapped their hands delightedly; but their cries of admiration were cut short by an angry shout from Jia Zheng:

'Ignorant young puppy! Just how many "old poets" and "old poems" do you think you know, that you should presume to show off in front of your elders in this impertinent manner? We let you have your little say just now in order to test your intelligence. It was no more than a joke. Do you suppose we are seriously interested in your opinions?'

They had been moving on meanwhile, and he now led them into the largest of the little thatched buildings, from whose simple interior with its paper windows and plain deal furniture all hint of urban refinement had been banished. Jia Zheng was inwardly pleased. He stared hard at Bao-yu:

'How do you like *this* place, then?'

With secret winks and nods the literary gentlemen urged Bao-yu to make a favourable reply, but he wilfully ignored their promptings.

'Not nearly as much as "The Phoenix Dance".'

His father snorted disgustedly.

'Ignoramus! You have eyes only for painted halls and gaudy pavilions – the rubbishy trappings of wealth. What can *you* know of the beauty that lies in quietness and natural simplicity? This is a consequence of your refusal to study properly.'

'Your rebuke is, of course, justified, Father,' Bao-yu replied promptly, 'but then I have never really understood what it was the ancients *meant* by "natural".'

The literary gentlemen, who had observed a vein of mulishness in Bao-yu which boded trouble, were surprised by the seeming naïveté of this reply.

'Why, fancy not knowing what "natural" means – you who have such a good understanding of so much else! "Natural" is that which is *of nature*, that is to say, that which is produced by nature as opposed to that which is produced by human artifice.'

'There you are, you see!' said Bao-yu. 'A farm set down in the middle of a place like this is obviously the product of human artifice. There are no neighbouring villages, no distant prospects of city walls; the mountain at the back doesn't belong to any system; there is no pagoda rising from some tree-hid monastery in the hills above; there is no bridge below leading to a near-by market town. It sticks up out of nowhere, in total isolation from everything else. It isn't even a particularly remarkable view – not nearly so "natural" in either form or spirit as those other places we have seen. The bamboos in those other places may have been planted by human hand and the streams diverted out of their natural courses, but there was no *appearance* of artifice. That's why, when the ancients use the term "natural" I have my doubts about what they really meant. For example, when they speak of a "natural painting", I can't help wondering if they are not referring to precisely that forcible interference with the landscape to which I object: putting hills where they are not meant to be, and that sort of thing. However great the skill with which this is done, the results are never quite . . .'

His discourse was cut short by an outburst of rage from Jia Zheng.

'Take that boy out of here!'

Bao-yu fled.

'Come back!'

He returned.

'You still have to make a couplet on this place. If it isn't satisfactory, you will find yourself reciting it to the tune of a slapped face!'

Bao-yu stood quivering with fright and for some moments was unable to say anything. At last he recited the following couplet:

'Emergent buds swell where the washerwoman soaks her cloth.
A fresh tang rises where the cress-gatherer fills his pannier.'

Jia Zheng shook his head:

'Worse and worse.'

He led them out of the 'village' and round the foot of the hill:

> through flowers and foliage,
> by rock and rivulet,
> past rose-crowned pergolas
> and rose-twined trellises,
> through small pavilions
> embowered in peonies,
> where scent of sweet-briers stole,
> or pliant plantains waved –

until they came to a place where a musical murmur of water issued from a cave in the rock. The cave was half-veiled by a green curtain of creeper, and the water below was starred with bobbing blossoms.

'What a delightful spot!' the literary gentlemen exclaimed.

'Very well, gentlemen. What are you going to call it?' said Jia Zheng.

Inevitably the literary gentlemen thought of Tao Yuan-ming's fisherman of Wu-ling and his Peach-blossom Stream.

' "The Wu-ling Stream",' said one of them. 'The name is ready-made for this place. No need to look further than that.'

Jia Zheng laughed:

'The same trouble again, I am afraid. It is the name of a real place. In any case, it is too hackneyed.'

'All right,' said the others good-humouredly. 'In that case simply call it "Refuge of the Qins".' Their minds still ran on the Peach-blossom Stream and its hidden paradise.

'That's even more inappropriate!' said Bao-yu. ' "Refuge of the Qins" would imply that the people here were fugitives from tyranny. How can we possibly call it that? I suggest "Smartweed Bank and Flowery Harbour".'

'Rubbish!' said Jia Zheng. He looked inside the grotto and asked Cousin Zhen if there were any boats.

'Four punts for lotus-gathering and one for pleasure are on order,' said Cousin Zhen, 'but they haven't finished making them yet.'

'What a pity we cannot go through!' said Jia Zheng.

'There is a very steep path over the top which would take us there,' said Cousin Zhen, and proceeded to lead the way.

The others scrambled up after him, clinging to creepers and leaning on tree-trunks as they went. When, having descended once more, they had regained the stream, it was wide and deep and distorted by many anfractuosities. The fallen blossoms seemed to be even more numerous and the waters on whose surface they floated even more limpid than they had been on the side they had just come from. The weeping willows which lined both banks were here and there diversified with peach and apricot trees whose interlacing branches made little worlds of stillness and serenity beneath them.

Suddenly, through the green of the willows, they glimpsed the scarlet balustrade of a wooden bridge whose sloping ramps led to a flat central span high above the water. When they had crossed it, they found a choice of paths leading to different parts of the garden. Ahead was an airy building with roofs of tile, whose elegant surrounding wall was of grey-plastered brick pierced by ornamental grilles made of semi-circular tiles laid together in openwork patterns. The wall was so constructed that outcrops of rock from the garden's 'master mountain' appeared to run through it in several places into the courtyard inside.

'This building seems rather out of place here,' said Jia Zheng.

But as he entered the gate the source of his annoyance disappeared; for a miniature mountain of rock, whose many holes and fissures, worn through it by weathering or the wash of waters, bestowed on it a misleading appearance of fragile delicacy, towered up in front of him and combined with the many smaller rocks of various shapes and sizes which surrounded it to efface from their view every vestige of the building they had just been looking at.

Not a single tree grew in this enclosure, only plants and herbs:

some aspired as vines,
some crept humbly on the ground;
some grew down from the tops of rocks,
some upwards from their feet;
some hung from the eaves in waving trails of green,
some clung to pillars in circling bands of gold;
some had blood-red berries,
some had golden flowers.

And from every flower and every plant and every herb wafted the most exquisite and incomparable fragrances.

Jia Zheng could not help but admire:

'Charming! But what *are* they all?'

'Wild-fig' and 'wistaria' was all the literary gentlemen would venture.

'But surely,' Jia Zheng objected, 'wild-fig and wistaria do not have this delectable fragrance?'

'They certainly don't,' said Bao-yu. 'There *are* wild-fig and wistaria among the plants growing here, but the ones with the fragrance are pollia and birthwort and – yes, I think those are orchids of some kind. That one over there is probably actinidia. The red flowers are, of course, rue, the "herb of grace", and the green ones must be green-flag. A lot of these rare plants are mentioned in *Li sao* and *Wen xuan*, particularly in the *Poetical Descriptions of the Three Capitals* by Zuo Si. For example, in his *Description of the Wu Capital* he has

> agastache, eulalia,
> and harsh-smelling ginger-bush,
> cord-flower, cable-flower,
> centaury and purplestrife,
> stone-sail and water-pine
> and sweet-scented eglantine ...

And then there are

> amaranth, xanthoxylon,
> anemone, phellopteron ...

They come in the *Description of the Shu Capital*. Of course, after all these centuries nobody *really* knows what all those names stand for. They apply them quite arbitrarily to whatever seem to fit the description, and gradually all of them – '

Once more an angry shout from his father cut him short:

'Who asked for *your* opinion?'

Bao-yu shrank back and said no more.

Observing that there were balustraded loggias on either side of the court, Jia Zheng led his party through one of them towards the building at the rear. It was a cool, five-frame gallery with a low, roofed verandah running round it on all sides. The window-lattices were green and the walls freshly painted. It was a building of quite another order of elegance from the ones they had so far visited.

'Anyone who sat sipping tea and playing the *qin* to himself on this verandah would have no need to burn incense if he wanted sweet smells for his inspiration,' said Jia Zheng dreamily. 'So unexpectedly beautiful a place calls for a specially beautiful name to adorn it.'

'What could be better than "Dewy Orchids"?' said the literary gentlemen.

'Yes,' said Jia Zheng. 'That would do for the name. Now what about the couplet?'

'*I* have thought of a couplet,' said one of the gentlemen. 'Tell me all of you what you think of it:

> A musky perfume of orchids hangs in the sunset courtyard.
> A sweet aroma of galingale floats over the moonlit island.'

'Not bad,' said the others. 'But why "*sunset* courtyard"?'

'I was thinking of that line in the old poem,' said the man:

> 'The garden's gillyflowers at sunset weep.

After all, you have already got "dewy" in the name. I thought the "sunset weeping" would go with it rather well.'

'Feeble! Feeble!' cried the rest.

'I've thought of a couplet, too,' said one of the others. 'Let me have your opinion of it:

> Down garden walks a fragrant breeze caresses beds of melilot.
> By courtyard walls a brilliant moon illumines golden orchises.'

Jia Zheng stroked his beard, and his lips were observed to move as though he was on the point of proposing a couplet of his own. Suddenly, looking up, he caught sight of Bao-yu skulking behind the others, too scared to speak.

'What's the matter with you?' he bellowed at the unfortunate boy. 'You are ready enough with your opinions when they are not wanted. Speak up! – Or are you waiting for a written invitation?'

'I can see no "musk" or "moonlight" or "islands" in this place,' said Bao-yu. 'If we are to make couplets in this follow-my-leader fashion, we could turn out a couple of hundred of them and still have more to come.'

'No one's twisting your arm,' said Jia Zheng. 'You don't *have* to use those words if you don't want to.'

'In that case,' said Bao-yu, 'I suggest "The Garden of Spices" for the name; and for the couplet:

> Composing amidst cardamoms, you shall make verses like flowers.
> Slumbering amidst the roses, you shall dream fragrant dreams.'

'We all know where you got *that* from,' said Jia Zheng:

> 'Composing midst the plantains
> Green shall my verses be.

We can't give you much credit for an imitation.'

'Not at all!' said the literary gentlemen. 'There is nothing wrong with imitation provided it is done well. After all, Li Bo's poem "On Phoenix Terrace" is entirely based on Cui Hao's "Yellow Crane Tower", yet it is a much better poem. On reflection our young friend's couplet seems more poetical and imaginative than the original.'

'Oh, *come* now!' said Jia Zheng. But they could see he was not displeased.

Leaving the place of many fragrances behind them, they had not advanced much further when they could see ahead of them a building of great magnificence which Jia Zheng at once identified as the main reception hall of the Residence.

> Roof above roof soared,
> Eye up-compelling,
> Of richly-wrought chambers
> And high winding galleries.
> Green rafts of dark pine
> Brushed the eaves' edges.
> Milky magnolias
> Bordered the buildings.
> Gold-glinting cat-faces,
> Rainbow-hued serpents' snouts
> Peered out or snarled down
> From cornice and finial.

'It is rather a showy building,' said Jia Zheng. But the literary gentlemen reassured him:

'Although Her Grace is a person of simple and abstemious tastes, the exalted position she now occupies makes it only right and proper that there should be a certain amount of pomp in her reception. This building is in no way excessive.'

Still advancing in the same direction, they presently found themselves at the foot of the white marble memorial arch which framed the approach to the hall. The pattern of writhing dragons protectively crouched over its uppermost horizontal was so pierced and fretted by the sculptor's artistry as to resemble lacework rather than solid stone.

'What inscription do we want on this arch?' Jia Zheng inquired.

' "Peng-lai's Fairy Precincts" is the only name that would do it justice,' said the literary gentlemen.

Jia Zheng shook his head and said nothing.

The sight of this building and its arch had inspired a strange and unaccountable stir of emotion in Bao-yu which on reflection he interpreted as a sign that he must have known a building somewhat like this before – though where or when he could not for the life of him remember. He was still racking his brains to recall what it reminded him of, when Jia Zheng ordered him to produce a name and couplet for the arch, and he was quite unable to give his mind to the task of composition. The literary gentlemen, not knowing the nature of his preoccupation, supposed that his father's incessant bullying had worn him out and that he had finally come to the end of his inspiration. They feared that further bullying might once more bring out the mulish streak in him, thereby provoking an explosion which would be distasteful for everybody. Accordingly they urged Jia Zheng to allow him a day's grace in which to produce something suitable. Jia Zheng, who was secretly beginning to be apprehensive about the possible conquences of Grandmother Jia's anxiety for her darling grandson, yielded, albeit with a bad grace:

'Jackanapes! So even you have your off moments it seems. Well, I'll give you a day to do it in. But woe betide you if you can't produce something tomorrow! And it had better be something good, too, because this is the most important building in the garden.'

After they had seen over the building and come out again, they stopped for a while on the terrace to look at a general view of the whole garden and attempted to make out the places they had already visited. They were surprised to find that even now they had covered little more than half of the whole area. Just at that moment a servant came up to report that someone had arrived with a message from Yu-cun.

'I can see that we shan't be able to finish today,' said Jia

Zheng. 'However, if we go out by the way I said, we should at least be able to get some idea of the general layout.'

He conducted them to a large bridge above a crystal curtain of rushing water. It was the weir through which the water from the little river which fed all the pools and watercourses of the garden ran into it from outside. Jia Zheng invited them to name it.

'This is the source of the "Drenched Blossoms" stream we looked at earlier on,' said Bao-yu. 'We should call it "Drenched Blossoms Weir".'

'Rubbish!' said Jia Zheng. 'You may as well forget about your "Drenched Blossoms", because we are not going to use that name!'

Their progress continued past many unexplored features of the garden, viz:

> a summer lodge
> a straw-thatched cot
> a dry-stone wall
> a flowering arch
> a tiny temple nestling beneath a hill
> a nun's retreat hidden in a little wood
> a straight gallery
> a crooked cave
> a square pavilion
> and a round belvedere.

But Jia Zheng hurried past every one of them without entering. However, he had now been walking for a very long time without a rest and was beginning to feel somewhat footsore; and so, when the next building appeared through the trees ahead, he proposed that they should go in and sit down, and led his party towards it by the quickest route possible. They had to walk round a stand of double-flowering ornamental peach-trees and through a circular opening in a flower-covered bamboo trellis. This brought them in sight of the building's whitewashed enclosing wall and the contrasting green of the weeping willows which surrounded it. A roofed gallery ran from each side of the gate round the inner wall of the forecourt, in which a few rocks were scattered. On one side of it some green plantains were growing and on the other a weeping variety of Szechwan crab, whose pendant clusters of double-flowering carmine blossoms hung by stems as delicate as golden wires on the umbrella-shaped canopy of its boughs.

'What magnificent blossom!' exclaimed the literary gentlemen. 'One has seen plenty of crab-apple blossom before, but never anything as beautiful as this.'

'This kind is called "maiden crab",' said Jia Zheng. 'It comes from abroad. According to vulgar belief it originally came from the Land of Maidens, and that is supposed to be the reason why it blooms so profusely. Needless to say, it is only the ignorant sort of persons who hold this ridiculous belief.'

'It certainly has most unusual blossoms,' said the literary gentlemen. 'Who knows, perhaps there *is* something in the popular belief.'

'Surely,' said Bao-yu, 'it is much more probable that poets and painters gave it the name of "maiden crab" because of its rouge-like colour and delicate, drooping shape, and that the name was misunderstood by ignorant, literal-minded people, who made up this silly story to account for it.'

'That must be it!' said the literary gentlemen. 'Most grateful for the explanation!'

While they were speaking they were at the same time arranging themselves on some benches in the gallery.

'Has anyone an original idea for a name?' said Jia Zheng when they were all seated.

One of them proposed 'Storks in the Plantains'. Another suggested 'Shimmering Splendour'.

' "Shimmering Splendour",' Jia Zheng and the others repeated, trying out the words. 'That's good!'

'A lovely name!' said Bao-yu. But a moment later he added: 'Rather a pity, though.'

'Why "rather a pity"?' they asked.

'Well,' said Bao-yu, 'there are both plantains and crab-apple blossom in this courtyard. Whoever planted them must have been thinking of "the red and the green". If our name mentions only one and leaves out the other, it will seem somehow inadequate.'

'What do you suggest, then?' said Jia Zheng.

'I suggest "Fragrant Red and Lucent Green",' said Bao-yu.
'That takes account of both of them.'

Jia Zheng shook his head:

'No, that's no good!'

He led them inside the building. Its interior turned out to
be all corridors and alcoves and galleries, so that properly
speaking it could hardly have been said to have *rooms* at all.
The partition walls which made these divisions were of
wooden panelling exquisitely carved in a wide variety of
motifs: bats in clouds, the 'three friends of winter' – pine,
plum and bamboo, little figures in landscapes, birds and
flowers, scrollwork, antique bronze shapes, 'good luck' and
'long life' characters, and many others. The carvings, all of
them the work of master craftsmen, were beautified with in-
lays of gold, mother-o'-pearl and semi-precious stones. In
addition to being panelled, the partitions were pierced by
numerous apertures, some round, some square, some sun-
flower-shaped, some shaped like a fleur-de-lis, some cusped,
some fan-shaped. Shelving was concealed in the double thick-
ness of the partition at the base of these apertures, making it
possible to use them for storing books and writing materials
and for the display of antique bronzes, vases of flowers,
miniature tray-gardens and the like. The overall effect was at
once richly colourful and, because of the many apertures, airy
and graceful.

The *trompe-l'œil* effect of these ingenious partitions had
been further enhanced by inserting false windows and doors
in them, the former covered in various pastel shades of gauze,
the latter hung with richly-patterned damask portières. The
main walls were pierced with window-like perforations in the
shape of zithers, swords, vases and other objects of virtù.

The literary gentlemen were rapturous:

'Exquisite!' they cried. 'What marvellous workmanship!'

Jia Zheng, after taking no more than a couple of turns inside
this confusing interior, was already lost. To the left of him was
what appeared to be a door. To the right was a wall with a
window in it. But on raising its portière he discovered the door
to be a bookcase; and when, looking back, he observed – what
he had not noticed before – that the light coming in through

the silk gauze of the window illuminated a passage-way leading to an open doorway, and began walking towards it, a
party of gentlemen similar to his own came advancing to meet
him, and he realized that he was walking towards a large
mirror. They were able to circumvent the mirror, but only to
find an even more bewildering choice of doorways on the
other side.

'Come!' said Cousin Zhen with a laugh. 'Let me show you
the way! If we go out here we shall be in the back courtyard.
We can reach the gate of the garden much more easily from
the back courtyard than from the front.'

He led them round the gauze hangings of a summer-bed,
then through a door into a garden full of rambler roses.
Behind the rose-trellis was a stream running between green
banks. The literary gentlemen were intrigued to know where
the water came from. Cousin Zhen pointed in the direction of
the weir they had visited earlier:

'The water comes in over that weir, then through the grotto,
then under the lea of the north-east "mountain" to the little
farm. There a channel is led off it which runs into the south-
east corner of the garden. Then it runs round and rejoins the
main stream here. And from here the water flows out again
underneath that wall.'

'How very ingenious!'

They moved on again, but soon found themselves at the
foot of a tall 'mountain'.

'Follow me!' said Cousin Zhen, amused at the bewilder-
ment of the others, who were now completely at sea as to their
whereabouts. He led them round the foot of the 'mountain' –
and there, miraculously, was a broad, flat path and the gate by
which they had entered, rising majestically in front of them.

'Well!' exclaimed the literary gentlemen. 'This beats everything! The skill with which this has all been designed is quite
out of this world!'

Whereupon they all went out of the garden.

*

Bao-yu was now longing to get back to the girls, but as no dismissal was forthcoming from his father, he followed him

along with the others into his study. Fortunately Jia Zheng suddenly recollected that Bao-yu was still with him:

'Well, run along then! Your grandmother will be worrying about you. I take it you're not still waiting for more?'

At last Bao-yu could withdraw. But as soon as he was in the courtyard outside, he was waylaid by a group of Jia Zheng's pages who laid hands on him and prevented him from going.

'You've done well today, haven't you, coming out top with all those poems? You have *us* to thank for that! Her Old Ladyship sent round several times asking about you, but because the Master was so pleased with you, we told her not to worry. If we hadn't done that, you wouldn't have had the chance to show off your poems! Everyone says they were better than all the others. What about sharing your good luck with us?'

Bao-yu laughed good-naturedly.

'All right. A string of cash each.'

'Who wants a measly string of cash? Give us that little purse you're wearing!' And without a 'by your leave' they began to despoil him, beginning with the purse and his fan-case, of all his trinkets, until every one of the objects he carried about him had been taken from him.

'Now,' they said, 'we'll see you back in style!'

And closing round him, they marched him back to Grandmother Jia's apartment in triumphal procession.

Grandmother Jia had been waiting for him with some anxiety, and was naturally delighted to see him come in apparently none the worse for his experience.

Soon after, when he was back in his own room, Aroma came in to pour him some tea and noticed that all the little objects he usually carried about his waist had disappeared.

'Where have the things from your belt gone?' she said. 'I suppose those worthless pages have taken them again.'

Dai-yu overheard her and came up to inspect. Sure enough, not one of the things was there.

'So you've given away that little purse I gave you? Very well, then. You needn't expect me to give you anything in future, however much you want it!'

With these words she went off to her own room in a temper,

and taking up a still unfinished perfume sachet which she was making for him at his own request, she began to cut it up with her embroidery scissors. Bao-yu, observing that she was angry, had hurried after her – but it was too late. The sachet was already cut to pieces.

Although it had not been finished, Bao-yu could see that the embroidery was very fine, and it made him angry to think of the hours and hours of work so wantonly destroyed. Tearing open his collar he took out the little embroidered purse which had all along been hanging round his neck and held it out for her to see.

'Look! What's that? When have I ever given anything of yours to someone else?'

Dai-yu knew that he must have treasured her gift to have worn it inside his clothing where there was no risk of its being taken from him. She regretted her over-hasty destruction of the sachet and hung her head in silence.

'You needn't have cut it up,' said Bao-yu. 'I know it's only because you hate giving things away. Here, you can have this back too since you're so stingy!'

He tossed the purse into her lap and turned to go. Dai-yu burst into tears of rage, and picking up the little purse, attacked that too with her scissors. Bao-yu hurried back and caught her by the wrist.

'Come, cuzzy dear!' he said with a laugh. 'Have mercy on it!'

Dai-yu threw down the scissors and wiped her streaming eyes.

'You shouldn't blow hot and cold by turns. If you want to quarrel, let's quarrel properly and have nothing to do with each other!'

She got up on the kang in a great huff, and turning her back on him, sobbed into her handkerchief and affected to ignore his presence. But Bao-yu got up beside her, and with many soothing words and affectionate endearments humbly entreated her forgiveness.

Meanwhile in the front room Grandmother Jia was calling loudly for her beloved grandson.

'Master Bao is in the back with Miss Lin,' they told her.

'Ah, good!' said the old lady. 'Let us leave them alone together, then. It will be a nice relaxation for him after the strain of being so long with his father – as long as they don't argue.'

'Yes, milady.'

Finding herself unable to shake off Bao-yu's attentions, Dai-yu got up from the kang:

'I can see you are determined not to let me live in peace. I shall just have to go elsewhere.' And off she went.

'Wherever you go, I shall go with you,' said Bao-yu, taking up the purse and beginning to fasten it on again. But Dai-yu snatched it away from him.

'First you say you don't want it, and now you are trying to put it on again. You ought to be ashamed of yourself!'

Her anger dissolved in a little explosion of laughter.

'Dearest cuzzy!' said Bao-yu. 'Won't you please make me another sachet?'

'That depends on whether I feel in the mood or not,' said Dai-yu.

Chatting together they went out of the room and round to Lady Wang's apartment. Bao-chai was there already. They found everyone there in a state of great excitement owing to the fact that Jia Qiang had just arrived back from Soochow with the twelve child-actresses he had purchased there, together with their instructors and all the costumes and properties they would use in performing their plays.

Aunt Xue had now moved to a quiet, secluded apartment in the north-east corner of the mansion, and Pear-tree Court was undergoing alterations for use as a drama school where the instructors could train and rehearse their little charges. A number of female members of the Rong-guo staff who had some previous training in singing and acting – they were all grey-haired old women by now – were put in charge of the domestic arrangements. Pay and expenses and the provision of whatever was needed for the maintenance of the troupe was to remain in the hands of Jia Qiang, who was also to keep the accounts.

Simultaneously with this arrival, Lin Zhi-xiao's wife had come to announce that the selection and purchase of twenty-four little nuns – twelve Buddhist and twelve Taoist – had been successfully accomplished. Even the twenty-four little habits they would wear had now arrived brand-new from the tailor. But that was not all. It appeared that a young lady who had entered the church under half vows as an 'unshaved nun' might be persuaded to join them.

'She comes of a highly educated official family from Soochow,' Lin Zhi-xiao's wife told them. 'As a child she was always ailing and her parents paid for any number of "proxy novices" in the hope that she would get better; but all was of no avail. In the end there was nothing for it but for the young lady to take the great step herself – though as a lay sister, without the shaving of hair. And sure enough her illness got better immediately. She is now eighteen years of age. Her name in religion is "Adamantina". She lost both her parents some time ago and has only two old nurses and a little maid to look after her. She's said to be a great clerk and knows all the classics by heart. What's more, she is a very handsome young woman. She moved into this area with her teacher a year ago because of some relic of Guanyin she had heard about and because there are some old Sanskrit texts here that she wanted to look at. She has been living ever since in the Śakyamuni Convent outside the west gate. Her teacher was a great authority on the "Primordial" branch of the Tantra. She died last winter. As she lay dying she told Adamantina that she was not to go back home, but to wait here quietly for a call. That is why she stays on here and has never taken her teacher's coffin back.'

'We should certainly take advantage of this to invite her here,' said Lady Wang.

'We have tried asking her,' said Lin Zhi-xiao's wife, 'but the reply she gives is that noble households are given to trampling on other people's feelings, and she is not disposed to be trampled on.'

'She is bound to be rather a proud young woman, coming from a family of officials,' said Lady Wang. 'I don't see why we shouldn't make out a written invitation and request her formally.'

Lin Zhi-xiao's wife promised to see this done and hurried

off to ask one of the professional letter-writers in the family's employment to make out a formal invitation. Next day a carriage was sent round to fetch Adamantina to the mansion in a style befitting a young gentlewoman of tender susceptibilities.

But as to what happened thereafter: that will be disclosed in the ensuing chapter.

CHAPTER 18

A brief family reunion is permitted by the
magnanimity of a gracious Emperor
And an Imperial Concubine takes pleasure in the
literary progress of a younger brother

Just at that moment a servant came in to say that the workmen
needed some gauze for pasting on window-lattices and asked
Xi-feng if she would unlock the storeroom for them. Then
another servant arrived and asked her to take charge of some
gold and silver plate. Lady Wang and her maids also seemed
to be fully occupied. Thoughtful Bao-chai pointed out to
Bao-yu and the rest that they were getting in everyone's way,
and at her suggestion they all adjourned to Ying-chun's room.

Lady Wang's busyness in fact continued unabated until well
into the tenth month. By then the contractors had fulfilled
their contracts and the various buildings in the garden been
stocked with appropriate ornaments and antiques; supplies of
livestock – storks, deer, rabbits, chicken, geese, and so forth –
had been purchased and distributed to the parts of the garden
where they were to be reared; Jia Qiang's young ladies had
rehearsed and were word-perfect in twenty or thirty operatic
pieces; and the little Buddhist and Taoist nuns had mastered
the essential parts of their respective liturgies. Jia Zheng could
now feel reasonably well satisfied that things were as they
should be, and invited Grandmother Jia into the garden for a
final inspection in which she was to suggest any last-minute
alterations that might still be needed. When not the slightest
shadow of an imperfection could any more be found, he at
last sent in his written application for a Visitation. The
Gracious Reply arrived on the very same day:

> Her Grace will make a Family Visitation next year on the fif-
> teenth of the first month, being the Festival of Lanterns.

The receipt of this reply seemed to throw the Jia family into
an even greater frenzy of preparation than before, so that even
its New Year celebrations that year were somewhat scamped.

In no time at all the Festival of Lanterns seemed to be almost upon them. On the eighth of the first month a eunuch came from the Palace to inspect the layout of the Separate Residence and to establish where the Imperial Concubine would 'change her clothes', where she would sit to converse with her family, where she would receive their obeisances, where she would feast them, and where she would retire to when she wanted to rest. The eunuch Chief of Security also arrived with his eunuch minions and supervised a great deal of sealing-up and screening-off everywhere. He also instructed the members of the household in the regulations for leaving and entering, serving food and bringing messages, all of which had to be done through special entrances and exits and by special routes.

Outside the mansion the Chief Commissioner of the Metropolitan Police and a gentleman from the Board of Works were busy supervising the sweeping of the surrounding streets and the chasing away of all idlers, onlookers and other suspicious-looking characters.

Meanwhile Jia She and the consortium were putting up ornamental lanterns everywhere in the gardens and fixing fireworks in place for a pyrotechnic display in honour of the visit. By the fourteenth everything was finally ready. No one in the Jia household, whether master or servant, had a wink of sleep throughout the whole of that night.

By five o'clock next morning, when it was still dark night outside, all those in the family from Grandmother Jia downwards who held any sort of rank or title were already dressed in full court rig. In the Separate Residence

> painted phoenix and coiling dragon
> flapped and fluttered on drapes and curtains,
> gold and silver-work gleamed and glinted,
> jewels and gems made a fiery sparkle,
> subtle incenses smouldered in brazen censers,
> 'everlastings' blossomed in china vases;

– and all was so silent, that throughout the whole of that great garden not the sound of a cough was to be heard.

Jia She and the other menfolk drew themselves up outside the west gate. Grandmother Jia stood outside the main gate

with the female members of the family. They noticed that the
ends of the street and the entrances of the side-streets leading
into it had all been screened off.

Just as they were beginning to grow impatient, a eunuch
trotted up on horseback and was stopped and questioned by
Jia Zheng.

'Oh, you're much too early yet!' said the eunuch. 'Her
Grace won't be taking her lunch until one o'clock; then at two
she goes to divine service in the Bao-ling chapel. Five o'clock,
when she has an appointment to feast with the Emperor in
the Da-ming Palace and look at the New Year lanterns, is the
first opportunity she will have of asking permission to leave.
I should be surprised if she got started much before seven
o'clock this evening!'

'Well,' said Xi-feng to Grandmother Jia when she heard
this, 'you and Aunt Wang may as well go back to your room.
You will be able to come back later on nearer the time.'

Grandmother Jia and the other ladies took her advice and
went off, leaving Xi-feng to attend to whatever still needed
doing in the garden. Under her direction some of the stewards
carried off the eunuchs and treated them to food and wine,
while other servants fetched great bundles of wax candles to
illuminate the garden's many lanterns with.

Suddenly, as afternoon drew towards evening, a clatter of
many hooves was heard, and after a short pause, a group of
ten or so eunuchs rushed in out of breath, clapping their
hands as they ran. This was taken by the other eunuchs as a
sign that the Imperial Concubine was on her way, for they at
once jumped up and hurried to their prearranged places. The
family, too, took up their positions once more, Jia She and
the menfolk outside the west gate and Grandmother Jia with
the ladies outside the main entrance.

For a long time there was total silence. Then a couple of
eunuchs on horseback came riding very, very slowly up to the
west gate. Dismounting, they led their horses out of sight
behind the cloth screens, then returned to take up their stand
at the sides of the road, half-facing towards the west. After a
considerable wait, two more eunuchs arrived and went through
the same motions as the first pair. Then another two, and then

another, until in all some ten pairs were standing at the sides of the road, their faces turned expectantly towards the west.

Presently a faint sound of music was heard and the Imperial Concubine's procession at last came in sight.

First came several pairs of eunuchs carrying embroidered banners.

Then several more pairs with ceremonial pheasant-feather fans.

Then eunuchs swinging gold-inlaid censers in which special 'palace incense' was burning.

Next came a great gold-coloured 'seven-phoenix' umbrella of state, hanging from its curve-topped shaft like a great drooping bell-flower. In its shadow was borne the Imperial Concubine's travelling wardrobe: her head-dress, robe, sash and shoes.

Eunuch gentlemen-in-waiting followed carrying her rosary, her embroidered handkerchief, her spittoon, her fly-whisk, and various other items.

Last of all, when this army of attendants had gone by, a great gold-topped palanquin with phoenixes embroidered on its yellow curtains slowly advanced on the shoulders of eight eunuch bearers.

As Grandmother Jia and the rest dropped to their knees eunuchs rushed up and helped them to get up again. The palanquin passed through the great gate and made for the entrance of a courtyard on the east side of the forecourt. There a eunuch knelt beside it and invited the Imperial Concubine to descend and 'change her clothes'. The bearers carried it through the entrance and set it down just inside the courtyard. The other eunuchs then withdrew, leaving Yuan-chun's ladies-in-waiting to help her from the palanquin.

The courtyard she now stepped out into was brilliant with coloured lanterns of silk gauze cunningly fashioned in all sorts of curious and beautiful shapes and patterns. An illuminated sign hung over the entrance of the principal building:

FILLED WITH FAVOURS BATHED IN BLESSINGS

Yuan-chun passed beneath it into the room that had been prepared for her, then, having 'changed her clothes', came out again and stepped back into the palanquin, which was now borne into the garden.

Her first impression was a confused one of curling drifts of incense smoke and gleaming colours. There were lanterns everywhere, and soft strains of music. She seemed to be entering a little world wholly dedicated to the pursuit of ease and luxury and delight. Looking at it from the depths of her palanquin she shook her head a little sadly and sighed:

'Oh dear, this is all *so* extravagant!'

At that moment a eunuch knelt beside the palanquin and invited the Imperial Concubine to proceed by boat. Stepping out onto the waiting barge she saw an expanse of clear water curving between its banks like a sportive dragon. Lanterns of crystal and glass were fixed to the balustrades which lined the banks, their silvery radiance giving the white marble, in the semi-darkness, the appearance of gleaming drifts of snow. Because of the season, the willows and apricot trees above them were bare and leafless; but in place of leaves they were festooned with hundreds of tiny lanterns, and flowers of gauze, rice-paper and bast had been fastened to the tips of their branches. Other lanterns made of shells and feathers, in the form of lotuses, water-lilies, ducks and egrets floated on the surface of the water below. It would have been hard to say whether the water below or the banks above presented the more brilliant spectacle. Together they combined to make a fairyland of jewelled light. And to these visual delights were added the many charming miniature gardens on the barge itself – not to mention its pearl blinds, embroidered curtains, and the carved and painted oars and paddle with which it was furnished. While Yuan-chun was still admiring all this, her boat approached a landing-stage in a grotto, above which hung a lantern-sign inscribed with these words:

SMARTWEED BANK AND FLOWERY HARBOUR

Stone's Note to Reader:

You may find it surprising that 'Smartweed Bank and Flowery Harbour', 'The Phoenix Dance' and those other names, which in the last chapter we showed Bao-yu inventing in an aptitude test imposed at random by his father, should actually have been used on the occasion of the Imperial Concubine's first visit to her family. Surely, you will say, a household as long established and highly cultivated as the Jias' must have had several well-known talents at its disposal which it could have called upon for such important purposes as these? These were no wealthy parvenus whose vulgarity would be satisfied with the effusions of a gifted schoolboy for filling in the gaps where inscriptions are felt to be *de rigueur*.

The answer lies in Yuan-chun's special relationship with Bao-yu. Before Yuan-chun entered the Palace, she had been brought up mainly by Grandmother Jia; and when Bao-yu appeared on the scene (at a time when his mother was already middle-aged and unlikely to have any more children) she had lavished all her affection on this little brother who spent all his time with her at their grandmother's. When he was still a very little boy of only three or four and had not yet begun his schooling, she had taught him to recite several texts and to recognize several thousand characters. Although they were brother and sister, their relationship was more like that of a mother and her son; and even after she entered the Palace, she was always writing letters to her father and her male cousins in which she expressed concern for the little boy who was so constantly in her thoughts. 'I beg you to be most careful in your handling of this child,' she once wrote. 'If you are not strict with him, he will never grow up into a proper man. But if you are too strict, you may endanger his health and cause Grandmother to be distressed.'

When, some months previously, Jia Zheng received a favourable report from Bao-yu's schoolmaster in which his creative ability was commended, he had used the visit to the garden as a means of trying him out. The results were not, of course, what a great writer would have produced in similar circumstances, but at least they were not unworthy of the family's literary traditions, and Jia Zheng resolved that his daughter should see them, so that she might know that the progress made by her beloved younger brother fully came up to the measure of those ardent hopes she had so often expressed in her letters.

– Incidentally, Bao-yu had, in the intervening time, supplied many more inscriptions for the places they had been unable to cover on that first occasion.

Stone

When Yuan-chun saw the words 'Smartweed Bank and Flowery Harbour' she laughed.

'Surely "Flowery Harbour" is enough by itself? Why "Smartweed Bank" as well?'

At once an attendant eunuch disembarked and rushed like the wind to tell Jia Zheng, who immediately gave orders to have the inscription changed.

By this time the barge had drawn alongside the bank and Yuan-chun disembarked and stepped once more into her palanquin. Soon she was borne into that part of the garden where

> 'Roof above roof soared
> Eye up-compelling . . .'

and saw the white marble memorial arch which had so strongly affected Bao-yu when *he* first saw it. It now bore a temporary inscription:

PRECINCT OF THE CELESTIAL VISITANT

Yuan-chun gave orders that the words 'The House of Reunion' should be substituted.

She now ascended the terraces and entered the open-fronted hall of audience.

> From a ring of cressets against the night sky
> a fragrant scatter dropped on the flagstones;
> and candelabra like fiery fir-trees
> gleamed festively in the gilded casements;
> there were blinds looped and fringed like a prawn's belly,
> there were rugs in rows like an otter's offering;
> and tripods smoked with perfumes of musk and borneol,
> and behind the throne waved fans of pheasant feathers.

It was a scene no whit less splendid than that fairy palace of which the poet sings:

> The abode of the Princess has cassia halls and orchid chambers.

'How is it that this place has no name?' asked Yuan-chun.

'This is the principal hall of the Residence, Your Grace. The family dared not give it a name without consulting you first.

Her Grace nodded.

A eunuch Master of Ceremonies now requested her to seat herself upon a chair of state in order to receive the obeisances of her family. Music struck up from a band stationed at either side of the steps as two eunuchs conducted Jia She and Jia Zheng onto the terrace beneath. The other male members of the family ranged themselves behind them and the whole party then began to advance in formation up the steps into the hall.

'Excused!'

A lady-in-waiting came forward and uttered this single word as an indication that the Imperial Concubine wished to absolve them from the ceremonial, and with a slight bow they withdrew.

It was now the turn of Grandmother Jia ('the Dowager Lady Jia of Rong-guo' they called her) and the ladies of the household to make their obeisance. The eunuchs led them up the steps at the east side of the terrace on to the platform in front of the hall, where they ranged themselves in order of precedence.

Once more the lady-in-waiting pronounced the absolving word and they, too, withdrew.

After tea had been offered three times as etiquette prescribed, the Imperial Concubine descended from her throne, the music stopped, and she withdrew into a side room to 'change her clothes'. A less formal carriage than the imperial palanquin had been prepared which carried her from the garden to her family's own quarters.

Inside Grandmother Jia's apartment Yuan-chun became a grandchild once more and knelt down to make her kotow. But Grandmother Jia and the rest knelt down too and prevented her from prostrating herself. She ended up, clinging to Grandmother Jia by one hand and Lady Wang by the other, while the tears streamed down her face, too overcome to say anything. All three of them, in fact, though there was so much they wanted to say, seemed quite incapable of speech and stood there holding each other and sobbing, apparently unable to stop. The others present – Lady Xing, Li Wan, Wang Xi-feng, Ying-chun, Tan-chun and Xi-chun – stood round them weeping silently. No one spoke a word.

Yuan-chun at last restrained her sobs and forced a smile to her tear-stained face:

'It hasn't been easy, winning this chance of coming back among you after all those years since I was first walled up in That Place. Now that we are seeing each other at last, we ought to talk and be cheerful, not waste all the time crying! I shall be leaving again in no time at all, and Heaven only knows when I shall have another chance of seeing you!'

At this point she broke down once more and had to be comforted by Lady Xing. When she had composed herself, Grandmother Jia made her sit down while the members of the family came forward one at a time to greet her and say a few words. This was an occasion for further tears. Then the senior menservants of both the Rong-guo and Ning-guo mansions assembled in the courtyard outside and paid their respects. They were followed by the womenservants and maids, who were allowed to come inside the room to make their kotow.

Yuan-chun asked why her Aunt Xue and her cousins Bao-chai and Lin Dai-yu were missing.

'Relations outside the Jia family are not allowed to see you without a special invitation, dear,' Lady Wang told her.

Yuan-chun asked them to be invited in immediately, and Aunt Xue and the two girls arrived after a few moments. They would have kotowed to her in accordance with court etiquette had not Yuan-chun hurriedly excused them from doing so. The three of them went up to her, and niece and aunt exchanged news of the years that had elapsed since they last met.

Next Lutany and the other maids who had accompanied Yuan-chun into the Palace came forward to make their kotows to Grandmother Jia. The old lady at once motioned to them to rise and gave instructions to her own servants to entertain them in another room.

The senior eunuchs and the ladies-in-waiting were now led off by members of the staffs of Jia She's household and the Ning-guo mansion to be entertained elsewhere, leaving only three or four very junior eunuchs in attendance. Yuan-chun was at last free to chat informally with her mother and the other female members of her family and learned for the first time about many personal and domestic events that had occurred in the household since she left it.

Then there was her interview with Jia Zheng, which had to take place with her father standing outside the door-curtain of the room in which she was sitting. Now that she was the Emperor's woman, this was the nearest to her he could ever hope to get. The sense of deprivation struck home to Yuan-chun as she addressed him through the curtain.

'What is the use of all this luxury and splendour,' she said bitterly, 'if I am to be always separated from those I love – denied the tenderness which even the poorest peasant who seasons his bread with salt and pickles and dresses in hempen homespun is free to enjoy?'

With tears in his eyes the good man delivered the following little speech to the daughter he could not see:
'Madam.
That a poor and undistinguished household such as ours should have produced, as it were, a phoenix from amidst a flock of crows and pies to bask in the sunshine of Imperial favour and shed its reflected beams on the departed representatives of our ancestral line must be attributable to the concentration in your single person of the quintessences of all that is most admirable in celestial and terrestrial nature and the accumulated merit of many generations of our forebears, and is an honour and a blessing in which my wife and I are proud to be participators.

'Our beloved Emperor, who embodies in his own Sacred Person those life-giving forces which are always invisibly at work in the natural cosmos, has showered down upon his grateful subjects a gracious kindness unprecedented in the annals of recorded history – a kindness which even the expenditure of our life's blood to the veriest ultimate drop would be wholly inadequate to repay and which only the most unremitting pains and unswerving loyalty in the discharge of those duties to which it has pleased him to call us could adequately express.

'It is our earnest prayer that His Sacred Majesty may continue long to reign over us, a blessing to all his peoples; and that Your Grace should feel no anxiety concerning the welfare of my wife and myself during our now declining years, but should rather cherish and sustain your own precious person, in order to be the better able to serve His Sacred Majesty with care and diligence, seeking by that service to be worthy of the tender regard and loving favour which he has been graciously pleased to bestow upon you.'

To this formal speech the Imperial Concubine made a formal reply:

'Sir. It is of course desirable that you should exercise the utmost diligence when engaged upon business of state, but it is to be hoped that you will take sufficient care of your own well-being whenever not so engaged, and will under no circumstances vex yourself with anxiety on our behalf.'

'The inscriptions at present displayed on the pavilions and other buildings in the garden were composed by Bao-yu,' said Jia Zheng. 'If there are any places in the garden which particularly take your fancy, we hope you will name them for us.'

The news that Bao-yu could already compose inscriptions evoked a smile of pleasure.

'He *has* made progress, then!'

Jia Zheng withdrew.

'But why is Bao-yu not with us?' she added.

'The menfolk of the family are not supposed to see you without special reason,' Grandmother Jia explained.

Yuan-chun at once gave orders that he should be summoned, and presently he was brought in by one of the little eunuchs. When he had completed his kotow she called him over, and stretching out her arms, drew him to her bosom where she held him in a close embrace, stroking his hair and fondling the back of his neck.

'What a lot you have grown—!' she began. But the rest was drowned in a flood of tears.

You-shi and Xi-feng now approached to announce that a feast awaited her in the Separate Residence. Yuan-chun rose to her feet, and bidding Bao-yu lead the way, walked with the rest of the company to the gate of the garden. There, in the light of the innumerable lanterns, all kinds of spectacles had been prepared for her entertainment. The route led through 'The Phoenix Dance', 'Fragrant Red and Lucent Green', 'The Hopeful Sign', and 'The Garden of Spices'. This time the inspection was no perfunctory one. Yuan-chun insisted on looking inside the buildings and climbing up and down their stairs. She crossed bridges, she walked round each tiny 'mountain', and every once in a while she stopped to look about her and admire the view. All the places she visited were so beautifully furnished and so ingeniously planned, that she could not conceal her delight. But there was a faint note of censure in her praise:

'You really mustn't be so extravagant in future. This is *far* too much!'

They had now come to the main hall. Having first decreed that they should dispense with court etiquette – which would have prevented the older ladies from sitting down at all – she took her place at the main table, while Grandmother Jia and the rest sat at little tables on either side, and You-shi, Li Wan and Xi-feng moved to and fro, dispensing wine and helping with the service.

While they were still drinking, Yuan-chun sent for writing materials, and taking up a brush, began in her own hand to write out some names for the parts of the garden she had liked the best. The name she chose for the garden as a whole was 'Prospect Garden', and she composed the following couplet to go outside the main reception hall:

For all earth to share, his great compassion has been extended,
    that children and humble folk may gratefully rejoice.
For all ages to admire, his noble institutions have been promoted,
    that people of every land and clime may joyfully exult.

She altered 'The Phoenix Dance' to 'The Naiad's House', and she renamed 'Fragrant Red and Lucent Green' 'Crimson Joys and Green Delights' and named the building in its grounds 'The House of Green Delights'. The buildings belonging to 'The Garden of Spices' she named 'All-spice Court'. Those of 'The Hopeful Sign' she gave the name 'Washbrook Farm'. The main hall became 'Prospect Hall' with separate names for the high galleries on either side: 'The Painted Chamber' for the one on the east side, 'The Fragrance Gallery' for the one on the west. Among the other names which she invented for various other parts of the garden were:

'The Smartweed Loggia', 'The Lotus Pavilion', 'Amaryllis Eyot', and 'Duckweed Island'. She also composed inscriptions for some of its prospects, including 'Pear-tree blossom in springtime rain', 'Paulownia leaves in autumn wind', and 'Rushes in the winter snow'. The couplets composed by Bao-yu were to remain unaltered.

Having finished with the inscriptions, she proceeded to write out the following quatrain of her own composition:

> Embracing hills and streams, with skill they wrought:
> Their work at last is to perfection brought.
> Earth's fairest prospects all are here installed,
> So 'Prospect Garden' let its name be called!

'There!' she said with a smile to the girls. 'I'm no genius, as you all well know, and I have never been much of a poet. But tonight I thought I really must write *something*, for this beautiful garden's sake. Later on, when I have more time to spare, I intend to write a *Description of Prospect Garden* and a set of verses to be entitled *The Visitation* in commemoration of this wonderful night. But meanwhile I should like each of you girls to compose an inscription that could be used somewhere in the garden, and also a poem to go with it. Just write anything that comes into your heads. I don't want you to restrict yourselves by trying to make your poems in any way relate to my own poor effort. As for Bao-yu: I am *very* pleased that he is able to compose verses so well, and I want him to write me an octet for each of the four places in the garden I like best: the Naiad's House, All-spice Court – those are my two favourites – the House of Green Delights, and Washbrook Farm. The couplets he has already written for them are very good, but these are four such special places, that I feel they deserve to have something more written about them. And apart from that, if Bao-yu can show me these four poems while I am here, I shall feel that the efforts I made at teaching him when he was a little boy were worth while.'

Bao-yu could scarcely refuse, and went off to rack his brains for some good lines.

Tan-chun was by far the most gifted of the Three Springs and joined Bao-chai and Dai-yu in writing octets. Li Wan,

Ying-chun and Xi-chun, none of whom had any talent for versification, contented themselves with a quatrain apiece, but found even four lines a considerable effort.

When the girls had all finished, Yuan-chun took up the papers one by one and examined the results of their labours. Here is what they had written:

Ying-chun: *Heart's Ease*

The garden finished, all its prospects please.
Bidden to write, I name this spot 'Heart's Ease'.
Who would have thought on earth such scenes to find
As here refresh the heart and ease the mind?

*

Tan-chun: *Brightness and Grace*

Water on hills and hills on waters smile,
More bright and graceful than the Immortal Isle.
Midst odorous herbs the singer's green fan hides;
Her crimson skirt through falling petals glides.
A radiant jewel to the world is shown,
A fairy princess from her tower come down:
And since her steps the garden's walks have trod,
No mortal foot must desecrate its sod.

*

Xi-chun: *Art the Creator*

The garden's landscape far and wide outspreads;
High in the clouds its buildings raise their heads;
Serene in moonlight, radiant in the sun –
Great Nature's handiwork has been outdone!

*

Li Wan: *All Things Bright and Beautiful*

The finished garden is a wondrous sight.
Unlettered and unskilled, I blush to write.
Its marvels are not in one phrase expressed,
Yet 'Bright and Beautiful' I judge the best.

*

Xue Bao-chai: *Auspicious Skies*

West of imperial walls the garden lies;
The sun beams on it from auspicious skies.
Its willows orioles from the vale invite;
Tall bamboos tempt the phoenix to alight.
Poetic arts this night must celebrate
Filial affection dressed in robes of state.
Dare I, who have those jewelled phrases read,
Add more to what She has already said?

*

Lin Dai-yu: *The Fairy Stream*

To fairy haunts far from the world's annoy
A royal visit brings a double joy.
A thousand borrowed beauties here combined
In this new setting new enchantment find.
Its odours sweet a poet's wine enrich;
Its flowers a queenly visitor bewitch.
May she and we this favour hope to gain:
That oft-times she may pass this way again!

*

As soon as she had finished reading the poems, Yuan-chun praised them all warmly. 'But Cousin Lin's and Cousin Xue's poems are *specially* good,' she said. 'Our Jia girls are no match for them!'

Dai-yu had confidently expected that this night would give her an opportunity of deploying her talents to the full and amazing everyone with her genius. It was very disappointing that no more had been required of her than a single little poem and an inscription; and though she was obliged to confine herself to what the Imperial Concubine had commanded, she had composed her octet without enthusiasm and in very perfunctory manner.

Meanwhile Bao-yu was far from finished with *his* consignment. He had finished composing the poems for the Naiad's House and All-spice Court and was still in the middle of a

poem on the House of Green Delights. Bao-chai took a peep
over his shoulder and noticed that his draft contained the line

Some wear sheathed skirts of lucent green curled tight.

When no one was looking she gave him a nudge:

'You can tell Her Grace didn't like "lucent green" because
she only just now altered it to something else in your inscription. If you insist on using it in your poem, it will look as if
you are deliberately flaunting your difference of opinion.
There are so many allusions to plantain leaves you could use,
you shouldn't have much difficulty in substituting something
else.'

'It's all very well for *you* to talk,' said Bao-yu, mopping the
perspiration from his brow, 'but at this particular moment I
can't think of *any* allusion that would do.'

'Why don't you put "in spring green waxen sheaths" in
place of your "sheathed skirts of lucent green"?'

'Where do you get "green waxen" from?' said Bao-yu.

'Tut, tut, tut!' Bao-chai shook her head pityingly. 'If this
is what you are like tonight, Heaven knows what you'll be like
in a few years' time when you come to take the Palace Examination. Probably you'll find you have forgotten even the *Child's
First Primer of Rhyming Names*. It's from the Tang poet Qian
Xu's poem "Furled Plantains":

Green waxen candles from which no flames rise.

Do you mean to say you've forgotten *that*?'

The scales fell from Bao-yu's eyes.

'Good gracious, how *stupid* of me! The words are there
ready-made and I didn't think of them! I shall have to call you
my "One Word Teacher", like the poet in the story! I shan't
be able to treat you like a sister any more, I shall have to say
"sir" when I speak to you!'

'*Sister!*' said Bao-chai with a little laugh. 'Stop fooling
about and get on with your poem! That's your *sister*, sitting up
there in the golden robe. *I'm* no sister of yours!'

Fearing that he would waste more time if she stayed, she
slipped quietly away.

The poem finished, Bao-yu had now completed three out

of the four commanded. At this point Dai-yu, who was still full of dissatisfaction because her talent had been under-employed, noticed that Bao-yu was struggling and came over to the table at which he was working. Observing that 'The Hopeful Sign' still remained to be done, she told him to get on with the copying out in fair of the three poems he had already completed while she thought of something for 'The Hopeful Sign'. When she had completed a poem in her head, she scribbled it out on a piece of paper, screwed it into a little ball, and tossed it in front of him. Bao-yu smoothed it out on the table and read it through. It seemed to him to be ten times better than the ones he had written himself. He copied it out in neat *kai-shu* after the other three and handed the finished task to Yuan-chun for her inspection.

This is what she read:

The Phoenix Dance

> Perfected now at last, this place is fit
> For Bird of Paradise to enter it.
> Each graceful wand lets fall a dewy tear;
> Each glossy leaf breathes coolness on the air.
> Through narrow-parted blocks the pent stream leaps;
> Through chinks of blind the incense thinly seeps.
> Let none the checkered shade with violence rude
> Disrupting, on the slumberer's dreams intrude!

*

The Garden of Spices

> Fragrance of flower-drifts in these quiet confines
> Mingles with headier scents of eglantines,
> And summer's herbs in a soft, spicy bed
> Their aromatic perfumes subtly spread.
> Light mist half screens the winding walks from view,
> Where chilly verdure soaks the clothes with dew.
> Here, slumbering quietly at the fountain's side,
> The dreaming poet all day long may bide.

*

The House of Green Delights

In this quiet plot, where peace reigns through the year,
Bewitching ladies rank on rank appear:
Some wear in spring green waxen sheaths curled tight,
Some carmine caps, that are not doffed at night.
Some from the trellis trail their purple sleeves,
Some lean on rocks, where thin mists cool their leaves.
Their Mistress, standing in the soft summer breeze,
Finds quiet content in everything she sees.

*

The Hopeful Sign

An inn-sign, through the orchards half-discerned,
Promises shelter and a drink well-earned.
Through water-weeds the pond's geese make their way;
Midst elms and mulberry-trees the swallows play.
The garden's chives are ready to prepare;
The scent of young rice perfumes all the air.
When want is banished, as in times like these,
The spinner and the ploughman take their ease.

Yuan-chun was genuinely delighted.

'You really *have* made progress!' she said. She singled out 'The Hopeful Sign' as the best of the four and changed the name 'Washbrook Farm' back to 'Sweet-rice Village' by way of acknowledgement. She made Tan-chun copy all ten poems – Bao-yu's and the girls' – on to a sheet of fancy paper and sent a eunuch to show it to the gentlemen outside. Jia Zheng and the others were very complimentary, and Jia Zheng presented a eulogy of his own composition entitled *The Visitation*. Yuan-chun also ordered Bao-yu and Jia Lan to be given presents of junket and mince, both of some special kind only made in the Imperial kitchens. At this period Jia Lan was still only a very little boy and did not really know what was going on. He was taken by his mother Li Wan into Yuan-chun's presence and stood beside his uncle Bao-yu to make his little bow of thanks.

All this time Jia Qiang and his troupe of girl players had been waiting impatiently below for an order to begin their performance. Just as they were reaching a peak of impatience, a eunuch came running down to them.

'They've finished writing poems,' he said. 'Quick, give me a play-bill!'

Jia Qiang hurriedly handed him a list of the pieces they had rehearsed, together with a brochure containing the stage names of each of the twelve players and some notes on the parts which each of them played. Four pieces were chosen: 'Shi-fan Entertains' from *The Handful of Snow*, 'The Double Seventh' from *The Palace of Eternal Youth*, 'The Meeting of the Immortals' from *The Han-dan Road* and Li-niang's death-scene from *The Return of the Soul*. Jia Qiang supervised the preparations, and soon the rock-splitting little voices and spell-binding movements of the actresses had taken over, and the stage was full of passions which were no whit less overwhelming for being counterfeit.

No sooner had they finished than a eunuch came round, bearing a variety of fancy cakes and sweetmeats on a gilded salver.

'Which is "Charmante"?' he asked, referring to the stage name of the little soubrette who had played the part of Li-niang's maid in *The Return of the Soul* and a dashing young huntsman in the 'play within a play' in *The Handful of Snow*.

Jia Qiang realized that the confectionery was a present for the little actress, and taking the salver from the eunuch, made Mademoiselle Charmante come forward and kotow her thanks.

'Her Grace says that she enjoyed Mademoiselle Charmante's performance the most and would like to see her in two more pieces,' said the eunuch. 'She may choose any two she likes.'

Having replied to the eunuch, Jia Qiang told Charmante that she ought to play two more pieces from *The Return of the Soul*: 'The Walk in the Garden' and 'The Dream'. But neither had a part suitable for a soubrette in it, and Charmante obdurately refused. She said she would do 'The Assignation' and 'The Altercation' from *The Bracelet and the Comb*, in which the part of the pert young maidservant would allow her comic talent a fuller scope. Jia Qiang failed to talk her out of this decision and had to let her do as she wished. Yuan-chun was delighted, and gave special instructions that Charmante was to be well treated and to have the best possible training. She also awarded her, over and above her share of the presents that the whole troupe would receive in commemoration of her visit, two dress-lengths of tribute satin, two embroidered purses, and some miniature gold and silver ingots.

The feast was now cleared away and Yuan-chun recommenced her tour of the garden, visiting those places which she had not had time to look at before dinner. When they came to the little convent nestling under its hill, she washed her hands and entered the shrine-hall to offer incense and pray before the image of the Buddha. She also wrote an inscription for the board which hung above the image:

THE SHIP OF MERCY ON THE SEA OF SUFFERING

and gave instructions for various extra presents to be bestowed on the little nuns in addition to those which, along with all the other members of the household, they were already due to receive in commemoration of her visit.

A list for the latter had already been drawn up and presently it was submitted to Yuan-chun by a kneeling eunuch for her approval. After reading through it in silence she approved its contents and asked that they should be distributed forthwith. The presents distributed were as follows:

> To Grandmother Jia:
>> one golden ru-yi sceptre
>> one jade ditto
>> a staff of carved aloeswood
>> a rosary of putchuk beads
>> four lengths of 'Fu Gui Chang Chun' tribute satin
>> four lengths of 'Fu Shou Mian Chang' tribute silk
>> ten medallions of red gold with a design showing an ingot, a writing-brush and a sceptre (which in the riddling rebus-language used by the makers of such objects meant 'All your heart's desire')
>> ten silver medallions with a design showing a stone-chime flanked by a pair of little fish (carrying the rebus-message 'Blessings in abundance')

Lady Xing, Lady Wang and Aunt Xue each received the same selection of gifts as Grandmother Jia with the omission of the sceptres, staff and rosary.

To Jia Jing, Jia She and Jia Zheng (each):
> two new books of His Imperial Majesty's own composition
> two boxes of ink-sticks (collector's pieces)
> one solid gold wine-cup
> one solid silver ditto
> silks and satins as above.

To Bao-chai, Dai-yu, Ying-chun, Tan-chun and Xi-chun (each):
> one new book
> one inkstone (collector's piece)
> two specially designed medallions in gold
> two ditto in silver

To Bao-yu and Jia Lan (each):
> one gold necklet
> one silver ditto
> two gold medallions
> two silver ditto

To You-shi, Li Wan and Xi-feng (each):
> two gold medallions
> two silver ditto
> four dress-lengths of tribute silk

(Also twenty-four lengths of silk and one hundred strings of unmixed Imperial Mint copper cash for the women-servants and maids in attendance on Grandmother Jia, Lady Wang and the girls)

To Cousin Zhen, Jia Lian, Jia Huan and Jia Rong (each):
> one length of tribute satin
> one gold medallion
> one silver ditto

There were also a hundred bales of variegated satins, a thousand taels of silver and an unspecified number of bottles of Palace wine for the senior servants of the Rong and Ning Mansions and Separate Residence responsible for construction and maintenance, attendance, theatre management, and lighting, and an additional five hundred strings of unmixed Imperial Mint copper cash for the cooks, entertainers and Miscellaneous.

When all had expressed their thanks, one of the eunuchs in charge announced that it was a quarter to three and time for Her Grace to return to the Palace. At once Yuan-chun's eyes filled with tears, and even though she forced herself to smile, she was unable to prevent a few drops from falling. Clinging to Grandmother Jia and Lady Wang as if she would never let them go, she begged them again and again not to grieve for her.

'Now you mustn't worry about me, my dears: just look after yourselves! Thanks to the Emperor's kindness, we are now allowed visits in the Palace once a month: so you see we can see each other quite easily. It is silly of us to be so upset! And if His Majesty is gracious enough to permit another Visitation next year, you really mustn't be so extravagant again on my account!'

Grandmother Jia and the others were now sobbing audibly and were much too overcome to reply. But Yuan-chun, however hard it was to leave her family, dared not infringe the regulations of the Imperial Household, and steeled herself to re-enter the palanquin which was to carry her away. It was all the rest of the family could do to restrain Grandmother Jia from making a scene, and when she was somewhat calmed, she and Lady Wang had to be led weeping from the garden in a state of near-collapse.

What followed will be told in the next chapter.

CHAPTER 19

*A very earnest young woman offers
counsel by night
And a very endearing one is found to
be a source of fragrance by day*

On the day following the Imperial Concubine's return to the Palace, she called on the Emperor to offer thanks and gave him a full account of her Visitation. The Emperor was visibly pleased by her report and commanded that bounties of gold, silver and silks should be issued to Jia Zheng and the other fathers of visiting ladies by the Inner Treasury.

But there is no need for us to pursue these matters in further detail.

*

The events of the last few days had taxed the energies of all the inmates of the Ning-guo and Rong-guo mansions to the utmost, and by now all of them were feeling both physically and mentally exhausted. Even so, Xi-feng forced herself to supervise the taking down and storing away of all the decorations and other movables from the garden – an operation which took another two or three days to accomplish.

Xi-feng's duties and responsibilities were so many that she could not evade them and seek recuperation in rest and quiet as the others did. At the same time, however, the anxiety to be thought well of and the shrinking fear of criticism that were a part of her nature made her take pains, even when she was at her busiest, to appear outwardly as idle and unoccupied as the rest.

Of those idle and unoccupied rest, the idlest and most unoccupied was Bao-yu. On this particular morning, Aroma's mother had been round first thing to report to Grandmother Jia that she was taking her daughter home for a New Year's party and would not be bringing her back until late that evening. After her departure Bao-yu played 'Racing Go' with the other maids. This was a game in which you moved your Go-piece across the board in accordance with the throw of dice, the object being to reach the opposite side before everyone else and pocket all the stakes.

He was already tired of sitting indoors and was beginning to find the game boring, when one of the maids told him that someone had just been round from Cousin Zhen's inviting him over to the other house to see their New Year lanterns and to join them in watching some plays. Bao-yu told the maids to fetch his going-out clothes and help him change. As he was on the point of leaving, someone arrived with a present of sweetened koumiss from the Imperial Concubine. He remembered how much Aroma had enjoyed this drink last time they had had some, and asked them to put it by for her. Then, having first called on Grandmother Jia to tell her he was leaving, he went over to the other house to watch the players.

The plays they were performing turned out to be very noisy ones: *Ding-lang Finds His Father*, *Huang Bo-yang and the Ghostly Army*, *Monkey Makes War in Heaven* and *The Investiture of the Gods*. All of them, but especially the last two, seemed to involve much rushing in and out of supernatural beings, and the sound of drums and cymbals and blood-curdling battle-cries, as they whirled into combat across the stage with banners flying and weapons flashing or invoked the names of the Buddha with waving of burning joss-sticks, was positively deafening. It carried into the street outside, where the passers-by smiled appreciatively and told each other that only a family like the Jias could afford theatricals that produced so satisfying a volume of noise.

To Bao-yu, however, a little of this kind of thing was more than enough, and after sitting for a short while with the rest, he drifted off to seek his amusement elsewhere. To begin with he went inside and spent some time in bantering conversation with You-shi and the maids and concubines in the women's quarters. When he went off once more through the inner gate, the women assumed that he was going back to the play and made no attempt to detain him. The menfolk – Cousin Zhen, Jia Lian, Xue Pan and the rest – were engrossed in games of guess-fingers and other convivial aids to drunkenness, and if they noticed his absence at all, assumed that he was inside with the ladies and did not comment on it.

As for the pages who had accompanied him: the older ones, estimating that he had almost certainly come over for the day, gave themselves time off to gamble and drink with their cronies or to visit friends and relations outside, confident that if they returned in the evening they would be in time for Bao-yu's departure. The younger ones wormed their way into the green-room to watch the excitement and get in the way of the actors. Bao-yu was left without a single one of them in attendance.

Finding himself alone, he began thinking about a certain painting he remembered having seen in Cousin Zhen's 'smaller study'. It was a very life-like portrait of a beautiful woman. While everyone was celebrating, he reflected, she was sure to have been left on her own and would perhaps be feeling lonely. He would go and have a look at her and cheer her up.

But as he approached the study, he experienced a sudden thrill of fright. A gentle moaning could be heard coming from inside it.

'Good gracious!' he thought. 'Can the woman in the painting really have come to life?'

He made a tiny hole in the paper window with his tongue and peeped through. It was no painted lady he saw, stepped down from her hanging scroll upon the wall, but Tealeaf, pressed upon the body of a girl and evidently engaged in those exercises in which Bao-yu had once been instructed by the fairy Disenchantment.

'Good lord!'

He cried out involuntarily, and kicking open the door, strode into the study, so startling the two inside that they shook in their clothes. Seeing that it was Bao-yu, Tealeaf at once fell upon his knees and begged for mercy.

'In broad daylight!' said Bao-yu. 'What do you think you're at? If Mr Zhen got to hear of this, it would be more than your life is worth.'

As he spoke, his eye fell upon the girl. She had a soft, white skin, to whose charms he could not be insensible. At the moment she was red to the very tips of her ears and stood there in silence, hanging her head with shame. Bao-yu stamped his foot impatiently:

'Why don't you go?'

The words seemed to bring her to herself, for she turned and fled immediately. Bao-yu ran after her, shouting.

'Don't be afraid! I won't tell anyone!'

Tealeaf, running out behind him, was frantic:

'My dear little grandfather, that's exactly what you *are* doing!'

'How old is she?' Bao-yu asked him.

'Not more than fifteen or so,' said Tealeaf.

'You don't even know her age!' said Bao-yu. 'You can do *this* to her without even knowing her age! She's wasted on *you*, that's evident. Poor girl! What's her name?'

'Ah *now*, that's quite a story,' said Tealeaf with a broad smile. 'She says that just before she was born her mother dreamed she saw a beautiful piece of brocade, woven in all the colours of the rainbow, with a pattern of lucky swastikas all over it. So when she was born, she gave her the name "Swastika".'

Bao-yu smiled back.

'She ought to have a lucky future ahead of her, then. Shall I ask them tomorrow if you can have her for your wife?'

Tealeaf thought this was a huge joke.

'Why aren't you watching the plays, Master Bao?' he asked. 'They're ever so good!'

'I did watch for quite a while,' said Bao-yu, 'but I got rather deafened and came out to walk around for a bit. That's how I found you here. But what are we going to do now?'

Tealeaf gave a sly little smile:

'What about going for a ride outside the city? If we slipped off quietly we could get there and back without anyone knowing.'

'Too risky,' said Bao-yu. 'We might get kidnapped or something. Besides, there would be terrible trouble if they found out. It'd better be somewhere nearer, so that we can get back quickly.'

'Who do we know near here that we could call on?' said Tealeaf. 'I can't think of anyone.'

'I know,' said Bao-yu. 'Why don't we go round to the Huas' house and see what Aroma is up to?'

'All right. But I've forgotten where they live,' said Tealeaf untruthfully. 'And suppose they *do* find out you've been gadding around outside' (he added the real reason for his hesitation) 'they'll say I put you up to it, and I shall get a beating.'

'I'll see you don't get into trouble,' said Bao-yu.

Reassured, Tealeaf fetched the horse, and the two of them slipped out by the back entrance.

Luckily the Huas' house was only a few hundred yards from the Ning-guo mansion, and in no time at all they had reached its gate. Tealeaf entered first and called out the name of Aroma's elder brother, Hua Zi-fang.

Aroma's mother was not long back from collecting the various nieces, on both her own and her late husband's side of the family, who had had to be fetched after she had been to call for Aroma, and the family had only just settled down to their tea when they heard this voice outside calling for Hua Zi-fang. To the latter's considerable surprise and mystification he found, on going outside to look, his sister's young master waiting at the gate with a servant. Having first lifted Bao-yu off his horse, he went back into the courtyard and bawled to the rest inside:

'It's Master Bao!'

Aroma was dumbfounded and came running out to discover the cause of this unaccountable visit. As soon as she saw him she clung to him anxiously:

'What is it? Are you all right?'

Bao-yu laughed carelessly.

'I was just feeling bored, so I came over to see what you were up to.'

'Stupid!' said Aroma, relieved to find that nothing was amiss. 'What did you *think* I would be up to?'

She turned to Tealeaf.

'Who else is with you?'

'Nobody,' said Tealeaf with a grin. 'Nobody else knows we're here.'

At this Aroma became alarmed once more.

'That's terrible! Suppose you were to run into someone? Suppose you were to meet the *Master*?' She glanced at Bao-yu fearfully. 'In any case, the streets are so crowded now, you could easily get ridden down or something. It would be no joke if you were to have an accident. You two certainly have a nerve!' She turned to Tealeaf again. 'You put him up to this, didn't you? Wait till I get back: I'll tell his nannies about you. They'll have you flogged like a felon, see if they don't!'

Tealeaf pulled a face.

'Don't go trying to pin the blame on me! Master Bao was cursing and swearing at me to make me go with him. *I* kept telling him not to come. Anyway, we'd better be going back now, if that's the way you feel!'

'You might as well stay, now you're here,' said Hua Zi-fang in a conciliatory manner. 'There's no point in quarrelling about it. The only trouble is, this is not much of a place we live in here: poor and cramped and not too clean and that. Hardly a fit place for the likes of Master Bao, I'm thinking.'

By this time Aroma's mother had joined them outside to welcome the visitors. Aroma took Bao-yu by the hand and led him in. He saw four or five girls sitting down inside who hung their heads and blushed when he entered. Despite their blushes, Hua Zi-fang and his mother insisted that Bao-yu should get up on the kang with them, as they were afraid that he would find their house cold. Having installed him on the kang, they bustled to and fro fetching things to eat and pouring tea.

'Now don't you two rush about, Mother,' said Aroma. '*I* know how to look after him. There's no point in your giving him a lot of things he won't be able to eat.'

As she said this she took her own cushion that she had been sitting on, put it on top of a little short-legged kang table, and made Bao-yu sit on it with his feet on her metal foot-warmer. Then she took a couple of rose-shaped perfume lozenges from a little purse she was wearing, opened up her hand-warmer, popped the lozenges onto the burning charcoal, and closing it up again, stuffed it into the front of his gown. Having at last got him settled comfortably and to her own satisfaction, she served him with tea which she poured out for him into her own cup.

Hua Zi-fang and his mother had by now finished laying an elaborate tea. The cakes, nuts and dried fruits were arranged on their plates, and the plates themselves on the table, with painstaking attention to symmetry and design. Aroma could tell at a glance that there was nothing there which Bao-yu could possibly be expected to eat. But her family must not be offended.

'Since you've decided to come,' she said to Bao-yu with a smile, 'we can't let you go without having tasted *something* of ours. You'll have to try *something*, just to be able to say that you have been our guest!'

She took a handful of pine nuts from one of the dishes on the table, and blowing away the skins, handed them to him on her handkerchief.

Bao-yu noticed that Aroma's eyes were slightly red and that there were recent tear-stains on her powdered cheeks.

'Why have you been crying?' He spoke the words in an undertone as she handed him the pine nuts.

'Who's been crying?' said Aroma with a feigned laugh. 'I've just been rubbing my eyes.'

Her little fiction was successful, for he made no further comment.

Bao-yu was wearing his dark-red gown with the pattern of golden dragons and white fox-fur lining, and a sable-lined slate-blue jacket with fringed edges.

'Fancy!' said Aroma, 'you got yourself all dressed up just to come and see *us*. Didn't anyone ask you where you were going?'

'No,' said Bao-yu. 'Actually I changed because I was going to Cousin Zhen's. He invited me over to watch the players.'

Aroma nodded.

'You'd better go back after you've sat a bit longer,' she said. 'This is really no place for you here.'

'*You* shouldn't be too long, either,' said Bao-yu with a smile. 'I've got something nice waiting for you when you get back.'

'Sh!' said Aroma. 'Do you want them all to hear you?'

As she said this, she reached out and took the Magic Jade from his neck.

'Here's something that will interest you all,' she said, holding it out to the others. 'You know how often you've spoken about that wonderful jade of Master Bao's and said how much you'd give for a look at it? Well, here it is! Now you can look to your heart's content. There you are, that's all it is! Not so wonderful, really, is it?'

They passed it from hand to hand, and when it had gone full circle and all had examined it, she hung it once more round his neck.

Aroma told her elder brother to go out and hire the cleanest, smartest-looking cab he could find to take Bao-yu home in.

'*I* can see him safely back,' said Hua Zi-fang. 'He won't come to any harm on horseback.'

'It's not a question of whether he'll come to any harm or not,' said Aroma. 'I'm afraid someone might see him.'

Hua Zi-fang hurried out to hire a cab. The rest of the company, realizing that Bao-yu had no real business to be there, made no effort to detain him and rose to see him off. Aroma snatched up a handful of sweetmeats for Tealeaf. She also gave him a few coppers to buy fireworks with.

'Mind you don't tell anyone about this visit!' she said. 'You'll be in trouble yourself if they find out about it.'

She escorted Bao-yu to the gate and saw him into the cab, pulling the blind down on him as soon as he was inside. Tealeaf and her brother followed behind it with the horse. When they arrived outside the Ning-guo mansion, Tealeaf told the cabbie to stop.

'We'd better go in here for a bit before going home,' he explained to Aroma's brother. 'Otherwise they might get suspicious.'

Hua Zi-fang acknowledged the sense of this precaution, and lifting Bao-yu from the cab, helped him up on to his horse.

'Thank you for your trouble,' said Bao-yu with a winning smile as he rode into the rear gate of the Ning-guo mansion.

And there, for the time being, we shall leave him.

*

When Bao-yu left his room for the other mansion, his maids were free to do exactly as they liked and threw themselves into their amusements with great abandon. Some played at Racing Go, some at Dice and Dominoes. Everywhere a litter of the spat-out skins of melon-seeds bore silent testimony to their indulgence.

It was unfortunate that Nannie Li should have chosen such a moment to come stomping in, stick in hand, to call on Bao-yu and to inquire how he was getting on. She could see that Bao-yu was out, and the uproar created in his absence by the maids was deeply offensive to her.

'Now that I've left service and don't come in very often,' she said with a sigh, 'you girls have got worse than ever. The other nannies can do nothing with you. And as for Bao-yu: he's like a six-foot lampstand that lights up others but stays dark itself; for he's always on about how dirty other people are, but look at the mess he allows you to make of his own room! It's a disgrace!'

Now the maids all knew that Bao-yu did not care about such matters. They also knew that Nannie Li was pensioned off now and had no more power over them. They therefore continued with their fun and took no notice of her. But Nannie Li was not to be ignored. 'How is Bao-yu eating nowadays?' 'What time does he go to bed?' She plied the maids with questions which they answered either cheekily or not at all. One of them even said, quite audibly and in her hearing, 'Old nuisance!'

'What's in this covered bowl?' Nannie Li went on. 'It's junket, isn't it? Why don't you offer it to me?' She picked up the gift of koumiss and began to drink it.

'Don't you touch that!' said one of the maids. 'He was keeping that for Aroma. He'll be angry when he gets back and finds out about that. You'd better tell him yourself you took it. We don't want you getting *us* into trouble!'

Nannie Li was angry and embarrassed at one and the same time.

'I won't believe it of him,' she said. 'I won't believe he would be so wicked as to grudge his old Nannie a bowl of milk. Why, he *owes* it to me. And not only a bowl of milk, either. Much more precious things than that. Do you mean to tell me that Aroma counts for more with him than I do? He ought to stop and ask himself how he grew up to be the big boy he is today. It's my milk he sucked, that came from my own heart's blood: that's what he grew up on. And you mean to tell me that now, if I drink one little bowlful of *his* milk – cow's milk – he's going to be angry with me? Well, I *will* drink it, so there! He can do what he likes about it. And as for that Aroma. I don't know what sort of a wonderful creature you think *she* is – a little bit of a girl I picked out myself and trained with my own hand!'

Defiantly she applied the koumiss once more to her lip and downed it to the last gulp.

One of the maids, politer than the rest, attempted to placate her:

'They shouldn't talk to you like that, Nannie! I'm not surprised you are cross. Of *course* Bao-yu isn't going to upset himself over a little thing like that. He's much more likely to send something nice round to you when he hears that you've been to see him.'

'Don't you try wheedling me with your airs and graces, young woman!' said Nannie Li implacably. 'You think I don't know about Snowpink being dismissed that time over the tea? You needn't worry. If he makes a fuss about it tomorrow, *I* shall take the blame.'

She went off in dudgeon.

Presently Bao-yu returned and sent someone off to fetch Aroma. He noticed Skybright lying motionless on the day-bed.

'What's the matter with her?' he asked. 'Is she ill? Or has she lost the game?'

'She was winning,' said Ripple. 'Then Nannie Li came along and put her off her stroke and she started losing. She got so cross that she had to go and lie down.'

'You shouldn't all take the old girl so seriously,' said Bao-yu. 'Just leave her to do as she likes and take no notice!'

Just at that moment Aroma arrived and said 'hullo' to everyone. She asked Bao-yu where he had eaten and what time he had got back. She also gave her mother's regards to the other maids. When she had finished changing out of her holiday attire and taken the 'going-out' ornaments from her hair, Bao-yu asked someone to fetch the koumiss. There was a chorus of replies from the maids:

'Nannie Li drank it!'

Bao-yu was about to say something when Aroma cut in with a smile:

'So *that*'s what you were saving for me! It was a very kind thought; but last time I had some of that stuff I took too much, being so fond of it, and gave myself a terrible stomach-ache. It didn't go away until I'd brought it all up again, and it's put me off it ever since. It's a good job really that she *did* drink it. It would only have got left around and gone bad. Now what I'd *really* fancy are some dried chestnuts, if you'd like to be peeling them for me while I make up your bed on the kang.'

Bao-yu was completely taken in by this little ruse, and forgetting all about the koumiss, went off for some chestnuts and sat down by the lamp to peel them. He and Aroma were now alone in the room together. Glancing up with a smile from his peeling he said,

'What relation of yours was that girl in the red dress today?'

'That's my mother's sister's child.'

Bao-yu made appreciative noises.

'What are you "oo-ing" and "ah-ing" about?' said Aroma. 'No, don't tell me! I know how your mind works. You think she's not *good* enough to wear red.'

'No. On the contrary,' said Bao-yu. 'If *she*'s not good enough to wear red, I shouldn't think *anyone* is. No, I was merely thinking what a beautiful girl she is and how nice it would be if we could have her to live with us here.'

'Because I have the misfortune to be a slave,' Aroma said bitterly, 'does that mean that all my relations ought to be slaves too? I suppose you think every pretty girl you see is just waiting to be bought so that she can be a servant in your household!'

'How touchy you are!' said Bao-yu. 'Having her to live

with us doesn't have to mean as a servant, does it? It could mean as a bride.'

'Thank you, I'm sure!' said Aroma. 'But my folk are not quite grand enough for that!'

Bao-yu was unwilling to pursue a conversation that had become so unpleasant and went on peeling in silence.

'Why don't you say something?' said Aroma. 'I suppose I've upset you now. Well, never mind! Tomorrow you can go out and buy the lot of them, just to spite me!'

'I don't see what answer I *can* give when you say things like that,' said Bao-yu. 'I only said what a nice girl she was. I think she is exactly suited to live in a big, wealthy household like ours. Much more so than some of the lumbering idiots who *do* live here.'

'She may not have that much good fortune,' said Aroma; 'but for all that she has been very delicately brought up – the apple of my aunt's and uncle's eye. She was seventeen this holidays, and her trousseau is all ready for her to be married next year.'

'Hai!'

An involuntary expression of regret broke from him when he heard that the girl in red was to be married. Already Aroma's words had made him uneasy; but worse was to follow.

'I haven't been able to see much of my cousins during these last few years,' she said with a sigh, 'and now it looks as if they will all have left home when I do go back.'

There was obviously a good deal more that lay behind this remark. Startled, he threw down the chestnut he was peeling and asked her:

'How do you mean, "when you do go back"?'

'Today I heard my mother discussing it with my elder brother. They want me to hold out this one year more, then next year they will see about buying me out of service.'

Bao-yu was becoming more and more alarmed.

'Why should they want to buy you out of service?'

'Well upon my word, that's a funny question to ask!' said Aroma. 'I'm not one of your house-born slaves, my family lives elsewhere. I'm the only member of my family away from home. There's no future for me here. *Naturally* I want to rejoin them.'

'You can't if I won't let you,' said Bao-yu.

'I never heard of such a thing!' said Aroma:

> 'Even in palace hall
> Law is the lord of all.

A bond is a bond. When their term of service has ended, you *have* to let people go. You can't force them to stay in service for ever and ever – especially a household like yours.'

Bao-yu thought a bit. What she said seemed reasonable enough.

'But suppose Grandmother won't let you?'

'Why shouldn't she?' said Aroma. 'If I were a very exceptional sort of person, it's quite possible that she and Her Ladyship might feel upset at the idea of losing me and offer my family money to let me stay on. But as it is I'm only a very ordinary sort of maid. There are any number much better than me. I started off with Her Old Ladyship and served Miss Shi for a few years. Then I was transferred to you, and I've already been quite a few years with you. They would think it quite natural that my family should want to buy me out now. In fact, I wouldn't be surprised if they let me go as a kindness without even asking for the money. If you think they wouldn't let me go because I've served you so well, that's just ridiculous. Serving you well is no more nor less than what I'm supposed to do. It's my job. There's nothing remarkable about that. There'll be plenty of other good ones to take my place when I'm gone. I'm not irreplaceable.'

Everything Aroma said pointed to the reasonableness of her going and the unreasonableness of her staying. A kind of desperateness began to seize him.

'That may be so,' he said, 'but if I'm absolutely determined to keep you, I'm sure Grandmother would speak to your mother about it. If Grandmother had a talk with your mother and offered her a really large sum of money, surely she wouldn't refuse?'

'I'm sure my mother would never insist,' said Aroma. 'And I don't only mean if you spoke to her and gave her a lot of

money. Even if you didn't speak to her about it and didn't
give her any money at all, but simply made up your minds to
keep me here against my will and say nothing, I'm sure she
wouldn't dare object. But your family has never gone in for
throwing its weight about like that in the past, and I don't
believe it is going to start doing so now. It would be different
if I were just an object you'd taken a fancy to and they could
get it for you without any danger of upsetting the owner by
simply offering him ten times the price. But I'm not an object.
If you were to keep me here without rhyme or reason against
my will, you'd not only be doing yourselves no good, you'd
be breaking up someone else's family; and that's something
I'm quite sure Her Old Ladyship and Her Ladyship would
never be willing to do.'

For some time Bao-yu reflected in silence. At last he spoke:

'The long and short of all this is that you are definitely
going, is that right?'

'Definitely.'

'Who would have believed that so sweet a person could be
so faithless and unfeeling?' he thought to himself. But all he
said was:

'If I had known all along that in the end you would go away
and leave me on my own, I should never have let you work
for me in the first place.'

And with those words he took himself off to bed in a
thoroughly bad humour and composed himself for sleep.

Now Aroma's mother and elder brother *had* spoken earlier
that day about their intention of buying her out of service, but
Aroma had at once stated that she would never go back home
as long as she lived.

'When you sold me in the first place,' she said, 'it was
because you had nothing to eat and I was the only thing you
had left in the house which was worth a bit of money. I
couldn't have refused to go and watched my own mother and
father starve. But now, fortunately, *I*'ve got a good situation
– one in which I'm not beaten and sworn at all day long and
where I'm fed and clothed as well as the masters themselves –
and the rest of you, in spite of losing Father, have managed to
get in the clear again and are as well off now as you've ever

been. If you were still hard up and wanted to buy me out so that you could raise a bit of money by reselling me, there would be some point in it. But you're not. What do you want to buy me out *for*? Why don't you just pretend that I'm dead, then you won't need to think about buying me out any more?'

And after that she had had a little cry.

Seeing her so adamant, her mother and brother had naturally resigned themselves to her continuing in service. They did so the more readily as Aroma's contract was, in point of fact, for life. In seeking to redeem her they would have had to rely on the customary generosity of the Jias, who, as soon as they were approached on the subject, would in all probability restore not only the person of Aroma but also the body-price offered for her, but who were certainly not under any obligation to do so.

Another consideration which predisposed them to let her stay was the well-known fact – already mentioned by Aroma – that the Jia household did not ill-treat its servants and relied more on kindness than coercion in its dealings with them. Indeed, the 'inside maids' – those who, like Aroma, were in personal attendance on members of the family (and this was true of *all* of them, no matter in whose apartment they were employed) were the *crème de la crème* of the household staff and were even regarded as a cut above the free daughters of poorer households outside.

Later, when Bao-yu unexpectedly arrived on the scene and they saw how it was between him and Aroma, the reason for her reluctance to leave service at once became apparent. It was a factor they had not foreseen; but now they recognized it, it was a great weight off their minds, and it was not without feelings of relief that they abandoned all further thought of attempting to purchase her freedom.

But to return to our story.

Since early youth Aroma had always been aware that Bao-yu's character was peculiar. His naughtiness and intractability exceeded those of normal boys, and in addition he had a number of extraordinary eccentricities of his own which she could scarcely even have put a name to. Recently he had taken advantage of the comparative immunity from parental control, afforded him by the all-encompassing protection of his doting grandmother, to become even more wild and self-indulgent and even more confirmed in his aversion to serious pursuits than in previous years, and all her attempts to remonstrate with him met with the same obstinate unwillingness to hear. Today's talk about buying her out of service turned out to be providential. By employing only a minimum of deceit, she could use it as a means of ascertaining his real feelings towards her and of humbling his spirit a little, so that he might be in a suitably chastened frame of mind for the lecture with which she was preparing to admonish him. She judged from his going off silently to bed that he was shaken and a little unsure of himself. Evidently she had succeeded in the first part of her plan.

Aroma had not really wanted the chestnuts. She had pretended to do so because she was afraid that the matter of the koumiss might blow up into an incident like the earlier one involving Snowpink and the tea. By pretending to want chestnuts she had deflected him from pursuing it further. She now told the younger maids to take them away and eat them themselves, while she went over to rouse up Bao-yu. The face that he lifted from the pillow was wet with tears.

'Now what do you want to go upsetting yourself like that for?' she said with a smile. 'If you *really* want me to stay, of course I won't go.'

Bao-yu at once brightened up.

'Tell me!' he said. 'Tell me what I must do to *prove* to you how much I want you to stay, since nothing I say myself seems any good!'

'I know we're both fond of each other,' said Aroma. 'That doesn't need any proving. But if you want to be sure of my staying here, it mustn't only be because of that. There are three other things I want to talk to you about. If you will promise to obey me in all of *them*, I shall know that you really and truly want me to stay; then nothing – not even a knife at my throat – will ever make me leave you!'

'Tell me what they are!' he said impetuously. 'I promise to obey you. Dearest Aroma! Sweetest Aroma! Never mind two or three: I would promise if it were two or three *hundred*! All I

ask is that you shouldn't leave me. If the day ever comes
when nothing remains of me but floating particles of ash – no,
not ash. Ash has form and substance and perhaps consciousness
too. Say smoke. A puff of thin smoke dissolved upon the
wind. When that is all that remains of me, and you can no
longer fuss over me because there is nothing left to fuss over,
and I can no longer pay attention to you because there is
nothing left to pay attention with – when that time comes, you
may go or stay as you please!'

'My dear young gentleman,' said Aroma exasperatedly,
clapping her hand over his mouth to prevent him saying any
more, 'it's precisely this way of carrying on that I was going
to talk to you about, and here you go, ranting away worse
than ever!'

'Right,' said Bao-yu. 'Right. I promise never to talk that
way again.'

'That was the *first* thing I wanted you to reform.'

'I've reformed already,' said Bao-yu. 'If I ever talk that way
again, you can pinch my lips! Then what?'

'The second thing is this,' said Aroma. 'I don't care
whether you really like studying or not, but even if you don't,
I'd like you at least to pretend that you do when you're with
the Master or any other gentlemen, and not always be making
sarcastic remarks about it. If you could only put on an appearance of liking it, he would have less cause to be angry with
you, and could even take a bit of pride in you when he was talking to his friends. Look at it from his point of view. Every
generation of your family up to now have been scholars. Then
suddenly *you* come along. Not only do you hate studying –
that's already enough to make him feel angry and upset – but
on top of that you have to be forever making rude remarks
about it – and not only behind his back but even when he's
there. According to you anyone who studies and tries to improve himself is a "career worm". According to you the *Illumi-
nation of Clear Virtue* or whatever it's called is the only genuine
book ever written and all the rest are forgeries. No wonder the
Master gets so angry with you. No wonder he's every minute
of the day wishing he could lay his hands on you and give you
a thrashing.'

Bao-yu laughed.

'All right. I won't say such things any more. In any case, these are all things I used to say when I was younger and didn't know any better. I don't say things like that nowadays. What else?'

'You must leave off forever going on about people's appearance and interfering with their make-up – and you *must* give up that filthy habit of stealing people's lipstick and eating it on the sly. That's *most* important!'

'I'll reform! I'll reform! Is there anything else, now?'

'Nothing else, really. Just to be a bit more careful about things in general and not always letting yourself get carried away by your whims and fancies. But if you will really keep your promise about these three things I've mentioned, *I* will promise never to leave you – even if they send a bridal chair and eight strong bearers to carry me away!'

'Oh, come now! Isn't that stretching it a bit?' said Bao-yu with a laugh. 'For eight bearers and a handsome husband I bet you'd go!'

'It wouldn't interest me in the least,' said Aroma haughtily. '"Kind sir, for such blessing I am not willing." Even if I *did* go, I should take no pleasure in it.'

Their dialogue was interrupted by Ripple, who just at that moment entered the room.

'It's nearly midnight, you two. You ought to be in bed. Her Old Ladyship just now sent one of the nannies round to ask about you and I told her you were asleep.'

Bao-yu asked for his watch and looked. The hand was pointing to half past eleven. He washed and cleaned his teeth all over again, and taking off his outer clothes, settled down once more to sleep.

*

When Aroma got up first thing next morning she felt heavy and unwell. Her head ached, her eyelids were puffy and her whole body was afire. At first she dragged herself round performing her usual tasks, but eventually she could hold out no longer and had to lie down fully clothed on the kang. Bao-yu at once informed Grandmother Jia, who called in a doctor.

Having taken Aroma's pulses, the doctor informed them that she had 'merely contracted a severe chill and would be all right after taking a few doses of medicine to relieve the congestion,' and left after writing a prescription. Bao-yu sent out for the materials prescribed, and when they had been duly boiled up and the first draught taken, made her cover herself with a quilt to bring on a perspiration. Then he went off to see Dai-yu.

Dai-yu was at that moment taking a midday nap. Her maids had all gone off about their own affairs. Not a sound could be heard from the inside room. As Bao-yu lifted the embroidered door-curtain and entered, he could see her lying asleep inside and hurried over to rouse her:

'Sleeping after you've just eaten, coz? That's bad! Wake up!'

His voice woke her. She opened her eyes and saw that it was Bao-yu.

'*Do* go away and play for a bit! I'm so dreadfully tired. I didn't get any sleep last night and I haven't been able to rest until now.'

'Never mind how tired you are,' said Bao-yu. 'You'll do yourself much more harm by sleeping after a meal. I'll stay and amuse you to keep you awake if you feel sleepy.'

'I'm not sleepy, I'm *tired*. I want to *rest* for a bit. Can't you go and amuse yourself somewhere else for a few minutes and come back later?'

Bao-yu gave her another shake.

'Where else *can* I go?' he said. 'I'm so *bored* with everyone else.'

'Chee-ee-ee!' Dai-yu exploded in a little laugh. 'All right. I suppose now you are here you may as well stay. You can sit very, very quietly over there and we will talk.'

'I should prefer to lie down,' said Bao-yu.

'All right, lie down then!'

'There isn't a pillow. We shall have to share yours.'

'Don't be ridiculous!' said Dai-yu. 'Look at all those pillows in the next room. Why don't you get yourself one of them?'

Bao-yu went into the outer room for a look but came back empty-handed.

'I don't want any of *them*,' he said genially. 'How do I know some dirty old woman hasn't been sleeping on them?'

Dai-yu opened her eyes very wide.

'You really are the bane of my life!' she said. 'Here, take this!' She pushed the pillow she had been lying on towards him and got up to fetch another one of her own to replace it with. The two of them then reclined, facing each other, at opposite ends of the bed.

Glancing up from her recumbent position, Dai-yu noticed that there was a blood-spot about the size of a small button on Bao-yu's left cheek. She bent over him to examine it more closely and touched it lightly with her finger.

'Whose nails was it this time?'

Bao-yu lay back to avoid her scrutiny and laughed.

'It isn't a scratch. I've just been helping them make rouge. A little of it must have splashed on to my face.' He rummaged for a handkerchief to wipe it off with.

Dai-yu wiped it off with her own, clicking her tongue censoriously as she did so.

'So you're up to *those* tricks again? You might at least refrain from advertising the fact! Even if Uncle doesn't see you himself, someone else might who thought it an amusing story to go around gossiping about. He could easily get to hear about it in that way, and that would make it unpleasant for *all* of us.'

But her words were lost on Bao-yu. He was preoccupied with a subtle fragrance which seemed to emanate from Dai-yu's sleeve – a fragrance that intoxicated the senses and caused one to feel rather limp. He seized hold of the sleeve and demanded to know what perfume she was wearing.

'Perfume? At this season?' said Dai-yu with a laugh. 'I'm not wearing any. "In the cold winter none smells sweet"!'

'Well, where *does* it come from, then?'

'I don't know myself where it comes from,' said Dai-yu. 'I suppose it might have come from the wardrobe.'

Bao-yu shook his head.

'I doubt it. It's a very unusual scent. Not the kind you would get from a scent-cake or a perfume-ball or sachet.'

'I hope you don't imagine it's some exotic perfume given me by the Immortals of the Isles. Even if I had the recipe, *I* have no kind elder brother to get together all those flowers and stamens and things and make it up for me. *I* have got only the ordinary, vulgar sorts of perfume!'

'Whatever I say, you are always dragging in things like that,' said Bao-yu. 'Very well. You will have to be taught a lesson. From now on, no mercy!'

Half rising, he pretended to spit on his hands, then stretching them out before him, began to waggle his fingers up and down in the region of her ribs and armpits. Dai-yu had always been the most ticklish of mortals, and the mere sight of his waggling fingers sent her off into shrieks of laughter which soon ended in breathlessness:

'Oh! Oh! Bao-yu! No! Stop! I'll be angry!'

'Will you say things like that any more?'

'No,' said Dai-yu, laughing weakly, 'I promise.'

She proceeded to pat her hair into place, smilingly complacently:

'So I've got an unusual fragrance, have I? Have *you* got a *warm* fragrance?'

For the moment Bao-yu was puzzled:

'*Warm* fragrance?'

Dai-yu shook her head pityingly.

'Don't be so dense! You have your jade. *Somebody* has a gold thing to match. Somebody has Cold Fragrance, *ergo* you must have Warm Fragrance to go with it!'

'I've only just let you off,' said Bao-yu, 'and here you go again, worse than ever!'

Once more he stretched out the threatening fingers and Dai-yu again began to shriek.

'No! Bao-yu! *Please*! I promise!'

'All right, I forgive you. But you must let me smell your sleeve.'

He wrapped the free end of that garment over his face and abandoned himself to long and prodigious sniffs.

Dai-yu jerked away her arm.

'I really think you ought to go.'

'Couldn't go if I wanted to. Let's lie down very quietly and genteelly and have a conversation.' And he stretched himself out again.

Dai-yu lay down too, and covered her face with a handkerchief.

He tried to arouse her interest with desultory chat – talking for the sake of talking. Dai-yu took no notice. He tried asking questions. How old was she when she first came to the Capital? What had the scenery been like on the journey? What places of historical interest were there in Yangchow? What were its inhabitants like? What were its local customs? Dai-yu made no reply. Still concerned that she might fall asleep and injure her health, he tried a ruse.

'Why, *yes*!' he said, as if suddenly remembering something. 'There's a famous story that took place near Yangchow. I wonder if you know about it.'

This was delivered with so straight a face and in so serious a tone of voice that Dai-yu was quite taken in.

'Oh? What?'

Mastering a strong inclination to laugh, he began to extemporize with whatever came into his head.

'Near the city of Yangchow there is a mountain called Mt Yu-dai, in the side of which is a cavern called the Cave of Lin.'

'That's false, for a start,' said Dai-yu. 'I've never heard of a mountain of that name.'

'There are a great many mountains in this world,' said Bao-yu. 'You could hardly be expected to know all of them. Leave your criticisms until I have finished my story.'

'Carry on,' said Dai-yu.

'Now in the Cave of Lin there lived a tribe of magic mice, and one year, on the seventh day of the last month, the Oldest Mouse climbed up on to his throne and sat in council with the rest of the tribe.

' "Tomorrow is Nibbansday," he said, "and everywhere in the world of men they will be cooking frumenty. Since our cave is at present short of dry provender, we should take this opportunity of replenishing *our* stores by raiding *theirs*." He took a ceremonial arrow from the receptacle in front of him and handing it to an able younger mouse, instructed him to carry out a reconnaissance. In due course the Able Younger Mouse came back and reported that, though he had looked positively everywhere, there were nowhere more plentiful stores to be found than in the temple at the foot of the mountain.

' "How many kinds of grain have they got there, and how many sorts of dried fruits?" the Oldest Mouse asked him.

' "There is a whole granary full of rice and beans," replied the Able Younger Mouse, "but only five kinds of dried fruits:

the first,	red dates
the second,	chestnuts
the third,	peanuts
the fourth,	caltrops
the fifth,	sweet potatoes."

'The Oldest Mouse was highly delighted, and picking up another arrow, he said,

' "Who will go to steal rice?"

'A mouse at once took the arrow and went off to steal rice.

' "Who will go to steal beans?" he asked, picking up another arrow.

'Another mouse took the arrow and went off to steal beans.

'One by one they departed on their missions until only the sweet potatoes had still to be arranged for.

'The Oldest Mouse took up another arrow.

' "Who will go to steal sweet potatoes?"

'A little puny, weak mouse replied,

' "I will!"

'Seeing how young and puny he was, the Oldest Mouse and the other members of the mousey tribe feared that he would be too lacking in training and experience and too timid and weak to carry out the task, and refused to let him go. But the little mouse said,

' "Although I am young in years and weak in body, I am eloquent and resourceful and possess unlimited magic powers. I can guarantee to carry out this mission even more expeditiously than the rest."

' "How will you do that?" asked the other mice.

' "I shan't rush at the job head-on like the others," said the little mouse. "By just giving my body a couple of shakes I shall change myself into a sweet potato; I shall *roll* myself into the pile of sweet potatoes without anyone seeing me; then – very, very gently – I shall *roll* the sweet potatoes away, one by one, until there aren't any more left. Isn't that a more expeditious way of doing it than the crude and headlong approach which the others have adopted?"

' "That's all very well," said the other mice, "but what about this transformation business? Let's see you do it first!"

' "Nothing easier!" said the little mouse with a confident smile. "Watch!"

'He gave his body a couple of shakes.

' "Hey presto!"

'And at once he turned into the most exquisitely beautiful young lady.

'The other mice all laughed.

' "No, no, no, you've made a mistake! That's not a sweet potato, that's a young lady you've turned into!"

'The little mouse resumed his own shape and smiled at them pityingly.

' "It is you who are mistaken. You have seen too little of the world to understand. The vegetable tuber is not the only kind of sweet potato. The daughter of our respected Salt Commissioner Lin is also a sweet potato. She is the sweetest sweet potato of them all." '

Dai-yu got up on her knees and, crawling over, planted herself on top of Bao-yu.

'I'll teach you to make fun of me, you hateful creature! I'll teach you!'

She seized his lips between thumb and finger and began to pinch and shake them.

'Help!' cried Bao-yu. 'Mercy! I won't do it again! It was smelling your beautiful perfume that put me in mind of the allusion.'

'*Allusion*?' said Dai-yu. 'You vilify someone else and then call it an allusion?'

Just at that moment Bao-chai walked in.

'Who's this talking about allusions? I must hear this!'

Dai-yu invited her to sit down.

'Look! Who else would you expect it to be? He says a lot of horrid things about me and then tells me it's an allusion!'

'Oh,' said Bao-chai. 'Cousin Bao. I'm not surprised, then. He is *full* of allusions. The only trouble is that he tends to forget them at the very moment when they are most needed. If he can remember allusions today, he *ought* to have been able to remember that allusion about the plantain the other night. But no, it just wouldn't come, and though everyone else was dying of cold, *he* was perspiring! Yet now his memory has come back again. Strange!'

'Now praised be!' said Dai-yu. 'I have a nice, kind cousin to stick up for me. You've met your match now,' she said to Bao-yu. 'Now you are going to get as good as you give! Now we shall see you paid in your own coin!'

Their conversation was interrupted by a burst of angry shouting from the direction of Bao-yu's room.

The occasion of it will be discussed in the following chapter.

CHAPTER 20

*Wang Xi-feng castigates a jealous attitude
with some forthright speaking
And Lin Dai-yu makes a not unattractive speech
impediment the subject of a jest*

We have shown how Bao-yu was in Dai-yu's room telling her the story of the magic mice; how Bao-chai burst in on them and twitted Bao-yu with his failure to remember the 'green wax' allusion on the night of the Lantern Festival; and how the three of them sat teasing each other with good-humoured banter.

Bao-yu had been afraid that by sleeping after her meal Dai-yu would give herself indigestion or suffer from insomnia through being insufficiently tired when she went to bed at night, but Bao-chai's arrival and the lively conversation that followed it banished all Dai-yu's desire to sleep and enabled him to lay aside his anxiety on her behalf.

Just then a sudden commotion arose from the direction of Bao-yu's room, and the three of them stopped talking and turned their heads to listen. Dai-yu was the first to speak:

'That's your Nannie quarrelling with Aroma,' she said. 'To think how that poor girl goes out of her way to be nice to the old woman, yet *still* she manages to find fault with her! She really must be getting senile.'

Bao-yu was for rushing over straight away, but Bao-chai restrained him:

'Don't go quarrelling with your Nannie, whatever you do! She's only a silly old woman. You have to indulge her a bit.'

'Of course,' said Bao-yu and ran off.

He found Nannie Li leaning on her stick in the middle of the room abusing Aroma:

'Ungrateful little baggage! After all I've done for you – and now when I come to call on you, you lie back there on the kang like a young madam and haven't even the grace to look up and take notice of me! You and your airs and graces!

All you ever think about is how to win Bao-yu over to you. Thanks to you he won't listen to me any more. He only does what *you* say. To think that a cheap bit of goods like you that they only paid a few taels of silver for should come along here and turn the whole place upside down! The best thing they could do with you would be to marry you off to one of the boys and send you packing. *Then* we'd see how you managed to play the siren and lead young gentlemen astray!'

Aroma at first thought that Nannie Li's anger arose solely on account of her failure to get up and welcome her, and had started to excuse herself on that supposition:

'I'm ill, Mrs Li. I've just been sweating. I didn't see you because I had my head under the clothes.'

But when the old woman proceeded to go on about leading young men astray and marrying her off to a servant and what not, she felt wronged and humiliated, and in spite of her efforts to restrain them, burst into tears of sheer helplessness.

Bao-yu had heard all this, and though too embarrassed to argue, could scarcely refrain from saying a word or two in Aroma's defence:

'She's ill. She's having to take medicine,' he said. 'If you don't believe me, ask any of the maids.'

This made the old woman even angrier.

'Oh yes! You stick up for the little hussies! You don't care about *me* any more! And which of them am I supposed to ask, pray? They will all take your side against me. You are all under Aroma's thumb, every one of you. I know what goes on here, don't think I don't! Well, you can come along with me to see Her Old Ladyship and Her Ladyship about this. Let *them* hear how you have cast me off – me that reared you at my own breast – now that you don't need my milk any more, and how you encourage a pack of snotty-nosed little maidservants to amuse themselves at my expense!'

She was in tears herself by now, and wept as she cursed.

By this time Dai-yu and Bao-chai had also arrived on the scene and did their best to calm her:

'Come, Nannie! Be a bit more forbearing with them! Try to forget about it!'

Nannie Li turned towards this new audience and proceeded

to pour out her troubles in an interminable gabble in which tea and Snowpink and drinking koumiss mingled incoherently.

Xi-feng happened to be in Grandmother Jia's room totting up the day's scores for the final settlement when she heard this hubbub in the rear apartment. She identified it immediately as Nannie Li on the rampage once more, taking out on Bao-yu's unfortunate maids some of the spleen occasioned by her recent gambling losses. At once she hurried over, seized Nannie Li by the hand, and admonished her with smiling briskness:

'Now, Nannie, we mustn't lose our tempers! This is the New Year holiday and Her Old Ladyship has been enjoying herself all day. A person of your years ought to be stopping other people from quarrelling, not upsetting Her Old Lady-ship by quarrelling yourself. Surely you know better than that? If anyone has been misbehaving, you have only to tell me and I'll have them beaten for you. Now I've got a nice hot pheasant stew in my room. You just come along with me and you shall have some of that and a drink to go with it!'

She proceeded to haul her off the premises, addressing a few words over her shoulder to her maid Felicity as she went:

'Felicity, bring Nannie's stick for her, there's a good girl! And for goodness' sake give her a handkerchief to wipe her eyes with!'

Unable to hold her ground, the old Nannie was borne off in Xi-feng's wake, muttering plaintively as she went:

'I wish I was dead, I really do! But I'd sooner forget meself and make a scene like I have today and be shamed in front of you all than put up with the insolence of those shameless little baggages!'

Watching this sudden exit, Bao-chai and Dai-yu laughed and clapped their hands:

'How splendid! Just the sort of wind we needed to *blow* the old woman away!'

But Bao-yu shook his head and sighed:

'I wonder what had really upset her. Obviously she only picked on Aroma because she is weak and can't defend herself. I wonder which of the girls had offended her to make her so . . .'

He was interrupted by Skybright:

'Why should any of us want to upset her? Do you think we're mad? And even if we *had* offended her, we should be perfectly capable of owning up to it and not letting someone else take the blame!'

Aroma grasped Bao-yu's hand and wept:

'Because *I* offended one old nurse, *you* have to go offending a whole roomful of people. Don't you think there's been enough trouble already without dragging other people into it?'

Seeing how ill she looked and realizing that distress of mind could only aggravate her condition, Bao-yu stifled his indignation and did his best to comfort her so that she might be able to settle down once more and continue sweating out the fever. Her skin was burning to the touch. He decided to stay with her for a while, and lying down beside her, spoke to her soothingly:

'Just try to get better, now! Never mind all that other nonsense! It's of no importance.'

Aroma smiled bitterly.

'If I had allowed myself to get upset about things like that, I shouldn't have lasted in this room for five minutes! Still, if we're *always* going to have this sort of trouble, I think in the long run I just *shan't* be able to stand any more. You don't seem to realize. You offend people on my account and the next moment you've forgotten all about it. But *they* haven't. It's all scored up against me; and as soon as something goes a bit wrong, they come out with all these horrible things about me. It makes it so unpleasant for all of us.'

She cried weakly as she said this, but presently checked herself for fear of upsetting Bao-yu.

Soon the odd-job woman came in with the second infusion of Aroma's medicine. Bao-yu could see that she had started sweating again and told her not to get up, holding the medicine for her himself and supporting her while she drank it. Then he told one of the junior maids to make up a bed for her on the kang.

'Whether you're going to eat there or not,' Aroma said to him, 'you'd better go and sit with Her Old Ladyship and Her Ladyship for a bit and play a while with the young ladies before you come back here again. I shall be all right if I lie here quietly on my own.'

Bao-yu thought he had better do as she said, and after waiting until she had taken off her ornaments and was lying tucked up in bed, he went to the front apartment and took his dinner with Grandmother Jia.

After dinner Grandmother Jia wanted to go on playing cards with some of the old stewardesses. Bao-yu, still worrying about Aroma, returned to his own room, where he found her sleeping fitfully. He thought of going to bed himself, but it was still too early. Skybright, Mackerel, Ripple and Emerald had gone off in quest of livelier entertainment, hoping to persuade Grandmother Jia's maids, Faithful and Amber, to join them in a game. Only Musk was left in the outer room, playing Patience under the lamp with a set of dominoes. Bao-yu smiled at her.

'Why don't you go off to join the others?'

'I haven't got any money.'

'There's a great pile of money under the bed. Isn't that enough for you to lose?'

'If we all went off to play,' said Musk, 'who would look after this room? There's *her* sick inside. And lamps and stoves burning everywhere. The old women were practically dead on their feet after waiting on you all day; I *had* to let them go and rest. And the girls have been on duty all day, too. You could scarcely grudge them some time off now for amusement. – Which leaves only me to look after the place.'

'Another Aroma,' thought Bao-yu to himself and gave her another smile.

'I'll sit here while you're away. There's nothing to worry about here if you'd *like* to go.'

'There's even less excuse for going if *you* are here,' said Musk. 'Why can't we both sit here and talk?'

'What can we do?' said Bao-yu. 'Just sitting here talking is going to be rather dull. I know! You were saying this morning that your head was itchy. As you haven't got anything else to do now, I'll comb it for you.'

'All right,' said Musk, and fetching her toilet-box with the mirror on top she proceeded to take off her ornaments and shake her hair out. Bao-yu took a comb and began to comb it for her. But he had not drawn it more than four or five times through her hair, when Skybright came bursting in to get some more money. Seeing the two of them together, she smiled sarcastically:

'Fancy! Doing her hair already – before you've even drunk the marriage-cup!'

Bao-yu laughed.

'Come here! I'll do yours for you too, if you like!'

'I wouldn't presume, thanks all the same!'

She took the money, and with a swish of the door-blind was gone.

Bao-yu was standing behind Musk as she sat looking at herself in the mirror. Their eyes met in the glass and they both laughed.

'Of all the girls in this room she has the sharpest tongue,' said Bao-yu.

Musk signalled to him agitatedly in the glass with her hand. Bao-yu took her meaning; but it was too late. With another swish of the door-blind, Skybright had already darted in again.

'Oh! Sharp-tongued, am I? Perhaps you'd like to say a bit more on that subject?'

'Get along with you!' laughed Musk. 'Don't go starting any *more* arguments!'

'And don't you go sticking up for him!' said Skybright gaily. 'I know what you're up to, you two. You don't deceive me with your goings-on. I'll have something to say to you about this when I get back later. Just wait until I've won some of my money back!'

With that she darted off once more.

When Bao-yu had finished combing her hair, he asked Musk to help him get to bed – very quietly, so as not to disturb Aroma.

And that ends our account of that day.

*

First thing next morning Aroma awoke to find that she had sweated heavily during the night and that her body felt very much lighter; but she would take only a little congee for breakfast in order not to tax her system too soon. Bao-yu saw that there was no further cause for concern, and after his meal drifted off to Aunt Xue's apartment in search of amusement.

Now this was the prime of the year, when the schoolroom is closed for the New Year holiday and the use of the needle is forbidden to maidenly fingers throughout the whole of the Lucky Month, so that boys and girls alike are all agreeably unemployed, and Bao-yu's half-brother Jia Huan, on holiday like all the rest, had also drifted over to Aunt Xue's place in search of amusement. He found Bao-chai, Caltrop and Oriole there playing a game of Racing Go, and after watching them for a bit, wanted to play too.

Bao-chai had always behaved towards Jia Huan in exactly the same way as she did towards Bao-yu and made no distinctions between them. Consequently, when he asked to play, she at once made a place for him and invited him to join them on the kang. They played for stakes of ten cash each a game. Jia Huan won the first game and felt very pleased. But then, as luck would have it, he lost several times in a row and began to get somewhat rattled.

It was now his turn to throw the dice. He needed seven to win, and if he threw anything less than seven, the dice would go next to Oriole, who needed only three. He hurled them from the pot with all his might. One of them rested at two. The other continued rather erratically to roll about. 'Ace! Ace! Ace!' cried Oriole, clapping her hands. 'Six! Seven! Eight!' shouted Jia Huan glaring at Oriole and commanding the die to perform the impossible. But the perverse wanderer finally came to rest with the ace uppermost, making a grand total of three. With the speed of desperation Jia Huan reached out and snatched it up, claiming, as he did so, that it was a six.

'It was an ace,' said Oriole, 'as plain as anything!'

Bao-chai could see that Jia Huan was rattled, and darting a sharp look at Oriole, commanded her to yield.

'You grow more unmannerly every day,' she told her. 'Surely you don't think one of the masters would cheat you? Come on! Put your money down!'

Oriole smarted with the injustice of this, but her mistress

had ordered it, so she had to pay up without arguing. She could not, however, forbear a few rebellious mutterings:

'Huh! One of the masters! Cheating a maid out of a few coppers! Even *I* should be ashamed! Look how much money Bao-yu lost when he was playing with us the other day, yet *he* didn't mind. Even when some of the maids took all he had left, he only laughed . . .'

She would have gone on, but Bao-chai checked her angrily.

'How can I hope to compete with Bao-yu?' said Jia Huan, beginning to blubber. 'You're all afraid of him. You all take his part against me because I'm only a concubine's son.'

Bao-chai was shocked:

'Please don't say things like that, Cousin! You'll make your-self ridiculous.'

Once more she rebuked Oriole.

Just at that moment Bao-yu walked in, and seeing the state that Jia Huan was in, asked him what was the matter. But Jia Huan dared not say anything.

Bao-chai, familiar with the state of affairs, normal in other families, which places the younger brother in fearful subjec-tion to the elder, assumed that Jia Huan was afraid of Bao-yu. She was unaware that Bao-yu positively disliked anyone being afraid of him. 'We are both equally subject to our parents' control,' he would say of himself and Jia Huan. 'Why should I create a greater distance between us by trying to control him myself – especially when I am the wife's son and he is the concubine's? People already talk behind our backs, even when I do nothing. It would be ten times worse if I were to start bossing him about.'

But there was another, zanier, notion which contributed to this attitude. Let us try to explain it. Bao-yu had from early youth grown up among girls. There were his sisters Yuan-chun and Tan-chun, his cousins of the same surname Ying-chun and Xi-chun, and his distaff-cousins Shi Xiang-yun, Lin Dai-yu and Xue Bao-chai. As a result of this upbringing, he had come to the conclusion that the pure essence of human-ity was all concentrated in the female of the species and that males were its mere dregs and off-scourings. To him, there-fore, all members of his own sex without distinction were brutes who might just as well not have existed. Only in the case of his father, uncles and brother, where rudeness and disobedience were expressly forbidden by the teachings of Confucius, did he make an exception – and even then the allowances he made in respect of the fraternal bond were extremely perfunctory. It certainly never occurred to him that his own maleness placed him under any obligation to set an example to the younger males in his clan. The latter – Jia Huan included – reciprocated with a healthy disrespect only slightly tempered by their fear of his doting grandmother.

But Bao-chai was ignorant of all this; and fearing that Bao-yu might embarrass them all by delivering a big brother's telling-off, she hastened to Jia Huan's defence.

'What are *you* crying about in the middle of the New Year holidays?' said Bao-yu to Jia Huan, ignoring Bao-chai's excuses. 'If you don't like it here, why don't you go somewhere else? I think your brains must have been addled by too much study. Can't you see that if there is something you don't like, there must be something else you *do* like, and that all you've got to do is leave the one and go after the other? Not hang on to it and cry. Crying won't make it any better. You came here to enjoy yourself, didn't you? And now you're here you're miserable, right? Then the thing to do is to go somewhere else, isn't it?'

In the face of such an argument Jia Huan could not very well remain.

When he got back to his own apartment, his real mother, 'Aunt' Zhao (Lady Wang was his mother only in name) observed the dejected state he was in.

'Who's been making a doormat of you this time?' she asked him, and, obtaining no immediate reply, asked again.

'I've just been playing at Bao-chai's. Oriole cheated me and Bao-yu turned me out.'

Aunt Zhao spat contemptuously:

'Nasty little brat! That's what comes of getting above yourself. Who asked you to go playing with that lot? You could have gone anywhere else to play. Asking for trouble!'

Just at that moment Xi-feng happened to be passing by outside, and hearing what she said, shouted back at her through the window:

'What sort of language is that to be using in the middle of the New Year holiday? He's only a child. He hasn't done anything terrible. What do you want to go carrying on at him like that for? No matter *where* he's been, Sir Zheng and Lady Wang are quite capable of looking after him themselves. There's no cause for *you* to go biting his head off! After all, he *is* one of the masters. If he's misbehaved himself, you should leave the telling-off to those whose job it is. It's no business of yours. Huan! Come out here! Come and play with me!'

Jia Huan had always been afraid of Xi-feng – more even than he was of Lady Wang – and hearing her call him, came running out immediately. Aunt Zhao dared not say a word.

'You're a poor-spirited creature!' Xi-feng said to him. 'How many times have I told you that you can eat and drink and play with any of the boys and girls you like? But instead of doing as I say, you hang about with these other people and let them warp your mind for you and fill it up with mischief. You've no self-respect, that's your trouble. Can't keep away from the gutter. You insist on making yourself disagreeable and then you complain that people are prejudiced against you! Fancy making a fuss like that about losing a few coppers! How much *did* you lose?'

'One or two hundred,' Jia Huan muttered abjectly.

'All this fuss about one or two hundred cash! And you one of the masters!' She turned to Felicity. 'Go and get a string of cash for him, Felicity, and take him round to the back where Miss Ying and the girls are playing! And if I have any more of this nonsense from you in future, young man,' she went on to Jia Huan, 'I'll first give you a good hiding myself and then send someone to tell the school about you and see if *they* can knock a bit of sense into you! It sets your Cousin Lian's teeth on edge to see you so wanting in self-respect. He'd have disembowelled you by now I shouldn't wonder, if I hadn't kept his hands off you! Now be off with you!'

'Yes,' said Jia Huan meekly and went off with Felicity.

When he had got his money, he took himself off to play with Ying-chun and the girls.

And there we must leave him.

*

While Bao-yu was enjoying himself with Bao-chai, a servant announced that Miss Shi had arrived, and he hurriedly got up to go.

'Wait!' said Bao-chai. 'Let's go and see her together!'

She got down from the kang as she said this, and accompanied him round to Grandmother Jia's apartment. Shi Xiang-yun was already there, laughing and chattering away nineteen to the dozen, but rose to greet them as they entered. Dai-yu was there too.

'Where have *you* been?' she asked Bao-yu.

'Bao-chai's.'

'I see' (very frostily). 'I thought *something* must have been detaining you. Otherwise you would have come flying here long since.'

'Is one only allowed to play with *you*,' said Bao-yu, 'and keep *you* amused? I just happened to be visiting her. Why should you start making remarks like that?'

'How thoroughly disagreeable you are!' said Dai-yu. 'What do I care whether you go to see her or not? And I'm sure *I* never asked to be kept amused. From now on you can ignore me completely, as far as I'm concerned.'

With that she went back to her own room in a temper.

Bao-yu came running after.

'What on *earth* are you upset about this time? Even if I've said anything wrong, you ought, out of simple courtesy, to sit and talk with the others for a bit!'

'Are you telling me how to behave?'

'Of *course* not. It's just that you destroy your health by carrying on in this way.'

'That's my affair. If I choose to die, I don't see that it's any concern of yours.'

'Oh, really, really! Here we are in the middle of the New Year holiday, and you have to start talking about *death*!'

'I don't care. I'll talk about death if I like. Death! Death!

Death! I'm going to die this minute. If you're so afraid of death, I wish you long life. A hundred years, will that satisfy you?'

'Do you think I'm afraid of dying when all you will do is quarrel? I wish I *were* dead. It would be a relief.'

'Exactly!' said Dai-yu. 'If I were to die, it would be a relief from all this quarrelling!'

'I said if *I* were to die,' said Bao-yu. 'Don't twist my words. It isn't fair.'

Just then Bao-chai came hurrying in.

'Cousin Shi's waiting for you!'

She took hold of Bao-yu's hand and pulled him after her, to the great mortification of Dai-yu, who sat with her face to the window and shed tears of pure rage.

After about as long as it would take to drink two cups of tea, Bao-yu came back again. During his absence Dai-yu's sobs seemed to have redoubled in intensity. Seeing the state she was in he realized that it would need careful handling and began turning over in his mind all kinds of soft and soothing things to coax her with. But before he could get his mouth open, she had anticipated him:

'What have you come for this time? Why can't you just leave me here to die in peace? After all, you've got a new play-mate now – one who can read and write and compose and laugh and talk to you much better than I can. Oh yes, and drag you off to be amused if there's any danger of your getting upset! I really can't imagine what you have come back here for!'

' "Old friends are best friends and close kin are kindest," ' said Bao-yu, coming over to where she sat and speaking very quietly. 'You're too intelligent not to know that. Even a simpleton like me knows that much! Take kinship first: you are my cousin on Father's side; Cousin Bao is only a mother-cousin. That makes you much the closer kin. And as for length of acquaintance: it was you who came here first. You and I have practically grown up together – eaten at the same table, even slept in the same bed. Compared with you she's practially a new arrival. Why should I ever be any less close to you because of her?'

'Whatever do you take me for? Do you think I want you

to be any less close to *her* because of *me*? It's the way I *feel* that makes me the way I am.'

'And it's the way *I* feel,' said Bao-yu, 'that makes me the way *I* am! Do you mean to tell me that you know your own feelings about me but still don't know what my feelings are about you?'

Dai-yu lowered her head and made no reply. After a pause she said:

'You complain that whatever you do people are always getting angry with you. You don't seem to realize how much you *provoke* them by what you do. Take today, for instance. It's obviously colder today than it was yesterday. Then why of all days should you choose today to leave your blue cape off?'

Bao-yu laughed.

'I didn't. I was wearing it this morning the same as usual; but when you started quarrelling just now, I got into such a sweat that I had to take it off.'

'Next thing you'll be catching a cold,' said Dai-yu with a sigh, 'and then Heaven knows what grumblings and scoldings there will be!'

Just then Xiang-yun burst in on them and reproved them smilingly for abandoning her:

'Couthin Bao, Couthin Lin: you can thee each other every day. It'th not often I get a chanthe to come here; yet now I *have* come, you both ignore me!'

Dai-yu burst out laughing:

'Lisping doesn't seem to make you any less talkative! Listen to you: "Couthin!" "Couthin!" Presently, when you're playing Racing Go, you'll be all "thicktheth" and "theventh"!'

'You'd better not imitate her,' said Bao-yu. 'It'll get to be a habit. You'll be lisping yourself before you know where you are.'

'How you do pick on one!' said Xiang-yun. 'Always finding fault. Even if you are tho perfect yourthelf, I don't thee why you have to go making fun of everyone elthe. But I can show you thomeone you won't dare to find fault with. I shall certainly think you a wonder if you do.'

'Who's that?' said Dai-yu.

'If you can find any shortcomings in Cousin Bao-chai', said Xiang-yun, 'you must be very good indeed.'

'Oh *her*,' said Dai-yu coldly. 'I wondered whom you could mean. I should never dare to find fault with *her*.'

But before she could say any more, Bao-yu cut in and hurriedly changed the subject.

'I shall never be a match for you as long as I live,' Xiang-yun said to Dai-yu with a disarming smile. 'All I can thay ith that I hope you marry a lithping huthband, tho that you have "ithee-withee" "ithee-withee" in your earth every minute of the day. Ah, Holy Name! I think I can thee that blethed day already before my eyeth!'

Bao-yu could not help laughing; but Xiang-yun had already turned and fled.

If you wish to know the conclusion of this scene, you must read the following chapter.

CHAPTER 21

*Righteous Aroma discovers how to rebuke her
master by saying nothing
And artful Patience is able to rescue hers by being
somewhat less than truthful*

As Shi Xiang-yun, fearful that Dai-yu would pursue her, turned and fled, Bao-yu shouted after her:

'She's tripped: you needn't worry! She'll never catch up with you now!'

And when Dai-yu reached the doorway where he was standing, he spread his arms across it to stop her getting by and laughingly begged an amnesty for Xiang-yun.

'Never!' said Dai-yu, endeavouring to tug one of his hands away from the door-jamb. 'I'll get that Yun if it's the last thing I do!'

With Bao-yu blocking the doorway and Dai-yu evidently unable to get past him, Xiang-yun deemed it safe to stop running, and turned to plead with her pursuer:

'*Pleathe* cousin, just this once – spare me!'

Just then Bao-chai appeared from behind her shoulder – the smiling peacemaker:

'I advise you two to make it up, for Cousin Bao's sake.'

'I *won't*!' said Dai-yu. 'You're all in league against me. You have all come here to make fun of me.'

'Oh, *really*!' said Bao-yu. 'Who would ever have the nerve to make fun of you? Yun only said what she said because you mimicked her in the first place. She'd never have dared to otherwise.'

It is hard to say how long the four of them might have remained there in this impasse had not a servant arrived at that moment and summoned them to dinner in Grandmother Jia's room. It was already lighting-up time and Lady Wang, Li Wan, Xi-feng, Ying-chun, Tan-chun and Xi-chun had also forgathered for the meal. When dinner was over, the company conversed for a while and then retired to their various rooms for the night – Xiang-yun to sleep with Dai-yu in what had once, in the days when she lived with Grandmother Jia, been her own bedroom. Bao-yu saw the two of them back to their room and stayed there talking until well after ten, in spite of frequent summonses by Aroma.

As soon as it was light next morning, Bao-yu was off again to the girls' room, shuffling along in his slippers and with a gown thrown loosely round his shoulders. The maids Nightingale and Kingfisher were not yet about, and their two young mistresses still lay fast asleep under the covers. Dai-yu was tightly cocooned in a quilt of apricot-coloured damask, the picture of tranquil repose. Xiang-yun, by contrast, lay with her hank of jet-black hair tumbled untidily beside the pillow, a white arm with its two gold bracelets thrown carelessly outside the bedding and two white shoulders exposed above the peach-pink coverlet, which barely reached her armpits.

'A tomboy, even in her sleep!' Bao-yu muttered ruefully as he gently drew the bedding up to cover her. 'She'll get a draught on those shoulders, and next thing she'll be complaining of a stiff neck!'

Dai-yu had by now awakened. She sensed that there was someone else in the room, and guessing that it must be Bao-yu, lifted her head up to look. Sure enough, it was he.

'What are *you* doing here at this early hour?'

'Early? Get up and have a look and then tell me if you think it's early!'

'You'd better go outside a minute if you want us to get up,' said Dai-yu.

Bao-yu went into the outer room. Dai-yu got up as soon as he had gone out and roused Xiang-yun. When the two girls had slipped into some clothes, Bao-yu came inside again and sat himself down beside the dressing-table. Presently Nightingale and Kingfisher came in to help the girls with their toilet. Xiang-yun finished washing first. Kingfisher was on her way out to empty the basin, when Bao-yu called her back:

'Just a moment! While you are about it I may as well wash too and save myself the trouble of going back to my own room.'

He came over to where she stood, and bending his head

down over the basin, scooped up two handfuls of water and began washing his face. Nightingale handed him some scented soap.

'It's all right,' he said, 'there's lots in here already.'

Then he asked for a towel.

Kingfisher pursed her lips up derisively:

'You haven't changed much, have you?'

Ignoring the sarcasm, he demanded crude salt to clean his teeth with, and after rubbing it all round them vigorously with a finger, he rinsed his mouth out with water. That part of his toilet completed, he observed that Xiang-yun had just finished doing her hair and wandered over to where she was sitting.

'Coz dear, do my hair for me, will you?'

'I'm afraid I can't,' said Xiang-yun.

Bao-yu smiled coaxingly:

'Go on, be a dear! You used to do it for me once.'

'Well, I can't any longer,' said Xiang-yun. 'I've forgotten how to.'

'It doesn't need very much doing to it,' said Bao-yu. 'I'm not going out anywhere today. Just a few plaits.'

He continued to coax and wheedle until at last she gave in, and taking his head in her hands, sat him down in her place at the dressing-table and proceeded to comb and dress his hair.

Bao-yu never wore any head-covering when he was at home. Instead he had his side-hair done up in a number of little plaits which were looped round over his ears and brought together by means of red silk thread into a single large queue at the back. It was fastened by a golden clasp at the end and by four pearl clips at regular intervals between the clasp and the crown of his head. As Xiang-yun plaited, she noticed that a pearl appeared to be missing.

'What's happened to this clip?' she said. 'I'm sure it used to be the same as the other three. Where has its pearl gone?'

'I lost it,' said Bao-yu.

'I expect it fell off somewhere outside and somebody picked it up,' said Xiang-yun. 'Lucky old somebody!'

'Who knows whether or not he *really* lost it?' said Dai-yu

scoffingly. 'For all we know he may have given it to someone to have remounted as a keepsake!'

Bao-yu made no comment, but sat fiddling with the toilet articles that crowded the dressing-table on either side of the mirror. He picked up a pot of rouge, almost without realizing what he was doing, and sat with it poised in his hand, wanting to put it to his lips for a little taste, but afraid Xiang-yun would rebuke him. While he hesitated, Xiang-yun leaned forward from where she was sitting and administered a sharp slap to his hand, causing the rouge-pot to fall from it on to the dressing-table.

'*Nasty* habit!' she said. 'It's time you gave it up!'

The words were scarcely out of her mouth when Aroma entered. She concluded from the scene that met her eyes that Bao-yu had already completed his toilet, and went back again to attend to her own. Soon after this Bao-chai dropped in.

'Where's Cousin Bao?' she asked.

' "Cousin Bao" has no time to spend in *here* nowadays,' said Aroma bitterly.

Bao-chai immediately understood.

Aroma sighed.

'I say nothing against being friendly,' she said. 'But this hanging around there morning, noon and night is another matter. However, nothing I say makes any difference. It's just a waste of breath.'

Bao-chai was impressed.

'One mustn't underestimate this maid,' she thought to herself. 'She is obviously a girl of some intelligence.'

And she sat down on the kang with her for a chat. In the course of conversation she inquired casually about her age, family, and various other personal matters, paying careful attention to her answers and gaining from them and from the tone in which they were uttered an increasing respect for this uneducated maid.

Presently Bao-yu came in, whereupon Bao-chai got up and left. Bao-yu commented on her departure:

'Cousin Bao-chai seemed to be very thick with you just now. Why should she suddenly rush off when *I* come into the room?'

There was no reply, so he repeated his question.

'Are you asking *me*?' said Aroma. '*I* don't know what reasons you all have for your comings and goings.'

The expression on her face as she uttered these words was angrier than he had ever seen her look before.

He laughed.

'Oh dear! Are you in a rage again?'

Aroma laughed mirthlessly.

'It's not for the likes of me to get into rages. But I wish that from now on you would stop coming into this room. After all, you *have* got people to wait on you elsewhere. You don't really need my services. I shall go back to serving Her Old Ladyship, like I used to before.'

With that she closed her eyes and lay back upon the kang.

Bao-yu was alarmed to see her in such a state and impulsively rushed over to the kang to soothe her. But Aroma kept her eyes tightly shut and would take no notice. Bao-yu did not know what to do. Just then Musk chanced to enter and he turned to her for help:

'What's up with Aroma?'

'How should I know?' said Musk. 'You'd do better to ask yourself that question.'

Bao-yu was so taken aback that for a while he said nothing. Then, finding their combined hostility too much for him, he got up with a sigh from his suppliant position on the kang.

'All right, ignore me then! I'm going off to sleep, too.'

And he slid from the kang and went off to his own bed to lie down.

For a long time there was no sound from him except for a gentle snoring. Judging that he must be really asleep, Aroma rose from the kang and took a large travelling-cloak to cover him with. A moment later she heard a gentle thud. He had whipped it from him and thrown it to the floor as soon as her back was turned. But when she looked, his eyes were closed as before and he was still pretending to be asleep. The significance of the gesture did not escape her. She nodded slowly and regarded the feigned sleeper sarcastically:

'All right, then! There's no need for *you* to get angry. From now on I'll just pretend I'm dumb. I won't say another word of criticism. Will that satisfy you?'

This was too much for Bao-yu. He sat bolt upright on his bed.

'What am I supposed to have done this time? And what's all this "criticism" you're talking about? If you *had* been criticizing me it wouldn't be so bad; but when I came in just now, you didn't say *anything*: you simply ignored me. You went and lay down in a huff without my having the faintest idea what it was all about, and now you accuse *me* of behaving unreasonably! I haven't heard a single peep out of you yet to explain what it is that you are angry about!'

'Your own conscience ought to tell you that,' said Aroma. 'You don't need me to tell you.'

They were still arguing when Grandmother Jia sent a servant round to summon him to lunch. He went off to the front apartment, but returned almost immediately after bolting a single bowlful of rice. He found Aroma asleep on the kang and Musk sitting beside her playing Patience with some dominoes. He had long known that Musk was a close ally of Aroma's, so ignoring them both, he marched past them into the inner room, raising the door-curtain for himself as he passed through. Musk followed him automatically, but he pushed her out:

'No, no, I wouldn't presume to trouble you!'

She laughed and went back to her Patience, having first ordered a couple of the younger maids to wait on him in her stead.

In the inner room Bao-yu took up a book and reclined on the kang to read. For a considerable while he remained engrossed in his reading. When eventually he did look up, intending to ask someone for some tea, he saw two little maids waiting there in silence, one of whom – evidently the older by a year or two – was an attractive, intelligent-looking girl. He addressed himself to her:

'Isn't your name "Nella" something or other?'

'Citronella.'

'Citronella? Who on earth gave you that name?'

'Aroma, sir. My real name is "Soldanella", but Miss Aroma altered it to "Citronella".'

'I don't know why she didn't call you "Citric Acid" and have done with it,' said Bao-yu. '*Cit*ronella! – How many girls are there in your family, Citronella?'

'Four,' said Citronella.

'And which of the four are you?'

'I'm the youngest.'

'Right!' said Bao-yu. 'In future you will be called "Number Four". We're not going to have any more of these floral fragrances around here. It's an insult to decent scents and flowers to give their names to you lot!'

Then he asked her to pour him some tea.

Listening attentively in the outer room, 'Flowers' Aroma and her Musky ally – for whose ears this gibe was intended – were nearly bursting themselves in their efforts not to laugh.

All that day Bao-yu stayed in his own room, seeing no one. It was gloomy on his own, with nothing but reading and a little writing for amusement, but he refused to make use of any of his usual attendants and would have only "Number Four" to wait on him. Though he did not realize it, she was a designing little minx and endeavoured by every artifice at her command to get her hooks into him while she had the chance.

After dinner Bao-yu came back flushed and slightly tipsy, having taken a few cups of wine with his meal. Normally this would have been the occasion for an evening of hilarity with Aroma and the rest, but today he would have to sit by his lamp alone in cheerless isolation. The prospect was a depressing one. Yet if he were to go running after her, it would seem too much like a capitulation, and her nagging would thenceforth become insufferable. On the other hand, to frighten her into some sort of compliance by asserting his mastery over her would be heartless. There was nothing else for it: he would just have to grin and bear it.

'Suppose they were all dead,' he said to himself. 'I should have to make do on my own *somehow* or other!'

The thought was strangely comforting. He was able to stop worrying. He even began to feel quite cheerful. Having instructed Number Four to trim up the lamp and brew him a pot of tea, he settled down to a volume of *Zhuang-zi*. Presently he came to the following passage in the chapter called 'Rifling Trunks':

Away then with saints and wise men, and the big thieves will cease from despoiling. Discard your jades, destroy your pearls, and the little thieves will cease from pilfering. Burn your tallies, smash your seals, and the common people will revert to their natural integrity. Break all the bushels and snap all the steelyards, and they will have no further grounds for dispute. Obliterate those 'sacred laws' by which the world is governed, and you will find yourself at last able to reason with them. If you confuse the pitch-pipes, break up the organs, unstring the zithers and stop up Shi Kuang's ears, people will begin to make proper use of their own hearing. If you abolish all intricacy of design and brilliancy of colouring and glue up Li Zhu's eyes, people will begin to make proper use of their own eyesight. And if you destroy your arcs and lines, throw away your compasses and set-squares and break the fingers of Chui the Cunning, people will begin to make proper use of their own skill . . .

The words wonderfully suited his present mood. He read no further. Impulsively picking up a writing-brush, and with the inspiration lent him by his tipsiness, he added the following lines in the margin:

Away then with Musk and Aroma, and the female tongue will cease from nagging. Discard Bao-chai's heavenly beauty, destroy Dai-yu's divine intelligence, utterly abolish all tender feelings, and the female heart will cease from envy. If the female tongue ceases from nagging there will be no further fear of quarrels and estrangements; if Bao-chai's heavenly beauty is discarded there will be no further grounds for tender admiration; and if Dai-yu's divine intelligence is destroyed there will be no further cause for romantic imaginings. These Bao-chais, Dai-yus, Aromas and Musks spread their nets and dig their pits, and all the world are bewitched and ensnared by them.

Having written these lines, he threw down the brush and went straight to bed.

He was asleep almost as soon as his head touched the pillow and remained dead to the world throughout the whole of that night. Waking with the first light next morning, he sat up in bed to find Aroma lying fully clothed beside him outside the covers. He roused her with a gentle shake, all yesterday's unpleasantness now quite forgotten:

'Go to bed properly! You'll get cold, sleeping like that!'

Aroma had not, on the day previous to this, openly criticized Bao-yu for disporting himself at all hours of the day and night with his girl cousins because she knew from experience that criticism was powerless to change him. To alert him to the error of his ways she had instead adopted a more passive approach. She had confidently expected this new method to produce a speedy repentance, followed by a swift return to normal relations; so that when, contrary to her expectation, a whole day went by without his having manifested the looked-for change of heart, she was left with no further resources, and as a consequence had been too worried to sleep properly for the greater part of that night.

But now here he was addressing her normally once more. He must have undergone a change of heart during the night. She forced herself to ignore him still, in order to drive the lesson home.

Meeting with no response, Bao-yu reached out his hand to help her get undressed; but he had got no further than undoing the first button when she pushed his hand away and did it up again. He was at a loss to know what to do with her. With a gentle smile he took her by the hand:

'Now – what's the matter?'

He had to repeat the question several times. She fixed her eyes on him angrily:

'Nothing's the matter. But now you're awake, hadn't you better hurry over to the other place to get washed? If you delay much longer, you might not be in time.'

'What other place?' said Bao-yu.

Aroma smiled coldly.

'Why ask me? How should *I* know? Go wherever you like for your toilet! Let's make a clean break from now on, you and I, and perhaps we'll have a bit less of all this bickering and making ourselves ridiculous in front of the others. I mean to say, even if you get tired of going *there*, you've always got your Number Fours and Number Fives back here to wait on you.

But as for the rest of us: even our names are "an insult to decent scents and flowers"!'

Bao-yu laughed:

'Do you still remember that?'

'I'll remember that if I live to be a hundred!' said Aroma. 'I'm not like you: treating everything *I* say like so much wind and forgetting in the morning what you said yourself the night before!'

There was something about her pretty face suffused with anger that Bao-yu found infinitely touching. He snatched up a jade hairpin that was lying beside the pillow and snapped it in two.

'So be it with me if I ever fail to listen to you again!' he said.

'What a way to carry on at this hour of the morning!' said Aroma, hurriedly picking up the pieces. 'Whether you listen to me or not is up to you. There's no need to get into such a state about it!'

'You don't know how worried you make me,' said Bao-yu.

'So *you* feel worried, do you?' said Aroma smiling. 'Now perhaps you'll have some idea what *I* feel like most of the time! – Come on, let's get washed!'

With that the two of them got up and began their toilet.

Later, after Bao-yu had gone off to the front apartment, Dai-yu looked in unexpectedly, and not finding Bao-yu in, began idly turning over the books that were lying on his desk. Chancing to light on the volume of *Zhuang-zi* that he had been reading the night before, her eye was drawn to the lines he had written in the margin. They both vexed and amused her, and she could not resist picking up a writing-brush and adding the following quatrain on the remaining blank space:

> What wretch would here, with scurrile pen,
> The text of *Zhuang-zi* plagiarize,
> And, heedless of his own great faults,
> Fright others with his wicked lies?

That done, she went to the front apartment to see Grand-mother Jia, and from there on to Lady Wang's.

*

She found everyone at Lady Wang's in a great to-do. Xi-feng's baby daughter was ill. The doctor had been called and had just finished taking her pulses.

'Convey my congratulations to Her Ladyship and Mrs Lian' – the doctor's diagnosis was couched in the strange language which custom decrees in such cases – 'I am happy to inform them that the little girl's sickness is the small-pox!'

Lady Wang and Xi-feng at once sent back to inquire whether the child was in any danger. The doctor made the following reply:

'Variola is, of course, a dangerous disease, but provided there are no complications, most cases of it are recuperable. Let the ladies lay in a plentiful supply of *sanguis caudae*, or pig's tail blood, and plenty of essence of mulberry-worm. Applied externally these will ensure a satisfactory development of the pustules.'

Xi-feng immediately became very busy. A room had to be swept out and prepared for the worship of the Smallpox Goddess. Orders had to be given to the servants to avoid the use of all fried and sautéed cookery. Patience had to be told to move Jia Lian's clothes and bedding to a room outside – for sexual abstinence, too, was enjoined on the parents of the sufferer. A length of dark-red cloth had to be procured and made up into a dress for the child by the combined labours of the nurses, maids and female relations most closely associated with it. Finally, a ritually purified room had to be made ready for the two doctors who would take it in turns to examine the little patient and make up her medicines, and who would not be permitted to return to their own homes until the customary period of twelve days had elapsed. These arrangements having been completed, Jia Lian went off to the outer study which was from now on to be his bedroom, while Xi-feng and Patience joined Lady Wang in the daily worship and propitiation of the Smallpox Goddess.

Jia Lian was the sort of man who will begin getting up to mischief the moment he takes leave of his wife. After only a couple of nights sleeping on his own he began to find abstinence extremely irksome and was reduced to slaking his fires on the more presentable of his pages. But other relief was at hand.

Among the domestic staff at the Rong-guo mansion was a certain drunken, dilapidated cook, by surname Duo, who, because of his weakness of character and general uselessness, had acquired the nickname of 'Droopy Duo'. Two years previous to this date Droopy's father had provided him with a wife. She was now just turned twenty, a fine, good-looking young wanton, always eager to throw herself at whatever partners opportunity might place in her way. Droopy Duo raised no objection to her infidelities. As long as he had meat to eat and wine to drink and money in his pocket he saw no reason to concern himself about anything else. Consequently there was scarcely an able-bodied male in the Ning-guo and Rong-guo mansions who had not at one time or another sampled her wares. Because of her pneumatic charms and omnivorous promiscuity this voluptuous young limmer was referred to by all and sundry as 'the Mattress'.

Jia Lian, now separated from the wife of his bosom and fairly frying with unsatisfied desires, had for some time past been aware of the Mattress's charms; but though his mouth had long watered to enjoy them, what with fear of his jealous young wife on the one hand and fear of his fancy boys on the other, he had so far found no opportunity of approaching her.

The Mattress, too, had for some time past had her eye on Jia Lian, and it was a source of regret to her that he had so far proved unapproachable. Learning that he had now moved to his study outside, she managed to find excuses for passing by that way three or four times in a day, provoking Jia Lian to a pitch of frantic eagerness only to be compared with that of a starving rat confronted by some food. He was obliged to seek the advice of his pages and to promise them rich rewards if they could procure her for his pleasure. The pages were ready enough to oblige – the more so as they were themselves old customers of hers – and the request for an assignation was no sooner made than granted.

At about ten o'clock that night, when all were abed and Droopy Duo lay collapsed on the kang in drunken slumbers, Jia Lian slipped noiselessly into the room for his pre-arranged meeting with the Mattress. The mere sight of her proved so potent a stimulant that without wasting any time on tender preliminaries, he took down his trousers and set to work at once.

Now this wife of Duo's had a physical peculiarity which was that as soon as the man's body came into contact with her own she felt a delicious melting sensation invading her limbs, rendering her body soft and yielding to that of her partner, so that he had the impression of lying on a heap of down; and in addition to this natural endowment she knew more tricks of posture and more ways of exciting a man with murmured lewdnesses and amorous cries than a professional prostitute.

As Jia Lian lay on top of her, wishing he could melt into her body from sheer excess of pleasure, she began to exercise this last accomplishment.

'Your little girl's got the smallpox,' she murmured. 'While they're worshipping the Goddess, you are supposed to keep yourself pure. Naughty man! You're making yourself unclean because of me. You must leave me! Go away!'

Jia Lian's movements became more violent.

'You are my only goddess!' he said, panting heavily. 'I care for no other goddess but you!'

At this the Mattress began to grow even more reckless in her incitements and Jia Lian to reveal the more disgusting of his sexual accomplishments.

They lay a long time together when it was over, exchanging oaths and promises, unable to break apart. From that day onwards there was a secret understanding between them.

A day arrived when the smallpox poison had spent itself and Baby's pustules showed signs of drying up. After the twelfth day the Smallpox Goddess was ceremoniously ushered off the premises, the entire family joined in a service of thanksgiving to Heaven and the ancestors, and there was much burning of incense in discharge of vows made on the child's behalf by various of its members, and much exchanging of congratulations and paying out of rewards. When all this was over, Jia Lian returned once more to the matrimonial couch. 'A night after absence is better than a wedding night' as the proverb crudely puts it, and certainly the affection shown that night by Jia Lian for his lady was of more than usual intensity.

Early next morning, when Xi-feng had gone off to Grandmother Jia's, Patience began putting away the clothes and bedding that had been brought in from the outer study. To her surprise she felt something strange in the cover of Jia Lian's head-rest, and after groping inside it, fished out a black, silky tress of woman's hair. Quick to understand its significance, she hid it in her sleeve and going across to the other room, showed it to Jia Lian and asked him what it was.

As soon as he saw the hair, Jia Lian rushed forward to snatch it from her. She darted away, but he seized hold of her, and forcing her on to the kang, attempted to wrest it from her grasp.

'Mean thing!' said Patience. 'After I've gone to the trouble of asking you about it behind her back, you have to start being rough!'

Just at that moment they heard Xi-feng coming. Jia Lian didn't know whether to let go of Patience or make a final effort to obtain the hair. Finally, with a muttered entreaty, he released her:

'Angel! Don't let her know!'

Patience managed to get up just as Xi-feng was entering.

'Quick!' said Xi-feng. 'Open up the chest and find that pattern for Her Ladyship!'

'Yes madam,' said Patience.

While Patience was looking for the pattern, Xi-feng caught sight of Jia Lian and suddenly thought of something else.

'Have we got the things back from the outer study yet?'

'Yes,' said Patience.

'Was there anything missing?'

'No,' said Patience. 'I went through them very carefully, but there was nothing missing.'

'Was there anything there that *shouldn't* have been?'

Patience laughed.

'Isn't it enough that there was nothing missing? Why should there be anything extra?'

Xi-feng laughed, too.

'He was nearly a fortnight outside. I wouldn't bank on his

having kept himself clean all that time. There might have been something left behind by one of his little friends: a ring or a sash or something.'

Jia Lian turned pale with fright. He grimaced piteously at Patience from behind Xi-feng's back, and drawing a finger across his throat, silently entreated her to keep her discovery hidden.

Patience affected not to notice him.

'It's funny you should say that, Mrs Lian. Exactly the same thought occurred to me; but though I went through his things very carefully, I didn't find anything suspicious. If you don't believe me, you can have a look yourself.'

'Silly girl!' said Xi-feng. 'Do you imagine that if there were really anything there he would *let* us look?'

And taking the pattern from her she went out again.

Patience pointed a finger at her own nose and wagged her head from side to side.

'How are you going to thank me for that?'

'You're a sweet little darling!'

He beamed delightedly and lunged forward to embrace her. Patience dangled the hair in front of him:

'You'll have to watch your step from now on,' she said. 'Now I've got something to keep you in order with. If you misbehave . . .!'

'All right, you look after it, then. But' – his tone became entreating – 'don't, whatever you do, let her find out!'

He said this to put her off her guard. As soon as her defences were relaxed he made a quick grab and snatched it from her.

'Perhaps you'd better not have it, after all,' he said with a grin of triumph. 'If I have it I can burn it, and then it's all over and done with.'

He stowed the hair in the side of his boot as he said this. Patience clenched her teeth in anger.

'You're *mean*! Burn the bridge when you're safely over the river – that's your way, isn't it? All right then, you needn't expect me to tell lies for you in future!'

In Jia Lian's lascivious eyes her anger made her adorable. He felt himself becoming excited, and throwing his arms around her, he asked her to let him take her. But Patience struggled free and ran from the room, leaving him doubled up in a fury of frustrated desire.

'Little cock-teaser!' he shouted after her. 'You deliberately provoked me, and now you run away!'

'Who provoked you?' Patience giggled from outside the window. 'You shouldn't be so randy! Do you expect me to make the Mistress hate me just for the sake of making you feel comfortable?'

'You needn't worry about her,' said Jia Lian. 'One of these days when I get my temper up I'm going to lay into that jealous bitch and break every bone in her body. Then perhaps she'll know who's master round here. She watches me like a bloody thief. *She* can talk to men when she likes, but I'm not supposed to talk to women, oh no! If I'm talking to a woman and just happen to get a bit close, she immediately starts suspecting something. But if *she* wants to go chattering and larking around with Bao or Rong or any other bloody male on the premises, *that*'s supposed to be all right! You wait! One of these days I'll stop her seeing anyone at all!'

'She's every right to watch you,' said Patience, 'and *you*'ve no right at all to be jealous of *her*. She's always been perfectly straight and above board where men are concerned; but you – whatever you do you've got something nasty in mind! You make even *me* worried, never mind about her!'

'Oh, shut up!' said Jia Lian. 'You're all perfect, aren't you? It's just me that's always up to something nasty! One of these days I'll make a clean sweep of the lot of you!'

Just at that moment Xi-feng stepped into the courtyard and saw Patience standing outside the window.

'If you want to talk,' she said, 'why not talk inside the room? What's the idea of running outside and bawling through the window?'

'Don't ask *her*!' said Jia Lian's voice from inside. 'She thinks there's a tiger in the room and she's afraid of being eaten!'

'He's in there on his own,' said Patience. 'What should I be doing in there with him?'

'All the more reason for being in there, I should have

thought, if he's on his own,' said Xi-feng, smiling rather spitefully.

'Is that remark intended for me?' said Patience.

'Who else?' said Xi-feng.

'You'll make me say something I shall feel sorry for in a minute,' said Patience; and instead of standing aside and raising the door-blind for her mistress, she entered ahead of her, dropped it rudely in her face, and marched angrily through the sitting-room to one of the rooms at the back.

'What's the matter with Patience? The girl's gone mad!' said Xi-feng when she had raised the blind again and let herself in. 'I really do believe she is trying to displace me. You'd better look out, my friend: I'll have the hide off you!'

'Bravo! Good for Patience!' said Jia Lian, who had retreated on to the kang and was applauding the comedy from that safer eminence. 'I didn't know she had it in her. In future I shall take that girl more seriously.'

'It's you who've let her get above herself,' said Xi-feng. 'I hold you directly responsible for this!'

'*Oh* no!' said Jia Lian. 'If you two want to quarrel, I'm not going to stand between you and take all the knocks. I'm getting out of here!'

'I'm sure I don't know where you think you'll go to,' said Xi-feng.

'Don't you worry, I've got somewhere to go to,' said Jia Lian, and he began to go; but Xi-feng stopped him.

'No, don't go! There's something else I want to talk to you about.'

But if you want to know what it was, you will have to wait for the next chapter.

CHAPTER 22

*Bao-yu finds Zen enlightenment
in an operatic aria
And Jia Zheng sees portents of doom in
lantern riddles*

Hearing that Xi-feng wanted to consult him about something, Jia Lian halted and asked her what it was.

'It's Bao-chai's birthday on the twenty-first,' said Xi-feng. 'What do you think we ought to do about it?'

'How should I know?' said Jia Lian. 'You've managed plenty of big birthday celebrations before in your time. Why have you become so helpless all of a sudden?'

'There are fixed rules for everything when you are planning a big grown-up celebration,' said Xi-feng; 'but in Bao-chai's case she's neither exactly grown-up nor exactly a child any longer. That's why I wanted your advice.'

Jia Lian lowered his head and thought for a moment.

'Why, you're being stupid!' he said presently. 'There's a precedent right in front of you. What about Dai-yu? All you've got to do is find what arrangements you made in the past for her and do exactly the same for Bao-chai now.'

'Do you suppose I didn't think of that?' said Xi-feng with scorn. 'I'm not *that* stupid! The point is that yesterday, because of something Grandma said, I started asking them all their birthdays and ages, and it seems that on this birthday of hers on the twenty-first Bao-chai is going to be fifteen. Now that doesn't qualify for a full-scale celebration, but it *is* a sort of coming-of-age, and when Grandma heard about it she said she wanted to sponsor something for it herself. So obviously, whatever we do, it can't be quite the same as what we've done in the past for Dai-yu.'

'Well in that case,' said Jia Lian, 'take what you did for Dai-yu as a basis and just add on a bit.'

'That's what I'd thought of doing,' said Xi-feng; 'but I wanted to see what *you* thought before doing anything definite, because I didn't want to go adding extras on my own initiative and then have you complaining that you hadn't been properly consulted.'

'You can cut that out!' said Jia Lian – though not ill-humouredly. 'You know you don't really mean a word of it! Just stop snooping on me all the time, that's all I ask. You won't hear any complaints from me then about not being consulted!'

With that he walked off: but whither, or to whom, our narrative does not disclose.

It tells us instead that Shi Xiang-yun, having spent a considerable part of the New Year holiday with the Jias, was now on the point of returning home, but was urged by Grandmother Jia to wait for Bao-chai's birthday and not go back until she had seen the plays. Xiang-yun agreed to stay and sent someone home with instructions to tell them that she would be returning a little later than planned and to fetch a couple of pieces of her own embroidery that she could give to Bao-chai as a birthday-present.

Ever since Bao-chai's first arrival, Grandmother Jia had been pleasurably impressed by her placid and dependable disposition, and now that she was about to spend her first 'big' birthday in the Jia household, the old lady resolved to make it a memorable one. Taking twenty taels of silver from her private store, she summoned Xi-feng and directed her to spend it on providing wine and plays for a celebration. Xi-feng made this the occasion for a little raillery.

'If the old lady says she wants her grandchild's birthday celebrated,' she said, 'then celebrated it must be, and we must all jump to it without arguing! But if she's going to start asking for *plays* as well, all I can say to that is that if she's in the mood for a bit of fun, I'm afraid she's going to have to pay for it. She's going to have to cough up something out of those private savings of hers she's been hoarding all these years – not wait until the last minute and then fish out a measly little twenty taels to pay for the party: that's just another way of telling us we've got to pay for it ourselves. I mean, if you were really hard up, it would be another matter: but you've got boxes and boxes of boodle – the bottoms are dropping out of them, they're so full! It's pure meanness, that's what it is! You forget, Grannie, when you go to heaven young Bao-yu won't be the only one who'll walk ahead of the hearse. You've got other grandchildren too, don't forget! You don't have to leave *everything* to him. The rest of us may not be much use, but you mustn't be *too* hard on us. Twenty taels! Do you really think that's enough to pay for a party *and plays*?'

At this point the entire company burst into laughter, which Grandmother Jia joined in herself.

'Just listen to her!' she said. 'I thought *I* had a fairly sharp tongue, but I'm no match for *this* one: "Clack-clack, clack-clack" – it's worse than a pair of wooden clappers! Even your mother-in-law daren't argue with *me*, my dear! Don't pick on *me*!'

'Mother-in-law is just as soppy about Bao-yu as you are,' said Xi-feng. 'I've got no one to tell my troubles to. And you say I'm sharp-tongued!'

Xi-feng's mock-lugubriousness set the old lady off in another squall of laughter. She loved to be teased, and Xi-feng's bantering put her in great good humour.

That night, when the young folk had finished paying their evening duty and were standing round her laughing and talking a while before retiring to their own apartments, Grandmother Jia asked Bao-chai what sort of plays she liked best and what her favourite dishes were. Bao-chai was well aware that her grandmother, like most old women, enjoyed the livelier, more rackety sort of plays and liked sweet and pappy things to eat, so she framed her answers entirely in terms of these preferences. The old lady was delighted.

Next day presents of clothing and various other objects, to which Lady Wang, Xi-feng, Dai-yu and the rest had all contributed, were sent round to Bao-chai's. Our narrative supplies no details.

At last the twenty-first arrived. A dear little stage had been erected in the courtyard outside Grandmother Jia's apartment and a newly trained troupe of child actors able to perform both *Kun-qu* and the noisier *Yi-qiang* type of plays had been engaged. In the apartment's main sitting-room a semicircle of little tables were arranged facing outwards towards the stage and laid in preparation for a feast. No outsiders were invited. The guests of honour were Aunt Xue, Shi Xiang-yun, and Bao-chai herself. All the others invited were members of the family.

Early that morning Bao-yu, not seeing Dai-yu around, went to look for her in her room and found her still reclining on the kang.

'Get up and have something to eat!' he said. 'The players will be starting shortly. Tell me some play you like so that I shall know which one to choose!'

'If you're so anxious to please me,' said Dai-yu coldly, 'you ought to hire a troupe specially and put on all my favourites. It's a cheap sort of kindness to treat me at someone else's expense!'

'Never mind!' said Bao-yu. 'When we hire a troupe for you, you'll be able to return the compliment.'

He hauled her up from the kang, and the two of them went off hand in hand together.

As soon as they had eaten, it was time to talk about choosing the plays and Grandmother Jia called on Bao-chai to begin. Bao-chai made a show of declining; but it was her birthday, and in the end she gave in and selected a piece about Monkey from *The Journey to the West*. Grandmother Jia was pleased.

Aunt Xue was now invited to pick a play, but as her own daughter had just chosen, she refused. Grandmother Jia did not press her and passed on to Xi-feng. Xi-feng would normally have refused to take precedence over her aunt and mother-in-law, who were both present, but Grandmother had commanded and must be obeyed. As she happened to know that the old lady's partiality for lively plays was particularly strong in the case of those which had lots of jokes and clowning in them, she selected a piece entitled *Liu Er Pawns His Clothes* in order to make sure that this element was not lacking from the programme. As she had anticipated, Grandmother Jia was even more delighted by this second choice.

Next Dai-yu was asked to choose. She deferred to Aunt Xing and Aunt Wang; but Grandmother Jia was insistent:

'I've brought you young people here today for some fun,' she said. 'I want you to enjoy yourselves. Never mind about *them*! I didn't go to all this trouble just for *their* sakes! They are

lucky to be here at all, having all this good food and entertainment for nothing: you surely don't think that *on top of
that* I'm going to let them choose the plays?'

The others all laughed, and Dai-yu chose a play. Then
Bao-yu, Shi Xiang-yun, Ying-chun, Tan-chun, Xi-chun and
Li Wan each chose a play in turn, after which the little players
proceeded to perform them in the order in which they had been
selected.

When the time came to bring in the wine and begin the
feast, Grandmother Jia invited Bao-chai to choose again.
This time she asked for *Zhi-shen at the Monastery Gate*.

'Why do you keep choosing plays like that?' said Bao-yu.

'To hear you talk, it doesn't sound as if all your years of
play-going have taught you much,' said Bao-chai. 'This is an
excellent play, both from the point of view of the music and
of the words.'

'I can't stand noisy plays,' said Bao-yu. 'I never could.'

'If you call this a noisy play,' said Bao-chai, 'it *proves* that
you don't know what you're talking about. Come over here
and I'll explain. This *Zhi-shen at the Monastery Gate* is a "Ruby
Lips" sequence in the Northern mode. That means, musically
speaking, that it is in a vigorous, somewhat staccato style.
In fact the musical excellence of this piece goes without
saying. But apart from that, the libretto is good, too. The words
of Zhi-shen's "Clinging Vine" aria, which is the last but one
in the sequence, are particularly fine.'

Bao-yu was interested, drew his chair closer, and begged
her to let him hear them. Lowering her voice so as not to disturb the others, she half-sang, half-recited them for his benefit:

> 'I dash aside the manly tear
> And take leave of my monkish home.
> A word of thanks to you, my Master dear,
> Who tonsured me before the Lotus Throne:
> 'Twas not my luck to stay with you,
> And in a short while I must say adieu,
> Naked and friendless through the world to roam.
> I ask no goods, no gear to take away,
> Only straw sandals and a broken bowl,
> To beg from place to place as best I may.'

Bao-yu listened enthralled, tapping his knee and nodding his head in time to her singing. When she had done, he agreed enthusiastically about the excellence of the words and congratulated her on the extraordinary breadth of her knowledge.

'Sh!' said Dai-yu, looking round crossly in Bao-yu's direction. 'Can't you be a bit quieter and attend to the play? This is *Zhi-shen at the Monastery Gate* we're supposed to be listening to, not *Jing-de Acts the Madman*!'

Xiang-yun found this very funny.

They continued to watch plays until the evening. Grandmother Jia had taken a particular fancy to the little player who had acted the heroine's parts and the one who had played the clown, and when the last performance was over, she asked for them to be brought in to see her. She found them very 'sweet' – even more so on a closer inspection – and asked them their ages. The leading lady turned out to be eleven and the clown only nine! There were murmurs and exclamations from all present when they heard this, and Grandmother Jia told someone to give them delicacies from the table and a present of money each, in addition to what they would receive as members of the troupe.

Meanwhile Xi-feng appeared to be very much amused about something.

'The way that child there is made-up makes him look *so* like someone we know,' she said. 'Haven't any of you noticed?'

Bao-chai knew whom she was referring to, but merely nodded her head slightly without replying. Bao-yu, too, nodded, but did not dare to reply. Only Xiang-yun was tactless enough to say anything:

'Oh, I know!' she blurted out. 'Like Cousin Lin, you mean?'

Bao-yu shot a quick glance in her direction; but it was too late. Xiang-yun's reply had prompted the others to look more carefully, with the result that they all instantaneously burst out laughing, so striking was the resemblance. Shortly after this the party broke up.

During the evening Xiang-yun ordered Kingfisher to start packing. Kingfisher remonstrated:

'What's the hurry? Why not wait till we're going? There'll be plenty of time before we go.'

'We're going first thing tomorrow,' said Xiang-yun. 'What's the point of staying any longer? You can see from the looks on their faces that we are not welcome here.'

Bao-yu chanced to overhear this remark and hurried in to her:

'You're wrong to be offended with me, coz. The others all know how sensitive Cousin Lin is, and they wouldn't answer because they were afraid of upsetting her. When you suddenly spoke up without realizing, I knew she was *bound* to be upset, and that's the reason why I looked at you like that. I was worried for *your* sake, because I was afraid she would be offended with *you*. That *you* should now get angry with *me* is really rather unfair. If it had been anyone else but you, I shouldn't have minded whether they offended her or not. I shouldn't have felt that much concern about them.'

Xiang-yun silenced him with an imperious wave of her hand:

'You can save your fine speeches for someone else. They're wasted on me. Obviously I'm not in the same class as your Cousin Lin. It's all right for other people to laugh at her; but as soon as *I* say anything about her, I'm at once in the wrong. I'm not really worthy to speak about her at all. She's the young lady of the house. I'm only a little nobody!'

'I was only thinking of you,' said Bao-yu in great agitation, 'yet now you put me in the wrong. May I straightway turn into dust and be trodden beneath ten thousand feet if I had any but the kindest intentions!'

'You are too glib with your ridiculous oaths,' said Xiang-yun. 'This is no time for swearing. You can keep that kind of talk for that sensitive, easily upset person you were talking about. She knows how to handle you. Don't try it on me: it makes me *thick*!'

With these words she walked off into the inner room of Grandmother Jia's apartment and lay down on the kang in a rage.

Very much out of countenance, Bao-yu went off to look for Dai-yu. She must have been waiting for him, for just as he was entering the room, she pushed him out again and shut the door. Totally at a loss to understand her behaviour, he called to her softly through the window:

'Dai, dear! Dai!'

But she took no notice.

Bao-yu stood there disconsolately, hanging his head in silence. Nightingale knew what was happening, but judged the time not ripe for her to intervene; so he continued to stand there like an idiot, until at last Dai-yu thought he must have gone back to his own room, and opened the door again. When she saw him still standing there, she had not the heart to shut the door on him a second time, and allowed him to follow her back into the room.

'There's always a reason for everything,' he said. 'If you tell people what it is, they don't feel so bad about it. You can't suddenly get angry with me for no reason whatever. What *is* all this about?'

'Don't ask *me*!' said Dai-yu coldly. '*I* don't know. I'm only a figure of fun – the sort of person you might compare with a child actor in order to get a good laugh from the others.'

'I never made the comparison,' said Bao-yu hotly, 'and I never laughed at you. Why should you be angry with *me*?'

'You would *like* to have made the comparison; you would *like* to have laughed,' said Dai-yu. 'To me your way of *not* comparing and *not* laughing was worse than the others' laughing and comparing!'

Bao-yu found this unanswerable.

'However,' Dai-yu went on, '*that* I could forgive. But what about that look you gave Yun? Just what did you mean by that? I think *I* know what you meant. You meant to warn her that she would cheapen herself by joking with me as an equal. Because she's an Honourable and her uncle's a marquis and I'm only the daughter of a commoner, she mustn't risk joking with me, because it would be so degrading for her if I were to answer back. That's what you meant, isn't it? Oh yes, you had the *kindest intentions*. Only unfortunately she didn't *want* your kind intentions and got angry with you in spite of them. So you tried to make it up with her at my expense, by telling her how touchy I am and how easily I get upset. You were afraid she might offend me, were you? As if it were any business of *yours* whether she offended me or not, or whether or not I got angry with her!'

When Bao-yu heard her say this, he knew she must have overheard every word of his conversation with Xiang-yun. He reflected that he had only acted in the first place from a desire to keep the peace between them: yet the only outcome of his good intentions had been a telling-off by either party. It put him in mind of something he had read a day or two previously in *Zhuang-zi*:

> The cunning waste their pains;
> The wise men vex their brains;
> But the simpleton, who seeks no gains,
> With belly full, he wanders free
> As drifting boat upon the sea.

and of another passage from the same book about timber trees inviting the axe and sweet springs being the cause of their own contamination. The more he thought about it, the more dejected he became.

'If I can't even get on with the few people I live with now,' he asked himself, 'how am I going to manage later on . . .?'

At that point in his reflections it seemed to him that there was no further point in arguing, and he turned to go back to his room.

Dai-yu realized that he must have thought of something upsetting to go off like this. But not to be answered was altogether too provoking. She felt the anger mounting inside her.

'All right, go!' she shouted after him. 'And don't ever come back! And don't ever speak to me again!'

Bao-yu ignored her. He went straight back to his own room, threw himself on the bed, and lay staring at the ceiling. Aroma knew what the trouble was but dared not, for the time being at any rate, refer to it. She tried distracting him with talk of other matters.

'I suppose there'll be more plays after today, won't there? Miss Bao is sure to give a return party, isn't she?'

'Whether she does or not,' said Bao-yu, 'what concern is it of mine?'

This was certainly not the sort of answer Aroma was used to getting. She tried again, smiling breezily:

'That's no way of looking at it! This is the New Year holidays, when their ladyships and the young ladies are all enjoying themselves. We can't have you mooning around like this!'

'Whether their ladyships and the young ladies are enjoying themselves or not,' said Bao-yu, 'what concern is it of mine?'

Aroma laughed.

'Seeing that they're all doing their best to be agreeable, couldn't you try to do likewise? Surely it's much better all round if everyone will give and take a bit?'

'What do you mean, "give and take a bit"?' said Bao-yu in the same lack-lustre voice as before. '*They* can give and take a bit if they like. *My* destiny is a different one:

> naked and friendless through the world to roam.'

A tear stole down his cheek as he recalled the line from the aria.

He continued to ponder its words and to savour their meaning, and ended up by bursting into tears and crying outright. Jumping up from the bed, he went over to his desk, took up a writing-brush, and wrote down the following lines in imitation of a Buddhist *gāthā*:

> I swear, you swear,
> With heart and mind declare;
> But our protest
> Is no true test.
> It would be best
> Words unexpressed
> To understand,
> And on that ground
> To take our stand.

After writing it, he was still not satisfied. Though now enlightened himself, he feared that someone reading his *gāthā* might not be able to share his enlightenment. Accordingly, with the words of the 'Clinging Vine' aria still running in his head, he added another set of verses after it to explain his point. That done, he read the whole through to himself out loud, then, with a wonderful feeling of liberation, went to bed and fell fast asleep.

Curious to know the sequel to Bao-yu's departure, Dai-yu, on the pretext of wanting to see Aroma about something, eventually came round herself to have a look. Aroma told her that Bao-yu was already in bed asleep. She was on the point of going back again when Aroma smilingly detained her:

'Just a moment, Miss! There's a note here. Would you like to see what it says?'

She handed her the sheet of paper containing Bao-yu's *gāthā* and the 'Clinging Vine' poem. Dai-yu could see that they must have been written under the influence of their recent quarrel and could not help feeling both amused by them and a little sorry. But all she said to Aroma was:

'It's only a joke. Nothing of any consequence.'

She took it with her back to her own room and showed it to Xiang-yun. Next day she showed it to Bao-chai as well. Bao-chai glanced at the second poem. This is what Bao-yu had written:

> You would have been at fault, if not for me;
> But why should I care if they disagree?
> Free come, free go, let nothing bar or hold me!
> No more I'll sink and soar between gloom and elation,
> Or endlessly debate the depth of our relation.
> What was the point of all of that past pother?
> When I look back on it, it seems scarce worth the bother.

Then she read the *gāthā*. She laughed.

'I'm afraid this is all *my* fault. It must have been that aria I told him about yesterday which started it all. Those Taoist writings and Zen paradoxes can so easily lead people astray if they do not understand them properly. I shall never forgive myself if he is going to start taking this sort of nonsense seriously and getting it fixed in his head. It will all be because of that aria!'

She tore the paper into tiny pieces and gave them to one of the maids:

'Here, burn this – straight away!'

Dai-yu laughed at her.

'You needn't have torn it up. If you will both come with me and wait while I put a question to him, I can guarantee to drive this nonsense from his mind once and for all.'

The three girls went round to Bao-yu's room together.

'Bao-yu,' said Dai-yu, addressing him in a heavily mock-serious manner, 'I wish to propound a question to you: "*Bao*" is that which is of all things the most precious and "*yu*" is that which is of all things the most hard. Wherein lies your preciousness and wherein lies your hardness?'

Bao-yu was unable to think of an answer. The girls all laughed and clapped their hands.

'Ha, ha, ha! He can't reply. For a student of Zen he does seem *remarkably* obtuse!'

'You say in your *gāthā*,' Dai-yu continued,

> '". . . It would be best
> Words unexpressed
> To understand,
> And on that ground
> To take our stand."

Now that's all right as far as it goes, but it doesn't go far enough. I should like to add a few lines to it. Like this:

> But, I perpend,
> To have no ground
> On which to stand
> Were yet more sound.
> And there's an end!'

'Ah, that's better!' said Bao-chai. 'That sounds like a *real* "insight". When the Sixth Patriarch Hui-neng first came to Shao-zhou looking for a teacher, he heard that the Fifth Patriarch Hong-ren was living at the monastery on Yellow-plum Mountain, so he found employment there in the monastery kitchen. When the Fifth Patriarch wanted to choose a successor, he ordered each of the monks to compose a *gāthā*. The Elder Shen-xiu recited this one:

> "Our body like the Bo-tree is,
>   Our mind's a mirror bright.
> Then keep it clean and free from dust,
>   So it reflects the light!"

Hui-neng happened to be hulling rice in the kitchen at the time, and he shouted out, "That's not bad, but it's still not quite right." Then he recited this *gāthā* of his own:

> "No real Bo-tree the body is,
> The mind no mirror bright.
> Since of the pair none's really there,
> On what could dust alight?"

The Fifth Patriarch at once handed him his robe and bowl as a sign that he was to succeed him. Your improvement on Cousin Bao's *gāthā* is on very much the same lines, Dai. There's just one thing, though: what about that "koan" of yours he couldn't answer? Surely you're not going to let him get away with it?'

'Failure to answer means defeat,' said Dai-yu. 'In any case, if he were to answer *now*, it would hardly count. The only condition I impose as victor is that he should henceforth be forbidden to talk any more about Zen. You see,' she told Bao-yu, 'even Bao-chai and I know more about it than you do. It's too ridiculous that you should set yourself up as a Zen authority!'

Bao-yu *had* in fact believed that he had attained an Enlightenment; but now suddenly here was Dai-yu propounding koans he couldn't answer and Bao-chai quoting with easy familiarity from the *Sayings of the Patriarchs* – though neither had shown any evidence of these accomplishments in the past. It was clear that their understanding of these matters was far in advance of his own. He consoled himself with the reflection that if they, whose understanding was so superior, were manifestly still so far from Enlightenment, it was obviously a waste of time for *him* to go on pursuing it. Having reached this comfortable conclusion, he accepted Dai-yu's condition with a laugh:

'Who wants to be an authority on Zen? It was only a joke, any way!'

*

Just then it was announced that the Imperial Concubine had sent someone round from the Palace with a lantern-riddle which they were to try and guess. After they had guessed the answer, they were each to make up a riddle of their own and send it back to her.

As soon as they heard this, the four of them hurried to the reception room in Grandmother Jia's apartment, where they found a young eunuch with a square, flat-topped lantern of white gauze specially made for hanging riddles on. There was one hanging on it already which they crowded round to read while the eunuch gave them their instructions:

'When the young ladies have guessed, will they please not tell anyone the answer, but write it down secretly. The answers will be collected and taken back to the Palace in a sealed envelope so that Her Grace can see for herself who has guessed correctly.'

Bao-chai went up to the lantern and looked at the riddle, which was in the form of a quatrain. It was not a particularly ingenious one, but she felt obliged to praise it, and therefore remarked that it was 'hard to guess' and pretended to have to think about the answer, though in truth it had been obvious to her at a glance. Bao-yu, Dai-yu, Xiang-yun and Tan-chun had also guessed the answer and were busy writing it down. Presently Jia Huan and Jia Lan were summoned, and they too wrote something down after a good deal of puzzling. After that everyone made up a riddle about some object of their choice, wrote it out in the best *kai-shu* on a slip of paper, and hung it on the lantern, which was then taken away by the eunuch.

Towards evening the eunuch returned and reported what the Imperial Concubine had had to say about the results:

'Her Grace's own riddle was correctly guessed by everyone except Miss Ying and Master Huan. Her Grace has thought of answers to all the riddles sent her by the young ladies and gentlemen, but she does not know whether or not they are correct.'

He showed them the answers written down. Some were right and some were wrong, but even those whose riddles had been incorrectly answered deemed it prudent to pretend that the answers they had received were the right ones.

The eunuch proceeded to distribute prizes for answering the Imperial Concubine's riddle. Everyone who had guessed correctly received an ivory note-case made by Palace craftsmen and a bamboo tea-whisk. Ying-chun and Jia Huan were the only ones who did not receive anything. Ying-chun treated the matter as a joke and rapidly dismissed it from her mind, but Jia Huan was very much put out. To make matters worse, the eunuch went on to query Jia Huan's own riddle:

'Her Grace says that she has not answered Master Huan's riddle because she could not make any sense of it. She told me to bring it back and ask him what it means.'

Intrigued, the others crowded round to look. This is what Jia Huan had written:

'Big brother with eight sits all day on the bed;
Little brother with two sits on the roof's head.'

There was a loud laugh when they had finished reading it. Jia Huan told the eunuch the answer: a head-rest and a ridge-end. The eunuch made a note of it and, after taking tea, departed once more.

Fired with enthusiasm by Yuan-chun's example, old Lady Jia decided to hold a riddle party. A very elegant lantern in the form of a three-leaved screen was hurriedly constructed on her orders and set up in the hall. When that had been done, she told all the boys and girls to make up a riddle – being careful to keep the answers to themselves – write it on a slip of paper, and stick it on her lantern-screen. Then, having prepared the best fragrant tea to drink, a variety of good things to eat, and lots of little gifts to serve as prizes, she was ready to begin. Jia Zheng observed the old lady's excitement when he got back from Court and came along himself in the evening to join in the fun.

There were three tables. Grandmother Jia, Jia Zheng, Bao-yu and Jia Huan sat at the table on the kang, while below, Lady Wang, Bao-chai, Dai-yu and Xiang-yun sat at one table and Ying-chun, Tan-chun and Xi-chun at another. The floor below the kang was thronged with old women and maids in attendance. Li Wan and Xi-feng had a table to themselves in an inner room.

'Where's my little Lan?' said Jia Zheng, not seeing Jia Lan at any of the tables.

One of the serving-women went into the inner room to ask Li Wan. She rose to reply out of respect for her father-in-law:

'He refuses to come because he says his Grandpa Zheng hasn't invited him.'

The others were much amused when the woman relayed this answer back to Jia Zheng.

'He's a stubborn little chap when he's made his mind up!' they said. But they thought none the worse of him for that.

Jia Zheng quickly sent Jia Huan with two of the old women to fetch him. When he arrived, Grandmother Jia made him squeeze up beside her on her side of the table and gave him a handful of nuts and dried fruits to eat. The little boy's presence provided the company with something to laugh and talk about. But not for long. Bao-yu, who normally did most of the talking on occasions like this, was today reduced by his father's presence to saying no more than 'yes' and 'no' to remarks made by other people. As for the rest: Xiang-yun, in spite of her sheltered upbringing, was normally an animated, not to say indefatigable talker, but this evening she too seemed to have been afflicted with dumbness by Jia Zheng's presence; Dai-yu was at the best of times unwilling to say very much in company from a sort of aristocratic lethargy which was a part of her nature; and Bao-chai, whose punctilious correctness made her always sparing in the use of words, even though on this occasion she was probably the least uncomfortable of those present, said little to advance the conversation. As a consequence, what should have been a jolly, intimate family party was painfully unnatural and restrained.

Grandmother Jia knew as well as everyone else that this state of affairs was entirely owing to Jia Zheng's presence, and after the wine had gone round for the third time, she attempted to drive him off to bed. Jia Zheng, for his part, was perfectly well aware that he was being driven away so that the younger people could feel freer to enjoy themselves and, smiling forcedly, appealed against his banishment:

'When they told me earlier today that you were planning to give a riddle party, I specially prepared a contribution to the feast so that I might come and join you. You have so much affection for your grandchildren, Mama. Can you not spare just a tiny bit for your son?'

Grandmother Jia laughed:

'They can't talk naturally while you are here. All you are doing is making it gloomy for *me*. I can't abide it. Well, if you've come to answer riddles, I'll give you a riddle. But if you can't guess the answer, you will have to pay me a forfeit.'

'Yes, of course,' said Jia Zheng eagerly. 'And if I guess right, I shall expect to be given a prize.'

'Of course,' said Grandmother Jia. 'The monkey's tail reaches from tree-top to ground. It's the name of a fruit.'

Jia Zheng knew that the answer to this hoary old chestnut was 'a longan' (long 'un), but pretended not to, and made all kinds of absurd guesses, each time incurring the obligation to pay his mother a forfeit, before finally giving the right answer and receiving the old lady's prize. Then he propounded a riddle of his own for her:

> 'My body's square,
> Iron-hard am I.
> I speak no word,
> But words supply.

– It's a useful object.'

He whispered the answer to Bao-yu, who, readily understanding what was expected of him, surreptitiously passed it on to Grandmother Jia. The old lady, having thought for a bit and decided that it sounded all right, said:

'An inkstone.'

'Bravo, Mamma! Right first time!' said Jia Zheng, and turning round to address the servants, he asked them to bring in the presents for Lady Jia. There was an answering call from the women below, and presently a number of them came forward bearing trays and boxes of various shapes and sizes which they handed up onto the kang. Grandmother Jia examined them one by one. They all contained traditional Lantern

Festival presents, but in new and exquisite designs and of the very highest quality. The old lady was obviously pleased.

'Come, children!' she commanded jovially. 'Give the Master a drink!'

Bao-yu stood up and poured wine from the wine-kettle into a little cup and Ying-chun handed it ceremoniously to her uncle.

'Have a look at the riddles on the screen,' said Grandmother Jia when Jia Zheng, with equal ceremony, had drained the cup. 'They were all made up by the children. See if you can tell me the answers.'

Jia Zheng rose from his seat and went up to the lantern-screen. The first riddle he saw was Yuan-chun's:

> At my coming the devils turn pallid with wonder.
> My body's all folds and my voice is like thunder.
> When, alarmed by the sound of my thunderous crash,
> You look round, I have already turned into ash.
> An object of amusement.

'Would that be a firework?' said Jia Zheng.

'Yes,' said Bao-yu.

Jia Zheng looked again, this time at Ying-chun's:

> Man's works and heaven's laws I execute.
> Without heaven's laws, my workings bear no fruit.
> Why am I agitated all day long?
> For fear my calculations may be wrong.
> A useful object.

'An abacus?'

There was a laugh from Ying-chun:

'Yes.'

The next riddle was Tan-chun's:

> In spring the little boys look up and stare
> To see me ride so proudly in the air.
> My strength all goes when once the bond is parted,
> And on the wind I drift off broken-hearted.
> An object of amusement.

'It looks as if that ought to be a kite,' said Jia Zheng.

'Yes,' said Tan-chun.

The next riddle he looked at was Dai-yu's:

> At court levée my smoke is in your sleeve:
> Music and beds to other sorts I leave.
> With me, at dawn you need no watchman's cry,
> At night no maid to bring a fresh supply.
> My head burns through the night and through the day,
> And year by year my heart consumes away.
> The precious moments I would have you spare:
> But come fair, foul, or fine, I do not care.
>> A useful object.

'That must be an incense-clock.'
Bao-yu answered for her:
'Yes.'

Jia Zheng looked at the next riddle:

> Southward you stare,
> He'll northward glare.
> Grieve, and he's sad.
> Laugh, and he's glad.
>> A useful object.

'Very good!' said Jia Zheng. 'If the answer is "a mirror", it is a very good riddle.'

Bao-yu laughed:

'That *is* the answer.'

'Who is it by?' said Jia Zheng. 'There is no name on it.'

'I expect that one is by Bao-yu,' said Grandmother Jia.

Jia Zheng said nothing and passed on to the next one in silence. It was by Bao-chai:

> My 'eyes' cannot see and I'm hollow inside.
> When the lotuses surface, I'll be by your side.
> When the autumn leaves fall I shall bid you adieu,
> For our marriage must end when the summer is through.
>> A useful object.

Jia Zheng knew that the answer must be 'a bamboo wife', as they call those wickerwork cylinders which are put between the bedclothes in summertime to make them cooler; but a growing awareness that all the girls' verses contained images of grief and loss was by now so much affecting him that he felt quite unable to go on.

'Enough is enough!' he thought. 'What can it be that makes these innocent young creatures *all* produce language that is so tragic and inauspicious? It is almost as if they were all destined to be unfortunate and short-lived and were unconsciously foretelling their destiny.'

The gloom into which this reflection plunged him was evident in the melancholy expression on his face and in his bowed and dejected stance. Grandmother Jia noticed it but attributed it to fatigue. She feared that in this melancholy mood his continued presence would place an even greater restraint on the young folk's gaiety.

'I think you really *oughtn't* to stay,' she said. 'Why don't you go and lie down? The rest of us will sit up for a bit, but I don't expect we shall go on very much longer.'

'Yes,' said Jia Zheng, roused from his reverie by her voice. 'Yes, of course.'

But he forced himself to resume his former jovial manner and to drink another cup or two of wine with her before finally retiring. Back in his own apartment, he became lost in reverie once more; but whichever direction his thoughts took him in, he remained melancholy and troubled.

Meanwhile the party he had just left was proceeding somewhat differently.

'Now, my dears, you can enjoy yourselves!' Grandmother Jia said as soon as he had left the room; and the words were no sooner out of her mouth than Bao-yu leaped up from his seat and over to the screen and began criticizing the riddles on it – this one had a line wrong here – that one's words didn't suit the subject – pointing with his finger and capering about for all the world like a captive monkey that had just been let off its chain.

'Can't we sit down and enjoy ourselves quietly, as we were doing just now,' said Dai-yu, 'instead of all this prancing about?'

Xi-feng put in a word too, emerging from the inner room to say it:

'You ought to have Uncle Zheng with you every day and never budge an inch from his side!' She turned to the others: 'What a pity I didn't think of it at the time: we ought to have got Uncle to make him compose some more riddles for us. *Then* we should have seen him sweat!'

Bao-yu was greatly exasperated by this remark and tried to seize hold of her. Xi-feng tried to ward him off, and the result was that the two of them became locked in a sort of playful wrestling-match.

Grandmother Jia continued for a while to laugh and joke with Li Wan and the girls, but soon began to feel tired and sleepy. The night-drum was sounding, and when they stopped to listen they found it was already the beginning of the fourth watch. She ordered the food to be cleared away, telling the servants that they might have what was left over for themselves.

'Time for bed, children!' she said, rising to her feet. 'We can do this again tomorrow, if you like; but now we must have some sleep.'

With that the party gradually broke up and they all dispersed to their rooms.

What happened thereafter will be told in the following chapter.

CHAPTER 23

Words from the 'Western Chamber' supply
a joke that offends
And songs from the 'Soul's Return' move a
tender heart to anguish

Some time after her return from the Visitation the Imperial Concubine commissioned Tan-chun to make her a copy of all the poems about Prospect Garden that had been written during her visit, and having rearranged them in what she considered to be their order of merit, further instructed that they should be engraved on stone in the Prospect Garden itself – a lasting memorial to the precocious talent of her gifted family. In pursuance of these instructions, Jia Zheng ordered his people to look out the best craftsmen available to prepare and engrave the stone and delegated Cousin Zhen to supervise the work with Jia Rong and Jia Qiang as his lieutenants. As Jia Qiang proved to be fully occupied with his twelve young actresses – not to mention their costumes, properties and other paraphernalia – three other junior members of the clan, Jia Chang, Jia Ling and Jia Ping, were called in to supervise the labour in his stead. In due course the preliminary stages of waxing, scratching and 'redding in' had commenced, and work on the memorial proceeded according to plan. We pass from this to other matters.

The twenty-four little Buddhist and Taoist nuns having now been moved out of the two miniature temples in the garden, Jia Zheng had been thinking of dispersing them among various temples and convents about the city, when a certain Zhou-shi, the widow of a poor relation of the Rong-guo Jias who lived near by in North Dukes Street, chanced to get wind of this matter and saw in it the possibility of some employment.

Zhou-shi had for some time past been meaning to ask Jia Zheng if he would find her boy Jia Qin a job – no matter how small a job as long as it would bring them in a little income – and now, hearing this news about the nuns, she drove incontinent forth to Xi-feng as fast as cab could carry her and besought her to use her influence on the boy's behalf.

Xi-feng had always found Zhou-shi a pleasant, unassuming sort of body and was disposed to help her. Having agreed to do so, and having rehearsed her line of approach, she went in to Lady Wang and broached the matter with her in the following manner.

'These little Buddhist and Taoist nuns,' she said, '– we definitely ought not to send them away. We shall need them again if Her Grace ever comes on another visit, and it will be a terrible job getting them together again if they have all been dispersed. If you ask me, the best thing would be to move them to the Temple of the Iron Threshold where they would still be under our control. It would only be a question of sending someone out there every month with a bit of money to pay for their housekeeping; then if there *is* ever any question of needing them again, we have only to say the word and they can be with us immediately without any trouble.'

The suggestion pleased Jia Zheng when it was in due course relayed to him by Lady Wang.

'Of course. That is just what we should do. I am glad you reminded me.'

From Jia Zheng a summons arrived for Jia Lian while he and Xi-feng were at dinner. He laid down his chopsticks and rose to go, but Xi-feng put a hand out and detained him:

'Not so fast! Listen to me! If it's anything else, never mind; but if it's about those little nuns . . .' – and she went on to tell him exactly what he should say in that event and to impress on him how important it was that he should say it.

Jia Lian smiled and shook his head:

'Sorry, nothing doing! You'll have to ask him yourself – if you think you know how to!'

Xi-feng's back stiffened. She laid down her chopsticks and looked at Jia Lian. There was a glint in her eye and a dangerous little smile on her face when she spoke:

'Do you mean that, or are you joking?'

'That boy of my cousin's widow who lives in West Lane, Jia Yun, has been on at me two or three times about getting him a job, and I promised to do something for him if he would wait. Now here at last a job comes along and, as usual, you want to snap it up yourself.'

'Don't worry!' said Xi-feng consolingly. 'Her Grace has mentioned that she wants a lot of planting done – pines and cypresses – in the north-east section of the garden, and she has also asked for more shrubs and flowers to be planted round the foot of the main hall. I promise you that as soon as that job comes up your Jia Yun shall be placed in charge of it.'

'Oh well, in that case all right,' said Jia Lian. 'Just one thing, though' – he dropped his voice and smiled at her slily – 'Why did you keep pushing me off like that last night? I only wanted to try a change of position.'

A quick flush overspread Xi-feng's face and she exploded in a little laugh. Then with a 'pshaw!' in his direction, she lowered her head again and went back to her meal.

Jia Lian laughed and slipped away. On entering Jia Zheng's presence he found that the subject was, as Xi-feng had anticipated, the arrangements for accommodating the little nuns, and he replied as Xi-feng had instructed him:

'Jia Qin is a promising young fellow. I think *he* could be entrusted with the job. In any case, he would be drawing the allowance from Accounts each month when all the other payments are made, so we should be able to keep an eye on him.'

Jia Zheng never took much interest in these trivial domestic matters and agreed readily enough to Jia Lian's suggestion. The latter returned to his apartment and reported to Xi-feng. Xi-feng sent someone to inform Zhou-shi; and soon Jia Qin himself had arrived and was pouring out his gratitude to the two benefactors. With a show of conferring further favours, Xi-feng 'begged' Jia Lian to allow Jia Qin three months' payment in advance. A receipt was written for this amount and Jia Lian's seal affixed to it, and there and then Jia Qin was issued with a tally and sent to the counting-house to collect the money.

When the three hundred taels of shining silver had been weighed and counted and handed over, Jia Qin picked up a piece at random and tossed it to the cashiers to 'buy themselves a cup of tea with'. He had a boy to carry the money back home for him, and after taking counsel with his mother he hired a stout little donkey for himself to ride on and four or five covered mule-carts for the nuns, and conducting the carts round to the side gate of the Rong-guo mansion, he called forth the twenty-four little nuns and packed them all inside. Then off they set, with Jia Qin on his donkey at the head of the procession, to the Temple of the Iron Threshold outside the city. And there we leave them.

*

Yuan-chun's editing of the Prospect Garden poems had given her a vivid recollection of the garden's beauties. She was sure that her father, out of a zealous reverence for the Emperor and herself, would have kept it all locked and closed since her visit and would have allowed no one else to enter, and she felt this to be a waste and a shame – the more so when her family contained so many poetical young ladies who would have found inspiration in its scenery – not to mention the benefit their presence would have bestowed on the garden itself: for, as is well-known,

> When lovely woman smiles not,
> All Nature's charms are dead.

Assuredly, the girls must be allowed into the garden. It should become their home. And if the girls, why not Bao-yu? He had grown up in their midst. He was different from other boys. If he were not allowed into the garden as well, he would consider himself left out in the cold, and his distress would cause Lady Wang and Grandmother Jia to feel unhappy too. Unquestionably she should ask for him to be admitted along with the girls. Having reached this decision, she summoned the eunuch Xia Bing-zhong and ordered him to convey the following Edict to Rong-guo House:

Bao-chai and the other young ladies of the household are to reside in the Garden. The Garden is not to be kept closed. Bao-yu is to accompany the young ladies into the Garden and to continue his studies there.

The Edict was received by Jia Zheng and Lady Wang. When Xia Bing-zhong had gone, they reported it at once to Grandmother Jia and sent servants into the garden to sweep and prepare its buildings and rehang the blinds, portières and bed-curtains in readiness for occupation.

No one was more excited by the prospect of this move than Bao-yu. He was discussing it animatedly with Grandmother Jia (it was a discussion in which the words 'I want' recurred rather frequently) when suddenly a maid came in and announced that he was wanted by his father. At this bolt from the blue his countenance fell and all his animation drained away. Clinging to his grandmother with the gluey persistence of a toffee twist, he made it abundantly plain to her that he had no wish to obey. The old lady did her best to comfort him:

'There, there, my lamb! You'd better go and see him. Grannie will see to it that he doesn't hurt you. He wouldn't dare. Besides, look at all those lovely poems you wrote: I expect that's why Her Grace is letting you inside the garden. I'm sure that's all he wants to see you about. Probably he just wants to warn you against getting up to mischief after you have moved in. You only have to answer nicely and promise to do as he says. You'll be all right.'

To make sure, she sent a couple of old nannies along as well with strict instructions to watch over him:

'See that his Pa doesn't frighten him!' she told them, and the old women promised their protection.

Obliged to go, yet still reluctant, Bao-yu contrived to do so at so dawdling a pace that each step can have advanced him only a few inches upon his way. It so happened that Jia Zheng had gone for the purpose of discussing these matters into Lady Wang's room and Lady Wang's maids Golden, Suncloud, Sunset, Avis and Avocet were standing outside under the eaves. Their amusement when they caught sight of Bao-yu advancing at this snail's pace into the courtyard was evident from the expression on their faces. Golden seized him by the hand, and thrusting out a pair of heavily carmined lips, she said to him in a whisper:

'Look at that *byootiful* lipstick! I've only just put it on. Wouldn't you like a taste of it?'

Suncloud, with a suppressed giggle, pushed her off him:

'Can't you see how scared he is? It's mean of you to tease him at a time like this! He's in a good mood,' she said to Bao-yu. 'You'd better go in straight away, while it lasts!'

Bao-yu entered in a sort of sideways crouch, the picture of a submissive son – a gesture that was wasted, however, since his father and mother were in the inner room at the back. Aunt Zhao raised the inner room's portière to admit him. He bowed to her and entered. Jia Zheng and Lady Wang sat facing each other on the kang talking. Ying-chun, Tan-chun, Xi-chun and Jia Huan were sitting on a row of chairs below. Ying-chun remained seated at his entrance, but the other three rose to their feet.

Jia Zheng glanced up and saw Bao-yu standing before him. The lively intelligence that shone in the boy's every feature, his almost breath-taking beauty of countenance contrasted strikingly with Jia Huan's cringing, hang-dog looks and loutish demeanour, and Jia Zheng thought suddenly of his other son, Jia Zhu, his Firstborn, whom he had lost. He glanced at Lady Wang. Of the children she had borne him Bao-yu was now the only surviving son. He knew how much the boy meant to her. He thought of himself, too: ageing now, his beard already grey. And as he thought, much of his customary dislike of Bao-yu slipped away, so that for the time being perhaps only ten or twenty per cent of it still remained. After what seemed to Bao-yu a very long time, he said:

'Her Grace has expressed a fear that by spending your time in constant amusement outside you may become an idler and a dullard, and she has directed that you and the girls should be moved into the garden so that you may be kept more closely at your books. See to it that you work hard and diligently! If I detect any signs of your former unruliness and disobedience, you will be in for trouble!'

Bao-yu assented meekly. Lady Wang took his hand and drew him up beside her on the kang. Now that he was seated, Jia Huan and the other two sat down once more in their chairs. Lady Wang stroked Bao-yu's neck affectionately:

'Have you finished those pills I sent you the other day yet?'

'There's still one left,' said Bao-yu.

'You must come for some more tomorrow. I'll give you another ten. You must get Aroma to give you one every night before you go to sleep.'

'Yes. You told Aroma, Mother. She's been giving me one every night, as you said.'

'Who is this "Aroma"?' asked Jia Zheng sharply.

'A maid,' said Lady Wang.

'I suppose there are no limits to what a maid may be called,' said Jia Zheng, 'but who would have picked an outlandish name like that to give her?'

Lady Wang could see that he was displeased and did her best to cover up for Bao-yu:

'I think it was Lady Jia who gave her the name.'

'Mother would never think of a name like that,' said Jia Zheng. 'It must have been Bao-yu.'

Bao-yu saw that a frank avowal was now unavoidable and rose to his feet:

'This maid has a surname which means "Flowers". There is a line in an old poem I happened to remember

> The flowers' aroma breathes of hotter days

and so I named her after that.'

'When you get back you must change the name at once,' said Lady Wang hurriedly to Bao-yu. 'Come, Sir Zheng' – this to her husband – 'you aren't going to get angry about a little thing like that?'

'It doesn't really matter,' said Jia Zheng, 'and there is no need for him to change the name; but it demonstrates what I have always said about the boy: he is fundamentally incapable of caring about serious matters and preoccupies himself with poetic frivolities and other such airy-fairy nonsense as a substitute for solid learning. Wretched fellow!' he shouted at Bao-yu. 'What are you waiting for?'

'Go now, go now!' said Lady Wang in a flutter. 'Grandma is probably waiting to begin her dinner.'

Bao-yu murmured a reply and retired, rather more slowly than was necessary. Emerging from the outer door, he grinned and stuck his tongue out at Golden, then shot off like a puff of smoke, the two old nannies hurrying after him. Arriving at the entrance of the covered passage-way he came upon Aroma leaning in the doorway. Her face lit up when she saw him returning unscathed and she asked him what his father had wanted to see him about.

'Oh, nothing much,' said Bao-yu. 'He just wanted to say a few words about not getting up to mischief after we've moved into the garden.'

Having answered Aroma, he went in to see his grandmother and told her about the interview. He found Dai-yu with her and asked her which part of the garden she planned to live in. It appeared that she had just been considering this question herself, for her answer was a prompt one:

'I've been thinking how nice it would be in the Naiad's House. I love all those bamboos and the little winding, half-hidden walk. It is so quiet and peaceful there.'

Bao-yu clapped his hands delightedly:

'Just what I would have chosen for you! I was *hoping* you would want to live there, because *I* want to live in the House of Green Delights – which means that we should be neighbours. And both places are quiet and tucked away.'

They were still discussing their plans when a servant arrived from Jia Zheng with a message for Grandmother Jia. It was to say that the twenty-second of the second month being a Lucky Day was the date on which Bao-yu and the girls were to move into the garden. Servants were to be allowed inside in the interim in order to make the rooms ready for them. It was finally settled that Bao-chai should have All-spice Court, Dai-yu the Naiad's House, Ying-chun the building on Amaryllis Eyot, Tan-chun the Autumn Studio, Xi-chun the Lotus Pavilion, Li Wan Sweet-rice Village, and Bao-yu the House of Green Delights. Each set of rooms was allotted two old women and four maids in addition to the occupant's existing maids and nannies, and there were other servants whose sole duty was sweeping and cleaning. On the twenty-second of the second month everyone moved in. The silent, deserted garden suddenly came to life –

> Live flowers on silk-embroidered flowers up-glanced,
> And unguent scents the scents of spring enhanced

as the bevy of gaily-dressed, chattering girls spread themselves
through its quiet walks.

*

But to return to our hero.

Life for Bao-yu after his removal into the garden became
utterly and completely satisfying. Every day was spent in the
company of his maids and cousins in the most amiable and
delightful occupations, such as

> reading,
> practising calligraphy,
> strumming on the *qin*,
> playing Go,
> painting,
> composing verses,
> embroidering in coloured silks,
> competitive flower-collecting,
> making flower-sprays,
> singing,
> word games and
> guess-fingers.

In a word, he was blissfully happy.

One product of this period was a set of four *Garden Nights*
poems which, though they have little claim to poetic merit,
give a fairly accurate impression of the mood and setting of
those carefree days:

I. *Spring*

> Behind silk hangings, in warm quilts cocooned,
> His ears half doubt the frogs' first muted sound.
> Rain at his window strikes, the pillow's cold;
> Yet to the sleeper's eyes spring dreams unfold.
> Why does the candle shed its waxen tear?
> Why on each flower do angry drops appear?
> By uncouth din of giggling maids distressed
> He burrows deeper in his silken nest.

II. *Summer*

> A tired maid sleeps at her embroidery.
> A parrot in its gilt cage calls for tea.

Pale moonbeams on an opened mirror fall,
And burning sandal makes a fragrant pall.
From amber cups thirst-quenching nectar flows.
A willow-breeze through crystal curtains blows.
In pool-side kiosks light-clad maidens flit,
Or, dressed for bed, by open casements sit.

III. *Autumn*

In Red Rue Study, far from worldly din,
Through rosy gauze moonlight comes flooding in.
Outside, a stork sleeps on moss-wrinkled rocks,
And dew from well-side trees the crow's wings soaks.
A maid the great quilt's golden bird has spread;
Her languid master droops his raven head.
Wine-parched and sleepless, in the still night he cries
For tea, and soon thick smoke and steam arise.

IV. *Winter*

Midnight and winter: plum with bamboo sleeps,
While one midst Indian rugs his vigil keeps.
Only a crane outside is to be found –
No orioles now, though white flowers mask the ground.
Chill strikes the maid's bones through her garments fine;
Her fur-clad master's somewhat worse for wine;
But, in tea-making mysteries deep-skilled,
She has with new-swept snow the kettle filled.

The indifferent quality of these poems did not prevent
members of that class of worldlings who see merit in a name
and excellence in a title from copying them out and proclaiming
them everywhere as miracles of precocious talent when they
discovered that their author was the thirteen-year-old heir
apparent of Sir Jia of Rong-guo House. There were also a
number of bright young things who professed an extravagant
liking for the *deliciousness* of the poems, and who copied them
on to fans and wall-spaces and recited them on the least
provocation (or none at all) at social gatherings. Soon Bao-yu
was being besieged with requests for more poems, for specimens of his calligraphy, for paintings, for inscriptions. He
began to feel himself a lion and was kept constantly busy with
these dilettantish 'duties'.

Then, quite suddenly, in the midst of this placid, agreeable existence, he was discontented. He got up one day feeling out of sorts. Nothing he did brought any relief. Whether he stayed indoors or went out into the garden, he remained bored and miserable. The garden's female population were mostly still in that age of innocence when freedom from inhibition is the fruit of ignorance. Waking and sleeping they surrounded him, and their mindless giggling was constantly in his ears. How could *they* understand the restless feelings that now consumed him? In his present mood of discontent he was bored with the garden and its inmates; yet his attempts to find distraction outside it ended in the same emptiness and ennui.

Tealeaf saw how it was with him and racked his brains for a remedy. Unfortunately all the things he could think of seemed to be things that Bao-yu had already tried and grown tired of. But no, there *was* something he had not yet tried. As soon as Tealeaf thought of it, he set off to the book-stalls and bought a pile of books – books of a kind Bao-yu had never heard about – to give as a present to his young master. His purchases included

> *Old Inklubber's Stories Old and New*
> *The Secret History of Flying Swallow*
> *Sister of Flying Swallow*
> *The Infamous Loves of Empress Wu*
> *The Jade Ring Concubine, or Peeps in the Inner Palace*

and a heap of playbooks – mostly romantic comedies and the like.

Bao-yu took one look at this gift and was enraptured; but Tealeaf uttered a warning:

'Don't take these into the garden! If you do, and anyone finds out about them, I'll be in *real trouble* – more than just a bellyful!'

The injunction was one with which Bao-yu was most unwilling to comply. After a good deal of hesitation he picked out a few of the chaster volumes to keep by his bed and read when no one was about, and left the cruder, more forthright ones behind, hidden somewhere in his outer study.

One day after lunch – it was round about the Midwash of the third month, as our forefathers, who measured the passage

of time by their infrequent ablutions, were wont to say –
Bao-yu set off for Drenched Blossoms Weir with the volumes
of *Western Chamber* under his arm, and sitting down on a rock
underneath the peach-tree which grew there beside the bridge,
he took up the first volume and began, very attentively, to
read the play. He had just reached the line

The red flowers in their hosts are falling

when a little gust of wind blew over and a shower of petals
suddenly rained down from the tree above, covering his
clothes, his book and all the ground about him. He did not
like to shake them off for fear they got trodden underfoot,
so collecting as many of them as he could in the lap of his
gown, he carried them to the water's edge and shook them in.
The petals bobbed and circled for a while on the surface of
the water before finally disappearing over the weir. When he
got back he found that a lot more of them had fallen while he
was away. As he hesitated, a voice behind him said,

'What are you doing here?'

He looked round and saw that it was Dai-yu. She was
carrying a garden hoe with a muslin bag hanging from
the end of it on her shoulder and a garden broom in her
hand.

'You've come just at the right moment,' said Bao-yu,
smiling at her. 'Here, sweep these petals up and tip them in
the water for me! I've just tipped one lot in myself.'

'It isn't a good idea to tip them in the water,' said Dai-yu.
'The water you see here is clean, but farther on beyond the
weir, where it flows past people's houses, there are all sorts of
muck and impurity, and in the end they get spoiled just the
same. In that corner over there I've got a grave for the flowers,
and what I'm doing now is sweeping them up and putting
them in this silk bag to bury them there, so that they can gradually turn back into earth. Isn't that a cleaner way of disposing
of them?'

Bao-yu was full of admiration for this idea.

'Just let me put this book somewhere and I'll give you a
hand.'

'What book?' said Dai-yu.

'Oh . . . The *Doctrine of the Mean* and *The Greater Learning*,' he said, hastily concealing it.

'Don't try to fool *me*!' said Dai-yu. 'You would have done much better to let me look at it in the first place, instead of hiding it so guiltily.'

'In your case, coz, I have nothing to be afraid of,' said Bao-yu; 'but if I do let you look, you must promise not to tell anyone. It's marvellous stuff. Once you start reading it, you'll even stop wanting to eat!'

He handed the book to her, and Dai-yu put down her things and looked. The more she read, the more she liked it, and before very long she had read several acts. She felt the power of the words and their lingering fragrance. Long after she had finished reading, when she had laid down the book and was sitting there rapt and silent, the lines continued to ring on in her head.

'Well,' said Bao-yu, 'is it good?'

Dai-yu smiled and nodded.

Bao-yu laughed:

> 'How can I, full of sickness and of woe,
>   Withstand that face which kingdoms could o'erthrow?'

Dai-yu reddened to the tips of her ears. The eyebrows that seemed to frown yet somehow didn't were raised now in anger and the lovely eyes flashed. There was rage in her crimson cheeks and resentment in all her looks.

'You're *hateful*!' – she pointed a finger at him in angry accusal – 'deliberately using that horrid play to take advantage of me. I'm going straight off to tell Uncle and Aunt!'

At the words 'take advantage of me' her eyes filled with tears, and as she finished speaking she turned from him and began to go. Bao-yu rushed after her and held her back:

'Please, *please* forgive me! Dearest coz! If I had the slightest intention of taking advantage of you, may I fall into the water and be eaten up by an old bald-headed turtle! When you have become a great lady and gone at last to your final resting-place, I shall become the stone turtle that stands in front of your grave and spend the rest of eternity carrying your tombstone on my back as a punishment!'

His ridiculous declamation provoked a sudden explosion of mirth. She laughed and simultaneously wiped the tears away with her knuckles:

'Look at you – the same as ever! Scared as anything, but you still have to go on talking nonsense. Well, I know you now for what you are:

"Of silver spear the leaden counterfeit"!'

'Well! *You* can talk!' said Bao-yu laughing. 'Listen to *you*! Now *I'm* going off to tell on *you*!'

'You needn't imagine you're the only one with a good memory,' said Dai-yu haughtily. 'I suppose I'm allowed to remember lines too if I like.'

Bao-yu took back the book from her with a good-natured laugh:

'Never mind about all that now! Let's get on with this flower-burying!'

And the two of them set about sweeping together the fallen flower-petals and putting them into the bag. They had just finished burying it when Aroma came hurrying up to them:

'So there you are! I've been looking for you everywhere. Your Uncle She isn't well and the young ladies have all gone over to visit him. Her Old Ladyship says you are to go as well. You'd better come back straight away and get changed!'

Bao-yu picked up his book, took leave of Dai-yu, and accompanied Aroma back to his room.

And there, for the moment, we shall leave him.

*

With Bao-yu gone and the girls evidently all out, Dai-yu began to feel lonely and depressed. She was on her way back to her own room and was just passing by the corner of Pear Tree Court when she heard the languorous meanderings of a flute and the sweet modulation of a girlish voice coming from the other side of the wall, and knew that the twelve little actresses were at their rehearsal inside. Although she was paying no particular attention to the singing, a snatch of it chanced suddenly to fall with very great clarity on her ear, so that she was able to make out quite distinctly the words of two whole lines of the aria being sung:

> 'Here multiflorate splendour blooms forlorn
> Midst broken fountains, mouldering walls –'

They moved her strangely, and she stopped to listen. The voice went on:

> 'And the bright air, the brilliant morn
> Feed my despair.
> Joy and gladness have withdrawn
> To other gardens, other halls –'

At this point the listener unconsciously nodded her head and sighed.

'It's true,' she thought, 'there is good poetry even in plays. What a pity most people think of them only as entertainment. A lot of the real beauty in them must go unappreciated.'

She suddenly became aware that her mind was wandering and regretted that her inattention had caused her to miss some of the singing. She listened again. This time it was another voice:

> 'Because for you, my flowerlike fair,
> The swift years like the waters flow –'

The words moved her to the depth of her being.

> 'I have sought you everywhere,
> And at last I find you here,
> In a dark room full of woe –'

It was like intoxication, a sort of delirium. Her legs would no longer support her. She collapsed on to a near-by rockery and crouched there, the words turning over and over in her mind:

> Because for you, my flowerlike fair,
> The swift years like the waters flow . . .

Suddenly she thought of a line from an old poem she had read quite recently:

> Relentlessly the waters flow, the flowers fade.

From that her mind turned to those famous lines written in his captivity by the tragic poet-emperor of Later Tang:

> The blossoms fall, the water flows,
> The glory of the spring is gone
> In nature's world as in the human one –

and to some lines from *The Western Chamber* which she had just been reading:

> As flowers fall and the flowing stream runs red,
> A thousand sickly fancies crowd the mind.

All these different lines and verses combined into a single overpowering impression, riving her soul with a pang of such keen anguish that the tears started from her eyes. She might have remained there indefinitely, weeping and comfortless, had not someone just at that moment come up behind her and tapped her on the shoulder. She turned to look and saw that it was –

But if you wish to know who it was, you must read the next chapter!

CHAPTER 24

*The Drunken Diamond shows nobility of character
in handling his money
And the Quiet-voiced Girl provides material for
fantasy by losing her handkerchief*

As Dai-yu continued to crouch there, a prisoner of her own sorrowful thoughts and emotions, someone suddenly came up behind her and tapped her on the shoulder:

'What are you doing here all on your own?'

She looked round with a start. It was Caltrop.

'You silly girl!' said Dai-yu. 'You gave me quite a shock, creeping up on me like that. Where have you just come from?'

Caltrop laughed mischievously:

'I've been looking for our young lady, but I can't find her anywhere. Your Nightingale is looking for you too, by the way. She says Mrs Lian has sent you – I think it's some kind of tea. Shall I go with you?'

She took her by the hand and accompanied her back to the Naiad's House. The present from Xi-feng she had mentioned was waiting there when they arrived: two little cylindrical containers of a new tea supplied to the Palace for the Emperor's own use. The two girls sat down and discussed the relative merits of various pieces of embroidery, played a little Go, and looked at one or two books. Then Caltrop went off again.

Our narrative leaves them at this point and passes to other matters.

*

Recalled to his own apartment by Aroma, Bao-yu arrived back to find his grandmother's maid Faithful reclining on the couch examining Aroma's needlework.

'Where have you been?' she said, as soon as she saw him enter. 'Her Old Ladyship is waiting for you. She wants you to go next door to see how your Uncle She is getting on. You'd better hurry up and get changed!'

Aroma went into the next room to get his clothes. Bao-yu sat on the edge of the couch and kicked his shoes off. While he was waiting for his boots to come, he turned and scrutinized Faithful. She was wearing a pale strawberry-coloured dress of silk damask, a sleeveless black satin jacket, stockings of eggshell blue, and dark-red embroidered slippers. Her neck, which was towards him as she bent down once more to inspect the needlework, was encircled at its base by a reddish-purple silk scarf. A fascinating neck. He bent down over it to sniff its perfume and stroked it softly with his hand. It was as smooth and white as Aroma's. With an impish chuckle he threw himself upon her and clung like sticky toffee about her person:

'Come on, Faithful darling, give us a taste of your lipstick!'

Faithful called out to Aroma in the next room:

'Aroma, come in and look at this! All the years you've been with him now – haven't you managed to cure him yet?'

Aroma came in with her arms full of clothes.

'I don't know what's the matter with you,' she said to Bao-yu. 'Heaven knows, I've *tried* hard enough to cure you! If you go on much longer like this, you're just going to make it impossible to go on living here any longer.'

She hurried him on with his dressing. When he was ready, he accompanied Faithful to the front apartment to see Grandmother Jia. Going outside again, he found horse and servants ready waiting and was about to get into the saddle, when he noticed Jia Lian dismounting opposite, having just returned from *his* visit. The two cousins went up to each other and exchanged a few words. Just at that moment a figure emerged from the side of the courtyard and greeted Bao-yu:

'Uncle Bao! How are you?'

Bao-yu turned. It was a tall, thin youth of eighteen or nineteen who had spoken, with a thin, handsome face and an air of great natural refinement. Although his face was familiar, Bao-yu could not for the moment remember his name or which part of the clan he belonged to.

'You look very puzzled!' said Jia Lian amusedly. 'Surely you know who this is? This is Jia Yun – Cousin Bu-shi's boy, who lives in West Lane.'

'Yes, of course,' said Bao-yu. 'I can't think what made me forget! – How's your mother?' he asked Jia Yun. 'What business brings you here today?'

Jia Yun pointed to Jia Lian:

'I came here to have a word with Uncle Lian.'

'You've grown very good-looking since I saw you last,' said Bao-yu with a grin. 'You could almost be my son.'

'You've got a nerve!' said Jia Lian laughing. 'Your *son*? He's five or six years older than you.'

'How old *are* you then?' Bao-yu asked him.

'Eighteen.'

Being a sharp-witted young man who knew how to make the most of an opportunity, Jia Yun was quick to turn Bao-yu's jest to good account.

'There's a saying about "grandsires in cradles and babbies with beards", you know; and even if I *am* older than you, "the highest mountain can't shut out the sun"! I've had no one to care for me during these last few years since my father died, and if you don't mind having so stupid a person for your son, I should certainly be very happy to have you for a father.'

'You hear that?' said Jia Lian. 'Now you've got yourself a son! You'll find that parenthood is no laughing matter, I can tell you!'

He left them and went inside, chuckling to himself.

Bao-yu smiled at his new 'son':

'Next time you're free, come and see me. Don't waste your time trying to join in *their* little intrigues! I'm afraid I'm not free at the moment, but if you will come round to my study tomorrow, we can spend all day together, and I shall be able to show you round the garden.'

With these words he mounted his horse and set off, his pages at his back, for Jia She's.

Bao-yu found that his uncle was suffering from nothing more serious than a chill. He delivered his grandmother's message first and then asked after his uncle on his own behalf. Jia She stood up to hear what his mother had to say, and when Bao-yu had finished, ordered a servant to take him to his Aunt Xing's room. Bao-yu withdrew and followed the servant through the back and across the courtyard to the main reception room. Seeing him enter, Lady Xing rose to her feet to ask after Grandmother Jia, then sat down again to be asked after in turn by Bao-yu. Then she drew him up to sit beside her on the kang and asked him about the others, at the same time giving orders for tea to be served.

While they were still sipping the tea, little Jia Cong, the son of one of Jia She's concubines, came in to say 'hullo' to his Cousin Bao.

'Where did this little ragamuffin come from?' Lady Xing scolded. 'I don't know what that Nannie of yours can be thinking of to let you get in such a state! I declare, your face is as black as a crow! No one would ever think to look at you that you were an educated little boy and came from a good family!'

While she scolded, Jia Huan and Jia Lan arrived, their duty call on Jia She evidently just completed. Lady Xing made them sit on chairs below the kang. Seeing Bao-yu up on the kang with Lady Xing and sharing her cushion, and observing how she fondled and petted him, Jia Huan soon began to feel uncomfortable and made a sign to Jia Lan indcating that they should go. As Jia Huan was his uncle, Jia Lan had to do as he said, so the little boy and the big one rose together to take their leave. Bao-yu said he would go with them, but Lady Xing stopped him with a gracious smile:

'You sit where you are! I've got something else to say to you.'

He was obliged to stay. Lady Xing turned to the other two:

'When you get back, do each of you give my regards to your mothers. I won't ask you to stay to dinner because I've already got the girls here and they are making so much rumpus that it's given me a headache.'

Jia Huan and Jia Lan promised to convey her greetings and went out.

'Where *are* the girls, then?' Bao-yu asked after they had gone. '*I* haven't seen them.'

'Oh, I don't know,' said Lady Xing nonchalantly. 'They only sat here for a few moments, then they went round to the back. They're round the back somewhere or other.'

'You said there was something you wanted to talk to me about, Aunt. What was it you wanted to tell me?'

'Oh, nothing at all!' said Lady Xing gaily. 'I only said that because I wanted you to stay and have dinner here with me and the girls. And I've got something nice for you to take back with you afterwards.'

Bao-yu and his aunt chatted away, and before long it was time for dinner and the three girls were called in. A table and chairs were arranged, the table was laid, and Lady Xing, her daughter Ying-chun, her two nieces and her nephew sat down to their meal. When it was over, Bao-yu went in to take his leave of Jia She, after which he and the girls returned to their own side of the mansion. There they first went in to see Grandmother Jia and Lady Wang and then returned to their own apartments for the night.

So much for Bao-yu and the girls.

Let us return to Jia Yun who, after his encounter with Bao-yu, had gone in to see Jia Lian and ask him if there was any prospect of a job.

'A job turned up only the other day,' said Jia Lian, 'but unfortunately your Aunt Feng was very anxious that I should give it to Jia Qin and I'm afraid I let him have it. However, she did mention that there will soon be a lot of planting to do in the garden, and she promised that as soon as that work turns up we shall definitely hand it over to you.'

Jia Yun was silent for some moments, then he said:

'All right. I'll just have to go on waiting, then. But would you mind not mentioning this visit to Auntie? I can tell her about it myself, if need be, next time I see her.'

'*I* shan't mention it,' said Jia Lian. 'I've got better things to do with my time than go running after her to talk about things like this! Tomorrow I have to go to Xing-yi, by the way. I have to get back on the same day – but perhaps you'd better wait until the day after tomorrow before coming round again. In fact, you'd better wait until the *evening* of the day after tomorrow – some time after the beginning of the first watch. Any time before that I shall be busy.'

He terminated the interview by going into the inner room to change his clothes.

Jia Yun went out of the Rong-guo mansion and set off for home, ruminating as he went. A plan at last formed in his mind. Instead of returning home, he struck off for the house of his maternal uncle.

His uncle's name was Bu Shi-ren. He was the proprietor of a perfumery, and when Jia Yun arrived had only just got back from the shop. Seeing his nephew enter, he asked him what he had come about.

'I'm on to something which needs your help,' said Jia Yun. 'Please Uncle, could you possibly let me have four ounces of Barus camphor and four ounces of musk on credit? I promise faithfully that you shall have the money by Autumn Quarter-day.'

Bu Shi-ren 'humph-ed' scornfully:

'Don't talk to me about credit! A while ago we let one of the assistants have several taels' worth of goods on credit for one of his relations, and we haven't seen the money for it yet. We had to share the loss between us. We've got a written agreement now that in future if any of us gives credit to a friend or relation, he is liable to a fine of twenty taels of silver to be shared out among the rest.

'In any case, we're short of stock on those two items. I doubt we've got that much in the shop, even if you could pay cash down for it. We'd have to try to raise it for you else-where.

'And for another thing: what do you want it for, anyway? I don't expect it's for any serious purpose. Even if I let you have it on credit, I expect it would only get thrown away on some foolishness or other.

'And don't you go saying that your Uncle's always on at you when you come to see him! You young people just don't know what's good for you. If only you could pull yourself together and earn a bit of money, no one would be happier for you than I should.'

Jia Yun smiled:

'What you say is no doubt perfectly true, Uncle. But when Father died I was too little to understand what was going on, and according to what Mother has since told me, it was you who stepped in and took care of everything. Now you know as well as I do that it wasn't *I* who spent all the money that came from selling off our little bit of property, and I don't see what I am supposed to do without any capital. Even the cleverest housewife can't make bread without flour! You're lucky you've only got *me* to contend with. Anyone else in my position would be pestering the life out of you. They'd be round here scrounging all the time: a pound of rice one day, a quart of beans the next. Then you *would* have something to grumble about!'

'My dear boy,' said Bu Shi-ren, 'if I had it to give, you should have it and welcome! Your trouble is, though, as I'm always telling your Aunt, you won't *think ahead*. If only you'd pull yourself together and go and have a word with your Father's folk at the big house – or if you can't get to see them, put your pride in your pocket and make yourself agreeable to some of the stewards there – get yourself a job of some kind! When I was on my way out of the city the other day, I ran into that cousin of yours from North Street riding on a donkey with four or five carriages behind him and fifty or sixty nuns on his way to your family temple out in the country. Now that's a shrewd young fellow! You can't tell me he got *that* job by doing nothing!'

Exasperated by his uncle's nagging, Jia Yun got up to go.

'What's the hurry?' said Bu Shi-ren. 'You can have something to eat before you go –'

'Are you crazy?' his wife's voice cut in from the kitchen. 'I *told* you we haven't got any rice in the house. I've just bought this half a pound of noodles that I'm cooking for you now. I don't know what you're acting so lordly about, asking people to dinner. The boy'll only go hungry if he stays!'

'Buy another half a pound, woman, and put it in with the rest!' said Bu Shi-ren.

'Goldie!' Mrs Bu shouted to her daughter. 'Go over to Mrs Wang's house across the road and ask if she can lend us a few cash. Tell her we can pay her back tomorrow!'

But before she had finished, Jia Yun, with a muttered 'Don't bother!' had slipped quietly away.

Angrily leaving his uncle's house behind him, he was on his way back home, eyes fixed on the ground as he brooded miserably on his affairs, when he walked head-on into a drunkard. The man seized hold of him with a curse:

'You sodding blind, bumping into me like that?'

The voice was a familiar one. Looking closer he saw that it was his neighbour Ni Er, a racketeer who made most of his money from high-interest loans supplemented by what he took off other players in the gambling dens. He drank too much and was always getting into fights. At this particular moment he was on his way back from paying a little 'call' on one of his debtors – evidently a lucrative one, for he was already half-seas-over. He did not take kindly to being bumped into, and it would have gone badly with Jia Yun if he had not immediately identified himself:

'Ni, old chap, don't strike! It's me! I wasn't looking where I was going.'

Hearing the voice, Ni Er opened his bleary eyes a little wider, saw that it was Jia Yun, released him – lurching heavily as he did so – and gave a crapulous laugh:

'Oh,' he said, 'young Mist' Jia. Parm me. Wherra you jus' come from?'

'Don't ask me!' said Jia Yun bitterly. 'I've just been given the bird!'

'Nemmind!' said Ni Er. 'Anyone been bothering you, Mist' Jia, jus' tell me and I'll settle accounts with him for you! You know me. Ni Er. The Drunken Diamond. Old Dime'll look after you. Anyone this part of the town troubling neighbour of Dime's, don't care who he is, guarantee put him out of business.'

'Look, Diamond, if you'll promise not to get angry, I'll tell you what happened,' said Jia Yun, and proceeded to give him an account of his interview with Bu Shi-ren. Ni Er was hugely incensed:

'Damn fella! Give the damn fella piece of my mind if he wasn't a relation of yours. Make my blood boil. Damn fella! Nemmind. Dome be downhearted. Got a few taels of silver here. If you can use it, help yourself! Good neighbour of Dime's. Here y'are. Interest-free loan.'

'This man's a racketeer,' Jia Yun thought to himself, 'but he's been known to do a good turn before now – in fact, he's got quite a reputation in some quarters as a champion of the poor. If I don't accept his offer, he may turn nasty and I shall be in trouble. Better accept the money and pay back double the amount when I can.'

Having made the decision, he thanked Ni Er with a smile:

'You're a real sport, Diamond! Since you've been kind enough to make the offer then, I won't refuse. I'll make you out a proper IOU for it when I get home.'

Ni Er roared with laughter:

'There's only fifteen taels and six pennyweights of silver here. If you're going to go writing IOUs, I won't lend it to you!'

Jia Yun laughed too and took the money from him:

'All right, Diamond, anything you say! Let's not fall out about it!'

'That's more like it!' said Ni Er. 'Getting dark now. Won't keep you for a drink. Still got a little business to do. You go on home. Like you to give a message to my old woman, be so kind. Not going home tonight. If there's anything to tell me about, she can send my daughter round first thing tomorrow. Find me at Bandy Wang, the horse-dealer's.'

With these words he went on his way, lurching horribly.

The encounter left Jia Yun somewhat bemused.

'That Ni Er's certainly a character!' he thought. 'The trouble is, it may only have been the drink that made him generous. Perhaps when he's sobered up tomorrow he'll want his money back with a hundred per cent interest. What am I going to do then?'

Then he suddenly remembered what the money would enable him to do:

'Of course! It doesn't matter! If I get the job, I can pay back the loan *and* a hundred per cent interest easily.'

With that thought uppermost in his mind he went into a money-changer's to have the silver weighed. To his great delight it turned out to be exactly the amount Ni Er had said, not a pennyweight less. Then he went home, calling at Ni Er's house on the way to give the message to his wife. Entering his own house he found his mother on the kang spinning. She looked up as he entered:

'Where have you been all day?'

He did not like to mention that he had been to see her brother in case she was angry. He only said:

'Been at Rong-guo House waiting for Uncle Lian. Have you had supper yet?'

'Yes, I've had mine. I put something aside for you.'

She called to their little slavey to fetch it for him. Except for her work-lamp it was already dark indoors, so after finishing his supper he got himself ready for the night, unrolled his bedding, and settled down to sleep.

Rising early next morning, he went off as soon as he had washed to the shops in Central Street outside the south gate of the Inner City and bought camphor and musk at a perfumer's. From there he went to Rong-guo House, and having first ascertained at the gate that Jia Lian was out for the day, he made his way to the Lians' apartment at the back. Outside the gateway leading to their courtyard a number of page boys were sweeping the ground with long-handled brooms. Suddenly Zhou Rui's wife came out and addressed them:

'Stop sweeping now! The Mistress is coming.'

Jia Yun hurried up to her with a smile of greeting:

'Where is Aunt Lian off to, then?'

'Her Old Ladyship wants her,' said Zhou Rui's wife. 'I think it's to see about some tailoring.'

As she spoke, the subject of his inquiry emerged from the gateway, surrounded by a bevy of attendants. Jia Yun was well aware that she had a weakness for flattery and the showier forms of deference. Bringing his hands together in an exaggerated salute and stepping briskly forward, he made her a tremendous bow and wished her in good health.

Xi-feng continued to walk on and, without actually looking at him or turning her head, inquired after his mother's health and asked why she never came to visit.

'She's not been very well, Auntie. She's always thinking about you and meaning to pay a call, but when it's come to it, she just hasn't been able to get out.'

'You're a wonderful liar!' said Xi-feng with a laugh. 'I don't suppose she's ever thought about me until this moment!'

'I'm too much afraid of lightning to lie to my superiors,' said Jia Yun. 'Mother *was* talking about you only last night, as a matter of fact. She said, "Your Auntie Lian is only a single weak woman, yet she has all those responsibilities. It's a good thing she has the will-power to keep everything running so smoothly, because if that should go, she'd be worn out in no time."'

Xi-feng was now all smiles, and halted in spite of herself to hear more.

'And why should you and your mother be chewing over *my* affairs behind my back, pray?'

'That's a long story,' said Jia Yun. 'A very good friend of mine who runs a perfumery and had quite a bit put by in savings decided to invest his money in a government post and bought himself the place of an Assistant Sub-Prefect. Well, a few days ago his posting came and it turns out to be for somewhere down in Yunnan. He's taking his family with him, so of course he won't be able to keep on the shop, and he's been going over all his stock deciding what to give away and what to put in his clearance sale. He decided to give the more valuable stuff to friends and relations. My share was a whole quarter of a pound of Borneo camphor and another quarter of musk, and I was discussing with Mother last night what we ought to do with it. We don't know anyone who could afford to buy it; and it seems a shame to sell it at less than the price; and even if we *gave* it away, we couldn't think of anyone who would want so much. But then I suddenly thought of you and the packets of money you've spent on this kind of thing in years past, and I thought to myself that this year, what with Her Grace in the Palace and the Double Fifth already not far off, you're sure to be using ten or twelve times the usual amount. So, to cut a long story short, we decided to make a present of it to you. There you are, Auntie – a little token of my esteem!'

As he spoke, he took out a small brocade-covered box and respectfully raised it in both hands to offer her.

Now Xi-feng *was* just beginning to think about the problem of purchasing aromatics for the Double Fifth festival, and it pleased her very much to be relieved of the trouble of doing so – especially when it was in so agreeable a manner. She smiled at him graciously before turning to her maid:

'Felicity, take my nephew's present and give it to Patience to take care of!'

The smile was directed once more on Jia Yun:

'You are very thoughtful. I'm not surprised your Uncle speaks so highly of you. He's often told me what a well-spoken, sensible young man you are.'

They seemed to be sailing into harbour. Jia Yun took a step closer:

'Has Uncle been talking to you about me then?' – The tone in which he asked the question was deliberately meaningful.

Xi-feng was on the point of telling him that he would get the tree-planting job when she reflected that by doing so she would be cheapening herself in his estimation. He would almost certainly suppose that she was promising it in return for the perfume. In replying to his question she therefore confined herself to a few insipid civilities, avoiding all mention of jobs and trees, and presently continued on her way to Grandmother Jia's.

Obviously Jia Yun was in no position to raise the subject if his aunt was not willing, so he was obliged to return in the same uncertainty in which he had come. Back home he remembered Bao-yu's invitation of the previous day, and as soon as he had finished his meal, he returned once more to Rong-guo House and made his way to Sunset Studio outside the gateway leading to Lady Jia's quarters. He found the pages Tealeaf and Ploughboy sitting over a game of chess and arguing about a piece that one of them had just taken. Other pages – Trickles, Sweeper, Cloudy and Storky – were up on the roof looking for fledgelings. Jia Yun entered the court-yard and stamped his foot:

'Come on, you young rapscallions! Can't you see you've got a visitor?'

The pages, except Tealeaf, melted away. Jia Yun went into the study and sat down in a chair.

'Has Master Bao been here yet?'

'He hasn't been here yet today,' said Tealeaf. 'If you want to talk to him, I'll have a look and see if he's about.'

With that he, too, vanished.

For about the time it would take to eat a meal, Jia Yun gazed at the paintings, calligraphic scrolls and antiques which adorned the room. At the end of that time, as there was still no sign of Tealeaf, he took a look outside to see if there were any other pages whom he could ask to take a message; but they had all gone off to play elsewhere. Dejectedly he went back once more to wait.

'Tealeaf!'

A soft and thrilling voice was calling from outside. Craning out to look he saw a fifteen- or sixteen-year-old maid standing near the entrance to the study. She was a neat, pleasant-looking girl with a pair of limpid, intelligent eyes. Seeing a strange man in the room, she quickly shrank back out of his line of vision. At that very moment Tealeaf walked back into the courtyard.

'Ah, good!' he said, catching sight of the maid. 'I was beginning to wonder how I'd ever get a message to him.'

Jia Yun ran out to question him:

'Well?'

'Waited for ages,' said Tealeaf, 'but no one came by. *She*'s from his room, though' – he indicated the soft-voiced maid – 'Listen, dear,' he said addressing her. 'Can you take a message for us? Tell him that Mr Jia from West Lane is here.'

On learning that the visitor was a member of the clan, the maid became less concerned about concealment and engaged the limpid eyes in bolder scrutiny of his features. The object of her scrutiny now addressed her:

'Don't bother about the "West Lane" stuff! Just say that "Yun" has called!'

The girl reflected for some moments, then, with a half-smile, she said:

'If I were you, Mr Jia, I'd go home now and come again tomorrow. I'll try to get a message through to him this evening if I get the chance.'

'What's the idea?' said Tealeaf.

'He didn't have his nap today,' said the maid. 'That means he'll be having dinner early. Then suppose he doesn't go out after dinner: are you going to let Mr Jia wait here all day without eating? It would be much better if he went home now and came again tomorrow. Even if I succeed in getting word through to him as soon as I get back, he'll probably only send an answer to the message. I don't expect he'll actually come over.'

Her words were sensible and to the point and were spoken in the same thrilling tone that had first attracted him. Jia Yun would have liked to ask her name, but etiquette forbade that he should do so now that he knew she was one of Bao-yu's maids. He just said:

'I'm sure you're right. I'll come again tomorrow, then.'

He turned to go.

'I'll get some tea for you, Mr Jia,' said Tealeaf. 'Have a cup of tea before you go.'

'No thanks,' said Jia Yun, looking back over his shoulder but continuing to go. 'I've got other business.'

The words were for Tealeaf, but the look which accompanied them was directed at the soft-voiced maid, who was still standing there.

Jia Yun went back home and returned next day as she had advised. On his way in he ran into Xi-feng outside the main gate. She was about to visit Jia Lian's parents next door and had just got into her carriage. Seeing Jia Yun, she made her attendants call to him to stop.

'Yun!' She smiled at him through the window of the carriage. 'You've got a nerve, my lad, playing a trick like that on me! I see now why you gave me that present. It's a job you were after. Your Uncle told me yesterday. Apparently you've been on to him about it already.'

Jia Yun smiled back ruefully:

'I'd rather we didn't go into my dealings with Uncle, if you don't mind! I'm beginning to wish I'd never spoken to him about it. If I'd realized earlier what the situation was, I should have gone straight to you in the first place. I'm sure if I had, it would all have been settled long ago. I'm afraid Uncle has let me down.'

'Humph!' said Xi-feng. 'So that's why you came to me yesterday, is it? You'd had no success with the husband so you thought you'd try your luck with the wife!'

'That's most unfair, Auntie!' Jia Yun protested. 'It was a purely disinterested present. I wasn't thinking at all about a job when I gave it to you. If I had been, why do you suppose I didn't take the opportunity of asking you about it at the time? However, since you do now know that I'm looking for one, I'd like to forget about Uncle and throw myself on *your* kindness instead.'

'You have a very devious way of going about things,' said Xi-feng with a hint of malice in her smile. 'Why couldn't you have spoken up sooner? A little thing like this is hardly worth so much delay. We still need some more trees and shrubs planted in the garden, and I've been trying to think of someone to do the job. If you'd spoken up earlier, it could all have been done by now.'

'You can set me to work tomorrow, Auntie. I'll be ready.'

Xi-feng thought for a while.

'I don't know that it's a very suitable job for you. Perhaps we'd better wait until next New Year and put you in charge of lanterns and fireworks. That's a much bigger job.'

'Look, Auntie: you give me this planting job now, then; if you're satisfied with the way I do it, you can give me the other job later on.'

Xi-feng laughed:

'You certainly know how to fish with a long line! – All right, then! It's not really my affair, but I suppose as your Uncle has mentioned it to me — I'm only going next door now and I shall be back again after lunch. Come round a little after midday to get the money and you shall start your planting the day after tomorrow.'

She told the servants to harness the carriage and drove off to make her call.

Beside himself with joy, Jia Yun now continued on his way to Sunset Studio to look for Bao-yu. In point of fact Bao-yu had gone off first thing that morning to call on the Prince of Bei-jing; but no one seemed to know about this, and Jia Yun sat waiting expectantly throughout the whole of the morning. Having waited until noon, he inquired whether Xi-feng was back yet, and being informed that she was, he wrote out a form of receipt, took it round to the Lians' apartment, and sent in word that he had called for his tally. Sunshine came out in response to his message and asked him for the receipt, which he took indoors. Presently he reappeared and handed it back to Jia Yun with the date and amount filled in in the blanks he had left for this purpose, together with the precious tally which would enable him to draw the money. Glancing at the receipt as he took it from him, Jia Yun was delighted to observe that the figures entered were for a payment of two hundred taels of silver. He hurried off to the counting-house to collect it, then home once more to share the joyful news with his mother.

Next day he was off long before daylight to look up Ni Er and pay him back the loan. That done, he took another fifty taels of the silver with him and called on a nurseryman outside the West Gate called Fang Chun, from whom he bought a large number of trees.

At this point our narrative abandons Jia Yun's affairs and returns to Bao-yu.

When Bao-yu, in the course of his meeting with Jia Yun, had invited Jia Yun to drop in and spend the following day with him, the invitation was of the careless, half-serious kind that is unfortunately typical of young gentlemen of his class. As he had made no real effort to remember it at the time, it naturally slipped his memory the following day. Returning now, two evenings later, from the palace of the Prince of Bei-jing where he had been all day, he called first on his grandmother and his mother and then returned to his own rooms in the garden and changed back into his everyday clothes.

He decided to take a bath; and since Aroma was out, having been 'borrowed' by Bao-chai to make braid buttons on a dress, Ripple and Emerald had gone off to see about the water. Of the other senior maids, Skybright had been fetched home for her cousin's birthday and Musk was away ill; and the few heavy-work maids left in attendance had all assumed that their services would not be required and had gone off in search of their gossips. For a quarter of an hour Bao-yu was left entirely on his own. It chanced that precisely at this moment he wanted someone to get him some tea. He had already called a couple of times without response and at his third call two or three old charwomen came hurrying in to see what was the matter.

'No, no: I don't need *you*!' – he waved them away impatiently. The old women retired, baffled.

Since there were no maids, Bao-yu saw that he would have to serve himself. He found himself a cup and was about to take up the pot to pour himself some tea when a voice started speaking right behind him:

'Let me, Master Bao! You might scald yourself.'

Bao-yu jumped. The owner of the voice hurriedly relieved him of the cup.

'Where have you been all this time?' he said. 'You gave me quite a start, coming up suddenly like that!'

She handed him his tea with a smile:

'I was in the back courtyard. I came in through the courtyard door at the back. Didn't you hear me coming?'

Bao-yu sipped his tea and observed her carefully. Her dress, though not shabby, was far from new. By contrast she had a magnificent head of raven-black hair which was done up in a simple bun. The face was rather long and thin; the build slender; the overall impression that of a tidy, clean, graceful person.

'Do you belong here then?' he asked her.

'Yes.' She seemed amused.

'If you do, how is it that I've never seen you before?'

She replied with some bitterness:

'There are quite a few of us you've never seen. I'm not the only one, by any means. How *could* you have seen me? I've never been allowed to wait on you or show myself in your presence.'

'Why not?'

'I don't think it's for me to say. – Oh, there's something I *do* have to tell you, though. Yesterday a gentleman calling himself "Yun" came to see you. I thought you probably wouldn't be able to see him at the time, so I told Tealeaf to ask him round this morning. Unfortunately by the time he came, you'd already gone off to see the Prince—'

Their conversation was interrupted by the giggles of Ripple and Emerald who had just entered the courtyard with a large bucket of water. Each of them held the bucket by one hand and lifted her skirts up with the other. They were staggering under the unaccustomed weight and slopping a good deal of the water about as they went. The maid hurried out to relieve them. By now the giggles had given way to recriminations:

'Look, you've soaked my dress!'

'You trod on my toe!'

They stopped to look at this person who had just issued from the young Master's room and saw with some surprise that it was Crimson. Putting down the water, they hurried indoors to look. Bao-yu was there on his own. The girls were indignant. As soon as they had prepared the bath and seen him undressed, they shut the door after them and hurried to the other side of the building to find Crimson.

'What were you doing in his room just now?' they asked her accusingly.

'I wasn't doing anything,' said Crimson. 'I couldn't find my handkerchief, so I went to look for it round the back. He was calling for some tea and none of you happened to be about, so I ran in and poured it out for him. And just at that moment you came back.'

Ripple spat in her face:

'Nasty, shameless little slut! When we asked you to fetch the water for us you said you were busy and made us go ourselves. You didn't waste much time, having got him to yourself, did you? You think you're on the way up, don't you? Step by step. Well, we can catch up with you, my fine lady! Why don't you take a look at yourself in the mirror and *then* ask yourself if you're a fit person to go serving tea to the Masters?'

'We'd better warn the others that when he asks for tea or anything in future they must stay where they are and let *her* go and get it!'

'In that case,' said Ripple, 'the rest of us may as well clear off and let her have him all to herself!'

They were still at their antiphonal taunting when an old woman arrived with a message from Xi-feng:

'Someone is bringing some workmen in tomorrow to plant trees, so you have all got to be extra careful. No hanging clothes out to dry all over the place! There will be screens put up along the line of the embankment and you are not to go running around outside.'

'Who's the person in charge of the workmen?' asked Ripple.

'A young chap called "Yun" from up the Lane,' said the old woman.

The name meant nothing to Ripple and Emerald, who went on to ask about other matters; but Crimson knew it must be the young man she had met the day before in the outer study.

Crimson's surname was 'Lin'. Her family had been retainers in the Jia family for generations. Nowadays her father worked as a farm-bailiff on the family's estates. She was sixteen. Along with many other servants, she had originally entered the Prospect Garden to carry out caretaking duties in the period when it was still unoccupied. The part of it she was assigned to was the House of Green Delights. She found it a very beautiful place to live in – very quiet and secluded. But this had changed when Bao-yu and the girls were commanded to move in and Bao-yu had chosen the House of Green Delights as his own residence.

Although Crimson was a very inexperienced maid, she had a measure of good looks and a determination to better herself. She was therefore constantly on the look-out for an opportunity of making herself known to Bao-yu and showing off her ability to serve him. Unfortunately the little group of body-servants who had accompanied him into the garden guarded their privileges with tooth and claw and were careful to allow no toehold to an ambitious outsider. Today she had at last found an opening, only to have her hopes immediately dashed by Ripple's malice. She felt very discouraged.

Still smarting with resentment, she heard the old woman say that Jia Yun was coming next day into the garden. The name provoked a momentary flutter in her breast; but she returned to her room with the same feeling of resentment bottled up inside her and went to bed to ponder moodily on the events of the day. As the thoughts pursued themselves round and round in her mind without object or conclusion, she suddenly heard her name being called very softly outside her window:

'Crimson! Crim! I've found your handkerchief!'

She quickly got up and went outside to look. To her surprise it was Jia Yun. A maidenly confusion mantled her comely cheek.

'Where did you find it?' she asked timidly.

Jia Yun laughed:

'Come over here and I'll show you!'

He took hold of her dress to pull her to him. Overcome with shame, she turned and fled, but her foot caught on the threshold and she fell on her face.

The conclusion of this adventure will be revealed in the following chapter.

CHAPTER 25

*Two cousins are subjected by witchcraft to
the assaults of demons
And the Magic Jade meets an old acquaintance while
rather the worse for wear*

We have seen how Crimson, after lying a long time a prey to
confused and troubled thoughts, at last dozed off to sleep;
and how later, when Jia Yun grabbed at her, she turned and
fled, only to stumble and fall on the threshold of her room.
At that point she woke in bed and discovered that she had
been dreaming. She did not get to sleep again after that, but
lay tossing restlessly throughout the night.

When daylight came at last, she got up, and shortly after
was joined by the other maids who shared with her the early
morning duties of sweeping the rooms and courtyards and
fetching water for the others' washing.

Crimson's own toilet was a simple one: a brief look in the
mirror while she coiled her hair, a quick wash, and she was
ready to join the others in their sweeping.

Her encounter with Bao-yu had made a stronger impression
on that impressionable young man than she realized. He had
even thought of asking for her by name to wait upon him,
but hesitated, partly from fear of offending Aroma and the
rest, and partly because he did not know what she was really
like and dreaded the unpleasantness of sending her away again
if she proved unsatisfactory. The question still preoccupied
him when he woke that morning. He rose quite early and sat
musing silently on his own, making no effort to begin his
toilet.

In a little while the paper-covered shutters were removed
and he was able to see clearly through the silken gauze of the
casement into the courtyard outside. He could see several
girls there sweeping, all of them heavily made-up and with
flowers and ornaments in their hair, but no sign of the quiet,
neat girl of the day before. He went outside in his slippers to

look around, pretending that he had gone out to inspect the flowers. He could see someone leaning on the balustrade in the south-west corner of the cloister-like covered walk, but she was half hidden by the crab-apple tree and he could not make out who it was. He approached and looked more closely. It was she, yesterday's girl, standing there on her own, apparently lost in thought. He was a little shy of addressing her at that particular moment and was still hesitating when Emerald came up and asked him to come in and wash. He had to go in again without having spoken to her.

While Crimson stood there musing, she suddenly became aware that Aroma was beckoning to her, and hurried up to see what she wanted.

'Our spittoon is broken,' Aroma said. 'Can you go to Miss Lin's and ask them if they will lend us one until we can get a replacement?'

Crimson hurried off in the direction of the Naiad's House. When she got to Green Haze Bridge, she stopped a moment to look around. She noticed that cloth screens had been set up all along the side of the artificial hill, and remembered that this was the day on which the workmen were coming into the garden to plant trees. She could just make out a knot of workmen digging a hole in the distance and Jia Yun sitting on some rocks supervising them. She would have liked to go over, but did not quite dare, and having collected the spittoon, returned, in very low spirits, and lay down in her own room to brood. The others all assumed that she must be feeling unwell and took no notice.

*

Next day was the birthday of Wang Zi-teng's lady. A message had already been received from that quarter inviting Grandmother Jia and Lady Wang to spend the day with her. Lady Wang would have liked to go but felt unable, even though the invitation was from her brother's wife, because she could see that Grandmother Jia did not want to. Wang Zi-teng's other sister, Aunt Xue, went instead, together with his niece Xi-feng, Bao-chai, Bao-yu and the three Jia girls. They did not return until the evening.

Not long before they returned, Jia Huan got back from school and Lady Wang gave him the task of copying out the text of that prolonger of life and highly efficacious prophylactic against sickness and misfortune, the *Dharani of the Immaculate Diamond*. He seated himself on Lady Wang's kang, called for a candle to be lit, and, with a great deal of self-important fuss, began his copying, one minute calling for Suncloud to pour him tea, the next requiring Silver to trim the wick of his candle, and shortly after that informing Golden that she was standing in his light. The maids all hated Jia Huan and took no notice – all, that is, except Sunset, who had always had a soft spot for him. She poured him a cup of tea and, observing that Lady Wang was engaged in conversation with someone elsewhere in the apartment, quietly counselled some restraint:

'Try not to throw your weight about so!' she said. 'It's silly to put people's backs up.'

Jia Huan scowled angrily:

'I know what I'm doing,' he said. 'Don't talk to me like a child! You're friends with Bao-yu nowadays, aren't you? You don't like me any more. I know. I've watched you both.'

Sunset clenched her teeth. She stabbed the air above his head with her finger:

'You ungrateful thing! You're like the dog that bit Lü Dong-bin: you don't know a friend when you see one.'

They were still exchanging words when Xi-feng came in, having just got back from the birthday party. Lady Wang wanted to know about the other ladies who had been invited, whether the plays had been any good, and what sort of things they had had to eat and drink.

In a little while Bao-yu, too, arrived, and after a few respectful words to his mother, asked the servants to take off his headband and gown for him and help him off with his boots. Disencumbered, he flung himself into his mother's bosom to be fondled and petted by her, then, worming his way up and nuzzling affectionately against her neck, he proceeded to add his own amusing commentary on the day's events.

'You've been drinking again, child,' said Lady Wang. 'Your face is burning. All this romping about will make you sick. Lie down quietly for a while over there!'

She made them bring him a head-rest, and he lay down behind her, towards the back of the kang. Sunset was instructed to massage him by gently patting his legs.

He tried to joke with Sunset as she knelt beside him, but she barely acknowledged his questions and answered frigidly, directing her eyes and all her attention upon Jia Huan. Bao-yu seized her hand:

'Come, my dear! You must take notice of me if I speak to you!'

He tugged at her hand as he spoke, but she snatched it from his grasp.

'If you do that again,' she said, 'I shall call out!'

Jia Huan heard every word of this exchange. He had always hated Bao-yu, and this flirting with Sunset – *his* Sunset – was the last straw. He must be revenged or burst. A moment's reflection suggested the means. He had only to feign a slight clumsiness of the hand and it was done. The candle, brimming with molten wax, toppled straight on to Bao-yu's face. There was a piercing cry, which made everyone else in the room jump. Quickly they brought standard lamps up from the floor below. By their light Bao-yu's face was seen to be covered all over in wax. Torn between anguish for him and anger with Jia Huan, Lady Wang urged the servants to remove it as quickly as possible, while alternately berating the other boy for his carelessness. Xi-feng scrambled up on to the kang to help the servants, grumbling at Jia Huan as she did so:

'Huan, you are *the* most cack-handed creature I have ever met! You are simply not fit for decent company. I don't know why Aunt Zhao hasn't taught you better.'

Her words reminded Lady Wang that she had been abusing a Master in front of the servants. She ceased rebuking Jia Huan at once and, summoning Aunt Zhao, directed all her wrath upon that luckless concubine:

'This is a fine son you bore us, I must say! He is a black-hearted little monster! You might at least *try* to teach him better. But no. Time and again I have overlooked this sort of thing, but instead of feeling sorry, you glory in it. You think that when I do nothing, you have got the better of me.'

Aunt Zhao was obliged to swallow her anger and endure

these taunts in silence. She climbed up onto the kang and made a show of helping the others with the injured boy. She looked at his face. The whole left side of it was badly blistered. It was a wonder that the eye had not been damaged. When Lady Wang saw it, she was both full of anguish for her son and at the same time, when she thought of the questioning to which she would inevitably be subjected by Grandmother Jia and wondered what she would say, terrified on her own account. To relieve her fear she turned once more on Aunt Zhao. Then, after tongue-lashing the concubine, she comforted her beloved son and applied Antiphlogistic Ointment to the blistered part of his face.

'It does hurt a bit,' said Bao-yu when she asked him, 'but nothing very terrible. When Grandma asks about it, we had better tell her that *I* did it.'

'She'll blame the rest of us for not looking after you properly, even if you say you did it yourself,' said Xi-feng. 'There'll be a row, whatever you say.'

Lady Wang told them to see him back to his room. It was a great shock to Aroma and the other maids when they saw him.

Dai-yu had had a dull time of it with Bao-yu away all day, and in the course of the evening sent several times round to his room to inquire whether he was back yet. It was in this way that she heard about his scalding. She hurried round immediately to see for herself how he was.

She found him with a mirror in his hand, examining the extent of the damage. The entire left side of his face was thickly plastered with ointment, from which she deduced that the injury must be a serious one. But when she approached him to look closer, he averted his head and waved her away. He knew how squeamish she was, and feared that the sight of it would upset her. Dai-yu for her part was sufficiently aware of her own weakness not to insist on looking. She merely asked him 'whether it hurt very badly'.

'Not so bad as all that,' said Bao-yu. 'A couple of days and it will probably be all right again.'

Dai-yu sat with him a little longer and then went back to her room.

Next day Bao-yu had to see Grandmother Jia. Although he

told her that he had burned himself through his own careless-ness, the old lady, as had been predicted, berated his attendants for having allowed the accident to happen.

Another day went by, and Bao-yu's godmother, old Mother Ma, called round. Mother Ma was a Wise Woman. Her special relationship with Bao-yu had been arranged in his infancy to ensure him the protection of her powers. She was shocked by her godson's appearance and, on being informed of the cause, shook her head and tutted sympathetically. She made a few signs over his face with her fingers, muttering some gibberish as she did so, after which she assured them that he would soon be better: the malignant aura that had caused the accident was of a transitory, impermanent nature. She turned to Grand-mother Jia:

'Bless you, my lucky lady! Bless you dearie! You don't know a half of the unseen harms and dangers the Scripture tells us of. All the sons of princes and great folks the moment they begin to grow up are followed round everywhere they go by troops of invisible little imps – spiteful little creatures who nip them and pinch them whenever they can. Some-times they knock the ricebowl from their hands when they're eating. Sometimes they push them over when they are walking. It's on account of these creatures that so many young gentlemen of good family don't live to make old bones.'

Grandmother Jia was anxious to know if the afflicted person could be freed from these unwelcome attentions.

'Easily,' said Mother Ma. 'By doing good works. Giving a bit more to charity on the young person's behalf. There *is* another way, though. According to what the Scripture says, there's a Bodhisattva of Universal Light living in the Para-dise of the West who spends his time lighting up the dark places where these evil spirits lurk, and if any believer, male or female, will make offerings to that Bodhisattva in a proper spirit of devoutness, he will grant their children and grand-children his holy peace and protect them from possession by devils and from the powers of darkness.'

'What sort of offerings do you make to this Bodhisattva?' Grandmother Jia asked her.

'Nothing very special. Apart from the usual incense offerings, we take a few pounds of sesame oil each day and make what we call a "sea of light" by burning wicks in it. We believe that this sea of light is the trans-substantial body of the Bodhisattva. It has to be kept burning night and day and never allowed to go out.'

'How much oil does it take to keep it burning for one whole day and night?' said Grandmother Jia. 'I should like to do this for the boy.'

'There's no fixed amount,' said Mother Ma. 'We leave it to our clients to decide how much they *want* to give. There are several members of the aristocracy among those I do this service for. Let's see ... There's the Prince of An-nan's lady. She's my biggest subscriber. Her subscription is for forty-eight pounds of oil and a pound of lampwicks a day. *Her* sea of light is pretty nearly as big as a cistern. Then there's the Marquis of Jin-xiang's lady: twenty pounds of oil a day. Oh, and there's some pays for ten pounds a day, some for eight pounds, three pounds, five pounds— all sorts. All of them I keep their seas of light burning for them, back at my house.'

Grandmother Jia nodded thoughtfully.

'One thing I should mention,' said Mother Ma (observing the thoughtfulness): 'if the offering is for an older person – a mother or father, say – it doesn't matter *how* much you subscribe; but if it's an older person making it for a younger one, like as it may be Your Ladyship for Bao-yu, you don't want to subscribe too much, or it would overload his luck and have the opposite effect. In the case of Your Ladyship subscribing for Bao-yu, I should suggest between five and seven pounds a day.'

'Make it five pounds a day, then,' said Grandmother Jia. 'We'll work out the total and send you a month's supply every month.'

'Amitabha, Merciful Buddha! Bless His Holy Name!' said Mother Ma.

As a further precaution Grandmother Jia called in some of Bao-yu's maids and told them that in future whenever Bao-yu went out anywhere his pages were to be provided with several strings of cash to give as alms to any itinerant monks or priests or any poor or afflicted persons they might meet upon the way.

After seeing Grandmother Jia, Mother Ma drifted round the mansion calling at various other apartments. Presently she came to Aunt Zhao's room. After they had exchanged greetings, Aunt Zhao told her little servant to pour the old woman a cup of tea. Aunt Zhao was pasting pieces of cloth together for soling shoes with, and Mother Ma observed that the kang around her was piled with miscellaneous remnants of material.

'I'm looking for something to make a pair of uppers out of, dearie,' said Mother Ma. 'I suppose you haven't got an old bit of silk or an old bit of satin that would do? It doesn't matter about the colour.'

Aunt Zhao heaved a long-suffering sigh:

'Take a look at this lot! You won't find anything much worth having here. Nothing worth having in this family ever comes *my* way. But you're welcome to pick out a couple of pieces if you don't mind the poor quality.'

Mother Ma rummaged around in the heap, and having picked out several pieces, stuffed them into her sleeve.

'I sent someone round to you the other day with five hundred cash to pay for an offering to the Medicine Buddha,' said Aunt Zhao. 'Have you managed to make it yet?'

'Oh yes. That was done days ago.'

'Holy Name!' said Aunt Zhao. 'I'd do it oftener if things were a bit easier; but you know the saying: "my heart is willing but my purse is lean".'

'Don't you worry about that!' said Mother Ma. 'You only have to hold out a few more years. When your Huan has grown up and got himself a job in the Service, you'll be able to afford all the good works you want.'

Aunt Zhao made a scornful sound in her nose:

'Hfn! Let's not talk about it! It'll be no different then from what it is now: Huan and I will never be able to compete with the Other One. It's like the Heavenly Dragon appearing when *he* comes on the scene. Mind you, I don't hold it against the child. He's a good-looking boy, is Bao-yu, and you can understand the grown-ups being silly about him. No, *this* is the one I can't stand.'

As she uttered the word 'this', she held up two fingers. Mother Ma guessed her meaning: 'Number Two' – the younger of the Rong mansion's two daughters-in-law.

'You mean Mrs Lian?' she said.

Aunt Zhao's face assumed an expression of terror. Motioning agitatedly to the other to remain silent, she got up, went to the door, raised the door-blind, looked around, and having satisfied herself that there were no eavesdroppers, came back and sat down again, her face close to Mother Ma's.

'She's a dreadful person – *dreadful*! If that woman doesn't end up by carrying off every stick of property belonging to this family to line her own nest with, my name's not Zhao!'

Mother Ma sensed interesting possibilities in this conversation, and was quick to explore them:

'It doesn't need you to tell me that,' she said. 'You surely don't think I haven't noticed *that*? I've often wondered why you all let her get away with it – though I suppose it's probably just as well you do.'

'My dear good woman,' said Aunt Zhao, 'we've no choice but to let her get away with it. Who would ever have the nerve to stand up to *her*?'

'Well,' said Mother Ma, 'I don't want to seem a trouble-maker, but if you don't mind my saying so, you do all seem to have acted a bit helpless about her – not that I'm blaming you, mind. But I mean to say, even if you daren't stand up to her *openly*, there are things you could do in secret. I'm surprised you haven't thought of it before.'

To Aunt Zhao the words seemed to contain a hidden promise. She concealed her pleasure.

'What do you mean: "things we could do in secret"?' she said. 'I'm willing enough to do them: it's just that I've never met anyone who could tell me how. If you would show me the way, I'd pay you. I'd pay a lot.'

Mother Ma could see that they understood each other, but she was taking no chances.

'Holy Name! Don't ask me about things like that! I don't touch that kind of business. No, no, no. That's wicked.'

'There you are!' said Aunt Zhao. 'That's all the help I ever get. And I thought you were such a kind person, always helping those in trouble. Are you prepared to stand by and watch me and my Huan being made mincemeat of by that scheming woman? I suppose it's because you think I wouldn't pay you.'

'If you was to say that I am too tender-hearted to stand by and watch you and your boy being wronged,' said Mother Ma, 'you would be saying no more nor less than the truth. But I don't know what you mean about *pay*. What have *you* got that you could tempt me with, dearie, even if I *was* willing to do it for pay?'

Aunt Zhao observed that her opposition to the very idea of helping her in the desired way had considerably weakened.

'For someone so clever,' she said, 'aren't you being rather stupid? If you help me and it works, with the two of *them* safely out of the way, everything in this household will be ours. You'll be able to ask for what you like. Fancy not thinking of that!'

Mother Ma lowered her head and reflected for a while in silence.

'When *that* time comes and you're safely landed,' she said eventually, 'you won't want to have anything more to do with *me*, dearie – not when I've got no proof to show what I done for you.'

'That's no problem,' said Aunt Zhao. 'I've got a few taels put by of my own savings, and I've got some dresses, and there's my jewellery. You can take some of each to be getting on with and I can give you an IOU promising to pay you so much later on. We can have a witness too, if you like.'

'Are you sure?'

'Why should I tell a lie?' said Aunt Zhao, and summoned a trusted crone into whose ear she whispered instructions:

'Ps-ps-ps-ps-ps-ps-ps-ps.'

The old crone nodded and went out, returning after a few minutes with a promissory note for five hundred taels of silver. Aunt Zhao made her mark on it and then went to the wardrobe to get out her savings. The white shine of silver and the signed and sealed IOU dispelled whatever residual

doubts the Wise Woman may have entertained, for she seized
and pocketed both with alacrity, giving hearty assurances of
her aid as she did so; then, after rummaging for some time in
the capacious waistband of her trousers, she fished out twelve
little paper cut-out figures – ten of them demons with green
faces and red hair and two of them plain human figures – and
handed them to Aunt Zhao. Dropping her voice to a whisper,
she instructed her to write the eight symbols of her victims'
nativity – two for the year, two for the month, two for the day
and two for the hour – on each of the human figures, wrap
five of the demons round each of them, and slip them somewhere under her victims' beds.

'That's all you have to do,' she said. '*I* shall be doing other
things at home to help you. It's sure to work – no question of
that. But you must be very, very careful. And you mustn't
be afraid.'

While she was still talking, one of Lady Wang's maids came
in looking for her.

'Oh, here you are! Her Ladyship is waiting for you.'

Mother Ma went off in the company of the maid.

And there we leave her.

*

Because of the injury to his face, Bao-yu had stopped going
out of doors since his accident and Dai-yu spent a good deal
of time in his apartment talking to him.

One morning after lunch she had settled down to read,
but after a couple of chapters grew bored with the book and
did some sewing instead with the maids Nightingale and
Snowgoose. When that, too, became boring, she stood for a
while leaning against the doorway, vacantly looking out. The
young bamboo shoots were just breaking through in the
forecourt, and after inspecting them, she drifted out into the
Garden. Everywhere the flowers were blooming, the birds
were singing, and the water splashed and tinkled, but not a
human soul was to be seen. Almost without thinking where
she was going, she made her way to the House of Green
Delights. A group of maids had fetched some water from the
well and were watching the white-eyes in the gallery giving

themselves a bath. A sound of laughter came from inside the house. Li Wan, Xi-feng and Bao-chai were there already. Their friendly laughter greeted Dai-yu as she entered:

'Another one! Come in! Come in!'

'What *is* this?' said Dai-yu, joining in the good humour. 'A party?'

'I sent someone round to you the other day with two caddies-full of tea,' said Xi-feng, 'but you were out.'

'Yes,' said Dai-yu. 'I'm sorry: I forgot to thank you.'

'Have you tried it?' said Xi-feng. 'What did you think of it?'

'I wouldn't ask, if I were you,' said Bao-yu, chipping in. '*I* thought it was rotten. I don't know what the rest of you thought about it.'

'I thought the flavour was all right,' said Bao-chai. 'The colour wasn't up to much.'

'That was tribute tea from Siam,' said Xi-feng. '*I* didn't like it at all. I thought it wasn't as nice as the tea we drink every day.'

'Oh, I quite liked it,' said Dai-yu. 'Your palates must be more sensitive than mine.'

'If you really like it,' said Bao-yu, 'you're welcome to have mine.'

'I've still got quite a bit left,' said Xi-feng. 'If you *really* like it, you can have it all.'

'Thank you very much,' said Dai-yu. 'I'll send someone round to fetch it.'

'No, don't do that,' said Xi-feng. '*I*'ll send it round to *you*. There's something I want you to do for me. The person I send round about it can bring the tea as well.'

Dai-yu laughed mockingly:

'Do you hear that, everybody? Because she's given me a bit of her old tea, I have to start doing odd jobs for her.'

'That's fair enough,' said Xi-feng. 'You know the rule: "drink the family's tea, the family's bride-to-be".'

Everyone laughed at this except Dai-yu, who turned her head away, blushing furiously, and said nothing.

'Cousin Feng will have her little joke,' Li Wan observed to Bao-chai with a smile.

'Do you call that a *joke*?' said Dai-yu. 'It was a silly, idle remark, and very irritating.'

She gave a snort of disgust by way of reinforcement.

Xi-feng laughed:

'What's so irritating about it? Look at him!' – She pointed at Bao-yu – 'Isn't he good enough for you? Good looks, good family, good income. There are no snags that *I* can see. It's a perfect match!'

Dai-yu rose and fled.

'Oh, Frowner's in a rage! Come back Frowner!' Bao-chai called out after her. 'If you go, it will spoil all the fun.'

She got up and went after Dai-yu to bring her back. At the doorway they ran into Jia Zheng's two concubines, Aunt Zhao and Aunt Zhou, come to see Bao-yu. Li Wan, Bao-chai and Bao-yu made them welcome and invited them to sit down and talk, but Xi-feng and Dai-yu conversed with each other and rather pointedly ignored them.

Bao-chai was in the middle of saying something to the rest of the group when a maid arrived from Lady Wang's to say that Wang Zi-teng's wife had come and the presence of the young ladies was requested. Li Wan and Xi-feng rose to go. Aunt Zhao and Aunt Zhou hurriedly took their leave.

'I can't go out,' said Bao-yu. 'For heaven's sake don't let Aunt Wang come over here! – Cousin Lin!' he called to Dai-yu. 'Stay here a bit! There's something I want to say to you.'

Hearing him, Xi-feng turned back to address Dai-yu:

'Do you hear that? Someone wants a word with you. You'd better go back and see what he wants to say!'

She gave her a push in the direction of the house; then she and Li Wan went off, both laughing.

When they were alone together, Bao-yu took Dai-yu by the hand. He smiled and smiled, but said nothing. Dai-yu felt herself blushing, and tried to break away.

'Aiyo!' he said. 'My head!'

'Good!' said Dai-yu. 'It serves you right!'

Then Bao-yu let out a dreadful cry, jumped two or three feet into the air, and began to shout and babble deliriously. Dai-yu and the maids were terrified and ran to tell Lady Wang and Grandmother Jia. Wang Zi-teng's lady was with them and hurried over with the rest to see him. By the time they arrived he had already tried several times to kill himself and was raving like a madman. His mother and grandmother were so stricken by the sight that for a few moments they stood mute and trembling. Then, breaking into loud weeping, they cried out to him piteously between their sobs: 'my son!', 'my child!', 'my darling!'

Soon the news had spread to the other parts of the Rong household and to the household next door and Jia She, Lady Xing, Cousin Zhen, Jia Zheng, Jia Lian, Jia Rong, Jia Yun, Jia Ping, Aunt Xue and Xue Pan – not to mention Zhou Rui's wife and a great bevy of domestics both high and low – came hurrying into the garden, adding numbers and confusion to the group of helpless spectators.

While they were still wondering what to do with Bao-yu, Xi-feng appeared, brandishing a gleaming knife in one hand and attacking whatever came in her path. She had already massacred several luckless dogs and hens and now, seeing people ahead, glared at them madly and would have rushed upon them too had not Zhou Rui's wife and a few hefty and resourceful womenservants advanced upon her while the others looked on helplessly, clasped her about the arms and body, wrested the knife from her hand, and carried her off to her room. Patience and Felicity wept piteously to see their mistress in such a state.

On this occasion even Jia Zheng's customary impassivity seemed to have deserted him, as he turned this way and that, uncertain on whom to direct his attention. And if Jia Zheng was distraught, the state of the others can be imagined. Most remarkable, perhaps, was the spectacle of Xue Pan fussing over his womenfolk, one moment afraid that his mother would be jostled in the crush, the next that Bao-chai might be ogled or Caltrop glad-eyed by some wanton male. Cousin Zhen, he knew for a fact, was a notorious womanizer. Then he caught sight of Dai-yu (whom he had never seen before) and forgot his anxiety in gawping admiration of that ethereal beauty.

Although no one knew what to do themselves, there were a great many opinions about what *ought to be done*. Some said an exorcist should be called in to *expel* the malignant spirits, some that it required a dancing medium to *draw* them out, some offered charm-sheets invoking the demon-quelling powers of the Heavenly Master and issued under the hand of the Taoist pontiff; yet in spite of prayers, incantations, divination, and all the expedients that faith and physic could provide, there was no visible improvement in the condition of the patients. At sundown Wang Zi-teng's lady took her leave and went home.

Next day she made another visit to inquire after them. This was followed by visits from the wife of Grandmother Jia's nephew the Marquis, from Lady Xing's brothers' wives, and from the wives of other marriage connections of the family. Bottled charm-water, wonder-working monks and Taoists and highly recommended physicians were also sent round to the mansion by various friends and relations.

But the cousins continued delirious and lay on their beds burning with fever and babbling incomprehensibly. At nightfall they became even worse, so that the maids and even the older women no longer dared go near them. The two of them had to be carried into Lady Wang's room on their beds and set down there side by side so that Jia Yun and a group of pages could watch over them in shifts throughout the night. Grandmother Jia, Lady Wang, Lady Xing and Aunt Xue stayed near at hand, refusing to budge, though unable to do anything but sit by and weep. Jia She and Jia Zheng, afraid that their mother's health would suffer, displayed their concern by keeping themselves and everyone else up throughout most of the night. There were lights burning everywhere and hardly anyone slept at all.

Jia She continued to hunt everywhere for monks and exorcists reputed able to cure diseases of the mind. Finally Jia Zheng, who saw that their methods were all useless, lost patience with him and tried to make him stop:

'Young people will die if they must. Nothing can alter fate. And that they are fated to die would appear from the fact that all efforts to cure them have been unavailing. I think we should allow them to die in peace.'

But Jia She took no notice, and the commotion continued as before.

By the third day the patients were so weakened that they lay on their beds motionless and their breathing was scarcely perceptible. The whole family had by now abandoned hope and were already making preparations for their laying-out. Grandmother Jia, Lady Wang, Jia Lian, Patience and Aroma had cried themselves into a state bordering on prostration. Only Aunt Zhao was cheerful – though she did her best to look miserable.

Early on the fourth day Bao-yu suddenly opened his eyes wide and spoke to Grandmother Jia:

'From now on I can no longer stay in this family. You must get my things ready and let me go.'

To the old lady the words were a tearing of heart from body; but Aunt Zhao, who also heard them, had the temerity to urge their acceptance:

'Your Ladyship shouldn't take it so hard. It's already all up with the boy. We should be getting his graveclothes ready so that he can go in peace. It will be better that way. If we won't let him go now, when he's ready, it will only make more suffering for him in the world to come . . .'

She would have gone on, but Grandmother Jia spat in her face. No empty gesture: it was a full gob of spittle.

'Evil woman! May your tongue rot! How do you *know* it's all up with him? You *want* him to die, don't you? But if you think you will gain by his death, you must be dreaming; because if he does die, I shall hold you responsible. It's your spiteful meddling that has forced him to do all this studying. You have reduced the poor child to such a state that the mere sight of his father makes him more scared than a mouse with the cat after it. *You* have done this, you and the others of your kind. And now I suppose, if you succeed in murdering him, you will be satisfied. But don't imagine you will escape me – *any* of you!'

She railed and wept. Jia Zheng was close at hand while she was saying all this and was deeply distressed by it. Peremptorily dismissing the concubine, he tried to calm his mother and reasoned against the injustice of her charges.

It was unfortunate that just at that moment a servant should have come in to announce that 'the two coffins that had been

ordered were now ready'. The words were as oil upon fire.
The old lady blazed.

'Who gave orders for those coffins to be made? Where is
the man who made them? Go and get the man who made
those coffins! Flog him to death!'

Suddenly, as she raged and stormed, the faint *tock tock* of
a holy man's wooden fish was heard upon the air and a high
monotone chant that kept time with the beat:

> 'Na-mah A-mi-ta-bha Bo-dhi-satt-va!
> Mer-ci-ful de-li-ve-rer!
> All a-fflic-ted and tor-men-ted,
> All a-ttacked by e-vil spi-rits,
> All de-mo-ni-ac po-sse-ssion,
> I cure,
> I cure,
> I cure.'

Grandmother Jia and Lady Wang at once sent someone
into the street to see who it was. The source of the chanting
proved to be a disreputable-looking Buddhist monk. *Stone*
describes him in the following quatrain:

> A bottle nose he had and shaggy brows,
> Through which peeped eyes that twinkled like bright stars.
> His robe was patched and torn, his feet straw-shod,
> His unclean pate blotched with unsightly scars.

He was accompanied by a lame Taoist, for whom a similar
quatrain has been supplied by our poetical *Stone*:

> Up, down he hopped on his unequal legs,
> From mud and puddle not a stitch left dry.
> Yet, if you asked him where his dwelling was,
> 'Westward of Paradise' he would reply.

Jia Zheng had them invited in and asked them what monastery they were from. The monk was genially dismissive:

'There is no need for Your Worship to waste time on
formalities. Suffice it to say that I heard you had sickness in
this house and have come to cure it.'

'Two members of this family have, indeed, fallen victims
to some kind of witchcraft,' said Jia Zheng. 'Might one
inquire what charm you intend to cure them with?'

'Charm?' The monk laughed. 'You already possess in your own house a precious object capable of curing them. What other charm is necessary?'

Jia Zheng gave a start.

'To be sure. My son was born with a piece of jade whose inscription makes some such claim – "Dispels the harms of witchcraft". But as you see, it does not appear to possess the power it lays claim to.'

'That is because the world and its temptations have confused it,' said the monk. 'It certainly *used* to have the power. If you will have the goodness to fetch it for me and allow me to hold it in my hand and say a wee prayer over it, I think I can undertake to bring the power back again.'

Jia Zheng took the Magic Jade from Bao-yu's neck and handed it to the monk, who held it on the palm of his hand and addressed it with a sigh:

'Thirteen years, old friend, since we first met under Green-sickness Peak! Time certainly flies. But you have not finished with this world yet, you know. Dear, dear, dear! You aren't the Stone you were, are you?

– Time was you lived in perfect liberty,
Your heart alike from joy and sorrow free,
Till, by the smelter's alchemy transformed,
Into the world you came to purchase misery.

By the bye, I am sorry you have been having such a disagreeable experience these last few days.

– Vain sensual joys the jade's sheen have besmirched;
The poor bird droops, in its close prison perched.
From drunken dreaming one day you'll recover:
Then, when all debts are paid, the play will soon be over.'

When the monk had finished apostrophizing the stone, he rubbed it and polished it between his hands and muttered some strange-sounding words over it.

'There! Its power has now been restored.' He handed it back to Jia Zheng. 'But you must be careful that it does not become contaminated again. Hang it above the threshold of the bedroom and let no women apart from the patient's own mother and grandmother go inside. If you will do that, I can guarantee a complete recovery in thirty-three days.'

Jia Zheng would have liked to detain the monk for tea and offer him some remuneration, but he and the Taoist slipped quietly away and could not be traced.

The monk's directions were scrupulously followed. Lady Wang guarded the doorway in person and prevented any unauthorized person from getting into the bedroom. By evening the sufferers had regained consciousness and said they were hungry. This news, so precious to the ears of Lady Jia and Lady Wang, who at once had rice gruel brought in to feed them with, was relayed to the girls in the outer room.

'Bless His Holy Name!' Dai-yu murmured fervently.

Bao-chai laughed, but said nothing. The others were mystified.

'Why do you laugh, Cousin Bao?' Xi-chun asked her.

'I was thinking how busy He of the Holy Name must be,' Bao-chai said. 'Apart from working for the salvation of all sentient beings, He has to protect the sick and hasten their recovery – not to mention watching over plighted couples to make sure that they marry and live happily ever after. What a lot He has to keep Him busy! Don't you find the thought rather amusing?'

Dai-yu affected scorn, but was blushing hotly.

'You are all horrid. Instead of following good examples, you all imitate Feng and make nasty, cheap jokes all the time.'

She raised the portière and went out.

But if you wish to know more, you will have to wait for the next chapter.

CHAPTER 26

*A conversation on Wasp Waist Bridge is a cover for
communication of a different kind
And a soliloquy overhead in the Naiad's House reveals
unsuspected depths of feeling.*

By the time the thirty-three days' convalescence had ended,
not only were Bao-yu's health and strength completely
restored, but even the burn-marks on his face had vanished,
and he was allowed to move back into the Garden.

It may be recalled that when Bao-yu's sickness was at its
height, it had been found necessary to call in Jia Yun with a
number of pages under his command to take turns in watching over him. Crimson was there too at that time, having
been brought in with the other maids from his apartment.
During those few days she and Jia Yun therefore had ample
opportunity of seeing each other, and a certain familiarity
began to grow up between them.

Crimson noticed that Jia Yun was often to be seen sporting
a handkerchief very much like the one she had lost. She nearly
asked him about it, but in the end was too shy. Then, after
the monk's visit, the presence of the menfolk was no longer
required and Jia Yun went back to his tree-planting. Though
Crimson could still not dismiss the matter entirely from her
mind, she did not ask anyone about it for fear of arousing
their suspicions.

A day or two after their return to Green Delights, Crimson
was sitting in her room, still brooding over this handkerchief
business, when a voice outside the window inquired whether
she was in. Peeping through an eyelet in the casement she
recognized Melilot, a little maid who belonged to the same
apartment as herself.

'Yes, I'm in,' she said. 'Come inside!'

Little Melilot came bounding in and sat down on the bed
with a giggle.

'I'm in luck!' she said. 'I was washing some things in the

yard when Bao-yu asked for some tea to be taken round to Miss Lin's for him and Miss Aroma gave *me* the job of taking it. When I got there, Miss Lin had just been given some money by Her Old Ladyship and was sharing it out among her maids; so when she saw me she just said "Here you are!" and gave me two big handfuls of it. I've no idea how much it is. Will you look after it for me, please?'

She undid her handkerchief and poured out a shower of coins. Crimson carefully counted them for her and put them away in a safe place.

'What's been the matter with you lately?' said Melilot. 'If you ask me, I think you ought to go home for a day or two and call in a doctor. I expect you need some medicine.'

'Silly!' said Crimson. 'I'm perfectly all right. What should I want to go home for?'

'I know what, then,' said Melilot. 'Miss Lin's very weakly. She's always taking medicine. Why don't you ask her to give you some of hers? It would probably do just as well.'

'Oh, nonsense!' said Crimson. 'You can't take other people's medicines just like that!'

'Well, you can't go on in this way,' said Melilot, 'never eating or drinking properly. What will become of you?'

'Who *cares*?' said Crimson. 'The sooner I'm dead the better!'

'You shouldn't say such things,' said Melilot. 'It isn't right.'

'Why not?' said Crimson. 'How do you know what is on my mind?

Melilot shook her head sympathetically.

'I can't say I really blame you,' she said. 'Things *are* very difficult here at times. Take yesterday, for example. Her Old Ladyship said that as Bao-yu was better now and there was to be a thanksgiving for his recovery, all those who had the trouble of nursing him during his illness were to be rewarded according to their grades. Well now, I can understand the very young ones like me not being included, but why should they leave *you* out? I felt really sorry for you when I heard that they'd left you out. Aroma, of course, you'd expect to get more than anyone else. I don't blame *her* at all. In fact, I think it's owing to her. Let's be honest: none of us can compare with Aroma. I mean, even if she didn't always take so much trouble over everything, no one would want to quarrel about *her* having a bigger share. What makes me so angry is that people like Sky-bright and Mackerel should count as top grade when every-one knows they're only put there to curry favour with Bao-yu. Doesn't it make you angry?'

'I don't see much point in getting angry,' said Crimson. 'You know what they said about the mile-wide marquee: "Even the longest party must have an end"? Well, none of us is here for ever, you know. Another four or five years from now when we've each gone our different ways it won't *matter* any longer what all the rest of us are doing.'

Little Melilot found this talk of parting and impermanence vaguely affecting and a slight moisture was to be observed about her eyes. She thought shame to cry without good cause, however, and masked her emotion with a smile:

'That's perfectly true. Only yesterday Bao-yu was going on about all the things he's going to do to his rooms and the clothes he's going to have made and everything, just as if he had a hundred or two years ahead of him with nothing to do but kill time in.'

Crimson laughed scornfully, though whether at Melilot's simplicity or at Bao-yu's improvidence is unclear, since just as she was about to comment, a little maid came running in, so young that her hair was still done up in two little girl's horns. She was carrying some patterns and sheets of paper.

'You're to copy out these two patterns.'

She threw them in Crimson's direction and straightway darted out again. Crimson shouted after her:

'Who are they for, then? You might at least finish your message before rushing off. What are you in such a tearing hurry about? Is someone steaming wheatcakes for you and you're afraid they'll get cold?'

'They're for Mackerel.' The little maid paused long enough to bawl an answer through the window, then picking up her heels, went pounding off, *plim-plam*, *plim-plam*, *plim-plam*, as fast as she had come.

Crimson threw the patterns crossly to one side and went

to hunt in her drawer for a brush to trace them with. After rummaging for several minutes she had only succeeded in finding a few worn-out ones, too moulted for use.

'Funny!' she said. 'I could have sworn I put a new one in there the other day . . .'

She thought a bit, then laughed at herself as she remembered:

'Of course. Oriole took it, the evening before last.' She turned to Melilot. 'Would you go and get it for me, then?'

'I'm afraid I can't,' said Melilot. 'Miss Aroma's waiting for me to fetch some boxes for her. You'll have to get it yourself.'

'If Aroma's waiting for you, why have you been sitting here gossiping all this time?' said Crimson. 'If I hadn't asked you to go and get it, she wouldn't have been waiting, would she? Lazy little beast!'

She left the room and walked out of the gate of Green Delights and in the direction of Bao-chai's courtyard. She was just passing by Drenched Blossoms Pavilion when she caught sight of Bao-yu's old wet-nurse, Nannie Li, coming from the opposite direction and stood respectfully aside to wait for her.

'Where have you been, Mrs Li?' she asked her. 'I didn't expect to see you here.'

Nannie Li made a flapping gesture with her hand:

'What do you think, my dear: His Nibs has taken a fancy to the young fellow who does the tree-planting – "Yin" or "Yun" or whatever his name is – so Nannie has to go and ask him in. Let's hope Their Ladyships don't find out about it. There'll be trouble if they do.'

'Are you really going to ask him in?'

'Yes. Why?'

Crimson laughed:

'If your Mr Yun knows what's good for him, he won't agree to come.'

'He's no fool,' said Nannie Li. 'Why shouldn't he?'

'Any way, if he *does* come in,' said Crimson, ignoring her question, 'you can't just bring him in and then leave him, Mrs Li. You'll have to take him back again yourself afterwards. You don't want him wandering off on his own. There's no knowing *who* he might bump into.'

(Crimson herself, was the secret hope.)

'Gracious me! I haven't got *that* much spare time,' said Nannie Li. 'All I've done is just to tell him that he's got to come. I'll send someone else to fetch him in when I get back presently – one of the girls, or one of the older women, maybe.'

She hobbled off on her stick, leaving Crimson standing there in a muse, her mission to fetch the tracing-brush momentarily forgotten. She was still standing there a minute or two later when a little maid came along, who, seeing that it was Crimson, asked her what she was doing there. Crimson looked up. It was Trinket, another of the maids from Green Delights.

'Where are you going?' Crimson asked her.

'I've been sent to fetch Mr Yun,' said Trinket. 'I have to bring him inside to meet Master Bao.'

She ran off on her way.

At the gate to Wasp Waist Bridge Crimson ran into Trinket again, this time with Jia Yun in tow. His eyes sought Crimson's; and hers, as she made pretence of conversing with Trinket, sought his. Their two pairs of eyes met and briefly skirmished; then Crimson felt herself blushing, and turning away abruptly, she made off for Allspice Court.

*

Our narrative now follows Jia Yun and Trinket along the winding pathway to the House of Green Delights. Soon they were at the courtyard gate and Jia Yun waited outside while she went in to announce his arrival. She returned presently to lead him inside.

There were a few scattered rocks in the courtyard and some clumps of jade-green plantain. Two storks stood in the shadow of a pine-tree, preening themselves with their long bills. The gallery surrounding the courtyard was hung with cages of unusual design in which perched or fluttered a wide variety of birds, some of them gay-plumaged exotic ones. Above the steps was a little five-frame penthouse building with a glimpse of delicately-carved partitions visible through the open doorway, above which a horizontal board hung, inscribed with the words

CRIMSON JOYS AND GREEN DELIGHTS

'So that's why it's called "The House of Green Delights"' Jia Yun told himself. 'The name is taken from the inscription.'

A laughing voice addressed him from behind one of the silk gauze casements:

'Come on in! It must be two or three months since I first forgot our appointment!'

Jia Yun recognized the voice as Bao-yu's and hurried up the steps inside. He looked about him, dazzled by the brilliance of gold and semi-precious inlay-work and the richness of the ornaments and furnishings, but unable to see Bao-yu in the midst of it all. To the left of him was a full-length mirror from behind which two girls now emerged, both about fifteen or sixteen years old and of much the same build and height. They addressed him by name and asked him to come inside. Slightly overawed, he muttered something in reply and hurried after them, not daring to take more than a furtive glance at them from the corner of his eye. They ushered him into a tent-like summer 'cabinet' of green net, whose principal furniture was a tiny lacquered bed with crimson hangings heavily patterned in gold. On this Bao-yu, wearing everyday clothes and a pair of bedroom slippers, was reclining, book in hand. He threw the book down as Jia Yun entered and rose to his feet with a welcoming smile. Jia Yun swiftly dropped knee and hand to floor in greeting. Bidden to sit, he modestly placed himself on a bedside chair.

'After I invited you round to my study that day,' said Bao-yu, 'a whole lot of things seemed to happen one after the other, and I'm afraid I quite forgot about your visit.'

Jia Yun returned his smile:

'Let's just say that it wasn't my luck to see you then. But you have been ill since then, Uncle Bao. Are you quite better now?'

'Quite better, thank you. I hear you've been very busy these last few days.'

'That's as it should be,' said Jia Yun. 'But I'm glad you are better, Uncle. That's a piece of good fortune for *all* of us.'

As they chatted, a maid came in with some tea. Jia Yun was talking to Bao-yu as she approached, but his eyes were on her. She was tall and rather thin with a long oval face, and she was wearing a rose-pink dress over a closely pleated white satin skirt and a black satin sleeveless jacket over the dress.

In the course of his brief sojourn among them in the early days of Bao-yu's illness, Jia Yun had got by heart the names of most of the principal females of Bao-yu's establishment. He knew at a glance that the maid now serving him tea was Aroma. He was also aware that she was in some way more important than the other maids and that to be waited on by her in the seated presence of her master was an honour. Jumping hastily to his feet he addressed her with a modest smile:

'You shouldn't pour tea for *me*, Miss! I'm not like a visitor here. You should let me pour for myself!'

'Oh *do* sit down!' said Bao-yu. 'You don't have to be like that in front of the *maids*!'

'I know,' said Jia Yun. 'But a body-servant! I don't like to presume.'

He sat down, nevertheless, and sipped his tea while Bao-yu made conversation on a number of unimportant topics. He told him which household kept the best troupe of players, which had the finest gardens, whose maids were the prettiest, who gave the best parties, and who had the best collection of curiosities or the strangest pets. Jia Yun did his best to keep up with him. After a while Bao-yu showed signs of flagging, and when Jia Yun, observing what appeared to be fatigue, rose to take his leave, he did not very strongly press him to stay.

'You must come again when you can spare the time,' said Bao-yu, and ordered Trinket to see him out of the Garden.

Once outside the gateway of Green Delights, Jia Yun looked around him on all sides, and having ascertained that there was no one else about, slowed down to a more dawdling pace so that he could ask Trinket a few questions. Indeed, the little maid was subjected to quite a catechism: How old was she? What was her name? What did her father and mother do? How many years had she been working for his Uncle Bao? How much pay did she get a month? How many girls were there working for him altogether? Trinket seemed to have no objection, however, and answered each question as it came.

'That girl you were talking to on the way in,' he said, 'isn't her name "Crimson"?'

Trinket laughed:

'Yes. Why do you ask?'

'I heard her asking you about a handkerchief. Only it just so happens that I picked one up.'

Trinket showed interest.

'She's asked me about that handkerchief of hers a number of times. I told her, I've got better things to do with my time than go looking for people's handkerchiefs. But when she asked me about it again today, she said that if I could find it for her, she'd give me a reward. Come to think of it, you were there when she said that, weren't you? It was when we were outside the gate of Allspice Court. So you can bear me out. Oh Mr Jia, please let me have it if you've picked it up and I'll be able to see what she will give me for it!'

Jia Yun had picked up a silk handkerchief a month previously at the time when his tree-planting activities had just started. He knew that it must have been dropped by one or another of the female inmates of the Garden, but not knowing which, had not so far ventured to do anything about his discovery. When earlier on he had heard Crimson question Trinket about her loss, he had realized, with a thrill of pleasure, that the handkerchief he had picked up must have been hers. Trinket's request now gave him just the opening he required. He drew a handkerchief of his own from inside his sleeve and held it up in front of her with a smile:

'I'll give it to you on one condition. If she lets you have this reward you were speaking of, you've *got* to let me know. No cheating, mind!'

Trinket received the handkerchief with eager assurances that he would be informed of the outcome, and having seen him out of the Garden, went back again to look for Crimson.

*

Our narrative returns now to Bao-yu.

After disposing of Jia Yun, Bao-yu continued to feel extremely lethargic and lay back on the bed with every appearance of being about to doze off to sleep. Aroma hurried over to him and, sitting on the edge of the bed, roused him with a shake:

'Come on! Surely you are not going to sleep *again*? You need some fresh air. Why don't you go outside and walk around for a bit?'

Bao-yu took her by the hand and smiled at her.

'I'd like to go,' he said, 'but I don't want to leave you.'

'Silly!' said Aroma with a laugh. 'Don't say what you don't mean!'

She hoicked him to his feet.

'Well, where am I going to go then?' said Bao-yu. 'I just feel so *bored*.'

'Never mind where, just go out!' said Aroma. 'If you stay moping indoors like this, you'll get even more bored.'

Bao-yu followed her advice, albeit half-heartedly, and went out into the courtyard. After visiting the cages in the gallery and playing for a bit with the birds, he ambled out of the courtyard into the Garden and along the bank of Drenched Blossoms Stream, pausing for a while to look at the goldfish in the water. As he did so, a pair of fawns came running like the wind from the hillside opposite. Bao-yu was puzzled. There seemed to be no reason for their mysterious terror. But just then little Jia Lan came running down the same slope after them, a tiny bow clutched in his hand. Seeing his uncle ahead of him, he stood politely to attention and greeted him cheerfully:

'Hello, Uncle. I didn't know you were at home. I thought you'd gone out.'

'Mischievous little blighter, aren't you?' said Bao-yu. 'What do you want to go shooting them for, poor little things?'

'I've got no reading to do today,' said Jia Lan, 'and I don't like to hang about doing nothing, so I thought I'd practise my archery and equitation.'

'Goodness! You'd better not waste time jawing, then,' said Bao-yu, and left the young toxophilite to his pursuits.

Moving on, without much thinking where he was going, he came presently to the gate of a courtyard.

> Denser than feathers on the phoenix' tail
> The stirred leaves murmured with a pent dragon's moan.

The multitudinous bamboos and the board above the gate confirmed that his feet had, without conscious direction, carried him to the Naiad's House. Of their own accord they now carried him through the gateway and into the courtyard.

The House seemed silent and deserted, its bamboo door-blind hanging unrolled to the ground; but as he approached the window, he detected a faint sweetness in the air, traceable to a thin curl of incense smoke which drifted out through the green gauze of the casement. He pressed his face to the gauze; but before his eyes could distinguish anything, his ear became aware of a long, languorous sigh and the sound of a voice speaking:

> 'Each day in a drowsy waking dream of love.'

Bao-yu felt a sudden yearning for the speaker. He could see her now. It was Dai-yu, of course, lying on her bed, stretching herself and yawning luxuriously.

He laughed:

'Why "each day in a drowsy waking dream of love"?' he asked through the window (the words were from his beloved *Western Chamber*); then going to the doorway he lifted up the door-blind and walked into the room.

Dai-yu realized that she had been caught off her guard. She covered her burning face with her sleeve, and turning over towards the wall, pretended to be asleep. Bao-yu went over intending to turn her back again, but just at that moment Dai-yu's old wet-nurse came hurrying in with two other old women at her heels:

'Miss Lin's asleep, sir. Would you mind coming back again after she's woken up?'

Dai-yu at once turned over and sat up with a laugh:

'Who's asleep?'

The three old women laughed apologetically.

'Sorry, miss. We thought you were asleep. Nightingale! Come inside now! Your mistress is awake.'

Having shouted for Nightingale, the three guardians of morality retired.

'What do you mean by coming into people's rooms when they're asleep?' said Dai-yu, smiling up at Bao-yu as she sat on the bed's edge patting her hair into shape.

At the sight of those soft cheeks so adorably flushed and the starry eyes a little misted with sleep a wave of emotion passed over him. He sank into a chair and smiled back at her:

'What was that you were saying just now before I came in?'

'I didn't say anything,' said Dai-yu.

Bao-yu laughed and snapped his fingers at her:

'Put that on your tongue, girl! I heard you say it.'

While they were talking to one another, Nightingale came in.

'Nightingale,' said Bao-yu, 'what about a cup of that excellent tea of yours?'

'Excellent tea?' said Nightingale. 'There's nothing very special about the tea we drink here. If nothing but the best will do, you'd better wait for Aroma to come.'

'Never mind about *him*!' said Dai-yu. 'First go and get me some water!'

'He *is* our guest,' said Nightingale. 'I can't fetch you any water until I've given him his tea.' And she went to pour him a cup.

'Good girl!' said Bao-yu.

'If with your amorous mistress I should wed,
'Tis you, sweet maid, must make our bridal bed.'

The words, like Dai-yu's languorous line, were from *Western Chamber*, but in somewhat dubious taste. Dai-yu was dreadfully offended by them. In an instant the smile had vanished from her face.

'*What* was that you said?'

He laughed:

'I didn't say anything.'

Dai-yu began to cry.

'This is your latest amusement, I suppose. Every time you

hear some coarse expression outside or read some crude, disgusting book, you have to come back here and give me the benefit of it. I am to become a source of entertainment for the *menfolk* now, it seems.'

She rose, weeping, from the bed and went outside. Bao-yu followed her in alarm.

'Dearest coz, it was very wrong of me to say that, but it just slipped out without thinking. Please don't go and tell! I promise never to say anything like that again. May my mouth rot and my tongue decay if I do!'

Just at that moment Aroma came hurrying up:

'Quick!' she said. 'You must come back and change. The Master wants to see you.'

The descent of this thunderbolt drove all else from his mind and he rushed off in a panic. As soon as he had changed, he hurried out of the Garden. Tealeaf was waiting for him outside the inner gate.

'I suppose you don't know what he wants to see me about?' Bao-yu asked him.

'I should hurry up, if I were you,' said Tealeaf. 'All I know is that he wants to see you. You'll find out why soon enough when you get there.'

He hustled him along as he spoke.

They had passed round the main hall, Bao-yu still in a state of fluttering apprehensiveness, when there was a loud guffaw from a corner of the wall. It was Xue Pan, clapping his hands and stamping his feet in mirth.

'Ho! Ho! Ho! You'd never have come this quickly if you hadn't been told that Uncle wanted you!'

Tealeaf, also laughing, fell on his knees. Bao-yu stood there looking puzzled. It was some moments before it dawned on him that he had been hoaxed. Xue Pan was by this time being apologetic – bowing repeatedly and pumping his hands to show how sorry he was:

'Don't blame the lad!' he said. 'It wasn't his fault. I talked him into it.'

Bao-yu saw that he could do nothing, and might as well accept with a good grace.

'I don't mind being made a fool of,' he said, 'but I think it was going a bit far to bring my father into it. I think perhaps I'd better tell Aunt Xue and see what *she* thinks about it all.'

'Now look here, old chap,' said Xue Pan, getting agitated, 'it was only because I wanted to fetch you out a bit quicker. I admit it was very wrong of me to make free with your Parent, but after all, you've only got to mention *my* father next time you want to fool *me* and we'll be quits!'

'Aiyo!' said Bao-yu. 'Worse and worse!' He turned to Tealeaf: 'Treacherous little beast! What are you still kneeling for?'

Tealeaf kotowed and rose to his feet.

'Look,' said Xue Pan. 'I wouldn't have troubled you otherwise, only it's my birthday on the third of next month and old Hu and old Cheng and a couple of the others, I don't know where they got them from but they've given me:

a piece of fresh lotus root, ever so crisp and crunchy, as thick as that, look, and as long as that;

a huge great melon, look, as big as that;

a freshly-caught sturgeon as big as that;

and a cypress-smoked Siamese sucking-pig as big as that that came in the tribute from Siam.

Don't you think it was clever of them to get me those things? Maybe not so much the sturgeon and the sucking-pig. They're just expensive. But where would you go to get a piece of lotus root or a melon like that? However did they get them to *grow* so big? I've given some of the stuff to Mother, and while I was about it I sent some round to your grandmother and Auntie Wang, but I've still got a lot left over. I can't eat it all myself: it would be unlucky. But apart from me, the only person I can think of who is *worthy* to eat a present like this is you. That's why I came over specially to invite you. And we're lucky, because we've got a little chap who sings coming round as well. So you and I will be able to sit down and make a day of it, eh? Really enjoy ourselves.'

Xue Pan, still talking, conducted Bao-yu to his 'study', where Zhan Guang, Cheng Ri-xing, Hu Si-lai and Dan Ping-ren (the four donors of the feast) and the young singer he had mentioned were already waiting. They rose to welcome Bao-yu as he entered. When the bowings and courtesies were over and tea had been taken, Xue Pan called for his servants to lay. A tremendous bustle ensued, which seemed to go on for quite a long time before everything was finally ready and the diners were able to take their places at the table.

Bao-yu noticed sliced melon and lotus root among the dishes, both of unusual quality and size.

'It seems wrong to be sharing your presents with you before I have given you anything myself,' he said jokingly.

'Yes,' said Xue Pan. 'What are you planning to give me for my birthday next month? Something new and out of the ordinary, I hope.'

'I haven't really *got* anything much to give you,' said Bao-yu. 'Things like money and food and clothing I don't want for, but they're not really mine to give. The only way I could give you something that would *really* be mine would be by doing some calligraphy or painting a picture for you.'

'Talking of pictures,' said Xue Pan genially, 'that's reminded me. I saw a set of dirty pictures in someone's house the other day. They were real beauties. There was a lot of writing on top that I didn't pay much attention to, but I did notice the signature. I think it was "Geng Huang", the man who painted them. They were really good!'

Bao-yu was puzzled. His knowledge of the masters of painting and calligraphy both past and present was not inconsiderable, but he had never in all his experience come across a 'Geng Huang'. After racking his brains for some moments he suddenly began to chuckle and called for a writing-brush. A writing-brush having been produced by one of the servants, he wrote two characters with it in the palm of his hand.

'Are you quite *sure* the signature you saw was "Geng Huang"?' he asked Xue Pan.

'What do you mean?' said Xue Pan. 'Of course I'm sure.'

Bao-yu opened his hand and held it up for Xue Pan to see: 'You sure it wasn't these two characters? They *are* quite similar.'

The others crowded round to look. They all laughed when they saw what he had written:

'Yes, it must have been "Tang Yin". Mr Xue couldn't have been seeing straight that day. Ha! Ha! Ha!'

Xue Pan realized that he had made a fool of himself, but passed it off with an embarrassed laugh:

'Oh, Tankin' or wankin',' he said, 'what difference does it make, anyway?'

Just then 'Mr Feng' was announced by one of the servants, which Bao-yu knew could only mean General Feng Tang's son, Feng Zi-ying. Xue Pan and the rest told the boy to bring him in immediately, but Feng Zi-ying was already striding in, talking and laughing as he went. The others hurriedly rose and invited him to take a seat.

'Ha!' said Feng Zi-ying. 'No need to go out then. Enjoyin' yourselves at home, eh? Very nice too!'

'It's a long time since we've seen you around,' said Bao-yu. 'How's the General?'

'Fahver's in good health, thank you very much,' said Feng Zi-ying, 'but Muvver hasn't been too well lately. Caught a chill or somethin'.'

Observing with glee that Feng Zi-ying was sporting a black eye, Xue Pan asked him how he had come by it:

'Been having a dust-up, then? Who was it this time? Looks as if he left his signature!'

Feng Zi-ying laughed:

'Don't use the mitts any more nowadays – not since that time I laid into Colonel Chou's son and did him an injury. That was a lesson to me. I've learned to keep my temper since then. No, this happened the other day durin' a huntin' expedition in the Iron Net Mountains. I got flicked by a goshawk's wing.'

'When was this?' Bao-yu asked him.

'We left on the twenty-eighth of last month,' said Feng Zi-ying. 'Didn't get back till a few days ago.'

'Ah, that explains why I didn't see you at Shen's party earlier this month,' said Bao-yu. 'I meant at the time to ask why you weren't there, but I forgot. Did you go alone on this expedition or was the General there with you?'

'Fahver most certainly *was* there,' said Feng Zi-ying. 'I was practically dragged along in tow. Do you think I'm mad enough to go rushin' off in pursuit of hideous hardships when I could be sittin' comfortably at home eatin' good food and drinkin' good wine and listenin' to the odd song or two? Still, some good came of it. It was a lucky accident.'

As he had now finished his tea, Xue Pan urged him to join them at table and tell them his story at leisure, but Feng Zi-ying rose to his feet again and declined.

'I ought by rights to stay and drink a few cups with you,' he said, 'but there's somethin' very important I've got to see Fahver about now, so I'm afraid I really must refuse.'

But Xue Pan, Bao-yu and the rest were by no means content to let him get away with this excuse and propelled him insistently towards the table.

'Now look here, this is too bad!' Feng Zi-ying good-humouredly protested. 'All the years we've been knockin' around togevver we've never before insisted that a fellow should have to stay if he don't want to. The fact is, I really *can't*. Oh well, if I *must* have a drink, fetch some decent-sized cups and I'll just put down a couple of quick ones!'

This was clearly the most he would concede and the others perforce acquiesced. Two sconce-cups were brought and ceremoniously filled, Bao-yu holding the cups and Xue Pan pouring from the wine-kettle. Feng Zi-ying drank them standing, one after the other, each in a single breath.

'Now come on,' said Bao-yu, 'let's hear about this "lucky accident" before you go!'

Feng Zi-ying laughed:

'Couldn't tell it properly just now,' he said. 'It's somethin' that needs a special party all to itself. I'll invite you all round to my place another day and you shall have the details then. There's a favour I want to ask too, by the bye, so we'll be able to talk about that then as well.'

He made a determined movement towards the door.

'Now you've got us all peeing ourselves with curiosity!' said Xue Pan. 'You might at least tell us when this party is going to be, to put us out of our suspense.'

'Not more than ten days' time and not less than eight,' said Feng Zi-ying; and going out into the courtyard, he jumped on his horse and clattered away.

Having seen him off, the others went in again, reseated themselves at table, and resumed their potations. When the party finally broke up, Bao-yu returned to the Garden in a state of cheerful inebriation. Aroma, who had had no idea what the summons from Jia Zheng might portend and was still wondering anxiously what had become of him, at once demanded to know the cause of his condition. He gave her a full account of what had happened.

'Well really!' said Aroma. 'Here were we practically beside ourselves with anxiety, and all the time you were there enjoying yourself! You might at least have sent word to let us know you were all right.'

'I was going to send word,' said Bao-yu. 'Of course I was. But then old Feng arrived and it put it out of my mind.'

At that moment Bao-chai walked in, all smiles.

'I hear you've made a start on the famous present,' she said.

'But surely you and your family must have had some already?' said Bao-yu.

Bao-chai shook her head:

'Pan was very pressing that I should have some, but I refused. I told him to save it for other people. I know I'm not really the right sort of person for such superior delicacies. If *I* were to eat any, I should be afraid of some frightful nemesis overtaking me.'

A maid poured tea for her as she spoke, and conversation of a desultory kind proceeded between sips.

*

Our narrative returns now to Dai-yu.

Having been present when Bao-yu received his summons, Dai-yu, too, was greatly worried about him – the more so as the day advanced and he had still not returned. Then in the evening, some time after dinner, she heard that he had just got back and resolved to go over and ask him exactly what had happened. She was sauntering along on the way there when she caught sight of Bao-chai some distance ahead of her, just entering Bao-yu's courtyard. Continuing to amble on, she came presently to Drenched Blossoms Bridge, from which a large number of different kinds of fish were to be seen swimming about in the water below. Dai-yu did not know what kinds of fish they were, but they were so beautiful that she had to stop and admire them, and by the time she reached the House of Green Delights, the courtyard gate had been shut for the night and she was obliged to knock for admittance.

Now it so happened that Skybright had just been having a quarrel with Emerald, and being thoroughly out of temper, was venting some of her ill-humour on the lately arrived Bao-chai, complaining *sotto voce* behind her back about 'people who were always inventing excuses to come dropping in and who kept other people staying up half the night when they would like to be in bed'. A knock at the gate coming in the midst of these resentful mutterings was enough to make her really angry.

'They've all gone to bed,' she shouted, not even bothering to inquire who the caller was. 'Come again tomorrow!'

Dai-yu was aware that Bao-yu's maids often played tricks on one another, and it occurred to her that the girl in the courtyard, not recognizing her voice, might have mistaken her for another maid and be keeping her locked out for a joke. She therefore called out again, this time somewhat louder than before:

'Come on! Open up, please! It's me.'

Unfortunately Skybright had still not recognized the voice.

'I don't care who you are,' she replied bad-temperedly. 'Master Bao's orders are that I'm not to let *anyone* in.'

Dumbfounded by her insolence, Dai-yu stood outside the gate in silence. She could not, however much she felt like it, give vent to her anger in noisy expostulation. 'Although they are always telling me to treat my Uncle's house as my own,' she reflected, 'I am still really an outsider. And now that Mother and Father are both dead and I am on my own, to make a fuss about a thing like this when I am living in someone else's house could only lead to further unpleasantness.'

A big tear coursed, unregarded, down her cheek.

She was still standing there irresolute, unable to decide whether to go or stay, when a sudden volley of talk and laughter reached her from inside. It resolved itself, as she listened attentively, into the voices of Bao-yu and Bao-chai.

An even bitterer sense of chagrin took possession of her. Suddenly, as she hunted in her mind for some possible reason for her exclusion, she remembered the events of the morning and concluded that Bao-yu must think she had told on him to his parents and was punishing her for her betrayal.

'But I would never betray you!' she expostulated with him in her mind. 'Why couldn't you have asked first, before letting your resentment carry you to such lengths? If you won't see me today, does that mean that from now on we are going to stop seeing each other altogether?'

The more she thought about it the more distressed she became.

> Chill was the green moss pearled with dew
> And chill was the wind in the avenue;

but Dai-yu, all unmindful of the unwholesome damp, had withdrawn into the shadow of a flowering fruit-tree by the corner of the wall, and grieving now in real earnest, began to cry as though her heart would break. And as if Nature herself were affected by the grief of so beautiful a creature, the crows who had been roosting in the trees round about flew up with a great commotion and removed themselves to another part of the Garden, unable to endure the sorrow of her weeping.

> Tears filled each flower and grief their hearts perturbed,
> And silly birds were from their nests disturbed.

The author of the preceding couplet has given us a quatrain in much the same vein:

> Few in this world fair Frowner's looks surpassed,
> None matched her store of sweetness unexpressed.
> The first sob scarcely from her lips had passed
> When blossoms fell and birds flew off distressed.

As Dai-yu continued weeping there alone, the courtyard door suddenly opened with a loud creak and someone came out.

But in order to find out who it was, you will have to wait for the next volume.

EXPLICIT PRIMA PARS LAPIDIS HISTORIAE

The 'Twelve Beauties of Jinling' and the 'Dream of Golden Days' Song-cycle

We know from Red Inkstone's Commentary that Xueqin's final chapter would have contained Disenchantment's *Roster of Lovers*, a table in which the sixty names of the novel's female characters would have been divided into five groups of twelve with the names inside each group arranged according to her own peculiar system of categorization. Thus the first place in each group would have been awarded for 'pure love', the second for 'conscientious love', and so on.

The pictures and verses in the three registers which Bao-yu looks at in chapter 5 contained cryptic indications of the fate in store for each of the thirty-six girls in the first three groups.

The first thing he looks at is the first page of the register for the third group. The picture, of a cloud-covered sky, and the verses 'Seldom the moon shines in a cloudless sky, etc.' refer to the sad fate of Bao-yu's maid Skybright – a simple play on the meaning of her name.

Next comes the second girl of the third group: Aroma. The bunch of flowers in the picture stands for her surname Hua, which means 'Flowers'. The mat, likewise, is a rebus for her Chinese name, Xi-ren. In the verses which follow, the 'sweetest flower' and the 'rich perfume' once more refer to her name, 'Flowers Aroma', and 'the player fortune favoured' is the female impersonator Jiang Yu-han whom she eventually married, in spite of her earlier insistence that she would remain unwed.

Bao-yu then turns to the Supplementary Register No. 1, which concerns the girls in the second group. This time he looks only at the first picture. It stands for Caltrop. The rebus, however, represents not 'Caltrop' but the name she was known by as a little girl before she was kidnapped: Ying-lian, which means 'lotus'. Caltrop was persecuted and, in the dénouement originally planned by Xueqin, finally done to death by Xue

Pan's detestable wife Xia Jin-gui, whose name means 'cassia'. The meaning of the picture is now self-evident. In the poem the mysterious 'two earths' and 'single tree' combine to make the Chinese character for *gui* 'cassia'. The meaning of the second couplet, therefore, is that when Xia Jin-gui appears on the scene, Caltrop's fate will be sealed.

The mysterious verses chanted by the monk in chapter 1 (p.56) at a time when Caltrop was known only by the name of Ying-lian, refer to her, rather perversely, as 'Caltrop':

> 'That caltrop-glass which shines on melting snow'.

The 'melting snow' refers to Xue Pan, whose surname, Xue, sounds the same as the Chinese word for 'snow'. She is called 'caltrop-*glass*' because in ancient times the caltrop motif was used in the ornamentation of mirror-backs.

Bao-yu next turns to the Main Register, which contains the fates of the twelve female characters in the first group. The order is the same as in the song-cycle 'A Dream of Golden Days' which is performed for Bao-yu's benefit on pp.139–44, viz.:

1. and 2. Lin Dai-yu and Xue Bao-chai
3. Yuan-chun
4. Tan-chun
5. Shi Xiang-yun
6. Adamantina
7. Ying-chun
8. Xi-chun
9. Wang Xi-feng
10. Qiao-jie
11. Li Wan
12. Qin-shi

First '1 and 2' needs explaining.

From various hints in the commentary we can deduce that Bao-chai and Dai-yu, unlike most of the book's female characters, are not modelled on real persons but represent two complementary aspects of a single ideal woman. In other words, Dai-yu is all the things that Bao-chai is not, and *vice-versa*. The ideal woman they add up to appears briefly in the person of little Two-in-one towards the end of Bao-yu's dream. This is probably the reason for the otherwise unaccountable fact that these two characters, the most important female characters in the book, have only a single picture and a single set of verses between them in the Register. In the song-cycle it is possible to say that the *First Song* is about Bao-chai and the *Second Song* about Dai-yu; but it would be equally possible to say that the first is about both and the second about Dai-yu only, or that the first and second are both mainly about Bao-yu; so even here there is a special treatment for which there must have been a special reason.

1. and 2. *Lin Dai-yu and Xue Bao-chai*

The picture is a simple rebus. Two trees make up the Chinese character for 'Lin', whilst 'jade belt' is an inversion of 'Dai-yu': the 'Dai' of Dai-yu's name really means 'eye-black', but it sounds the same as the word for 'belt', and *yu* means 'jade'. The pile of snow is a rebus for Bao-chai's surname Xue, which sounds the same as the Chinese word for 'snow'. 'Gold hairpin' is her name Bao-chai, which means 'precious hairpin'. The 'greenwood' in line three of the poem is Dai-yu's surname again (*lin* means 'forest').

In the *First Song* the 'marriage rites of gold and jade' refers to the marriage of Bao-chai (gold) and Bao-yu (jade). 'Stone' and 'flower' are, of course, the avatars of Bao-yu and Dai-yu. The 'crystalline snow' stands for Bao-chai's surname Xue, and the 'fairy wood forlorn' for Dai-yu's surname Lin.

The *Second Song* is self-explanatory.

3. *Yuan-chun*

I think the bow in the picture is intended to be a pun on the Chinese word for 'palace'. The word for 'citron' is *yuan*, a rebus for Yuan-chun. The 'three springs' are, of course, Ying-chun, Tan-chun and Xi-chun. 'Hare' and 'tiger' are two of the animal equivalents of the astrological signs by which Chinese years are named. Yuan-chun died at the end of a Tiger year and just before the beginning of a Rabbit one. If this were a real date it would have to mean 1735, but it is hardly likely to be.

The *Third Song* is puzzling in terms of what we are told about Yuan-chun elsewhere in the novel. The Imperial Concubine lives (and in the 40-chapter Supplement dies) not 'far from home' but in the Imperial Palace at Peking a few streets away. Xueqin evidently wrote the song-cycle at a stage in the novel's evolution when he was still sticking fairly closely to historical facts. For example, the whole of chapter 5 seems to assume that the place where Bao-yu's family lives is Jinling (i.e. Nanking). If we remember that the character of Yuan-chun is modelled on a daughter of Cao Yin who married the Manchu prince Nersu, it at once becomes clear why 'So far the road back home did seem'. The Caos lived in Nanking and Prince Nersu and his consort lived in Peking, a thousand miles away. There is nothing in Gao E's version about Yuan-chun appearing to her parents at the time of her death in a warning dream. Possibly Xueqin transferred the passage which contained this to fill out the rewritten account of Qin-shi's death. There is certainly something rather unconvincing about the words of the apparition that Xi-feng sees in chapter 13 coming from the mouth of a person like Qin-shi.

Xueqin) Shoo Chin

4. *Tan-chun*

Throughout the novel Tan-chun is repeatedly associated with the image of a kite. It is her leitmotiv. Thus in chapter 22 of this volume 'a kite' is the answer to the riddle she makes up for Grandmother Jia's party.

Tan-chun was the ablest and most intelligent of the Three Springs – a sort of junior version of Xi-feng without the crookedness and venom. Her fate was to be married off to a young man holding a post in a distant province, where she would have no hope of ever seeing her family again. The

Fourth Song simply repeats the imagery of the boat carrying the weeping bride away to her remote matrimonial exile.

5. *Shi Xiang-yun*

The picture is a rebus of Xiang-yun's name. Xiang is the river which flows northwards through the province of Hunan into Lake Dongting. *Yun* means 'cloud'. Chu was the ancient name of the Hunan-Hupeh area of which Lake Dongting is the centre.

Shi Xiang-yun was Grandmother Jia's little great-niece. Orphaned in her infancy, she was brought up by a harsh and unloving uncle and aunt. Her fate was to be blissfully happy in her marriage (almost the only young woman in the novel who was) but to lose her young husband a short time after it.

In the *Fifth Song* 'the clouds of Gao-tang' and 'the waters of the Xiang' allude once more to her name Xiang-yun. Gao-tang was the name of a mountain in the ancient kingdom of Chu which was believed to be the seat of a goddess. She was the patroness of lovers' embraces and of the nuptial couch. The lines about the Xiang's waters and the clouds of Gao-tang therefore refer also to the fleetingness of Xiang-yun's marital bliss.

6. *Adamantina*

Strictly speaking, the nun Adamantina's Chinese name means not 'diamond' but 'jade'. Hence the jade in the picture. She is the only one of the twelve not related in any way to the Jia family, though she lived for several years with Bao-yu and the others in Prospect Garden.

Adamantina had a mania for cleanliness and a morbid obsession with purity, but ended up in a brothel after being kidnapped and ravished by robbers. Neither the verses in the Register nor the words of the *Sixth Song* present any difficulties.

Shaodzoo=z

7. *Ying-chun*

Ying-chun, the eldest of the Three Springs, was married by her callous parents, despite protests from the rest of the family, to the unspeakable Sun Shao-zu, a drunkard, gambler and libertine who maltreated her. The 'old fable' refers to the well-known tale of Master Dong-guo and the wolf of Zhong-shan. The story appears in many versions and was even made into an opera by the sixteenth century playwright Kang Hai. It tells of a simple-minded Mohist scholar who saves a wolf from the huntsmen, only to be informed, when the huntsmen have gone, that the wolf is feeling hungry and intends to eat him for its dinner. The 'wolf of Zhong-shan' is therefore a symbol not only of ferocity but also of ingratitude. The implication is that Sun and his family were in some way indebted to the Jias. A family called Sun was in fact related to the Caos by marriage and the Caos had connections of some sort in Shansi, of which Zhong-shan is a part, so perhaps there is more in this riddle than meets the eye.

In the *Seventh Song* the Chinese words of the first line contain a play on the surname Sun which cannot, unfortunately, be reproduced in English. Literally it says 'Thou art a Zhong-shan wolf'; but the characters for 'thou' and 'art' combine together to make up the character for 'Sun'.

8. *Xi-chun*

Youngest of the Three Springs. Like her third cousin Bao-yu, she eventually renounced the world and entered a religious order.

9. *Wang Xi-feng*

Xi-feng's name means 'phoenix'. The iceberg is unexplained, but evidently has some reference to Xi-feng's sufferings after the family's fall. Various hints suggest that these included some sort of ordeal in the snow; but nothing of this is to be found in Gao E's version.

The interpretation of the rebus-language in line 3 has been much discussed by Chinese scholars. All I will venture to say here is that the message, whatever it is, appears to include the words 'cold' and 'divorce'.

The *Ninth Song* – fortunately – is more straightforward.

10. *Qiao-jie*   *Chiao-jie*

This is the name of Xi-feng's little girl. It was given her by Grannie Liu at Xi-feng's request and connects her with the Weaving Maiden of Chinese mythology whose feast-day has the same name. The Weaving Maiden gazes all the year at her starry lover, the Herd Boy, across the Milky Way, except on the night of the festival, when they are united. Like the Weaving Maiden, Qiao-jie married a farmer's son. She was rescued by Grannie Liu, when her wicked uncles would have sold her into concubinage, and offered an asylum in the country.

11. *Li Wan*

The surname Li means 'plum'. Li Wan was the mother of Bao-yu's little nephew Jia Lan, whose name means 'orchid'. Jia Lan evidently emerged from the wreck of the family's fortunes to become a high official, thus entitling his mother to wear court dress on ceremonial occasions. I think we are meant to infer from the second half of the quatrain and from the words of the *Eleventh Song* that Li Wan died shortly after her son's success.

12. *Qin-shi*

I have already explained in the Introduction that Xueqin originally intended Qin-shi to commit suicide by hanging herself in the Heavenly Fragrance Pavilion when her adultery with Cousin Zhen was discovered.

In the *Twelfth Song* the text of the sixth line is uncertain. I think it means no more than that Jia Jing was really most to blame for the shocking state of affairs in the Ning-guo household because of his refusal to shoulder his responsibilities as head of the family.

CHARACTERS IN VOL I

ADAMANTINA a genteel nun persuaded by the Jias to take up residence in Prospect Garden

AMBER one of Grandmother Jia's maids

AROMA Bao-yu's chief maid

AUNT XUE widowed sister of Lady Wang and mother of Xue Pan and Bao-chai

AUNT ZHAO concubine of Jia Zheng and mother of Tan-chun and Jia Huan

AUNT ZHOU Jia Zheng's other concubine

AVIS
AVOCET } maids of Lady Wang

BABY *see* QIAO-JIE

BAN-ER *see* WANG BAN-ER

BAO-CHAI *see* XUE BAO-CHAI

BAO-YU *see* JIA BAO-YU

BENEVOLENTIA young novice at Water-moon Priory

BIG JIAO an old retainer of the Ning-guo Jias

BRIGHTIE
BRIGHTIE'S WIFE } couple employed by Jia Lian and Wang Xi-feng

BU GU-XIU one of Jia Zheng's 'literary gentlemen'

BU-SHI Jia Yun's mother

BU SHI-REN a shopkeeper; maternal uncle of Jia Yun

CALAMITY a manservant in Zhen Shi-yin's household

CALTROP Xue Pan's 'chamber wife'; the kidnapped daughter of Zhen Shi-yin

CHARMANTE a child-actress; member of the Jia family troupe

CHENG RI-XING one of Jia Zheng's 'literary gentlemen'

CHESS Jia Ying-chun's maid

CITRONELLA *see* 'NUMBER FOUR'

CLOUDY one of Bao-yu's pages

COUSIN FENG *see* WANG XI-FENG

COUSIN ZHEN son of Jia Jing; acting head of the senior (Ning-guo) branch of the Jia family

CRIMSON one of Bao-yu's maids

DAI LIANG foreman in charge of the granary at Rong-guo House

DAI QUAN Eunuch Chamberlain of the Da-ming Palace

DAI-YU *see* LIN DAI-YU

'DARLING' a pupil at the Jia family school

DISENCHANTMENT an important fairy

DR ZHANG *see* ZHANG YOU-SHI

'DROOPY' DUO a drunken cook on the staff of Rong-guo House

'DRUNKEN DIAMOND, THE' *see* NI ER

EMERALD one of Bao-yu's maids

EUERGESIA prioress of Water-moon Priory

FAITHFUL Grandmother Jia's chief maid

FELICITY maid attendant on Wang Xi-feng

FENG *see* WANG XI-FENG

FENG-SHI Zhen Shi-yin's wife

FENG SU a farmer; Zhen Shi-yin's father-in-law

FENG TANG an old general; Feng Zi-ying's father

FENG YUAN Caltrop's first purchaser, murdered by Xue Pan's servants

FENG ZI-YING a family friend of the younger Jias

GEM a maid of Qin-shi's who committed suicide on the death of her mistress

GENERAL FENG *see* FENG TANG

GENERAL YUN *see* YUN GUANG

GOLDEN one of Lady Wang's maids

GOU-ER *see* WANG GOU-ER

GRANDMOTHER JIA née SHI; widow of Bao-yu's paternal grandfather and head of the Rong-guo branch of the Jia family

GRANNIE LIU an old countrywoman patronized by Wang Xi-feng and the Rong-guo Jias

'HORTICULTURAL' HU a landscape gardener entrusted with the planning of Prospect Garden

HU SI-LAI one of Jia Zheng's 'literary gentlemen'

HUA ZI-FANG Aroma's elder brother

INKY one of Bao-yu's pages

JEWEL maid of Qin-shi's who stood in place of a daughter at her mistress's funeral

JIA BAO-YU incarnation of the Stone; the eldest surviving son of Jia Zheng and Lady Wang of Rong-guo House

JIA CHANG a junior member of the clan given casual employment by the Rong-guo Jias

JIA CONG little son of one of Jia She's concubines

JIA DAI-RU an elderly scholar in charge of the Jia family school

JIA HUAN Bao-yu's half-brother; the son of Jia Zheng and his concubine, 'Aunt' Zhao

JIA JING father of Cousin Zhen and nominal head of the Ning-guo branch of the family living in retirement outside the city

JIA JUN a schoolboy attending the Jia family school

JIA LAN son of Li Wan and Bao-yu's deceased elder brother

JIA LAN (not to be confused with the above) a schoolboy attending the Jia family school

JIA LIAN son of Jia She and Lady Xing and husband of Wang Xi-feng

JIA LING junior member of the clan given casual employment by the Rong-guo Jias

JIA MIN younger sister of Jia She and Jia Zheng; wife of Lin Ru-hai; Lin Dai-yu's mother

JIA PING junior member of the clan given casual employment by the Rong-guo Jias

JIA QIANG a distant relation of the Ning-guo Jias patronized by Cousin Zhen; inseparable friend of Jia Rong

JIA QIN a junior member of the clan employed by the Rong-guo Jias to look after the little nuns from Prospect Garden

JIA RONG son of Cousin Zhen and You-shi

JIA RUI grandson of the schoolmaster Jia Dai-ru

JIA SHE Jia Zheng's elder brother

JIA TAN-CHUN daughter of Jia Zheng and 'Aunt' Zhao; half-sister of Bao-yu and second of the 'Three Springs'

JIA XI-CHUN daughter of Jia Jing and younger sister of Cousin Zhen; youngest of the 'Three Springs'

JIA YING-CHUN daughter of Jia She by a concubine; eldest of the 'Three Springs'

JIA YU-CUN a careerist claiming relationship with the Rong-guo family

JIA YUAN-CHUN daughter of Jia Zheng and Lady Wang and elder sister of Bao-yu; the Imperial Concubine

JIA YUN a poor relation of the Rong-guo Jias employed by Wang Xi-feng

JIA ZHEN see COUSIN ZHEN

JIA ZHENG Bao-yu's father; the younger of Grandmother Jia's two sons

JIA ZHU deceased elder son of Jia Zheng and Lady Wang; husband of Li Wan and father of little Jia Lan

JIN-GE see ZHANG JIN-GE

JING-QING 'school name' of QIN ZHONG sometimes used by Bao-yu in addressing him

'JOKEY' JIN a pupil in the Jia family school

KE-QING 'familiar' name of QIN-SHI, q.v.

KINGFISHER Shi Xiang-yun's maid

LADY JIA *see* GRANDMOTHER JIA

LADY WANG wife of Jia Zheng and mother of Jia Zhu, Yuan-chun and Bao-yu

LADY XING wife of Jia She and mother of Jia Lian

LAI DA Chief Steward of the Rong-guo mansion

LAI SHENG Chief Steward of the Ning-guo mansion

LENG ZI-XING an antique dealer; friend of Jia Yu-cun and son-in-law of Zhou Rui

LI GUI Nannie Li's son; Bao-yu's foster-brother and chief groom

LI WAN widow of Bao-yu's deceased elder brother and mother of Jia Lan

LIN DAI-YU incarnation of the Crimson Pearl Flower; daughter of Lin Ru-hai and Jia Zheng's sister, Jia Min

LIN RU-HAI Dai-yu's father; the Salt Commissioner of Yangchow

LIN ZHI-XIAO one of the stewards on the staff of Rong-guo House

LUCKY a maid in Zhen Shi-yin's household, later married to Jia Yu-cun

LUTANY a maid of Yuan-chun who continued to serve her mistress in the Imperial Palace

MACKEREL one of Bao-yu's maids

'MATTRESS, THE' nickname of 'Droopy' Duo's wife who subsequently became Jia Lian's mistress

MELILOT one of Bao-yu's maids

MOTHER MA a Wise Woman; Bao-yu's godmother

MRS HUANG Widow Jin's sister and wife of Jia Huang, a poor relation of the Jia family

MRS LIAN *see* WANG XI-FENG

MRS YOU You-shi's mother

MUSK one of Bao-yu's maids

NANNIE LI Bao-yu's old wet-nurse

NANNIE WANG Dai-yu's old wet-nurse

NANNIE ZHAO Jia Lian's old wet-nurse

NI ER 'The Drunken Diamond'; gangster neighbour of Jia Yun

NIGHTINGALE one of Dai-yu's maids

'NUMBER FOUR' one of Bao-yu's maids, formerly called CITRONELLA and before that SOLDANELLA

ORIOLE Bao-chai's maid

PATIENCE chief maid and confidante of Wang Xi-feng

PLOUGHBOY one of Bao-yu's pages

'PRECIOUS' a pupil at the Jia family school

PRINCE OF BEI-JING, THE *see* SHUI RONG

QIAO-JIE little daughter of Jia Lian and Wang Xi-feng

QIN BANG-YE father of Qin-shi and Qin Zhong

QIN-SHI wife of Jia Rong

QIN ZHONG younger brother of Qin-shi; Bao-yu's best friend

RIPPLE one of Bao-yu's maids

SAPIENTIA little novice at Water-moon Priory

SCRIBE Tan-chun's maid

SHAN PING-REN one of Jia Zheng's 'literary gentlemen'

SHI DING Marquis of Zhong-jing; nephew of Grandmother Jia and uncle of Shi Xiang-yun

SHI XIANG-YUN orphaned great-niece of Grandmother Jia

SHI-YIN *see* ZHEN SHI-YIN

SHINER one of Jia Lian's pages

SHUI RONG Prince of Bei-jing; princely connection of the Jias who befriends Bao-yu

SILVER one of Lady Wang's maids; Golden's sister

SIR JING *see* JIA JING

SIR SHE *see* JIA SHE

SIR ZHENG *see* JIA ZHENG

SKYBRIGHT one of Bao-yu's maids

SNOWGOOSE one of Dai-yu's maids

SNOWPINK one of Bao-yu's maids

SOLDANELLA one of Bao-yu's maids renamed first CITRONELLA by Aroma and then 'NUMBER FOUR' by Bao-yu

STORKY one of Bao-yu's pages

SUBLIMITAS monk-in-charge of the Temple of the Iron Threshold

SUNCLOUD maid of Lady Wang

SUNSET maid of Lady Wang favoured by Jia Huan

SUNSHINE page employed by Wang Xi-feng for clerical duties

SWASTIKA one of You-shi's maids

SWEEPER one of Bao-yu's pages

TAN-CHUN *see* JIA TAN-CHUN

TEALEAF ⎫
TRICKLES ⎬ pages of Bao-yu

TRINKET one of Bao-yu's maids

WANG BAN-ER Grannie Liu's little grandson

WANG GOU-ER a poor farmer; Grannie Liu's son-in-law

WANG REN Wang Xi-feng's elder brother

WANG XI-FENG wife of Jia Lian and niece of Lady Wang, Aunt Xue and Wang Zi-teng

WANG XING ⎫
WANG XING'S WIFE ⎬ couple on the staff of Rong-guo House

WANG ZI-TENG elder brother of Lady Wang and Aunt Xue

Genealogy of the Ning-guo and Rong-guo Houses of the Jia Clan

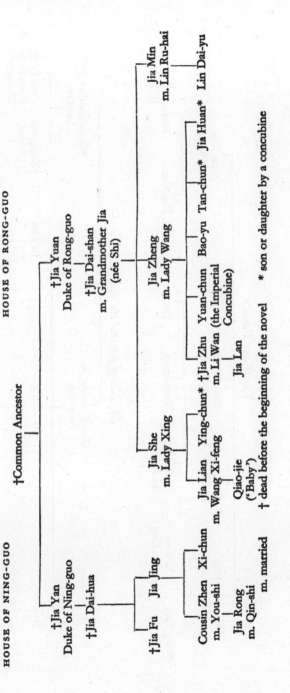

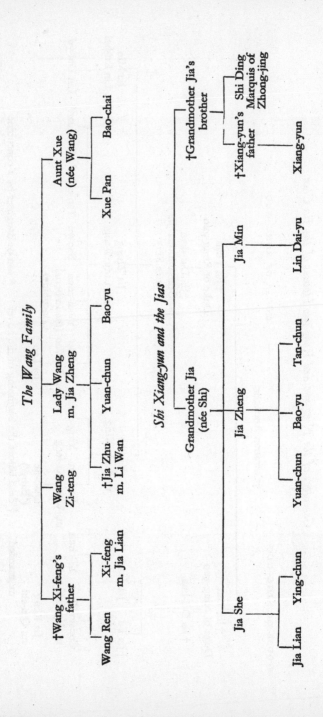

The Wang Family

†Wang Xi-feng's father — Wang Zi-teng — Lady Wang m. Jia Zheng — Aunt Xue (née Wang)

Wang Ren — Xi-feng m. Jia Lian

Jia Zhu m. Li Wan — Yuan-chun — Bao-yu

Xue Pan — Bao-chai

Shi Xiang-yun and the Jias

Grandmother Jia (née Shi) — †Grandmother Jia's brother

Jia She — Jia Zheng — Jia Min — Shi Ding Marquis of Zhong-jing

Jia Lian — Ying-chun

Yuan-chun — Bao-yu — Tan-chun

Lin Dai-yu

†Xiang-yun's father — Xiang-yun

1. 1 → 2 pm
2. 2 — 3 pm
3. 3 — 4 pm
4. 4 — 5 pm
5. 5 — 6 pm
6. 6 — 7 pm
7. 7 — 8 pm
8. 8 — 9 pm
9. 9 — 10 pm
10. 10 — 11 pm
11. 11ᵖᵐ — 12 am
12. 12 am — 1 am
13. 1 am — 2 am

TRY
TO
SLEEP
at 8pm